Wicked Christmas Nights

ALYSSA DRAKE   AMANDA MARIEL   ARI THATCHER

DAWN BROWER   LAUREN SMITH   NADINE MILLARD

TABETHA WAITE   TRACY SUMNER

Contents

THE DUKE'S SCANDALOUS CHRISTMAS WISH
ARI THATCHER

SMITTEN WITH MY CHRISTMAS MINX
DAWN BROWER

EXCERPT: SEARCHING FOR MY ROGUE

EXCERPT: THE VIXEN IN RED
DAWN BROWER

DEVIL AT THE GATES
LAUREN SMITH

SCANDAL IN THE SNOW
NADINE MILLARD

MISS PAGEANT'S CHRISTMAS PROPOSAL
TABETHA WAITE

TEMPTING THE SCOUNDREL
TRACY SUMNER

An Imperfect Introduction

ALYSSA DRAKE

One

A faint rattle pricked Wilhelmina's subconscious, pulling her from the darkened fog of sleep which suffocated her mind with petrifying images of ghosts, the nightmare born of an earlier conversation that evening, one she wasn't meant to overhear but had listened despite her mother's strong warning to stay away from the sitting-room, where the married women chattered about spirits and scandals behind closed doors.

She only intended to knock, to inform her mother she was retiring upstairs, exhausted from the long journey. She'd paused, her hand raised to rap on the sitting-room door when she heard her mother's quiet voice crawl out from the crack between the door and its frame.

"The maid swears she witnessed the spirit enter the room?"

Wilhelmina gasped, clamped her hand over her mouth, stifling the sound, and took a step backward, her heart pounding. She glanced over her shoulder, debating running for the stair-case, but proper decorum forced her to freeze. She waited, her breath caught in her throat, for the sitting-room door to rip open and chastisement to fall from her mother's tongue, but nothing happened. After a minute, she stepped toward the door again, curiosity overwhelming her engrained manners, and placed her ear against the crack.

"She claimed the spirit floated through the fireplace, paying her no attention, crossed the room, and passed through the window, as though it wasn't there," Aunt Isabelle replied. "She

3

pinched herself, later showing the mark, to prove she was awake." The collective sound of feminine gasps and a few inebriated titters met her admission.

"Was the girl sober?" Her mother's skeptical question silenced the room.

"She swore on her own life," Isabelle replied, her voice nearing the door. "The servants refuse to enter the room alone. Come, I'll show it to you. It's directly above us."

The handle twisted.

Wilhelmina jumped, spun mid-air, and was running before her feet touched the floor. She zipped up the staircase, darted down the hallway, and burst into the chamber she shared with her mother, where she spent the better part of the next hour huddled under the coverlet, trembling.

Now, as the faint scratching at the window transformed into a clawing sound, Wilhelmina was grateful they were sharing a bed. Her hand slid sideways, stopping just as the edge of her pinkie bumped into the warmth of her mother's arm. Wilhelmina's heart thudded out a sporadic rhythm of fear, and her head whipped left. She froze, her chest barely rising, as she stared at the heavy drapes covering the window.

The sound stopped.

After a long moment, she exhaled, her muscles relaxing, and she allowed herself a tiny chuckle at the absurdity of the situation—frightened by a sound, which was most likely a tree branch. She retracted her arm, careful not to wake her mother, and sat up. The best way to dispel fear was to meet it.

She climbed from the bed, shivering as the paltry warmth of the dying fire brushed over her skin, and pulled a wrap from the foot of the mattress. Draping the thin material around her shoulders, she padded to the center window, grabbed the heavy drape, her fingers curling around the edge, and took a deep breath. Exhaling slowly, she counted to three, then jerked the curtain aside.

A pale, distorted face appeared in the glass.

Wilhelmina opened her mouth to scream, but terror locked her throat, and no sound came from her lips. She dropped to the floor, scuttled beneath the windowsill, and pressed herself against the wall, her chest heaving.

What was that?

A very human yell answered her unspoken question, followed by a heavy thud, then a stream of profanity so perverse, the blush burning Wilhelmina's face threatened to combust into flames. She peered around the drape—certain her mother's disapproving glare waited on the other side—and exhaled a shaky breath as her mother's quiet snore replied. Encasing her body in the drape, Wilhelmina turned back toward the window and rose to her knees just as a deep voice hissed from below.

"What in the devil are you doing? You'll wake the house."

She leaned against the window, gasping as her skin touched the cold glass, and cupped her hands around her face, her gaze searching the moonlit grounds. Two men appeared below her, one lying on his back in a mound of snow and the other standing over him, their identities hidden beneath layers of clothing.

"It's Christmas," the second man replied, slurring the words together. He rolled side to side, his legs wiggling like a beetle stuck on its back.

"It is not Christmas for two more days," the first man corrected with no trace of annoyance. He leaned over and held out his gloved hand. "Come inside and warm yourself. I've had a room prepared for you."

"There's someone in it." The second man said the statement with such accusation, Wilhelmina bristled. She grasped the handle, intending to push open the window and correct the gentleman, but paused when the first man spoke.

"That was not your room. Your room is on the south side."

Another curse word followed.

"I should apologize." The second man scrambled to his feet, trudged beneath the window, and disappeared, then scraping sounds vibrated along the wall.

Trembling, Wilhelmina leaned away from the window. *He wouldn't dare. It would be inappropriate, unexplainable...* Her gaze darted to her mother's sleeping form.

"No." The stern command, given as one would speak to a child, stopped the second man's attempt to scurry up the side of the house, and he let go, dropping into the pile of snow which had broken his fall earlier.

"I may have given them a fright," he replied in a petulant tone.

"Of that, I am certain. However, another appearance at the

window will only cause further distress to the room's inhabitant," the first man grunted. Their boots crunched in the snow, the sound fading.

After a minute, Wilhelmina pressed her forehead to the frigid glass again. No evidence remained of the two men except two deep sets of footprints, which led from beneath her window, around the side of the house, then vanished.

The front door slammed, and a cacophony of curse words exploded in the entrance hall, the offensive vocabulary floating up from the first floor. Wilhelmina jerked her face from the window, scrambling to her feet, and raced for the bed, ripping the wrap from her body. She dove onto the mattress, dropped the wrap to the floor, yanked the coverlet over her body, and screwed her eyes shut, forcing her breathing to an even pace.

Her mother, her mouth half-open in a snore, started to awake, turned on her side, facing Wilhelmina, and expelled a heavy sigh, falling back into her deep slumber. Exhaling, Wilhelmina opened her eyes and stared at the ceiling, her gaze following the dancing shadows painted on the ceiling by the dying fire.

She strained her ears, listening for the late-night visitors.

The staircase creaked, complaining as they ascended the steps. One of them crashed into the wall—she assumed the second man—and riotous laughter followed, then two doors slammed in quick succession, and the house fell quiet again.

The man's face flashed into her mind. He was as astonished as she, and, though she was grateful he did not injure himself, she was thankful he hadn't managed to open the window. Surely, her mother wouldn't consider such an unfortunate mistake to be grounds for an engagement but, considering the shrinking number of gentlemen visiting their home, she might resort to more drastic means of trapping a husband.

It wasn't Mrs. James' fault to be certain, nor was it Wilhelmina's, but solely her father's, who chased away every suitor with two words, "No dowry."

That left the option of love—that a man might become so enchanted with her, he proposed marriage despite her lack of wealth. Wilhelmina had extraordinarily little faith in that possibility since every man thus far had heard those words and never returned.

She grimaced and twisted onto her side, tucking her arm under her head. She'd spent the final days of the season in front of the large window facing the street, painting flowers and tiny birds as the town promenaded past her. Between projects, when her mother was absent from the room, Wilhelmina worked on a small self-portrait, which she intended to give her mother as a gift after receiving a proposal, however, the season had ended without one. She debated holding onto the portrait until the next season, but clouds of doubt settled around her head, and she decided to give it to her mother for Christmas, hiding the portrait in the traveling chest between the layers of undergarments, when Mrs. Turner left the room.

Flipping onto her back again, Wilhelmina frowned at the dancing shadows. How would she hide it in the tree without anyone seeing her? She was never alone, not that any proper unmarried lady would strive to be on their own, but she wondered what kind of delight an hour of solitude would bring.

The inappropriate idea fluttering in her brain would only be inappropriate if she was caught, and since no one appeared after the noisy arrival of the two gentlemen, she doubted anyone would hear her light footsteps down the staircase. It wouldn't take long to dart down the steps, hide the portrait in the boughs, and run back to the room. It wouldn't be the hour she craved, but even a few moments of privacy…

Wilhelmina inhaled, her decision made, then holding her breath, she slid from beneath the coverlet. As she bent to collect the wrap from the floor, her mother shifted, murmuring in her sleep, and Wilhelmina dropped to the floor. She crawled toward the fireplace, keeping her head low, and stopped in front of the trunk at the foot of the bed. Rising on her knees, her eyes peeped over the mattress. Her breath catching in her throat, she lifted the trunk's lid, praying it didn't squeak. With her gaze locked on her mother, Wilhelmina stuck her left arm into the trunk and rummaged through the clothing.

Where was it?

She ducked her head, her gaze skimming over the disheveled undergarments. Shoving the clothing into the corner, her fingertips brushed over the portrait's rough canvas. She extracted the portrait from the trunk and set the lid down gently, but the lock slipped from her hand and slammed against the wood.

Her mother sat up with a gasp. Wilhelmina flattened herself to the floor, pressing her mouth against her arm to quiet her frantic breathing. The portrait, trapped beneath her body, dug into her ribs, the frame threatening to break.

A loud snore vibrated the room. Wilhelmina exhaled and rolled onto her side, ripping the portrait from its painful location. She pushed up, draped the wrap around her shoulders, and with no way to hold the portrait, held it between her teeth and crawled across the floor, then she stood, grasped the handle, and opened the door. After one final glance at her mother, she darted out of the bedroom, closing the door behind her.

Removing the portrait from her mouth, she checked it for damage, then turned and tiptoed down the corridor. It was strange, this feeling of independence that resulted from a most inappropriate decision. The feeling grew, a bubble of exhilaration increasing with each step until she nearly floated down the stairs.

In the entrance hall, beside the staircase, a large fir stood, decked out with glowing candles, colorful paper chains, and candies swinging from elegant ribbons. Wilhelmina walked around the tree, searching for the perfect spot to hide the portrait. Near the back of the tree, she found a break in the boughs that was just big enough to slide the canvas into.

"He'll never find it back there."

Wilhelmina screamed and glanced down. Crumpled on the floor, a man was lying on his back, his stocking feet poking out from beneath the tree's low boughs.

"Pardon me?" She jerked her hands back, tightening the wrap across her chest, aware of her inappropriate attire, and took one step backward, sliding her foot behind the first.

The man rolled his head toward her, his unfocused gaze finding her face. "I said, he'll never find it back there."

"Who won't?" She frowned, confused.

"The man you're hiding that for." He groaned and pushed himself into a sitting position, his body propped against the stairwell. The movement pulled his shirt, separating it at the neck and revealing more of his chest than she'd ever seen of any man.

The desire to touch the exposed skin rippled through her body, followed by astonishment at the realization she'd had that reaction.

His chest looked soft but hard, and her fingers twitched, curious what it would feel like beneath her fingertips. Wilhelmina swallowed and dropped her gaze to his feet, grateful he was wearing pants.

"I'm not hiding it for a man," she said, her tone harsher than she intended.

"Then, for whom are you hiding it?" he asked softly.

She lifted her head and locked eyes with his piercing blue stare.

"My mother."

"May I see it?" He held out his hand.

Nodding, Wilhelmina retrieved the small portrait from the tree and after a moment of hesitation, handed it to him. He patted the floor beside him. When she didn't move, he patted the spot again.

"The house is asleep. Who would witness this one transgression?" he asked and tilted his head, further mussing his unkempt chestnut hair. "Unless you're afraid of me…"

She should not have given in to his taunt, but since she'd already stolen out of her bedchamber, she supposed five more minutes of disobedience wouldn't cause any harm. She sank down beside him and jutted out her chin.

"No, I'm not."

"Excellent." He offered her a lopsided grin, then turned away and studied the small portrait. "Have you no husband to give such a fine gift to on Christmas?"

"I am not yet married," she replied, hating the disappointed tone of her statement.

"Engaged?" He glanced up.

She shook her head.

"Why?" The improper question hung between them.

"My father…" Wilhelmina's voice faltered, and she glanced down, folding her hands together and placing them on top of her legs.

"That is not an explanation," he said, handing back the portrait.

"There is no money for a dowry." The words tumbled from her lips before she could stop them. She sank her teeth into her lower lip, biting back the confession too late.

"I see." The man leaned his head back against the stairwell

and closed his eyes. A moment later, he slid down the stairwell, his body returning to its previously crumpled state.

"Sir?" Wilhelmina reached out and placed a tentative hand on the man's shoulder.

He opened his eyes with a gasp and reached up, grabbing hold of Wilhelmina. Pulling her down, he pushed his mouth to hers, igniting a spark that exploded through Wilhelmina's blood. Locked in his embrace, her mind went blissfully blank, a direct result of the soft pressure on her lips. He released her and fell back, his eyes rolling into his head.

"Hastings." A deep voice clucked from the staircase.

With a terrified squeak, Wilhelmina scrambled to her feet and pressed herself against the stairwell. There was nowhere to hide. Her gaze dropped to the man's unconscious form.

Hastings.

She'd heard the name before. The rumors circulating on the tongues of "polite" society members did not paint Mr. Edward Hastings nor his close companion, her cousin, Mr. Benjamin Reid, as honorable men. Scoundrel was the word most associated with both names.

That meant two things. One, her first kiss had been with a scoundrel, an inebriated one at that, and two, the man bearing down on her was Mr. Reid. She prayed he did not demand restitution. She couldn't imagine he'd want to force Mr. Hastings into marriage, especially considering the absurdity of the situation.

When Mr. Reid's face peered around the fir, he did not seem the least bit surprised to find Wilhelmina hovering uncertainly beside Mr. Hastings.

"Miss James, it is a pleasure to see you again." Mr. Reid greeted her with a formal bow, as though it were mid-day, and she was not hiding behind a tree, clad in only her nightdress and wrap. "I hope your mother is well."

"She is, thank you." Wilhelmina curtsied. Her gaze flicked to Mr. Hastings. "I found him this way."

"I have no doubt." Mr. Reid smiled—a pleasant lilt of his lips that caused many women to faint—and allowed Wilhelmina to dart out from behind the tree. He knelt and hooked Mr. Hastings' arm around his neck. "I have been tasked with returning Mr. Hastings to his chamber."

"Is he ill?" Wilhelmina asked as Mr. Reid hoisted Mr. Hastings to his feet.

"He is grieving," Mr. Reid replied. He half-dragged, half-carried Mr. Hastings toward the staircase.

"Would you like some assistance?" Wilhelmina asked, trailing after them.

Mr. Reid stopped on the third stair and glanced at her, his face darkening. "I have no intention of trapping my friend into marriage."

"And I'm most grateful for your discretion," Wilhelmina replied. She joined him on the step, lifted Mr. Hastings' other arm, and ducked beneath it. "However, since I was already awoken once this evening by Mr. Hastings—"

"It was your chamber." Mr. Reid grimaced. "Mr. Hastings offers his regrets for his inappropriate behavior this evening."

"Are you in the habit of apologizing for your friends?" Wilhelmina asked as they inched up the staircase one step at a time.

"When they've lost both their parents, I am." After they reached the landing, Mr. Reid jerked his head toward the corridor to his right. "It would be best for everyone if nothing was mentioned about your late-night meeting with Mr. Hastings."

"Of course." Wilhelmina pulled out from beneath Mr. Hastings' arm and leaned the whole of his weight on Mr. Reid. She curtsied again and turned, walking toward her chamber. As she opened the door, Mr. Reid's warning chased her inside.

"That includes him kissing you."

Two

hy are you still abed?" Her mother's shrill voice broke through Wilhelmina's fitful sleep.

She peeled one eyelid open and groaned, assaulted by the bright mid-morning light, let in when her mother yanked open the drapes. Last night's excursion seemed like a dream. She'd snuck back into the room and crawled back into bed without disturbing her mother. Her overstimulated mind focused on the kiss, replaying it over and over until she felt as if her lips would burst into flame, her last conscious thought that it might be entirely possible to kiss a woman senseless.

"I didn't sleep well," Wilhelmina replied and sat up, pulling the coverlet to her chest. She pressed her hand to her mouth, wondering if her mother could tell she'd been kissed.

"It's because we are in a strange place," her mother answered and waved her hand as if she knew her explanation to be the truth. She sat on the bed and took Wilhelmina's hand, clasping it in both of hers. A touch of sadness flashed through her mother's eyes. "I realize finding a suitable husband for you has been difficult—"

Wilhelmina forced a tight smile. It was too early to listen to all the excuses why she hadn't landed an acceptable suitor. No matter what her mother said, they both knew the reason she'd finished the season without a husband.

"However, I have a solution that will benefit both you and your fiancé," her mother said, her tone lightening.

"I don't have a fiancé, Mother."

"That's because he hasn't asked you yet." Her mother squeezed her hand in a reassuring gesture. "He must arrive first."

"Who must?" Wilhelmina frowned. This was the real reason she had been told to stay away from the sitting-room last evening. Her mother had been plotting with her aunt, and they didn't want her interfering with their plans.

"Your cousin, Oliver," her mother said as if Wilhelmina should have known the answer.

Wilhelmina almost snorted. She'd known Oliver since she was a toddling two-year-old. He was like a brother. "Oliver doesn't want to marry me."

"Of course, he does. You two have been amiable companions for years. He has no need of a dowry, and Isabelle told me he didn't make one proposal last season."

"Perhaps he doesn't want a wife," Wilhelmina replied, thinking that neither Mr. Hastings nor Mr. Reid seemed keen on the idea, either, and if the rumors were true, they were quite adept at remaining bachelors. However, if Mr. Hastings kept kissing women the way he did Wilhelmina, she was certain one of those featherheaded ninnies would figure out how to trap him into matrimony. Not that a life with Mr. Hastings would be uncomfortable. He didn't lack for funds, but a life with a drunkard… She grimaced. There were worse things than being a spinster.

"Wilhelmina!" Her mother's voice broke through the daydream.

"Of course, Mother," she said the words automatically, an instant reply whenever her mother shouted her name in that timbre. It meant the argument, if Wilhelmina even had one, was dead.

"Excellent. I'm pleased to hear you are so amenable to the idea. Truly, a late spring wedding would be ideal, early enough you aren't competing with other weddings, but late enough so not to look rushed."

What had she just agreed to?

"Don't frown, Wilhelmina. There are many benefits to having a husband." She leaned closer and dropped her voice to a whisper, "Not just financial but also physical."

"Mother!" Wilhelmina gasped, heat flooding her face. Her

mother's grip tightened on Wilhelmina's hand, and she wrenched her daughter forward.

"Oliver is a kind and gentle man. He will make your wedding night—and the consecutive nights afterward—enjoyable for you both, I have no doubt. After you fulfill your duty to bear children, you will have a comfortable home, and he will leave you to your own pursuits."

"He hasn't even proposed!" Wilhelmina jerked her hand from beneath her mother's. Anger vibrated through her body; her entire life plotted out without her participation.

"Josephine wrote that Oliver is considering the idea." Her mother waved her hand as if that were enough confirmation.

"Considering and doing are two different actions," Wilhelmina replied, unable to keep the bitter tone from her voice.

"Ungrateful child!" Her mother leapt off the bed, spun around, and stabbed the air in front of Wilhelmina's chest. "You should give thanks that your aunts and I are working to ensure your future instead of leaving you to sort out your affairs after your father passes. Do you think any man will want you at that age? What will you do for money? What ability do you have… painting?"

Shaking her head, Wilhelmina lowered her eyes in submission.

"Your uncle and his family will join us for today's luncheon. I expect you to dress as though you are already engaged." She reached out and hooked her finger under Wilhelmina's jaw, lifting it. "I know you disagree with my methods, but the life I want for you is better than the one I had." She fell silent, and her gaze flicked to the drapes, dropping to the corner that was pulled away from the wall.

Would she notice the exposed portion of the window?

Heart pounding, Wilhelmina flung back the coverlet and leapt from the bed, the sudden movement drawing her mother's attention.

"What is that?" Her mother reached out and detangled something from Wilhelmina's hair. Holding it up, the corner of her mouth pulled. Clutched in her fingers was a small bough from the fir tree in the entrance hall.

"I must have brushed against the tree at some point last

evening when I was helping Aunt Isabelle decorate." Wilhelmina twisted away, pretending as though the discovery of greenery in her tresses was a common occurrence.

"Of course," her mother replied, tapping the bough against her palm. She strolled to the fireplace, tossed the twig into the fireplace, and lifted her eyes to the mirror hanging over the mantle, finding Wilhelmina. "I expect you downstairs in twenty minutes, and when Oliver asks you to marry him, the only word I expect from your lips is yes. Are we in agreement?"

"Yes, Mother," Wilhelmina replied, her voice flat.

Without another word, her mother swept from the room.

Sighing, Wilhelmina dragged across the room to the window. She wasn't against the idea of marriage, or even against the idea of Oliver, but she wanted to fall in love, and after spending much of her life with Oliver, she was quite certain neither of them felt anything romantic toward each other.

She pulled aside the drape, pinning it beside the window, and placed her face against the cool glass, her gaze searching the grounds. No footprints were visible beneath her window, and she was thankful there was no evidence of Mr. Hastings' inexcusable attempt to crawl into her bedchamber, no matter how intoxicated the man was. She flushed as the memory assaulted her— Mr. Hastings' mouth on hers, the subtle taste of brandy coating his lips—and a rash of tingles rippled through her body.

She knew Mr. Hastings would not remember the incident— unless Mr. Reid reminded him, which she doubted, considering his abhorrence of matrimony—however, a tiny part of her wished

Mr. Hastings would remember. Not that she wanted to be forced into a relationship with the man, but it had been her first kiss, and the fact he wouldn't recall it was especially disheartening.

A light tapping indicated the lady's maid's arrival outside the door. Wilhelmina darted away from the window, leaping onto the mattress, then called for the woman to enter. The door crept open, and Mrs. Turner's thin face peered around the edge.

One lady's maid shared between her and her mother— another result of her father's mismanagement of his finances— whose responsibilities included the whole of the upstairs in addition to her lady's maid's duties. The older woman struggled to meet the exacting standards of her mother, often arriving in Wilhelmina's chamber with her hands quaking in terror.

"Good morning, Miss James." The words tumbled from Mrs. Turner's mouth as she bobbed her graying head and closed the door behind her. "Your mother instructed me to have you dressed in ten minutes."

Wilhelmina, accustomed to Mrs. Turner's anxious nature, climbed from the bed again and headed toward the chest. Lifting the lid, she knelt, pulling undergarments from her side of the trunk. She had already donned fresh underclothing and was pulling her corset over her head when Mrs. Turner appeared at her side, a blue skirt and bodice draped over her arm.

It took them eight minutes, with Wilhelmina shoving her stockinged feet into her slippers while Mrs. Turner pinned large sections of her hair in a simple hairstyle, to finish dressing. Just as Mrs. Turner stepped back, Mrs. James shoved the door open, a disapproving twitch on her lips. Her gaze swept over Wilhelmina, starting with her hair, and ending at the tips of her shoes, which peeped out from beneath the full skirt.

"I'm pleased to see the temporary accommodations have not disrupted your ability to perform adequate work." Her mother's eyes flicked to Mrs. Turner. "You are dismissed."

Mrs. Turner curtseyed, keeping her eyes on the floor, and darted around Wilhelmina. She vanished through the open doorway, her footsteps fading as she hurried down the corridor.

"He is here," her mother whispered excitedly. "He's already asked to speak with you in the library."

Wilhelmina nodded, her throat tightening.

"His sister will act as chaperone. I know you'll be more comfortable with her in the room." Mrs. James marched a half-circle around Wilhelmina, then her hands closed around Wilhelmina's shoulders, squeezing. "Your entire future rests on this conversation."

"I understand," Wilhelmina replied, her back ramrod straight. She pulled free of her mother's hands and passed through the open door, fighting the shiver which hovered between her shoulder blades, a lamb heading to slaughter.

"Cousin!" The joyful word echoed up the staircase as a blur of blonde hair and snow-coated skirts darted up the steps toward

Wilhelmina, who had barely enough time to fling open her arms before Cora crashed into her, knocking them both into the wall.

"Cora!" Aunt Josephine hissed from below, her voice dripping with disapproval. "While I am pleased to see Wilhelmina and her dear mother again,"—her gaze flicked to the left, focusing on Wilhelmina's mother, who'd appeared at the top of the staircase wearing a similar sour expression—"this behavior is unacceptable."

Cora detangled herself from Wilhelmina with a grin, smoothed her skirts, dusting the floor with a light blanket of snow, and offered Wilhelmina and her mother a proper curtsey.

"Mrs. Parrish, how delightful to see you again," Wilhelmina's mother gushed as she flowed down the staircase. "I was just remarking to Isabelle last night that I would happily place any wager on a game of cards, as long as you were my partner."

"Mrs. James," Cora's mother giggled, a faint blush crawling through her cheeks. "I'm honored to receive such a compliment from my husband's sister. Truly, it's your guidance that has helped me understand the game so easily."

"Then we are agreed. A sizable wager will be placed on tonight's game." Wilhelmina's mother wrapped her arm through Aunt Josephine's, and the two ladies strolled toward the sitting-room, their heads leaned toward each other.

"Cora," Cora's mother called over her shoulder, "please escort Wilhelmina to the library. Your brother is waiting to speak with her."

"Why does Oliver want to talk to you?" Cora whispered as she and Wilhelmina trudged toward the library.

"He is going to propose," Wilhelmina replied, curious why Cora wasn't aware of the impending marriage.

Cora frowned, chewing on her lip. "Are you certain?"

"Mother and Aunt Isabelle have been plotting since before you arrived, and I'm quite sure your mother is aware of their plans." Wilhelmina sighed.

"Is Oliver?" Cora asked, her frown deepening, then murmured to herself. "I didn't even know he was interested in marriage."

"Should I refuse your brother?"

"My brother is a fine man," Cora replied, glancing over, her clouded eyes clearing as she patted Wilhelmina's arm. "He will ensure your comfort."

But will he love me?

The question died on her lips as Cora pushed open the library door. Oliver stood in front of one of the shelves, his hands clasped behind his back, and his head tilted sideways as he read the titles. He spun when Cora cleared her throat, his brown eyes lightening as they landed on Wilhelmina.

"Good morning, ladies." He offered a formal bow, then gestured to one of a pair of long couches in the center of the room.

Wilhelmina, her heart hammering a rhythm of terror, crossed the floor, led by Cora, whose hand remained firmly wrapped through Wilhelmina's. When she reached her brother, she passed Wilhelmina's hand to him and gave him a deep curtsey.

"It appears, dear brother, I do not know your mind." With pursed lips, Cora wandered to the far corner of the room and perused the bookshelf.

A small wrinkle etched itself across Oliver's forehead. "She's angry with me."

"It's my fault." Wilhelmina's gaze flicked to Cora's back.

"We have only been here a few moments. What possible trouble could you have caused?" Oliver asked, amusement lacing his voice.

"I shared my concerns about an upcoming proposal."

Understanding passed through his eyes.

"A proposal my sister was not aware of?"

Wilhelmina nodded once.

"What are your concerns?" he asked, releasing her hand.

"I don't believe the gentleman is in love with me."

"He is not," Oliver replied, his voice even. "However, I don't believe you are in love with him, either."

"I'm not." Wilhelmina swallowed. "But love could grow with time."

"Much time has already passed since our introduction." His soft words swirled around her. "I don't believe a greater attachment will follow this particular union."

He was rejecting her before he'd even asked for her hand. Misery crawled through her heart. Her mother would never forgive her for this blunder. Lowering her head, Wilhelmina sniffed and discreetly daubed at the tears gathering in the corners of her eyes.

"Sweet cousin." Oliver's heavy sigh rolled over her. "Don't despair. It would be my honor to be bound to you for a lifetime, and I will fulfill that duty to you to the best of my ability, but,"—he reached out and cupped her face, lifting her chin until she stared into his eyes—"I'm reluctant to steal the opportunity to experience love from you."

"Have you ever been in love?" Wilhelmina whispered.

"He still is." Cora glanced up from her book, a silent conversation occurring between her and Oliver, then she returned her attention to the page she was reading.

"If you're interested in another person, why did you agree to—"

"Propose to you?" Oliver interrupted, his mouth twitching into a tight smile. "I will never be allowed to wed the person I love, and I cannot allow you to suffer through another season of unacceptable suitors... or worse. You are too kind to be attached to a brute."

"But you're giving up the possibility of happiness."

She shouldn't argue. She should be relieved Oliver was willing to make that kind of sacrifice for her, but she didn't want him to. She didn't want anyone to.

Oliver arched an eyebrow, clearly confused by her reluctance. "As are you."

"I could be happy with you," she countered and folded her arms.

Oliver made a nonsensical noise. Grasping her upper arms, he jerked her forward and pressed his mouth to hers. She squeaked, surprised by the sudden movement.

It was pleasant, the feeling of his warm lips pressed to hers, but that was all. Pleasant. Not a spark, not a smolder, and certainly not the explosion of flames that burned across her lips when Mr. Hastings kissed her. She felt empty.

Releasing her, Oliver stepped back. His unaffected gaze slid to Cora, who hadn't witnessed the quick exchange, then back to Wilhelmina.

"That was adequate," she said, unsure what one should say in this kind of situation.

He snorted. "I'm not going to propose to you today." .

Wilhelmina's chest constricted. "I—"

Oliver placed his finger to her lips. "I will ask you tomorrow. However, at the ball this evening, I ask you to consider a love match among your dance partners before you settle for a passionless marriage."

"My financial situation has not improved." Wilhelmina grimaced and turned away, a sob hovering in her throat. "No man wants a wife without a dowry."

"A man in love will," Oliver replied, glancing up as Cora appeared at his side.

"As much as I would enjoy having you as my sister," she said, wrapping an arm through Wilhelmina's, "I'd rather you found happiness. Therefore, I will assist you in your search for love."

"Why are you helping me?" Wilhelmina asked, her head swiveling between the siblings. Cora twisted away, her attention on the bookshelf.

After a long minute, Oliver replied, his voice filled with melancholy.

"Mother is insistent I marry you. It's all she has spoken of for weeks. However, if you were to become engaged to a more suitable man this Christmas, she'd be forced to find another acceptable young woman for me to marry, thus earning me a reprieve."

"Your mother will not be deterred," Wilhelmina said, wondering if all men detested marriage.

"Of that, I am certain, but she can be delayed,"—a delighted smile broke out across Oliver's face—"indefinitely."

Three

"You must have done something!" Mrs. James yanked a hairbrush through Wilhelmina's hair, her voice rising in pitch as she tortured her daughter's head.

Wilhelmina winced, her gaze flicking to the reflection of the open doorway in the mirror, and prayed her mother's shrill accusation hadn't been heard by the myriad of guests who'd arrived over the course of the afternoon.

"Have you ruined yourself?" Her mother jerked Wilhelmina's head straight, nearly breaking it from her shoulders.

"I would never make that mistake," Wilhelmina hissed, embarrassment crawling through her face. The whole section of the house must have heard her mother. "I'm never alone, and you have ensured a constant companion whenever I'm out of your sight. How would I have had the opportunity?"

Her mother released Wilhelmina's throbbing head, satisfied with the answer, and set about fixing the damage she'd caused during her tirade. No apology would come from her lips for the harsh treatment of her daughter's scalp, nor for the screeching allegations that reverberated down the corridor, which was closer to the truth than she expected. Wilhelmina *had* been alone last night when Mr. Hastings passionately kissed her and possibly ruined her for all other men... The blush darkened, a subtle reaction to the ghostly feeling of his lips brushing across hers.

"I don't understand," her mother murmured, drawing

Wilhelmina from her daydream, "Oliver was to propose this morning. What could have happened?"

"He will ask me tomorrow," Wilhelmina replied, repeating the same sentence she'd been saying for the past fifteen minutes.

"What difference will one day make?"

"Exactly, Mother," she said, grimacing as the hairbrush ripped through her tresses again. "If I am engaged to him tomorrow or today, we will still be married in the spring, just as you wished."

"He gave you no indication he'd changed his mind?" her mother asked, worry creeping into her tone. She set down the hairbrush and picked at the bristles. "Is there someone else he is considering?"

Yes.

"He said I was the only match Aunt Josephine approved." Wilhelmina fell silent, her heart giving a painful lurch. Oliver wouldn't be happy with her, and after years of forced attachment, the amiable feelings they shared for each other would be replaced by resentment. She glanced down, picking at her skirt.

"Oliver is young," her mother said and took up the hairbrush again. "He is likely suffering from the same nerves as you. I will speak with his mother."

"That won't be necessary," Cora announced from the doorway. She sailed into the room, her pale lemon dress brushing on the floor, and pirouetted once before joining Wilhelmina in front of the dressing table. She gestured for Wilhelmina to scoot over on the bench and sank into an elegant pose beside her. "Mother was extremely displeased with Oliver when she learned he had postponed the engagement."

"How displeased?" Wilhelmina asked, guilt fluttering in her chest. She swallowed the lump rising in her throat. It was her fault Oliver had decided not to propose this morning.

"He does not blame you, dear cousin." Cora placed her hand on Wilhelmina's forearm.

"You and your brother are quite close, are you not?" Wilhelmina's mother asked, her gaze on Wilhelmina's hair.

"Yes," Cora replied, her tone frank. "We have no secrets from each other."

"Then, you know the name of the other woman he is considering."

"You can't ask her that!" Wilhelmina's head whipped up, yanking a piece of hair from her mother's grasp.

"Of course, I can." Her mother clamped her hand on top of Wilhelmina's head, wrenching it toward the mirror, and retook the fallen tress. "I'm his aunt, and I should know if he's planning to propose to an unsuitable match." She stabbed a hairpin into Wilhelmina's scalp.

"Oliver has no desire to marry any other woman." Cora squeezed Wilhelmina's arm, holding her to the bench as two more hairpins joined the first. "He will propose to Wilhelmina tomorrow if she still desires to be wedded to him."

"Why wouldn't she want to be his wife?" Dropping the hairbrush on the table with a loud clatter, her mother leaned over and lowered her voice. "Is there a scandal? A child who bears his name?"

"No." Cora laughed, her amusement growing until it echoed around the room. She doubled over, her arms wrapped around her waist, and howled with laughter, tears streaming down her cheeks.

Irritation poured from Wilhelmina's mother, and she marched from the room without another word.

"She's gone to speak with Aunt Josephine about your lack of manners," Wilhelmina said, adding a small shake of her head; her cousin's inappropriate behavior was a favorite topic of Mrs. James.

Snickering, Cora rose and took up the hairbrush, moving behind Wilhelmina. "My mother will reply as she always does— it is the fault of my father's unruly blood, and she cannot do a thing to control it."

"If Oliver's idea is successful—"

"When his idea is successful," Cora corrected, pinning up the last portion of Wilhelmina's loose curls.

"You have a lot of faith in my charms," Wilhelmina replied as the corner of her mouth dipped.

Cora bent forward and wrapped her arms around Wilhelmina's shoulders, her face hovered beside Wilhelmina's, almost touching her cheek.

"Any man who cannot see your worth is a fool."

"Is your brother?"

"He is a man desperately in love and unable to act upon that desire." Cora turned toward Wilhelmina. "Yes, he's a fool."

"Do you approve of his paramour?"

"It is not my place to involve myself in my brother's affairs," Cora replied with a sniff and straightened, her voice adopting her mother's haughty tone, then she caught Wilhelmina's eye in the mirror and winked. "Don't be troubled. Oliver and I have discussed this matter at length. There are a number of suitable men attending tonight's festivities. Only one of them needs to fall in love with you."

"If it were so easy to change a man's heart, why haven't you married?" Wilhelmina turned toward her.

Cora grinned. "I've not found a man more courageous than my Henry."

"Or a man willing to spend more than five minutes in a room with the vicious pup," a familiar baritone voice added from the doorway.

"Oliver!" Cora chastised him as she spun around. "You shouldn't be in Wilhelmina's bedchamber."

"First," Oliver took one exaggerated step forward, "I'm not alone with her, you are here as a chaperone, and second,"—he took another step—"we will be engaged in one day. How much gossip could I cause?"

"What if another man passes the room?" Cora asked, storming toward him. She met him halfway across the floor. "Think of the damage that would cause in our endeavor to find her a love match."

"Only our families are residing on this side of the house," he replied and leaned around Cora, his gaze sliding over Wilhelmina. "Which you should be grateful to learn."

Wilhelmina grimaced. "You heard?"

"Every word." His eyes softened. No matter what Aunt Josephine thought of Oliver's behavior, she wouldn't express her displeasure with as much vulgarity as Mrs. James had. "I thought it would appease our mothers if I escorted you to the ballroom."

"No," Cora slid into his eye line. "If she arrives on your arm, the other gentlemen will assume she is unavailable."

"They will be intrigued," he replied, circling his sister. She moved with him, mirroring his steps in a bizarre dance. "How

24

unique must the woman be to capture the attention of Oliver Parrish?"

Cora narrowed her eyes. "If you think that is best…"

"I do."

She didn't argue, which was unusual for Cora. Wilhelmina wondered why her cousin had chosen that moment to withhold her opinion. Before she could think too much on the subject, Oliver approached, bowed, and held out his hand, lifting her from the bench. With Cora trailing behind them, he swept Wilhelmina out of the room toward the staircase. They paused at the top, listening to the faint music drifting from the first floor.

Wilhelmina inhaled slowly, her heart pounding. Her grip on Oliver's arm tightened, and he glanced down, sympathy flowing through his eyes.

"If you don't want to go through with this, I'll propose right now," he whispered. "I'd prefer to be miserable with you than with anyone else."

"If that is your proposal, then I refuse you," Wilhelmina muttered in return, and a bark of laughter burst from Oliver.

"As delighted as I am to hear your rejection, the only way you are leaving this house is as an engaged woman,"— Wilhelmina gasped at his candor—"and I'd prefer my favorite cousin married a man who is worthy of her affection… which, at the moment, is solely me."

Wilhelmina sighed, gathered her skirt in her free hand, and nodded.

"Because you are my favorite cousin,"—she felt Cora bristle behind her—"I will endure this evening's experiment in an effort to rescue you from that misery."

"You are rescuing yourself as well," he murmured as they descended the staircase.

"I can imagine a myriad of worse situations than to be your unloved wife," she said, her lips barely moving.

Oliver stopped, causing Cora to crash into the back of them. Turning to Wilhelmina, he pinned her with his intense stare. "You would be loved, but you would be unsatisfied, and I can't allow that."

"I—"

"Just like my sister, you intend to argue with me at every step." Oliver pressed one finger to Wilhelmina's mouth. "Accept there are matters which I understand and you do not because you are still innocent."

Wilhelmina glowered at him.

"That is a compliment to your modesty."

"She doesn't want your compliments," Cora growled and poked him in the center of his back.

Oliver glared at her. Returning his attention to Wilhelmina, he lifted his hand and cupped her face. "What did you tell me? Adequate?"

She nodded, sinking her teeth into her lower lip. Her gaze flicked to Cora, who vibrated impatiently on the staircase and back to him.

"Tell me when you discover fire." He retook her arm, turned, and escorted her down the steps without another word.

The whispers began as soon as they entered the ballroom, whipping across the floor like lightning before Wilhelmina managed two steps. It was the first time anyone had seen a woman other than Cora on Oliver's arm, and the excitement was more than the room could endure. A shiver rolled down Wilhelmina's spine, a direct result of the number of eyes following them around the outskirts of the dance floor.

Cora strolled behind them, keeping the respectable distance one would expect of a chaperone, but stopped to speak with her aunts and mother, who were cluttered in the nearest corner of the room, leaving Wilhelmina and Oliver to continue through the crowd alone.

"If you leave my side, too, I will—"

"Force me to marry you?" Oliver's mouth twitched. "Dance with me. It will be the last time I touch you this evening."

Wilhelmina's mouth popped open. "What do you mean?"

"Look around." He spun her in a half-circle and leaned close, his mouth almost touching her ear. "They're all watching, waiting for their chance."

"I think you overestimate my charms," she murmured.

Cora glanced up at the exact moment Wilhelmina whirled past her, drawing the attention of Mr. Hastings and Mr. Reid, who stood beside her, conversing on the sidelines. Mr. Hastings' gaze locked on her face, following her as Oliver spun her toward the far side of the room. She blushed, heat flaring in her cheeks, and glanced away.

As the last strains of the song died, Oliver lifted Wilhelmina's hand to his mouth and pressed his lips to her glove. "Thank you for the dance, Miss James." He barely had time to finish the words before another man appeared at his side, repeating the same deep bow.

"Mr. Parrish, may I request the next dance from your lovely partner?" The gentleman possessed slightly less stature than Oliver but was wider, as if he'd started at Oliver's height and had been squished down by a heavy weight.

"Miss James, may I present Mr. Nigel Mason? He would like the next dance… if you are free."

Smug. That was the look that passed across Oliver's face. Wilhelmina's eyes narrowed. If this inane idea worked, Oliver would never let her forget it. He abandoned her on the dance floor, leaving her with Mr. Mason, who bowed again, signaling the beginning of the next song.

"Miss James, I was astonished to see Mr. Parrish escorting you this evening," Mr. Mason said. His voice was a pleasing timbre, not deep but developed enough to indicate the man enjoyed reading aloud. "Does that mean Miss Parrish is available for courting?"

Wilhelmina frowned, a slight wrinkle creasing her forehead. "If you are asking if Miss Parrish would be willing to dance with you this evening, I would encourage you to ask her yourself."

"Of course." He smiled and spoke no more.

She sighed, her gaze searching the crowd for Oliver, who she couldn't find. However, it did stumble across Mr. Hastings again. He swayed on the edge of the dance floor, ignoring the discussion occurring around him. When he realized Wilhelmina was staring at him, he shook his head, rousing himself from his thoughts, and started across the floor, crashing into three couples before he reached Wilhelmina and Mr. Mason.

"May I have this dance?" The slurred words were barely audible above the music.

"I believe it's customary to wait until the current dance has completed before requesting the next one," Mr. Mason replied, irritated, and whirled her away from Mr. Hastings, who rushed after them, smacking into another couple in his chase.

"May I have the next dance?" Mr. Hastings' pressed, his blue eyes blazing.

"That choice is up to the lady." Mr. Mason moved in front of Wilhelmina, blocking her.

She placed a hand on Mr. Mason's shoulder and stepped around him, offering Mr. Hastings a genteel smile. "If the gentleman is willing to wait until his turn, I would be delighted to dance with him."

Mr. Hastings nodded and spun, stumbling away from them. He bumped into Mr. Asher Reid—Benjamin Reid's cousin—and his wife, Eleanor, who caught Mr. Hastings before he fell, each of them grabbing one arm. They carted him off the floor and deposited him in a chair on the sidelines.

"I think you should refuse Mr. Hastings," Mr. Mason said, drawing Wilhelmina's attention. "He's not in control of his senses this evening."

"Is it not better to placate the man and prevent a scene? He has suffered a great loss," Wilhelmina replied. "It is merely one dance."

"I was not aware of your generosity, Miss James." He stared at her as if meeting her for the first time. "I can see why Mr. Parrish is enamored with you."

Mr. Mason bowed when the song finished and escorted her to the fringes of the dance floor. They joined Asher Reid and his wife, who were conversing with Eleanor's younger sister, Lydia, and Mr. Allandale.

"Mrs. Reid, Miss Daniels." Wilhelmina curtsied to both women. "It's lovely to see you again."

Eleanor smiled with the genuine glow of happiness that accompanied a newly married woman, but her sister, Lydia, greeted Wilhelmina with a frosty twitch of the lips, which one could only attribute to a woman suffering from unrequited love. She wondered which young man had captured her attention.

"Wilhelmina," her mother's hand grabbed her arm, pinching the flesh as she pulled her from the group. "What are you doing?"

"What do you mean?" Wilhelmina panted as she ran to catch up with her mother, her arm throbbing where her mother's nails dug into the flesh.

"Why did you dance with Mr. Mason?" Her mother flung her into the dim corridor, lit only by the soft glow of the candles decorating the fir tree.

"He asked me." Wilhelmina rubbed her arm, backing away as her mother advanced on her.

"You. Are. Engaged."

"I'm not. No one has asked me."

Her mother's eyes bulged, almost bursting from her head. "Don't put your future—*our* future—at risk."

"I haven't." Wilhelmina took a step forward, lowering her voice. "Oliver told me to dance with whoever I chose this evening. I'm following the instruction of my intended fiancé."

Growling, her mother flung her hands in the air and stomped back into the ballroom, enveloped by the first notes of the next song. Wilhelmina darted after her mother, skidding to a respectable walk as she entered the room and clasped her hands in front of her. Her gaze slid over the swaying couples seeking Mr. Hastings, but his unkempt head of chestnut hair was nowhere to be seen.

Had he forgotten their dance? She chewed her lip. Why would he demand the next turn, then disappear?

"You look unhappy," Cora said from her left. Wilhelmina jumped.

"Mr. Hastings asked for a dance," she replied, her eyes searching the sidelines.

"That troubles you?"

"Only that he doesn't appear to have remembered it."

"Perhaps he is lost. Come! We shall seek him out." Cora grabbed Wilhelmina's arm and steered her toward the corridor.

"We cannot, we are expected to..." Wilhelmina dragged her feet, glancing over her shoulder as she passed through the doorway.

"A mystery, dear Cousin, requires our immediate attention, no matter the location," Cora replied, pulling her into the dim corridor. Her eyes sparkled. "If Mr. Hastings chooses to spend his requested dance hiding, then we must be amenable to his decision and seek him out."

"Do you not have a partner for this dance?" Wilhelmina asked, allowing Cora to drag her toward the fir tree. "I know Aunt Josephine ensured you had a full dance card tonight."

A smirk twitched across Cora's lips. "Mr. Hastings asked me as well."

Four

Wilhelmina's eyes widened, and a gasp stuck in her throat. What kind of man asked two women for the same dance? Was he truly scandalous enough to believe he could partner with them both simultaneously?

"Bugger you and your bollocks!"

Cora froze halfway across the entrance hall and spun around, a peculiar expression on her face as if she was unsure she'd heard the appalling phrase.

"Did you say something?" she asked, and Wilhelmina shook her head.

"Perhaps it was the ghost."

"There's a ghost?" Glee exploded in Cora's eyes.

"Last night, I heard Aunt Isabelle admit the servants refuse to enter the chamber at the end of our corridor because it's haunted," Wilhelmina replied, knowing Cora wouldn't reveal that Wilhelmina had been listening at the sitting-room door.

"Bastards!" The word echoed up the stairwell.

Cora and Wilhelmina's heads turned toward the fir tree simultaneously.

"That is not a ghost," she murmured, her heart sinking.

He couldn't be beneath the tree again.

Wilhelmina held up her hand, stopping Cora's progress, and inched toward the tree. She peered around the boughs, hoping not to see Mr. Hastings, but knowing that the man slumped against the wall was likely he. When she moved back, his eyes opened, and his unfocused blue gaze shifted to her face.

"You're in the tree." He slurred the words and pointed at the branches, squinting. "I see you here, and I see you there."

"Yes, Mr. Hastings." Her eyes flicked to the portrait and back to him. "I showed you the painting yesterday."

"You said my name." He offered her a dazzling grin, one she was certain he reserved for those ladies who fell prey to his seductive nature.

"And I told you the portrait was a secret." She ignored the fluttering in her stomach and pressed a finger to her lips. His eyes flicked to her mouth, following the movement of her hand.

"Apples," he murmured, his tongue darting out, moistening his lips. "You taste like sweet apples."

She dove forward, knocking his head into the wall as she clamped her hand over his mouth, her heart pounding in terror. Cora was listening. If she discovered Mr. Hastings had kissed Wilhelmina, she'd encourage the attachment to spare her brother.

"Do not speak, Mr. Hastings. We are not alone." After he nodded his consent, she peeled her fingers away from his face. Leaning around the tree, she gestured for Cora to come closer.

Tiptoeing across the entrance hall, Cora checked the doorway of the ballroom as she passed to confirm their solitude, then darted the rest of the distance to the fir tree.

"Who is it?" Cora whispered, craning around the boughs.

"Mr. Hastings," Wilhelmina replied from her crouched position.

"Yes," he sang, leaning around Wilhelmina. He lost his balance, slid down the wall, and collapsed on the floor, a soft snore following.

"We can't leave him here." Wilhelmina collected his jacket from the floor. Bunching it into a ball, she lifted his head and slid his jacket beneath his face.

"What do you propose we do?" Cora arched an eyebrow.

"I overheard Mr. Reid say their rooms were on the south side." Wilhelmina's breath caught as feminine voices echoed near the corridor. Cora scooted to her right, blocking Wilhelmina and Mr. Hastings from the ballroom's view.

"I'll distract them," Cora murmured. "Try to get him standing."

Wilhelmina nodded.

Spinning, Cora straightened her shoulders and strolled toward the ballroom. She held out her arms, catching her mother and Wilhelmina's mother before they entered the corridor and directing them back toward the dancefloor.

"Mr. Hastings." Wilhelmina poked his shoulder. His hand snapped up and captured her wrist as his eyes opened.

"Why are you in my chamber?" He flipped onto his back.

"We are not in your chamber."

"Where are we?" He dragged her down, pulling until she was sprawled across his chest, and enveloped her in a potent perfume of bourbon and musk.

"Beneath the fir tree." She forced the words through her lips, knowing if she shifted a millimeter, her mouth would brush across his.

"Is this a dream?" he asked, his other arm snaking around her waist and locking her against him.

"N—"

Mr. Hastings chose that exact moment to press his mouth to hers, and the heat which resulted from the kiss burned the sensitive skin of her lips.

She moaned.

The sound escaped by accident, drawn from some part of her that had been awakened by his passionate embrace. Mr. Hastings, encouraged by the noise, pushed his tongue into her mouth, sending a stream of tremors rippling through her limbs as if her body had burst into flames and was melting from her bones. Her arms, trapped between their torsos, lacked the strength to push away.

She had to stop before they were discovered, but the feelings coursing through her, so completely foreign to anything she'd experienced, were overwhelming and tamped down the fear of scandal until it became a quiet buzz in the back of her mind.

It was Mr. Hastings who broke the spell. He hiccupped. That amusing moment was enough time to allow Wilhelmina to return to her senses. She pushed off his chest, scrambled to her feet, and fluttered her hands over her skirt.

"How did you get him to stand?" Cora's hushed voice asked from behind.

Wilhelmina spun around just as Mr. Hastings took two swaying steps forward and draped an arm over Wilhelmina's shoulders. He rolled his head to the right, attempting to focus his gaze on Cora.

"She offered me apples." He laid his head on her shoulder. "I love apples."

Cora frowned, mouthing the word 'apples' at Wilhelmina, who responded with a shrug and a matching look of confusion.

"He's been mumbling nonsense since you left us," Wilhelmina motioned for Cora to duck under his other arm.

"We have little time." Cora lifted Mr. Hastings' arm and wrapped it around her neck. "Your mother is looking for you and Oliver."

"Do you think she believes we've disappeared together?" Wilhelmina grunted as they tugged Mr. Hastings from behind the fir tree. Instead of helping them, he dragged his feet, and the scraping sounds reverberated in the empty entrance hall.

"I believe she hopes that is true." Cora shifted Mr. Hastings' weight. "However, you can't be missing too long, or it will ruin any chance you have of finding another suitor."

"Would you like a suitor?" Mr. Hastings asked and turned his luminous blue eyes to Wilhelmina.

"I'm not interested in a scoundrel," Wilhelmina replied as they stopped at the base of the staircase. They would need Mr. Hastings' assistance to get up the steps. She inhaled a slow breath, her gaze catching Cora's, and the same look of trepidation crossed her cousin's face.

"Mr. Hastings, would you please lift your right leg?"

He frowned, as though he couldn't understand why Wilhelmina would make that request of him, but he nodded and complied, lifting his right leg.

"Excellent," she said, using the same tolerant voice she used with her father when helping him to bed. "Now, place your foot on the step directly in front of you."

"How do you know I'm a scoundrel?" He twisted toward her, leaning heavily on her shoulder as she and Cora maneuvered him up the staircase.

"You asked both Miss Parrish and me for the same dance,"

Wilhelmina panted. They stopped halfway up the staircase and repositioned him between them.

"Did I?" He narrowed his eyes and leaned toward Cora, shifting the balance of the trio. They floundered on the thin step to keep him upright. "I don't remember your face."

"You asked my mother," Cora replied. Her mouth twitched. Clearly, she was finding this adventure much more amusing than spending her evening in the dull ballroom.

"Bollocks. I asked the wrong mother." He swayed back toward Wilhelmina. "Did I ask your mother, too?"

His face was so earnest, Wilhelmina struggled to keep from laughing.

"No, Mr. Hastings. You asked my dance partner."

He paled. "While you were dancing?"

"Indeed, you were quite adamant."

"Did I miss our dance?"

"It is occurring at this very moment."

Mr. Hastings stopped three steps from the top of the staircase and glanced around, his face a mixture of confusion and embarrassment. "We are not in the ballroom."

"You took ill," Wilhelmina replied through gritted teeth and together with Cora, jerked him up the last of the steps.

He stumbled on the landing, pulling free of their grasp, and toppled forward, crashing into the wall with so much force, he rebounded with a groan and careened backward. Wilhelmina caught his arm before he could tumble down the staircase and yanked, spinning him toward Cora, who gave him a small shove and propelled him down the south corridor.

"Do you know which chamber is his?" Cora asked as they hurried after Mr. Hastings.

"I was hoping he did." As she spoke, Mr. Hastings opened a door halfway down the corridor and popped his head into the room.

Leaving the door open, he wandered into the room. A moment later, his vest flew through the open space.

"Is he undressing?" Cora made a sound that was a combination of a gasp and a giggle.

Mr. Hastings reappeared in the corridor, his shirt unbuttoned and gaping from his neck to his mid-chest. He pointed at the opened doorway, loosening his ascot with his free hand. "That isn't my room."

"Are you certain?" Wilhelmina asked, her chest constricting.

What were they going to do? Mr. Hastings was rapidly losing clothing, and they couldn't open every chamber until they discovered his room. Someone was bound to discover them, and no explanation would excuse entering another guest's bedchamber.

"Cora," she clapped her hands together to draw her cousin's attention. "Would you retrieve Mr. Reid from the ballroom? I believe this delicate matter may require his assistance."

"What about..." Cora's eyes shifted to Mr. Hastings, who had stopped undressing and was currently conversing with a portrait of their uncle. He glanced up and gestured for Wilhelmina to join him.

"I suppose I should greet Uncle Charles' picture," Wilhelmina replied with a shrug.

"Don't allow Mr. Hastings to leave this corridor," Cora said. Lifting her skirt, she darted around the corner, heading toward the staircase.

"Good evening, Uncle Charles," Wilhelmina said as she curtsied to the portrait, feeling every bit as foolish as one should when speaking to inanimate objects.

"I was just telling Mr. Stanton how grateful I am that he invited me to stay this week. I find the empty townhouse to be overwhelming," Mr. Hastings said, his tongue stumbled over the words.

"Too many memories?" she asked.

He turned toward her and stared as if she'd asked him to name off all his prior lovers. She twisted her hands together, regretting her question, and tried to think of something else to say, but her mind offered no suggestions.

"That is precisely the difficulty." He snapped his heels together and bowed low to the picture, wobbling once. "Mr. Stanton, if you would excuse me, I must request a dance from your captivating niece."

She'd never been called captivating in the whole of her life and hearing the words from Mr. Hastings sent a sharp, stabbing pain through the center of her chest. Marrying Oliver would ensure she'd never hear that word again. He was right, she wanted a love match, and instead of seeking it out, she was hiding, spending her evening caring for an inebriated, disarmingly handsome man.

"Mr. Hastings," Wilhelmina said in a firm voice, the same one she reserved for her father when he'd consumed too much drink. "You have already asked me for a dance."

He tilted his head, apparently trying to recall the memory of their dance. "Did I step on your toes?"

"You were unavailable to fulfill the request."

"My apologies, it was unintentional." Melancholy settled in his eyes, a deep sadness that had been momentarily thwarted and had returned.

"I would offer you another dance, but there is no music," she said, reaching out. She stopped, her hand hovering over his shoulder, uncertain if he would welcome her touch. She couldn't imagine the devastation that resulted from the death of one parent, but to lose both when he was barely a man himself... Her heart ached for him.

"Yes, there is." He moved closer, his sweet, musky scent overwhelming her. "Can't you hear it?"

She shook her head.

"Shut your eyes," he murmured.

After a moment of hesitation, she closed her eyes, straining to catch the faint sounds from the ballroom. They drifted up the staircase, carried by an invisible breeze. She swayed, her hips moving in rhythm with the music.

A burst of fire blazed up her arm, consuming the flesh, and her eyelids flew open. She gaped at her hand, encased in Mr. Hastings', unable to keep the shock from her face.

"Miss James, if you can't stand my touch, how are we to survive an entire dance?" he asked, dropping his arms to his sides.

"You startled me," she replied, unsure if he was jesting or truly offended by her reaction.

"Did you forget I was here?" He asked, his face unreadable.

"I was listening to the music."

"Can you still hear it?" He lifted his arms into position and stepped forward. Their bodies were millimeters apart, his hands hovering an inch above her skin. The heat from his palms burned through the thin material of her dress.

"Only when my eyes are closed."

"Then I suggest you shut them." The low rumble caused her breath to catch in her throat. Her body hummed in anticipation as she closed her eyes. He moved closer and murmured, "I'm going to touch you now."

His warning didn't prepare her for the explosion of heat that ricocheted through her body as soon as he wrapped his hand around her upper torso. Every inch of skin caught fire as if she'd stepped into the kitchen's fireplace and was standing directly above the logs.

Her eyelids fluttered.

"Keep them closed." His growled instruction caused her stomach to flip.

She nodded, her teeth worrying her lower lip. His intoxicating scent wafted over her. How close was he? If he kissed her again, she wouldn't have the strength nor the inclination to push him away, as she ought to. She found the thought equally disturbing and exhilarating.

His fingers repositioned themselves on her torso, lightly grasping her before he spun her in an unexpected circle, and Wilhelmina, whose mind was focused on the unusual sensation of being held in Mr. Hastings' arms, stumbled, and tripped over his feet.

Mr. Hastings' faulty equilibrium didn't allow him to catch Wilhelmina before she fell, nor did it prevent him from toppling over on top of her. It was in this tangled state of limbs and laughter that Cora and Mr. Reid discovered them.

"What the devil are you doing?" Mr. Reid charged toward them, leaving Cora chasing after him. He grabbed hold of Mr. Hastings' shirt collar, yanked him from on top of Wilhelmina, and flung him halfway down the corridor.

"It wasn't his fault." Wilhelmina scrambled to her feet and rushed after Mr. Reid as he advanced on Mr. Hastings. "We were dancing, and I tripped."

Mr. Reid paused, his fist raised, and glanced back at Wilhelmina. "Miss James, you are a graceful dancer, a compliment my mother has shared on numerous occasions. There is no need to protect his reputation."

"I'm protecting mine, Mr. Reid." Wilhelmina scooted between the two men, hiding Mr. Hastings' supine form behind her. "And I don't appreciate having my word doubted."

"Of course, Miss James." His formal tone indicated he didn't believe her statement. His gaze skipped to Cora as she joined Wilhelmina's side. "I thank you for bringing Mr. Hastings' plight to my attention. Few people would have given him that kindness. However, I must ask that neither of you share his difficulties with the household."

"We will not speak of the incident," Wilhelmina replied.

Cora agreed and looped her arm through Wilhelmina's, attempting to drag her down the corridor, but Wilhelmina pulled free and stepped toward Mr. Reid, keeping her body in front of Mr. Hastings.

"You're not going to strike him, are you?" she asked.

"Are you concerned for him?" Mr. Reid seemed surprised. His gaze skipped to Mr. Hastings, who had flipped onto his side and was lightly snoring, then back to Wilhelmina.

"I am." Her own words surprised her. She barely knew the man, apart from the scandalous rumors which swirled around his name, yet here she stood, offering to protect him from his friend.

"Miss James, I have spent much this year caring for Mr. Hastings. The only reason I would have to strike him was if he dishonored a young woman, which you have stated did not occur." He paused, waiting for her to nod her confirmation. "Therefore, unless you wish to alter your statement, my only concern is to ensure he sleeps in his bed instead of in the corridor."

She blushed, embarrassment crawling through her cheeks. Dropping her gaze, she curtsied again. "Please attend to your friend, Mr. Reid. Have a pleasant evening."

"Were you really dancing with Mr. Hastings?" Cora whispered as she dragged Wilhelmina down the corridor.

"He was upset he'd missed our dance." Wilhelmina glanced over her shoulder to see Mr. Reid ushering Mr. Hastings through the open doorway of the very room Mr. Hastings had previously claimed wasn't his. She rolled her eyes, returning her attention to Cora. "I thought it best to amuse him until you returned."

"Do you think—"

"He's not a love match," Wilhelmina cut off her cousin, earning a sour glance from Cora.

She raised her eyebrows and volleyed a reply. "Is Oliver?"

"Are you suggesting a match with a man who doesn't know his own mind is a better choice than your brother?" Wilhelmina asked as they descended the staircase.

"I'm merely stating that a man who wasn't in possession of his mental faculties remembered he wanted to dance with you. Solely you." Cora turned to Wilhelmina, offering a small smile. "How do you explain that?"

Five

Captivating. He'd called her captivating. The word swirled around her head long after the final notes of music had faded and the guests had retired for the evening. While her mother slumbered peacefully beside her, Wilhelmina spent a second night staring at the decorative ceiling of the Stantons' country home.

She debated another excursion downstairs. There was no reason for one, save to abate the restlessness of her mind, and wandering about without discovery would prove almost impossible now that all the chambers had been claimed. However, if she continued to roll over, her movements would eventually wake her mother, who'd then inquire why Wilhelmina found herself unable to sleep.

A faint creak echoed down the corridor, followed by an equally faint curse word.

Curiosity pulled her from the bed, and she was halfway across the floor before she stopped to consider the person sneaking down the corridor may not be Mr. Hastings, as she had hoped. However, the peculiar sound came again, and she hastened to the door, grasped the handle, and opened it a sliver, peering through the small space.

"Oliver?"

"Wilhelmina!" Oliver's hand whipped out, latched onto her wrist, and yanked her into the corridor, closing the door behind her. "What are you doing awake?"

"I was considering my dance partners," she replied, her voice trailing off as her gaze slid from his unkempt hair to his gaping shirt, which was split from his neck to stomach as if it had been ripped apart in haste. "Were you assaulted?"

A light red tinge colored his cheeks. "Yes."

"We should alert Uncle Charles,"—her head whipped left and right, searching for potential assailants, her voice pitched, driven by hysteria—"they'll need to search the grounds."

Oliver grabbed her upper arms, shaking her gently until she stopped babbling.

"I wasn't injured." He glanced over his shoulder, placed a finger over his lips, and led her down the corridor until they were standing between two chambers. Lowering his voice, he leaned forward. "I was meeting someone."

"The person you wish to marry but cannot?" she asked, keeping her voice at a whisper.

Oliver's eyes flicked up, staring at something on the far end of the corridor. When he replied, his lips barely moved. "The very same."

"When do you intend to propose to me?" Her question drew his attention.

"I hadn't decided upon a time." His eyes narrowed. "Why do you ask?"

"If you aren't offended, I would like the day to seek out a love match." The words rushed out in a torrent.

Stunned, it took him a minute to recover. "What has brought on this desire for delay?"

She licked her lips, wondering if Oliver would understand her reasoning.

"A gentleman,"—was that the proper term for Mr. Hastings —"requested a dance. When he did so, he called me captivating, and I realized if I married you, I would never hear that word again."

Oliver sighed and wrapped her in a tight embrace. Hooking his finger beneath her chin, he lifted her face until she stared into his eyes.

"If I were to make you my wife, I would make it a point to comment upon your captivating nature at least once per day."

"I wouldn't believe your pretty words."

41

"Which is why I will agree to your reprieve." He grinned and dropped his hand. "How was your evening?"

"Does your sister truly tell you everything?" She indicated Cora's chamber to the left of them.

"A question answered by a question." His eyes sparkled. Grasping her arm, he escorted her further down the corridor, the opposite direction of the staircase. He didn't speak until they reached the large window at the end. "I'm wholly interested in the events of last night."

"Cora and I swore we wouldn't speak on the subject," she replied as her gaze dropped pointedly to his hand.

He rolled his eyes and released her. Holding up his arms, he took two exaggerated steps backward. "Would you prefer my sister join this discussion? I can wake her if you are frightened of me."

"You're being foolish, Oliver."

"Am I?"

She took a step toward him, held up one finger, and stabbed him in the chest. "Swear you will not repeat one word to anyone, and when Cora tells you these details, you must act as if it is the first time you've heard it. Do you swear?"

"You're going to be a challenge, aren't you?" Oliver laughed. "If we do marry, I shall never be bored."

"Swear," she growled.

"I swear." He pressed his lips together, swallowing his smile.

"My evening was thwarted by Mr. Hastings. He requested the same dance from both your sister and me. Since neither of us could find him, we decided to search for him." Wilhelmina crossed her arms over her chest, shivering from the chill seeping through her thin nightdress.

"An adventure." Understanding warmed his brown eyes. "Was it the fault of Mr. Hastings, or did my dear sister ensnare you in one of her schemes?"

"Mr. Hastings was the original cause," she replied, her attention diverted by a shadow, which had darted—*if that was possible* —across the far end of the corridor.

Oliver shifted, blocking her view. "I assume the two of you discovered Mr. Hastings."

"He was incoherent and crumpled behind the fir tree," she replied, shifting her attention back to Oliver. "We decided it best to return him to his chamber before any attention was drawn to his predicament."

"Was that your idea or Cora's?"

Wilhelmina side-stepped his question. "Each of us took an arm, and we guided him up the staircase. It was quite a feat to manage."

"I suppose Mr. Hastings should be grateful for your intervention." Oliver tapped his finger on his lips, a thoughtful expression on his face. "However, you've left out an important part of your story… how did you know which chamber was his?"

"You said earlier this evening only our family was residing on this side of the house; I assumed his room was off the other corridor." Wilhelmina offered Oliver a small smile. "We hoped he would recognize his door."

"Without a chaperone, my sister and my future fiancée escorted an intoxicated man to his chamber." Oliver choked, struggling to keep from laughing, and his face contorted into a bizarre half-grin. "Did you find the room?"

"No." Wilhelmina's eyes narrowed, annoyed by Oliver's amusement. "He was too inebriated to assist us."

"What did he do?" The glee fell from Oliver's face, and his back straightened, his attitude snapping to that of a man who needed to defend the honor of his sister.

"He removed his vest and ascot, but nothing else." she quickly added the last part when Oliver's face darkened. "Then he conversed with a painting of Uncle Charles and asked me to dance."

"Did you dance with him?"

She wasn't sure which emotion passed behind Oliver's eyes, but she was certain it wasn't delight.

"Briefly. I tripped on his foot, stumbled, and fell down."

"Mr. Hastings could not catch you?" His soft question sent a ripple of terror rolling down her spine. Mr. Hastings would need protection from Oliver before the night was through.

"He fell also." She bit her lip to stop the words from flowing. Every statement only served to further infuriate her cousin.

"Where was my sister?" he asked.

"She had gone to retrieve Mr. Reid."

"To solve the problem of which chamber belonged to Mr. Hastings?"

Wilhelmina nodded.

"How long were you alone with Mr. Hastings?" A menacing undercurrent accompanied his words.

"Not five minutes," Cora's musical voice replied from behind him.

Oliver whipped around. "What are you doing awake?"

"There's a noisy discussion occurring outside my chamber." She tilted her head. "You couldn't wait until the morning to interrogate her?"

"She stopped me as I passed her chamber!" His indignation rolled down the corridor.

"Then the question should be, what are you doing awake, dear brother?" Cora wrapped her shawl tighter around her torso and tapped her foot, an expectant smirk on her face.

"My activities are not your concern."

"But mine are?" Wilhelmina burst out. "Either I am your fiancée, or I am not. You don't get to act like a jealous husband if you're not going to marry me."

His head twisted around, his eyes bulging. "You were alone with him. Any manner of things could have happened."

"In five minutes?" She arched an eyebrow, her skeptical expression matching Cora's.

Oliver snickered. "I withdraw my protest."

"Why?" She and Cora asked simultaneously.

"Since neither of you is aware of the damage a man can do within that time period, I have no grievance." He clasped his hands behind his back, satisfied with his answer.

But she was aware, well-aware of what Mr. Hastings could do with his mouth and his tongue in five minutes, he could render her completely senseless. The telltale heat crawled across the back of her neck, and she ducked her head, hiding the blush.

"Have a pleasant night, ladies," Oliver called over his shoulder as he strolled toward his chamber. "I shall join you in the dining room tomorrow for breakfast."

When his door closed, Cora dashed forward and grabbed Wilhelmina's arm, hissing as they walked back to Wilhelmina's chamber, "Why was Oliver in the corridor?"

"I don't know. I heard someone curse, and when I investigated the sound, I found your brother sneaking past my door."

"Did he say what he was doing?" Cora pressed.

"Only that he'd been visiting with the person he can't marry."

Pain flitted across Cora's face. "Of course," she replied, releasing her hold on Wilhelmina. "I should return to my chamber as well."

"Cora," Wilhelmina called as her cousin turned away. "Is there truly no way for Oliver to be with his love?"

"I've never met a man more unhappy in his situation." Cora sighed and offered a sad smile, pulling the edges of her shawl closer. "Tomorrow, we shall examine every gentleman's worth who is staying the week." She pressed an airy kiss to Wilhelmina's cheek and turned away without another word.

As Cora disappeared into her room, Wilhelmina wondered which woman had mesmerized Oliver with her charms. It must be someone who'd attended the ball. Crawling underneath the coverlet, she stared at the ceiling, her disquieted mind filtering through the faces of the young women she'd seen that evening. She didn't remember falling asleep.

Her first thought was hunger, accompanied by a low rumbling in her stomach which protested the paltry amount of food she'd consumed the previous day. She climbed from the bed and dressed quietly, taking care not to wake her mother as she slipped out of the room.

Following the mouth-watering smell of bacon, Wilhelmina floated down the staircase, hoping to sneak into the dining room, consume her breakfast, and escape before anyone joined her. As her foot touched the entrance hall floor, she grabbed the banister and swung in a half-circle, careening toward the corridor.

She was moving too quickly to prevent herself from crashing into the bundle of clothing standing beside the fir tree. Rebounding with a gasp, Wilhelmina's apology was out of her mouth before she realized the person standing before her was Mr. Hastings.

"Good morning." He bowed; the automatic response ingrained by society. "I was hoping to speak with you on a personal matter."

"I'm not accustomed to granting private audiences with men," she replied, edging toward the dining room. Her stomach growled. His eyes flicked down, a tiny smile on his mouth.

45

"Would you agree to a meal? We are the only two guests who are awake at this hour." He offered his arm.

She debated his request. What harm could come from sitting at the same table and consuming food? If the conversation became inappropriate, she could take her leave, hopefully with a bit of toast.

"I will agree to your request." She accepted his arm, and they strolled down the corridor. "What matter would you like to discuss with me?"

"I found your hair."

"My hair?" She frowned at him as they passed through the doorway into the dining room.

"Yes, Miss James. I know of no other guest whose hair is as black as the one I discovered this morning." He pulled out a chair, seating Wilhelmina. After taking the chair beside her, he leaned over and murmured, "Why was your hair on my shirt?"

"You fell on me." She pursed her lips, glancing over as a kitchen maid entered the room through a side door, carrying a silver coffee pot and two plates of food. The smell triggered Wilhelmina's stomach, which growled as the maid set a plate in front of her.

"I'm going to need a more detailed explanation," he muttered, his gaze following the maid as she leaned around him to place the second plate and the coffee pot.

Wilhelmina picked up her fork and poked her eggs, waiting to speak until the kitchen maid exited the dining room. "The explanation is simple, Mr. Hastings. You requested a dance, and while we were waltzing, I tripped over your foot and fell, pulling you down with me."

He grimaced. "Was this ungraceful display witnessed by many of the guests?"

"Only two." She set down the fork, selected a piece of bacon, and took a bite, grateful for the distraction of chewing.

Her reply drew a frown to his face. He poured himself some coffee and lifted the cup, his eyes on the steaming liquid.

"Who were the two people?"

"Mr. Reid and Miss Parrish."

"Why were only four of us in the ballroom?" he asked, his voice filled with confusion.

"We weren't in the ballroom." She wasn't going to look at

him, but the strangled cry that came from his throat caused her head to whip up.

"Did we do anything inappropriate?" His face paled, graying until she thought he would faint. The thought made her snicker, her lips pulling into a quick smile. His eyes narrowed. "Are you laughing at me?"

"Merely at the idea of a man fainting in front of me. However, you may put your mind at ease. We danced in the corridor before Mr. Reid escorted you into your chamber." She took a second bite.

"I'm pleased to know nothing improper occurred." He leaned back in his chair and sipped his coffee, his features relaxing. "I had a memory that was plaguing me, but it must have been a dream."

Wilhelmina stopped chewing and forced herself to swallow the bite. She glanced at him, her heart hammering, and asked in what she hoped was a nonchalant tone, "What was your recollection?"

"That I kissed you." He lifted the cup again and froze, his eyes widening, and he dropped the cup, splashing coffee across the table. "I did kiss you."

"Shh," she hissed, her head whipping back and forth. "Please, lower your voice, Mr. Hastings. No one knows."

"No one?"

"Mr. Reid may suspect it, but I haven't spoken about either time to anyone."

"Either?" His eyes were going to pop out of his head. "How many times have I kissed you?"

"Twice, both times under the fir tree." Her eyes flicked to the doorway.

"Why have you not demanded marriage?" He shoved back his chair, rose, and paced the room, dragging his hand through his hair. "I should propose."

"That is not necessary." She twisted around, gesturing for him to quiet down.

"Have you a fiancé already?" he moaned. "I must make amends."

"I'm not engaged," she replied and stood, marching over to him. "Nor do I wish to be connected to a man who loves the drink more than he loves his wife and family. I've experienced that life. Therefore, you don't need to think about what occurred yesterday. I have no desire to demand anything of you."

A thundercloud detonated across his face.

"Your opinion of me is lacking," he growled, stepping forward. The heat from his body rolled over her. "You shouldn't listen to gossip, especially the wagging tongues of last night's guests."

"My opinion is based upon what I've seen of your behavior, Mr. Hastings, which includes attempting to crawl into my bedchamber the night my mother and I arrived." She stretched to her full height, the top of her head coming even with his chin. "However, considering the extraordinary circumstances from which you are currently suffering,"—he flinched—"I'm willing to give you an opportunity to sway my mind."

His mouth twitched into a wolfish smile.

Challenge accepted.

"I look forward to the task, Miss James," he replied.

Their intimate moment dissolved as Mr. Asher Reid and his wife, Eleanor, entered the dining room. Eleanor's younger sister, Lydia, trailed behind them as she had the whole of the previous evening. When they caught sight of Mr. Hastings and Wilhelmina inches apart, they froze.

Spinning, Mr. Hastings greeted them in a booming voice. "Mr. and Mrs. Reid, Miss Daniels, a pleasure to see you this morning. I was hoping the three of you would be interested in playing games in the parlor after breakfast."

"That would be delightful," Mrs. Reid replied, giving her sister's hand a squeeze. The sour expression on Lydia's face disappeared. "We shall meet you in one hour."

"I do hope you will join us as well," Mr. Hastings said, lifting Wilhelmina's hand to his mouth. He pressed a blazing kiss upon her knuckles, his lips brushing across her skin. Releasing her hand, he returned to his seat mumbling, "I so love the taste of apples."

Heat exploded across Wilhelmina's cheeks.

Six

Each time someone passed through the parlor doorway, Wilhelmina glanced up from her cards. She looked up so many times, she thought her head would pop off her neck and roll beneath the table.

One hour. He said one hour, and after two hours crawled by without an appearance from Mr. Hastings, Wilhelmina was convinced he must have become inebriated again and forgotten. She slapped down her card, irritated at herself for wanting to see him and irritated at him for not following through on his word.

With a joyful noise, Cora captured the trick, ending the game. While she and Oliver collected the wagered coins from the table, Miss Daniels vibrated with annoyance. She'd been reluctant to accept Wilhelmina as her partner and had only agreed after Cora convinced Oliver to be hers, a choice Miss Daniels appeared to be regretting.

"Are you purposefully trying to lose, Miss James?" Her sour question was punctuated with a vicious glower.

Knowing her mother would hear of any disrespect, Wilhelmina swallowed her spiteful retort and shook her head, exercising incredible patience as she replied, "I'm attempting to play at your capability, but I am woefully lacking at this game. I hope you forgive me."

She lied.

Wilhelmina was quite skillful at whist, but her mind wasn't on the game, which was why she'd missed playing the queen at an earlier opportunity. However, explaining why her brain was focused on the Stantons' south wing and not on the cards in front of her wasn't an experience she wished to share with any of her tablemates, none of whom she believed had innocent motives for participating in this card game. Considering the covert glances Miss Daniels had been stealing at Oliver, Wilhelmina was certain the younger girl was nurturing a crush on him. Which meant the scowls she'd been shooting toward Wilhelmina likely had to do more with the rumor of Oliver's upcoming proposal and less to do with losing the game.

"Hastings, there you are!" Mr. Benjamin Reid's voice boomed, fueled by several rounds of Snapdragon. "Join us."

Wilhelmina's head whipped up just as Mr. Hastings stepped through the doorway. His gaze swept over the faces of the room's inhabitants, lingering on Wilhelmina's just long enough to entice the blush back into her skin before moving to Mr. Reid's side.

"Please excuse me," Cora murmured, her eyes on the corridor. She rose and hastened from the room, leaving her seat vacant. Wilhelmina stared after her, curious by her cousin's peculiar behavior.

"Do you need a fourth?" Mr. Hasting's deep voice interrupted her thoughts.

"Yes," Miss Daniels replied, her voice a breathy combination of lust and awe. She nearly fell out of her chair, indicating Cora' abandoned seat.

Wilhelmina clamped her hand over her mouth and twisted away, trying to hide her amusement at Miss Daniel's exuberance. Mr. Hastings caught the attempt to conceal her inappropriate reaction and wiggled his eyebrows, causing Wilhelmina to double over, ducking beneath the table, as she choked on her laughter.

"Miss James, are you ill?" Miss Daniels' worried question lacked the warmth one would expect from such an inquiry.

Fanning her face, Wilhelmina sat up, praying the heat would fade from her cheeks, and palmed a coin from the table, which she held up between her fingers. "I felt it strike my foot when I knocked it off the table."

The explanation seemed to satisfy Miss Daniels, who replied with a false smile of gratitude. "I'm grateful you rescued it. We don't have very many coins between us."

"Perhaps we could wager something other than money," Mr.

Hastings said. He plucked the deck from the table and shuffled the cards.

"What would you like to wager?" Oliver folded his hands on the table, a gesture Wilhelmina felt was more of a challenge than an agreement with Mr. Hastings' suggestion.

"The losing team must give the winning team a kiss."

"I agree." The words burst from Miss Daniels' lips the moment Mr. Hastings finished speaking.

Oliver glanced at Wilhelmina, reluctance spilling from his eyes. She shrugged. They would have to kiss in front of everyone eventually, so it might as well be due to a game of whist. He nodded once as if accepting his fate.

"You have a wager."

Miss Daniels beamed, her face glowing as Mr. Hastings dealt the cards. However, her expression changed into a sullen glower when she picked up her cards. Wilhelmina wasn't sure if that meant she had a terrible hand or an excellent one.

"Have you ladies had a lovely morning?" Mr. Hastings asked as Wilhelmina laid down her first card.

Oliver silently slid his beneath hers. The card of lower rank wouldn't capture the trick.

"It would be more delightful if we could win a game," Miss Daniels replied, setting a higher-ranking card on top of Wilhelmina's, capturing the trick from her partner.

Wilhelmina's eyes narrowed. That was a mistake a novice would make, but certainly not one someone as adept as Miss Daniels would choose to do… unless she was purposely making the error.

Her eyes lifted, catching a similar confused expression on Mr. Hastings' face. He turned toward her, the corner of his mouth pulling into a lopsided grin. "Would you like to forfeit, Miss James?"

"No." She set her card on the stack, winning the next trick, then played a low card, which Oliver did as well. When the turn came to Miss Daniels, she fiddled with her cards, unsure which to choose, and asked Oliver for his opinion, which he tried to give without peeking at her hand.

"Your partner doesn't share your tenacity," Mr. Hastings murmured just low enough only Wilhelmina heard him.

"She has her own plan," Wilhelmina muttered in return, her lips barely moving.

"Which is?" He leaned closer.

"To lose," she replied.

"Why would she want to do that?" he asked, his whispered question barely audible over the boisterous Snapdragon game.

"She wishes to express her interest in Mr. Parrish without causing a scene."

"Thank the Lord." Mr. Hastings exhaled loudly, relief washing over his face. "I suppose my arrogance is to blame."

"Your arrogance?"

"Yes, I thought it was me she wanted to kiss." He comically wiggled his eyebrows in an exaggerated movement.

Wilhelmina laughed. "You're safe."

"Am I?" He tilted his head. "Are you not both giving me a kiss?"

"Only if we lose."

"And if you win, then I am to kiss you?" He laid down his card, claiming the trick. "I fail to see how I can lose this game."

"You will also have to kiss Miss Daniels." Her soft murmur caused Mr. Hastings' to twitch, a tiny tic near the corner of his eye, which belied his gentlemanly façade.

"I would be honored to give a kiss to or receive one from any lady." He played a mid-range card and arched an eyebrow as if daring her to play over him, which she did.

Her gaze flicked to Miss Daniels as she leaned over, holding out her hand to Oliver, and pointed at two cards. When Wilhelmina's gaze slid back to Mr. Hastings, he smirked.

She set her cards facedown and glowered at him. "If Mr. Parrish is going to continue assisting Miss Daniels, it seems only fair you assist me."

"You wish to show me your hand?" Mr. Hastings asked, confusion evident on his features. "Perhaps I misunderstood your intentions. I was under the impression you wanted to win the game."

"I do," she hissed. Her gaze returned to Miss Daniels as she ignored Oliver's advice and played the wrong card, losing the trick to him. Wilhelmina rolled her eyes and returned her attention to Mr. Hastings. "You should show me your cards."

Plucking a card from his hand, he tapped it against his chin as if considering her request, then slowly turned it around, showing the value, and set it on the table, his intense gaze holding hers. "I don't need any help with my hand, and,"—he leaned closer, his deep voice swirled around her—"I intend to win."

"I'm surprised you chose to play cards, Mr. Hastings." Oliver interrupted their conversation. "I was given to believe Snapdragon was a game in which you excelled."

There was something in his tone that perturbed Wilhelmina as if Oliver's comment wasn't meant as a compliment. She was offended for Mr. Hastings, and her gaze flicked to the other side of the room.

Gathered around a table, their faces glowing with flickering blue light, were Misters Reid, Mrs. Reid, Mr. Mason, and several guests from last evening whose names had blended into a tangled mess of syllables. At that moment, Mr. Mason whipped his hand out and plucked one flaming brandy-soaked raisin from the bowl. He yelped and ripped his arm back, dropping the raisin on the rim of the bowl, then danced around in a small circle, blowing on his fingers.

Chuckling, Wilhelmina glanced back at Mr. Hastings, who had not replied to Oliver but shuffled the cards in his hand. After a minute, he set them down and lifted his eyes.

"It's the most peculiar thing, Mr. Parrish. Since I've arrived at your uncle's home, I have no taste for anything,"—he glanced at Wilhelmina—"save apples."

An inferno blazed across Wilhelmina's cheeks and crawled down her neck, coating her skin in bright pink. She glowered at him and slapped a card on the table, winning the trick. He stared back, refusing to look away, and licked his lips.

"I had the opportunity to enjoy the sweetest apple the other day, and I daresay, it has turned me off of all other food," he continued, his gaze sliding to Wilhelmina's mouth.

"I've never enjoyed apples," Oliver said and played his turn after Wilhelmina, unaware Mr. Hastings nearly fell out of his chair in delight.

"Never?" Mr. Hastings' managed.

Oliver responded with a deft shake of his head.

"Nor have I." Miss Daniels set down her card, feigning disappointment as Oliver collected the trick.

"Miss Daniels, perhaps the person assisting you shouldn't be your opponent," Wilhelmina said, unable to keep the annoyance from her voice.

Miss Daniels lifted her venomous gaze to Wilhelmina, forcing more horror into her inflection than Wilhelmina thought possible. "Do you believe Mr. Parrish would use my inexperience to his advantage?"

"What man wouldn't," Wilhelmina retorted. It was an inappropriate comment, to be certain, and quite insulting, and it earned a snarl from Oliver.

"Cousin, may I speak with you a moment?" he said, his voice tight.

Wilhelmina nodded and set down her cards. As she rose from her chair, Mr. Hastings offered her a sympathetic smile. She trailed after Oliver, who didn't speak until they reached the entrance hall.

He spun, his face dark.

"I'm aware of the careful instruction you've received from your mother, and I realize my sister has encouraged your recent improper behavior. However, know the freedom I give to her, I will not be extending to my wife. If we marry, you are only to speak on subjects suitable to your station, and you are never to oppose me, in public or private."

"Am I not allowed to speak my mind?" Wilhelmina asked, her eyebrows pulled together, confused by Oliver's sudden change in demeanor.

"No." He moved closer, his jaw clenching. "That is the sacrifice you will make; I will not tolerate impudence."

"I'm not a child." Wilhelmina stepped to him and lifted her chin, shaking with indigence.

"Yes, you are." His eyes blazed. "And you are wasting your day playing cards with me... Or have you relinquished the idea of a love match?"

She wanted to punch him in the middle of his smug face. The alien desire curled through her body, and her hand clenched into a fist.

"I do hope you're not thinking of striking me." Oliver's eyes flicked to her hand.

"I'm considering it," she replied, not because she knew the statement would rankle him but because it was the truth.

He reached down and took her wrist. Lifting her arm, he brought her fist to his face, pushing it against his cheek, and released her hand.

"I'll give you one opportunity."

She pulled her arm back and swung, crying out as pain radiated through her knuckles. She hit him just above his jawline, and the explosion of agony that radiated through her hand nearly brought her to her knees. She yanked her hand back, cradling it against her chest.

"You did it wrong." Mr. Hastings' deep voice sent a shiver sliding down Wilhelmina's spine. She turned as he stepped into the entrance hall.

"This discussion is not your concern." Oliver's narrowed eyes slid to Mr. Hastings.

"The lady has struck you. I cannot imagine anything more concerning than that." Mr. Hastings bared his teeth.

"Regardless of what your inebriated mind may have imagined, I did nothing to earn Miss James' ire." Oliver took a step forward, placing himself between Wilhelmina and Mr. Hastings.

"I am not drunk, and even if I was, Miss James seems a reasonable woman in possession of all her faculties. If she hit you, there must have been a reason." Mr. Hastings peered around Oliver. "Do you need any assistance?"

"Are you offering to strike Mr. Parrish for me?" Wilhelmina asked.

"If your honor requires it."

"It does not but thank you for your proposal."

"Miss James, if I proposed, you'd be unable to refuse." Mr. Hastings' taunting gaze returned to Oliver. "Miss Daniels is anxious to complete the game."

"We shall return momentarily." Oliver turned his back on Mr. Hastings, dismissing him, and grabbed both of Wilhelmina's wrists. "After our game finishes, you are to join the game of Snapdragon."

"I. Don't. Like. Brandy," she replied, enunciating each word, then yanked her arms free, and marched around Oliver, heading toward the parlor. If she had been less of a lady, she would have stomped on his foot as she passed.

She retook her seat and lifted her cards, refusing to glance at Oliver when he sat down. The rest of the game was played in silence, which was only broken when Miss Daniels realized, her voice pitching in hysterical theatrics, if they lost another trick, they'd lose the game. Then, she threw a three.

"Why are you growling at your cards, Miss James?" Mr. Hastings rumbled in her ear.

"My hand hurts," she murmured, not wanting him to know how irritated she was with Miss Daniels.

"If you want to know how to strike someone without injuring yourself, I'd be happy to teach you," Mr. Hastings' muttered in her ear.

She lifted her eyes, certain he was teasing, but his face was quite serious. "You're going to teach me how to hit a man?"

"Or a woman." He shrugged. "Whoever you wish."

"Why?"

"Shouldn't a woman be able to protect herself as well as a man can?" He tilted his head. "I've taught my sister."

Her mind sifted through the gossip her mother had been repeating since the death of Mr. and Mrs. Hastings earlier that year. *Had she mentioned a sister?*

"I don't believe I've met your sister," Wilhelmina replied. "Is she here?"

"Sammie?" Mr. Hastings laughed. "She's only twelve."

"But…" Wilhelmina paused, threw her last king, and won the trick, then threw a ten, the next highest card in her hand.

"But…" Mr. Hastings repeated, encouraging her to continue.

Wilhelmina glanced at Oliver. His attention was on Cora as she entered the parlor. She smiled at them both and ambled over to the game of Snapdragon, scooting in beside Mrs. Reid.

"You can ask me," he said, his voice soft. "No one ever asks me. They simply assume…"

"It's Christmas. Why aren't you spending it with her?" The question burst from Wilhelmina's mouth, and she blushed. "I apologize, Mr.—"

"Don't." He offered her a melancholy smile. "I wanted her to have a happy Christmas. It's best I'm not there."

"I can't imagine how lonely it must be to spend Christmas without your parents and your brother." Wilhelmina ground her teeth as Miss Daniels laid down a king.

"A brother who is a drunk?" Playing low, Mr. Hastings let the trick go to Miss Daniels.

"Your opinion of yourself is lacking." Wilhelmina refused to look at the card Miss Daniels had just played. "I've had a delightful time playing cards with you."

"It's unfortunate you've lost." He set down the knave.

Wilhelmina dropped her eyes to her last card, a nine. With a heavy sigh, she laid down the card. "I will accept defeat."

Miss Daniels squealed and leapt out of her chair, clapping her hands together. "I'll go first."

She began with Mr. Hastings, who pointed to a spot in the center of his right cheek. Miss Daniels bestowed the lightest of kisses upon him, then danced around the table to Oliver. He, too, chose the exact same spot on his cheek, and Miss Daniels, in her delight, toppled into his lap when she attempted to kiss him. He firmly deposited her back in the chair, foregoing his kiss, and turned to Wilhelmina, again pointing at the spot in the center of his cheek.

Rising from her chair, Wilhelmina shot him a glare and ambled around the table. When she reached his side, she bent down and placed a kiss on his cheek, moving away from him before he'd had an opportunity to react. She continued around the table and stopped beside Mr. Hastings, bending down.

He grinned, lifted one finger, and touched the tip to his mouth. Wilhelmina shook her head.

"We had a wager, Miss James."

"Perhaps when you teach me how to strike a man, it will be you I hit."

"That is quite possible." The corner of his mouth pulled into a smile. "I'd like to collect my winnings now."

She leaned down and pressed her mouth to his. It was as if her body had been set on fire, the heat blazing from his lips unimaginable. She was caught between wanting to wrap her arms around him to pull him closer and needing to push him away before someone realized she was moments away from causing the biggest scandal of the year.

Then she moaned.

Seven

Her low sigh went unnoticed by everyone else in the room except Mr. Hastings, whose mouth curved against hers. His tongue darted out, teasing the seam of her lips with impending incineration, and sent flames coursing through her body.

A scream echoed through the room, and Wilhelmina jerked back, fearing the worst as she yanked up her head, seeking the origin of the shriek. It was Cora, waving a handful of raisins and bouncing with delight. Exhaling the breath she didn't realize she'd been holding, Wilhelmina's gaze dropped to Mr. Hastings, who hadn't moved from his current position, astonishment glowing in his eyes, and something else, something she'd never seen in a man before... hunger.

Before he could rise, she raced from the parlor, mumbling a hasty apology over her shoulder as she fled. She skidded to a halt as she reached the entrance hall and froze. Voices echoed down the staircase as her mother descended, flanked by Josephine and Isabelle, a formidable trio of wills.

She should have met them at the bottom of the staircase, greeted them with the respect they deserved, and accompanied them to the sitting-room. However, that choice meant an hour of disappointed clucks and false reassurances of Oliver's intentions. Knowing she didn't possess the patience to endure that experience, she darted toward the fir tree and squeezed behind the boughs. Holding her breath, Wilhelmina squished herself into the corner, praying her mother wouldn't discover her hiding behind the fir tree, since there was no explanation she could think of to allay her mother's temper.

"Their wedding will be the envy of every young woman." Her mother's arrogant voice crawled around the tree, pregnant with enthusiasm.

"I insist we hold the wedding banquet at our home." Aunt Josephine adopted a similar high-pitched squeal of excitement.

Her mother and aunts passed beside the tree, their elaborate matrimonial plans assaulting Wilhelmina's ears. All three ladies' heads turned simultaneously to peer into the parlor as they strolled by the doorway.

"Did you see her?" her mother hissed in a loud whisper.

"No, but I didn't see Oliver either," Aunt Josephine replied. They giggled and entered Aunt Isabelle's private sitting-room, closing the door behind them with a light click.

Wilhelmina waited another minute, then exhaled and peeled herself off the wall. She leaned out from her hiding place, craned around the tree, and screamed.

A pair of blazing blue eyes waited on the other side of the boughs.

The sitting-room door ripped open. Mrs. James' anxious voice echoed down the corridor. "Wilhelmina?"

Wilhelmina grabbed Mr. Hastings by his jacket and yanked him behind the tree. Shoving him against the stairwell, she clamped her hand over his mouth and pressed against him, her body twisted so she could watch the entrance hall over her shoulder.

Her mother's shadow stretched across the floor, inching closer to their hiding place. After a moment, her footsteps faded, and she closed the sitting-room door again. Wilhelmina peeled her fingers away from Mr. Hastings' mouth, and she edged around the tree, checking to ensure her mother was gone.

"Is there a reason you've kidnapped me?" Mr. Hastings' amused question floated over her head.

She spun around. "I didn't kidnap you. I hid you."

"As you wish." He gestured to the tree with a fluid movement. "There are other places we could go if you want privacy."

"I have no intention of going anywhere with you."

"What are your intentions, Miss James?" He leaned against the stairwell and crossed his arms, looking as comfortable as one could be in the tiny space between the boughs and the wall.

"I have none."

"I don't believe that." He reached out and plucked a long, white ribbon from the fir tree, stroking it between his fingers. "Are yours to be married?"

"That is my mother's intention." Her gaze dropped to the ribbon as he wound it around his fingers, weaving it back and forth.

"I suspect she will get her wish." He lifted his eyes to her face. "But I didn't ask about your mother's desires. I asked about yours."

"No one is concerned with what I want." She stepped toward him.

"I am." He unwound the ribbon and draped it over the tree, then pushed off the wall, eliminating the chaste distance between them. He stared down at her, pinning her to the spot with his intense gaze.

"Why did you follow me?" she asked, hoping that the subject change would dispel the butterflies fluttering in her stomach.

"I like apples."

"You must not say that," she murmured, blushing. He was close enough that his musky smell overpowered the pine scent of the fir tree.

"Why?" He tilted his head. "It's the truth."

"It means something different to me than it does to other people."

"What does it mean to you?"

"Mr. Hastings…" She silently pleaded with him, begging him not to force her to admit he'd kissed her twice.

"Are you engaged to Mr. Parrish?" he asked, his voice soft. He brushed a loose hair from her face, and the caress of his fingertips sent a shiver rippling through her body.

"He is to ask me tonight," she replied, unable to tear her eyes from his.

"Do you intend to accept?" He leaned closer, his mouth millimeters from hers.

"I'm expected to."

"Again, that is not what I asked you." He stepped back, dissolving the intimacy between them. "Miss James, you seem quite adept at replying to questions yet not providing an answer. That is an intriguing skill. I wonder how often you share your true opinion."

She bristled at his statement. "I didn't lie to you."

"I haven't accused you of such." He glanced over his shoulder as voices neared the doorway to the parlor and took another large step backward. "I would enjoy another game of cards, the same wager as we previously agreed to... unless you are not allowed to deviate from Mr. Parrish's instructions."

Mr. Hastings was teasing, but his words sliced through Wilhelmina's chest, leaving a deep gash across her heart.

Did Oliver truly expect her to follow his orders without question?

Her mother would expect her to do exactly that. Wilhelmina grimaced and shifted her eyes away from Mr. Hastings' challenging gaze. Her attention fell on the colorful ribbons winding through the fir boughs. She hadn't noticed them decorating the rear of the tree yesterday morning, which meant someone must have added them after she hid the portrait. She hoped that person hadn't damaged the painting. Frowning, her eyes slid over the boughs, hunting for the portrait.

"What are you searching for?" Mr. Hastings asked and leaned forward, bewilderment on his face.

"The painting," she replied, dropping to her knees, and peered under the low-hanging branches, hoping the portrait had fallen through the boughs. "I hid it in the tree."

"What does it look like?"

She twisted her head toward him, an incredulous expression on her face.

"It looks like me."

"No," he chuckled and dropped beside her. "I wasn't insulting your artistic talent. I was asking for the shape and size of the frame. I will look under the tree. A lady shouldn't crawl on the floor."

Sighing, she pushed back onto her knees and held up her hands, indicating the measurement. He nodded and bent over, taking her place, then slithered beneath the boughs. The top half of his torso disappeared underneath the fir tree.

"I don't see anything." His muffled voice came from the

other side of the base. "Are you certain someone didn't move it to a different part of the tree?"

Wilhelmina stood, scooted out from behind the tree, and walked around the front, her gaze inspecting the branches.

"Mr. Hastings! What are you doing?" Cora, exiting the parlor on the arm of her brother, froze in the doorway, her gaze locked on Mr. Hasting's chestnut head, which poked out from beneath the boughs.

He crawled out from under the tree, rose, and brushed the needles from his sleeves nonchalantly as if the activity were a common occurrence for him.

"The portrait Miss James painted for her mother has vanished. She placed it on the tree yesterday morning and discovered it missing just now. She was distraught, so I offered to search under the boughs."

Hands clasped behind his back, Oliver strode across the corridor and stopped in front of Wilhelmina, his gaze sliding over her face. After a long minute, he reached out and detangled a piece of fir tree from her hair. His icy voice sent a tremor rolling down her spine.

"Did you find the portrait?"

She licked her lips, her gaze following his hand as it returned to his side. Oliver's proximity was unnerving. "We did not."

"Would you like my assistance?" There was a hidden taunt behind the question, and she found herself again wanting to strike Oliver in the face.

Why had she not noticed this domineering quality in him? It couldn't have grown overnight, and such a temperament wouldn't improve with time. Perhaps she ought to accept Mr. Hastings' instruction on punching.

She felt Mr. Hastings slide behind her, indicating he was near enough to hit Oliver if the occasion warranted the action, and she was quite certain Mr. Hastings would relish the opportunity, although she didn't know why there was animosity between them.

Inhaling a deep breath, she clasped her hands in front of her waist and adopted a submissive pose, but she couldn't lower her gaze. Her head refused to bow, no matter how many silent commands she gave it. The whole situation was comical, and she would have laughed aloud if she wasn't terrified of the burgeoning darkness blossoming across Oliver's face.

"Mr. Hastings has already crawled beneath the fir tree." She gestured at the broken boughs near her feet. "I cannot imagine if you repeat the process, you will discover the missing portrait."

Mr. Hastings, to his credit, didn't react. Oliver, however, nearly split himself in half with anger. His hand whipped out and closed around Wilhelmina's arm. Pinching the skin, he jerked her forward. She slammed against his chest.

"We've already spoken once today about your insolence."

"Oliver." Cora glided forward, her hand outstretched.

His cold eyes flicked to her. "Stay where you are."

"It's not her fault." Cora ignored his command and took two more steps.

"Whose is it?" Oliver twisted around. "Is it mine?"

"It is no one's." She placed her hand on her brother's shoulder. Dragging it down his arm, she stopped at his fingers and peeled them off Wilhelmina's wrist, one by one. "This is the arrangement that was made by Father. You must honor it."

He pouted, cajoled into silence, and stood in the center of the entrance hall like a sullen child. After a minute, he lifted his eyes to Wilhelmina. "If it is of import to you, then I shall find your portrait."

It was not an apology, and she had a horrible feeling there would never be an apology for any slight he administered over the course of their life together.

Spinning on his heel, he marched into the parlor and in a booming voice, requested all the inhabitants stop their games instantly and gather around the fir tree. They spilled into the entrance hall, wearing various degrees of confusion on their faces. The din drew Wilhelmina's mother and her aunts from the sitting-room, and they joined the fringe of the group gathered around the tree.

Oliver appeared beside Wilhelmina, inserting himself between her and Mr. Hastings, and clapped his hands together, silencing the crowd.

"I have an announcement." He paused, dragging out the silence. "The portrait Miss James intended to give to her mother is missing. It was placed upon the fir tree yesterday morning and is no longer among the boughs. We need your help to find it."

Wilhelmina caught the grimace her mother flashed as she turned and pushed past Aunt Isabelle, heading toward the sitting-room. The door slammed. A missing portrait was not the announcement she wanted to hear. Wilhelmina wondered if Oliver hadn't conceived this display to annoy both Mrs. James and his own mother, who flounced after Mrs. James, wearing the same grim expression.

There were murmurs of excitement from the guests at the idea of turning the search into a game. Mr. Mason suggested the man, or woman, who discovered the missing portrait should be allowed to choose the person they wished to partner with for the first dance of the evening. The scandalous suggestion was met with approval, and the group rapidly dispersed throughout the house.

"Hastings, a word." Mr. Benjamin Reid stopped beside Mr. Hastings and clapped a hand on his shoulder.

Mr. Hastings' gaze flicked to Wilhelmina as if requesting her approval, then back to Mr. Reid. He nodded once and followed Mr. Reid down the corridor toward the dining room.

Wilhelmina turned, expecting to find Oliver scowling beside her, but he had vanished, along with Cora. She was alone in the entrance hall, surrounded by snatches of laughter that echoed through the house.

She circled the tree again, her gaze moving glacially across the branches, inspecting each bough. She held little hope she would find it hidden in the tree, but she couldn't think of another place to search. No one knew the painting was there, save the person who added the ribbons... *and Mr. Hastings.*

The nagging thought popped into her mind. When she first discovered the portrait was missing, he seemed more than willing to assist her, even crawling beneath the tree, and soiling his jacket in his attempt to help.

Unless it was a ruse...

Chewing her lip, her eyes flicked to the staircase. If he had taken it, he would have hidden it in his chamber, the only logical place. Due to Mr. Reid's assistance last night, she knew which south wing chamber belonged to Mr. Hastings, and with Mr. Hastings distracted, this was the most opportune time to search through his chamber.

Gathering her skirt, she raced up the staircase, her head swiveling left and right as she darted around the corner and dashed down the empty corridor toward Mr. Hastings' chamber.

She skidded to a stop in front of the door and, before she could change her mind, ripped open the door and rushed inside. She closed the door behind her with a soft click, leaning against the smooth wood. Her hand tightened on the handle, reluctant to release the one tangible item preventing her from rifling through a stranger's possessions.

The room was shrouded in darkness, the drapes drawn across the windows. The only light was provided by a fire crackling in the fireplace, the heat emanating from the hearth indicating the fire had been recently tended.

Her gaze, once accustomed to the dimness, slid over the room, decorated in a similar fashion as the chamber she was sharing with her mother. At the base of the bed was a trunk, the lid partially open, and she decided that would be the best place to start her search. Crossing the room, she knelt in front of the trunk and lifted the lid. Inside, stacked in haphazard piles, were stockings, drawers, and linen shirts. She poked through the clothing, trying not to think of Mr. Hastings wearing the garments she was currently sorting through. Rising on her knees, she leaned into the trunk, digging toward the bottom.

"What the devil are you doing?"

Wilhelmina squeaked and spun around, her hand buried in the trunk. Mr. Hastings stood in the doorway, his face a blend of annoyance and amusement. She ripped her hand back, slammed the lid down, and stood.

"I was searching for my portrait."

"And you thought my trunk would be the ideal place to check?" He stepped into the room.

"You were the only person who knew where I hid it." She took a small step toward the doorway, unsure if his final reaction would be anger.

"That does seem to be a logical argument." He moved, blocking her escape. "I don't want you to marry Mr. Parrish."

"Are you offering yourself as a replacement?" She arched a daring eyebrow.

"I'm asking for an opportunity to prove that I am worthy of your attention."

"I have already told you, I have no interest in marrying a—"

"A drunk," he interrupted, "I remember your words."

65

"Then you understand why I must refuse you." She craned her head, peering around him at the empty corridor behind him.

"I've stopped," he replied.

"You've stopped?" Her gaze snapped back to his face.

"Yes."

"Is it that simple?"

"It is not." He offered a half-smile.

"How do I know you're telling me the truth?"

Mr. Hastings kicked the door closed, hooked his arm around her waist, and spun her in a circle, backing her into the door.

"I can prove it." His mouth descended and captured hers in a rough kiss.

Tracing the seam of her lips, his tongue teased her mouth open and plunged inside, tangling with her tongue. His hips pressed into her, his grip tightening around her body as he sucked her lower lip into his mouth, biting down gently.

She moaned, longing to curl into his arms, but the gravity of their situation overtook her, and she broke the kiss, her head spinning. Pushing against his chest, she pulled back, and her head smacked against the door.

"Why did you do that?" she panted, the heat fading from her skin.

"You don't like brandy," he replied and leaned forward, bumping his nose against hers. "And I no longer taste like it."

Her jaw dropped.

"I'm asking for an afternoon to change your mind."

His fingers slid up her side, skated dangerously close to the swell of her breast—her breath caught as tingles rippled across her skin. Eyes closing, her head tilted back, exposing her throat. He continued his slow blazing path upward, skimming his fingers over her collarbone and along her jawline, then grasped her chin and tugged it down. She opened her eyes, her heart thrumming.

"Will you give me that?" he asked, his voice thick.

"Do you swear to teach me how to strike a man?"

"A specific man?"

"I have no man in mind, Mr. Hastings." She struggled to keep her face expressionless.

"I think you do, Miss James." He brushed his thumb across her lips, sending another bout of tingles racing through her body.

What was it about his touch that robbed her of all capability for reason?
"One hour," she said.

"Two," he murmured. She must have nodded her ascent because he smiled. "Now, what shall I do about discovering you in my chamber?"

Eight

"I'm not in your chamber," she replied, conscious of a growing hardness pressing against her abdomen.

Keeping her body trapped against the door, Mr. Hastings glanced to his right and left in an exaggerated movement. When he returned his gaze to her, his eyes widened with mock fear.

"Whose chamber are we in?"

"You are in your chamber. I am elsewhere," she hissed.

"Where are you?" He trailed his knuckles under her jaw, leaving a path of fire across her skin, then leaned forward and touched his mouth to her ear, whispering, "Should I choose to seek you out, I'd like to know where to look."

She swallowed, her heart beating rapidly. The rumors about Mr. Hastings' roguish abilities were quite true and, as dangerous as he was to her resolve while intoxicated, his talents while sober would lead to ruin. She pressed against his chest, her attempt to distance herself destroyed by the sensation of his muscles moving beneath her fingers. She gasped.

He glanced down, amusement in his eyes, and captured her wrists, holding her hands against his chest. "Am I the only man you've touched?"

She lowered her eyes and mumbled, "Mr. Parrish kissed me."

"Did you enjoy it?"

Not able to tell his mood by his voice, she glanced up, catching a dark glower as it fluttered across his face.

"It was pleasant."

Mr. Hastings' snorted. "Did you tell him?"

"I did."

"Did you feel the same when I kissed you?"

"No." She licked her lips, debating the admission. "It was like fire."

"It was for me as well," Dipping his head, he pressed his mouth to hers.

The smoldering inferno that had previously blistered her lips exploded through her body, blazing every inch of skin. With a growl, he shoved her against the door, imprisoned her wrists above her head, and thrust his tongue into her mouth.

Need flowed through her, the unknown feeling driven by an all-consuming blaze coursing through her veins. She kissed him back, her tongue tangling with his as she jerked against the iron grip holding her arms above her head.

Releasing her arms, his hands slid down her torso, setting her body aflame, and wrapped around her hips. He yanked her forward, lifting her and pinning her against the door. Fingers tightening around her thighs, he pushed her legs apart, ground himself into her center, his tongue moving in rhythm with his hips.

Her fingers curled around his biceps, digging into the muscles as he rubbed himself between her legs, his hard length grinding through layers of clothing. It felt as though she would rip apart. Each movement intensified the remarkable sensation ricocheting through her body. His mouth wandered to her throat, trailing tiny nips across her skin.

Soft cries falling from her lips, her hips mirrored his rhythm, rocking each time he thrust forward. Her stomach clenched, winding tighter as her breath came in short gasps. He quickened his pace, grinding against her with such force, she thought their clothes would incinerate. Her body stiffened, her fingernails sank into his arms, and she cried out as her body ripped apart. His mouth covered hers, swallowing the sound while she convulsed against him.

When she stopped shaking, he broke the kiss and set her on her feet. Stepping a respectable distance back, he pulled his jacket from his shoulders and flung it at the trunk, his wary gaze on her as if she were a caged animal.

"Am I ruined?" Her meek voice barely crossed the space between them.

He laughed, then realizing her distress at his response, smoothed his face and replied with conviction, "No."

"But we…" She bit her lip and gestured at the door, heat blazing across her cheeks.

"We?"

"We had *intercourse*," she whispered the word, afraid the mere mention would summon her mother to the room.

"No, we did not." He strode to the armoire and pulled it open.

"Then…"

"There are ways to satisfy those desires that don't lead to children." He leaned around the open door, his gaze sliding over her body. "And as much as I would enjoy spending the afternoon teaching them to you, I don't think I'll be given that opportunity." He ripped a coat from the armoire, shook it out, and shoved his arms into the sleeves.

She took a step toward him, her hands outstretched in an awkward attempt to shush him. "It's improper to say those things. Someone will hear."

"We are alone."

"We shouldn't be. If we are discovered…"

"I came to my chamber to change my coat, which was stained with sap from the fir tree." He buttoned his coat. "And you, Miss James, by your own admission, were elsewhere. There is no need to worry about a scandal."

"Are you certain the third chamber is Mr. Hastings' room?" A high-pitched giggle echoed down the corridor.

"Yes, I saw him exit earlier this morning," a man's voice replied.

Wilhelmina's eyes rounded. Her terrified gaze locked on Mr. Hastings, who stood frozen in the center of his room, an incredulous expression on his face. He strode forward, placed a finger to his lips, and ushered Wilhelmina behind the door.

When the handle moved, Mr. Hastings grabbed it and yanked the door open, startling the person on the other side.

"Is there something I can assist you with, Mr. Mason?" Mr. Hastings asked, an unspoken threat in his question.

Mr. Mason stumbled over his tongue, struggling to find an

excuse to explain why he was opening the door to Mr. Hastings' chamber without invitation.

"Mr. Hastings," the feminine voice purred, "I'm so pleased we were able to find you. After our game this morning, I was hoping we could arrange another contest. I would be delighted to offer a repeat of our earlier wager."

Recognizing Lydia Daniels' breathy tone, Wilhelmina growled, grinding her teeth together. At the sound, Mr. Hastings reached out, his arm hidden behind the door, and placed his hand on her shoulder, giving it a light squeeze.

"I would be delighted to join the game, Miss Daniels, although it is a shame to leave off searching for Miss James' portrait after such a short time. I do hope someone discovered its location." The hand holding Wilhelmina's shoulder gave another gentle squeeze, then Mr. Hastings extended one finger and dipped it beneath her collar, tracing a light pattern across her skin.

She shivered, sinking her teeth into her lip to keep from making a sound, nearly crying out when his finger pushed lower and brushed over her breast.

"However, I fear it may be irreversibly lost," Mr. Hastings continued, giving no indication he was aware of the effect of his wicked finger as it teased her nipple.

"We fear the same thing," Mr. Mason replied, having apparently regained some of his composure.

"That is a shame." Mr. Hastings removed his finger, traced it down Wilhelmina's arm, then clasped her hand in a silent farewell, and stepped around the door, opening it wide enough to show the inside of the chamber but not enough to reveal Wilhelmina's hiding place. "Come. I shall help you seek out Miss James. Perhaps she would like to join our game."

Mr. Hastings strode through the doorway and closed the door behind him with a definitive click. As the trio tottered toward the staircase, he spoke vociferously of the upcoming festivities that evening, his voice carrying down the corridor. Once Wilhelmina could no longer hear him, she opened the door a sliver and peered into the corridor.

It was empty. She darted out of Mr. Hastings' chamber and shut the door behind her. Fear exploded in her chest when the door's heavy thud echoed down the corridor. She froze, pressing herself against the wall. When she was certain she was alone, she sprinted down the corridor toward the staircase. She debated concealing herself in her chamber for the rest of the day, but the thought of a confrontation with her mother was too much to bear, so she settled on the library as her destination, praying she could reach the room without notice, and avoid the invitation for another game of cards with Miss Daniels.

When Wilhelmina reached the staircase, she paused, her gaze sweeping over the entrance hall. It, too, was bereft of guests. She lifted her skirts and dashed down the steps. Her shoes slipped on the entrance hall floor as she flew around the corner, running pell-mell for the library.

The library held no appeal for any of the guests on this snowy day, save Wilhelmina, who crawled into the window alcove, partially hidden by the curtains, and sat on the cushioned bench, watching the flurries drift down like fluffy bits of cotton.

She was grateful for the silence, for it gave her the opportunity to think over what had occurred with Mr. Hastings. She flushed, recalling her wanton behavior and the extraordinary sensations he'd wrung from her body. While these thoughts were not conducive to finding her a suitable husband, she entertained them long enough to wonder how many other women Mr. Hastings had pleasured with the same method.

"Had you told me your whereabouts when I inquired about them, I wouldn't have spent the past twenty minutes searching for you." Mr. Hastings' deep voice reverberated in the library.

Wilhelmina spun on the bench, unable to keep the joyous smile from her face. "I assumed you had begun the game without me. Miss Daniels is an eager player."

"I daresay she will kiss every man in this house before the week is through," he murmured, then grinned, knowing his comment was inappropriate. "I surrendered my seat to Mr. Allandale. Your kiss is the only one I want to win." Crossing the room, he stopped in front of her, bowed low, and held out a thin box, which he'd been hiding behind his back.

"What is this?" she asked, setting the box on her lap.

"It's a gift."

She frowned, her fingers plucking the twine tied around the box. "When did you have time to make me a gift?"

"I stole it."

Her head whipped up. "From whom?"

"My sister." He grinned.

"You can't give me your sister's gift." She held it out.

"I will purchase another one for her." He pushed the box back. "She has enough books to keep her occupied."

"Books cannot replace love."

He flinched. "You and Mr. Reid share the same opinion."

"When was the last time you saw your sister?"

Mr. Hastings shuddered as if taken hold of by a terrible memory as his eyes slid to the window. "It's been a long time."

He offered no further words, and Wilhelmina, uncertain how to respond to his sullen attitude, dropped her gaze to the box. She untied the twine, pulling it free of the package, and dropped it beside her on the bench. Lifting the lid, she gasped. Nestled inside was an exquisite mahogany box that contained porcelain pans filled with a kaleidoscope of moist watercolors, brushes, scrapers, and storage tins. Beneath the paintbox was a stack of paper. Her head whipped up.

"I cannot accept this."

"You must." He glanced at her. "I've already told Mr. Reid I damaged his gift."

"His gift?" Wilhelmina's voice cracked. "Why would you do that?"

"Since I can't give you back your portrait, I will paint you a new one." He wiggled his eyebrows, his playful demeanor returning as he dipped a hand into the paintbox and retrieved a brush. He sat beside her on the bench and squinted at her, holding up his thumb as if he were judging the proportions of her face.

"Are you a skillful painter?" Wilhelmina asked, giggling as he extracted a sheet of paper.

"Not in the slightest." He set the box lid on his lap, placed the sheet of paper on top of it, and swirled his brush in the closest pot of color.

He gave her no direction, did not pose her body, or adjust curtains to alter the light streaming into the room. He just attacked the paper with broad, swift strokes. After fifteen minutes, she craned forward, inspecting his progress, and laughed.

"Mr. Hastings," she said as he lifted his head, "that is an apple."

He glanced down with a merry grin. "Indeed, it is."

"You were supposed to paint my face."

"Alas, I cannot." He sighed dramatically. "I had hoped, once the brush was in my hand, some of my sister's talents would pass to me. However, they did not, and as I attempted to paint your lovely face,"—Wilhelmina blushed at his words—"I realized it was impossible to recreate such beauty, so I painted the image that comes to mind whenever I think of you."

"Do you think of me often?" she asked, her skin threatening to adopt a permanent pink tinge.

"Every time I lick my lips," he murmured.

It was a scandalous statement, one that certainly would have set the gossiping tongues wagging, but there was no one to hear Mr. Hastings' inappropriate words. Even though the house was teeming with people, many of whom had paraded past the open library door since Mr. Hastings' had begun his portrait, not one person dared to step into the room.

He set down the paintbrush, and with a flourish, turned the painting around. It was a red circle, simple, not quite round, and lacking the definition a practiced artist would have had in regard to light and shadow. However, the glee splitting his face was immeasurable.

"We should hide it in the tree," he said, rising from the bench, and hastened from the room.

Wilhelmina chased after him, her shoes pounding in the corridor as she darted around the corner. He had vanished! She frowned, skidding to a stop in the entrance hall, and spun in a full circle searching for Mr. Hastings.

"Miss James," a hissed whisper came from the fir tree. Mr. Hastings popped out from the small alcove, his eyes shining, and waved her over.

"You will get sap on your coat again," she warned as she approached him.

"The only reason my coat was ruined was because I crawled under the tree." He grabbed her wrist, pulling her behind the boughs.

His mouth found hers, igniting the embers that had been floating through Wilhelmina's blood since earlier that day. She returned the kiss, wrapping her arms around his torso and pulling him closer, her body longing for the fire only he seemed able to provide. His hands tightened around her hips, digging into her flesh, his arousal apparent.

A soft squeak reverberated above them. They broke apart and glanced up, peering through the fir tree's high boughs at the staircase, but no other sound followed.

"Do you think anyone saw us?" she mouthed, terror pumping through her veins.

He shook his head, then pointed at the painting nestled among the greenery, and asked in a hushed voice, "Would your mother appreciate my talent?"

"My mother doesn't share the same humor," she whispered, stifling a giggle.

"Nor does she understand why you are currently hiding behind the tree." Her mother's icy voice sent a shiver of terror sliding down Wilhelmina's back.

Wilhelmina spun, clasped her hands in front of her waist, and curtsied. "Good afternoon, Mother. Have you had a pleasant day?"

"No." Mrs. James' critical gaze slid over Mr. Hastings, who hovered a respectable distance behind Wilhelmina. "I was expecting to hear of a marriage proposal."

"I'm certain you will by this evening," Wilhelmina replied. She stepped out of the alcove, offering her mother a pacifying smile.

"I thought you were spending the day with your cousins." Her mother glowered at Mr. Hastings over Wilhelmina's head.

"Mr. Hastings offered to help find your missing gift." She gestured at him. "He's been searching since we discovered the portrait missing."

"You've been hunting for it all day?" A peculiar expression crossed her mother's face as if she knew they weren't telling her the complete truth.

"We have." Mr. Hastings stepped forward and bowed low. Mrs. James' eyes flicked to him.

"Thank you, Mr. Hastings." Her dismissive tone rankled Wilhelmina, but Mr. Hastings merely nodded, apparently accustomed to the indifference. His gaze slid to Wilhelmina.

"I'm sorry we were not able to recover your original painting,

Miss James. I appreciate the time you spent with me today. It was most entertaining." He bowed again and spun on his heel, ambling toward the parlor.

"Come, Wilhelmina, we must find Oliver, I'm certain he has something of great import to ask you." Mrs. James, her face mottled with anger, wrapped her hand around Wilhelmina's arm and steered her toward the staircase, a low hum of chastisements falling from her tongue.

As her mother ushered her up the staircase, Wilhelmina glanced at the parlor. Before Mr. Hastings entered the room, he turned, his eyes finding Wilhelmina. He held her gaze a moment, then blew her a kiss.

Nine

"Oliver!" Wilhelmina's relieved voice echoed down the corridor. Her mother released her arm, melting into the shadows and vanishing down the staircase with a smug grunt.

He flinched upon hearing his name but refused to slow his speed, heading toward his chamber. Wilhelmina was faced with chasing him down or accosting him in his private quarters. She hoisted her skirt and darted down the corridor, flinging a threat at the back of his head.

"If you don't stop, I will tell your mother of your scheme to delay proposing indefinitely."

Oliver stopped, twisted around, and marched back down the corridor, his face a mask of fury. Meeting her halfway between his chamber and hers, he jabbed his finger into her shoulder, his eyes bulging.

"I gave you a reprieve, and you repay me with threats."

"You gave yourself the reprieve," she retorted, jutting out her chin, and smacked away Oliver's hand.

Oliver opened his mouth to argue and deflated, his shoulders rolling forward. "You're correct, I didn't make the decision for you…" A heavy sigh escaped him. "Tell me, did you find your fire?"

The soft question disarmed her, and she lifted her gaze, astonished to discover sadness leaking from his eyes. "It's an inappropriate match."

"Love doesn't care for propriety."

Wilhelmina forced a smile. "Are you cross?"

"My dear cousin, you are enamored with a man you cannot marry. Who understands my situation more than you?"

"But—"

"I have tried not to blame you, to accept that our marriage would benefit both of our families." Oliver grabbed her shoulders as if he meant to shake her but stopped before completing the forceful act. "I cannot forgive you for taking the place of the person I wish you to be, and I don't want to punish you for that fault."

He placed a finger over her lips, stopping her words.

"These past two days, I haven't acted as the cousin you knew and loved." He grimaced, acknowledging his rude behavior. "I've acted as my father expected and have treated you with indifference. Each time I spoke, I saw my words injure you, carving irreparable damage to your kind heart, yet I did nothing to stop your pain."

He sighed again, the melancholy sound filled with regret, and released her. Staggering backward, he bumped into a long, thin table and knocked it against the wall. He leaned on the table, wrapped his fingers around the edge, steadying himself, and lifted his gaze to her face.

"Can you forgive me?"

"Yes." Wilhelmina's reply was instantaneous.

Uncle Gilbert was an intimidating man whose imposing presence had her fleeing any room he entered, a childhood habit she carried into adulthood. If anyone could force Oliver to act outside of his character, it was her uncle.

After a moment of silence, Oliver lifted himself up, swinging on his arms as if testing the strength of the table, then sat in the center, his long legs dangling a foot above the floor. He patted the space next to him.

Wilhelmina shook her head.

"Cora would do it," he said, his eyes sparkling at the challenge.

"Cora doesn't have the same mother as I."

"I don't see your mother… or mine."

She grumbled at him, an unladylike response, but it encompassed her mood, and since Oliver had seemingly returned to the Oliver she remembered from her youth, she allowed herself the freedom.

Spinning around, she pulled up her skirt two inches, rose on her toes, and backed into the table, pinning the skirt between her legs and the table's edge. She placed her hands on both sides of her, curled her fingers around the smooth wood as Oliver had, and lifted herself, scooting back until she perched on the edge, and her shoes hung several feet above the floor.

"I'm thankful that you found me." Oliver reached out and placed his hand on top of hers, keeping his eyes on the portrait across from them. "It prevents me from having to seek you out tomorrow before I depart for the coast."

"You're leaving tomorrow?" Wilhelmina's head whipped toward him, but he refused to look at her.

"I intended to ask for your hand today, then retract my proposal in writing, claiming I had discovered an illegitimate child."

"Have you?"

"Certainly not." Oliver bristled and tore his gaze from the painting. "I've never been with a woman, and if I had, I would have married her straight away."

"How will you produce a child? Surely, some proof would be required." Wilhelmina pulled her hand from beneath his.

"By the time my father discovers the claim is false, you,"—he bumped her with his shoulder—"will be engaged to someone else."

"And if I'm not?"

Oliver's eyes flicked up. He stared at the end of the corridor as if he'd seen something, then returned his gaze to Wilhelmina without acknowledging the distraction.

"Miss James, I have no intention of asking for your hand this evening or any other evening. There is no purpose for us to continue this conversation." He pushed off the table, landed lightly on his feet, and twisted around, his face emotionless. "I don't want you as my wife, and I am willing to accept whatever punishment my father will award me for disobeying his instructions, including disownment."

He bowed, ignoring the astonished expression on Wilhelmina's face, and strolled down the corridor. Opening the door to his chamber, he entered and kicked the door closed behind him.

Wilhelmina stared, her jaw hanging open as the hopelessness of her situation crashed down on her. She sniffed, dabbing at the tears forming in the corners of her eyes.

Oliver had rejected her.

He was her last chance, the only man that would have her without a dowry, and he'd changed his mind, deciding exile was more acceptable than a life with her. Tears streaming down her face, she placed her palm against her mouth, biting down to keep her sobs from echoing in the quiet corridor. She'd failed her mother and herself. She was going to spend the rest of her life alone.

"Miss James?"

Mr. Hastings' tentative voice startled her. She glanced toward the end of the corridor, wiping her eyes, and struggled to crawl off the table without exposing herself. He ambled closer and stopped several feet away, keeping a respectable distance—and the length of the table—between them.

"Instead of watching my discomfort, you could assist me," she snapped.

"Why are you sitting on a table?" he asked, moving around the side. He stopped in front of her, his body not quite near enough to touch.

She licked her lips. "Mr. Parrish dared me."

"If I dared you to do something, would you?" He stepped closer, the heat from his body rolling over her skin.

"No." Her voice hitched as he leaned in.

"I don't believe you," he murmured, nudging her knees further apart with his hips.

"I don't trust your intentions." Her hands slid between them and pressed against his chest. She wasn't strong enough to push him away, but Mr. Hastings, understanding her intention, allowed her to regain some space between them.

"You shouldn't." His gaze dropped to her lips.

"Then, I'd like you to leave."

"I heard you crying," he replied with a frown. To prove his point, he dragged a fingertip beneath her eye, collecting the left-over moisture, which he held up.

"I wasn't crying."

Mr. Hastings pressed his lips together as if considering his next statement. She was certain, had he been Oliver, he would have lacked the patience to draw out the truth of her misery, but Mr. Hastings wiped the tear on his jacket lapel, making a grand gesture as he dragged his finger over the material, and tilted his head, a pleasant expression on his face, as if he had nothing else to occupy his time.

"Why was water staining your face?"

She meant to tell him it was exhaustion, fatigue from the day's activities that had left her in such a despondent state, but as she stared into his earnest blue eyes, she found the truth flowing from her lips.

"Mr. Parrish is no longer interested in forming an attachment with me. He has sworn he will never propose."

"That can be no great loss. I'm certain you have other suitors."

"I have already explained to you that I possess no dowry to entice any other gentleman." She glanced down, her gaze dropping to her lap.

"A gentleman in love doesn't need a bribe."

Her head jerked up. "A dowry isn't a bribe."

"Is it not?" He grinned, floating closer, and his intoxicating scent washed over her. "A father pays a man a generous sum of money to take his daughter from his household and to support her for the rest of her life. That sounds like a bribe."

Wilhelmina snorted. "I will not disagree with your definition, although I don't know any gentleman without the need of a bribe."

"I do." His eyes blazed.

"Mr. Reid is not interested in my hand."

A flash of darkness zipped through Mr. Hastings' eyes. "You would be as unhappy with him as you would have been with Mr. Parrish."

"Am I not fit to marry any man?"

"I can only think of one man who meets my qualifications." He leaned down, his mouth hovering millimeters from hers.

"Why are you doing this to me?" The words were through her lips before she could stop them.

"Doing what?" His soft voice wrapped around her, causing her heartbeat to triple in speed.

"You're not a husband," she murmured as her eyes dropped

to his sinful mouth. Her stomach clenched, anticipation flowing through her veins.

"I am not," he rumbled, the vibrations rippling over her skin. His proximity was confusing her mind.

"That is, you don't want to be a husband."

Could he hear her heart? It thrummed rapidly, threatening to burst from her chest.

"I don't?"

"Mr. Hastings—"

"Edward," he corrected. "That is the name I expect to hear the next time I bring you to release."

"You cannot say those things." She reddened, her entire body encased in embarrassment.

"I should not." He bumped his forehead against hers, sending a shiver of delight rippling through her body. "I can say whatever I wish."

"Why are you pursuing me?" she asked, her breath catching. The question was accompanied by a moan, a quiet admission that his hips worked their way between her thighs, and his arousal now dug enticingly into her center.

"I remember meeting you." He touched his mouth to her cheek, but instead of pulling back, his lips lingered on her skin, kissing a blazing path along her jawline.

Her body betrayed her, and her head tilted back, allowing him access to her throat. She was losing the battle to retain her senses.

"You were drunk." She forced out the words.

"I was, but I still recall every detail, from the boughs in your hair to the sweet taste of your lips." He leaned back, his eyes searching hers. "I thought you were a dream, a false image created by drink, and it brought on a depression so great, I returned downstairs to search behind the fir tree for any proof you existed."

"Did you find my painting?" she whispered.

He nodded once, a light pink tinge crawling into his face. "I'm ashamed to admit, I spent much of the morning conversing with your picture."

"You do that a lot."

"Whose portrait did you find me speaking with?" He leaned close again and inhaled slowly as if memorizing her scent.

"We had a lovely conversation with Uncle Charles."

His lips brushed hers, and the flames smoldering between them exploded. Mr. Hastings captured her mouth with a growl. His arms wrapped around her body, his fingers curling into her hips, and he yanked her against him as his tongue pushed past her lips, tangling with hers.

It was as if she were melting through the table. Her body, turned to molten lava by his wicked tongue, curled into his embrace, and she rubbed herself against him, craving the pleasure he'd introduced to her earlier that day. He obliged, grinding into her, his hips moving in rhythm with hers. Her stomach clenched, need unfurling in her stomach. Her hands inched forward and claimed his waist, her fingers digging into his hips.

Only Mr. Hastings had this effect over her, this peculiar ability to direct her body to respond to his every touch. Her muscles tensed, her legs parting further. One of his hands slipped between their bodies, navigating the layers of clothing. His fingers parted the slit of her drawers and brushed against her core. She cried out, wiggling against him, and his finger slid across her again. On the third pass, it pushed inside her. She broke the kiss with a gasp, her hands flying up to his chest, and dragged in a shaky breath.

"You're making it impossible for me to think clearly."

"Then I am doing it correctly." His eyes glowed with fire as he retracted his hand from beneath her skirts.

"We are in the corridor."

"Would you prefer somewhere more private?"

She squeezed her eyes shut. "I would prefer that your interest in me fades."

"Untruths don't become you, Miss James," he whispered.

"You will deter potential suitors."

"That is my intention."

Her eyes snapped open. "Why do you want to ruin my chances at happiness?"

"All I want is for the woman I love to be happy, and I can't picture her achieving that result with any other man, save myself."

"The woman you love…" She frowned. "Mr. Hastings, I'm flattered, but you hardly know anything about me."

"Matches are made on much less."

"You are drunk."

"I am not." His eyes narrowed. "I made a promise to you, an exceptionally difficult promise, and you agreed to give me an afternoon to compete for your affections."

"The afternoon has passed."

"Have I earned your affections?" He cupped her face and slid his thumb across her lower lip, and her mouth parted.

He leaned forward, moving slowly enough that Wilhelmina had ample time to protest. When she didn't, he pressed his mouth to hers. Her arms slid around his torso, bringing him closer, and she lost herself in his musky scent.

Somewhere in the back of her mind, her brain was screaming warnings from her mother. They were exposed, in a most compromising position, and bound to be found out if she didn't collect enough strength to push away Mr. Hastings, who seemed none-to-concerned at the prospect of being forced into marriage upon discovery.

"Wilhelmina!"

Mr. Hastings released Wilhelmina and jumped back, his head whipping toward the end of the corridor just as Mrs. James, her face purple with rage, stormed toward them. At her heels followed Miss Daniels, wearing an expression of haughty delight —it would be a matter of minutes before her gossiping tongue destroyed Wilhelmina's reputation.

"Mrs. James," Mr. Hastings stepped into her mother's path and bowed, preventing her from reaching Wilhelmina. "I'd like to request your daughter's hand in marriage."

Mrs. James' lips thinned. She glanced at Wilhelmina, who'd managed to crawl off the table and was smoothing her skirt down, then back to Mr. Hastings.

"I knew both your parents, and I'm sorry for the tragedy you suffered. As a mother, I am delighted at the prospect of a union between our families, and I'm thankful you are willing to take responsibility for your scandalous actions. Even though my daughter may not understand the repercussions of her behavior, I'm certain you do."

He nodded, his eyes flicking to Wilhelmina. She hovered between the two of them, unsure which person she should stand beside.

"However…" Mrs. James' voice adopted a dark tone. "It's

not my permission you require. It is my husband's, and until you receive it, you are not to speak with my daughter again. Good night."

"Of course, Mrs. James." Mr. Hastings bowed, his tone polite despite her dismissive scowl. "I shall request an audience with him tomorrow."

"Tomorrow is Christmas," Mrs. James replied, her voice icy.

"An excellent day as any for an engagement," he replied, undeterred by the fury flowing from Mrs. James. He glanced at Wilhelmina, offered her a tight smile, strode down the corridor, and vanished around the corner.

"You,"—Mrs. James pointed an accusing finger at Wilhelmina—"are to remain in our chamber for the rest of the evening, and you are to pray Mr. Hastings returns to claim you."

"Why wouldn't he?" Wilhelmina asked, her voice soft. Her eyes flicked to the end of the corridor.

Mrs. James leaned in and hissed, "Because you are worthless to him."

Ten

" I am not worthless!" Wilhelmina screamed, her voice echoing down the corridor.

Mrs. James arched an eyebrow as if to say that was exactly the kind of behavior she expected from someone she considered to be of no value. Her hand closed around Wilhelmina's arm, squeezing.

"Where is Oliver?" she hissed, enunciating each syllable.

"I presume he's in his chamber," Wilhelmina replied.

Her mother's eyes nearly exploded from her head. "He could have seen you!"

"He had already refused me before Mr. Hastings..." Her voice died upon catching the kaleidoscope of anger filtering across her mother's face.

Miss Daniels, who'd been trying to remain invisible while absorbing every humiliating detail of Wilhelmina's tryst, squeaked, her delight at the news apparent. Her hands flew to her mouth, stifling the inappropriate sound.

"That is not his choice to make!" Her mother snarled. Flinging Wilhelmina to the side, she stalked toward Oliver's room. She paused, her hand raised to rap, and lowered her arm, reconsidering bursting into her nephew's bedchamber. Scowling, she turned and marched back to Wilhelmina. "Don't leave that chamber until I discuss this new difficulty with your aunts."

"What of Mr. Hastings' proposal?" Wilhelmina asked.

Her mother's eyes narrowed. "Mr. Hastings' nature will be

his undoing. He will fail in his task, and once you've recovered from this bout of foolishness, your marriage to Oliver will proceed."

"Yes, Mother." Wilhelmina lowered her head.

Thwarted again. No matter what delay any of them threw in their mothers' paths, nothing deterred them from their matrimonial goal. Oliver's scheme to allege an illegitimate child was an act of desperation, one which would tarnish his family's reputation, further delaying any prospects for either him or Cora. However, once the paternal claim was proven to be false, they would be welcomed back into society, even celebrated for surviving such a horrific ordeal, and if Mrs. James had her way, Wilhelmina would be waiting at the altar for him within the month.

Grimacing, Wilhelmina scurried across the corridor and opened the door. As she darted inside, she heard her mother mutter a threat to Miss Daniels.

"If you speak one word about my daughter's inexcusable behavior this evening, I will reveal that you feigned an injury"—Miss Daniels choked at Mrs. James' accusation—"to steer Mr. Parrish into a scandalous situation, which would have resulted in a marriage proposal."

"I would never purposefully damage your daughter's reputation," Miss Daniels replied, the tone in her voice relaying the exact opposite message.

Considering the apparent amorous tendencies Miss Daniels was nurturing for Oliver, Wilhelmina suspected she would use any gossip to further her aspiration. However, Miss Daniels was shrewd enough to know not to cross Oliver's aunt, which was why she suspected the simpering young girl offered to escort Mrs. James downstairs under the pretense of concern for the older woman's nerves.

Rolling her eyes, Wilhelmina shut the door with a light click and leaned her head against the wood. She should be happy, or at least grateful, Mr. Hastings requested her hand instead of leaving her to face her mother's wrath alone. She knew little about the man, save his parents had died tragically, and he hadn't spent a day sober since their funerals.

Except for today…

Her mother believed Mr. Hastings incapable of that feat, just as she expected him to succumb to the temptation of an unfettered life and retract his proposal. A small part of Wilhelmina feared the same thing.

The fireplace glowed, coating her in the warmth of a crackling fire. A deep sigh escaping, she peeled herself away from the door, and paced the length of the chamber. When she reached the windows, she turned, intending to return to the fireplace, but a strange tapping sound drew her attention. Fingers curling around the drape, she yanked back the material and gasped.

Mr. Hastings' face appeared in the glass.

She screamed, stumbled backward, and fell, landing hard on her butt. Heart hammering, she spun around and stared at the door, expecting someone to burst into the room. No one appeared, and she exhaled, her muscles relaxing.

Flipping over onto her knees, she gathered her dress and rose, then crept over to the window, and peered through the frosted glass. Unlatching the window, she pushed it open and leaned out, her gaze sliding over the moonlit landscape.

"Mr. Hastings," she whispered.

Two hands grabbed onto the window ledge, and Mr. Hastings' chestnut head popped up from beneath her. He grinned.

"Good evening."

"What are you doing?"

"I'm kissing my fiancée good night."

"My father hasn't approved your request for my hand." She glanced over her shoulder at the chamber door. "And my mother may shoot you before that occurs."

"Your mother can use a pistol?" He paused, his chin resting on the window ledge.

"Yes, my father thought it important she could defend herself. Carriages make him ill, and he rarely travels with us. She always carries one."

Mr. Hastings squinted at the ground. "There's a fair amount of snow piled beneath your window. If I need to jump, I should survive."

"Is a kiss worth all this trouble?"

"Absolutely." He grunted, his shoes scraping the side of the house as he scrambled into the room, landing on his feet, and completing his athletic exhibition with a jaunty bow. "And I'm not concerned about proving my ability to provide for you."

The accomplishment surprised Wilhelmina, who expected him to end up in a ball of limbs on the floor, tangled in the drapes. His jacket, vest, and cravat were missing. She grimaced. He shouldn't be in her chamber, not with her mother prowling about, not with her reputation already dangerously close to ruin, and not with half his wardrobe missing. Licking her lips, she took a step backward.

"What are you concerned about, Mr. Hastings?"

"Edward."

The rumbled correction swirled around her, setting her blood on fire. He mirrored her step, moving forward, and closed the distance between them.

"Edward," she repeated as he crushed her in his embrace.

His head dipped, but before his mouth could touch hers, he stopped, and his head cocked to the right, then a strange expression crossed his face—fear. A moment later, a trio of footsteps thundered down the corridor.

"Oliver!" Uncle Gilbert's terrifying bellow was accompanied by the wrath of his fist, which threatened to break through the door separating him from his son.

There was no response.

Releasing Wilhelmina, Mr. Hastings crept across the floor and pressed his head to the gap between the door and the frame. He gestured her closer, placing his finger to his lips. As she joined him, Oliver's door crashed open, smashing into the wall, and causing the whole side of the house to vibrate with Gilbert's anger.

"He's gone!" Aunt Josephine's echoing announcement was followed by a muffled thud.

"She's fainted," Wilhelmina mouthed at Mr. Hastings, and he nodded his agreement.

"He may not have left. Perhaps he is conversing with Wilhelmina." Mrs. James' hope-filled suggestion crawled under the door.

Wilhelmina and Mr. Hastings darted to the opposite side of the room before hearing Uncle Gilbert's reply. Shoving Mr. Hastings behind the heavy drape in front of the window, Wilhelmina arranged it around his body, hiding him just as her mother opened the door.

Mrs. James' troubled frown slid across the chamber. When it

89

landed on Wilhelmina, a tiny spark of relief flashed across her mother's face, vanishing as quickly as it appeared. She stepped into the room and closed the door, cutting off the heart-wrenching wailing sound emanating from Oliver's room.

"Have you seen your cousin?" her mother asked, her voice pinched.

"Cora?" Wilhelmina pasted an innocent smile on her face and strode forward, meeting her mother halfway across the room.

"Oliver." Mrs. James jerked her hand in a small circle, indicating for Wilhelmina to turn around. Once Wilhelmina faced the opposite direction, Mrs. James unfastened her dress, loosening the material until she could pull it over Wilhelmina's head.

"I have not spoken with anyone since you exiled me to our chamber." Wilhelmina knew the phrase would irritate her mother. She shivered, a chill crawling across her exposed skin.

They'd forgotten to close the window!

She scooted closer to the warmth of the fireplace, dragging her mother with her, and prayed her mother wouldn't realize the cause of the chamber's cool temperature.

"Has something happened?"

Her mother paused, her fingers embedded in Wilhelmina's corset strings. "Oliver has vanished. No one has seen him, and there is no note explaining his whereabouts."

"Perhaps he is merely taking an evening stroll to clear his mind," Wilhelmina suggested, her tone brighter than she intended.

"In the snow?" Sarcasm dripped from her mother's voice. She grabbed hold of a petticoat, unfastened it, and worked it down Wilhelmina's legs, repeating the process as she removed several layers.

Wilhelmina's gaze shifted to the drape, which had moved aside, revealing Mr. Hastings, who seemed quite pleased to discover Mrs. James undressing her daughter. Wilhelmina waved her hand, directing him to cover himself again. He pouted, twisting his face into an exaggerated expression, then disappeared behind the material.

After ripping the corset over Wilhelmina's head, Mrs. James laid it, the petticoats, and the dress across the trunk at the foot of the bed. Her critical gaze swept across the room, stopping on the misshapen drape, and a line appeared in her forehead. She took a step toward it.

Wilhelmina's heart thudded, tripping over itself. If her mother discovered Mr. Hastings hiding behind the curtain, she'd ensure he never had the opportunity to request her hand. If she didn't shoot him, she'd shove him out the window—either solution resulting in the premature death of Mr. Hastings.

"If I should hear from him or see him, I will notify you immediately." Wilhelmina placed her hand on her mother's arm, giving it a gentle squeeze. "Aunt Josephine needs you."

"Can you unpin your hair without assistance?" Her mother asked, her eyes flicking toward the door.

"Ye—" Mrs. James had already rushed from the room before Wilhelmina completed the word.

"Do you know where Mr. Parrish went?" Mr. Hastings peeked around the drape.

"No." Wilhelmina's mouth twitched. "However, considering the depth of the snow, I suspect, since no one witnessed his departure, he made use of your observation."

"Why have they not asked his sister?" He shivered and spun around. Grasping the handle, he closed the window and latched it.

"I'm fairly certain if Oliver has disappeared, Cora has as well."

"I thought she supported your marriage to her brother."

"Her brother's happiness conflicted with the engagement." Wilhelmina's eyes returned to the fireplace. She wrapped her arms across her chest, shivering in the fire's warmth. "When Cora discovered Oliver was against the union, she attempted to find me a suitable match."

"Who was her choice?" he growled.

Wilhelmina glanced at him, alarmed by the dark expression on his face. "She failed in her endeavor."

"I'm extremely pleased to hear that." His posture relaxed, and he ambled across the room, stopping directly behind her. The heat rolling from his body rivaled that of the fireplace, melting the block of ice that had settled in her stomach. He leaned forward and murmured in her ear, "I would loathe disposing of another suitor."

Wilhelmina turned around, her arm brushing against him, and

her stomach flipped over at the contact. She placed her hand on his chest—the tips of her fingers stroking the exposed skin between his open shirt—and froze as if she intended to push him away. He glanced down, his mouth curving into a smile, and inhaled slowly, the movement causing her fingers to slide beneath his shirt.

"Did you threaten Mr. Parrish?" Her brain, focused on the sensation of his skin moving under her fingers, could barely force her tongue to form the words.

"Certainly not. However, I did consider it on several occasions." He wrapped his arms around her waist, drawing her nearer, his eyes glittering like sapphires. "Have I told you how lovely you look this evening?"

"I'm only wearing a chemise."

"Have your drawers gone missing?" He wiggled his eyebrows and leaned back, his gaze sliding down her torso. "I don't recall seeing your mother remove them."

"I have those on as well," she mumbled, embarrassment blazing through her body. She dropped her eyes to her hand, then realizing the position she was in, jerked her hand away from his chest and tucked it behind her back.

"Edward?"

He sulked, apparently displeased by the absence of her hand. When it became apparent she didn't intend to put it back on his chest, he asked, "What is your question?"

"If we marry,"—a low rumble vibrated in his throat at her supposition, but he held his tongue—"what would you expect of me?"

"I'd like to answer you properly, but I'm not certain I understand the purpose behind your query."

"Am I allowed to speak my thoughts?"

A peculiar expression crossed his features, and his eyes pulled into a confused frown. "Do you wish to swear?"

"No." She laughed. "Oliver—instructed by Uncle Gilbert—set forth strict parameters regarding the expectations of my behavior as his wife."

"You may say whatever you want to me," Edward murmured, drawing her body flush against his. The chemise rode up her legs, encouraged by Edward, who bunched a section in his hand and pinned it to her waist. He lowered his head, pressing his mouth to the sensitive spot on her neck, and sent a wave of tremors rippling through her body.

Her fingers latched onto his arms, curling as his mouth brushed tingles across her throat. She arched her neck, her eyes closing, and rubbed herself against his growing arousal, her body craving the fire he'd coaxed from her earlier.

Growling, Edward wrapped his hands around her hips and lifted her from the floor, winding her legs around his waist. His mouth claimed hers, his tongue pushing past her lips as he staggered across the room. He deposited her in the center of the bed, following her to the mattress, and settled his hips between her legs. Palming her breast through the thin material, his fingers teased her nipple, which pebbled under his ministrations. She moaned, clawing at his shirt.

Breaking the kiss, Edward sat back on his legs, yanked his shirt from his trousers, and flung it aside. Gathering her chemise, he dragged the material up her torso and ripped it over her head. Before she could react, his warm mouth closed over her breast, and she cried out, arching against him.

Skating down her torso, his hand scattered goosebumps across her flesh. It slipped between their bodies, seeking the slit in her drawers leading her center, and finding it, brushed a soft caress across her apex. She came off the mattress with a moan and pulled away from him, her body a perplexing combination of desire and fear.

Edward's hand stilled, and he lifted his head, his eyes searching hers.

"I won't hurt you, but I don't want you to be frightened. There are things a man does with a woman that can be satisfying for both, and as your husband, it will be my pleasure to introduce you to those delights. However, that doesn't need to occur tonight. If you tell me to leave, I will."

"I don't want you to leave." She didn't quite understand the gravity of her words but knew her decision would cause irreversible damage to her heart.

Locking his eyes on her, and he slid his finger across her center. She gasped, her body jerking from the simple caress. His finger skated across her again, eliciting another gasp. Leaning forward, Edward pressed his mouth to hers, his lips parting hers, and his tongue dove forward at the same moment he dipped one finger into her warmth.

Wilhelmina's eyes flew open, but his hand didn't stop its seduction. His thumb pressed against her center, moving in rhythm with the finger sliding in and out of her, stoking the inferno threatening to scorch her limbs until they crumbled into ashes. She ground herself against his hand, her stomach winding tighter with need, but he refused to speed up, his fingers continuing their slow, maddening torture.

She was going to explode, and Edward was doing nothing to ease the growing pressure between her legs. She growled, her fingers clawing at his arms. He grinned against her mouth and complied with her unspoken demand. Her head fell back, guttural cries pouring from her lips as her release crashed down. It kept rolling through her, bringing wave after wave of pleasure until it felt as though she was going to tear into tiny pieces.

Edward retracted his hand, crawled up her body, and nuzzled his face in her hair. His musky scent clung to her skin like perfume. Boneless, she stared at the ceiling, her ears ringing with the memory of her release.

"As much as I'd like to stay, I fear if your mother discovers me in your chamber when she retires for the evening, you will become a permanent spinster."

"When will you return?" she asked, drawing the coverlet over her body.

"Tomorrow, once I receive your father's approval." Edward placed a searing kiss to her mouth, lingering long enough to rekindle Wilhelmina's need. She grumbled when he crawled from the bed.

"Tomorrow is Christmas," she replied, unable to hide her disappointment as he pulled his shirt over his head.

"And I intend to spend it with you." He reached his hand into his pocket and extracted a small rectangle. He stared at it a moment, then held it out to her.

She accepted the rectangle, flipped it over, and gasped. "My portrait! Where did you find it?"

"It was in the bottom of my trunk." A deep pink tinge crept into his face.

"Was it there when I was searching for it?" she asked, staring at him over the top of the painting.

"It was."

"Why did you take it?" she whispered.

"I didn't think a woman such as you would consider me worthy of her affections." He rose and lifted her hand to his mouth, his lips hovering over her skin. His eyes locked on her. "However, as you haven't given me an answer, perhaps I am undeserving after all."

"Yes." She replied before she was aware the word had leapt from her mouth. "Yes, I will marry you."

"I cannot promise marriage to me will be easy, but I swear I will spend every day of my life ensuring the taste of brandy never touches your lips, and I will use each opportunity afforded me to seduce you in the manner befitting my reputation."

She blushed and chewed her lower lip, worry crawling into her mind. "What if I cannot allay the demands of your character?"

He appeared as though he would laugh, as Oliver had done, but Edward's face melted into that of kindness.

"My character demands solely you; there is nothing you could do to dishearten that craving." He leaned forward and cupped her face, pressing a soft kiss to her lips. "You were the best present hidden under the tree this year."

Thank You

Thank you for reading *An Imperfect Introduction*. If you enjoyed this historical holiday romance, please leave a review wherever you purchased the story, it really does make a difference. If you are interested in learning more about new releases, behind-the-scenes author secrets, sales, and giveaways, sign up for my newsletter.

I invite you to return to Wiltshire to spend more time with the Hastings' family. Ensnare yourself in the mystery and discover the nefarious truth behind the deaths of Edward's parents in *A Perfect Plan (Wiltshire Chronicles #1)*.

♥ Alyssa

A Perfect Plan – Chapter One (Sneak Peak)

He stared pitilessly, his mouth twisted in a cruel smirk as Mr. Matthew Hastings writhed on the mahogany desk, his arms flopping independently of his body—a muffled thudding that did nothing to alert the household of their master's early morning plight.

"It's unfortunate I had to resort to this unpleasantness." The man shook his head with feigned sadness. He paused, deep in contemplation, then spoke calmly as if explaining an important lesson to a child. "I did caution you—several times—over the past few months. However, you refused to heed my warnings." Leaning over, the man slid his fingers through Mr. Hasting's hair, mostly black but highlighted by the graying of age, tightened his grip, and wrenched Mr. Hastings' head sideways. Pressing his lips to Mr. Hastings' ear, he hissed, "You have something I want, something promised to me when I was much younger. Since you are unwilling to relinquish possession…" He indicated a half-empty glass of brandy near the edge of the desk, just out of reach of Mr. Hastings' twitching hand. The amber color glistened ominously; a poisonous concoction concealed by an innocent refreshment.

Mr. Hastings' blue eyes spun, threatening to burst from their sockets as the toxin caused his body to spasm in a gruesome dance, like a marionette with invisible strings. His tongue remained paralyzed, locked to the roof of his mouth, unable to form one simple word.

Help.

The man released Mr. Hastings' head, abruptly dropping it on the desk and savoring the flash of anguish that exploded in Mr. Hastings' eyes as his face crashed to the wood.

"This poison is quite painful." The man drew one finger down Mr. Hastings' contorted cheek. "I must admit, I chose it because I knew it would cause great suffering... and you deserve to suffer."

Mr. Hastings moaned. His flopping body beat its slow rhythm again. His mouth opened and closed, akin to a fish gasping for its last breath of air. The raspy breathing echoed in the study. Although the sound was not loud enough to draw the servants to the study, the man's eyes flicked over to the closed door, confirming their privacy. Grabbing Mr. Hastings by his hair again, he yanked up, crushing Mr. Hastings' mouth with his hand.

"Stop that nonsense, this moment," he snarled.

Jerking his body out of the man's grasp, Mr. Hastings threw his torso forward and stretched out his arm toward the poisoned snifter. His fingers brushed against the glass, sliding down the side. The glass scooted further away, teetering on the edge of the desk. Groaning, Mr. Hastings extended his fingers and wrapped his hand around the glass, then exhaled, his body slumping across the desk.

The man relaxed, his gaze sliding over Mr. Hastings' body, searching for any hint of movement. The smug chuckle tickling his lips ceased when his gaze landed on the snifter clutched in Mr. Hastings' fist.

"From the moment I met you, you have undervalued my intelligence." The man clucked his tongue. "Once again, I have proven myself the better man, and since I can't have the constable investigating your death..."

Prying the glass from Mr. Hastings' stiff hand, the man dumped the remaining liquid into the fireplace. The fire hissed, burned red for several minutes, then returned to its normal color. Wrapping the snifter in a handkerchief, the man tucked it into his coat and patted the pocket twice before lifting his gaze to meet Mr. Hastings' gaze.

"I am sorry to steal you so young from your lovely wife. The loss will devastate her." A horrid smile stretched across the man's lips. "Please don't concern yourself with the well-being of your dear wife or your children. I intend to take good care of your family."

The End

A Perfect Plan (Wiltshire Chronicles #1).

About the Author

USA Today Bestselling Author Alyssa Drake has been creating stories since she could hold a crayon, preferring to construct her own bedtime tales instead of reading the titles in her book-shelves. A multi-genre author, Alyssa currently writes a blend of historical romance, paranormal romance, and romantic suspense. She adores strong heroines with quick wit, and often laughs aloud when imagining conversations between her characters.

She believes everyone is motivated by love of someone or something and is always curious to discover what's hidden beneath the first layer. When she's not whipping up chocolate treats in the kitchen, Alyssa can be found searching for fairy houses and mermaid eggs.

http://www.alyssadrakenovels.com

Also by Alyssa Drake

AN IMPERFECT ENGAGEMENT (book 2)

A PERFECT DECEPTION (book 3)

~ Coming Soon ~

AN IMPERFECT SCOUNDREL (book 4)

Earl of Edgemore

AMANDA MARIEL

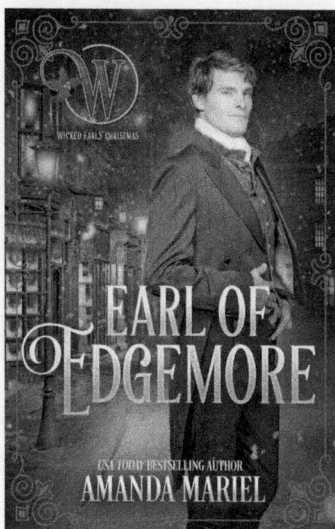

For my husband—You are my favorite reformed rogue. I love you!

Christmas has never been more wicked...

The Earl of Edgemore, Blake Fox, does as he pleases and he would not dream of apologizing for it. His only weak spot is his sister, Lady Minerva. Little does he know the minx has match-making on her mind, and Christmas provides the perfect opportunity.

Does Blake stand a chance against his meddlesome sister, mistletoe, and Christmas magic?

One

England, 1816

"Bullocks," Carstine Greer cussed as her ankle twisted beneath her. She dropped to the frozen ground at the side of the road and inhaled sharply at the ensuing pain. Reaching for her hem, she began pulling up her skirt to inspect her injury.

"Ach," she seethed as she worked to free her foot from the confines of her boot. Every movement sent unpleasant jolts of white-hot pain through her ankle and up her leg. She glared at the offending icy patch that had caused her misery.

Tossing her boot aside, Carstine feathered her fingers over the angry red and swollen skin of her ankle. Despite the pain she knew would follow, Carstine forced herself to wiggle her toes then flex her foot.

Good, the bone hadn't fractured, but she was in a great deal of pain nonetheless. She'd earned herself a nasty sprain to be sure.

She'd wager this would not have happened if her parents had allowed her to remain in Scotland.

Why the devil had Mother been so insistent that Carstine come to England? She did not care about English society, nor was she in any hurry to wed. She wasn't opposed to husband-hunting, but saw no reason why she couldn't do it in the highlands. A braw Scottish man would suit her best, she thought, as she put her boot back on with care.

The pounding of horse hoofs pulled her from her misery, and she glanced down the snow-blanketed road. A rider presently raced toward her at break-neck speed. She caught a glimpse of the gentleman as he flew past, the tails of his greatcoat flapping in the wind, before bringing his mount to a halt then turning back toward her.

Carstine stared unabashedly as the rider made his way back to her. He was tall and muscular beneath his greatcoat with broad shoulders, a strong jaw, and curious blue eyes framed in thick lashes. The man sat expertly upon a great chestnut beast of a horse. A fine specimen indeed—both the horse and its rider.

Carstine gave a slight grin then nodded as the stranger met her gaze.

The man nodded in return before moving his attention to her ankle. His eyebrows scrunched as he inspected her. "You're injured."

"Aye." She nodded then cringed as she finished pulling her boot back on. "I slipped on the ice. It's a wee sprain. Nothin too serious."

The man dismounted. He strolled toward her with long confident strides. "Allow me to assist you home?"

Carstine shook her head. She wasn't foolish enough to mount a horse with a strange man. Certainly not in a country she wasn't familiar with. "I haven't far tae go. Fox Grove Hall is just around the bend. I can see myself there," Carstine said.

"Nonsense," he insisted, then met her gaze with a confident smile. "Blake Fox, Earl of Edgemore at your service." He gave a sweeping bow. "You must be Lady Minerva's new maid?"

Carstine narrowed her eyes on him. The man did bear a striking resemblance to Lady Minerva. His coloring was fairer, but the almond shape of his eyes and high cheekbones were precisely the same. She cleared her throat. "It's a pleasure to meet ye, my lord, though I fear ye are mistaken about Lady Minerva."

"Nonsense." He waved his hand. "My sister would have my hide if I left her maid out in the snow, and injured at that. Come along." He reached his hand out to her.

Maid? The word echoed in her mind, and Carstine narrowed

her eyes. Whatever would make him think she was a servant? She glanced down at her wet skirt and muddied boots. She may be a bit disheveled, but she was no maid.

"Don't be stubborn." Lord Edgemore wiggled his fingers impatiently. "Come, I'll help you onto the horse."

"Nae." Carstine shook her head. "I'll not be ridin with ye."

"But of course you will. You are in my sister's employment and, therefore, my responsibility." He took a step closer, the crisp breeze stirring the golden locks that hung near his shoulders. "I know you Scots are used to the cold, but you'll freeze if you stay out much longer." He captured her arm and nudged her to stand. "Don't be stubborn."

Carstine's cheeks flamed with angry heat. She jerked away, then pushed to her feet. "I told ye already. It's nothin. Yer assistance is not needed."

He'd insulted her, and she could not help but be upset. And what did being Scottish have to do with anything? Did he think her to be less than him because of her heritage? Is that why he instantly decided she was a servant?

It was on the tip of Carstine's tongue to correct his misguided beliefs. However, the thought of watching his smugness crumble once they were properly introduced proved too tempting, and she swallowed back her words.

He deserved his comeuppance and the embarrassment that was sure to follow. What's more, she would delight in every uncomfortable moment he suffered. A smile stretched her lips as she imagined the look that would no doubt overtake his handsome face.

She was a wicked lass, indeed.

Carstine squealed as the earl lifted her off her feet and swung her onto his saddle. She glared at him, her chin notched defiantly. "I'll not be ridin with ye." She began lowering herself from the horses back, sliding toward the edge of the saddle. "Ye canna force me."

Lord Edgemore reached up, gripping her waist and holding her in place. "I dare say I do not understand your objection. Nor do I care. I'll not leave you here to freeze, nor will I allow you to further your injury by walking on that ankle." He spared a glance at her boot. "You will ride."

"Nae—"

"That is an order." He pushed her more firmly onto the saddle. "And I warn you now; I'll brook no further argument."

Carstine huffed an irritated sigh. "Then ye will guide the horse," she tossed the reins down at him. "As ye walk."

Satisfaction flooded her as Lord Edgemore took the reins and began leading the horse toward Fox Grove Hall. The high-handed, smug lord may have insulted her, but at least in this, she'd gotten the best of him. The knowledge that there was more to come vastly improved her mood.

Carstine turned her attention to the countryside as she relaxed in the saddle. She would soon have the full measure of her revenge.

Two

Blake Fox, fourth Earl of Edgemore, led his horse Crusader and its angry parcel down the drive of Fox Grove Hall. He was fully intent on delivering the feisty, if not beautiful, woman to the servant's door, then retreating to his billiards room for a much-needed brandy.

His bones were chilled to the marrow. No doubt, the woman suffered as well. Blake could not help but wonder if the woman enjoyed brandy too. If she were not so cross with him, he'd invite her to join him for a glass.

He hazarded at a glance at Crusader's rider. She sat high in the saddle, her arms crossed over her ample bosom, and her head held high. Based on her appearance, she was handling the winter chill far better than he. Perhaps it was her angry disposition that kept her warm?

He'd heard Scottish woman were a different breed, though he'd never believed the tattle. Not when the Scots he'd met did not seem much different from their English counterparts, but this woman...

She was all fire and brimstone hidden beneath a fair complexion and captivating eyes. A plaited crown of dark auburn hair created the effect of a halo on top of the little devil's head, while her heart-shaped face was equally deceiving.

He wanted her.

The realization startled him, and he turned his attention back to the drive. But then why shouldn't he want the lass? She was stunning and fiery. No doubt, the chit would make a splendid bedfellow.

Assuming, of course, that he could sway her opinion of him.

Charm her out of both her desire to hang him and her skirts.

Blake turned his gaze back to her. "What is your name?"

She smirked as though she held a secret, then said, "Miss Carstine Greer."

"Ah, a beautiful name for an equally stunning woman."

She notched her chin a fraction higher, indignation swimming in her bright green eyes. Despite her apparent distaste for his flattery, a small grin curved her lips.

Blake could not help but tease her. "It seems you are not accustomed to flattery. A pity to be sure."

"On the contrary, my lord. I have suffered far more flowery praise than any lady should," Carstine held his gaze, her stare hard, but not altogether unfriendly.

At that moment, he made up his mind. The insolent Carstine would be in his bed by Christmas. She'd be begging for his compliments and craving his kisses. She would be his, and it would be a Merry Christmas, indeed.

Leastwise, a vastly pleasurable one.

"Dear God! What happened, Carstine?"

Blake stilled at the high pitch sound of his sister Minerva's voice. He pivoted slightly to see her racing toward them.

"Why are you riding Blake's horse? Are you hurt?" Minerva called out as she continued toward them, her chestnut curls bobbing with each footfall.

"I slipped on a patch of ice and twisted my ankle. A wee sprain. 'Tis nothing. Dinna fash yersel." Carstine answered.

Blake turned to a footman that had followed Minerva from the house and said, "Do help the woman down. Take her below stairs and see that she is tended to."

"Below stairs!" Minerva squealed with indignation. "Why ever would you send her there?" Minerva looked at the footman. "His lordship is mistaken. Please take Miss Carstine to her guest room and see that Mother is informed."

"Guest room?" Blake raised a brow in question.

"Yes, her guest room. Carstine is Mother's guest. Her ward actually." Minerva narrowed her gaze on him. "Who did you think she was?"

"He thinks I serve you, milady," Carstine said.

"My servant?" Minerva swatted his arm. "You're an idiot. Did you not think to ask her who she was?"

Blake glanced from Minerva to Carstine. His Mother's ward? Why the devil hadn't she said as much. And why the deuce was she dressed like a fishmonger's wife?

Heat rose up, flaring across his chilled skin. A mixture of anger at being deceived and embarrassment over his mistake coursed through him. He heaved a sigh as he returned his attention to Minerva. "I was more concerned with her injury than her identity," Blake confessed.

"On the contrary," Carstine said as the footman carried her toward the front steps. "He was too highhanded tae care. I attempted tae tell him, but he wouldna listen."

"Blake!" Minerva scowled at him.

He shot the lass a dubious glare. She had bested him to be sure. She'd made a fool of him and seemed rather pleased with herself for it. He'd wager that smug look would disappear quickly once he had her in his bed.

This was war!

Minerva elbowed him, bringing him back to the moment.

Blake glared at his indignant sister.

"Apologize," Minerva demanded.

"Very well." Blake turned toward Carstine, and in three long strides, he'd reached her. Rather than speaking, he took her from the footman. She immediately stiffened in his arms but did not put up a fuss. "I'm sorry for my mistake. Allow me to make amends by seeing you to your chamber," he said in a cool flat tone.

"That is not at all proper," Minerva called out from behind him, but Blake ignored her as he carried his burden into the manor house.

He knew he was acting uncivilized, but at the moment, he did not care. He'd make it up to Minerva latter. Presently, he had a point to prove.

Carstine needed to recognize that he was not a man to be trifled with. He was lord of the manor.

Blake mounted the stairs two at a time, his hold on Carstine firm. The feel of her lush body in his arms wreaked havoc on his senses. His pulse increased as desire took hold threatening to overwhelm his good sense.

For her part, the minx acted unaffected. Her gaze cold and body still but for the jostling caused by his movements. The fact only served to further grate on his nerves. He started down the hall, his gaze trained on the doors that lined either side of the corridor. "Which room?" He spoke the question through clenched teeth.

"Third one on the right," Carstine answered as though there was nothing amiss with their current situation.

Blake hastily made his way to the door she'd indicated, then shoved it open with his hip before strolling inside. He marched over to the large four-post bed. Once there, he took a moment to bring his mouth close to her ear and whisper, "This is not over, beauty."

Before she could react, he deposited her in a heap and turned to take his leave.

Like an angry little shadow, Minerva was at his elbow. She wrapped her hand around his arm and tugged. "We must talk."

Blake allowed his sister to lead him from the room, but once they stepped into the hallway, he took control, turning them toward the billiards room.

He would allow her to talk all she pleased. He never denied Minerva anything—never could. But while she filled his head with her chatter, he'd be filling his gut with good brandy.

When they reached the billiards room, Blake held the door so Minerva could enter. "Be a dear and pour me a glass of brandy before you gnaw my head off," He said as he dropped onto the sofa nearest the hearth.

Minerva waved her hand. "I have no intention to gnaw off heads today." Minerva strolled toward the cherry wood sideboard. "Certainly not my favorite brother's."

"I am your only brother," Blake drawled.

"Then, it is little wonder that you are also my favorite." She picked up a crystal decanter and poured a measure of its amber liquor into a tumbler.

Blake could not help but grin. Minerva had a way of making him smile even when it was the last thing he wished to do.

She crossed the room and handed him the tumbler before seating herself beside him.

He took a long sip, enjoying the way the brandy heated his insides, then turned his attention to her. "If you do not intend to yell at me, then what is it you wish to discuss?"

"Carstine, of course." Minerva smiled sweetly.

Blake sighed. "Indeed," he said before lifting the tumbler back to his lips. He feared one glass would not be nearly enough to sustain him.

"It seems the two of you have gotten off on the wrong foot," she said.

"To say the least." Blake swirled the liquor in his glass.

"I want you to give her a chance. To show her you are truly sorry and make nice with her. It would please me if the two of you got along." Minerva said, her eyes imploring.

"And how do you suppose I am to accomplish that?" Blake asked before taking another long drink.

Minerva tipped her head to the side, her gaze turning thoughtful.

Blake braced himself for what was to come. If he knew his sister at all, and he was confident he knew her better than most, she would devise a cake worthy scheme.

One, he would have no choice but to enact if he wished to escape her ire.

She smiled as she clapped her hand onto his arm. "I've got it."

"Oh? Do go on," Blake offered false enthusiasm, then brought his brandy back to his lips. No doubt, this would be a whopper.

"You will invite her on an outing."

"I will?" Blake arched an eyebrow.

Minerva's smile broadened. "You will. A sleigh ride, perhaps?" Her gaze turned speculative for a moment, then she smiled. "Yes, a sleigh ride shall be the perfect way for you to get to know each other."

Blake drummed his fingers on the arm of the sofa. "Perfect?" Utterly harebrained is what he'd wanted to say, but he could not bring himself to further upset his sister.

"Yes, perfect," Minerva repeated. "It is a respectable way for the two of you to be alone. That will allow you to apologize again as well as show her what a delightful gentleman you can be."

Minerva grinned. This time the jubilation reached her sky-blue eyes. "She is a splendid girl. If you just give her a chance, you'll see. Carstine is impossible to dislike."

Blake drained his tumbler before turning his attention back to Minerva. "I fear the die has been cast in this case."

"Nonsense, brother." She slid closer, her gaze locked on his. "Do it for me. For Mother as well. She'd not wish for you to dislike her guest. She is rather fond of Carstine, you know."

"Actually, I wasn't aware," he drawled.

"Well she is. Carstine happens to be the daughter of her dear friend, Mrs. Leticia Greer. Surely you remember Mother speaking of her."

Blake searched his mind but could not recall the name. "I fear not."

Minerva took his tumbler, then stood and started toward the sideboard. "They were school friends. Leticia is English born, but she married a Scottish landowner. She and Mother have stayed in contact all these years despite the miles and miles that separate them." Minerva rotated her wrist, twirling her hand. "When Leticia wrote to Mother sharing her desire for Carstine to have a London season, Mother could scarcely stop herself from offering to sponsor the girl."

"How very much like Mother." Blake accepted the glass, then ran his finger around the edge as he considered what Minerva had told him. Carstine was a Scottish lass with English blood and the daughter of his mother's dear friend. He sighed. As much as it pained him, he would have to make an attempt at mending their relationship.

"Indeed, Mother has always enjoyed this sort of thing, and so you see why she would want the two of you to get on well?"

Blake held up a hand in resignation. "You've won, dear. There is no need to continue on."

"Then, you will invite her on a sleigh ride?"

"As soon as she is mended," Blake agreed, then took another long, slow sip of his brandy.

Bedding the feisty lass was entirely out of the question. He'd have to find a more civilized way to even the score between them. He tipped his glass to his lips.

No, he'd have to give up his revenge.

Swallowing another deep drink, he could not help but think

that his previous assessment had been wrong. This would not be a Merry Christmas, not even close. It would, no doubt, be an irritating one, indeed. The women in his house would see to it as sure as the snow would fall.

"Blake?"

He turned his attention back to Minerva. "What?"

"Are you quite, alright?"

"Indeed." He waved her off as he relaxed back against the sofa. "Be a dear and deliver my invitation."

Minerva beamed. "With pleasure."

Three

Blake's breath caught for a heartbeat when Carstine appeared on the porch. He'd thought her to be a beauty before, but now, dressed as a proper lady and not the least bit disheveled...she was captivating.

His gaze traveled from the fur-lined hood of her sapphire-colored cloak all the way to her toes and back, not missing a single curve or flair. Her eyes were sparkling, pink lips plump, and her cheeks held a slight flush, likely from the crisp winter air.

He swallowed past the dryness in his mouth as she approached, then extended his hand. "Allow me."

Carstine met his gaze but did not take his hand. "I believe ye have a bit more crow tae swallow before I consent to go anywhere with ye." Her sweet smile belied her words.

Blake was instantly reminded as to why he didn't like the woman. She was annoying, snarky, and sharp-tongued. He'd not stand for the abuse—not even for Minerva.

He released an exasperated breath and shook his head. "I am only doing this for Minerva, but if you do not have the same care for my sister and mother, you are welcome to return to the house."

Carstine's eyes narrowed before she tossed her head back and laughed.

Laughed! The insolent woman found him amusing. What the devil was wrong with her?

On second thought, he didn't care to know. Blake shoved his hands in his pockets and pivoted to stride away.

"Wait," she called to his retreating backside. "I'm sorry. Let us do our duty tae yer family."

He turned back, a scowl pulling at his lips.

"Come now, we may even enjoy ourselves." Carstine strolled over and laced her hand through his arm. "Dinna be sour. I promise tae be nice henceforth."

He pinned her with his gaze. "You had better be, or I'll leave you in the snow to fend for yourself."

She smirked. "Ye wouldna dare. Ye said so yerself yesterday."

"That was before I knew you." He smiled with amusement as he led her back to the sleigh.

"I said I was sorry," she protested as he handed her up.

Blake went around the sleigh, then climbed in and settled beside her. "As did I, but my apology did nothing to stem your obnoxiousness." He slanted his gaze at her. "Now, I am to simply forgive you even though you have not forgiven me?"

"Nae, yer wrong." She waved her hand with a little flourish. "I forgave ye the moment I saw the embarrassment over yer assumptions color yer cheeks."

His jaw slackened as he took up the reins and set the sleigh into motion. "Then why did you give me a hard time just now?"

"For tae fun of it. Yer rather cute when ye are cross, ye ken." Her laughter rang out, filling the air around them with a whimsical, contagious melody.

She thought him cute? He fought a grin at the revelation, and shot her a reproachful look. "I am not the least bit amused."

"Ye and Beira seem to be of tae same mood."

"Beira?" Blake arched a brow in question.

"Aye, the goddess of winter." Carstine held out a glove covered hand and caught several fluffy snowflakes that swirled in the air around them. "Ye've not heard of her?"

"I'm afraid not," Blake answered.

"She's a haggard old woman with ash-colored skin and one eye. Beira rules over winter, and when she is displeased, she makes it known."

"You are comparing me to a haggard old woman?"

"Aye, but only in temperament." Carstine tucked her hand

back into the blanket, covering her lap. "She's been in a mood tae be sure. 'Tis why we've seen so much snow and wind of late."

"I'm not in a mood." Blake shook his head.

"Nae?" Carstine slanted her head to study him. "Then why do ye keep scowling?"

"I don't."

Her smile grew, the corners of her eyes crinkling. "Yer doing so now."

"I'm not." Blake forced a smile.

Carstine began laughing again. "Ye look like a statue about to crack into a thousand pieces."

Blake imagined he must look as she'd described for his efforts were hurting his face. He no doubt appeared downright ridiculous, and why? Because a slip of a lady was jesting with him?

Ridiculous indeed!

He chuckled at the pure lunacy of it.

"Much better," she said as she playfully nudged him. "Ye ken, Minerva is rather fond of ye. She near tae blathered my ears clean off talking about ye. Insisting that ye were a good sort, and I must give ye a chance tae redeem yerself."

That did indeed sound like his sister. Blake gave a genuine smile. "She did the same to me in your regard."

"A suborn lass, tae say the least." Carstine shuffled on the seat, turning to face him more fully. "I say we forget our first meeting and all that has followed."

"Indeed, we should," Blake agreed.

"Aye." Carstine nodded, then held out her hand. "I am Miss Carstine Greer."

Blake hesitated for a moment before bringing the sleigh to a stop and taking her hand. "Blake Fox, Earl of Edgemore at your service." He took her hand and drew it to his mouth, placing a kiss on her glove covered knuckles.

"Tis a pleasure to meet ye, my lord." She grinned, her green eyes vibrant as she studied him.

"I assure you, the pleasure is all mine." Blake gave a roguish grin. "Now do, tell me all about yourself."

"As I'm well aware, ye ken, our mothers are old friends…"

Blake took up the reins and set the horses back into motion as Carstine chatted. She told him how her parents met and married and how she was born and raised in Scotland, but her mother always did what she could to make sure Carstine was also exposed to her English heritage. He hung on her every word, finding her more than a little captivating.

"And so, ye see why Mother wished for me tae have an English season."

"I do." Blake nodded. There was something in her voice, and the way her eyes seemed to dim that made him suspect that Carstine did not share her mother's wishes. He gave her a slight smile and asked, "Am I right in thinking that you do not share her wish?"

Carstine sighed, a tiny laugh escaping her as she shook her head. "What gave me away?"

"Nothing, really."

"Come now." She nudged him with her elbow.

Blake chuckled. "Very well. Your voice seemed to carry a note of sorrow, and your eyes changed for a fraction of a heartbeat."

"And ye noticed that?" She fiddled with the edge of her lap blanket. "I dare say, ye are a surprise. And not an altogether unpleasant one."

"Some would most certainly disagree with that assessment. I am a renowned rogue, you know?" He winked, relishing the fresh blush that crept across her cheeks.

She burst into another fit of laughter, and Blake found himself chuckling as well.

By the time they returned to the house, he had long forgotten his earlier frustration with the woman. Carstine, though a pain in his arse, was an unusual and captivating woman. One he wished to know better. She was like a decadent treat made of many layers—some hard, perhaps even a bit tart, and others sweet and soft. He wished to devour her one layer at a time. Uncover all of her flavors and textures, savoring each and every one.

A startling realization to be sure.

Four

It seemed that Carstine's sponsor intended to waste no time in her introduction to English society for the countess had filled the house near to bursting.

It proved to be an awkward affair as Carstine was herded into the parlor and introduced to one gentleman after another. The countess told each that Carstine had been sent from Scotland so that she might enjoy an English season. Carstine suspected a bit more than that had been said in private for the men appraised her as one might inspect livestock for sale.

Exasperated, Carstine turned a forced smile on the countess. "Thank ye for takin tae time tae introduce me, but I fear all the excitement has gotten to me. Might I have a few minutes tae collect myself?"

The countess patted her arm. "Of course, dear."

Carstine wasted no time joining Minerva in a far corner. She released an exasperated sigh as she stood next to her friend. "Yer mother seems tae be on a mission."

"Indeed." Minerva turned a sympathetic gaze on Carstine. "I should have warned you."

"Aye, but Dinna fash yersel. I'll survive."

Minerva scanned the parlor, then brought her gaze back to Carstine. "If it is of any consolation, this gathering has as much to do with me as it does you." She offered a sympathetic grin. "Mother thinks it wise for me to meet every eligible gentleman in Britain before my first season begins. She believes it will allow me to marry both well and fast."

Carstine cringed. "How dreadful, lass."

"Indeed." Minerva took Carstine's hand and squeezed. "Though I must admit that I am pleased, no, overjoyed, to have you by my side. It means we can endure it together."

"Aye, misery does enjoy company," Carstine gave a conspiratorial grin.

"There's Blake." Minerva waved at her brother.

Carstine turned her head to find Lord Edgemore strolling toward them. Her pulse quickened as he drew closer.

The man was something to behold in his fine-cut evening clothes. His black coat hugging his muscular frame and long legs flexing beneath the fabric of his trousers held Carstine captive. But what enthralled her most was the boyish grin tilting his lips.

She tried to look away but found it an impossible task as her gaze seemed to roam back to him of its own accord.

He gave an exaggerated bow. "How lucky am I to begin my evening standing beside the two loveliest ladies in the room."

"Flattery will get you everywhere." Minerva beamed at her brother.

Lord Edgemore turned his attention to Carstine, took her hand, and dropped a kiss to the back of it before meeting her eyes. "Tell me, Miss Carstine, does my sister speak the truth?"

"Nae, my lord." She shook her head. "It will get ye nowhere with me."

"You wound me, fair lady."

Carstine let a small trickle of laughter escape her. "I doubt that very much."

Minerva grabbed Carstine's arm, her gaze sparkling with mischief. "I have an idea."

"God help us," Lord Edgemore said.

"Not at all." Minerva swatted his arm with her fan.

"Dinna keep us in suspense." Carstine stared at Minerva.

"Blake can save you from the masses by pretending an interest in you. Leastwise, for the holiday."

"No," Lord Edgemore and Carstine blurted in unison.

Minerva pouted. "Why ever not?"

"Because," Lord Edgemore said flatly.

Minerva stared at him. "But it's the perfect plan. If the

gentlemen Mother invited believe you have an interest in her, they will back away."

Lord Edgemore shook his head. "I'll not be a party to it."

"For goodness sake, Blake. It's not like I'm suggesting you marry her." Minerva turned pleading eyes on Carstine. "Surely, you can see the merit in my plan?"

Carstine bit her lip as she considered. She could not argue Minerva's point, so instead, she said, "Lord Edgemore barely tolerates me."

"Nonsense," he said.

Minerva's face lit, her eyes sparkling. "Good, then you'll do it!"

He gave a resigned nod.

Carstine stared dumbstruck at the earl. Finding her voice, she asked, "Are ye certain?"

"Yes, it has been a long time since I played a role in a good lark." He shot her a grin. "In fact, now that I have considered the idea, I'm rather looking forward to it."

"Then, it's decided." Minerva took Carstine's hand and placed it on Lord Edgemore's arm. "You can begin by promenading her around the parlor."

She shot a pointed look at Carstine, then her brother. "And do pretend to enjoy yourselves."

Before either could argue, Minerva had swept herself off to join another group.

"Is she always like that?" Carstine asked.

Lord Edgemore arched a golden eyebrow. "Like what?"

Carstine strolled beside him with slow, easy steps as she considered the best way to describe Minerva. She settled on a word and said, "Mischievous."

Lord Edgemore chuckled. "Ah, that. Yes. As well as scheming and calculating." His steps faltered.

Carstine slid her gaze to him. "What is it?"

"I believe we have just played into the minx's hand." He frowned as his gaze moved to where Minerva stood.

Carstine gave a slight tug on his arm, and he resumed walking. "How so?"

"She does not wish to spare you." He looked at Carstine and cringed. "She wishes to match you."

"With ye? Absurd!" Carstine's eyes rounded. "Ye canna be serious."

"Oh, but I am."

"Then we shall stop this farce at once," Carstine made to release his arm, but he placed his hand over hers, holding it in place.

"As neither you nor I wish to marry—certainly not to each other—what is the harm?"

Carstine considered his words. What was the harm indeed?

She slanted her gaze to him. He was handsome, and for the most part, charming, but he was also right, she did not have any desire to wed him.

But then, desires often changed. "I canna argue yer point. But do ye think it wise to hold our feet to the fire? We may find them missing before we ken what happened."

Lord Edgemore chuckled. "You say the oddest things."

Carstine peered at him, but she could not deny the humor bubbling up in her as well. "Be that as it may." She waved her hand in dismissal.

"And now you sound like a proper English lady," he said, amusement laced through his voice.

"Aye. It is a gift that comes with having an English mother and a Scottish father. Like a Pomeranian and a bloodhound's offspring, I reap the benefits of both parents. Prim and proper one moment, and savage the next." Carstine laughed.

Lord Edgemore chuckled as well before saying, "I'll not argue with that." He met her gaze, then said, "Back to the topic at hand. Will you go along with the scheme in order to save us both?"

"Aye." She exhaled, her gaze moving to Minerva before returning it to him. "So long as we agree that it is only a farce."

Lord Edgemore gave a satisfied if not amused grin. "You needn't fear me, lass. Marriage is the last thing on my mind."

Carstine swallowed back any further objections. Indeed, what harm could ensue when they both understood the game they played?

All the same, an uneasy feeling crept through her, and she prayed she'd not come to regret her actions.

It did not take Carstine long to see the glaring error in their plan for the following day guests once again joined them.

It seemed the countess had planned to surround her—all of them—with marriage-minded merchants, peers, and local gentry for the duration. The woman was undoubtedly determined.

The evening had begun in the receiving room, where guests and family alike gossiped and chatted as they awaited dinner.

When she entered the dining room, Carstine breathed a sigh of relief to find herself seated beside Lord Edgemore and across from Minerva. And as luck would have it, the countess had placed a handsome and successful merchant, Mr. Kingston, to her left.

Unfortunately for Carstine, Mr. Kingston seemed to take a shine to her.

"Your eyes are like glittering emeralds," Mr. Kingston said.

Carstine forced an amicable grin. "Thank you, Mr. Kingston."

Lord Edgemore leaned forward, looking past her to Mr. Kingston. "Rubbish, they are like lush green grass on a sunny spring day."

Carstine's cheeks warmed as the gentleman debated the color of her eyes. An argument that lasted until after the final course was served when the gentleman left the ladies to go indulge in brandy and cigars.

The worst part of all was how much Lord Edgemore seemed to enjoy the exchange. Carstine determined to make him pay for that at a later time.

For now, she was content to retire to the parlor, and in doing so, escape the gentleman. Leastwise, for a little while.

As it turned out, her reprieve lasted but three-quarters of an hour. She gave Lord Edgemore a practiced smile as he entered the room then strolled directly to her side.

He gave her an amused look and said, "Dinner was surprisingly entertaining."

"The devil it was," she admonished. "How could ye encourage Mr. Kingsley to continue that ridiculous argument?"

"Eyes so captivating a man could drown in them," Lord Edgemore emulated Mr. Kingsley's earlier statement.

"Stop it." Carstine elbowed him hard enough to make him gasp. "Yer not the least bit funny."

"I beg to differ, my dear." He nodded to the far edge of the room. "Brace yourself, it seems your Mr. Kingsley is headed this way."

"He is most defiantly not my anything," she seethed as she wrapped her hand around Lord Edgemore's elbow. "Assume your role."

Just then, Minerva hoisted herself onto a chair. She stood tall and smiled at the gathering. "I would like to invite anyone who wishes to join myself, Lord Edgemore, and Miss Carstine for parlor games to adjourn to the blue parlor at once."

Carstine looked to Lord Edgemore. "Were ye aware of this?"

"No, but it seems we have no choice." He patted her hand then led her out of the room and down the hall to the blue parlor.

It was there that Minerva pulled a deck of cards from a nearby table and announced, "I have the inclination to play *The Chance Kiss*."

"I dinna like the sound of that," Carstine said, her worried gaze on Lord Edgemore.

"As well, you shouldn't. That is unless you have to kiss me." He winked.

"Hurry," Carstine's cheeks burned as she swatted his arm, "suggest another game. One that does not involve kisses."

Lord Edgemore glanced across the room. "It's too late. She's already passing the cards out."

Carstine considered fleeing the parlor, but she had no wish to make a spectacle of herself. Instead, she asked, "How does the game work?"

Lord Edgemore answered, "You will kiss the gentleman whose card matches yours. The king of hearts will kiss the queen of hearts, and so on. But fear not, there are only eight cards involved. You may not receive one."

Minerva handed a card to a dark-haired gentleman, then turned toward them, mischief in her blue eyes.

"Forget what I said. You are most certainly about to receive a card." Lord Edgemore gave an apologetic grin.

"I'd expect nothing less," Carstine said in a quiet voice. "And I'd wager it matches yours."

"Knowing Minerva, we can count on it."

Carstine narrowed her eyes. "I always ken there was a reason the Scots fought the English, though I must confess that I am only now starting tae understand said reason."

Lord Edgemore chuckled. "Do not forget who won."

"Aye," Carstine said a moment before Minerva reached them.

After handing them both a card, Minerva returned to the hearth and faced the room at large. "Reveal your cards," she announced.

Lord Edgemore turned his card around for all to see. "King of spades," he announced in a dry tone.

"Who holds the queen of spades?" Minerva asked, though her gaze did not stray from Carstine.

Carstine bit her lip as she turned her card around.

Minerva clasped her hands excitedly. "Then the two of you must exchange a kiss."

Carstine had known what was coming. What she hadn't bargained on was the jolt of pure desire that shot through her when Lord Edgemore pressed his lips to hers.

It was not a romantic kiss by anyone's standards, but it nearly swept her off her feet all the same.

A soft brush of his lips to hers that lasted nary a heartbeat, but would be imprinted on her soul for eternity.

She averted her gaze as she wondered if he had felt it too.

Nothing to fear, her arse!

Five

Blake watched Carstine as she strolled beside Minerva and another young lady, the three of them chatting like magpies without a care for the weather.

Despite the continuous snowfall and brisk winter wind, Minerva had insisted they go out to collect decorations. He could hardly argue with her considering that tomorrow was Christmas Eve. Therefore, he'd pulled on his greatcoat, hat, and gloves then followed the group out of the house.

Strangely enough, the sight of Carstine sent warmth through him, keeping the chill at bay.

The kiss they had shared affected him more than he cared to admit and left him wanting more. He'd had a devil of a time sleeping last night because of it. He wondered what it might feel like to hold her in his arms—to caress her and explore her body. Would her hair be silken as he twined his fingers through it? What would she taste like? Honey and sweetness, or would she be pleasingly tart?

He'd wager no matter her taste, it would be intoxicating.

"Rather blustery, is it not?" Mr. Kingston said as he came up beside Blake.

"Indeed," Blake answered, his tone flat. He'd never had an ill opinion about the man in the past. In fact, he'd rather enjoyed his company, but Kingston suddenly set Blake's nerves on end.

"Though it does put a rather becoming blush on our dear Miss Carstine's fair cheeks." Kingston winked.

And that was the very reason Blake had come to dislike, Kingston. Blake ground his teeth, both irritated with the man's observation and himself. He had no business raising his hackles over a woman he did not intend to wed, regardless of how captivating she was. In fact, if he were a true gentleman, he'd encourage Carstine to let Kingston woo her.

But then, he'd never claimed to be a true gentleman and saw no reason to start now. He slanted his gaze at Kingston, his ire increasing when he noted that the man was staring at Carstine. "I do not believe her cheeks are your concern."

"Come now, Edgemore. I've never known you to be territorial." Kingston said, pulling his greatcoat tight around his neck. "Do you intend to ask for her hand?"

"Gads no!"

"Then perhaps I will." Kingston returned his gaze to Carstine's backside.

"She is a beguiling creature."

Blake elbowed him. "Like hell, you will."

Kingston turned his head, his eyes narrow. "Are you quite alright, Edgemore?"

"Yes," Blake sliced the air with his hand, "We have a misunderstanding is all."

Kingston's eyes narrowed further as he stared at Blake in speculation. "It would seem so."

"What I should have said was that I am not ready to ask for her yet, but I may well in the future." Blake increased his stride, very much in want of ending this ridiculous conversation.

"Then I would suggest you not wait overlong," Kingston called out as Blake strode ahead.

Blake ignored the man, his sights set on Carstine.

"There." Minerva pointed, excitement ringing in her voice. "I see holly." She turned toward a cluster of bushes and trees.

Blake hurried to Carstine's side and reached for her elbow as the rest of the group followed Minerva.

She turned her startling green eyes on him. "What is it?"

Blake smiled as he released his hold on her. "I thought we might go in search of ivy and mistletoe. I happen to know that it grows over there." He nodded his head in the opposite direction of that which the others had gone.

Carstine nodded, a slight grin playing at her lips, then

followed him for a few silent minutes as he led her into a thicket of evergreens.

"Wait." She stopped and turned around. "Shouldn't we call for a footman tae carry what we gather?"

Blake shook his head. "That won't be necessary." He started walking again but stopped when he noticed she wasn't moving. He turned back to her and said, "Are you coming?"

She slanted her head, studying him. "I suspect there isna any mistletoe, nor ivy tae be had."

He tried not to look chagrined as he answered, "You would be correct in your suspicion."

She strolled closer, a mischievous grin pulling at her mouth. "Why did ye say there was?"

"I wanted to spend a moment alone with you." He inwardly cringed at his confession. He should have told her something else —anything else.

Her smile widened, amusement lighting her eyes. "We'll start a scandal."

"If anyone notices, we'll say you took ill."

"Then I would miss the evenings' activities." She stooped down and gathered a handful of snow. "I have no wish tae spend the evening alone."

She stood as she packed the snow she'd gathered into a ball, then launched it at him.

Blake dodged the projectile, but before he could do much else, she flung another. The ball collided with his shoulder.

Carstine laughed, her green eyes full of merriment as she reached for more snow. "Perhaps we shall say that ye became ill after having an unfortunate accident in the snow." She pulled back her arm, then launched the snowball.

Blake ducked his head as it flew past. "Is that so?" He asked as he took long strides in her direction.

"'Tis a perfect plan," Carstine said as she let another snow-ball fly from her hand. She laughed uproariously as it hit his chest and burst into a small storm of white powder.

Blake charged at her, wrapping his arms around her. Her laughter infected him, and he chuckled as he swung her in a circle. "I've captured you, minx."

She tossed her head back, her loose red curls fanning out as he spun her.

Blake brought her close against him and stared into her eyes. The urge to kiss her overwhelming.

Carstine smiled up at him, her cheeks rosy and lips slightly parted. "And now that you have, what do you intend to do with me?" She asked, a playful lilt in her voice.

All thought fled his mind. He brought his mouth down on hers, pressing his lips to hers, demanding more.

Need and anticipation tangled within him as he deepened the kiss, desperate to taste her.

He pulled her closer, one hand at the small of her back while his other cupped her neck as he slid his tongue along the crease of her lips.

She parted them for him, her tongue darting out to slide and twirl against his as she wound her arms around his shoulders.

She was intoxicating. Better than the finest brandy. Sweeter than the most decadent treat, and more alluring than any woman he'd ever kissed before.

And he was lost.

Six

Carstine sighed as she leaned against the stable wall. She could not say why, but for some reason, she found herself homesick. Thoughts of Mother, Father, and Scotland had run through her mind all day and into the evening. Perhaps it was merely because today was Christmas Eve. That and the merriment of those around her left her feeling—alone.

Ridiculous when she was surrounded by people, but true all the same. She inhaled a slow breath and let her head fall back against the wall. What were Mother and Father doing right now?

Likely sitting before the fire and enjoying a glass of fine Scottish whisky.

A hand touched her shoulder, and she jumped, her eyes flying open to find Blake gazing at her. "Ye startled me! What are ye doin out here?"

"I came to ask you that very thing." He let his hand drop from her shoulder. "I saw you slip away and followed. You've not been yourself today."

She should be angry that he'd intruded on her, but her heart warmed at the concern reflected in his blue eyes. "I'm fine."

"You do not look fine." He stroked the back of one long finger over her cheek.

Carstine closed her eyes and leaned into his touch.

"Tell me what's been bothering you," Blake said in a soothing voice.

Carstine opened her eyes and met his. "It's silly. Ye shouldna concern yerself with me." No sooner did the words leave her mouth than she wished to take them back.

Her heart hitched, because at that moment she realized that she'd fallen in love with him. Completely and irrevocably in love with a man who only pretended to court her.

"Nonsense." He stared into her eyes, tenderness in his gaze. "Now, tell me what's wrong."

The way he looked at her melted her insides. Such tenderness and something else too... perhaps longing? Or was she merely seeing what she wished to see?

"Carstine, you can confide in me. I promise not to laugh at you," Blake continued.

She forced a smile, then said, "It's nothin dire. I've just been missin my family." She nibbled her lip.

Blake took her by the hand and led her to a pile of fresh hay. He drew her down to sit beside him. "Tell me about them?"

"My family?"

He nodded.

Carstine folded her hands in her lap and stared across the stable to where a sliver of the night sky revealed itself.

For the first time in nearly a sennight, no snow fell, and stars could be seen sparkling against the inky sky. "I don't ken where tae start," she said, without looking at him.

"Do you have siblings?" Blake asked.

Carstine shook her head. "I had a brother, but he died from an illness when he was just a wee bairn."

"I'm sorry." Blake reached out and started rubbing her back.

Carstine sighed. "Don't be. It was a long time ago. I was but a lass of six myself. I barely remember it other than how sad Mother was afterward. But that too has long passed."

She turned to Blake. "We don't celebrate Christmas like yer family does."

"Right. Not since Scotland banned it nearly two hundred years ago." His gaze turned thoughtful for a moment, then he said, "But your mother is English."

"Aye, and she does have fond memories of the holiday as a lass, but she adopted the Scottish ways when she married Father." Carstine grinned. "All but one." She paused, her gaze turning wistful. "Mother always insists on a fine Christmas dinner with plum pudding, syllabub, and roasted goose as well as other English dishes."

"Which is your favorite?" Blake asked.

"Yorkshire pudding." She wet her lips at the thought.

"I did notice you take a second helping tonight." Blake teased.

Carstine smiled, laughter bubbling up in her.

"I've always been partial to sweets as well." Blake returned her smile.

She slid closer, her gaze on his—searching. "And what is yer favorite?"

"Kisses. But only those that come from a red-haired, green-eyed lass." He winked roguishly.

Her stomach fluttered as her heart swelled. He'd been watching her at dinner and now he unashamedly told her he liked her kisses.

Blake may not love her, but he most certainly desired her, and the thought thrilled her to her toes.

She beamed at him as she asked, "Will any red-haired, green-eyed lass do?" her tone teasing.

"Nae," he answered, his Scottish accent terrible but more than a bit endearing.

She turned toward him, her head angled upward and pressed her lips to his.

He welcomed her kiss, slanting his mouth over hers, his tongue slipping into her mouth, stroking and demanding as passion flared within her. Blake lowered her to the hay, his lips never leaving hers. He kissed her until nothing else remained save for the two of them, here, together, consumed with need.

When he trailed kisses across her cheek to the column of her neck, she whimpered with pure bliss. Carstine feathered her fingers over his shoulders. She cursed the clothing that separated her skin from his as she brought her fingers to tangle in his thick blond hair.

Desire swamped her causing a throbbing need to drive her actions as she arched against him—pressing her body to his. "Please. Please, Blake," she whimpered. "I need…"

He pressed his hand to the mound between her legs. Putting pressure and friction right where she needed it most.

"Ohh…aye." She rubbed against his hand, the tension building.

He brought his lips back to hers in a devastating kiss as he pulled her skirts up her thighs, leaving a trail of tingling skin in his wake.

Carstine clung to him, desperate for more. For him. For his skin on hers, his mouth against hers…

He found the curls at the apex of her thighs then smoothed one finger along the crease of her passage.

She jerked as a jolt of pleasure shot through her, then arched her hips in an effort to feel the glorious sensation again.

Blake slid his finger into her moist heat, and she moaned, "Yes, Blake, aye." She rocked against him, kissing him and pulling him close.

Mindless with overwhelming need and lost to passion, she slid her hand between them, searching. When she found the hard ridge of his manhood, she clasped her fingers around it.

"I want everything," she said on a sigh as she fumbled to unbutton his trousers.

Blake nipped at her lower lip. "Then, you shall have it." He pulled back, his hands going to the buttons she'd been working to undo. Then in an instant, he was pushing his trousers down his muscular thighs.

Carstine's pulse thrummed in unison with the pulsing need between her legs, and she reached for him, drawing him back to her.

Blake positioned himself between her thighs, and on instinct, she pressed her core against his cock, taking him into her.

Carstine's need was so great that she barley flinched at the burning discomfort that resulted.

BLAKE STIFFENED AND TURNED AWAY FROM HER. "YOU'VE NOT done this before?" He asked, accusation ringing in his voice. Anger surged through him. He did not need her to answer to know she was a bloody virgin!

He'd felt the evidence of it.

Why the devil hadn't she told him? He started to pull out, to leave her, but she arched against him, pulling his cock back into her slick heat and rendering him powerless.

She clung to him, her hips moving against him. "I need… Ah…This," she sighed. Her breathes coming in pants.

He well knew what she needed, and at this point, he was in the same state.

Blake hesitated before pulling back and plunging into her again. He should stop, but then the damage had already been done.

"Aye, Blake. Yes," she called out as she moved with him. Her slick passage stretching and pulsing around him. He was powerless in the face of her sweet seduction. He brought his lips back to hers, drowning her moans with his kisses. Blake thrust into her again and again until she threw her head back and broke apart in his arms.

He thrust a couple more times, then pulled out, spilling his seed across the creamy flesh of her mound. His heartbeat a crescendo as he rolled onto his back to stare at the stable ceiling.

His instincts told him to pull on his trousers and leave at once, but his breeding insisted he offer marriage. Blake blew out a slow breath as his mind battled over what should be done.

How had he let this happen? Him. A renowned rogue.

He'd had more than his share of liaisons. How had he misjudged her so grievously?

Her wanton actions and silky words had muddled his thinking. She'd seduced him. This travesty was of her making. Why should he be made to pay for her sins?

Anger heated his blood, overriding the final troughs of passion. He stood then retrieved his trousers and pulled them on before turning to her.

For a moment, he was rendered speechless at the sight of her stretched out on the bed of hey, her red hair streaming around her shoulders and bare legs stretched out.

Satisfaction was written all over her face. It reflected in the gentle parting of her kiss swollen lips and lazy droop of her eyelids, as much as it did in the flush covering her exposed skin.

Blake swallowed past the lump in his throat and averted his gaze. "I'll not marry you."

"I never asked ye tae," she said, her tone firm but voice shaking.

He brought his gaze back to her as she stood, her skirts billowing down to cover her shapely legs. "You should have told me."

"Ye never asked," she said, then gathered her skirts in her hands and fled into the night.

Blake started to go after her, then stopped. There was nothing else to say. Nothing else to do. He did not want a wife. Leastwise, not now. Certainly, not a wife who had tricked him into ruining her.

No, he'd not allow himself to be dog walked into the parsons' noose. He'd done the right thing, given the circumstances.

Blake had been honest, which was more than he could say for her.

So why did his heart ache?

He drew in a deep breath and closed his eyes. Momentary insanity. Nothing more. He'd not allow it to be more.

He'd not allow himself to love her.

Seven

Carstine gathered her courage as she approached the countess' private sitting room. She'd spent the previous two nights and all of Christmas Day considering what she should do. The time to act had come, and she'd made a decision.

Part of her was furious with Blake for how he'd treated her, but she also understood his reaction. He'd not been wrong.

She should have told him she was chaste. But why the devil had he thought otherwise?

And regardless, he should have given her some consideration rather than simply declaring he'd not marry her.

What if she had no wish to marry him?

Had he even considered that possibility? No. He'd been too worried about his freedom, his reputation, his—whatever the rogues' concern was—to speak to her with any kind of respect.

The truth was, had he offered for her, she would have accepted. But she'd not let him bed her with marriage in mind.

Carstine had never intended to trap him. She'd been carried away with emotion at the realization that she loved him and driven mad with passion.

Carstine stiffened her resolve. She had no regrets, save one: he didn't love her.

Carstine knocked at the door, then waited.

"Enter," the countess called out.

Carstine pushed the door open and stepped into the elegant room.

"Come, sit." The countess patted the spot beside her.

Creamy Aubusson carpet padded Carstine's footfalls as she moved to the yellow brocade sofa.

She gave the countess a forced smile as she sat beside her. "I'm sorry tae interrupt yer reading." Carstine glanced at the leather-bound book in the older woman's hand.

"Nonsense." the countess closed the volume and sat it on the cherry-wood table beside her. "I welcome the visit."

"I fear ye will soon change yer mind on that count." Carstine's stomach twisted over what she was about to reveal.

"I very much doubt that, dear." The countess gave a warm smile as she reached for Carstine's hand. "No use in putting the storm before the rain. Out with it then."

"I wish tae return tae Scotland." Carstine averted her gaze to the fire crackling in the marble hearth.

"Oh," the countess said.

Carstine returned her gaze to the older woman. "At once."

"I see." The countess looked speculative for a moment before she spoke again. "I fear your mother would be most displeased. She has her heart set on you experiencing a London season, and I dare say, she harbors some hope that you will marry an English gentleman."

"That isna possible."

"But of course, it is." The countess studied her for a heartbeat before continuing. "You've not yet been to London, and I assure you the gentlemen you've met here are but a small sampling of what awaits you there. Surely you will meet a man that catches your fancy."

Carstine fought against the moisture pooling in her eyes and blurted, "I'm ruined."

"Ruined," the countess repeated, her eyes going wide before her expression went blank. She gave Carstine's hand a slight squeeze, and said, "Then we shall see that the blackguard marries you." She leaned closer to Carstine, her eyes warm. "Who is responsible for this?"

"I am," Carstine said on a whisper as the first tear spilled from her eyes.

"Surely not." The countess brought her hand to rest on her

chest. "A woman is never to blame in these things." She met Carstine's gaze. "Give me his name."

Carstine shook her head as she dashed the tear away. "It's not important as I have no wish tae wed him."

She stood and turned toward the door, then stilled. "And no-one else will have a ruined woman. Not if they ken she is ruined, and I won't lie."

The countess placed her hand on Carstine's shoulder and turned her back to face her. "You must marry at once. What if you are with child?"

A bairn? No. Carstine shook her head. Blake had not spilled within her.

"You'd not sentence your child to live life as a bastard? Some blackguards by blow." The countess shook her head. "Surely not." She pulled Carstine into her embrace and hugged her. "I know this is hard, but you must marry. And you must do so with haste."

Carstine swallowed, her stomach lurching at what she must do. The countess was right. If even the tiniest chance existed that she carried a bairn, she had to marry.

Carstine nodded her consent. "Aye." If she could not marry the man she loved, then she saw no harm in marrying one she did not. After all, she'd made the bed she now laid in.

The countess stepped back, placing her hands on Carstine's shoulders and meeting her gaze. "I want you to be at your most charming tonight. The ball will be a perfect venue for us to find you a match."

Carstine nodded though she hardly heard a word the countess was saying. Her mind remained on the possibility of a bairn and how she'd come to be in this position.

How she'd lost her heart to Blake, then foolishly gave him her virtue.

"Mr. Kingston seems to be enamored with you. I'll see to it that he is cast into your path as often as possible. He'd make a splendid husband. Don't you agree?" The countess grinned.

Carstine bobbed her head and sighed.

The absurdity of the suggestion was not lost on her. She hardly knew Mr. Kingston, for she'd spent the entirety of their acquaintance trying to avoid his attentions.

Not because she was opposed to his suite so much as she was opposed to marrying any English man.

Though she had to admit that he was handsome and so far as she could tell an upstanding sort.

"He's not a lord, mind you, but he is very wealthy. He'll take fine care of you, dear." The countess released Carstine's shoulders and gave her a broad smile. "All will be well. You'll see, dear."

"Aye. I'm certain you are right." Carstine hoped against hope that the countess was indeed correct. That she wasn't about to make another colossal mistake.

The countess nudged Carstine toward the door. "Off with you now. If you're to be at your best tonight, you'll need the rest of the day to prepare. Start with a nap, then a bath. And be sure to have your maid ready your best gown."

Carstine nodded. "Thank you."

"You can thank me by getting yourself betrothed." The countess gave a conspiratorial wink.

Carstine gave her a forced smile then stepped into the hallway, closing the door behind her. She pivoted to start down the corridor, then froze.

Blake. Had he heard their conversation? Had he been eavesdropping? She stiffened her back and held her head high.

She didn't care if he had.

Blake reached out and captured her arm as she strolled past him.

Carstine stopped but did not look at him. She nibbled her lower lip as she waited for him to either speak or release his hold on her. When neither happened, she jerked her arm free and started walking once more.

"Wait."

She turned back to him, her gaze meeting his.

Blake took two steps in her direction, then stopped. "We should talk."

Carstine notched her chin defiantly and peered at him. "I have nothin tae say."

Blake's brow drew together, and he averted his gaze for a heartbeat before returning it to her. "In that case… Allow me to thank you for what you did in there." He nodded toward the countess' sitting room, his expression unreadable.

"Dinna Fash. It had nothin tae do with ye. My actions were for myself." Carstine pivoted away, then hurried down the hall. She had no desire to cause herself more pain and even less for him to discover that he'd broken her heart.

Eight

Blake lifted a glass of champagne off a passing servant's tray as he peered at Carstine and Kingston.

He huffed in disgust. The swain held her far to close as they danced. It almost looked as if she belonged to him. She most certainly did not belong to Kingston, but then, neither did she belong to Blake. He brought the flute to his lips and took a long drink.

He should be pleased that Carstine had not trapped him, but instead, her actions left him with an unidentified ache in his soul.

He'd tried to ignore her over the past two days. Tried to keep himself from thinking about her—from remembering what they had shared, but it was to no avail.

Kingston drew Carstine close and held her too tight for Blake's liking as he led her through a waltz. When the man's hand roamed indecently low on her back, Blake scowled. Why the deuce was he so bothered by the pair?

Jealousy.

Bloody hell, he was jealous. Blake had not experienced that particular emotion in years. Not since he was a green lad.

He brought the crystal flute to his lips and drained the contents. His heart pounded and ached as he sat the flute aside then strode toward the ballroom entrance.

He had to escape the sight of Carstine and Kingston before he did something stupid. Before he let his jealousy show, or God forbid, proposed.

"Blake," Minerva smiled as she captured his elbow, "Surely you were not planning to leave before dancing with your favorite sister?"

He leveled his gaze on her. "You are my only sister."

"Bother that." She tugged him toward the polished dance floor. "It's all the more reason why we must dance."

Blake groaned inwardly, but he did not resist. He turned a charming smile on Minerva and said, "Indeed."

Having reached the crowded dance floor, he twirled Minerva then brought her close. She met his eyes, concern reflecting in hers. "I could not help but notice you acting odd these past days."

"Me? Odd? Never." He smiled.

"Rubbish." She tilted her chin, stubbornly. "You have been morose and standoffish. And don't think for one moment that I haven't noticed you staring at Carstine."

Minerva's gaze wandered to where Kingston and Carstine danced before returning to Blake. "Whatever is going on?"

Blake arched a curious eyebrow. "You did not ask her?"

"Oh, I did." Minerva pursed her lips and peered at him. "She would only say that she'd determined to marry and as such, no longer required your help."

"Well, there you have it." Blake twirled her, buying himself a moment of silence before bringing her close again.

"You don't honestly expect me to believe such nonsense." Minerva studied him for a heartbeat, her gaze searching. "She was determined not to marry this season. What changed her mind?"

"How should I know?" Blake grinned. "Women are fickle creatures. Perhaps Kingston has quite swept her off her feet." His heart squeezed as he spoke, a lump forming in his throat.

He knew perfectly well that Carstine did not fancy the merchant.

"Hells bells, Blake!" Minerva's eyes narrowed. "Don't play the fool with me. I perfectly well know that you and Carstine have feelings for each other. I dare say you're in love. And love is the only reason she'd change her mind about marriage."

There it was. The emotion he'd refused to acknowledge and clearly done a poor job of hiding.

Love.

153

He'd refused to consider it. Refused to name the emotions he felt for Carstine. But dammit, he did love her.

Blake's jaw twitched with the effort it took to control himself. To keep from speaking.

When had Minerva become so astute?

And why the devil did she insist on meddling?

Minerva poked her finger into his chest. "Go ahead. Deny your feelings for her." She peered at him through knowing eyes. "I dare you."

"It hardly signifies at this point."

Minerva's expression softened. "Love is everything. A rare gift granted only to the luckiest among us. Don't throw it away."

"When did you become such a romantic?" Blake shook his head.

Minerva gave him a reproachful look. "We are not discussing me, and I'll not allow you to change the subject." She glanced at Carstine and Kingston. "Tell me what you intend to do about Carstine?"

"Nothing," Blake said, his voice so low it could have been a whisper.

"You cannot be serious," Minerva argued.

He released a breath then said with conviction, "Carstine made her choice, and I shall honor it."

"Of all, the…the…ignorant things to say." Minerva frowned. "I won't allow it."

"Is that so?" Blake chuckled as he spun Minerva around. "And how do you intend to change a situation you do not understand?"

"I'll find a way," she said, confidence and stubborn determination in her tone. "I'll not allow you to throw away happiness."

The quartet struck the final cords of the waltz, and Blake led Minerva from the dance floor.

"I admire your determination, Minerva, but I must insist that you stay out of this." He turned to face her, then placed his fingers beneath her chin and tipped her head so that their gazes meet. "Rather, I demand that you do."

"But, Blake—"

"No arguing, Minerva." He met her determined stare with a stern one of his own. "There is nothing you can do. Nothing Carstine, nor I wish for you to do."

"You cannot be serious."

"Oh, but I am."

Minerva released a shallow breath. "But you love her, and she loves you."

A stab of pain shot through his heart, followed by a surge of hope at Minerva's words.

Carstine loved him. Was it true? Did it matter one way or another? After all, she'd deceived him. More than that, she'd choose Kingston. But how could he blame her for her choice when he'd given her no other option?

"Bloody hell." He ran his hand through his hair and sighed. What a colossal mess.

"You needn't curse, Blake," Minerva chastised. "If you insist on being stubborn, then I shall leave you to your misery." She pivoted and strolled away but not before he saw the spark of mischief in her blue eyes.

Heaven help him.

Nine

"He's here," Minerva announced as she stepped into the library. "Mother said you should come at once."

"Thank ye." Carstine stood and smoothed her skirts. "I just need a moment."

"I'd not thank me. Not when we both know you are making a mistake." Minerva stepped closer and took Carstine's hands. "You cannot marry Mr. Kingston. Not when you are in love with Blake," she implored.

Carstine pulled her hands free and turned toward the hearth. "Ye dinna ken what ye are sayin."

"Rubbish." Minerva placed her hand on Carstine's shoulder. "Don't be a fool. Go to Blake. Go now. Tell him how you feel."

Carstine turned back, her gaze meeting Minerva's. "Ye are a dear friend, but yer mad. I dinna love Blake. I will marry Mr. Kingston. He's a fine match."

Minerva sighed, her shoulders rising and falling with the effort. "You are as stubborn as my brother, and mark my words; you will both pay a heavy price for your bullheaded natures."

She waved her hand at the door. "Well, go then. Don't let me stand in the way of your happiness."

Carstine cringed, her heart hitching. She knew that Minerva spoke the truth. She would always regret spending her life without the man she loved, but there was nothing for it.

She could scarcely force Blake to love her, and forcing him to marry her would only breed indifference, if not hate. She could not do that to him—to herself.

She inhaled a steadying breath then nodded before strolling from the room.

Perhaps Minerva was wrong. Maybe she and Mr. Kingston would have a wonderful future together. One that would remove all thoughts of Blake from her mind.

Not bloody likely. No matter how good a husband, Mr. Kingston, turned out to be, Carstine would always love Blake. But that did not mean she would pine for the rest of her days.

She could find a way to be happy. Her stomach twisted even as she tried to convince herself that she was doing the right thing, and she knew it was rubbish. Just as Minerva had said.

But nonetheless, it was rubbish she had committed to. With each step that brought her closer to the parlor, her heartbeat more furiously, and her stomach twisted.

By the time Carstine reached the parlor door, she was fighting tears. She leaned against the wall and wrapped her arms around her stomach. *Breath. Just breath*, she told herself.

After taking a moment to clear her head and school her features, Carstine entered the parlor.

"My dear, Miss Carstine." Mr. Kingston bowed over her hand before depositing a kiss to the back of her knuckles. "You are a vision."

Carstine gave a forced smile and prayed it did not ring false. "Good afternoon, Mr. Kingston."

The countess approached, her smile broad and eyes sparkling. "It is a splendid day indeed," she announced.

The countess turned her smile on Mr. Kingston. "I believe we have concluded our business, so I'll leave you to speak with Carstine." She gave Carstine an encouraging nod, then turned and strolled to the far corner of the parlor.

Carstine swallowed hard as she met Mr. Kingston's warm gaze. He truly was a handsome man, and well mannered too. She certainly could do worse.

So why was she so distraught? This was, after all, what she wanted. Wasn't it?

Mr. Kingston reached for her hands. "It is no secret that I am enamored with you. I have been from the first moment I laid eyes on you."

Her mind screamed at her to stop him. To prevent this madness before it went too far, but instead, Carstine pressed her lips together and gave a small nod.

Mr. Kingston gave her a warm smile before continuing. "My dear…may I use your given name?"

Carstine gave another nod, her stomach twisting, and throat swelling.

His smile grew, his eyes lighting. "My dearest Carstine, will you make me the happiest man in all of Britain by consenting to be my wife?"

Speak, she urged herself. *Say yes.* "I…" She choked on the words. "I…"

The parlor door swung open. Startled, she turned to face the entrance as Blake sauntered in. Her breath hitched.

BLAKE COULD NOT SAY WHAT CHANGED HIS MIND, BUT WHEN Minerva told him Kingston had come to propose all thought fled his mind, save for one, Carstine could not marry Kingston.

He'd downed the tumbler of whisky in his hand, slammed the glass on the sideboard, and made haste for the parlor.

Dammit, he did love her. He hadn't planned to. Hadn't wanted to. But he did love her, and if there was a chance that she returned his feelings…

He could not allow her to commit to another man.

Blake did not pause when he reached the parlor door. He pushed it open and stormed into the room. "Wait." His gaze went to Carstine, his heart hammering.

"You cannot marry Kingston," he said, his tone frantic.

Carstine stared at him, her lips slightly parted and eyes wide.

Blake went to her and took her hands from Kingston's. "You cannot marry him. Not when I am in love with you."

She inhaled sharply, her green eyes hazed with moisture. "You love me?"

"I do," Blake said with all of the conviction he felt, and he lifted a silent prayer that she saw it too. "I love you with all I am, and I want to marry you. I want to take you to wife and spend the rest of my days redeeming myself. I want to have children with you and hold your hand in old age. I want to protect you and care for you. Carstine, marry me."

A rogue tear slid down her cheek and he reached out to brush it away. "Carstine?"

She closed her eyes and wet her lips.

"Do not punish us both for my idiotic choices. Marry me, Carstine. Allow me to redeem myself."

She opened her eyes, her gaze locking on his, searching. And just when he thought he could take no more of the silence, she spoke. "I love ye tae."

Blake pulled her into his arms and hugged her close. The scent of her, vanilla and jasmine, wrapped around him, warming his soul as he dropped a kiss to the top of her head.

She pulled back to look at him, and he captured her lips with his in an all-consuming kiss. When he pulled away, she placed her hand on his chest and smiled mischievously. "I did not answer yer question yet."

His heart seemed to stop as her words sank in. She hadn't said yes. But she had said she loved him.

Was love enough? He drew in a breath, his gaze never leaving hers, then asked, "Will you marry me?"

Her smile broadened. "I will."

Minerva rushed forward, wrapping her arms around the pair of them. "I knew you'd come to your senses. I'm so happy for you!"

"Ahem." Mother cleared her throat, and Minerva stepped away from Carstine and Blake, as Mr. Kingston quietly slipped from the parlor.

She glanced from Blake to Carstine and back again. "I must admit that I am rather surprised." Mother drew closer. "But happy nonetheless." She gave them a bright smile and said, "You have my blessing."

Carstine stepped away from Blake and went to Mother. "Thank you, my lady."

"There will be no more of that. Not when I am to be your mother-in-law." Mother pulled Carstine into a warm embrace.

Blake feared he would explode with happiness as all of the past day's frustrations and heartache melted away.

He reached for the golden pin he wore on his lapel and gave it a twirl. The symbol for the Wicked Earls' Club. He'd not be needing it anymore, for he'd found his forever.

Ten

New Years Day

"I now pronounce you husband and wife, Earl and Countess of Edgemore."

Blake pulled his wife into his arms and pressed his lips to hers amidst an uproar of cheers.

All of the local families, as well as Carstine's parents, and of course, his mother and sister, were present. All of them were watching as well, but Blake did not mind one bit. He intended to kiss his wife at every opportunity and welcomed any ensuing scandals.

"Yer indecent." Carstine laughed when he, at last, pulled his mouth from hers.

Blake gave a roguish grin. "And you love every second of it."

"Aye." She winked as she took his proffered arm.

Blake escorted her from the parish church, then handed her into his carriage—their carriage. A moment later, he was seated beside her. "Come here, wife." He held his arm out, inviting her to come close.

Carstine slid over on the leather seat, snuggling against him as he wrapped his arm around her. She nuzzled his chest, and not for the first time today, Blake regretted that they wore clothing.

She grinned up at him. "It seems fortuitous that we are starting our life together on the same day we start a new year."

He pulled her onto his lap. "One more thing to celebrate, Countess." He brushed his lips across hers and reveled in the little sigh that escaped her. Blake deepened the kiss as he moved one hand beneath her skirt, searching.

When he found the soft curls between her thighs, he stroked his fingers along the crease. She was already hot and so wet. His cock twitched at the discovery, a desperate need growing within him.

Carstine turned in his lap so that her thighs pressed to either side of his. She reached between them, undoing the buttons of his trousers.

He trailed kisses across her jaw to the hollow of her throat. Lapping and suckling her creamy flesh as she writhed and moaned against him.

Carstine gave him a satisfied smile when his cock sprung free from the confines of his breeches. Her passion-filled gaze held his as she bent to kiss him, desperate and sensual.

She placed his cock where she wanted it then sank down onto him.

A hiss of satisfaction tore from Blake's gut as he entered her. So tight, so warm, so his. She belonged to him, and he to her.

He cupped her bottom as she rocked back and forth, both giving and taking pleasure.

His angel, his everything.

Blake brought her mouth back to his, kissing her soundly as he lifted her, then laid her across the carriage seat.

He came down over her, his cock sliding back into her warmth as he worked to free her breasts from the confines of her gown. He wanted to see all of her, to feel every silken inch of his wife's bare skin.

She arched and ground against him as he brought his lips to one of her rose-colored nipples and drew the pebbled tip into his mouth.

Carstine moaned and panted her pleasure as he worshipped her. Thrusting in and out of her heat at the same time, he kissed and suckled her breasts as though he'd never get enough of her.

And perhaps he wouldn't. He'd not been complete without her. Blake had gone through the motions of life and drowned his boredom with his club.

He'd not complained because he hadn't known he'd been missing anything.

But now?

Now he knew he'd been missing her—his Carstine. His other half.

"Blake, oh, Blake," she moaned, her breaths coming in pants and sighs.

He slipped his hand between them to stroke the tight nub at the top of her sex, and she bucked against him, greedily seeking her release.

"Aye, yes. Blake dinna stop."

He thrust into her again, bringing his mouth close to her ear and saying, "Come for me, angel."

Another flick of his thumb over her hard nub and she came apart beneath him.

Her passage pulsed around his cock as he took his own pleasure before rolling off of her more sated than he'd ever been.

Blake pulled her into his arms as he lounged against the carriage seat, his heart pounding and blood warm with satisfaction.

Carstine feathered her fingers over his chest and grinned. "Do ye think we shall ever make love in a bed?" She asked, her gaze teasing as much as her tone.

Blake gave her a roguish look and answered, "We shall." He stroked his hand over her bare chest. "I intend to make love to you every chance I get, no matter the location."

Her cheeks colored as she arched one red eyebrow. "No matter where?" She questioned.

"You may rely on it, love." Blake kissed her again, his mind roaming to all of the possible ways, and many places, where he could make love to his wife.

She gave a devilish grin. "Will ye make love to me in the library?"

He nodded.

"And what of the billiards room?"

"Without question." He flicked his thumb over her nipple, and her breath caught.

"Will ye take me home and make love to me in our bed?"

"Now?" He asked, his cock already hardening with renewed need.

"Aye." She bit her lower lip and stared at him, her gaze sultry.

"I will do anything you wish. You need only ask."

"Will ye love me for the rest of yer life?" She asked through hooded eyes.

"With every beat of my heart," he said, and he knew it to be the truth the same as he knew he'd never deserve her. But he would spend the rest of his days trying to be good enough. Endeavoring to be the man she deserved.

"Ye are a lucky man for I love ye too, and with every breath I draw, I shall love ye more."

Blake nuzzled his face against her soft hair. He was a lucky man, indeed. Carstine was his every desire, his every fantasy, and most importantly, she was his soulmate.

USA Today Bestselling author Amanda Mariel dreams of days gone by when life moved at a slower pace. She enjoys taking pen to paper and exploring historical time periods through her imagination and the written word. When she is not writing she can be found reading, crocheting, traveling, practicing her photography skills, or spending time with her family.

Visit www.amandamariel.com to learn more about Amanda and her books. Sign up for Amanda's newsletter while you are on her website to stay up-to-date on all things Amanda Mariel and receive a free eBook!

Text AmandaMariel to 38470 to be notified by SMS/text message *ONLY* when there is a new release or book sale. Bonus: Receive a free eBook when you subscribe!! **At this time SMS/text notifications are only available in the US and Canada**

Amanda loves to hear from her fans! Email her at amanda@amandamariel.com or find her on social media:

Also by Amanda Mariel

His Perfect Hellion

Coming next to the A Rogue's Kiss series

Her Perfect Scoundrel

Standalone titles

One Moonlit Tryst

One Enchanting Kiss

Christmas in the Duke's Embrace

One Wicked Christmas

On preorder now

A Lyon in her Bed

Courting Temptation

Mists of Babylon series

Love's Legacy

One Wanton Wager

Forever in Your Arms

Wicked Earls' Club

Titles by Amanda Mariel

Earl of Grayson

Earl of Edgemore

Coming next to the Wicked Earls' Club

Earl of Persuasion

Fated for a Rogue

A Wallflower's Folly

Coming next to the Fated for a Rogue series

One Fateful May Day

Connected by a Kiss

These are designed so they can standalone

How to Kiss a Rogue (Amanda Mariel)

A Kiss at Christmastide (Christina McKnight)

A Wallflower's Christmas Kiss (Dawn Brower)

Stealing a Rogue's Kiss (Amanda Mariel)

A Gypsy's Christmas kiss (Dawn Brower)

A Duke's Christmas Kiss (Tammy Andresen)

Box sets and anthologies

Visit www.amandamariel.com to see Amanda's current offerings.

Thank you so much for taking the time to read Earl of Edgemore.

Your opinion matters!

Please take a moment to review this book on your favorite review site and share your opinion with fellow readers.

USA Today bestselling author

~Heartwarming historical romances that leave you breathless~

The Duke's Scandalous
Christmas Wish

ARI THATCHER

One

November 1816
Camborne House

Richard Foote, Duke of Alconbury winced at the crash ringing from the nursery above his friend's study and reflexively ducked his head. "You didn't consider the noise your darling hellions could produce when you chose this room as your sanctuary, I take it."

Ephraim Willoughby, Viscount Camborne, who sat in a chair near the fire, set down his newspaper and chuckled. "The children weren't born when we moved here, but now I understand why Father's room was in the other wing. Our Sammy has become much more active since the weather turned cool. They've been rather quiet today, though."

Shaking his head, Richard returned to gazing out the window overlooking the frozen kitchen garden. A young woman wearing a drab gray gown, unadorned black cloak and equally plain bonnet paced back and forth in one corner. There was nothing about her to hold his attention, but he continued to watch. She looked like a servant who was afraid to face the housekeeper's stern scowl.

Suddenly she turned, shielding her eyes from the ray of sunlight breaking through the clouds, and looked directly at him.

Recognition dawned as he took in the heart-shaped face of the viscountess' sister, Miss Milly Hudson. He hadn't seen her in more than a year, when they were at the small gathering of family and close friends following her fiancé's funeral. The harsh color of her half-mourning garb washed away any bloom in her features, leaving her wan. Such a pity, given the striking beauty she was. The Christmas season was clearly still difficult for her to face without Tobias.

"Well, at least she won't spend it alone," Richard muttered aloud.

"Who won't spend what alone?" Ephraim asked.

"What?" Richard walked back to the seat he'd vacated a short time ago. "I didn't realize I'd spoken aloud. Milly is in the garden. She appeared sad. I thought it kind of Arnetta to invite her here so she's not alone over the holidays."

"Sad? I wouldn't use that word to describe Milly. She came to keep Arnetta company during her confinement with Billie. Milly is in charge of the holiday festivities, and my housekeeper is none too pleased," Ephraim added with a laugh.

"Isn't Arnetta the one who would be displeased? It's her household."

Ephraim shrugged, setting the newspaper on the small table beside him. "Arnetta was more than happy to relinquish the duties this year. She isn't fully recovered from Billie's birth, and since Sammy and Ann are now old enough to participate, she wants us to take part in all the traditions her family celebrates."

"All the traditions? What does that mean? Am I going to wish I'd decided to delay my arrival until Christmas Eve?"

"I'm not quite certain, to be honest. Milly and Arnetta have many more customs than we are used to, I'll wager. It should be interesting, at least."

Richard's lips twisted to one side as he considered what lay ahead for him over the next few weeks. As he had no family of his own, he didn't normally celebrate the holidays, much less the entire month before Christmas. But his estate didn't need him there; his steward performed his job competently and enjoyed giving out the Boxing Day gifts. While he'd never admit to lone-liness, Richard appreciated that Ephraim and Arnetta—Arnetta, most especially, enjoyed having him stay with them. "I hope the ladies don't expect me to participate in anything more than eating mince and pies. Those other traditions are for children."

"Arnetta would understand, but I'll let *you* tell Milly. She assumes everyone is as excited about the holiday as she is."

A *thud* shook the ceiling, followed by a small child's laughter. The noise was so loud Richard fully expected to find plaster covering his sleeves. "Have you invited the entire village to play in your nursery? What are they doing up there?"

"Using up their endless energy, I imagine. You should go upstairs and visit with them. They've missed you."

"Perhaps later, if it's not too cold, I can join them in the park so they can run." The idea of being in a closed room with those wild urchins was more intimidating than staring down an angry bull. "It's apparent they don't require my company to enjoy themselves."

Laughing, Ephraim leaned back in his chair. "You are afraid of them. I never would have guessed it."

"I am not afraid. I prefer 'astutely cautious.' I know Arnetta has them well trained enough to be civilized when guests are present, but they're still too young to be trusted in their native habitat."

"You aren't a guest, you are family," Ephraim argued. "We've known each other since we were mere lads."

"My point exactly—they can't be trusted around me. As I said, I'll visit with them out of doors."

A tap came from the doorway followed by a sweet voice. "Am I interrupting?" Milly asked.

"Come in." Ephraim motioned for her to join them. "Richard just arrived, and we were catching up on news."

"It's good to see you again, Your Grace," Milly said. "You've arrived just in time for stir up."

Whatever that was, it could explain all the noise in the nursery. Those children were definitely stirred up. "Stir up?" Richard asked as he rose to greet her.

"Of course. We must stir up the plum puddings today so they may age properly before Christmas."

She wanted him to help bake plum puddings? He'd grown up with a staff to cook his meals. He failed to see how he could contribute, nor did the idea sound intriguing. "Ah, well then, I'm sure the cook will be busy this afternoon."

She stood beside the desk, her smile growing, one hip cocked to the side in a casual stance. With her cloak and bonnet removed, she looked slightly less severe, although her ashy brown hair styled in its simple twist did nothing to soften her features. She'd been pretty once, before the light left her eyes. "But we all must stir the pudding at least once, for luck."

"For luck?" Ephraim beat him to the question.

"Yes, luck for the entire household." She met Richard's gaze. "We wouldn't wish anything bad to happen to Ephraim and Arnetta's family, would we?"

Richard shifted uncomfortably, growing warm under her scrutiny. She would have him cast as the Christmas villain for his lack of cooking skills, would she? But he wasn't going to play her game. "Of course not. I fail to see how my not stirring the pudding would bring bad luck. My parents' cook managed well without me all these years."

"It's tradition. Every year on the Sunday before Advent, the vicar reads the Book of Common Prayer. 'Stir up, O Lord, we beseech thee—'"

Ephraim cleared his throat. "We know the passage, Milly. No need to recite it for us."

A flattering shade of peach crept over Milly's cheeks. She studied them as if they spoke a foreign language. "Didn't your families have Christmas traditions?"

Pushed by a sudden, inexplicable need to defend his family, Richard responded. "Naturally. We went to church that morning and had a special supper with roast goose and yes, plum pudding for dessert. And not once did the cook require our assistance in the preparation of any of it."

She walked toward him, her head tilted to one side as she studied his face. "That's all? You don't do anything more to celebrate?"

"Well, we exchanged gifts. And Mother gave out baskets to our neighbors on St. Stephen's Day," Richard said.

"I imagine she also saw that the greenery had been gathered to place about her home, and supervised any other decorating. This is my favorite time of year. I love the way the house smells when it's filled with evergreen branches."

She was correct. Before his parents died, when he arrived home a day or two before Christmas the work had already been done. And the house had had a crisp, fresh scent to it, now that he thought about it. He hadn't paid much attention to that while growing up. And he hadn't been home for Christmas in the three years since his parents died in a carriage accident. He spent as little time as possible there.

Milly turned to Ephraim. "Perhaps you two will find a suitable Yule log."

Ephraim held up a hand and shook his head. "I have no objection to greens, but even the kitchen hearth isn't big enough for an entire tree. I say no Yule log."

"But it brings so much good luck," she argued. "You must spread the ashes in the fields for the crops and put some in the well to be certain the water stays safe."

Richard hadn't realized she held to such superstitions. He wasn't aware there were so many superstitions around Christmastide. "Do you truly believe in luck? And that it can be manipulated by such pagan rituals?"

Her smile faded, revealing hollows in her cheeks he hadn't noticed before. Her chin lifted slightly in a very stubborn set. "I'm not a simpleton, nor a pagan. I don't believe stirring the Christmas pudding for luck means I may run barefoot in the rain without my cloak. The gods wouldn't really punish us for not burning the Yule log. But so many things in life are left to chance. Who does it hurt to continue the traditions? If we lose them, we lose some of the richness of our lives."

"Children do enjoy the little rituals," Ephraim said. "I have fond memories of the season when we were young. Receiving gifts on St. Nicholas Day awakened the anticipation of more to come."

Milly folded her arms across her chest and stretched to her full, yet insignificant, height. "Well, we are about to gather in the kitchen for stir up. Your children expect you to join us."

With that, she left. Richard watched her glide through the doorway, and he chuckled. "When did she become such a harridan? She'd have the Iron Duke quaking in his boots."

Rising, Ephraim laughed. "She never yells. She simply makes one feel guilty if one dares to disregard her wishes."

"We'd better hurry, then." Richard followed the viscount below stairs, the sound of happy voices and laughter growing louder as they neared the kitchen.

Arnetta and the children already waited there, gathered at a long table. Two-year-old Ann knelt on a bench, eyeing the ingredients with wonder while newborn Billie slept in his mother's arm. The pinkish circles below Arnetta's eyes spoke of her lack of sleep.

Four-year-old Sammy tugged on his aunt Milly's skirts. "Can I put the silver in the puddings?"

"We shall ask Cook if she'll allow it. She's not happy when we get in her way."

"I shan't get in her way, I promise. I'll drop the threepence in and jump away like this." Sammy sprang into the air to demonstrate.

Milly squeezed his shoulders and pressed her cheek to the top of his head, her features glowing, a soft chuckle escaping her smiling lips. "I don't believe we'll need to go to that extreme. Simply stepping aside should do."

From his position at the end of the long, rough table farthest from the fire, Richard observed the others. The cook's assistant pulled the dark turnspit chain at the hearth, rotating a large joint of meat on the spit over the flames. The footmen in their olive green livery gazed about with bored, vacant stares but they stood at attention in a corner in front of the large hutch. The butler kept glancing at the doorway as if he judged his chances of making an escape.

On the table were several enormous bowls filled with brown, speckled batter. Milly picked up the wooden spoon sitting nearby. "Let's begin. Arnetta, do you want to recite the blessing?"

Sammy climbed onto a stool and peered into the bowl. "I know it. Mama taught me. 'Stir up, we b'seech thee, O Lord, the wills of thy faithful people; that they, plenshusly bringing forth the fruit of good works, may of thee be plenshusly rewarded.'"

Milly and the others chuckled at his earnest recitation. "Very well done, Sammy, thank you. You may be the first to stir. Don't forget to make a wish." She lifted Sammy closer to the bowl to take his turn.

Ephraim and Arnetta stirred and stepped out of the way. Richard stepped forward and reached for the spoon.

"Don't forget to make a wish," Milly repeated, her raised brow daring him to argue.

As he took the spoon, certain she wouldn't know whether he

wished or not, he noted the slight shadows beneath her eyes, and the lack of sparkle within. All his bravado left him, his stubborn insistence in only making the minimal effort to keep the peace. He sighed. What would it cost him to make a wish? He barely needed to think on it. *I wish for Milly to be truly happy again.* He ran the spoon around the bowl.

When they proceeded through the servants one by one and the last one had a turn, Arnetta thanked them all. "Shall we have some biscuits in the nursery?" she asked the children.

Sammy and two-year-old Ann clapped and cheered. "Yes please."

"Come have biscuits," Sammy pleaded, tugging on Richard's hand.

"I must read some papers I brought with me," he replied, although he squeezed the boy's fingers with fondness.

Ephraim picked up Ann and walked toward the hallway. "Surely you can have one biscuit and a glass of milk," he called over his shoulder to Richard.

Richard sighed. He didn't care for sweets, and liked milk even less. "Very well. One biscuit before work."

As they left the kitchen, Milly spoke to Mrs. Avery. "Biscuits are more appealing than adding the coins to the batter, it would seem. Here are the threepence for you to add. I leave you to your work."

"Thank you, miss," Mrs. Avery said, her relief evident in her tone.

Richard trudged up the stairs at the slow speed of the four-year-old boy. All that pomp for ten minutes' worth of batter stirring. What other rituals did Milly have in store over the next few weeks? He might regret agreeing to spend the entire month in the viscount's household.

Two

A few mornings later, as Milly had her toast and tea in the dining room, Richard joined her, his face colored by his early morning ride. She greeted him as he piled eggs onto a plate from the warming dish on the sideboard. "Did you get caught in the downpour? Between that and the cold, you won't need coffee to shake off your night's sleep."

"I'd just returned when the worst of it hit. My ride was very refreshing," he commented.

"Thank goodness. It would be horrid if you caught a chill and became ill over Christmas."

"That would be bad luck, wouldn't it? And we can't have that."

Milly looked up to see if he teased her, but his back was to her.

Richard turned, his face showing no expression, and sat opposite her. He placed the linen napkin in his lap before lifting his fork. "Have the others eaten already?"

"Ephraim has. I imagine Arnetta is eating with the children in the nursery."

His lips pulled down as he set down his coffee cup. "She's brave."

"It pleases her to be with them. I think it perfectly natural to want to spend as much time as one can with one's children." If Milly had children of her own, she would do the same.

Richard ate in silence. When he'd cleaned his plate, he asked, "What plans do you ladies have for us today?"

"Does this mean you intend to participate?" That sounded sharper than she intended. "Forgive me, I didn't think our preparations appealed to you."

"I took part in the stirring thing." He took a sip of coffee, never breaking eye contact.

"So you did. Please don't feel you must join in our traditions if you don't wish to." Arnetta had encouraged her to do as she wanted with the preparations, but Milly hated to think she was lessening someone else's enjoyment of the season.

He patted his mouth with his napkin. "If the children enjoy it, I don't mind playing along. Advent begins Sunday. Shouldn't we gather branches and holly to decorate the house?"

"No, it's bad luck—" She broke off, suddenly certain he teased her. "You make sport of me."

Richard held up his hands in a defensive posture. "I didn't. I was quite earnest. I wasn't aware there's a schedule for these things."

"Yes, the greenery mustn't be brought in until Christmas Eve."

"Most likely to keep them from drying out before Christmas," he offered. "I remember a few house fires in the village on St. Stephen's Day or the following week, when we were young."

"Possibly. I only know Mama didn't allow it."

"Did she enjoy the holiday as much as you and Arnetta?"

Memories flooded her with delight. "Oh, yes. She made each of us a small gift, monogrammed handkerchiefs or lace-trimmed bonnets. I'm afraid I don't take after her in skill, but I enjoy making what I can. Aunt Sophie and I will be shopping today for St. Nicholas gifts, and a few things I need to finish the ones for Christmas."

"Now there's a tradition I'm familiar with. Perhaps I should accompany the two of you. I haven't bought anything yet."

She was surprised he hadn't shopped in London before he came to Little Bookham. The variety there would make choosing a gift easier. As he sipped his coffee, Milly studied him. His straight black hair remained neatly in place, swept to one side off his face, even after wearing his hat and riding in damp weather. She'd always felt he was the more handsome of the two men, although Ephraim laughed more and was easier to be around. Richard was very rigid in his manner, saw things only in the black and white rules he'd likely been taught as the son of a duke. Arnetta had chosen well in marrying Ephraim, just as Milly had in choosing Tobias Dobney.

Just thinking her former fiancé's name brought a sigh, but that was an enormous improvement over the wrenching agony and tears she'd suffered immediately after his death. At first, she'd thought her own life had ended, but lately she recalled their happiest times with fondness. She was richer for having loved him, even for such a short time.

Tobias wasn't as handsome as Richard, either, if she was honest. He'd had a kind, pleasant face. Richard's straight nose and full lips could have been sculpted in marble—well, for all she knew he probably did have a likeness of himself in a grand gallery in Alconbury, as well as a few portraits hanging among those of his ancestors. Suddenly she wondered if he'd smiled in any of them. His smile was a thing of beauty in itself.

Richard rose from the table, bringing Milly out of her reverie. Straightening his waistcoat, he said, "If you'll excuse me, I believe I'll challenge Ephraim to a game of chess."

"If he doesn't wish to play, I would love to," Milly responded. "If you are game?"

"Of course. I've played against ladies in the past. I can play against him another time."

Milly led the way into the drawing room toward the front of the house. "But have you lost to many ladies?"

He laughed, coming to walk beside her when they entered the room. "You are very sure of yourself. We'll see how your tune changes after we've played."

As she sat, Milly grabbed a pawn from each side, dropped them in her lap where he couldn't see, and cupped one in her hand. "Black or white?"

"White."

She held up her hand to show the white piece. "Excellent, you will start the game. I prefer being black."

He pulled back his arm without taking his turn. "Don't tell me. Black is your lucky color."

What was his obsession with luck? "Of course not. I rely on skill when I play chess. I just prefer the black pieces."

184

"How interesting. You feel strongly enough about luck to adhere to a strict schedule when it comes to decorating for Christmas, but you have no rituals for other activities in your daily life?" He slid a pawn forward a space.

Milly made her move without much thought. "What you call rituals, I call tradition. It's common practice to prepare puddings the week before Advent, so they may age properly. We add silver coins as a treat for the children and servants. While tradition says finding the coin promises wealth in the coming year, it's also a simple way to bring joy to others. The same with St. Stephen's Day."

Richard moved another pawn to a new position. "St. Stephen's Day brings good luck?"

"Wouldn't you say the families receiving the boxes of food and trinkets feel lucky?"

"I suppose so. I'd never considered it." He waited for her to move a piece.

Milly pondered whether the dowager duchess had given out boxes or baskets the day after Christmas as was the custom, then remembered he'd said she had. Hadn't she involved her son in the task? Richard had no artificial airs about him, but he seemed unaware of how the poor survived. How sad it was to think he could have reached adulthood with such a narrow window on the lives of the people around him. Who was looking out for his tenants and servants now?

She grew tired of talking about luck, so she changed the subject as she took her turn. "Do you remain in London throughout the winter?"

"Yes, I'll return there after the holiday." He lifted his gaze from the chessboard, his pale-blue eyes catching her off guard.

She was unable to look away and hesitated while searching for conversation. All thought had left her mind. "I can't imagine there are many families there to call upon. What do you do with yourself?"

His lips spread wide, reiterating just how breathtakingly handsome he was. "I do the same things as the rest of the year. I read. Go to my club. I box with Gentleman John a few times a week."

"But during the Season you attend assemblies, the opera, the theatre," she prodded. She wanted to know him better.

Wished to be free to talk to him as they had before she'd met Tobias.

"If I must. I really have no need to go about in Society. Soon enough, I'll feel the pressure of my age and submit to the marriage mart, but not yet." He was thirty-one years old. Many men were married by that age. Certainly, the need for an heir had to be in his thoughts.

"By now everyone has gone home to their country houses. We've received invitations to local assemblies. This will be a busy few weeks."

He took his turn, then sat back, again watching her. "Will these be your first social gatherings since you left mourning?"

She lowered her gaze to the board and feigned working out her next move. "Yes." Noticing her gray wool sleeve when she reached for her knight, she realized she needed a new gown or two, as most of her wardrobe was half-mourning colors.

"It will be good to see you dance again."

Milly was compelled to look up at Richard. Nothing but sincerity showed in his features. Suddenly self-conscious, her heart beat stronger and she grew warm. "Thank you."

They continued their small talk as they played, and Milly relaxed in his company. This was how her life had been before Tobias. The duke and viscount had called on her sister often in the summer when Ephraim was courting Arnetta. After Arnetta and Ephraim married, Milly was often visiting when Richard came to call. They'd developed an easy friendship.

Studying the board, she realized he'd left an opening she couldn't pass up. The opportunity to best him was too perfect, even though it would end the game so soon. Setting her bishop in place, she said, "Checkmate."

Richard's mouth turned down at the corners and his brows grew together. "That's not possible."

"It's very possible. Do you see a move you have open?"

His lips pressed together. "I do not."

She tried very hard to keep the gloating smile under control. "You have now been beaten by a woman."

RICHARD STOOD IN THE ENTRY HALL THAT AFTERNOON WHEN Milly descended the stairs with her aunt. Already wearing his cloak, he held his hat and gloves in hand, eager to leave. He couldn't explain his excitement. He rode through Greater Bookham daily when he stayed at Camborne, and there was nothing in the village to draw his interest. He cared little for shopping, although picking up a toy or two always brought pleasure in anticipation of Sammy or Ann's reaction.

He could find no explanation for his increasing desire to spend time with Milly. To see her smile. He remembered when he'd first met her at some gathering his family held. She'd accompanied her sister. The entire week she'd been at his home, he'd never seen her without a smile. Her laughter rang out constantly in the background. He thought her the happiest person alive.

Enough time had passed since then that he could admit to having had a small attraction to her. The feeling hadn't really faded, but the time hadn't been right for him to act on his attraction, and she'd soon found love elsewhere.

He greeted Milly's aunt when they reached the ground floor. "Lady Sophie, thank you for letting me join you this afternoon."

"Think nothing of it." She pulled on her gloves. "There's plenty of room in the carriage."

When the ladies were bundled under their lap robes and Richard was settled on the opposite, rear-facing, seat, Milly asked, "What will you buy for the children, Your Grace?"

"I don't have any idea. What do they lack? Another ball or wooden boat? Does Ann enjoy ribbons for her hair?"

Milly laughed. "We can't keep them in her hair long enough to know. She doesn't enjoy sitting still while her hair is brushed."

"What do you suggest?"

"She has shown interest in her dolly in recent months. A new one would always be welcomed."

He nodded. "And Sammy?"

"Either of the toys you suggested would work, although he might expect to take his boat to the pond right away."

"Good thought. I shall have to see what else is available."

The selection in the all-things shop was not grand, but the variety was interesting. He followed Milly about, curious to see what she chose. "That's a pretty shade of pink. Is the ribbon for you or Ann?"

"I haven't decided yet." Milly reached for another color.

"That's yellow matches one of Arnetta's gowns."

"Yes, it does," she said simply. She moved down the counter to the laces.

"Will you trim an old bonnet or buy a new one?"

Her arms drooped momentarily and her lips thinned. "I don't know yet."

"You should buy a new one to wear to the upcoming balls you've been invited to."

She gave him a sharp glance before turning away. "I would rather spend my money on the children." Her voice was nearly as sharp as her glare.

He strolled after her when she moved to the shelves filled with toys. "Do you think Ann's old enough to enjoy this baby house?"

The miniature house was of fine enough quality to be displayed in most drawing rooms. A Palladian-style four-room replica, it held tiny, intricately detailed furnishings, several mantelpiece paintings and floral carpets.

Milly came to examine it and sighed. "It is beautiful, isn't it? I fear Ann would break the legs on those chairs, or swallow those dishes. Perhaps in a few years you might consider it."

Richard lifted a doll from the shelf and questioned Milly, followed by a wooden horse on a wheeled platform, a wood diabolo for Sammy, and a kite. He could tell from her expression which toys were a wise purchase, before she responded to each. She seemed more eager to discuss purchases for the children than herself.

When Milly moved to the perfume section he followed, asking questions about Arnetta's tastes. He held up a small bottle, which she took and set back down. "May I choose the gifts for you, if you are still uncertain what to buy?" Her tone rang with exasperation.

He hung his head, realizing how bothersome he must seem, then offered her a wry smile. "I'm behaving like Sammy, aren't I? You have my apologies for being inconsiderate of your need to shop. I will venture to make some choices on my own." He walked off to another corner of the shop.

A few moments later he heard Milly approach. "I did not mean to sound so abrupt. I would be more than happy to assist you."

"I value your advice but have no desire to be a nuisance."

"You aren't a nuisance. But I do believe that anything you select will be welcomed. You might decide a few sweets would satisfy the children for St. Nicholas Day. The ladies enjoy them too."

He caught a question in her gaze, but she didn't express it. Most likely it had to do with his behavior, and he was grateful she held back. He didn't have the answer for why he followed her about like a love-starved puppy.

Was he worried that she mourned too long? She was not his responsibility, and her loss didn't concern him. She was not his problem to correct. At best, he should leave her to her sister to worry about.

She offered a weak smile, her lips trembling. "If you do need my help, feel free to ask." With that, she marched to the counter where her sewing goods lay.

Three

Ephraim and Arnetta's nearest neighbors, the Farnhams, held a ball every year on St. Nicholas Day. While not as outlandishly formal as a gathering in London, it gave Milly an excuse to take extra care with her toilette. Her maid had woven red ribbons in the braid that wrapped around her head, and Milly had used that same ribbon to update one of Arnetta's velvet gowns. The hem was just barely long enough and the bodice a bit snug over her breasts. She should have taken the time to let out the seams where needed, and she would certainly do so on the other gowns Arnetta had given her before she wore them.

Ephraim, Richard and Milly joined Aunt Sophie and Uncle James in attending, while Arnetta remained home. She'd complained she was still too tired to stay awake very late, but insisted on Ephraim going. Wearing a deep shade of green instead of gray or lavender elevated Milly's mood, as did the cup of wassail she'd drunk while watching the others dance.

Richard strolled up looking exceedingly grand in his navy cutaway coat that revealed his trim waist, and tan breeches that molded to his muscular thighs. "You aren't dancing."

She tore her surprising thoughts away from the cut of his clothes. "Neither are you," she countered.

"We may correct that problem with the next set." He raised an eyebrow. "If you will dance with me?"

"Thank you, I will."

He hadn't danced at the assemblies they'd attended in the past. He usually played cards or spoke with other gentlemen. Was he self-conscious over some perceived lack of grace? The young ladies present would hardly notice any misstep, she judged from the twittering that followed him about. Why did he pick tonight to change his habit? Perhaps he was bored. "Is Ephraim in the card room?" she asked.

"He was there when I left."

"I'm surprised you aren't playing. I don't believe I've ever seen you dance."

He looked away, clasping his hands behind his back. "I thought I'd inquire if you had a dance open. I expected you'd have a partner for all the sets by now, but decided to take a chance."

He was an odd creature. And he must be up to something. He was being too nice, hovering underfoot as if he were afraid she was still fragile over Tobias' passing. She would let him know she'd recovered as fully as possible, but not here. "No one has asked me to dance. The gentlemen might be afraid I'm still in mourning. Some women do avoid pleasurable activities long after a year has passed."

"I will be pleased to show them you are living your life fully again." A curious note hovering in the background of his voice had her wondering if he meant more than dancing.

The song ended and the dancers went in search of their next partners. Richard offered his elbow and led her into the center of the room where a few other couples waited. "I wonder what the next dance will be?"

The familiar tempo of a waltz filled the room. Milly placed one hand in his, the other resting on his arm, and allowed him to sweep her away.

The movement felt glorious, his strong arms lifting her to the heavens so her feet barely brushed over the polished marble floor. They glided as one. Somehow, she intuitively knew when to expect his turns. At the point when she thought she would burst from enjoyment, a laugh escaped her.

Richard's smile spread slowly. "Now everyone knows you are no longer in mourning." His voice was husky.

"Is it shameful of me to enjoy waltzing so much?"

"Not at all." He turned them in a small circle. "Even Tobias would approve."

"He would, wouldn't he? He lived his life to the fullest and would want me to do the same." She looked at Richard again and stumbled when she found his eyes peering deep within her. How could a simple look feel so intimate in a room filled with people?

But that was no simple look. It held something she couldn't name, something she wanted to feel again. And often. The music faded away and Milly pulled free from his grasp, self-conscious in her sudden need to know him better.

Know him better? Was that possible? He was like a brother-in-law these five years since Arnetta had married Ephraim. He liked his coffee black, his toast unbuttered. He tolerated the finer meals Mrs. Avery prepared, but was happiest when eating her roast pork and boiled potatoes. He was generous with his laughter, and frugal with his opinions—at least where everyone else was concerned. He'd certainly been outspoken about her desire to celebrate a traditional Christmas season.

Had she known Tobias as intimately as she knew Richard? No, she realized. She hadn't had the chance. They'd never stayed under the same roof, never talked of silly things that didn't really matter but were the foundation of a friendship. She'd expected to spend the rest of her life knowing Tobias better. Melancholy threatened to settle in her bones.

Richard led her to the refreshment table, his black eyebrows slashing harshly downward. "Are you overtired? Was the dancing too much for you?" Was she so transparent?

Pulled from her thoughts, she took the cold punch he handed her. "I am well. Perhaps a bit overwhelmed after doing so little for so long." She sipped the punch.

"Are you sure? I can find your aunt and uncle and have the carriage brought around."

"And miss the rest of the ball? Please don't make me leave."

He studied her for a moment, his gaze dancing over her face. He features didn't relax when he exhaled loudly. "Very well, we shall stay. I won't be the one to spoil the first winter ball for you."

One of their hosts' sons approached. "May I dance the next country dance with you, Miss Hudson?"

"I'd like that, Mr. Farnham."

"I haven't learned to waltz yet. Mother says I'm too young to do so." He looked about eighteen, and probably hadn't been allowed to join the adults until the last year or so.

When their turn came, he performed the steps with much enthusiasm, and while she enjoyed the dance, Milly didn't lose herself in this one. Her next two partners had the same result, pleasant but not memorable. Perhaps she was more tired than she realized. Certainly Richard wasn't the cause.

Her partner returned her to Aunt Sophie, who chatted with several other matrons. Her aunt grasped Milly's hand. "There you are. I was afraid you'd retired to a withdrawing room, I hadn't seen you in so long."

"I've been dancing. And having fun."

"That's wonderful, darling." Pleasure shone in Aunt Sophie's eyes.

"And she owes me another dance." Richard's voice came from behind Milly.

She turned, pretending her breath didn't catch at hearing his familiar timbre. "Are you up to a cotillion?"

"The dance tutor Mother hired was relentless in his task. I won't embarrass you, if that's your concern." His wink was so quick, she wasn't sure she'd actually seen it.

"I was thinking more of your aging limbs, sir. This must be quite exhausting to a man of your years."

"Do I hear a challenge? Shall we see who can dance longer?"

Milly threw a glance toward her aunt, who'd returned to her own conversation. "I don't believe causing a scandal on the night I return to Society would be wise. I can offer you this dance, and perhaps one more later."

Richard chuckled. "Just my luck, to have you conform to the rules when I'm eager to toss them aside."

"There are other ladies who'd be pleased to partner with you."

He looked around as if considering whom to ask next. He spoke softly near her ear. "But it pleases me to dance with you."

She nearly asked what game he was playing, but they had to take their places in line with the other dancers. The lively steps of the cotillion made conversation difficult, but were so familiar to Milly, her mind wandered.

Mama had written to ask if she would care to go to London

in the spring, which meant Mama thought it time she looked for a husband. As difficult as it was to consider, she knew she needed to do so eventually. She refused to be a burden on Arnetta and Ephraim if something happened to her parents.

Having loved once, she could relax her standards and consider an amiable friendship rather than a true passion. A kind husband and several boisterous children would fill her days with joy. In time, she'd grow to love him and that was enough.

By the end of that set of dances, she regretted her choice of a velvet gown. A trickle of sweat ran down the side of her face and she swiped at it with the back of her hand. The room was quite warm, but it was much too cold outside to have doors or windows open.

"Shall we have more punch? I confess to needing a rest," Richard said.

"I told you, you are too old for this." She kept mum on her own weariness.

"My age has nothing to do with it." He motioned to where the young Mr. Farnham blotted his face with a handkerchief. "I am faring better than some."

Milly took a cold glass of punch off the table and drank. "Your gracefulness contributes to that, I would wager. You dance very well for one who prefers the card room."

He bowed his head. "Thank you. It's easy to do so with a partner like you."

"When I go to London next Season, you must attend some of the same assemblies as Mama and I so I may show the gentlemen there what a desirable partner I am," she said in an offhand manner.

Richard's smile faded. He took a sip of his punch. Meeting her gaze, he asked, "Now, why would I want to do that? It would mean I have to wait in line for a chance to dance with you."

She played along. "I could fill in your name on the dances of your choice as soon as I receive my dance card."

He looked out toward the other dancers. "I suppose that would be slightly more tolerable. But what if I didn't want to share you with every bumbling swain in Town?"

Her stomach quivered, but she quickly tamped it down. He was being silly, that was all. He wasn't flirting with her. *Oh, please, let him be flirting with me.* "You make assumptions that any of the gentlemen would want to dance with a lady who is so close to being on the shelf. My partners will all be white-haired widowers with nine children still at home."

"On the shelf? You?" He shook his head. "Weren't you a Diamond in your Seasons? That hasn't changed. Once you smile at them, they will fall at your feet."

She laughed at the mental picture. "That will make dancing rather awkward. I truly will require your assistance in exhibiting my grace, won't I? You're apparently the only man capable of withstanding my beauty."

Richard's lips twisted as if he'd bitten into a lemon. "Why must you exhibit? Why go to London at all? If you require a husband, why not marry me?"

Now she laughed. "That's kind of you. Are you afraid no one would offer for me? I'm not an objectionable companion, I don't think. There's no need to sacrifice yourself like that."

"It's not a sacrifice. Do not belittle yourself so."

Her head was spinning. He had to be teasing her; there was no other reasonable explanation. But why? People around them might hear and mistake their conversation as something earnest. "This isn't the place for such talk, no matter how lighthearted. We must find another topic."

"You are correct. How ill-mannered of me. Let me take you back to your aunt." He offered his arm, which she accepted.

LATER, AS SHE LAY IN THE DARK IN HER BED, SHE TRIED TO MAKE sense of the conversation. The problem was it was as nonsensical as they came. Marry Richard? What could he be thinking?

THE NEXT DAY, MILLY HAD SOME QUIET TIME WITH HER SISTER IN the morning room while the nanny tended the children. When Arnetta finished reading the letters she'd received, she set them aside. "How was the ball last evening?"

Milly marked the page in her book before closing it. "The same as previous years. Everyone came, everyone danced."

"And did you dance?"

"I did." Remembering the joy she'd felt made Milly smile. "I'd forgotten how pleasurable dancing can be. Oh, and this will surprise you. Richard danced, too."

Arnetta's eyes widened. "He did?"

"Well, a few times. And only with me. I suggested he dance with others, but he said it pleased him to dance with me."

Sitting forward, Arnetta folded her hands in her lap. "How intriguing. He asked the other day how I thought you were recovering from your loss. He seemed quite concerned. At the time, I just took it as brotherly interest."

"That's how I would describe our situation. He's another brother to me, like Ephraim. But he flirted with me last night. Suggested I didn't need to go to London with Mama when I could marry him."

"What?" Arnetta's voice reached heights like those young Ann favored. "He asked you to marry him?"

"That was the gist of the conversation, although the question was why not marry him. I would have laughed along with him, had he been laughing. He appeared so sullen. What do you make of this?"

"I'm all agog. I don't know what to make of it. Richard does have a sense of humor, but he would never jest about something like marriage. This is very curious." Her hand went up to her mouth. "What did you tell him?"

"I said he needn't make such a sacrifice. I'm certain I can find an amiable man to marry."

Arnetta's laugh was quickly covered by a cough. "Oh my."

"Did I say the wrong thing? I did acknowledge it was kind of him to suggest it." Oh dear. If Arnetta was surprised by Milly's reply, it must mean she thought he'd been earnest. "No, you can't believe he meant to ask me. Why would he say it that way?"

"He probably didn't mean to say it at all, at least not in such a setting. Were you two alone?"

"Heavens no. We were near the refreshment table. Right where anyone and everyone might have heard." Milly leaned back in her chair. "What do I do now? How should I behave? I must apologize for brushing him aside."

"No, I think it better you say nothing. Act as if nothing happened." Arnetta studied her for a few moments. "Do you wish to marry Richard?"

"I never considered the idea. I honestly don't know."

"Do you care for him? Could you love him?"

Milly drew in a slow breath to slow the whirling thoughts in her head, and glanced at the doorway before answering. "I—I can't answer that, even to myself. I'm Miss Harris and he's a duke. Oh, don't look at me that way. I'm not...I've never had aspirations of having a titled husband or a grand estate."

"Or three," Arnetta added, biting the corner of her mouth.

"Three? I never paid attention to any of that, you recall. Neither of us perused Debrett's, even when Mama pushed it our way. None of that matters to me."

"But does he?"

Milly gnawed on her lower lip, which did nothing to help her think. Finally, she blew out a breath and smoothed the creases she was making on her gown. "This is silly. He misspoke, that is all. Nothing will come of his words."

Four

Richard slipped quietly down the staircase two days after the Farnham's ball. No one else stirred in the house, from what he could tell. He stepped lightly across the entry hall toward the front door.

"Going riding this early?" Ephraim called from his study.

He was caught. He detoured to the open doorway of the room where his friend sat. "Some business has come up in Town."

"You weren't planning to tell me you were leaving?"

"I left a note. I didn't realize you were up."

"And I didn't realize the post arrived this early." Ephraim raised an eyebrow. "Or did a messenger come during the night bearing an urgent request for your assistance?"

Richard sat opposite Ephraim's desk. "You know no such message came. I need some time on my own. I'll be back before Christmas Eve."

Ephraim's brow creased. "Does this have anything to do with the ball?"

His chest tightening, Richard forced himself to breath. Milly had mentioned it. Or had her aunt or uncle overheard their conversation? He should play it all off as a jest. "Did Milly enjoy the ball? I did my best to assure she did."

"She had a pleasant enough time. She mentioned some rather interesting conversations with you."

Richard tugged at his cravat. "Yes, we laughed a bit."

"And nothing was said that might have been…misconstrued?"

He closed his eyes. Was Ephraim going to insist they marry? What did Milly think of that? "Perhaps…I, uh, might have suggested she didn't need to go to London next Season to look for a husband."

Ephraim nodded slowly. "I see. Then what Arnetta said is true."

"I'm not certain what came over me while watching her laugh and dance with other men. It can't be jealousy." He toyed with the bottom button of his waistcoat. "I went to the ball to make certain she had a pleasurable evening. I wanted to see her happy again, like before."

"Before Tobias died."

"Yes," Richard agreed. "Or before she met him, even. She was always such a joy to be around. She could find reason to laugh on the gloomiest day."

"That she could. She still does, but the laughter is quieter now. She's recovering from her loss, if that's your concern."

"I suppose it is. That's what I keep telling myself." He rose, unable to sit still and paced toward the window where the sun streamed. "I've made a cake of this."

"No, not completely. If you don't wish to marry her, we'll laugh it off as a scheme to improve her confidence."

He turned toward Ephraim. "I don't like the idea of making her think marrying her could be considered a joke."

"She'd be hurt less than if you say nothing. Arnetta said Milly wasn't sure what to make of your suggestion."

"I don't know what to tell her. The idea of marrying her is growing on me. That's why I thought I should go away for a time. If all I feel is pity on top of the friendship we have, that should fade when I'm away from her, shouldn't it?" He returned to his chair and sat.

"Perhaps. But if it's truly only pity, I think being around her and seeing how happy she is would do a better job of curing your concerns."

Could he do that? Stay close to her and not do something stupid? Say something imbecilic? He was normally a sensible man. He kept himself involved in the running of his properties, and didn't just fill his seat in Parliament. He had no excuse for his present behavior. "Very well, I will remain here for the time being. I do need to spend a few days in Town before Christmas, but can see where my leaving now could be misconstrued."

"Wonderful." Ephraim reached for his pen. "Arnetta mentioned taking the sleigh out this afternoon. You might want to join Milly for a trip down the lane."

Richard stood, realizing he still wore his cloak. "In the meantime, I'll take my morning ride, as I am dressed for it." He could use the time to think before seeing Milly.

THE SUN'S LIGHT REFLECTING OFF THE SNOW DIDN'T PROVIDE enough heat to melt it, or to warm the air. Richard helped Milly arrange the lap robes over them in the sleigh, then Milly tucked her hands into her fur-trimmed muff. Taking the reins, Richard urged the horse to a walk. "We're lucky the clouds have moved on. My ride this morning was intolerably cold."

"Why do you ride so early, knowing it will be cold?"

"It clears my head. I use the time to review what must be done that day."

"What do you think about on days when you aren't working?"

Days like this morning, when he considered how to handle the sleigh ride conversation. A rather ironic touch. "I let my mind wander." It wasn't actually a lie. His thoughts had gone from the near proposal of that recent night to what life might be like married to Milly.

"Where do you go in your wanderings?"

"Myriad places. Comparing life here in Little Bookham to London, for instance. You've stayed in Town during the Season. Do you prefer your home in Shottermill or the activity of city life?"

"You make it sound as though we do nothing in Shottermill. We call on friends or receive calls daily, attend numerous parties, and host dinners quite regularly."

"I didn't mean to sound condescending. I rarely do those

things in London. One hears the Season described as a social whirl, so I assumed life in a village dulled in comparison. I went from Oxford to London, so I have nothing to compare."

"Life is only dull if you let it be. One can be quite dull in London."

Was that directed at him? "I find it difficult to be pleasant and charming at a supper aimed at illustrating how beautiful my hostess's daughters are."

Milly laughed. "You poor dear. You've always been at the top of the list of desirable matches. For those parents seeking a son-in-law, of course," she added quickly, as if to clarify not her own list.

"You don't believe someone might think I could be a good husband even without my dukedom?" The implication hurt more than he wanted to think about.

"Of course not. I merely meant most of the matchmaking mamas aspire to a titled son-in-law. How can they see your good qualities when you work so hard to avoid being seen."

"I do no such thing."

"You do keep to yourself during the Season. You admitted as much the other day."

She had him there. "I fail to see how that makes one a poor prospect for a husband. Many wives complain theirs spend too much time in the clubs. One would think a wife would appreciate him preferring to stay at home."

A breeze kicked up and Milly adjusted the lap robes. "Why are you so determined to believe I feel you'd make a poor husband?"

She obviously didn't connect her lack of response to his awkward proposal to his poor mood. Still, she didn't deserve his churlishness. "Forgive me. Let us speak of other things. Have you finished making your gifts for Christmas?"

"I have. And have you completed your shopping?"

"No. I planned to return to London today for a brief stay, but Ephraim suggested I wait."

"Wait for what?"

There it was. He'd managed to skirt around the issue so far only to land right in the middle of it. "He felt now was not a good time for me to leave."

"Oh?"

"Yes." How much should he say? This hedging about accomplished nothing. "Miss Hudson, I feel I must apologize for my behavior at the Farnham ball."

"This is serious, if you are calling me Miss Hudson. You always call me Milly."

She'd always been a sister to him, thus they'd always used familiar names. Sometime in the past he'd stopped thinking of her as a relative, but he couldn't say when it happened. Slipping into formal conversation meant he wanted to distance himself from the closeness he now felt. He wasn't supposed to pour out his heart now, but wait until he knew himself better. He should admit to himself his feelings for her were simply pity. They were, weren't they? "I was inconsiderate to discuss marriage in such a public setting, regardless of whether or not I was making sport of the matter."

"And were you making sport?"

No, he hadn't been. As he sat beside her, he knew that in his heart. "It certainly wasn't a proper offer for your hand."

"I think most ladies would think any offer from the right man was proper."

Was he the right man? He tried to study her from the corner of his eye, but the brim of her bonnet hid her face. He had no clue what she might be thinking. "I would enjoy dancing with you when you come to London."

"We do dance well together, don't we? I had so much fun that evening."

"I did too."

"You see?" She turned her head and looked up at him. "You should try attending some of those assemblies you avoid. You might have fun."

He growled in disagreement. "I still believe it's the company involved that makes it pleasant, not being in a large crowd. Some people can make any task enjoyable."

"And some have a tendency to make misery wherever they go."

This conversation wasn't helping his insecurity at all. Did she think he was miserable? Why couldn't he speak directly to the matter? *Miss Hudson—Milly—do you find me pleasant company?* "We have known each other for some time."

"Six years, I believe."

"We've had some happy times."

"That is true."

"I hope we can continue to spend time together in the future." He'd done it again, skirted the matter completely. He deserved to spend his evenings alone while Milly danced with every swain in London. Some young buck with more confidence than sense would propose to her, she'd accept, and she'd be gone from his life forever.

He turned the sleigh on an open piece of road, and they rode back to the house in silence.

THE WEEK RICHARD WAS GONE STRETCHED ENDLESSLY FOR MILLY and she quickly ran out of activities to distract herself. While Arnetta stitched a bonnet for Ann, Milly stood at the large window overlooking the snow-covered drive. "I wish it were spring."

"You would miss Christmas. I thought this was your favorite time of year."

"Normally, yes. But I grow tired of being indoors. Of my boots becoming damp when I do venture outside. I want to plant a garden."

"If you go to London for the Season, you'd have to trust the servants to nurture your garden."

"I'm not certain I wish to go to London after all. I haven't written Mama yet, although I should write soon so I may wish her a happy Christmas." Feeling the need to move about, she strolled around the room. "Maybe it's too soon to think about marrying. It's only been a year since I loss Tobias."

"No one's rushing you and you don't need to have another Season to find a husband. We have several friends who are unmarried. We could host a dinner party or two this winter. You have friends of your own you may visit and widen your circle of acquaintances." Her lack of mentioning Richard was glaring.

"Yes, you are right. Those are much more sensible ideas than London, although it would be nice to visit with Aunt Dixon again. Mama and I could stay a week with her, rather than the entire Season." Milly returned to her seat. "I feel better now. I shall write Mama this afternoon."

Arnetta laughed. "You are more flighty than Ann. I don't remember you being this restless. I thought perhaps Richard was responsible for your nerves, but he's away now."

"He might have caused me some distress when he belittled all our traditions, but that is past."

"I remember a time when you were quite fond of him."

Milly tilted her head and gazed at the lamp between them. "He was the most handsome man I'd ever seen, when I met him. He still is, truthfully," she added, her voice lowering so as not to be overheard by any passing servants.

"And the two of you got on well."

"We did. It was easy to speak to him. I hadn't come out in society yet and had little thought of marrying at eighteen, so I didn't care what he thought of me."

"I can see where he might have fallen in love with you. You don't put on airs, and you weren't trying to trap him into anything."

Fallen in love with her? Arnetta had never mentioned such a thing. "What do you mean? He wasn't...isn't in love with me."

"There was a time I thought he was. I caught him watching you and Tobias on more than one occasion. He looked so...disappointed."

"You are mad. He said he was pleased to see me so happy with Tobias."

"Yes, he wanted what was best for you, even if he wasn't the man to give you that joy."

Richard? He didn't come across as so selfless. In recent weeks she'd grown to realize how much of himself he kept hidden. "Why didn't he say anything?"

"Perhaps he didn't realize it until too late."

"That's ridiculous. It can't be true." Would she have chosen differently if he'd said something before Tobias proposed? She would never know.

Arnetta tipped her head to one side. "You can say that, in light of recent events?"

"Oh Lord, what have I done? I believe I laughed at the suggestion I marry him. No wonder he won't speak to me now.

Arnetta, what do I do to correct this? I can't have his feelings hurt, yet I'm not certain he honestly wants to marry me."

"Don't do anything until you know your own mind. You didn't want him offering for you out of pity. He deserves the same consideration."

Milly jumped up to pace the room again. Richard would return the next day. She had some decisions to make.

Five

E phraim had the sleigh and wagon readied early on Christmas Eve, and Milly was excited to finally gather the greenery to decorate the house. Richard had returned the night before and he joined Millie, Ephraim, and Sammy in their trek to the woods. When they climbed down from the sleigh, Sammy pulled Ephraim one way and Milly went another, with Richard following her.

"What are we looking for?" Richard asked, using the blade end of a saw to push aside a bush for her.

"Yew and holly, as much as we can gather."

"That was rather obvious, I suppose. The evergreens."

"Yes." She remembered a spot where she and Arnetta had found what they needed in the past and tried to locate it. "Did you get your business taken care of?"

"I did. Oh, look. Here we are. I found some greens to harvest." Richard approached a leafless oak tree and reached for a low branch. He balanced the saw above the branch and hoisted himself in the air.

"What are you doing? That's an oak."

"It's not the oak I'm after."

She planted her hands on her hips. "Well, what else do you expect to find by climbing one?"

"This." He tossed a clump of leaves at her feet.

Mistletoe.

"Oh. Yes, I see." She couldn't prevent the warmth that

coursed inside her. She hadn't thought of finding any of that. A sudden thought slipped into her head. What would his kiss be like?

Richard dropped from the tree and landed gracefully on his feet. "What's a Christmas celebration without mistletoe?" He bent and picked it up.

"Indeed."

He stood too close and made no move to continue their search. His eyes were in shadow with the sun behind him, making it impossible to read his expression. "Tradition says Roman soldiers believed mistletoe brought peace." He held the mistletoe over their heads and his voice grew husky. "Enemy soldiers would throw down their weapons when they met under the mistletoe."

Her gaze lowered to his full lips, which held her transfixed. "But we aren't enemies."

"No, we are not." Richard leaned in, hesitated briefly, then brought his mouth down to hers. His lips were cool, his breath hot on her cheek.

Closing her eyes, Milly lost herself in the scent of his soap, the warmth of his body brushing against hers, and the fluttering of her heart. His lips pulled away, then captured hers once more, and suddenly the warmth was gone.

Her eyelids fluttered open to find him watching her. She smiled and, suddenly overcome with shyness, forced herself not to look away. "I am glad we aren't enemies."

"Can I hope we are much more?"

A mad urge struck her to scream *yes* while wrapping her arms about his neck and kissing him again, but it lost out to her prim and proper upbringing. "Ephraim will wonder where we are. I am surprised Sammy hasn't dragged him this way."

Milly hurried in the direction she hoped the holly bush was and tried to get her thoughts in order.

Disorder still reigned in her head when Milly helped Arnetta tie bundles of holly and mistletoe to hang about the house. Arnetta put her finger in place to hold the ribbon while Milly finished a bow. "We haven't had mistletoe in a few years. How wise of you to think of it."

"I didn't," Milly confessed. "Richard cut it down before I realized what he was up to."

"He did? Well, that shines a new light on the subject."

"Why is that?"

"I've never seen him take advantage of having mistletoe in the house."

Milly rolled her eyes. "Do not make too much of it. Who would he have kissed? You?"

Arnetta simply grinned and gathered more holly in her hands.

Milly knew that expression too well. "What?"

Arnetta rocked her head from side to side in her *I'm smarter than you are* manner. "You implied he has someone to kiss this year."

"I said no such thing." She couldn't stop the heat creeping up her face.

"You didn't need to, and your blush confirms it. You hope he will kiss you."

Milly grew even warmer.

Her sister gasped. "He has kissed you! Tell me now."

Two footmen worked in the far end of the room laying the larger yew branches on the shelves to either side of the fireplace. Milly glanced their way and lowered her voice. "He did, when he collected the mistletoe."

"I told you he cares for you."

"I admit it must be true. He wouldn't risk Ephraim's wrath by kissing me if he didn't."

"This will be the best Christmas," Arnetta said with a sigh.

"It's certainly starting out that way."

Ephraim entered the drawing room, stopping to watch the footmen work before finding his wife. "How are the decorations coming?"

"We are almost done with these, and then we'll add the holly to the yew branches."

"Excellent," Ephraim said. "The room will look festive when we gather in here after supper."

"It's looking festive already." Richard joined them at the small table. The crease between his eyebrows was noticeably less pronounced. He picked up one of the mistletoe bundles, and glanced toward the extra mistletoe still uncut. "I see I could have left most of this on the tree."

Ephraim laughed. "Perhaps we can smuggle some into the Smyth's Twelfth Night party and make it merrier."

"You'll do no such thing," Arnetta replied. "Shame on you for thinking it."

Ephraim nudged Richard with his elbow. "Don't worry. They make their wassail strong enough to make their company quite tolerable."

"Ephraim! That's quite enough." Arnetta insisted.

He winked at Milly. "Come, Richard. Let's leave them to their preparations. Ladies, we'll see you at supper."

As they left, Arnetta shook her head and whispered, "Honestly. At least you know what to expect if you do accept Richard's offer."

Milly threw a quick glance at the door but the men were gone. "Shh. He hasn't made an offer and I don't know that he will."

"You worry too much. You should be thinking on what you plan to say when he asks you."

Milly pushed her chair back from the table. "Let us place the holly around and hang the mistletoe so we may change for dinner. And say no more on the subject!"

MRS. AVERY HAD OUTDONE HERSELF WITH THE MEAT PIE SHE prepared, and the custard for dessert. Richard scraped the last of the pudding from his bowl and sighed with satisfaction. "I will miss these meals when I return to London."

"We are lucky to have Mrs. Avery, that's certain." Ephraim nodded to Arnetta.

She rose, setting her napkin on her plate. "Come, sister, we shall leave these two to their cigars."

Milly followed her sister to the drawing room. "Ephraim is so silly at times, acting as if he were lord of the manor."

Arnetta sat on the settee near the fire. "In case you've forgotten, he *is* lord of the manor. Such as it is."

"But must we leave them alone to talk every evening, when they've had the entire day to speak behind our backs?" Milly took her usual position in a side chair.

"I seem to recall your insistence that we follow traditions," Arnetta said, and laughed. "You'll become accustomed to the little things that please your husband. And at times like this when he's home day after day, you might appreciate the quiet moments when nothing's expected of you but your absence."

Milly was used to hiding away in her books, so she couldn't imagine needing to escape her family. Perhaps when she had three children in the nursery she might feel otherwise. "I can't wait to see how Sammy likes the tin soldiers I bought him."

"He will love them. I worry he won't sit through the service at church in the morning, he's so eager for his gifts."

"He gets that from his father," Ephraim announced as he entered. He sat beside Arnetta and kissed her cheek. "What did you buy me?"

"You will find out tomorrow, just as Sammy will."

"And what did you buy me, sister?" Ephraim asked Milly.

She opened her eyes wider. "I was supposed to buy you a gift?" She couldn't maintain the innocent look and broke into laughter.

Richard strolled over and stopped in front of her. "Care for a game of cards?"

Butterflies fluttered about inside her. "I'd be delighted."

They sat at the same table where she and Arnetta had bundled the mistletoe just hours before. That thought brought back Richard's kiss. Milly's fingertips pressed against her lips and she inhaled, wishing she could smell his scent again. They were close enough to hold hands across the table but far enough apart to prevent anything her mother might frown upon, if she were present. When they'd played chess, the distance hadn't seemed too great, but after his kiss, it was greater than the English Channel.

Pay attention. What game had he suggested when he dealt? Seeing two cards before her, she guessed *vingt-et-un*. "When do you return to London?"

"I will ride back on Tuesday."

She only had two more days with him. How sad. She forced herself to remember she might see him in May when she and Mama went to stay in Town.

"Will you be there in the spring?" he asked.

"I imagine so," she said. "I will discuss it with Mama when I see her."

"Well. Perhaps I'll see you then."

Some old part of her awakened and she couldn't resist flirting with him. "You see me now, don't you?"

"Naturally. Your hair picks up a beautiful reddish-gold gleam in the candlelight. Your smile is more relaxed than when I first arrived on stir up day."

Milly wanted to duck her head from his thorough examination and she shifted in her seat. She strove to lighten the mood. "You were so vexing that day. As though standing in the kitchen for ten minutes was beneath you."

He chuckled and lay down his cards. "My mother used to chase me out of the kitchen when I was young. Our cook kept the biscuit jar full somehow in spite of me."

Dealing the next hand, he continued. "What did you wish for?"

"I beg your pardon?"

"When you stirred. You did stir the pudding, didn't you? You were so busy making certain we all took a turn, yet I don't recall seeing you do so."

She nodded. "I did, after everyone. I wouldn't want to chance the bad luck of not stirring."

"What did you wish for?" he repeated.

"I cannot say. It doesn't come true if you speak a wish."

He leaned forward with his forearm resting on the table. "I think that rule was decided by the man who wanted to be able to change his wish."

She grinned. "Why would he do that?"

"So he can claim to have gotten his wish, when no one else had. And everyone would believe him, because they didn't know what he wished for."

"You are such a cynical man. I never would have imagined it to be true of you. What made you so?"

He shrugged. "I've always been so. I call it seeing men for what they are."

"I refer to pretend they are as I wish they are."

His eyes locked on hers and she froze, her lips parted. He kept her pinned there, breathless, waiting for what, she didn't know. When he smiled, her lips did, too. He spoke so only she would hear. "Between us, we have a balanced outlook. We are a perfect match."

She swallowed but was unable to respond. His quiet tones were more intimate than his kiss had been. She longed to feel his lips on hers again.

Suddenly remembering what night it was, she cringed. Christmas Eve, and she was nearly begging to be kissed. When had she become so scandalous?

"Shall I tell you what I wished for?" he asked.

"It won't come true. If you don't care whether it comes true or not, you may tell me."

"Very well. I will keep it to myself." He studied his cards, then looked up at her. "Have I made you even the least bit curious?"

"You are cruel. You had no intention of telling me."

"I did, but you don't wish to know."

She rolled her eyes, trying hard not to laugh. "If you must tell me, you may do so. But only after your wish has come true."

He raised one eyebrow and his lips pulled back on one side, making him look quite victorious. "Agreed."

Six

S ammy chattered the entire drive home from church on
Christmas morning. His excitement was contagious, and
by the time they'd removed their cloaks and gloves,
Richard was just as eager for them to eat so they could open
their gifts.

"Can't we open first?" Sammy begged in a whiney voice.

"You've been told we must eat first. Mrs. Avery will be planning on it." Arnetta removed Ann's bonnet and handed her to
the nanny.

"But I'll open them real fast, like this." Sammy waved his
arms in a mad flurry.

"You might break your gifts if you did that," Ephraim
warned.

"One gift?"

Ephraim turned to Arnetta, who turned to Milly. Milly
nodded. "I don't mind. Why not let him open one and take it up
to the nursery with him?"

"Very well, but only one." Arnetta led the others into the
drawing room where the packages lay on a table. She chose one
and handed it to Sammy.

He opened the box and pulled out a carved horse and wagon
toy. "Huzzah! Look at that. May I go play now?"

"Yes, we'll send for you when you may open more."

Richard walked over to the table as Sammy ran out into the
hallway in the nanny's wake. Picking up one package wrapped in

paper and tied with pretty, pale pink ribbon, Richard announced, "One more before we dine."

Arnetta frowned. "But Sammy has already gone."

"This one isn't for him." Richard approached Milly, holding out the gift.

"For me? But I can wait until everyone opens theirs."

"I can't. Please, open this." He hoped she didn't notice how his hand shook.

She studied him before accepting the gift. "If you wish." She untied the ribbon and removed the paper, setting both on the table. "A book, how nice."

"There's an inscription," Richard urged, eager for her to open the cover.

She read it aloud. "Turn to page 164." Frowning, she looked up. At his nod, she turned to the page he'd instructed.

He'd marked a passage halfway down the page, after reading it repeatedly until he had it memorized. *"I know now how mistaken I was,"* said the hero. *"I didn't recognize my feelings for what they were. My heart is yours, as it always has been."*

Milly's lips moved as she read, and Richard couldn't refrain from reciting the final line he'd marked. "Please tell me if you return the feelings."

The book shook in her hands. She closed it and faced Richard. It took a lifetime for her to ask, "Am I understanding this correctly?"

"If you understand it to say I hope you care for me, then yes."

"And by 'care", you mean as more than a friend?"

"Much more. I wish for you to be my wife."

"You do? Then you weren't teasing when you suggested I marry you."

"I surprised myself when I said it, I admit, but I would never tease about such a thing."

Arnetta's voice reminded him they were not alone. "I think he's waiting for your answer, sister, not a discussion about how he asked."

Closing her eyes, Milly drew in a breath as her cheeks turned that delicious shade of peach. Once more she met Richard's gaze, this time with a wide smile. "Yes, I will have you as my husband."

Richard set her book aside and grasped her hands. "Ephraim, don't you two have somewhere to be?"

The viscount cleared his throat. "Arnetta dear, I believe dinner is served." He led her out of the room.

Milly's mouth opened and closed a few times before she finally spoke. "I am so ashamed of the way I treated you that night. I had no notion you cared for me as anything more than Arnetta's sister."

"How could you? By the time I realized it, you were engaged to Tobias."

"Even then? You never let on."

"Of course not. You were so happy with him."

"Can we not talk about him? He's gone now and I have closed the book on him. Let's read this new one together, shall we?"

"Yes, let's do." He tugged gently on her hands and drew her into his arms. Cupping her face, he bent and kissed her. His Milly. His love. And one day soon, his wife.

When she pulled away, she rested her head on his shoulder as if she did so daily. "You know, I don't know if I've ever been this happy."

He stroked his hand down her back, feeling the warmth of her beneath her woolen gown. "Are you certain?"

Lifting her head, she searched his face. "You don't believe I know when I am happy?"

Richard laughed. "No, I was simply surprised to hear you say so. May I tell you my wish now?"

"I warned you—"

He smiled. "It's quite all right, it has come true."

"How sweet. You wished I would marry you."

"I hoped you would, but that wasn't the wish I made on stir up day. When I took the spoon from you in the kitchen, my only wish was to see you as happy as you were when I first met you."

Milly's eyes quickly glistened. "You are too good to me. I don't deserve it."

"You deserve that and more. I'm sure you were just as selfless with your own wish."

She looked away, shaking her head, apparently chagrinned. "I had the same wish you did."

"You wanted my happiness?"

She shook her head again. "My own. I was tired of being sad, and I hoped for an end to my sorrow."

Richard clasped her fingers and pressed them to his heart. "But ending your sadness guarantees my happiness. Your wish was altruistic without you even knowing."

"Why did it take me this long to see what a good man you are?"

"Because it took loving you to make me so."

"I am glad you love me, Richard."

"And I'm happy our wishes came true. Shall we join Ephraim and Arnetta before our dinner is cold? The sooner we do, the sooner we'll discover who will find the lucky silver coin in the pudding."

She held his hand as they walked to the dining room. "Maybe we should let one of them find it. I can't imagine being any richer than I am now."

Richard squeezed her hand. "Neither can I. You've made me the luckiest man alive."

LATE CHRISTMAS NIGHT, AFTER THE OTHERS HAD RETIRED, MILLY was unable to sleep. Richard loved her! She smiled and hugged herself, then rose from her bed and pulled on her wrapper. She couldn't decide which was more surprising, that he loved her, or that she'd felt that strongly for him without realizing it.

Milly had nothing to read, having left the book he'd given her downstairs, so she picked up her candlestick and tiptoed down to the drawing room. The embers in the fireplace offered only enough light to see the furniture sitting nearby, but she spotted her book right away. She padded silently across the rug, picked up the book, then froze, hearing a sound in the darkened half of the room. She pulled her wrapper tighter, hoping it wasn't a footman or the butler she'd stumbled on. "Who's there?"

Richard's voice called out just before he entered the dim light. "I couldn't sleep," he confessed as he walked toward her.

Hugging her book, she said, "Nor could I. It was such a lovely day."

He didn't stop until he was directly in front of her...close enough to touch.

She didn't even try to stop her hand from reaching out and pressing her palm against his lapel. Once, with another man, she'd been comfortable this close, but this was all so new.

Richard covered her hand with his. "Can you feel my heartbeat?"

"No."

"It's pounding. I'm surprised you can't hear it. It's so loud in my ears I'm afraid I'll shout to be heard over it."

She giggled. "Don't you dare. You'll wake Ephraim."

Reaching out to wrap his free hand around her, he pulled her closer. "We're engaged, what will he do?"

"You haven't spoken with my father yet—"

When his lips touched hers, Milly forgot how to speak. How to think. She could only feel. His soft lips. The rough whiskers brushing against her cheek. The heat of his hand on her back, only separated from her skin by two fine layers of linen.

His other hand cupped her shoulder, and flames radiated down her arm and across her breasts. His lips continued to knead against hers, then she felt his tongue trace the seam of her mouth. Her lips parted and Richard groaned and slid his tongue into her mouth.

The sensation was odd, yet she hungered for more. Her tongue met his and he pulled her even closer to him.

She wanted more, but had no idea what that was. She dropped the book and freed her arms from where they were trapped between their bodies, her hands gliding under his jacket and around to his back. She felt his taut muscles, and now she noticed his pounding heart.

One of Richard's hands cupped her breast and Milly thought she'd burst with need. She felt her breast swell against his palm, her nipple tingling with demands of its own. She whimpered.

Without releasing his hold on her, Richard whispered, "Is it too much? I should wait—"

"No," she said pleadingly. Rising on her toes, she found his mouth and kissed him hard, her tongue finding his immediately, touching, stroking. What was he doing to her sanity? Her entire body ached for his touch.

He dropped his hand to cup her hip, kneading gently, then she felt him tug at her gown, lifting the hem. Cold air hit her legs, but it wasn't enough to cool the heat inside her. He tugged again and his hand found the skin of her thigh. Her hips rocked. "Richard…"

"I'm sorry—no, I'm not sorry! I want you, Milly. I need to feel you."

"I want you, too. Please, Richard…" She didn't know what to ask for. She prayed he knew.

"You're certain?"

"Yes! Please do not stop. I feel as though I'd die without your touch."

As if he'd been freed from the rules of propriety, Richard lifted her into his arms and carried her to the nearest chair. Setting her on her feet, he stepped back, but she closed the space again, trying to kiss him. He laughed, the sound low and sexy. "Wait, my darling, soon."

She realized he was unbuttoning his breeches, but before she could see the rigid part of him she'd felt pressing so hard against her belly, he'd sunk onto the chair and lifted her onto his lap in one quick move. Her bare legs straddled him, her gown was wrapped above her waist, and that delightfully erect cock pressed against her.

Milly gasped.

"Should I stop?"

"No," she cried again. She was damp there, where his cock stroked, and she burned with an urgency she couldn't express.

His fingers found her first, stroking, pressing against a spot that made her jump. "Oh!"

His answer was a moan, and he took her right breast into his mouth, gown and all, and flitted his tongue against the nipple. His finger matched the tempo, and the knot inside her kept tightening.

"I want—"

"I know," he murmured against her skin, his hand still driving her mad where it touched her.

Then she felt she would shatter, and she did shatter, arching and rocking against his hand. His finger had slid inside her and its thrusts drove her on, sending wave after wave of delight through her body.

And when his hand left, she pouted, but only for the moment before his cock began to fill her. So big. So hard, and she wasn't complete until she'd taken all of him in. It hurt a bit, but his finger touched her nub again and all thought of discomfort fled.

"I'm trying to go slow. I don't want to hurt you," he whispered, his voice taut with restraint.

"I'm all right, love," she whispered back.

His cock twitched when she said *love*. With his hands beneath her buttocks, he lifted her slightly, then let her sink down again, repeating until she had the rhythm.

She was in control then. On her knees, straddling his lap, with that delicious rod inside her, she took control of how deep, how fast, his thrusts were. His hand moved madly over her body, touching, pinching, squeezing, and his hips rose to meet her. Just as the new knot inside her began to burst, Richard froze, grunting, and his hands held her in place with his cock buried deep.

His breaths came in small gasps, and he quivered once more, before his body seemed to melt into the chair. And hers melted onto him.

She rested her head on his chest, feeling the rapid rise and fall that matched her own heavy breathing, hearing his heart as it began to calm down.

Milly pressed a kiss against his waistcoat.

Richard pressed a kiss on the top of her head and rested his cheek there.

She was uncertain how long they remained thus, but her thighs grew cold, forcing her to react. She didn't want to leave his lap, but knew they must return to their separate bedchambers before someone noticed them missing. She shifted her weight to rise.

Richard started as if he'd fallen asleep. "Are you well?"

She smiled. "I am very well, darling."

"Not too sore? Can I get you something?" When she stood, he began to fasten his breeches.

"I must return to my bedchamber in case my maid comes to stoke the fire or something."

Richard bent to pick up her book, then handed it to her. "I'll wait a bit after you go so no one will suspect we were together. And, if I don't see you at breakfast, I won't see you for several days."

Milly frowned. He could leave her after what they'd just shared? "I see."

He took her shoulders in his hands, buried his nose in her flowing, tousled hair, and inhaled deeply. "I don't want to, but I must. I'll speak to your father, then get a special license. I cannot let an extra moment pass before I can call you my wife."

Lifting her chin, he kissed her gently and broke off before either of them could deepen the contact.

"I shall miss you, Richard."

He grinned. "I much prefer it when you call me darling."

Milly bit her lip, then admitted, "If I call you that again I might demand to feel you inside me."

Hugging her tightly, he sighed. "What a fool I was to never see how important you were to my happiness. But I've learned my lesson. I love you, Millie. I always will."

"And I love you. No more regrets about time we lost. We have an eternity to make up for it."

It took more willpower than she thought she owned, but Millie turned away, picked up her candle, and crossed the room, looking back once more to mouth, *I love you*, before silently making her way to her bedchamber. Richard Foote, Duke of Alconbury, was hers now and forever, and she couldn't wait to live every moment of her future beside him.

About Ari Thatcher

USA Today Bestselling author Ari Thatcher is the naughty side of sweet romance author Aileen Fish. Ari has always loved sexy romance where love takes the leading role. Reviews have called her work "captivating" and "compelling", and her characters "intelligent, intriguing and realistic."

Stay up to date through her website http://arithatcher author.com, and social media.

facebook.com/arithatcher

twitter.com/arithatcher

Smitten with My Christmas Minx

DAWN BROWER

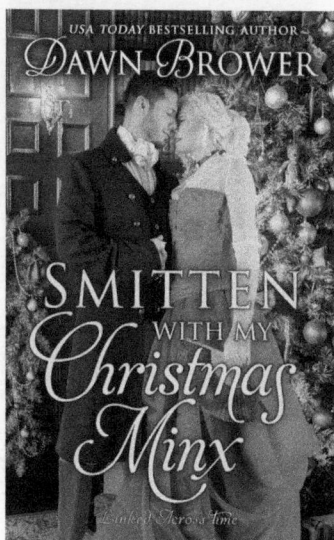

For everyone who makes a wish for love, and especially, for those that wish for someone to share the holidays with. May this story warm your heart.

Prologue

December 1865

Lady Adeline Carwyn stared out the window of the library at Whitewood Abbey. Snow fell from the sky in big fluffy flakes and landed on the ground in soft piles. Flurries filled the night sky making the stars almost indistinguishable against the blinding white snowflakes. Still she stared, hoping a wishing star might make an appearance.

Because…she needed one.

She was tired of being unloved. All right, that was a slight over-dramatization. Her family adored her. Her parents were the best a girl could have, and her grandparents were doting. Her little brother, as annoying as he was, loved her too. But that wasn't the same as being in love. She was one and twenty and had yet to feel anything resembling romantic love for a man. Adeline wanted what her parents, the Duke and Duchess of Whitewood, had. Perhaps that was too much to ask.

"What is so interesting outside?" her little brother, Jamie asked. He was named after their grandfather, James Kendall, the Duke of Weston. He was eight years her junior, and from what she understood, a complete surprise to both her parents. They thought they wouldn't have any more children.

"Nothing," she answered lightly. He was three and ten and had the curiosity of any young boy. "The storm seems to be going strong. I hope it doesn't prevent anyone from visiting for

Christmas." They were having a house party that would last until the new year. Two weeks with family and friends they hadn't seen in a while. She was looking forward to seeing her younger cousin, Francesca Kendall. Jamie would be excited to see their other cousins, Spencer Kendall and Oliver Rossington. Both boys were younger than Adeline, but older than James, and like her little brother, the heirs to the title their fathers' held. Francesca was three years younger than Adeline.

"It better not," he said mulishly. "Mother promised we'd have a grand time with everyone and even promised I could come to the Christmas ball."

"Really?" she said as she lifted a brow. "The entire night?"

"No," he said and sighed. "I can only stay until we decorate the tree and after the first dance is completed."

They usually decorated the tree as a family, but this year her mother, Elizabeth, had decided to break with tradition. They would have a day of creating decorations for the tree, and then the night of the ball everyone would put their creations on it before the festivities began. "That sounds more like what mother would agree to."

He wrinkled his nose. "I don't care to stay for dancing anyway. That's something girls like."

"Oh," she began. "I don't know about that. You might feel differently when you're older. Some gentlemen enjoy dancing very much." And some avoided it altogether...

"Not me," he replied stubbornly. "I'll never like it."

Adeline leaned down and ruffled his hair with her hands. They both had the same golden blond locks and blue eyes like their parents. Jamie was starting to look a lot like a younger version of their father, and Adeline favored her mother. No one would look at either of them and doubt who their parents were. "I believe you." Their father didn't care for dancing much either. He only gave in when their mother wished it. The duke would do anything for his duchess. Their love shined from them both, and it made Adeline envious. She glanced back out the window, but no star dared to shoot across the sky. Perhaps she should make a wish anyway. It might still come true.

"Have fun staring out the window," Jamie said. "I'm going to do something productive."

"Such as?" she asked with curiosity.

"I'm whittling a few pieces of wood for gifts. I have to finish the horse I'm making for grandpa." That was a brilliant idea. Adeline wished she had a similar skill so she could make something creative as a gift. Jamie was very talented, and it was part of his special abilities. He was tactile and got impressions from items after people touched them. Adeline, unfortunately, in her estimation was an empath. She felt too much and sometimes when she was around individuals their emotions became hers. It made socializing difficult and also falling in love. It made her mistrust her own feelings.

"I can't wait to see them." She lifted her lips into an affable smile. "Go finish your gifts. I'm going to sit here a little while longer."

"I'll show you when I'm done," he promised, then skipped out of the room.

Adeline turned back to the window. The snow had lightened and wasn't blowing around as much. The sky was more visible, and the stars seemed to blink at her. She sighed. What did that mean? She decided not to question it any longer. There was no reason to keep waiting for a shooting star. It was an impossible expectation, and it didn't mean her wish would come true.

Instead of hoping for the impossible, she closed her eyes and sent her hopes and dreams out into the world. She wanted love, even if it only existed for one night alone, it would be enough, she promised.

It wasn't too much to ask, at least she prayed it wouldn't be. A handsome man who saw her, and not her father's title and fortune. Someone that would kiss her until she lost the ability to breathe, touch her as if she were irresistible, and speak sweet words to her until her heart pounded inside her chest. A moment of love and a lifetime of memories. It would be enough. God, she hoped it would be…

Adeline opened her eyes and stared up at the sky. Nothing had changed outside, and she didn't feel any different inside. Maybe her wish had been for nothing, but she didn't think so. Guests should start arriving tomorrow, and perhaps, if her wish had been heard, it would include someone for her to love.

And maybe his love would be real, and not generated by a wish from a fanciful lady desperate for something tangible.

One

Two days later...

Devon Hayes, the Earl of Winchester, stared out the carriage window and sighed. He couldn't believe his best friend, Zachariah Barton, the Marquess of Merrifield, had convinced him that attending this Christmas ball was a good idea. He hated house parties, and Christmas had never been much of a joyous occasion to him. The only time he ever enjoyed the holiday season was when he had been fortunate enough to spend it with Zachariah's family when they were still attending Eton.

"I promise it will not be that bad," Merrifield said for the hundredth time in the past several hours. "Try to at least pretend you're willing to enjoy yourself. There will be other individuals there that you're acquainted with."

Devon turned to him and lifted a brow. "And who pray tell might that be?"

"Goodland and Lindsey for sure," Merrifield replied. "Maybe Hampstead. He never decides until the last second, but his sister is supposed to attend and she'll need a chaperone. I'm willing to wager his mother will make him attend."

Jonah Adams, the Viscount of Goodland; Matthew Grant, the Duke of Lindsey; and Daniel Andrews, the Earl of Hampstead were their close friends, but that still didn't mean Devon was remotely excited to be attending this fortnight of frippery cheerful nonsense. It was enough to make his stomach turn. "You're telling me what you think I want to hear." He glared at his friend. "None of them are going to attend, are they?"

"They might," Merrifield insisted.

All three of their other friends would most likely be returning home to celebrate with their families. They still had parents that doted on them. It was just Devon and Merrifield that were orphans. Merrifield at least still had his mother, but he avoided her at all costs. His friend didn't mix well with the frosty glares the old dame shot his way.

Devon had been on his own since he was five years old. His governess had raised him and then he'd been sent off to school when he'd come of age. After that he dealt with solicitors for guardians and servants as companions. While Merrifield's mother delivered cold dressing downs without batting an eyelash, Devon had no one to bother even being disapproving. His life was barren except for his friends, and he liked it that way. He had no desire to expand his social circle or search for a wife. There was only one place in his life for a woman, in his bed pleasing him, and he didn't need to shackle himself to one for the rest of his life for that.

"That's what I thought." Devon ran his hand through his dark brown hair. "You lied to me."

"I did not," Merrifield said. He almost sounded offended for Devon calling him on his malarkey. "They might and that's the truth. They told me they would come later, after their family celebrations."

"So," Devon began. "Their attendance might be for a day or two and we'll be stuck here for fourteen. That's hardly a fair arrangement." If he didn't like Merrifield, Devon might consider murder...or a maiming at least. Either way, he'd make his friend pay for the torture he was forcing Devon to endure.

"I still think you're acting like a spoiled child," Merrifield told him. Frustration was etched through his voice. "I had to come to this you know that. Would you really have left me to suffer alone?"

Devon sighed. Again. He might keep repeating that annoyed release several times over the next several days. Merrifield was right. He would not have left him to attend the house party on his own. His friend did not have control of his purse as yet. He wouldn't until he reached his majority in three more years, or he married. The man in charge of Merrifield's funds was making him attend the festivities. Merrifield had to make an appearance twice a year so the Duke of Whitewood could have a chat with him and ensure he had done nothing stupid, then he'd approve his allowance for the next quarter, and Merrifield hated every second of it.

"You could marry and be done with Whitewood and his constant interrogation," Devon goaded him.

"You're really in a surly mood, aren't you?" Merrifield kicked him in the shin from across the carriage. "What are you going to suggest next?" He lifted a brow. "That I marry the duke's daughter?"

"Is she a marriageable age?" He might regret the direction the conversation had taken, but now that he'd started he couldn't stop. "He might look at you more kindly if his daughter falls in love with you."

"Not a chance in hell," Merrifield said in disgust. "I'd rather eat mud pies for the next several months than…" He shuddered. "Marry his plain daughter."

Devon had never met the duke's daughter. He didn't even know her name and didn't want to find out either. Becoming acquainted with any eligible female was not even at the bottom of his list of endeavors. It didn't rate an addition to begin with. "Plain isn't ugly," he said. Merrifield might punch him next…

"It isn't exactly beautiful either." He blew out an exasperated breath. "The point is moot either way. She could be the loveliest woman I've ever had the pleasure of meeting, and I still wouldn't marry her. You do not understand what the duke is like. He's a bloody pirate out of time. I'd swear he would love to take me out to sea and make me walk the plank if that was still acceptable."

"Now you're exaggerating. No one would do that, and a duke wouldn't resort to piracy to begin with. I don't believe he's as bad as you're making him out to be."

"All right maybe he isn't a pirate but he'd make a good one. He has all the characteristics. I don't know how my father ever became friends with him and thought he'd make a suitable guardian for me. He's insane I tell you."

"I will reserve judgement," Devon said. The more he heard

about this pirate like duke, the more he wanted to meet him. He really didn't believe he could be as horrid as Merrifield believed.

ADELINE HAD WORN HER OLDEST GOWN AND BORROWED AN APRON from one of the maids to hang decorations in the library. It was her favorite room in the manor, and she wanted to give it her personal touches. She stepped off the ladder after she finished hanging boughs of holly along the beams on the ceiling. Adeline wiped sweat from her brow and stared up at her work. It looked even and gorgeous against the dark wood. The holly was evenly dispersed. Now all she had to do was hang the mistletoe in the center of the room. Her mother had this silly notion that they needed lots of mistletoe throughout the entire house. Did she really believe everyone would give in to the urge to kiss because of the tradition? That would be scandalous, and Adeline would not find herself caught in anything that might lead to her ruin. But her mother wanted them, and Adeline wouldn't disappoint her.

"It looks lovely," her mother, Elizabeth, the Duchess of Whitewood said. "You're a miracle worker. I might have you supervise the ballroom decorations for the dance when its time."

"If you would like me to, then yes, I'd be happy to assist." Adeline lifted her lips into a congenial smile. "I enjoy being creative."

Her mother wiped her nose. "You have a little dust gathering on your face. You should finish up in here and take a bath. I wouldn't want you looking like a servant at dinner."

"A bath would be nice," she admitted. "I have a few more things to do in here, and then I'll head up to my chambers and do that." Adeline hated leaving anything unfinished. It drove her a bit mad if something was out of place or rearranged. She had to fix it immediately before she left the room.

"I'll leave you to finish. Guests are starting to arrive and I need to ensure they're greeted and shown to their rooms."

Adeline nodded. "If you need help with anything let me know. I'll be happy to entertain some of the guests." This was her home, and she wanted everyone to love it as much as she did.

Though to be fair she didn't think that was possible. There were so many memories in the manor that couldn't be appreciated unless they had been experienced. No one would truly love it as much as she did, except her family. One day it would be long to Jamie, and if she never married she'd be nothing more than a spinster dependent on her brother's generosity.

"I'm sure it'll all be fine," her mother said. "But if I need your assistance, I'll send a servant to fetch you." She kissed her cheek. "Be a good girl and take care of yourself first." With those words, her mother turned and left the room.

"Lady Adeline," Sally, a maid said. "Is this how you want it hung?"

She turned toward Sally and studied how she was hanging the holly along the wall. "Yes," she said, "But straighten it a bit. It's uneven."

The maid followed her directions, and it was perfect. "Like this?" she asked.

"Yes," Adeline said. "Like that."

"Are you certain," a man asked. His tone was rich and warm, like hot honey and whisky.

Adeline turned to meet his gaze and swallowed hard. He had to be the handsomest man she'd ever laid eyes on. His hair was a rich burnished brown that appeared sun kissed even in the middle of the winter, and his eyes were a stunning gold that mesmerized her. "My apologies," she began. Her voice cracked a little as she spoke. "Do you not think it looks good?"

"Oh," he said, and grinned widely. "It looks all right. I wouldn't know if it was bad or not. I only inquired if you were certain it is how you want it. You were nibbling on your bottom lip as if you wanted to fix it yourself. It was adorable really."

Gentlemen didn't talk to her. They ignored her, and Adeline didn't know how to react to this one. Though to be fair she rarely attended balls or interacted in society. She'd had one terrible season and given up. Socializing wasn't for her, and she always messed up. "I'm sure it is how I wanted it to be." She somehow kept her voice from cracking as she spoke. That in itself was more of a miracle than she expected. "Are you lost?" That sounded stupid... "I mean, have you been shown to your bedchamber yet?"

"Are you offering to escort me there?" He wiggled his

eyebrows suggestively. "I could pretend that I'm lost if you want to join me there."

Adeline opened her mouth and closed it several times. Had he just propositioned her? Her cheeks heated and she must be as red as the ribbons decorating the boughs of holly. "Um…" She couldn't find words. Her brain had gone completely blank. "Lord…"

"Devon," he said. "Please call me Devon. I do believe we will be too intimate for formalities."

He was a rogue… She'd bet her entire inheritance on that. He would take advantage of her and use her in the worst way if she allowed it. Was it bad that his suggestion tempted her? "I'm Addie," she said. "And I'm all right with using your given name, but that's as intimate as we'll ever be."

"We'll see." He winked. "Pretty Addie, my sweet, we'll see." He turned on his heels and walked away from her. She blinked several times, thinking she must have imagined the entire encounter. Devon was wicked, and too gorgeous for his own good, and she had a feeling he was right. He'd worm his way into her heart and break it before he was done; however, she had never been excited at losing a piece of herself before. Adeline wanted him, even if it was a mere moment in time, and nothing more. Just once she wanted to feel as if she could be loved, and this might be all the wish she'd thrown out a couple nights garnered her. She would not waste it…

Two

D evon whistled as he strolled toward the gaming room. He'd agreed to meet Merrifield there to play billiards after they settled in. The manor was larger than Devon expected it to be, and he had taken a wrong turn. He was glad he had though, or he'd never have discovered the lovely maid hanging decorations in the library. She was a golden beauty that made his blood stir. Perhaps this house party wouldn't be so bad. He could lure Addie to his bed and it would go a long way toward alleviating his boredom.

She had blushed when he flirted with her. He found that refreshing. That meant she didn't give her favors lightly and also made her more appealing to him. Devon had no problem seducing her into being with him. She was a gift he never expected to find, but would appreciate all the same.

He turned a corner and located the gaming room. Devon pushed open the door and entered the room. Merrifield was on the far side of the room in a deep conversation with an older man. He had golden blond hair tied back with a leather band and startling blue eyes. Something about him seemed familiar, but he couldn't discern what it could be. Devon headed toward them and stopped when they both turned to meet his gaze.

"Ah, Winchester," Merrifield said. Relief was etched through his voice. "I'd like you to meet the Duke of Whitewood." Ah… the guardian. "Your Grace this is my closest friend, the Earl of Winchester."

The duke nodded at him. "I trust you've settled in all right."

More than all right... Devon tilted his lips upward as he remembered his encounter with Addie. If he could chase her up the stairs and make love to her in the linen closet, he would have. She hadn't been ready for that type of aggressive behavior. Perhaps after he'd had her a couple of times, he could swoop her up and carry her to a nearby secluded area to ravish her. She'd probably be ready and willing for that type of play then. He forced himself to stop envisioning her naked and opening her arms to accept him and met the duke's gaze. "I have your grace," he told him. "Your home is quite..." He searched for the right word. "...impressive."

The duke chuckled lightly. "This manor is my wife's project. She wanted something grand and I find I'm unable to refuse her anything." He slapped Devon's shoulder lightly. "I'm glad you find it impressive. I'll have to tell her you used that word specifically. I do believe it might amuse her."

What was he supposed to say to that? He hadn't met the duchess yet, and he prayed his description of her home didn't offend her. While he couldn't wait to find Addie again, he couldn't very well do that if he had to leave because he insulted the duchesses home. "It appears she's gone all out for the holidays. The bows of holly I see in every nook and cranny are a nice touch." That was lame, but he had nothing else to add. "I got turned around and stumbled into the library earlier. That's quite a collection of books you have."

The duke laughed. "That's my daughter's hideout. You probably saw her when you wandered in."

He'd remember if he had met an insufferable duke's daughter. If that was where she liked to spend her time, Devon was grateful he'd missed her. "I'm afraid I didn't. There were some maids decorating, nothing more."

He nodded. "She probably finished and went up to prepare for dinner." The duke grinned. "There's plenty of time to make everyone's acquaintance later. I'll leave you alone for now. Play some billiards before it's time to dress for dinner." He walked away from them but stopped at the door and turned back. "And Merrifield think about what we discussed. I'd like an answer from you before you depart at the end of the fortnight." After those parting words, the duke left the game room.

"What did he say to you?" Merrifield had been rather quiet through Devon's conversation with the duke. "You don't seem thrilled about it."

"I'd rather not discuss it." His friend's face was awash with resentment. "It's absurd."

"Is that so?" He lifted a brow, mocking him. "But you had such high expectations on how well this visit would go." Sarcasm practically dripped from each word as he spoke. "How much worse could it possibly be?"

"Don't..." Merrifield held up his hand. "It's bad. Trust me."

"Always," he said reflexively. "There's no one else that I do." He slapped his shoulder lightly. "So why don't you do the same and explain what is so bloody bad."

"He suggested I court his daughter," he admitted. Merrifield narrowed his eyes. "He must be desperate to unload her on someone."

"The plain girl you were telling me about on the way here?" Devon shook his head in disbelief. "And if you don't?"

"Nothing," he said, then shrugged. "It was a suggestion. But you know he holds all the power. If I say no he could make my life even more miserable than he already does. I don't want to marry his precious daughter, so it's a hell no, and no thank you several times over." He kicked the table. "I need a drink."

"Do you think that's wise?" Devon wouldn't mind a few glasses of brandy, but he didn't want to encourage his friend down the path to bad behavior. At least not on the first day. "Maybe we should wait until after dinner."

He'd rather search for Addie, but if his friend needed him, Devon would be by his side the entire time. Merrifield ran his fingers across the side of the billiard table. "You're right, of course. I need not give him any more reasons to be difficult." He met Devon's gaze. "How about you? Do you want to tell me what put that smile on your face that nearly lit up the room when you entered."

Devon grinned. "I met the prettiest little maid and I intend to make her mine. So if you don't need me after dinner, I'll be otherwise occupied."

Merrifield laughed. "Of course you found a willing woman already. Leave it too you..." He shook his head. "I'll be fine. You are free to find your pleasure with the maid. If you'll excuse me I don't much feel like billiards."

"Will you be at dinner?"

He shrugged. "I haven't decided."

Devon wished he could make this easier on his friend somehow. He didn't stop Merrifield as he left the game room. If he needed some time alone, Devon wouldn't deny him it. Later he'd find him and ensure he was all right, but probably not until after he found Addie...

ADELINE HAD TAKEN HER MOTHER'S ADVICE AND TOOK A LONG bath. Though it had ended up much longer than she had expected. She'd fallen asleep in the tub and woke up to tepid water and wrinkled skin. In short, she was a mess, and she'd slept right through the evening meal.

She had pulled herself out of the tub and instead of dressing in her gown, put on her nightrail. There was no reason to bother going downstairs and interrupting the ladies in the drawing room. Besides, she didn't want to explain to her mother why she had skipped dinner. Later, she'd sneak down to the kitchen and get something to eat. No one would be around to interrogate her, and she could go to the library to eat and enjoy her meal. It sounded like a good plan to her.

So now, hours later, her stomach rumbled to remind her she hadn't eaten anything. She'd been caught up in her latest novel and lost track of time. At least everyone would be retired for the evening. Still, she couldn't walk down the stairs in only her nightrail. Adeline stood up and retrieved a robe that covered her entirely. It was dark red velvet and tied in the middle with a silk ribbon. After she had it secured, she slid her feet into her slippers and headed downstairs. In the kitchen she would locate a candelabra and light some candles. She'd carry it with her to the library to help her find her way in the dark.

She took the servants' stairs to the kitchen and went to the larder. She was in luck... There was cold ham, cheese, and bread. She sliced some and put them on a plate, then took them to the library. Once she was there, she lit a fire in the hearth and poured some brandy into a glass. Her parents didn't mind if she drank liquor that was normally considered a man's drink. Neither one of them believed in confining her to society's rules. They wanted her to make decisions for herself.

Addie set the candelabra on the table next to the settee. She sat on the settee and sipped her brandy. It burned as it traveled down her throat. Addie grabbed her plate and set it next to her, then opened her book to the page she'd marked. She kept her brandy in her left hand as she alternated flipping pages and snacking on her late night meal.

Candlelight flickered over her book, and she nibbled on a piece of cheese. She was engrossed in the story and didn't even stop to consider someone might disturb her. Everyone was asleep. Heat spread through her and she pushed her robe off. No one would notice…

"Well, well," a man said. "I didn't expect to find you in her. What a lovely surprise."

Addie gasped and almost dropped her glass of brandy. It was almost empty, at least. "Devon…" She wished he'd told her his full name. It didn't seem right to address him intimately.

"Addie…" When he spoke her name it sounded almost decadent. He seemed to savor it and enjoy enunciating every syllable. It sent shivers down her spine and tingling at her core.

"What are you doing here?"

He sauntered into the room. "I could ask you the same thing." He plucked her glass from her hand and drank the remaining brandy. He swallowed and then said huskily. "A woman with taste. Is there more where this came from?"

She nodded and gestured toward the decanter to her left. She hadn't intended to have more than one glass, but had left it out on a nearby table in case she changed her mind. "Help yourself."

"You're generous with the duke's brandy." He chuckled lightly. "Does he know you sneak down here late at night and imbibe at your pleasure?"

She shrugged. "I couldn't say." Her father didn't keep tabs on her. He allowed her as much freedom as she liked. "I doubt he considers what I do with the brandy worth his notice." At least he hadn't in the past. He might have words with her for spending an evening nearly undressed in a gentleman's company, though. She should excuse herself immediately.

"You don't care if he discovers you like this."

She swallowed hard. "Well," she began. "I'm sure he'd have some unpleasant words if he discovered me at this particular moment." She tilted her chin upward. "But, in general, no. He doesn't own me and I make my own choices."

He chuckled lightly. She had to leave before she did something foolish. Adeline stood, and Devon took advantage of her new position. He pulled her into his arms and leaned down. "You're lovely."

Her heart beat faster and faster. His arms felt good wrapped around her, and she enjoyed being near him far more than she should. "You should let me go."

"Do you really want me to?" He lifted a brow. "If you truly do, I'll do it, but I think you want me to hold you."

Adeline nearly groaned. How could he read her so easily? "It doesn't matter what I want. It's what is proper, and this isn't." She boldly met his gaze. "And it's past time I retired for the evening."

"All right, have it your way, but before you do, there's something I have to do." He had a mischievous glint in his eyes that unsettled her.

Adeline was almost afraid to ask, "What?"

"This," he said cryptically, and then leaned down to press his lips to hers. Pleasure shot through her and she had to resist the urge to deepen the kiss. He made her feel...so much. He lifted his head and met her gaze. His lips tilted upward into a sinful smile. "I couldn't let that mistletoe go to waste." He let her go and stepped back. "Have pleasant dreams, Addie." With those words, he left her alone.

Adeline couldn't discern what game he was playing. What did he hope to gain by this flirtation? Was he trying to seduce her? Did he even know who she was? He had to. She'd told him her first name, and no one else attending had a name similar to hers. She shook her head and grabbed her robe. She'd leave her dishes for a servant to take care of in the morning. Addie couldn't stay a moment longer in the library. After she blew out the candles she rushed out of the room and went back to her bedchamber.

He wished her pleasant dreams. They were not pleasant; they were filled with wants, desires, and pleasure she didn't realize she needed. Devon had awakened something in her, and it wouldn't be suppressed any longer. God help her…

Three

Devon strolled through the halls of the Whitewood estate, hoping to run into his minx. The maid had more daring and boldness in her than he could have ever imagined. He couldn't believe his luck when he'd found her in the library the night before drinking brandy and snacking on pilfered food from the kitchen. Did the duke really allow his servants to act so brazenly? It was hard to believe he did. Especially the way Merrifield spoke of him. Addie seemed to think she wouldn't be reprimanded, and he wouldn't inquire about her actions with the duke to find out. He didn't want to cause her any problems if she happened to be wrong about the duke.

He turned the corner and almost ran into the duke. Did he conjure him by thinking about him? "Your Grace," Devon greeted him.

"Winchester," the duke nodded. "Are you lost again?"

Devon chuckled. "I may be. How did you know?" He couldn't very well admit he was searching for his pretty little maid.

"You have that look about you as if you are trying to find something but nothing seemed familiar. Where are you heading?"

"I'm wandering more or less," he admitted. "I was searching for Merrifield, but he seems to have found a nice little hidey hole."

The duke frowned and didn't say anything right away. After a moment he met Devon's gaze and said, "I'm concerned about him. He seems a little lost in the real sense. He has no direction or idea what he wants to do with his life. Being a peer isn't only about wealth and privilege. He needs a purpose or he'll be truly lost one day."

Devon didn't think Merrifield's problems ran that deep. He was young still, and he had time to figure it out. "He'll be all right. I wouldn't worry too much." Was this why he suggested Merrifield marry his daughter? Did he think that would give him this so-called purpose? "He won't disappoint you." Devon had every faith in that.

"I hope so." He grinned. "In the meantime, may I suggest you consider the conservatory to wander over to. It has some of the lushest plants, and my wife has somehow managed to grow oranges in there."

He doubted that his little minx had gone into the conservatory, but for lack of anything else to do he would take the duke's suggestion. "That is quite the feat." Devon tilted his lips upward into a congenial smile. "Your wife must be quite the talented gardener."

"She has many talents," the duke said and grinned. There was almost a wicked gleam in his eye. In that moment Devon could see why Merrifield called him a pirate.

"What do you know about pirates?" Devon asked before he could stop himself.

The duke jerked back, startled by the question. "Why do you ask?"

"It's something Merrifield said. He suddenly developed an interest in them on our journey here. Made me curious about what it takes to be a pirate and if it is as romantic as some books make it out to be."

The duke frowned and shook his head. "There's nothing romantic about piracy. It is a dirty, bloody business. Not for the weak of heart, or for someone unwilling to do what it takes to survive. That isn't you, and it definitely isn't Merrifield." He slapped him on the shoulder. "Do me a favor and stick to what you know and leave the piracy to those too cold-hearted and desperate to do anything else."

Devon frowned. "You almost sound as if you speak from experience."

"What if I am?" He lifted a brow. "Would you think differently of me if you knew I was a former pirate captain?"

He couldn't be serious… Was he? Why would a duke ever resort to piracy? Most pirates existed a hundred years earlier, not in the nineteenth century. Devon couldn't think of one known pirate alive. That didn't mean they didn't exist; it was just not a widely practiced activity. "I am not familiar enough with you to have an opinion one way or the other, and even if I was, it's not my place to judge your life choices." He really didn't want to insult his host. As much as he hadn't wanted to come to the house party, he didn't want to leave early even more. Merrifield would be quite angry with him.

"Well said," the duke replied. "And a refreshing outlook. If only some gossipmongers of the ton practiced the same restraint. Everyone's life would be so much easier."

He glanced away and looked down the hall. Almost as if he was expecting someone or something to reveal itself. The duke was…odd. He didn't understand why he was telling him all this, but it would be rude to walk away now. He had to stay and finish listening. "Some rumors can shred a person down to their core, that's true." He'd heard enough about himself to give him pause.

"You're wise for someone so young." The duke grinned. "I'll tell you a secret and take it however you will." He met Devon's gaze and didn't waver once. "There are things in this life that will constantly surprise you, and there are mysteries that you may never solve. Expect the unexpected and it'll make every decision you make that much easier." He grinned. "And I truly was once a pirate captain, but you'll not find my name in history books; however, if you ask my wife nicely, she might tell you the story her mother told her as a little girl about the pirate who saved her grandmother's life." He turned and walk away. He stopped momentarily, and added, "The conservatory is down the hall to your left if you're still interested." With those words, he left Devon alone.

He couldn't be telling the truth. Devon didn't believe it. The duke used to be a pirate? That didn't even seem possible… He shook his head and headed toward the conservatory. Maybe visiting the greenery would help clear his head.

ADELINE DIPPED HER PAINTBRUSH INTO THE GOLD PAINT AND THEN drew a swirl over the ornament she was making for the tree. Everyone had been invited to create decorations and encouraged to make their own ornament. She would much rather have created her own in private. She hated being part of a large gathering. That was why she had been so unsuccessful in her first and only season. She hid in the corner as much as possible. Adeline had probably been the only newly launched lady who wanted to be a wallflower. She had agreed to one season at her mother's urging. If she hated it as much as she proclaimed she would, then she'd be free to do as she pleased and stay home. She had hoped that the one season she'd agreed to endure would lead her to her one true love. Sadly, that hadn't happened. Which was why she'd thought to wish for him to find her instead. Adeline didn't think she could ever suffer another season again. This was her last chance to have love in her life.

Was Devon that man? Could she trust he would love her? Adeline wanted to believe he could be. That was what she wanted more than anything. To love and be loved in return. The kiss he'd given her the night before certainly had sparked something in her she'd never felt before.

She dipped her brush into the paint, then added one more flourish. There, it was perfect. She put the brush down and then went over to a nearby tray and set it carefully down to dry. She'd painted an angel on a circular piece of clay. They'd add a ribbon to it later so they could hang it on the tree.

"Are you already finished," Francesca asked. "I'm not nearly done."

"I am." She smiled at her cousin. "I'm weary and am going to lie down until dinner."

She must look like a fright too. She had paint all over her hands and the apron she pilfered from the servant's closet. They had to be getting irritated with her taking them so often. She'd make it up to them later, after all the guests left.

"Will you be joining us for tea?" Francesca asked. She brushed a lock of her strawberry blonde hair behind an ear.

"I am uncertain," she told her. Francesca had already turned her attention back to her ornament. "But don't expect me. I may stay in my chambers longer depending on how I feel."

"All right," Francesca said absentmindedly. "Have a nice rest."

Adeline grinned and walked away. One of the things she adored about her cousin was how uncomplicated she was at times. She had an innate sense of purpose and understanding where people were concerned. She didn't impose her expectations on to them.

As she headed to her chambers, she decided to head to the conservatory instead. She wanted to check on the orange trees her mother had planted. They might have ripe fruit, and if so, she wanted to grab some to take for a snack. The kitchen would be a nightmare this time of day as they prepared for the last meal of the day.

She hummed to herself as she strolled into the conservatory, then turned toward the grove her mother had added a while ago. She stopped immediately when she realized someone else was in the room. Devon was leaning down and staring at the orange trees. He glanced up and his lips tilted upward when he met her gaze. "Addie," he said. That rich timbre of his sent shivers down her spine. She loved the way he said her name.

"Devon," she squeaked out his name. She, on the other hand, was a nervous ninny. "Do you have an interest in oranges?"

"I didn't until the duke mentioned them earlier." He glanced back at the tree. "I've never had an orange," he admitted.

She lifted a brow. "Never?"

"Not at all," he said. "How does one tell if they're ready to eat?"

So that was why he'd been studying them. Adeline smiled and moved past him, examined the fruit on the dwarf tree. Luckily, it had grown a little more than her height. They were a nice bright orange, and definitely ripe enough. She pulled it off the tree and handed it to him. "Peel it and find out."

He chuckled. "You really are not afraid of displeasing the duke."

She shrugged. "He wouldn't care either way. These are not his babies after all." The conservatory was her mother's beloved project.

"That's right," he said as he peeled the orange. "He mentioned his wife planted the trees. So you don't think she'd mind."

Adeline shrugged. "Probably not." Her mother wouldn't be too concerned if a few pieces of fruit were stolen. She liked to grow things. "As long as someone finds enjoyment in her efforts, she's usually quite amiable."

"They seem like wonderful people—the duke and duchess, that is."

"I may be biased, but I think so." She wrinkled her nose. "That might not be true for others."

He nodded. "I can understand that, and it's probably true for anyone. We all see people differently. The duke is a little terrifying." He finished peeling the orange and broke it in half. "Earlier he told me he used to be a pirate captain."

"He did?" Adeline was shocked. "He rarely tells anyone that."

"So it is true?" His tone held an edge of shock. "I thought he was bamming me."

Perhaps she shouldn't have confirmed it… "There are stories, but they were before my time. I don't know how much truth they hold." She couldn't say more than that. Devon probably didn't believe in time travel. It was a closely held secret in her family, and she didn't know him well enough to impart secrets to him yet.

He tore off a piece of the orange and held it out to her. "Try it with me." He slid a slice into his mouth and moaned. It did funny things inside her stomach.

She took the slice he offered her and took a bite. Juice slid down her fingers. He took her hand and licked the juice, then sucked her finger to make sure he didn't miss a drop. It was decadent, and she had no idea how she should proceed…no one had licked her finger before. "I'll leave you to your orange. I…" She swallowed hard. "Have things I need to do."

"I'll let you run away now, Addie, my sweet," he called after her. "But I do intend to find you later."

Adeline didn't turn around or respond. Instead she went straight to her bedchamber. Her heart pounded inside her chest. What was he doing to her?

Four

Devon stared at the billiards table and frowned. He had promised Merrifield, Hampstead, Goodland, and Lindsey he would stay while they finished their game, but he wanted to leave. It was no fun to watch them play. Especially when there was a pretty maid that he'd like to play with instead. He had no idea what part of the house Addie usually worked in, but he hoped to finally discover that answer that day. He had looked all over the house but hadn't found her. It was almost as if she were hiding. The only place he hadn't looked was where all the ladies were spending their time. Devon shuddered. He was not brave enough to enter a drawing room filled with eligible ladies to find his little minx. It would be his luck that she was actually there. He supposed she could have had the day off... He could resume his quest after the billiards match finally ended.

"Why are you sulking in the corner?" the Duke of Lindsey asked. His tone held a hint of amusement in it. "If you wanted to play, you should have spoken up before we started."

"I don't need any chastisement," Devon drawled. He met Lindsey's gaze. "Since when did you decide to act like an old matron dropping unwanted advice?"

Hampstead chuckled. "He has you there Lindsey. None of us particularly like to hear anything resembling advice." He leaned over the table and took a shot, then stood to watch the balls roll

250

across the table. "Besides, he'd play horribly. He's too distracted."

"Is that so?" Lindsey turned toward Devon. "Who is she?"

Of course he'd land right on the problem. There was only one thing that would gain Devon's attention this much. He would not tell the duke about his maid though. He might try to find her, then seduce her right out from under Devon. He would not allow that to happen. She was his. "None of your concern," he said coldly. "Don't you have a game to finish?"

Lindsey's laughter echoed through the room and irritated Devon, but he refused to let the duke know that. "That makes it more fun," he said as he leaned down to take his shot on the table. "Thanks for making it more interesting."

"You're asking him to pummel you," the Viscount of Goodland said. "We might as well find some place to hold a match now. It will end in a sparring match with the winner getting the spoils."

The Earl of Hampstead lifted a brow. "You believe it'll end that way?"

"It will," Merrifield said and laughed. "As soon as Lindsey discovers the identity of Winchester's maid all bets are off."

Devon was going to kill them all. His irritation was so high he was ready to hit a wall. He might not actually commit murder, but he'd definitely hit one of them if they didn't stop talking. He counted to ten in his head, then said in a congenial tone, "Lindsey can meet her. I'm sure his title'll impress her. It isn't as if she's ever met a duke before." He snapped his fingers. "That's right, she's probably met at least two considering the duchess is also the daughter of another duke."

"But neither one of those dukes are eligible," Lindsey replied. "They all think they can convince me to marry them."

That was unlikely to happen, ever. Lindsey was as against marriage as the rest of them were. He wouldn't marry until he had no choice, and only to beget an heir. Devon had no intention of marrying even for that. He snorted. "They're not all that ignorant." He shook his head. "They know you won't marry them. They want you to fall in love with them, though. Maybe even hope you'll make them your beloved mistress. The actual ladies…" He grinned. "They don't care about love, they want your title. You should at least get your malarkey straight."

"You're stalling," Lindsey said. "What is your maid's name?"

He shrugged. "I cannot recall. She has red gold hair and ice-blue eyes that'll freeze you with one glance. She works in the kitchens." Devon grinned and outlined a silhouette with his hands that would gain all their attention. "With a body so curvy it'll make your mouth's water at the idea of exploring it." His Addie was all golden and blue eyed with a lean, lush body that begged to be loved. He wasn't sure if there was a kitchen maid that fit that description and, quite frankly, didn't care. As long as it gave Lindsey something to go searching for. "I doubt she'll give you a second look. She has one of those no nonsense attitudes."

"She's making you chase her and you haven't caught her yet," Lindsey said as he lined up his shot. "I won't have to work so hard."

Arrogant arse… He sighed. "Fine, have it your way." He threw up his hands in defeat. "Pursue her if you must. If she chooses you, I'll bow out gracefully." If Lindsey laid one finger on Addie, he'd beat him black and blue. "Finish your game and see if you can locate her. I've looked all day and have had no luck. I suspect it is her off day."

"Perhaps," Lindsey agreed. "Or she doesn't want you to find her. I'll be happy to locate her and keep her for myself." He hit the cue ball and sank his shot. "And that's how it is done, gentlemen." He rubbed his hands together. "Now that the game has concluded, I do believe I have a special lady to seduce into my bed." He waved at them and then left them alone in the game room.

"Sometimes I truly hate him," Devon said.

"Are you really going to let him win?" Merrifield asked with a bewildered expression on his face.

"Absolutely," Devon said in earnest. If there was a strawberry blond woman on the estate Lindsey was welcome to her. "He'll do whatever he wants anyway." He grinned. "And I don't feel like making it into much of a competition. That'll only ensure he makes it more difficult for me. Now I think I'll leave you three to entertain yourselves. I've had enough games for the evening." With those words, he left. He wasn't done for the night. Devon would find his maid, even if it took all night.

ADELINE HAD HOPED TO SEE DEVON, BUT HE SPEND HIS DAY WITH a group of gentlemen that had arrived later than anyone else had. Her mother had thought they had decided not to attend the house party and had been surprised when they showed up. Adeline thought it was rude of them to arrive days after the party had started. From a distance she'd studied them and then had been surprised when Devon and the Marquess of Merrifield had greeted them. There had been a lot of nodding and large grins expressed by the group. It was almost sickening to watch. They fit in. She did not. Would that be a deterrent for Devon when he realized she didn't like crowds and hated socializing?

She stayed with the ladies and had tea while everyone gossiped. Adeline had hated every second of it and had left at the first chance she could escape. She'd sent her regrets for dinner and instead had a tray sent to her room. There was only so much socializing she could handle before the need for being alone overtook her. She had always done better on her own. Her family was wonderful, and she loved them dearly, but even with them she felt overwhelmed at times.

Now it was late, and she'd finished another book. Her father had stocked the library with the latest fiction for her. She flew through books and then she'd be scrambling for something to read, and she read almost anything that would stimulate her mind. When she ran out of entertaining stories, she turned to nonfiction and studied ancient Greek and mathematics. She was not tired at all... Perhaps she should go to the library and grab another text to read. One that might make her sleepy and not want to keep reading through the adventure or love story. Yes, that was exactly what she needed.

Adeline pushed the blankets off of her and grabbed her wrap. She grabbed the book and left her room. It was dark, but she knew the house well and didn't bother grabbing a candle. She had blown hers out after she finished reading and hadn't wanted to bother lighting it again. It didn't take her long to reach the library. She pushed open the door and was surprised to find there were candles already lit.

"I had hoped you would visit the library again," Devon said

253

huskily. "I took a chance, and it looks as if it may have worked out in my favor."

Adeline had not tied her wrap closed because she had believed everyone would be asleep. She'd been foolish… "Wha…" She swallowed the lump in her throat. "You were waiting for me?" She had almost asked what he was doing there, but that would have been an idiotic question. He had already said he had been there for her.

He moved close to her. "I am." Devon took another step toward her. "It's been a long wait too." He took one more step and there wasn't much distance separating them. "Are you not glad to see me?"

"It's not that…" She did want to see him. Adeline craved being near him. She just didn't trust herself to be near him, alone. He was a temptation that she couldn't afford to give in to. "Being alone with you…it's not proper."

"Do we need propriety between us?" He lifted a brow. "I thought we were beyond those strict rules and firmly in the bonds of friendship."

Adeline moved past him. She needed to think and when he was near she lost all ability to form simple sentences. He made her want…him. The rules be damned. Her reputation was already in tatters from her lack of social skills. No one expected her to marry anyway. Why not give in to her desire for him and take what she wanted for the first time in her entire life? Because her parent's would be disappointed in her…

She went to the shelf where the book she'd been reading belonged and placed it in the correct spot. When she turned around, she found Devon staring at her. "Have I frightened you?" he asked.

"Not at all," she told him. Adeline lifted her chin. "I'm not afraid of anything."

"Brave words little minx." He stepped toward her. "You're not under the kissing bough now, but I'd still like to kiss you." He closed the distance between them. If he took one more step, they would be flush against each other. "May I?"

She took a deep breath and nodded. Her decision had been made. Consequences did not matter to her at the moment—she wanted to do everything with Devon, and would. There would be no regrets come morning. If he couldn't love her, at least she'd have this one night. One where she could look back with fondness. There may never be another opportunity to experience pleasure again. Gentlemen had all but forgotten about her existence and no one was knocking at the door to court her.

Devon leaned down and pressed his lips to her. The kiss had started chaste and then he pushed his tongue into her mouth to deepen the kiss, and fire burst through her entire body. As their tongues danced against each other her need grew. Her core tingled with expectation and she wanted to press herself against him and rub herself all over him like a cat seeking attention. She practically purred like one too as he stroked her back.

He bent down and trailed kisses down her neck. She leaned back to give him better access, wanting him to press his hot mouth all over her naked flesh, and he didn't disappoint. He pushed her wrapper to the ground and untied the ribbons in front of her nightrail. Devon leaned down and sucked one of her nipples into her mouth. Adeline groaned at the feel of his mouth on her sensitive flesh. This was so much more than she could have imagined.

Devon lifted his head and met her gaze. They were glossy with desire that matched her own. "I want to love every inch of you. Please say yes..."

"Yes," she answered without hesitation. "I want you to kiss me again."

"I want to do more than kiss you." He pushed her nightrail over her shoulders and let it float down to her ankles. "You, my minx, are magnificent." Devon trailed his fingers down her side, then cupped her arse in his hands. "I will enjoy giving you pleasure."

"You may begin when you're ready," she said breathlessly. "The moment I stepped into the library I knew what I wanted, and that is you."

He groaned. "You will undo me." Devon picked her up and carried her to the settee. "But it'll be worth it." He kneeled before her and spread her legs, then kissed her sensitive nub as he stroked her core. She squirmed beneath him as the pleasure overtook her. Adeline hadn't known what to expect, but this had not been it. He licked her until a pressure built up inside her. She didn't know what it was, but she needed it to reach its peak or she'd scream with frustration. He sucked the sensitive bud into his mouth and she moaned as she shattered beneath his ministrations.

Devon lifted his head and grinned. "That's my girl." He stood up and removed all his clothes, then joined her on the settee. Once he was settled between her thighs, he pushed himself inside her. She screamed as he pushed through her maidenhead. Adeline should have warned him she was a virgin. He stopped and stared at her. "You were innocent. Why…"

"I'm sorry if you want to stop we can." She hurt a little, but she wanted to finish this. Adeline had to know what it all was like. Until that moment, it had felt wonderful.

He shook his head. "It's past time for stopping. If you're all right, we can continue."

"I'm fine," she said, not wanting to discourage him.

Devon leaned down and pressed his lips to her. He kissed her, and kissed her until she softened beneath him, then he rocked back and forth inside her. It didn't take long for that pressure to build up inside her again. He lowered his hands to lift her hips to meet his thrusts. He moved faster and faster inside of her until she convulsed in his arms, and he followed soon after, spilling himself inside of her.

He rolled them to the side and wrapped his arms around her and closed his eyes. Their lovemaking had exhausted him. Adeline took the moment to study him. He was such a gorgeous man. Her Devon… She had stupidly fallen in love with him in a short time. He had not given her any promises and had been honest with her every step of the way. This would not have happened if she'd said no. Adeline wanted to be with him in every way. She would not blame him if he wanted to leave her, but oh, she hoped he'd stay. How could she not? She curled against him and reveled in his warmth. It was perhaps a mistake, but she closed her eyes too. It felt too good to leave him yet…

Five

Every muscle in Devon's body ached, mostly in a good way. He wrapped his arms around Addie and pulled her closer to him. She'd been a virgin. He still couldn't believe she hadn't told him. If he'd known… he might not have taken it as far as it had gone. As a general rule he didn't get involved with innocents, and while she might be a maid, she was still untouched. He preferred more experienced women, but there had been something about Addie that he found enchanting. He had needed to be with her, around her, have her…

Her eyelids fluttered open, and she met his gaze. Those blue eyes of hers were so expressive. He should have known she wasn't experienced in the art of love. Devon had seen what he had wanted to when he looked at her. She'd been in the library in her nightrail, and nothing more, and that led him to believe she was free with her charms. He'd been wrong. Now he didn't know what to do or say to her. He hoped she didn't want more than he could offer her.

"We fell asleep," she said. Her voice was a little raspy as she spoke.

He kissed her forehead. "We did and we should move before someone finds us." Devon had no idea how long they had slept, but servants were bound to start moving soon. Addie might have to be somewhere, too. He still wasn't sure where she worked in the house. "Where did we leave your nightrail."

"It's…" Addie sat up and glanced around. She tucked a

257

strand of hair behind her ear and bit down on her bottom lip. Devon was tempted to pull her back down and make love to her all over again. "Oh, I see it." She stood, and he groaned. There was enough light for him to appreciate the sight of her backside. She lifted her nightgown and slid it over her head. Addie turned toward him and asked, "Are you going to get dressed?"

"I might," he said. "But right now I'm enjoying the view."

She giggled and he couldn't tell in the low light, but she might be blushing too. "I can't stay."

"I can't entice you to shirk your responsibilities?" He adored her, and he intended to have her again before he left the house party. "At least a little while longer."

"I think you've already enticed me far too much as it is." Her lips tilted upward into a wanton smile. "I'm too sore for anything else you have in mind."

He sat up on the settee and reached for his trousers, and slipped them on, leaving the buttons undone, then stalked forward. He pulled her into his arms and pressed his lips to hers. The kiss was sensual and sweet, just like her. "There is plenty we can do that won't overtax your gorgeous body."

She nibbled on that bottom lip again. His minx was teasing him, and she probably did not understand what she was doing. "As wonderful as that sounds, I will have to still say no."

"How about another kiss then," he said huskily. Devon leaned down and whispered in her ear. "I'll need a little more of your sweetness to keep me going through the rest of the day. Please kiss me, Addie girl."

Addie stepped on her tiptoes and wrapped her arms around his neck. "One kiss, then I have to go."

He would not waste the opportunity. Devon wanted to ensure she thought about him all day as she went about her work. When she was free, he hoped she'd search for him, and perhaps he could sneak her into his room. It would be nice to make love to her all night long without worrying that they'd be discovered. He leaned down and pressed his lips to hers. Every time he kissed her, it was better than the last. Devon was staring to believe that he'd never tire of kissing her.

"What the hell is going on here," a man shouted. It broke the magic, and they both turned to stare where the sound had come from.

Addie gasped and stepped out of his arms. She shuffled her feet and Devon thought he understood why. The Duke of White-wood was a formidable man, and he looked as if he would lose it. She probably didn't like the idea of disappointing the man who she depended on for her position. Devon felt awful for causing her any discomfort. "Your Grace," he began. "It's not…"

"What it looks like?" The Duke lifted a brow. "So you're not having your way with my daughter?"

"Your daughter?" He turned to Addie and frowned. He had to have heard him wrong. He did not make love with the duke's daughter. She was a maid…

"Daddy…" She crossed the room and stopped in front of the duke. "I don't need any lectures. This was my decision to make, and you always said I could live my life as I pleased."

The duke opened and closed his mouth several times. Devon couldn't blame him. He was at a loss for words too. This was surreal…it had to be a mistake. It had to be. Duke's daughters didn't dress like maids and make love to a gentleman in their father's library. It was…it…he couldn't even think in complete sentences.

"And if it is a mistake?" The duke frowned. "He's going to hurt you. His reputation precedes him, and trust me Adeline, he is not the marrying kind. I could force…"

Like hell he could… Devon was not marrying anyone.

"No you cannot," Adeline said. Addie…Adeline…it was starting to make sense, and he suddenly felt sick. "I will not marry him. You know I won't and there is only one thing that would convince me to tie myself to a man for the rest of my life. No marriage has a chance of working if it starts out wrong."

Devon could almost love her for sticking her ground…if he were capable of loving anyone. He had to leave. Staying in the library, no staying at the same house where Addie lived…he couldn't do it. Not knowing now who she was and that he could never have her again. It wouldn't work, and it sickened him. He'd never made such a colossal mistake before. How could he have been so wrong about her?

"Do you have anything to add?" the duke asked.

He shook his head. What could he say that would ease any of the duke's concerns? Instead of putting that into words, he snatched his shirt off the floor and pulled it over his head. It would take too long to put his boots back on. He could just carry them to his bedchamber, and after he packed, he'd be gone. Merrifield would have to be told. His friend probably couldn't leave, but that was all right. Devon could take a hired coach back to London.

"Devon," Addie said. There was something in her tone that made him stop. She sounded…hurt. He'd done that to her and it gutted him. "Are you leaving?"

He wanted to tell her he'd stay, but he didn't lie. He'd never mislead her, and if he'd known she was the duke's daughter, he never would have grown close to her to begin with. "I don't see any reason I should stay."

"You don't?" She glanced away as if looking at him was too difficult. He was a first rate arse. "All right then." She picked up her wrapper and put it on. "You never made me any promises. You're free to do whatever you wish."

"And if I made promises?" He lifted a brow. "Then you'd make demands on me?" What was he doing? Why was her dismissal making him angry? He should be happy she was letting him go without a fight, but he wanted her…to what? Fall on her knees and beg him to love her?

"I'd hope I wouldn't have to make demands on someone who made me any sort of promise. That man," she began. "Won't want to leave me. He'd love me enough to stay and love me every day of his life. You're the one terrified of any commitment."

"I'm not the one who lied," he said heatedly. "You're the one that misrepresented yourself. I thought you were a maid." He knew she had not actually lied to him. She never claimed to be anything. He had been the one to make the mistake, but he couldn't let it go.

"I did nothing of the sort," she said with eerie calm. "I've never distorted the truth. You never asked me anything other than my name. I don't even know who you really are. You introduced me with your given name, and I did in return."

The duke lifted a brow. "You don't even know he's the Earl of Winchester." Her father shook his head and laughed. He turned to Devon and said, "You messed up quite a bit, boy. You do not deserve my daughter."

He was right. Devon didn't deserve her. That was why he

was leaving. He'd already hurt her. If he stayed it would be far worse. "You're right. It's all my fault. So it's good I'm leaving. You will not have to concern yourself with me ever again."

"You're selfish." She stalked forward until there was not much space between them. "I love you. I don't know why, but I fell for you hard and fast. It's foolish, and I wish I didn't still have all these tremendous feelings for you, but they're there and they're not going away." She stabbed him in the shoulder with her finger. "You find out one little thing about me that makes you uncomfortable and you're ready to run away like a scared little boy. We'll that's fine. I don't need some weak-willed man at my side. I'm better off without you."

"I'm not weak."

"You're not?" She laughed a little maniacally. "I think the evidence speaks for itself."

"There is no evidence. You're not making any sense and you're growing a little hysterical." He wanted to pull her into his arms and kiss her senseless. It was clear they were both losing their damned minds.

"I'm making perfect sense." She pushed him, and he stumbled a little but remained upright. "Love isn't perfect. It's flawed and risky, and in time there is always the chance that it might lead to nothing but disappointment. But I was willing to take a risk with you in case this was my chance to find the one person who was meant for me. That gamble could have paid off, and I was willing to risk regretting you for the rest of my life. That is how much you mean to me." She swallowed hard. "Well, I guess I found out sooner rather than later, that I will regret ever meeting you. I will regret loving you, and there won't be a day that goes by that I will not think of you, but I'll never regret giving you my heart. Because not loving you would have been a mistake. I'm not afraid of taking a risk. That is *your* fear and I won't fall victim to it." She brushed past him and started to leave. He should stop her, but he was momentarily frozen in place. Her words hit him hard, and he didn't know what to do with them. She stopped at the door and said, "I hope you have a good life and you find something that makes you happy. There's sadness in you, and I can't help you erase that. You have to overcome your doubts yourself, and maybe when you do it won't be too late for us. My fear is that it *will* be." With those words, she left the library.

The duke stepped closer to him. He'd been unusually quiet during the exchange. He said in a low menacing tone, "You have two choices. You either profess your love for Adeline and beg her to marry you or you pack your belongings and leave my house in the next hour. If you do the first, I welcome you to the family, if you fail to do the second you won't live to see another day. You hurt my daughter and you're lucky I haven't ended your life already." He met Devon's gaze, and he could believe the duke had been a pirate that made men walk the plank. "I pray you fail to leave on time so I get the pleasure of gutting you. Please do give me that pleasure. I'm almost tempted to not give you the chance to leave."

Devon swallowed hard. "I won't disappoint you."

"See that you don't."

With those words, the duke left Devon alone in the library. He had a lot to think about and he had no idea what he wanted to do.

Six

D evon sat down on the settee and stared at his discarded boots. He should put them on and go to his bedchamber. He should already be packing to depart at first light…which was soon. There were a lot of things he should do, but none of that mattered in comparison to the things he should never have done. He couldn't go back and change anything, and if he were to be honest with himself, he didn't want to. Spending the night with Addie in his arms was the best moments of his life. He would always remember them.

But he couldn't marry her.

He was no good to any woman, and he refused to ruin her life by attaching himself to her. His family hadn't been the best, and he didn't know if he would make a good husband. She said she'd been willing to take a risk, that she might regret him for the rest of her life. He'd hurt her and nothing could ease that ache. Even if he dropped on his knees before her and begged her to marry him that hurt would always still be there. He could never erase that wounded expression from his memory. Devon had done that to her, and he had to live with that guilt.

What was he going to do? He glanced over at the boots and sighed, then picked them up. He shoved his feet into them and then stalked out of the library. There was only one solution. He had to leave, and fast. He didn't particularly want to die, and he suspected the duke hadn't been lying when he said he'd gut him. He's already wasted a quarter hour wallowing in his uncertainty.

He didn't need to squander any more of the hour he'd been allotted.

He rushed up the stairs and nearly knocked a maid over in his haste. "My apologies," He said and helped her steady herself.

"It's all right, my lord," she said and smiled at him. She was pretty enough with soft brown hair and hazel eyes. Before he'd met Addie, he might have tried seducing her. Addie had changed everything. "Did you need something?"

Was she flirting with him? He could no longer tell. Devon was a complete and utter mess. "No, yes…" He blew out a breath. "Do you know who Lord Merrifield is?"

"I do," she answered and flashed him a sly smile. He had a feeling she knew Merrifield quite intimately.

"Wonderful. Can you tell him to meet me in my chambers immediately? I need to leave." Devon didn't have any time to lose, and he had to pack fast. They had come in Merrifield's carriage. He would need to borrow it to go into town to find a hired hack to take him to London.

"I will," she said and curtsied. "Right away, my lord." Then she scurried off to do as he had asked.

Devon continued his trek to his bedchamber. Once there, he started throwing his clothing into the trunk. He really didn't care if any of it wrinkled. The door swung open and hit the wall with a loud thud. Merrifield wobbled in and fell into a chair. "What is this about leaving? The maid had to have heard wrong."

"No, she understood correctly," Devon replied and threw a shirt into the trunk. "I'm leaving as soon as everything I brought is back in my trunk." He tossed in more clothing items. How much had he brought with him?

Merrifield sat forward and leaned his elbows on his knees. "Say what?"

"You heard me." Merrifield was either still inebriated or hadn't completely woken up yet. Devon was willing to bet Merrifield had drank his fair share of brandy and then had a wild night with one of the many maids at the estate, maybe even the one he'd sent to fetch him. "I. Am. Leaving." Devon enunciated each word clearly so Merrifield's addled brain understood.

"Bloody hell…" Merrifield scrubbed his hands over his face. "What happened after you left the game room last night?"

He'd had the best night of his life… "I don't want to discuss it." Devon didn't even want to think about it. "Suffice to say that I messed up, and quite badly, and the duke has requested my departure."

"You're going to have to talk more slowly because I think I didn't hear you correctly…" He paused a moment and then continued. "Did you say the duke told you to leave?"

"Ordered it or he'd gut me. If I'm not gone in the next quarter hour, I'm a dead man." He had to move faster. "I will need your carriage."

"This can't be happening. I can't leave…"

"You can stay. I'm going to go to town. Maybe the inn has a room and I can stay there until you're ready to leave." He'd prefer to go to London, but he'd wait in town if it made everything easier for Merrifield. He had reasons for being at the house party, and he hated that his actions made it more difficult for him.

"All right, but I'll go with you to town. I could use some fresh air and a little distance from this house. On the way you can tell me what you did to make his grace the arse so angry."

He didn't want to admit that he'd seduced the duke's daughter, Adeline, his Addie. The minx that he couldn't erase from his mind or his soul. She'd come to mean so much to him in a short time. For the thousandth time he couldn't help asking himself how he could have messed up so horribly. "All right," he resigned himself to dredging up the horrors of finding out Addie was no maid, but a lady he never should have touched intimately. "But please hurry. I don't doubt the duke would gut me if I'm here longer than I am supposed to be."

"Take your trunk down and order my carriage. I won't be long." With those words, Merrifield left the room.

Devon grabbed his trunk and went to the entrance and asked for Merrifield's carriage. Once it was ready Merrifield joined him in the foyer and they left the Whitewood estate. Devon didn't stop to look back or regret his decision. It was for the best…

ADELINE STARED OUT THE WINDOW AS THE CARRIAGE HEADED down the drive. He was actually leaving. She had told him she didn't regret loving him. A part of her had hoped that grand speech would reach him. He loved her. She believed that to the depth of her soul, but it hadn't been enough. That wish she'd made had come true, but it hadn't been enough. Finding love didn't mean it would stay forever. No one had made her any guarantees, and she'd lost the one man that she would always love.

She pushed the curtains back. They had reached the end of the driveway and soon they would be out of sight. She couldn't watch anymore. Devon, the Earl of Winchester, was leaving her. He had decided loving her was too much for him and he'd run away. Did he even consider staying? She didn't think he had because he had certainly left as fast as he possibly could. It hadn't even been an hour, and he was rushing down the stairs and calling for the carriage. It showed how little she'd meant to him. He'd made love to her and it had been wonderful…until it all came crashing down around her.

"Is something wrong?"

Adeline turned toward her mother. She hadn't heard her come into the sitting room. Why was she even there so early? It was barely past dawn and most of the guests were still asleep. "Why do you ask?"

"Dear," she said and brushed a strand of Adeline's hair behind her ear. "Do you really think your father would keep something from me?"

Of course he wouldn't…and to think Adeline had taken great pains to dress in a simple day gown without her maid's assistance to make herself presentable. She had even plaited her hair and left it hanging down the middle of her back. No one would question the style. She did her hair herself often enough they were accustomed to it. But none of that mattered if her father spilled her shame to her mother. "I wish he would have."

"Do you?" Her mother frowned. "You have nothing to be embarrassed about. You took a chance and while it didn't go as you would have liked, the important thing is that you risked your heart when you could have run away. He is the one that should be ashamed. If he were any sort of gentleman, he'd have stayed and taken responsibility for his actions."

"He never made me any promises." Devon made her feel better about herself without even trying to. She had always felt out of place in society. Around Devon, she didn't notice anything but him. She never stopped to think about what was happening around her. There were a few times that they had been alone and none of that mattered, but still… He brought something out of her no one else could. "He didn't have to stay."

"He didn't have to ruin you either," her mother said. There was a harshness in her tone, but Adeline knew her mother didn't think unfavorably toward her. She reserved that anger for Devon.

"I made my choice. You can't blame him for everything."

"That may be true," she began. "But you're my daughter and I'll always fight for you first. I hope he realizes his mistake… for your sake. No one else knows of this, but there could be consequences that would make that moot."

"Consequences?" Adeline lifted a brow, then gasped. She hadn't considered… "Oh, my…" What if one night with Devon meant she'd end up a mother several months down the road. What would she do with a baby and no husband? Her mother was right. She'd be completely ruined.

"We won't worry about that now. It might be nothing." She hugged Adeline. "No matter what, you need to know that your father and I are here for you. This doesn't have to change anything for you. Tell me if…" Her voice trailed off.

"I will," she promised. Adeline would have to tell someone if she found herself enceinte. Should she tell Devon if that happened? Would he want to know if he were going to be a father? There was still so much she didn't know about him, and she wished she had the time to discover it all.

"Good. I'm going to go reassure your father you're not falling apart. He worries…" Her mother sighed. "He used to run a pirate ship. You would think he could handle a little emotional upheaval."

Adeline smiled. "He doesn't have the stomach for emotions. They have no place on a pirate ship, and he was the captain. Everyone was supposed to follow his orders."

"This is true," her mother said and chuckled. "You are all right, aren't you?"

"I am truly," she said. "But I doubt that I'll ever willingly risk my heart again. It hurts too much." Devon was her one love. No one else could replace him in her heart. If he couldn't love her enough to stay and fight for her, then she didn't need him.

"Oh, sweetie," her mother said. There was sadness in her voice, and Adeline wished she wasn't the cause of it. "Don't say that. This was one hiccup in a sea of them. Don't give up now." She hugged her again, then stepped back to meet her gaze. "Besides your gentleman could surprise you. A lot of men run scared, and then they wise up and realize that they're about to lose the one good thing in their life. Lord Winchester feels something for you. I dare not call it love, but there's something there. Don't lose hope completely."

"I don't know…"

"I do," her mother said firmly. "Now go up to your chambers and rest. We have a long day ahead of us with the tree trimming and the ball. You won't make it through it all with no sleep."

"All right," Adeline agreed, and left the sitting room. There was no reason to remain awake anyway, and her mother was right. It was going to be a long day. At least sleep allowed her to escape reality for a little while.

Seven

D evon leaned against the side of the carriage and closed his eyes. The little bit of sleep that he'd managed while holding Addie in his arms hadn't been nearly enough. The morning's activities had exhausted him mentally and physically—and that didn't take into account making love to Addie. It was everything after that…it had changed how he saw his minx. She could never be his. Not really… As a maid he could have played with her until he left and that was all he'd wanted. He hadn't come to the house party looking for anything permanent. He hadn't really been looking for anything at all, and yet, he found Addie. She was the gift he didn't deserve and wanted to keep, but knew he couldn't.

"Are you going to finally explain to me what happened?" Merrifield asked. His voice was infused with exasperation and exhaustion all at once. "This all seems dramatic even for you."

"I don't want to dredge out all the details. Can't you accept that I offended the duke and leave it at that?" It was unlikely that Merrifield would allow him to not divulge any of the details, but he had to try.

"I cannot and you know why." Merrifield groaned and leaned back. "Bloody hell. You couldn't wait until a decent hour to get the boot. What did you do that was so terrible?"

It was time to say the words he'd been avoiding since Merrifield came into Devon's bedchamber earlier. His friend could be relentless and he had to accept that. Devon took a deep breath and then said, "I made love to his daughter."

"Pardon me…" Merrifield sat up straight and met his gaze. He opened and closed his mouth several times. The confusion and disbelief was etched all over his face. "Can you repeat that?"

God, he didn't want to. "I ruined his daughter." Maybe if he said it a different way, it would penetrate Merrifield's addled brain.

"And he didn't murder you on the spot?" He shook his head. "I don't understand? Just so we're clear Lady Adeline is the one you seduced?"

His Addie… It wasn't until that moment that he realized Merrifield had never said her name aloud before. When she introduced herself as Addie he might have made the connection. No, he wouldn't have. He'd been too taken with her. She should have clarified who she was, and maybe that would have made a difference. "Lady Adeline Carwyn. the daughter of the Duke of Whitewood with lovely golden blond hair and deep blue eyes. Yes, that would be her."

"But I thought you were smitten with a maid?" He couldn't blame Merrifield for being confused. Devon had been in a constant state of confusion since he discovered her identity.

"I thought she was a maid, yes." He sighed. "When I met her, she was all dusty and wearing an apron. They had been hanging decorations in the library." He'd fallen for her in that moment. Devon had wanted to know more about her, and with each new thing he learned, the more he'd become enamored with her.

"I'm…" Merrifield paused. "I have no words. You were right to leave. It would have been a mistake and if you had stayed you would have ended up tied to her for the rest of your life. That would have ruined your life."

Devon wasn't so sure about that. He was more inclined to believe he would have ruined Addie's life. He was not a good man, and she deserved someone worthy of her. Addie was special and wonderful. "It doesn't matter if it would have been or not. This is the choice I made and I don't regret it."

"Are you certain you don't?" Merrifield asked. "You don't sound resigned."

"How do I sound?" Devon wasn't certain about anything. He

believed he made the right choice. "I didn't realize there should be a certain tone I should inflect when I speak of the scandal I created." It was going to be another wonderful Christmas—alone. He couldn't remember the last time he spent a holiday with anyone. It was one of the reasons he'd wanted to refuse to attend the house party. Perhaps he had sabotaged it unconsciously.

"Now you're being churlish." Merrifield chuckled lightly. "My friend, I say this with a heavy heart…but you fell in love with her. I still think you made the right choice in leaving, but you don't. If you honestly love her why are you running away?"

"You know why." Devon had lost all hope for happiness a long time ago.

"Your parents' mistakes are not yours. Don't let their foolishness create any more havoc on your life." He threw up his hands. "I don't understand how you could have fallen for Lady Adeline, but the heart wants what it wants." The carriage came to a stop outside an inn. "We're here, but we are not supposed to leave for a couple more days. Take the time to think about what you really want. If you truly think you and Lady Adeline are better off apart—stay here and I'll retrieve you after I leave the duke's estate, but if you love her I think you should fight for her. Come to the ball tonight."

"I'll consider it." He wouldn't. Devon rarely changed his mind after he made a decision, and he was unlikely to do so now. "I'll see you in a couple days."

"I doubt that." Merrifield grinned. "I expect you'll find your way back to the ball later. I'd even wager on it." He looked far too smug for his own good, and Devon wanted to punch that grin off of his face.

"Don't bet on a losing hand," Devon said. He stepped out of the carriage and retrieved his trunk, then went into the inn. He had no intention of returning and claiming Adeline as his own. No matter how much he wanted to…

DEVON STARED AT THE CEILING OF HIS ROOM AT THE INN. HE'D been in luck and they had a room available. Most people were home with their families for the holidays. He felt a little bad having to stay at the inn and making them work when they normally wouldn't have to. He was a horrible person, and that wasn't the first time he thought in the past several hours.

Guilt overwhelmed him and it grew exponentially with each passing moment. Was Merrifield right? Should he go to the ball and get on his knees before Addie and beg her to marry him? Would that make the guilt go away or would it make it all worse? Devon didn't know what he should do, and he ached in places he didn't know he had inside of him.

Maybe if he ate something, he'd feel better. Which sounded stupid, but he had to do something. He was going a little crazy on his own, and he didn't understand why. This wasn't the first time he'd been on his own. He was actually quite accustomed to it.

Devon left his room and went down to the main room. It was empty. That didn't surprise him, but he thought someone would be around. Could he even order anything to eat? He turned around and considered going back to his room. He deserved to starve anyway.

"Can I help you, my lord?" a woman asked.

He turned toward the sound of her voice. She had dark hair streaked with silver and hazel eyes. Her clothes were a little threadbare, and she was on the thin side. Looking at her made him slightly uncomfortable. "I had hoped to find something to eat."

"We have a nice mutton stew if that will satisfy your needs," she said. The woman turned her head to the side. "If you don't mind me saying…you look a little rough around the edges. Are you all right?"

Devon feared he'd never be all right again. "Mutton Stew is fine." He didn't know how to respond to her assessment of his appearance.

"I'll have one of the girls bring it out." She paused and glanced at him. "Unless you prefer it be brought to your room."

"No," he said after a moment of thought. "I'd prefer to eat here."

He sat down at a table and waited for her to bring him his stew. A younger girl came out with it along with a pint of ale and a chunk of bread. It was a simple meal, but he didn't mind that.

The girl set it on the table before him. "Will there be anything else my lord?"

"No thank you," he said. "This is perfect."

With those words, she left him alone to enjoy his meal. He dipped the bread into the stew and took a bite. It was good. Perhaps the best mutton stew he'd ever eaten. After he finished, he pushed the empty bowl to the side and lifted the ale up and sipped it. He didn't much care for ale, but he didn't mind it once in a while.

"Not to your liking is it?" Devon didn't like how much the older woman saw right through him. He never believed he was that obvious, but she cut through him like a hot knife slicing butter.

"The stew was wonderful," he told her.

"I'm not talking about the stew." She said and pulled out a chair to sit with him. She gestured toward the ale. "It's not your fancy brandy."

"I don't like brandy that much either," he admitted. He had a love hate relationship with spirts...mostly hate. It had to do with how his father died. "But I do still drink it upon occasion." He had nights where he'd imbibed too much celebrating with his friends. But the taste had never appealed to him. "Why do you think I appear...rough?" He might regret asking her, but he had to know.

"That may not be the best description." She tilted her head to the side and studied him. "You're full of uncertainty." Her words were cryptic, but strangely on point.

She was not wrong. He had been full of doubt since he left the duke's estate. Merrifield had given him a lot to consider as well. "I may be." He didn't like admitting that aloud, but he didn't know what to do. Perhaps talking to a stranger would help him sort through his feelings.

The woman chuckled. "Even in this you're conflicted. You don't know which way to turn." She shook her head. "I can only tell you this... follow your heart. If you ignore what is inside of it, then you'll only find misery, but if you follow your deepest desire, you should find happiness. Don't ignore what is right in front of you."

She was right. "So I should return." That's what he thought

she was suggesting, but he had to clarify. In the past several hours, he'd done some rather foolish things...

"I don't know of what you speak," she said. Her lips tilted upward into a smile. "But if you left your heart behind, you best retrieve it." With those words, she stood and left him alone.

Devon didn't stay in the main room of the inn long. He hopped to his feet and went to his room, then prepared for a long walk in the snow. He had no other way to reach the duke's estate. He had been a fool to leave Adeline behind. Hopefully, it would not be too late and she would forgive him for being a complete arse. He loved her and he had to tell her that. Even if she kicked him out of the house and her father gutted him for returning. The risk was worth it. He should have listened to her when she told him she loved him. But he'd been foolish and run away. He could only pray that he wasn't too late to tell her he loved her too...

Eight

The ball would start soon. Not that Adeline cared much, but it was important to her mother. That was the only reason she even bothered to prepare for it. Adeline's heart was broken and nothing could heal it. She'd taken that risk and it hadn't worked out as she would have liked. Now she had to live with that disappointment.

Adeline sat down and pulled her stockings up, then secured them in place. Her maid walked in at that moment. Usually Adeline like to do most of her dressing on her own. She enjoyed having a little independence, but the gown she had fashioned for the ball was not one she could slip into on her own. The corset alone would require a lot of attention. Everything made for the ball down to her undergarments was a brilliant scarlet. It didn't have any elaborate decorations. The silk shimmered in the light and the lines were simple and elegant. Adeline felt pretty in the gown…at least she had when she'd worn it for her fittings. Now she would rather leave it in her armoire and stay in bed for the evening.

"Are you ready for the gown, my lady?" her maid Edith asked.

"I am," Adeline replied. "Can you retrieve the gown so I can slip into it after my stays are laced."

Edith went to the armoire and pulled the scarlet gown out, then placed it on the bed. With that task done, she came to help

Adeline with her corset. "All right, let's get your ribbons tied." Edith laced the corset and then pulled it tight until it closed. She tied the end and tucked the loose ribbons underneath. "There, now it is time for the dress."

"Indeed," Adeline agreed, but there was no emotion in her voice as she spoke. She couldn't muster up even a tiny bit of enthusiasm. "At least we already decorated the tree." That normally was one of the things she looked forward to most, but this year there hadn't been any joy in it.

Edith retrieved the dress and held it out. "All right, step in and I will pull it up." Adeline did as Edith instructed. This was not anything new, but Edith always had to explain what she would do. It was a habit Adeline doubted Edith would break, and at the moment she was grateful for it. The normalcy of the routine helped her get through dressing for the ball. She prayed she wouldn't fall apart. Perhaps she would bow out early and claim fatigue or a headache. Her mother wouldn't argue with her over it. Both her parents were aware of Adeline's misgivings about attending.

"There," Edith said as she pulled the dress up. "Now time to fasten all those buttons. I'm glad you're a patient young lady."

"It's the least I can do." It wasn't as if she had any reason to throw a fit or be demanding...most of the time. Edith didn't have to do very much for her at all. "You help me when I need it."

"I wish you needed it more." Edith slipped a button through a hole. "You might attract a young gentleman if you care enough for your appearance."

Adeline was tempted to laugh hysterically. She'd been on the verge of it for hours now. Edith didn't know about Devon. If she had she would never have suggested that to her. Her maid meant well. She wanted Adeline to be happy and have a family of her own. That was unlikely to happen for her. Not after her night with Devon.

"There is no reason to bother with such things," she told Edith. "No gentleman will want me either way."

"That's nonsense," Edith said, then sighed. "You're a beautiful woman and have an enormous dowry. Why wouldn't a gentleman want you for his wife?"

Because she was ruined... She couldn't say that to Edith though. It was better if her secret wasn't shared with too many people. That way it was more likely to stay a secret. The problem was, she didn't know what she could say for Edith to let it go. "Because I do not want them to." Perhaps that would be enough...

"Nonsense," Edith said, dismissing her statement. "You just have not found one that interests you enough to try is all." She leaned down and straightened her skirts. "There you're ready. Do me a favor and at least try to find a gentleman to dance with. This dress is too pretty to be hidden in a corner." She lifted her hand and placed a finger under Adeline's chin. "And you're far too beautiful to hide from the world."

"I cannot make any promises," Adeline said. Especially since she didn't intend to stay long at the ball. She would find a way to escape as soon as possible. Perhaps after the first dance... Someone would ask her. There was a lot of family at the ball, and one of them might take pity on her.

"All right, I suppose that's all I will manage to get from you tonight. Try to smile. You're so much prettier when you do." Edith sighed. "I'll leave you to finish. I'll help with the dress when you're done at the ball." With those words, Edith left her alone.

Adeline sat at her vanity and stared at her reflection. The sadness didn't seem as evident to her, but perhaps she didn't know what to look for. Her hair was pulled back loose so her curls were hanging wildly around her. A strand had come loose and framed her face. She should fix it, but decided against it. Adeline didn't want to be someone she wasn't, especially tonight. The world would get her how she was whether they liked it or not. She didn't owe any of them anything, and she would never let society's rules bother her again. Maybe Edith was right. It was time to stop hiding and face the world. At least she could thank Devon for that much. One night with him had awakened her to all the possibilities. She might not have love, but then she didn't think she needed it so much after all.

Devon shivered as he walked through the snow toward the Whitewood Estate. Surely it must be close by now. It seemed as if he had been walking forever and the bloody cold was not helping at all. He had to reach Addie. Once he told her he loved her and begged her to marry him, it would all be worth it.

He tripped over a fallen tree branch in the road and hit the ground hard. Devon cursed under his breath and fumbled around trying to get a foothold. He slipped again, and his face hit the snow this time. He spat the stuff that had gotten into his mouth out and shuddered. This was hell. Not the burning inferno people claimed it was, but this. Cold, wet, white flakes of torment…that was what he considered to be hell. He would much rather have a hot summer day.

Devon pulled himself up and managed to stay on his feet. Every inch of him was soaked through, and he might catch his death on his way to the manor. What was worse…he had nothing to change into. All his clothes were back at the inn. It would all be worth it though once he reached Addie. He needed his pretty little minx. Devon never should have left her.

He pushed himself to keep moving by sheer will alone. Finally, he reached the entrance to the drive. He blinked several times to clear his vision and breathed a sigh of relief. Thank heavens he'd arrived. Now he just had to find Addie. He ran to the door and opened it up. With all the guests arriving, no one would question his entrance. At least not at first… If the duke saw him before he found Addie, he would have a fight on his hands.

"What the blazes are you doing back here?"

Devon closed his eyes and internally cursed his luck. Had he conjured the duke by thinking about him? "I came for Addie."

"Have you now?" The duke raised an eyebrow. "That's too bad. You can't have her. You made your decision clear when you ran away. Now you best go the way you came before I gut you as I promised."

"I am not leaving. Not without her." His breathing was ragged. "I will never be separated from her again."

"Fancy words," the duke drawled. "But I don't believe you. You're weak, and my daughter deserves better than the likes of you. If you won't leave willingly, then so be it." He took off his coat and set it on a nearby chair. He started to roll up his sleeves.

"Good of you to make it interesting. It's been a while since I've pummeled a man. Gutting is too good for you now that I think about it. I'd much rather you live in agony…knowing Adeline will never have anything to do with you."

He refused to believe that would be his future. "I don't want to fight with you." Devon hoped to marry Addie, and having any discord with her father would not help his cause. "Please don't do this. Just let me talk to her."

"That is not going to happen." The duke took a step forward. "You do not deserve her and I will not have you hurting her again."

Devon took a step back and fell to the floor. The duke loomed over him, and he had no doubts he intended on hitting him. Devon closed his eyes and braced for the duke's fist to slam into his face, but the hit never landed.

"You would have let me hit you," the duke said, then sighed. Devon opened his eyes and met his gaze. The duke held out his hand for him. "Come on. If you're that determined, I suppose I'll let you talk to her. But if she asks you to leave, I expect you to honor her wishes."

Devon hadn't expected that… He stood next to the duke and frowned. "I am confused."

"I'm not surprised, the duke said. You're an idiot. I'd expect nothing less from you." He slid his sleeves back down and then picked up his jacket. "What are you waiting for? Go find her."

Devon didn't have to be told twice. He also didn't want the duke to actually hit him. Explaining why they were in the midst of fisticuffs in the middle of the foyer would not go over well… with anyone. Devon rushed toward the ballroom and flung open the doors. He didn't see her immediately and his heart sunk. Where was she? He scanned the ballroom, but she wasn't anywhere inside. Did she go somewhere else? Where would she be?

The library…

That was her favorite room. She would go there for some solitude. It was the one place he had known she'd go, but would she go there now? It was also where he'd seduced her and broke her heart. He had to check. He would search the entire house if necessary, but he would find her.

He paused outside the library door and took a deep breath,

then pushed it open. Devon stopped short, unable to breathe properly. Addie stood under the mistletoe in a red gown. Her blond hair framed her beautiful face, but she had a haunted expression on her face. He'd done that to her. She turned toward him and met his gaze. "You're here," she said softly.

"I'm here," he repeated her words. His voice was hoarse with emotion. "I should never have left."

A tear slipped from her eye and trailed down her cheek. "Why did you come back?"

He crossed the room and pulled her into his arms. "I love you. I thought I could walk away, but I was a fool. Even if I could why would I want to." He wiped the tear from her cheek. "I'm so sorry. Can you ever forgive me?"

"I don't know if I should."

Devon nodded. "I wouldn't blame you if you told me to leave." He went to his knees. "But please. I'm begging you…marry me."

"Did someone make you do this?" She took a step back. "I don't want a forced marriage. I want one that starts with love."

Devon didn't know what he could do to reassure her. He wanted her to marry him and he'd wait as long as it took for her to say yes. "No one made me come here. I walked from town in a snowstorm because I couldn't wait a moment longer. I. Love. You." He had to make her understand. "If I didn't, nothing could force me to be here."

"I want to believe you." She turned away from him and stared out the window. The snow was coming down hard now, and there was no visibility. "You actually walked in that?"

"I did," he said. "But to be fair, it wasn't that bad. I could see where I was walking." Devon wanted to always be honest with her. "I was afraid of what I felt for you. Love is a foreign emotion to me. I didn't experience it with my parents, and they sure as hell didn't have anything remotely resembling that with each other. I believed I had nothing to offer a woman. I thought I was protecting you." He took a deep breath then continued, "I realize now I was a coward. You are right. Love is a risk and if you are lucky enough to have it, you should fight for it. I hope I'm not too late." He crossed over to her. "So please, believe me when I say this. From the moment I met you, it has been one wonderful moment after the next. I cannot imagine not living the rest of my life with you by my side. Please marry me and ensure that we'll have the grandest of adventures together, and I promise, I'll love you every second of it."

She placed her hands on his cheeks. "I love you so much it hurts. I made a wish the night before the house party started. I wanted someone to love me, truly love me, for who I was and not who they thought I'd be. I never expected it to unfold as it did. You didn't know I was a lady, and that changed the dynamics between us. If I was a lowly maid, would you still want to marry me?"

He wanted to say yes, but he didn't know the answer. "In another lifetime social status wouldn't matter. You're not a maid and your question is moot. Maybe I would have, or maybe I'd have left you. I'd like to believe I'd have been more honorable, but I've not always been a good man."

She smiled. "Kiss me."

Addie still hadn't agree to marry him, but he wasn't going to tell her no. He wanted to kiss her. Devon craved it. He leaned down and pressed his lips to hers and his body came alive as it did every time he touched her. He deepened the kiss, and she moaned. Devon wanted to strip that provocative gown off of her and make love to her again, but instead he broke the kiss and stepped back. His breathing was ragged. "I can't keep kissing you or this will go farther than either of us want it to."

Her lips tilted upward into a wanton smile. "My love," she said. "Who said that I didn't want more than a kiss? I'll always want more."

He shook his head. "Not unless we're married. I rather like breathing, and if we make love again outside of the bonds of matrimony, I'm certain your father will murder me."

"He might," she said and then chuckled. "It's lucky then that I'm going to marry you isn't it." She wiggled her finger to him. "I'm standing under the bough of holly. It's against tradition not to kiss me."

Devon grinned. "I wouldn't want to break tradition." He closed the distance between them. "Will you dance with me?"

"A waltz without music?" Addie lifted a brow. "My favorite kind."

He pulled her into his arms and swirled her around the floor in something resembling a waltz, but it was more swaying and kissing that happened between them than anything else. He'd won the heart of his Christmas minx. This was the best Christmas he could ever hope for. Devon couldn't wait to marry her...

Epilogue

Six months later...

Devon had wanted to court Adeline properly. Even though they'd already made love and she'd agreed to marry him. Adeline deserved to be treated like the proper lady she was. So he spent the months after they met taking her to the theater, or out for a drive, and dancing with her at balls. He especially loved dancing with her.

They announced their betrothal in the Times and had the bans read at her grandfather, the Duke of Weston's, chapel. They were to be married there amongst her family and friends. He certainly didn't have any family to invite, but his closest friends would be there. Merrifield would be by his side the entire time.

Now, finally, he was going to marry her. Addie would be his minx forever, and he couldn't be happier. In a short time they would say their vows and then their adventure together would begin in truth.

"Are you ready for this?" Merrifield asked. He buttoned his waistcoat and then slipped on his jacket. "After this there is no going back. You'll have that bloody duke as a father-in-law."

"The duke isn't as awful as you make him out to be." Devon grinned. "He's been pleasant since Addie agreed to marry me."

"Before that he was a bloody arse," Merrifield said and shook his head. "I saw how he treated you in the foyer. Well...I saw the end. But you know what I mean."

Devon had been unaware of anyone else being there, but his focus had been on finding Addie. So it was no surprise he hadn't been aware Merrifield had witnessed his embarrassment. "He had every right to be angry with me. I did ruin his daughter and run away. I would have done the same to any man who treated my daughter so carelessly." Devon believed the duke had actually shown a great deal of restraint. If he was blessed with a daughter, he'd never allow a man to treat her the way he had treated Addie. "I was the one who was the true arse. I'm glad I realized my mistake and came back for her. I do love her and I am happy that we're about to be married."

"Then it's time we went to the altar and waited for your bride."

Devon chuckled. "Lead the way, my friend."

They walked out of Weston Manor and strolled toward the chapel. It was near the cliffs the estate had been built upon. The chapel was large enough to hold all the guests that had been invited to the ceremony. The wedding breakfast would be much larger in attendance, and the ball later that night would be packed. It wasn't every day the daughter of the Duke of White-wood and granddaughter of the Duke of Weston got married. It was one of the season's premiere events. It would be grand, and Devon was grateful they waited long enough to plan it properly.

Devon stood at the altar and waited for Addie to join him. When the chapel doors opened and revealed her his breath caught in his throat. She wore a dress the color of blush pink that almost matched her skin tone. She seemed almost...naked. His minx was making a statement of some sort, but he didn't know what it was. All Devon knew with certainty was she was lovely and he loved her.

She marched down the aisle toward him with a seductive smile on her face. They hadn't made love in months, and tonight, he would strip that lovely gown off her and make her moan with pleasure. God, he loved her. She joined him at the altar and they both turned toward the vicar.

"We're here to celebrate the joining of these two individuals in the bonds of matrimony..."

The words the vicar said became nothing but a blur in his

mind. Devon only had eyes for Addie. They said their vows, but he barely remembered those either. His entire focus was on his bride, the love of his life.

"I now pronounce you man and wife," the vicar said. "You may now kiss the bride."

"It'll be my pleasure," he said huskily and leaned down to press his lips to hers. He wanted to deepen the kiss, but he didn't want to shock her family. His friends would not have been surprised. He stepped back and said, "Are you ready for the next part of our adventure?"

"Darling," she said. Bliss was etched through her voice as she spoke. "There's nothing I want more…"

They walked out of the chapel together hand in hand. Love enveloped him as they stepped out into the morning sunlight. Happiness warmed his heart, and he couldn't believe how fortunate he'd been to fall for Addie…his wife. He'd been smitten with her since the moment he first met her, and he expected that would remain true for the rest of their lives.

Afterword

Thank you so much for taking the time to read my book.
Your opinion matters!
Please take a moment to review this book on your favorite review
site and share your opinion with fellow readers.

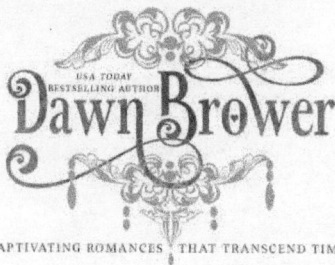

USA TODAY
BESTSELLING AUTHOR
Dawn Brower

CAPTIVATING ROMANCES THAT TRANSCEND TIME

www.authordawnbrower.com

About The Author

USA TODAY Bestselling author, DAWN BROWER writes both historical and contemporary romance. There are always stories inside her head; she just never thought she could make them come to life. That creativity has finally found an outlet.

Growing up she was the only girl out of six children. She is a single mother of two teenage boys; there is never a dull moment in her life. Reading books is her favorite hobby and she loves all genres.

BB bookbub.com/authors/dawn-brower

f facebook.com/1DawnBrower

twitter.com/1DawnBrower

instagram.com/1DawnBrower

g goodreads.com/dawnbrower

Also by Dawn Brower

One Wicked Kiss

Earl In Trouble

All the Ladies Love Coventry

One Less Scandalous Earl

Confessions of a Hellion

Coming Soon

The Vixen in Red

Marsden Descendants

Rebellious Angel

Tempting An American Princess

How to Kiss a Debutante

Loving an America Spy

Marsden Romances

A Flawed Jewel

A Crystal Angel

A Treasured Lily

A Sanguine Gem

A Hidden Ruby

A Discarded Pearl

Novak Springs

Cowgirl Fever

Dirty Proof

Unbridled Pursuit

Sensual Games

Christmas Temptation

Linked Across Time

Saved by My Blackguard

Searching for My Rogue

Seduction of My Rake

Surrendering to My Spy

Spellbound by My Charmer

Stolen by My Knave

Separated from My Love

Scheming with My Duke

Secluded with My Hellion

Secrets of My Beloved

Spying on My Scoundrel

Shocked by My Vixen

Smitten With My Christma Minx

Heart's Intent

One Heart to Give

Unveiled Hearts

Heart of the Moment

Kiss My Heart Goodbye

Heart in Waiting

Coming Soon

A Heart Redeemed

Heart Lessons

Broken Curses

The Enchanted Princess

The Bespelled Knight

The Magical Hunt

Ever Beloved

Forever My Earl

Always My Viscount

Infinitely My Marquess

EternallyMyDuke

Kismet Bay

Once Upon a Christmas

New Year Revelation

Acknowledgments

This is where I thank my editor and cover artist, Victoria Miller profusely. She helps me more than I can ever say. I appreciate everything she does and that she pushes me to be better...do better. Thank you a thousand times over.

Also to Elizabeth Evans. Thank you for always being there for me and being my friend. You mean so much to me. Thanks isn't nearly enough, but it's all I have, so thank you my friend, for being you.

Excerpt: Searching for My Rogue

LINKED ACROSS TIME TWO

Dawn Brower

SEARCHING
FOR MY
Rogue

Linked Across Time

One

∞

September 5, 2015

"Aly, have you seen my shoes?"

Alys Dewitt rolled her eyes. "Did you check under the bed?" Her younger sister, Regina, was constantly losing something. They both sat in Regina's chamber wearing their undergarments covered by a silk robe. If it wasn't one thing, her sister would make something up so the attention would fall back to where she believed it belonged—on her.

Alys plopped down into one of the fancy retro chairs next to the window and pulled a nail file from her overstuffed purse. She slid it across her nails to even them out. Maybe she would get lucky and Regina would find her shoes without asking for help.

"You can help me, you know," Regina whined. "You *are* my maid of honor."

No such luck...

With a sigh, she dropped the nail file back in her purse. She should have known better. Regina couldn't do anything on her own. Drama queen? Her sister put the very idea to shame. Men loved her though. They weren't able to look past her perfect frame and flawless heart-shaped face. That Regina's face was draped with platinum blonde hair and aquamarine eyes didn't hurt and was enough to give Alys a complex. Her perfect sister...

In truth, Alys was tired of people comparing them. She was content with how she looked and her life choices. So what if she was still single and her sister appeared to have found the man of her dreams. Someday, she'd find a man worth spending the rest of her life with, and if she didn't, well, that was perfectly fine too.

At least that's what she kept telling herself. *Complex—ugh— okay, I may have one.*

"I'm more than aware of my status in your wedding." The person in charge of making sure she showed up and radiated her perceived perfectness. Just because she organized things down to the last detail didn't mean she should have to do it. Her sister was lucky she loved her. She pasted a bright smile on her face and turned toward Regina. "I can't wait to watch you walk down the aisle and marry Trenton."

Alys couldn't wait for this wedding to be over with.

She loved her sister. Honestly. But her attitude grated on her nerves. Regina's spoiled princess demeanor drove her insane. Alys could only spend so much time with her before she felt her fingers start to twitch. A desire to wrap them around her sister's neck and squeeze filled her, and it took all of her self control not to act on it.

"You don't look very happy about it. Don't you want to be part of my wedding?" Regina pouted. "Your fists are clenched at your side, and you've been bitchier than usual."

Alys tilted her head heavenward, silently praying for patience. She turned her attention to her overwrought sister. "I promise I want to be part of your big day." She crossed her heart and blew her a kiss. "Now think, where was the last place you saw your shoes?" *For once, please remember...* So she wouldn't have to mess up her own hair digging around for her sister's shoes.

Regina bit her lip and a small tear slid down her cheek. "I don't know."

Alys took a deep breath and braced herself for the stream of tears about to descend. "It will be fine, Gina. Let me take a look. I'm sure they're here." She crossed the room and patted her on the back. Alys turned and scanned the room. No, her shoes weren't any place obvious. It appeared as if she'd have to do some serious searching.

"Thank you," Regina's voice wobbled. "You are the best sister, truly."

That's what she was to everyone: the one they could always

depend on. What would they do if she suddenly disappeared? Maybe she should. Teach them all they would have to learn to do for themselves sometimes. Alys couldn't really do it though. Meanness, along with selfishness, wasn't her go-to attitude. That was what made people lean on her so much. She was an easy target to get roped into doing everything. She walked around the room and looked under the furniture. No shoes. There was only one place left to check. Alys headed toward the closet.

Alys sat down in the walk-in closet and rifled through a pile of clothes. She tossed them to the other side in an effort to reach the bottom. Of course, lying in the middle of it all was a pair of white stilettos with clear crystals decorating the toes and along the side. Regina loved shoes and allowed everyone to choose their own style for the wedding. Alys had a similar pair; a bridesmaid gift from her sister. Her reasoning for the modern footwear was no one would see them under their long gowns. Everything else was Regency period accurate for the wedding.

She couldn't believe how careless Regina was being with her wedding attire. If it were her wedding, she'd have taken better care of her shoes. Looking perfect for her big day would top her list, along with meeting her intended in front of everyone and saying her vows. Regina tended to be a tad unorganized. Why would she need to keep track of her belongings when she had everyone else doing it for her?

"Found them," she called out from the back of the closet. "You hid them from yourself under a pile of clothes." Alys grabbed the shoes and stood. She left the closet and found her sister sitting on the edge of the bed, a forlorn expression on her face.

"Hey, are you all right?" Alys rubbed her shoulder. "What's bothering you?"

"Do you think I'm making a mistake?"

"Oh, honey, it's not my place to say." Was her sister having doubts? Didn't all brides on some level? How could she make it better for her? "You love Trenton, don't you?"

"I do..."

Good, that gave her something to work with. "Then what's the real issue?"

"I always jump in without thinking. When he proposed, I said yes before he finished asking me. I was so excited and could already see how our future would go, but now..." Regina bit her lip. "I think I may have feelings for somebody else."

Oh dear...

"Who?" Alys waved her hand, dismissing her question. "Never mind, I don't want to know. Let me put it like this. When you close your eyes, who do you picture as the man you want to grow old with, build a family with, and wake up each day to their face lying next to yours?"

Regina closed her eyes. Her face remained calm and unmoving, lips parted as she breathed in and out. "Trenton." A soft smile formed on her beautiful face. "I see him with me each day."

"Then you don't need to worry about your choice. You've already made it."

Thank God... If Regina cancelled the wedding—Alys didn't want to think about the backlash from it. Her mother, bless her heart, would be apoplectic. Crisis diverted, she needed Regina to finish dressing for her upcoming nuptials.

"I'm sorry I'm such a mess."

Alys smiled. "From what I understand these feelings are quite normal." She sat on the bed next to her sister and pulled her into a hug. "Now, I think we need to fix your makeup and get you into that lovely gown you picked out."

Regina rested her head on Alys's shoulder. "I know, you're right, but can we sit here for a minute?"

Alys wanted to give her whatever she desired, but they couldn't stay in their current position for very long. The wedding was scheduled to start in a half-hour. If they were going to be ready on time, they would have to start moving.

"Of course." Alys rubbed her arm. "Only a moment though. Mama will come barreling in any minute and go a little cray cray at the sight of us. Neither of us is ready."

Regina sighed. "Let's get me ready."

Alys stood up and held her hand out to her sister. "Come on, go sit at your vanity. Time to make you even more beautiful than you already are."

Regina sat and started fixing her face. Alys went to the closet and grabbed both of their dresses and laid them across the bed. She settled herself next to Regina at the vanity, watching her apply her makeup. Her hair had been arranged earlier in a perfect chignon with curls framing her face. After more than thirty minutes, her sister sighed and set down her makeup brush and turned toward her.

Alys shrugged. At least her sister hadn't taken as long as she usually did to put on makeup. This maid of honor thing was not something she wanted to experience ever again. Regina was her only sister, so chances of it happening again were slim.

"I'm ready to get dressed now," Regina stated.

"Good. I have your dress right here."

Alys held up the Regency inspired wedding gown. Her sister had decided on a themed wedding. They were all to wear period dresses or suits—even the guests. Alys loved her dress. It had a high empire waist with lace along the edge of the bodice and intricate beading at the base of the skirt. The fabric was silky and shown in a brilliant, pure white. The bridesmaid dresses were similar, but in varied shades. Alys's dress was a brilliant emerald. Regina wanted to dress Alys in a color to match her eyes—and she approved of the choice. When she tried it on, complete bliss overtook her.

Alys helped her sister into her gown and helped her tie the sash around the front. It all had to be historically accurate. No zippers for any of the wedding party. Lucky for Alys, hers slipped on and only had a few ties under the bodice. A complicated dress would have made getting out of it rather difficult considering she didn't have a groom to help her out of it at the end of the evening.

"All ready." Alys smiled. "It's time to go downstairs."

Regina nodded and wound her arm around Alys's. They left the room and descended the stairs. Their father awaited them at the bottom, along with the best man, Bradford Kendall, the current Duke of Weston. He also happened to be Trenton's stepbrother. The wedding was taking place on his estate in Kent. Alys sucked in a breath at the sight of him in his period attire. The man was gorgeous. There was no other word for it. His jet-black hair was brushed back, and his dark blue eyes shot upward as he watched them walk down. To be accurate, he watched Regina. Could he be the other man her sister had feelings for?

They reached the bottom. Their father kissed them each on the cheek. "You both look lovely." He looped his arm around theirs, one of them on each side of him. "You ready for a wedding?"

"I am." Regina giggled.

Bradford joined them, his gaze never leaving Regina's face. "It's a beautiful day for one. Every seat is filled."

"I can't wait to marry Trenton."

Alys watched Bradford. He sucked in a harsh breath at her sister's words. The duke had feelings for Regina. That would make for some awkward family dinners. She frowned. It was too bad really. The man could have any woman he wanted—except Regina—and now, well, her. Alys didn't want a man besotted with her sister.

"Yes, but you should let Bradford and I go on before you. Why don't you spend a few minutes with Daddy while we walk to the church?" Alys wanted to put some distance between the two of them. If Bradford was given an inch, he'd try to talk Regina out of marrying his brother. She couldn't allow him to destroy her sister's wedding. "We will be patiently waiting to see you walk down the aisle."

"I don't…" Bradford started to say, but stopped when Alys pinched his side, hard.

He glared at her, his eyes promising retribution.

"Leave Regina alone," Alys whispered. "She needs some quality time with our father. We have other things to take care of." She looped her arm around his and raised an eyebrow. "What are you waiting for? You're to escort me down the aisle, right?"

"Archaic," he grumbled. "I can't fathom why she wanted such an old-fashioned wedding."

They exited the house and headed toward the church located on the estate.

Alys shrugged. "I don't know. I find it rather charming."

"You would," he replied, sarcasm in his voice.

Alys stopped in her tracks and stared up at him. "What's that supposed to mean?"

He tucked a stray curl behind her ear. "You have a romantic heart. Probably comes from all that whimsical romance you bury yourself in."

Heat filled her cheeks. "So, what you're saying is because I read romance novels I have unhealthy expectations?" How *dare* he? He didn't even know her. They were barely acquaintances. To think she'd thought he was handsome when they first met. Way to ruin her fantasies... She should thank him for the wakeup call. For a brief moment she'd considered him a possibility. Rogues were all fine and good in romance novels. In real life they were such a letdown. Only in make believe were they redeemable. This man left a bad taste in her mouth.

So what if she'd been searching for a rogue of her own for some time now...It was time to wake up and realize she'd never find one worth fighting for.

"Your words, not mine." He shrugged. "I think we need to keep moving."

What an ass.

"Because I want a man to *love me* doesn't mean I have unreasonable expectations." She wanted to punch him and break his perfect nose.

"Love is for fools."

Wait... That meant he didn't love her sister.

"So what about your feelings for Regina?"

A deep throated chuckle filled the air. "Oh, sweetheart, that's not love. It's lust, pure and simple."

He needed to be taken down a peg or three... "Someday you will meet someone who takes your breath away. Your very existence moot without them by your side—every breath, every heartbeat, will be only for them. If you're lucky enough, they will feel the same. Either way, I hope I'm around to see you fall. It will be a damned beautiful sight. The great Duke of Weston on his knees before a mere woman."

He pinned her in place with a scathing look. Such striking blue eyes... "Not bloody likely."

Alys smirked. "Maybe not, still, it would be amusing to watch."

Bradford stared down at her with condescension. He tilted his head to the side as he studied her. His lips twitched and formed one of his cocky smiles. Whatever light bulb had gone off inside of his head, Alys did not know, but she didn't like how he was looking at her.

"Tell me, Alys, have you ever been in the gallery on my estate?"

Where was he going with this? "No, I've only been here since yesterday. Not a lot of time for a tour. You do have a very large home."

"Pity." He glanced down at her through hooded eyes. "You might have seen something interesting in there."

Like what? Bradford was confusing her. He wasn't flirting, but he wasn't exactly being standoffish either. Alys didn't know what game he was playing and didn't really care either. She was putting a stop to it before it went any further. "I'm sure it has a lot of lovely art, but I'm not generally drawn to pretty pictures." Books, on the other hand, were a craving she couldn't kick.

"Oh, it isn't a bunch of pretty pictures. Most of them are of my family."

The man was talking foolishness. Why would she care about portraits of his family? Alys shrugged. "I'm failing to follow your logic."

His lips tilted into an evil grin. "You remind me of someone in the portraits. Uncanny really. Remind me later, and maybe I will take the time to show you."

Was this his version of *"let me show you my etchings?"* Alys wasn't going to fall for his plans of seduction. She wasn't born yesterday. "No thanks. I won't be staying long enough to bother."

They had stopped just outside the church. The walk over had been enlightening. As far as Alys was concerned she wouldn't be repeating it. Bradford was a conundrum she didn't want to figure out. Soon Regina would be married to his step-brother. Alys wouldn't have to deal with him, but she hoped her sister knew what she was getting into. Bradford might just come between her and Trenton. He didn't seem like the type of man to step aside willingly.

"Suit yourself." He opened the church door and led her inside.

"Is Regina on her way?" Her mother rushed to their side. "It's time to start."

"Yes, she's coming over with Daddy. She should be here any minute. Go ahead and let them begin. Bradford and I can head down now."

Her mother didn't say a word and left them at the end of the aisle. The music started as Regina and her father entered the church. Bradford wound her arm around his, and together they marched down the aisle. They took their places and waited for the bride.

Regina came down the aisle with their father, tears falling down her cheeks as she approached Trenton. They said their vows—all of it a blur. Soon the wedding came to an end, and they were leaving the church. A reception was scheduled to immediately follow the nuptials.

Alys shook her head. For some reason, everything swam before her. A hammer seemed to pound against her skull—something wasn't right. She needed her purse. She'd have something in there to help whatever was going on. If she could get through the day, she could spend a week in bed if necessary. *Please, let me see Regina's wedding until the end...*

Alys followed everyone out blindly. She wanted a few minutes to herself. Maybe she could take a breath and find that time inside the manor. The people around her suffocated her, and she still couldn't get over Bradford's attitude. He would have ruined Regina's wedding for a brief affair. Who was this man? How had he come to discard love so easily? Jaded, cynical, and one of the current rogues in England—Dover, to be more precise—Bradford did what he wanted and didn't give it a second thought. Alys shouldn't have been surprised at his words, yet she couldn't help feeling disappointed at the same time.

He was right about one thing. Alys did read a lot. She loved romance novels and had a soft spot for the rogues written on the pages. She wanted a rogue of her own, provided he left his scandalous past behind and promised to love her forever. That's part of what had attracted her to Bradford. He'd reminded her of a romantic hero. Too bad he turned out to be a bad seed all around and in love with her sister. He claimed he only lusted after her, but Alys didn't believe it was just that. The duke had protested too much. Bradford wasn't the rogue for her.

Maybe someday she would get her wish and find the rogue meant only for her. Doubtful...

She walked up to her room and grabbed her heavy purse, sliding the strap over her shoulder. It had everything she could possibly need in it. If she could have taken it down the aisle with her, she would have. It relieved her to have it with her. Alys liked to be in control as much as possible. She hated to be unprepared for anything. So she carried a purse filled with items that could potentially solve any problem that might arise. Not everything was so easily fixed, she knew that, but it didn't stop her from trying. Her purse was a kind of security blanket. It made her feel like she could do anything. Plus, it had one very important item inside: her reading tablet.

I better get down to the reception before someone misses me.

Once outside, she breathed in the fresh air. The cliffs alongside the large manor were breathtaking. Maybe she could take a minute to enjoy the sea before returning to the party. She made a beeline toward the cliff's edge. When she got there, she stopped and absorbed the view. So beautiful... As much as she loved it though, she had obligations she needed to see to. Her sister would never forgive her if she bailed on the rest of her big day. Alys turned, took two steps and stopped.

Was that a white rabbit at the edge? The poor thing was going to fall off. Maybe she should shoo it away. Alys, dazed, stumbled toward it. It was so blurred... *Why did everything suddenly look so hazy?*

That was the last thought she had before the wind was knocked out of her. Her feet slipped and her arms flailed against the breeze, desperate for something to grab onto. She kept falling and falling... Only one thing going through her mind—*Damn rabbit's fault.* She was about to die.

Two

September 5, 1815

Moonlight acted as his guide as the boat moved across the English Channel. The trip home both grueling and exhausting, James couldn't get there soon enough. A deep burn filled his gut as he stretched. The wound on his side ached with each movement.

Bloody hell...

In the distance, he could see the shoreline. Soon, he'd be able to crawl into his own bed. France could go to the devil. The battle at Waterloo had left its mark on his soul. If he wanted a reminder, all he would have to do is look down on the jagged protruding scar on his abdomen. The images swam before his eyes—all the death, blood, and agony screaming through his mind.

If only he could forget...

To think many considered him lucky. The battle hadn't ended for him when the cease-fire had been called. It began when a saber slid into him, leaving a trail of blood and pain in its wake. The sawbones hadn't thought he'd make it through the night, but James had a mind of his own. He hadn't wanted his life to end on a dirty cot in the middle of a foreign countryside. For the first month, fever had raced through him as his body fought off the infection raging through his body. He'd finally been able to sit up and feed himself when news of his brother's death reached him—his presence was demanded back in England.

His boat hit the beach along the cove. James jumped out and attempted to pull it farther onto the beach. He fell backward, hitting the sand with a hard thud.

"Bloody rotten piece of..."

James stopped short of wishing it to fall into oblivion. It wasn't the boat's fault he wasn't at full strength. He'd leave it where it was and have a servant deal with it once he returned to Weston Manor.

With a deep breath in, then out again, James calmed himself.

"No time like the present to go home." And fall into a warm comfortable bed and sleep for a week. Crossing through France to get home had been treacherous even though Napoleon had been defeated at Waterloo. Smugglers still used the channel to import illegal goods and most of them didn't have any qualms about dispatching witnesses into the great beyond.

James took several steps along the sandy beach, stopped, and stared down the path leading to the caves built into the cliff. Someone was sprawled across the ground outside the entrance. Weary, and mistrustful, James took slow steps toward the entrance. He wouldn't put it past someone to be lying in wait to accost him before he made it home.

He closed in and kneeled before the person lying before him. Why, it was a woman... James placed his fingers at the base of her neck—a steady pulse beat against his skin. She was alive at least.

Her eyes fluttered open. "Bradford?"

Who the hell was Bradford? Was he responsible for the lady's condition? What kind of bastard would abandon a lady on the beach for anyone to find? James would have to take her up to Weston Manor.

"Miss, do you think you can walk?"

Please be able to walk... James wanted to help her, but his strength wasn't what it should be. He'd only had six weeks of healing before he'd been summoned home. The trip left him weaker than he'd like.

"I don't know... Where am I?" she mumbled, her eyes drifting closed. "Help me."

He nodded, though she didn't see him. "I will. Tell me who can I contact to let them know you're all right?"

"Weston." The word was barely coherent.

James stumbled back, startled at her words. Did she know his brother? Was she in search of him? Had she actually said, Edward, not Bradford? Her words were so garbled he could have heard her wrong. She couldn't be looking for *him*; James had never set eyes on her before.

"Miss..." James shook her. Her eyes opened into tiny slits. "What's your name? Do you know my brother, Edward?"

Her eyes fluttered closed, but not before she muttered, "Alys"

She didn't deny knowing Edward, but she hadn't admitted it either. "Well, Alys, I will make sure you get up to the manor. We can sort this out later."

He glanced around the area. A pair of shoes like he'd never seen before lay near her feet. They had spikes at least three inches long on the end. *How can she walk in those?* She probably couldn't, and that's why they laid near her feet instead of on them. A bag was lying across her mid-section, the straps across her shoulder. Was she running away from something? He picked up the shoes and put them inside her bag. He couldn't make out the contents in the dark. Perhaps he would take a look inside later. There might be some clues as to her identity and what she was after inside. When she was conscious he would question her further.

James stared down at her. He dreaded carrying her up through the tunnels to Weston Manor. The burning in his side intensified with each movement. It would only get worse if he were to lift her and carry her on the long trek up the cliff, but he couldn't leave her on the beach. He wrenched his arms underneath her lush frame and gathered her tightly against him. Her head fell onto his shoulder, cradling nicely in his embrace; it felt so...intimate.

Her eyes fluttered open and met his. They were a deep, rich green that seared his soul. "Thank you. Maybe you're not so bad after all." Her head lopped down on his shoulder, a long sigh escaping from her pretty pink lips. "Thought I was dead—maybe I am."

Who the hell was she speaking of? The lady was clearly delusional. Perhaps she'd hit her head and was seeing things. James pushed it out of his mind. He would deal with it all later. He needed to get her up to the manor and fetch a doctor to take a look at her. She must have been injured.

The hike up the side of the cliff through the tunnels was grueling on a good day. On a dark night, with no lantern guiding him and a heavy parcel, it was ten times worse. Once he breached the top and pushed through the hidden entrance he had to set Alys down to catch his breath. Sweat poured down his face and his arms shook from the exertion. His goal was clear in his sight. The manor nearly glowed in the moonlight. He merely needed to get himself, and Alys, a little bit farther. James took a deep breath and picked her up again.

"Almost there, sweetheart."

"You're so warm. Don't leave me here."

James groaned. *Poor thing—abandoned and cold on the beach.* "Stay with me. I will fetch a doctor to look you over once we're back at Weston Manor."

"Because you want to show me the infamous gallery of Weston Manor, Your Grace?" Her lips tilted into a soft smile. "I'm not so easily seduced."

James sucked in a breath. She was so lovely, but she wasn't for him. James wasn't in the market for a wife. She *must* have known Edward, and he didn't want a woman already taken by his deceased brother. He'd see her taken care of and leave her alone. It was all he could offer her.

And why did she mention the gallery? She was talking nonsense again. Why would she want to look at the family portraits? James kept moving. He made it to the entrance and pounded on the door. It flew open and his gaze landed on the head butler. "Wilson, help me."

"Yes, Your Grace." He nodded. "How may I be of assistance?"

"The lady was on the beach." James gestured toward the woman in his arms. "I need to get her settled. What room is immediately available?"

Wilson tilted his head. "There are only two chambers unoc-cupied and prepared."

James raised an eyebrow. "She's not as light as she looks, man. Which ones?"

"Yours and..."

James groaned. "Wilson, please, have mercy."

"The other chamber is for the future Duchess of Weston. Your brother ordered it readied before he..."

"Say no more," James stopped him. "I know where you're going. It will have to do for now. I will take the young miss there. Send for a doctor to have her looked over."

James carried her up the stairs and past the ducal chambers. He kicked open the door and strolled over to the bed. He laid her on top of the coverlet. A lantern would need to be lit so the doctor would have light to examine her. He located one on the table by the door. Once it was lit, a soft glow filled the room. James carried it over to the bed and set it on the nightstand. He stared down at Alys. His brother always did have good taste. Luxurious honey gold hair, soft pink lips, cheeks flushed with a rosy glow—Alys was simply exquisite. Too bad she could never be for him...

"Your Grace, I sent a footman for the doctor. Is there anything else I can do for you before he arrives?"

It was going to take a bit longer before he became used to his new title. Damn it, Edward, why did you have to go and get yourself killed? James didn't want to be the bloody Duke of Weston. It came with way too many responsibilities. The second son wasn't supposed to be tied down with the duties of the dukedom. With the death of his brother, he'd been left with little choice. His commission as a cavalry officer had to be resigned, and he headed home to take up the mantle his brother left for him.

"Have a bath set up for me in my chamber. I need to wash off the grit of the journey home." He paused to regain some momentum. He was so tired. "Have my belongings been transferred? Oh, and before I forget, my boat is on the beach. Send someone down to anchor it."

Wilson nodded. "Yes, Your Grace."

"What about a valet?" He'd had no use for one in battle, but as the Duke of Weston he would need one. "Is there someone here who can take over the duties for me?"

"Your brother's valet is still in residence. Would you like me to wake him to attend to your needs?"

James shook his head. "No, don't bother him tonight. Let him know I will need his services in the morning. Tonight, I only want to bathe and rest." The last thing he needed to deal with was a well-meaning servant. He was more than capable of washing himself and dressing for bed. The valet would simply deal with taking care of his discarded clothes and organizing his belongings.

"Very well, Your Grace." Wilson turned to leave. He halted in the doorway. "I will await the doctor in the parlor. One of the maids will bring up the hot water for your bath. I will instruct them to let you know when it's fully prepared."

James slumped down in a chair near the bed. "All right. I will wait here for now. I don't want to leave her alone."

"You should know that Rosanna is in residence. She arrived from London earlier this morning."

James gaze flew to Wilson's. He didn't want to deal with his sister, but it looked like he didn't have a choice. She was being sent off to finishing school the last time he saw her. "I take it she hasn't found a suitor yet."

"I wouldn't presume to know, Your Grace. Perhaps it's something she wants to discuss with you."

James scrubbed his hands over his face. One more thing he'd never thought to deal with. His life was falling apart before his eyes—or at least the life he'd planned for himself. "Very well, Wilson. Do me a favor and don't tell her I've arrived yet. I will deal with her once I'm fully rested."

"As you wish." Wilson inclined his head. "I will leave you with the young miss to await the doctor's arrival."

James shouldn't be left alone with Alys. It wasn't proper at all. The gossipmongers would shred them to pieces if they ever found out. Who was she? Would her family descend on him and demand he marry her? Hell, he should offer to do it. It was the right thing to do, but fool that he was, he wanted to pick his own wife. This lovely lady wasn't meant for him—she already cared for another, and it wasn't him.

Alys sighed and clutched her bag at her waist. Perhaps he should remove it. It couldn't be comfortable wrapped around her petite frame. James stood and hobbled over to the bed. His side itched and burned with each movement. He hissed as pain shot through him, but ignored it as best he could. Alys rolled over, making it easier for him to untangle the bag from her shoulder. He yanked it and stumbled backward. The bag hit the floor, some of the contents spilling out. The strange shoes, a weird tube, and a set of keys—Alys moaned loudly diverting his attention so he shoved it all back inside.

Alys moaned again.

James rushed to her side. "Alys?"

Her sea-green eyes met his. "You're a beautiful man. Have I ever told you that? No, why would I?" She cupped his cheek with the palm of her hand. "Tell me, do you still believe love is for fools?"

James sucked in a breath. "Yes, I do." How had she known?

"Love is a dream—a whimsical journey constantly surprising you. It's not meant for fools. At least, not in the way you believe. True love is a journey you willingly leap into." She sighed. "You'll see one day. I will help you."

She pulled his head down and touched his lips to hers. Fire spread through him, lighting him up, burning him from the inside out—he had to stop her. He stumbled backward, putting distance between them. When he looked back down at her, her eyes were closed again.

"What kind of madness is she driving me to?"

"Your Grace, the doctor is here." Wilson called from the entrance.

"Very well. I will be in my chambers if you need me."

James hurried out of the room. His breathing heavy and tapered with each step he took. That had been way too close. What was the chit after? Was she truly mad, or did she believe he was his brother? An easy mistake to make—they were identical twins.

Oh, Edward, why did you have to die?

James punched the wall. He slid to the floor and cradled his head in his hands. Tears he hadn't allowed himself before fell down his cheeks. His body shook, he groaned as agony overtook him. So much loss, too much responsibility, and not enough of him to go around—weariness set through him.

A bath was suddenly too much for him to bear. He told the maid to leave it until morning. He needed to rest. James's life had just become inherently more difficult. He lusted after the woman he believed loved his brother. James could not, would not, give in to those urges.

He would take care of Alys, but he would not give her his

heart. If he did, she'd own him. They hadn't even had a real conversation—he doubted she'd even seen him when she opened her eyes. Whoever she had seen, he couldn't live up to those expectations. She was wrong... Love, indeed, was for fools, and James would never play the fool.

Excerpt: The Vixen in Red

BLUESTOCKINGS DEFYING ROGUES BOOK
EIGHT

DAWN BROWER

Dawn Brower

The Vixen
in
Red

One

The sun was high in the sky and the wind blew lightly across Lady Charlotte Rossington's face. The garden at her father's, the Marquess of Seabrook's, London house had started to bloom. The flowers were mere buds, but they showed promise of being true beauties when they reached their peak. She reached down and brushed her fingers over the tiny buds and smiled.

"Are you certain this plan of yours is wise?" Her closest friend, Lady Pearyn Treedale asked. Her dark locks were pinned back into an intricate chignon, but a few tendrils had escaped in the breeze. Her blue eyes were the same shade as the sky. She was a true beauty and one day would be a duchess, if her fiancé ever deigned to return to England. Pear didn't mind his absence. She'd enjoyed being out in society without having to bother with finding a suitor. In some ways Charlotte envied her. She very much did not want to partake in any society events.

"It's the only way I can make my mother understand my wishes. Her only desire is to see me married and having babies." Charlotte wrinkled her nose in distaste. "I have more wants and desires than can be found in wedding vows and a lifetime of marriage. She may have found happiness with my father, but I would prefer to have much more than love to sustain me in my future." Maybe one day she wouldn't mind finding a man to give her heart to, but not for a long time. Charlotte wanted time to be alone, explore *who* she was deep inside, and write. She had so many ideas, and she wanted to have time to put the stories inside her head down. Sharing those stories with the world was her greatest dream. She would not be able to do any of that if her mother forced her to participate in the season.

Pear took a deep breath. "I understand, I do, but I cannot help wishing there was a better way." She twisted her mouth into a frown. It was not a pretty look on such a lovely face. "The scandal…"

"Is the reason I'm doing it at all," she reminded her friend. "My mother won't have any choice. She'll have to let me return to Seabrook. There I can weather the scandal and I'll be left in peace to write my first novel. It will work, I know it will." Her mother, Rosanna, the Marchioness of Seabrook, would be livid.

"I still do not like it. With you at Seabrook I'll be left alone in London all season. I'll miss you." Pear sighed. "And with you in seclusion your mother will not have a house party as she usually does. The one at Weston Manor will also be off limits for you. This seems extreme. Is writing your book worth being without any social interactions for months?"

She nodded her head vigorously. "Yes, yes, and yes," Charlotte said. The very thought of being alone to write…it filled her heart with happiness. "It won't be so terrible. We can still write each other and I'll have my family. Well, mother and father. I'm not certain what Rhys will decide to do. He might spend time in London with his wife."

Before her brother Rhys, the Earl of Carrick had married Lady Hyacinth, Charlotte had been thrilled at the idea of attending balls, soirées, musicals, anything that involved society. Her young heart had seen it as an opportunity, and in some ways it had been. The first year had been wondrous. Until she thought she'd fallen in love, and the rogue broke her heart. She gave up on finding someone. It hurt too much when the gentleman of her dreams crushed her fragile heart. She'd much rather take control of her life, and this scandal was the first step.

Pear tapped her fingers on the bench she sat on as Charlotte paced the garden path near it. "I suppose you wish for me to accompany you on this endeavor of yours."

"I would like it if you would," she said. "It gives my statement credence." The ton would notice Charlotte either way, but with Pear they would also gain the attention of any gentleman that happened to be nearby. Considering her affianced state it drew them all to her side. They thought they might coax her in breaking her engagement. What they didn't understand was that she liked being engaged; however, Pear had no desire to actually be married. She didn't want love any more than Charlotte did.

"Very well," she agreed. "I'll be glad to assist you in ruining yourself." She sighed heavily. "It is all quite dramatic. I hope that the end result is as you hope. I would hate for this elaborate scheme to be for naught."

"So you have mentioned several times." Charlotte grinned. "You truly are the greatest friend a lady could have." Then she clapped her hands with excitement. "I cannot wait."

"I can," Pear said dryly. "Once this is done I'll not likely see you until Christmastide."

"Don't be sour," Charlotte chastised her. "It is unbecoming."

"Now you *sound* like your mother," Pear said distastefully. "I don't think you're as unalike as you claim."

They might have some similarities, but there were not many. "We don't even look much alike. My coloring is more like my father's." Her hair had the same golden hue as her father's but her eyes were a blue shade somewhere in-between her mother and father's. Even her brother favored their father in looks. It was odd that neither one of them looked much like their mother. "Mother has complained about that often enough. She once said that if she hadn't given birth to us she wouldn't have believed us to be her children. It was very crass of her to say aloud." She giggled. "Though to be fair we were being minxes at the time."

"I do not doubt that," Pear told her. "You can be quite the hellion from time to time." She narrowed her gaze. "After this they'll consider you more of a vixen. Are you prepared for all the negative gossip?"

She had thought long and hard about it. Charlotte wouldn't enjoy what some in society would openly say about her. Some of it might even...sting. "It won't be anything resembling enjoyment, but I do believe I can withstand even the harshest of criticisms." Most of which would come from her own mother's sharp tongue. "Once I'm back at Seabrook I won't be privy to it any longer. So I can pretend they aren't saying anything at all. I'll be peacefully writing and forgetting the scandal. I will be all right."

She smiled at Pear. "I do appreciate your concern for my welfare."

"Since you are resigned," Pear began. "Then we should prepare for this scandal of yours. I'll have the stables prepare our horses. Meet me there after you've made your wardrobe adjustments."

"Perfect," Charlotte said. "I'll meet you in the stable in twenty minutes. It should not take me long. We need to be away from the house and in Hyde Park before my parent's return from their luncheon with the Duke and Duchess of Weston."

"Shoo," Pear replied and waved her hands at her. "There isn't a moment to lose."

Charlotte sprinted to the house and ran up to her bedchamber. Once there she stripped her gown, chemise, and shift off. Then she proceeded to change into a pair of her brother's old breeches, linen shirt, waistcoat, and jacket. She had been lucky enough to locate an old pair of his riding boots as well. Charlotte let her hair down from the chignon and plaited it, then twisted it in a knot at her nape. Once her hair was secured she slid a gentleman's hat on top her head. If not for her bosom and curves she might have been mistaken for a man at first glance. Satisfied with her handiwork she rushed down the stairs; careful to ensure no one noticed her, then went out to the stable.

Pear was already seated on her horse, and a groomsman held the reins to Charlotte's mare. She didn't ask him for assistance mounting. Charlotte strode to the block and slid on to the horse herself. Breeches were so freeing! She would have to figure out ways to wear them more often. She could ride like a man and not worry over a sidesaddle. Charlotte had instructed Pear to request a regular saddle. She was glad to see the groom had followed her directions. She turned to Pear and asked, "Are you ready?"

"Are we taking a chaperone?"

"That would defeat the purpose don't you think?" She nibbled on her bottom lip. "Are you worried about your reputation?" Charlotte didn't want to cause her friend any harm.

"I will be all right either way," Pear told her. "I don't have to worry about securing a good match. I'm flush with funds and I even have a fiancé if he decides traveling the continent is boring and returns to England. I was uncertain how much of a scandal you wished to cause is all."

"Well if you don't mind…"

"I do not," Pear reassured Charlotte, then pressed a knee into the side of her horse and guided the mare into a walk. Charlotte did the same, and then they started on their path to Hyde Park.

They did not converse for most of the trek to the park. Charlotte was too nervous to find words. So far everything had gone as planned. The rest had to follow suit. Otherwise the entire scheme would have been for nothing. She pressed her lips into a line as she anxiously rode beside Pear. Finally, they reached the park and steered the horses to the correct path. Hyde Park was the place to be seen and a large portion of the ton showed up to walk or ride in the late afternoon. There were perhaps not as many in the park as usual, but that was in large because it was not yet the full season. Early in spring was still early for the Season, as the gentry would not start to fully return to town until May. Still, there was enough of the upper crust in Hyde Park for Charlotte's purpose.

"Are they all looking at us?" she said in a loud whisper to Pear.

"Oh, yes," she reassured her. "There are quite a few discussions, and a few pointed glances, and fingers in your direction."

She hated being the center of attention. Charlotte had never wanted to be the belle of the ball. It would be much more to her liking if she could dance a couple of times, then retreat to the library. Occasionally a ball could be fun, but more often than not she'd hated them. "Good." The influx of gossipmongers would ensure that she would be at Seabrook by the end of the week… maybe sooner.

"You were right," Pear said. "Wearing men's clothing certainly caught their attention. Probably more than you anticipated." There was a bit of awe in her voice as she glanced around the park. "You still want to do one full round around the loop?"

"Yes," she said. "It has to be complete."

Though she was starting to wonder if she had lost her mind. The more they moved through the park the more the members of the ton started to talk…and loudly. She heard several unkind words she had wished she hadn't. Charlotte reminded herself that this had been what she wanted. It didn't hurt any less…

They reached the end of the path and the exit to the park was finally in sight. She froze. Her parents were strolling into the park with the Duke and Duchess of Weston. Charlotte had not anticipated that outcome. She thought she'd have time to go home and change. Then let the gossip come to them. Her mother's eyes widened, and her father turned toward her. His eyes glittered with disappointment. That hurt more than the harsh words. She hated displeasing her father…

Charlotte swallowed hard and held her head high. The time for turning back had passed the moment she left the townhouse in men's breeches. She had done this on purpose and now she had to pay the price for it…whatever that may be.

Two

The commotion in the park should have drawn Collin, the Earl of Frossly's attention. It normally would have, but he had too much on his mind. He'd rode into the park more out of habit than because he had any desire to do so. His stallion blew out a breath and lifted his head as if nodding at a nearby horse. That amused him. Were the two horses exchanging some sort of greeting?

Collin pulled on the reins and brought his horse to a halt. His good friend, Cameron, the Duke of Partridgdon came to a stop beside him. They had been riding together in communicable silence. Neither one of them had much to say, and seemed to have found comfort in not having to carry a conversation. The duke had returned to England for a short trip. He stayed out of the country more often than not—his way of avoiding the marriage his family had forced him to agree to. If he hadn't the dukedom would have been in ruins. The betrothal had guaranteed early fund from the chit's dowry to sustain it. Cameron hated the contract and the idea of marrying a woman he'd been tied to for almost two decades. She'd been a mere child when the contracts had been signed.

Collin's situation didn't appear to be much better...

"What do you suppose that is all about?" Cameron broke the silence.

He shrugged. "I'm sure we don't wish to know."

"You're probably correct," Cameron agreed. He narrowed

his gaze and stared across the park. "The one chit looks familiar."

Collin turned to glance in the direction of the commotion. He didn't recognize the two ladies. He frowned. "Is the blond chit wearing breeches?"

What had the lady been thinking? He could not ascertain one reason for a woman to dress so brazenly. Although he had to admit he was rather curious about her now. Had that been her purpose? Did she hope to attract a gentleman's attention? It was still not the correct way to behave. If she'd hoped to gain notice she had certainly done so, but he doubted it would be the kind she wanted. She would attract every rakehell and scoundrel the ton boasted.

"She is," Cameron said. "Do you know them?"

He shook his head. "I try to stay out of polite society. My sister would probably recognize them. If she were here I'd ask." His sister, Kaitlin, had been happily married to the Earl of Shelby more than fifteen years now. She had three children that kept her occupied...two sons, and a precocious daughter. "But as she isn't available I do not dare guess." He turned to Cameron. "Why are you interested?"

Cameron frowned. "The other lady," he began. "Not the one in the breeches," he clarified. "She might be my fiancée."

"Ah," Collin said suddenly understanding. "We should make haste then. Wouldn't do for her to realize you're in England would it."

"No," he agreed, then frowned again. "She's lovelier than I remember." The last bit was spoken in a mere murmur, but Collin had heard it, nonetheless.

Had this little outing given Cameron something to consider? The dark haired lady was indeed beautiful. At least what he could see of her. The blonde though...the daring one...something about her appealed to him. The fact that he could see every one of her curves outlined in those breeches certainly didn't leave much to the imagination either. She hadn't thought this scheme of hers through. Any red-blooded male would find her attributes appealing, and Collin was far from saintly.

"Oh, no," Collin said. The Duke and Duchess of Weston, along with the Marquess and Marchioness of Seabrook strolled into the park. Only then did he realize exactly who the blonde chit was, or more importantly who her parents were. "The commotion is about to take a turn for the worse."

Cameron lifted a brow. "I do not understand."

He gestured toward the front of the park. "I do believe the Marchioness of Seabrook is about to strangle her only daughter." Cameron glanced at the two couples then over to the two vixens causing the uproar.

"Ah," his friend said, and then grinned. "It might be worth it to sit back and witness the scene unravel." He shook his head. "Not sure if I want to risk it though. It's a pity we cannot stay."

"True," Collin agreed. "The Duchess of Weston may prove to be the voice of reason. She works with my cousin, Marian, and she's not the normal lady of the ton. She has more… progressive ideas."

Cameron sighed. "It's best we make haste. The ton is too busy gossiping over what's before them, and we can make a quick exit."

"Lead the way," Collin told him.

He'd much rather return to his Uncle Charles's, the Earl of Coventry's, house anyway. He had to discern the best way to handle his current situation. If Cameron hadn't shown up unexpectedly he would have stayed in the study perusing the ledgers of his estate. His estate manager had up and quit, and from what he could tell, the man had left everything in ruins. He'd siphoned funds from the estate coffers and didn't do any of the repairs. Collin might have to go to Peacehaven and live at his manor until they were all done to his liking. He didn't trust leaving it to anyone else to complete.

Collin still had to talk to the authorities about tracking the man down. He hated that he'd lounged in London living a mercurial life while he'd been robbed blind. What a fool he'd been. He should have gone to his estate a long time ago. If there was not too much pain involved regarding his ancestral home he might have. He hadn't returned to Peacehaven since his parent's death. He wasn't certain he could go without his heart ripping into pieces, but it seemed he had little choice. No one else could do it for him, and it was time he grew up and stopped avoiding his responsibilities.

They exited the park without anyone noticing. Collin glanced back one last time at the lady in breeches. Part of him hoped they crossed paths again. He wanted to ask her about her adventure and reasoning. It would be an interesting tale... He would be unlikely to see her again though. Soon he'd be in the country buried in house repairs, and farming updated. None of that would have anything to do with an unconventional lady that dared to ride her horse in the park in men's clothing...

CHARLOTTE PACED HER BEDROOM. SHE'D BEEN BANISHED THERE upon returning home. Once there she'd stripped off the borrowed men's clothing and redressed herself in her own undergarments and gown. Her mother would have a fit if she came downstairs still wearing breeches. For a moment she had thought her mother might strangle her in the park. She couldn't recall ever seeing the Marchioness of Seabrook that angry before. Her face had been so red it rivaled a Kingston Black apple for coloring.

Her parent's had been incredibly angry. Far more livid than she had anticipated... This scheme of hers had seemed like such a good way to get what she wanted. Now she questioned the veracity of what she had believed. She hated disappointing her parents. Especially her father...she'd always admired him and how brave he'd been during the war. If she ever married she hoped the gentleman she gave her heart to could be equally as courageous. Not that she hoped the country experienced anything resembling a war, but she still wanted the quality to be deep inside her fictitious love before she gave him her heart. It didn't seem like too much to ask...

The door to her bedchamber flung open. A maid stepped inside and curtsied. "Pardon me, milady," she said. "Your mother and father request your presence in the salon."

Her heart beat heavily in her chest. This was it. The reckoning she'd caused would gain her permission to travel back to Seabrook. She would have the freedom to work on her novel and not worry about any social engagements. Charlotte swallowed hard and took a fortifying breath. "Thank you, Mildred," she said to the maid. She was proud of how even she spoke. Her voice didn't show the nervousness that rattled through her entire body. It was a miracle she wasn't shaking uncontrollably. Somehow she doubted *request* had been the tone her parent's had used—more like ordered or demanded. Request implied she had a choice. Charlotte was pretty certain the correct word to describe what her parent's desired of her was more of a demand.

She stopped outside of the salon and took another breath. Somehow she thought she'd need it for the upcoming confrontation. Charlotte took a tentative step and then entered the salon. She kept her head held high. It wouldn't do her any good to show weakness. Her parent's, as much as she loved them, were merciless. They'd have her weeping and running back to her room if she allowed them to gut her with their words. That wasn't to say they were unkind. Her parents were loving and nurturing to her as she grew from a child to a young woman, but they also didn't suffer fools. Charlotte would wager they considered her deeds beyond foolish. "You wished to see me?" Her mother looked serene without one strand of her midnight locks out of place. There wasn't even any color in her skin. Gone was the dark red blotches and nothing but creamy skin remained.

It wasn't really a question, but somehow it slipped out as one...

"Please have a seat," her father said gesturing to a chair near the settee they were already seated at. Her mother calmly poured a cup a tea and put two lumps of sugar in it. She sipped it as if she wasn't about to deliver a punishment to her daughter. Merciless...

"We're not going to discuss your actions," her father began. His golden blond hair was disheveled. He must have run his hand through his locks several times in frustration. "It's pointless to repeat the details of the incident. What is done is done." He lifted a glass filled with amber liquid and took a sip. No tea for her father...that was brandy he had in his glass. She'd driven her dear father to drink. "What we are going to discuss is what we have decided to do about the situation."

Her mother picked up a scone and slathered it with jam and took a bite. Was she going to ignore Charlotte for the entirety of the conversation? Somehow that hurt...worse. "I understand," she answered. Somehow she managed to keep her tone void of emotion. So far she was handling it all without issue. She could do this.

"Do you have anything to say for yourself?"

She shook her head slowly. It wouldn't do any good to defend her actions. Charlotte had dressed as a man and rode through Hyde Park…on purpose. There was no excuse that would be acceptable. "I don't wish to compound anything with any defense of my actions. I'll accept what you decide." There was only one place she would be sent.

"That is wise of you," her father told her. "Especially as you don't have a choice."

That didn't sound…good. A foreboding settled deep inside her gut. "All right…" She swallowed hard. "What have you decided?"

"We had a couple of options," her father began. Couple? There was only one…Seabrook… What did he mean? "Seabrook is always an option, but if we sent you home you wouldn't learn any profound lessons. So that won't do at all."

Her heart sank and her stomach started to hurt. What was happening? Where were they going to send her? This was wrong, all wrong. "If I'm not to go home where will I go?"

A smile formed on her mother's face. It was almost…menacing. "I thought that was what you wanted." She set her tea down and met Charlotte's gaze. "You're going to stay with your Great Aunt Seraphina. She lives alone and it'll be a benefit to her to have you with her for the next several months."

Aunt Seraphina…was ancient. All right that was perhaps an exaggeration. Charlotte didn't want to spend the next several months with her aunt as company. She'd want to talk and have social engagements; all the things Charlotte had wanted to avoid. This had not gone as planned, but she couldn't go back and change anything. She had done this to herself, and she'd have to make do with the situation. How bad could it be?

Devil at the Gates

LAUREN SMITH

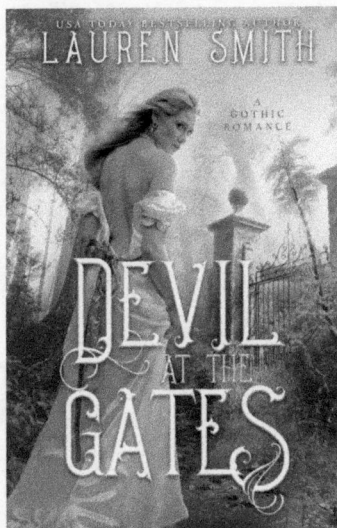

Prologue

Dover, England – 1793

The Duke of Frostmore stirred fitfully in his bed. The sheets that clung to his skin were damp and fresh with terrible dreams that had jolted him awake. He'd never slept well when it rained, even as a boy when he'd simply been known as Redmond Barrington. There was something about the sound, the way it plinked against the windows as the wind whined through the cracks in the stones of the large old medieval manor house.

He rubbed his eyes and squinted at the darkened bedchamber. Something had awoken him, something outside his door. A soft cry came, echoing through the gloom. Redmond turned in his bed to see if his wife had been disturbed. But the bed was cold, empty.

The duchess was gone.

He shoved back the covers and pulled on his dressing gown.

"Millicent?" He wondered if she'd perhaps gone to her bedroom, which was next door. He'd agreed to the tradition of allowing his wife to have a separate room, but he'd told her from the start that he longed to share his bed each night with her. She'd been hesitant, like many a new bride, but he'd cajoled her into agreeing at last to share in the intimacy of remaining in his bed after they'd made love. Whatever had drawn her from his bed tonight? Had she fallen somewhere, gotten hurt while walking in the dark?

The stones beneath his feet were ice cold, but he didn't mind. He liked the cold, liked the way it stirred his senses and kept him alert. He cracked open his bedchamber door and peered out into the corridor. The sound came again, but he saw nothing to indicate where it was coming from. He eased farther into the hall, still listening. Finally, he traced the sound to a bedchamber down the hall, the one belonging to his younger brother, Thomas.

"Thomas?" Redmond rapped at the door and pressed his ear to listen. There was a rush of hushed voices, followed by silence. Redmond's heart fluttered as his mind made the terrible connection as to his missing wife and the voices coming from his brother's room.

"Red?" Thomas finally asked as he opened the bedroom door. His hair was mussed, and he was only half-dressed. "What are you doing up? It's late…"

"Are you alone? I heard a crying sound. I'm worried Millicent is hurt. She wasn't in bed when I awoke. Will you help me find her?"

Thomas swallowed hard, and his gaze darted to the left as he began to craft a lie. Redmond had practically raised his younger brother and knew right away when Thomas wasn't being truthful. Which meant…he knew where Millicent was.

Redmond's heart hardened as he faced the betrayal by his own blood.

"She's with you, isn't she?" Redmond's veins filled with ice as he spoke what he hadn't wanted to admit had been true for months.

It hadn't been a cry of pain he'd heard but one of *passion*. A sound he'd never been able to coax from his wife since they'd married six months ago. She'd remained gentle and still beneath him in bed, and each time he'd tried and failed to excite her. Most of the time, he'd given up and rolled away from her, his heart pained by his failure.

Thomas's eyes refused to meet his. "She is."

Redmond kept his rage reined in, but barely. He loved his brother, but Thomas was a fool who would follow his heart right into the bed of a married woman, even the wife of his own brother.

"Redmond, please...let me explain," Thomas began again, but unable to find the words, he sighed and stepped back, letting Redmond enter the room.

Millicent peered around the edge of the changing screen in the corner of the room, her eyes wide with fear.

"Millicent." Redmond spoke her name softly, and even that gave a stab of pain to his chest.

"I'm sorry," she whispered. He saw the truth glimmering in her pretty blue eyes as they filled with tears. "I love him, Red. I think I've always loved him."

"Yet you accepted my proposal?" Redmond rubbed at his temples as a headache began to pound the backs of his eyelids. How had he been so bloody blind to let this slip of a young woman fool him into thinking she cared about him? Because he'd wanted to be loved, to be cherished for himself and not his title.

"My father said I had to accept you...to have a duchess in the family. He...he was so proud of me." The words trembled on her lips.

Thomas stepped between them. His stance was casual, but Redmond knew his brother was ready to protect Millicent should he fly into a rage. But the rage that brewed inside him was not directed at her. The pretty young woman was only nineteen, married to him less than six months and clearly too young to make a decision that would affect the rest of her life. No, Redmond was furious with himself. He was twenty-five, old enough to know he should have sensed Millicent's attraction to his title and not to him.

My damnable pride, he thought darkly.

Redmond walked over to the crackling fire in the hearth and braced one hand on the marble mantel. His thoughts raced wildly until they jerked to a halt. He turned around to face the exposed couple. Thomas had his arm around the girl's shoulders, and tears streamed down her face.

"You want Thomas?" he finally asked. Each word cost him much to even speak. A world-weary sorrow began to leach into his anger, eating away at him until he felt nothing at all. He was as hollow as the old dead trees in the woods beyond his estate.

Millicent nodded, the girlish hope in her gaze only deepening the emptiness inside him. She'd never looked at him that way, with hope.

"Then I give you my blessing. I will contact my solicitor tomorrow. We will have to demand an annulment which won't be easy. But know this—once this is settled, neither of you must return here ever again." He couldn't bear to see them, even his beloved brother. The pain would be too great. To annul a marriage meant he'd never consummated his love for his wife, but he had. Everything was built upon more lies now.

Thomas's lips parted as though he wished to speak, but then he seemed to reconsider and answered with a nod.

"Thank you, Redmond... I...," Millicent started, but her words died as Redmond stared at her.

"Don't," he warned before she could say another word. Redmond stalked from the room. He could not stand to listen to her thank him for letting her break his heart.

He didn't go back to bed. There would be no sleeping now. He headed to his study and sat in the moonlit room as he retrieved a bottle of scotch from his liquor tray by his desk. He didn't bother with the glasses. He simply drank from the bottle until his stomach revolted and he choked on the liquid. Then he leaned back in his chair and stared out the tall bay window overlooking the road that led to the cliffs. The sea would be harsh this time of year, the fall winds giving way to icy winter. He could simply go, walk out into the night and head to the cliffs. No one would see. No one would stop him. No one would care.

Thomas would become the Duke of Frostmore, and all would be well. Thomas had always been the favorite, the more handsome, more charming, more likable brother. He'd heard the whispers all his life: *Why couldn't Thomas have been born the first son?* Even his own parents had preferred Thomas. Redmond was quiet, intense, gruff at times, and not everyone understood him. Now it had cost him what little happiness he had carved out for himself.

Why had he ever thought Millicent would choose him when Thomas was at his side? From the moment he'd met the girl, her laughs had been for Thomas, her smiles, even her cries of passion. Redmond had never stood a chance.

Because I wanted to be loved, fool that I am.

He stared out at the cliffs a long time before he made a decision. A divorced man would have few options—no decent woman would ever be enticed by his title to become a second duchess after such a scandal broke. There was only one way to end this. He rose from his chair and grasped the bottle of scotch, taking another long, burning swallow.

"I never wished to be a bloody duke anyway," he muttered as he walked unsteadily out the door of Frostmore, his ancestral home. "Good riddance."

He stumbled a little but kept walking toward the cliffs until he could hear the crashing sound of the waves. There was nothing more beautiful or haunting than the sea when she was angry. Rain lashed his face and blinded his eyes to all but the lightning splitting the skies overhead. He moved numbly across the cold grass until he felt the rocky ledge was beneath his feet, and he wavered at the edge, his breath coming fast and his head spinning from grief and alcohol. All he wanted in that moment was for it to be over, to lose himself in the dark violence of the sea below. Then he took that final step toward the craggy abyss…

One

✻

Faversham, England – Seven Years Later

The bedchamber in Thursley Manor was dark except for a few lit oil lamps. The wind whistled clearly through the cracks in the mortar in between the stones. Harriet Russell tried to ignore the storm outside as she clutched her mother's hand. This old house, with its creaks and groans in the night, had never been a home to either of them, yet Harriet feared it would be her mother's last resting place.

"Harriet." Her mother moaned her name. Pain soaked each syllable as her mother coughed. The raspy sound tore at Harriet's heart.

Harriet brushed her other hand over her mother's forehead. "Rest, Mama." Beneath the oil lamp's glow, her mother's face was pale, and sweat dewed upon her skin as fever raged throughout her body.

"So little time," her mother said with a sigh. "I must tell you…" Harriet watched her mother struggle for words and the breath to speak. "Soon… You will be twenty. Your father…"

Harriet didn't correct her, but George Halifax had *never* been her father. No, the man who held that title had died when she was fourteen. Edward Russell had been a famous fencing master, both in England and on the continent. He'd also been a loving man with laughing eyes and a quick wit whom she missed with her whole heart.

"Yes, Mama?" She desperately needed to hear what her mother had to say.

"George is your guardian, but on your birthday, you will be free to live your life as you choose."

Free. What an amazing notion. How desperately she longed for that day to come. George was a vile man who made her skin crawl whenever she was in the same room as him, and she wished every day that her mother hadn't been desperate enough to accept his offer of marriage. But fencing masters, even the greatest ones, did not make a living that could sustain a widow and a small daughter.

"Mama, you will get better." Harriet dipped a fresh cloth in clean water and placed it over her mother's brow.

"No, child. I won't." The weary certainty in her mother's voice tore at her heart. But they both knew that consumption left few survivors. It had claimed her father's laugh six years before, and now it would take her mother from her as well.

The bedchamber door opened, and Harriet turned, expecting to see one of the maids who had been checking on them every few hours to see if they needed anything. But her stepfather stood there. George Halifax was a tall man, with bulk and muscle in equal measures. The very sight of him chilled her blood. She'd spent the last six years trying to avoid his attentions, even locking her door every night just to be sure. She may be only nineteen, but she had grown up quickly under this man's roof and learned to fear what men desired of her.

"Ah…my dearest wife and daughter." George's tone sounded outwardly sincere, but there was the barest hint of mocking beneath it. He moved into the room, boots thudding hard on the stone. He was so different from her father. Edward had been tall and lithe, moving soundlessly with the grace of his profession in every step.

"Mother needs to rest." Harriet looked at her mother, not George, as she spoke. Whenever she met his gaze, it made her entire body seize with panic, and her instincts urged her to run.

"Then perhaps you want to leave her to rest?" George challenged softly.

Harriet raised hateful eyes to his. "I won't leave. She needs someone to look after her."

"Yes, you will leave, daughter." He stepped deeper into the room, fists clenched.

"I'm not your daughter," Harriet said defiantly. His lecherous gaze swept over her body.

"You're right. You could be so…much…more." He paused between the last three words, emphasizing what she knew he had wanted for years.

"George…," her mother, Emmeline, gasped. "No, please…"

"Hush, my dear. You need your rest. Harriet and I shall have a little talk outside. About her future." He came toward her, but Harriet moved fast, despite the hampering nature of her simple gown. She'd been trained by the best to never be caught flat-footed.

"Stop!" George snarled and grabbed her by the skirts as she ducked under his arm. With a sudden jerk, she hit the ground, her left shoulder and hip hitting the pine floorboards hard. A whimper escaped her as he dragged her to her feet and slapped her across the face.

Her mother made a soft sound of distress from the bed, and she heard the whisper as though from a vast distance away.

"Harriet…go…*run!*"

Harriet kicked George in the groin as hard as she could. He released her to clutch himself.

"Get her!" George shouted in rage.

Two hulking men she didn't recognize from among the household staff of Thursley Manor rushed into the room. She tried to dodge them, but they trapped her in the corner and dragged her from the room by her arms.

"Lock her up!" George's shout followed them down the corridor.

Her mother called out weakly for her, but no matter how Harriet screeched and fought, they wouldn't let go. She was taken to an empty bedroom and shoved inside. The door was locked with a clack of cold iron. Shivering hard, her shoulder and hip still sore from her fall, Harriet threw herself at the door, but she was too small to break the sturdy oak.

Her mother's warning had come too late. She wouldn't turn twenty for another month, and George was already taking control of her, just as she feared he would. There was nothing he couldn't do to her, stranded as she was at Thursley. They were too far from the town of Faversham for anyone to come this way except on purpose. She had no friends, no one who would worry about her, which she now suspected with dread was what George had wanted all along.

The dark bedchamber was bracing in its chill. No fire had been lit in the small hearth, and she knew no one would come to see to the task. There was only one small oil lamp on the side table next to the bed. She dug around in the drawers of the side table until she found a pair of steel strikers. She used the strikers to light the lamp. The light blossomed into a healthy glow, but it offered no warmth. Outside the storm seemed to build as rain joined the howling winds.

She had to escape. Harriet attempted to pry the windows open, but nails were driven deep into the wooden frames. She even studied the lock of the door, trying to use a hairpin to see if she could twist the tumblers in a way that would set her free, but nothing worked.

A few hours later, footsteps echoed in the corridor. A key jangled in the lock, and a latch lifted. She tensed, her muscles tightening as she expected to see her stepfather or one of his men. But she saw only the cook, Mrs. Reed.

"Thank God you're all right, lass." The tall Scottish woman placed one hand on her bosom. "I was worried to death when I found out he had locked you up." Mrs. Reed spoke in a whisper and glanced down the darkened hall behind her, as though fearful of being overheard.

"Mrs. Reed… My mother… Is she…?" Harriet choked on the words.

"No, not yet, lass, but there's no time. You must go. *Now*." The cook came into the room and cupped her face the way Harriet's mother used to. "I know you dinna want to go, but you must."

"I can't leave Mama here, not with him."

"You can and you will. Your mother told me when she fell ill that she feared she wouldna be around to protect you. She made me promise that I'd help you escape," Mrs. Reed insisted. "The master has plans for you. Plans I cannot abide, you ken. He means to hurt you, to use you like a…" She shook her head as though the rest of what she might have said was too awful. "He wanted me to drug you.

But I drugged him and his men instead. We dinna have long." The cook put an arm around her shoulders and dragged her back down the servants' stairs and into the kitchens. A scullery maid named Bess was cleaning a pot and looked up at them as they entered.

"How are they, lass?" Mrs. Reed asked the girl.

"Still asleep," Bess whispered, her eyes wide with fear. "Mr. Johnson has the coach ready. He thinks he can take Miss Russell as far as Dover, despite the storm."

"Dover?" Harriet repeated in shock. That was so far away.

"Aye, lassie. You'll take this." Mrs. Reed pulled a leather pouch of coins from a pocket in her dress. "Buy passage to Calais."

"France?" Harriet trembled. To travel alone as a single woman was to invite trouble, possibly even danger.

"France will be safe. The master could have you tracked from here all the way to the bloody Isle of Skye in the north. 'Tis best if you leave England."

Harriet swallowed hard and nodded. She knew some French and could learn more when she was there. Her father had relatives in Normandy, second cousins. Perhaps she could reach them and find work. She tried to do what her mother had taught her, which was to focus on a plan of action rather than let fear freeze her in place.

Mrs. Reed pulled a heavy woolen cloak off of a nearby coatrack and wrapped it around her shoulders. "We have no time to delay." She led Harriet to the servants' entrance, which took them to the back of the house where the stables were. George's coach stood waiting, and the driver huddled near the horses, which pawed the ground uncertainly.

The rain came down in thick sheets, and Harriet splashed through the mud to the waiting coach.

"Take this." Mrs. Reed followed her and handed her a basket of food before she climbed into the vehicle.

"Mrs. Reed…" There were a thousand things she wanted to say, and a dozen new fears assailed her at what her life would become now as she fled. But only one thing truly mattered above all the rest. Her mother was still dying, and Harriet was abandoning her.

"I know, lass." The cook squinted in the rain and squeezed

LAUREN SMITH

her hand. "I know, but you canna stay here." She turned to head back to the servants' entrance.

"Take care of my mother. Tell her I made it to a ship and sailed for Calais," Harriet called out from the coach as Mr. Johnson, the driver, shut the door, sealing her inside. She wanted her mother to believe she had escaped, even if she never made it. It might be the last comfort anyone could give her. Harriet's bottom lip trembled, and she fought off a sob.

Mrs. Reed waved at her and then ducked back inside the house. Harriet began to shake as the wet woolen cloak weighed her down. An extra chill settled into her skin from her soaked clothes.

The coach jerked forward, and the basket of food in Harriet's lap nearly toppled over. She set it down on the floor and closed her eyes, trying to calm herself.

"Oh, Mama… I wish I didn't have to leave you."

But if she had stayed, the horrors she would have endured were unthinkable. And to suffer a life trapped beneath George's control… She knew he wouldn't honor her twentieth birthday—that must have been what her mother wished to tell her. That she would be free of him as a guardian, but she would need to escape him before he could stop her. Harriet collapsed back onto the seat and silently sobbed for her mother, for the life of the last person she'd loved in the world.

"Dry your eyes, kitten." Her father's voice seemed to drift from the past as old memories of her childhood came to her. She closed her eyes, imagining how he used to find her when she'd fallen and scraped a knee. He'd curl his fingers under her chin and gently make her look up into his smiling, tender face.

"Papa," she breathed, feeling more like a child now than she had for years. She clung to the vision of him inside her head.

"You are my daughter. You do not cower when life becomes difficult. Face every challenge with courage, and refuse to accept defeat."

Harriet's eyes flew open as she thought for a moment that she felt a caress on her cheek. But the ghost of him vanished just as quickly as it had come. She wiped her eyes and tried to steady herself, lest she burst into tears again.

She remembered how her father used to counsel the young lords he taught fencing. Harriet used to hide behind a tall potted plant, tucking her skirt up under her knees as she watched her

344

father move about the large room with a dozen young men wielding fencing foils. He would call out the positions, and the men would fall in line, raising their blades and performing. When they began to tire, he would call out, *"Clear eyes, steady hands, you shall not fail."*

She would need that advice and more to find a new life in Calais.

She leaned against the wall of the coach, listening to the rain and wondering what the dawn would bring.

Two

Rain whipped at the coach windows as Harriet attempted to catch a few hours of sleep. Thunder shook the road so hard that more than once Harriet was jostled awake in fright. She rubbed her eyes, fatigue hanging heavy in her limbs. It was close to midnight, and they still had a ways to go before they reached Dover. In good weather it would take at least two hours, but with the roads muddied and visibility hampered, that time might double.

With a quiet sigh, she wrapped her black wool cloak tight about her shoulders; it was freezing in the carriage. Her toes were already numb and her fingers icy as she twisted them beneath her skirts to try to keep them warm. She turned her thoughts to what would happen when she reached Calais. Harriet was completely alone and had no one to help her find her way, but surely with her passable French she could find a coach to Normandy. With the coins Mrs. Reed had given her, she should be able to afford a room at an inn before she journeyed ahead.

Caution would be crucial, however, because she knew she would be a target for men. Alone, and just shy of destitution, she would be easy prey if she wasn't careful. Harriet's only hope now was to trespass on the kindness of her father's distant cousins until she could find suitable work. She'd attended a finishing school for young ladies until her father had died, and she'd been a prized pupil of the instructors there. Perhaps she could find her way as a governess? If that didn't work, she might have a chance to be a seamstress. She wasn't completely useless with a needle and thread.

The storm only worsened as midnight passed, and the rains flooded the road. More than once, Mr. Johnson slowed the coach to allow the horses to walk through deeper pools of water that had gathered on the road. Harriet pressed her forehead against the coach window and peered into the darkness. She glimpsed nothing until a flash of lightning lit up the roads, and she was at last able to see what obstacles the horses were facing.

The poor beasts, they were risking their lives to save hers. They didn't even have the comfort of stopping here, because the countryside around Dover wasn't a safe place, at least according to the gossip she'd heard in Thursley Manor.

Harriet prayed that they would make it to Dover's harbor without a reason to stop. They were passing through the Duke of Frostmore's country, and Harriet feared meeting up with him. Redmond Barrington was known as the Dark Duke or the Devil of Dover by the servants at Thursley, and rumors followed his name like shadows cast by gravestones.

Harriet knew all the stories, of course. The duke feasted on naughty children who did not abide by the wishes of their parents; he stole the virtue of unsuspecting maidens foolish enough to travel alone in his lands. Perhaps the most gruesome tale was that he had killed his younger brother, Thomas Barrington, in a duel after Lord Frostmore discovered his brother bedding his new bride. They said he cast his wife off the cliffs before he shot Thomas in the stomach and watched him slowly bleed to death. Harriet knew that the younger brother was in fact dead, according to parish records, but no one knew the truth of how he'd met his end other than that he had been shot.

George had often bragged at dinner that he was well acquainted with Lord Frostmore, and that only made Harriet's fears of being caught in Dover that much stronger. What if the duke discovered she was here and returned her to George?

Regardless of the veracity of the grim tales, Harriet knew it was not wise to be caught alone on the duke's lands, especially when the cliffs of Dover were so close. Flights of imagination led Harriet toward visions of carriages plummeting over the cliffs and crashing into the sea below.

LAUREN SMITH

She shuddered at the notion of gasping for air and breathing in only icy seawater. Harriet tried to dismiss her fears as much as she could, and instead focused on thoughts of her father. She was almost asleep again when the carriage suddenly lurched and toppled onto its side.

Harriet's head struck the wall of the coach when the carriage overturned, and something warm began to trickle into her eyes. For a long moment she was paralyzed with pain and confusion as her vision blurred. Finally, her sight cleared enough for her to get up. Her right arm felt oddly numb after a violent pain. She lay against the window of the coach, which was now pressed into the muddy ground. Broken glass cut her palms as she tried to rise, and she winced as her shoulder suddenly flared with fresh pain.

"Mr. Johnson?" she called out.

There was a cry, muffled beneath the crash of thunder. Harriet shoved at the door above her so she could climb out of the side of the carriage, now the ceiling. Her hem tore as she jumped from the carriage, and her arm twinged as she braced herself to land. She sank almost instantly into several inches of oozing mud. The road was dark; moonlight was unable to pierce the storm clouds. In a brief flash of lightning, she saw Mr. Johnson clutching his leg, his face twisted in pain. Harriet ran over to him, hunching over to get a better look.

"Are you able to ride, Mr. Johnson?"

"Afraid not, Miss Russell." Mr. Johnson winced as he tried to stand, but fell back to the ground. "You should take a horse, ride to find help. I'll stay with the coach."

"We have to get you to a doctor," Harriet insisted. Lightning tore across the sky, and in the distance a mountainous edifice was momentarily revealed. "What place is that, Mr. Johnson?" She pointed in the direction of the distant building.

The driver's face darkened. "That is Lord Frostmore's estate."

"The Dark Duke?" Harriet's heart jumped in her chest.

"Yes, miss. I know you to be a brave lady, but you mustn't go there." Mr. Johnson grasped her arm as though to prevent her from going for help.

Harriet pried his fingers off her arm gently. "Is there nowhere else close enough to reach?"

"Not in this weather," the driver admitted.

"Then I must go to the duke."

"Miss, please…," the driver protested, but she shook her head.

"Do not worry about me, Mr. Johnson. Now come, let me help you up. You can rest inside the carriage until help arrives. You mustn't catch a chill in this storm."

Harriet forced him up and got him inside the carriage with some difficulty. After Mr. Johnson was secured, Harriet loosed one of the horses and pulled herself up onto the beast's back, grasping the long reins. She hadn't ridden a horse since she was a child, and while she was uncertain as to her skill now, she knew Mr. Johnson depended on her.

Her torn and muddied skirts split easily as she straddled the horse. Wrapping the reins tight around her fingers, she kicked the horse's sides. It didn't need any other urging to fly across the soaked road toward the distant estate. Her cloak flew out behind her as she dug her muddy boots into the horse's flanks again, spurring it toward the dark, shadowy edifice she'd glimpsed moments before.

Harriet rode the horse hard all the way to the gates. The heavy wrought-iron structure was open just enough for her horse to pass, but Harriet lingered at the entrance, taking in the sharp spiked tops of the gates and the stone carved with the name of "FROSTMORE" near the gates.

A pair of devilish gargoyles crouched menacingly on either side of the entrance pillars. And when the lightning flashed over them, Harriet nearly screamed as she swore they moved. More pain lanced through her shoulder, and she cried out, clutching her injured shoulder.

The large mansion lay in the gloom beyond. There within its walls was the Dark Duke. Could she pass these gates and brave the risks? Harriet thought of Mr. Johnson and his injuries, and she remembered her father's fencing lessons. She was capable of defending herself if it came to it, assuming he wasn't like her stepfather, with men hired to trap her, so she spurred her horse again and rode through the gates, ready to risk her life in order to help her driver. But she would do her best to beg for help from the servants who would answer the door, and hopefully they wouldn't share with their master that she was here. It was a small hope, but she clung to it, nonetheless.

The manor house was dark; only a few lights were lit near the main entrance. She abandoned her horse and ran up the stone steps, beating on the heavy oak door with the knocker. After a few minutes, a middle-aged man with a somber face opened the door. He was in his nightclothes, with a candle raised near his head. His bleary eyes focused on her in surprise and confusion.

"Please, sir. My coachman is injured. Our carriage over-turned on the road to Dover. He cannot walk or ride without assistance!" Harriet blurted out quickly.

The man took in her dirty, drenched appearance and opened the door wider. "Come in, my child. Quickly now," the man whispered in a soft tone. Harriet followed him, and he led her through darkened halls until they reached a small sitting room. The man lit fresh kindling under the logs in the hearth with his candle and turned to her.

"Now, more slowly, tell me exactly what has happened." He gestured for her to sit on the settee. She did her best to recount the accident on the road.

"I will see to his retrieval and care at once. Please remain here. Do not leave this room—it is better that no one but myself and a few others know you are here," the old man warned. There was a shadow of concern in his eyes that urged her compliance. He must wish to hide her arrival from the duke, and that was quite fine with her. But if the carriage was broken, she had no way to reach the port of Dover...and George may already be looking for her.

After the butler left her alone, Harriet stood up and walked to the fire, holding her hands out to warm them over the meager flames. Her shoulder still ached with a dull, agonizing pain, but she didn't want anyone to know she'd been hurt. Weakness in a woman traveling alone was even more dangerous.

A few minutes of dead silence passed with nothing but the ticking of a grandfather clock before she heard a stirring in the hall. She looked up to see a large black dog standing in the door-way. The silhouette of the creature was startling, like the inter-ruption of a dream by a hellhound. It let out a low growl, its white teeth bared. It was nearly as tall as her chest. The dog took a step toward her, its growl deepening to a deadlier tone.

Harriet brushed her hood back and shoved wet locks of

blonde hair away from her face so she could better make eye contact. Her stepfather had several mean-spirited hounds back at Thursley, which she'd had to defend herself against more than once. She did not back away or show fear. She braced her hands on her hips and leaned menacingly toward the dog. The dog took another step forward, its brown eyes boring into her blue ones. It let out a snarl and trotted toward her.

"Sit!" Harriet shouted in a commanding tone.

The massive dog froze, the growl dying in its throat. In mild confusion, it slowly lowered its back haunches so it now sat two feet away from her. For a long moment she continued to glare at the beast, which as she got a better look at it appeared to be some kind of hound...a schnauzer? But she had never seen one this large. It had a noble black beard, a strong and well-formed body, and a glossy coat.

Harriet carefully extended her hand to the creature, who craned its neck forward, brushing its wet black nose over her fingertips in a cautious but friendly manner. It snuffled loudly but made no move to bite her as she stroked its great head. The hairs on the back of her neck rose, and a sense of being watched prickled along her skin, sending little tremors down her spine.

"You are the first person Devil hasn't bitten upon first meeting," a cold voice said from the doorway.

Harriet's head flew up, and she saw a tall man leaning in the doorway. His head was afire with deep-red hair that was cut a tad too long, and his hazel eyes gleamed with the fire's distant glow like topaz. His face was carved with perfect masculinity, but there was a hint of cruelty that hung about his sensuous lips, and anger radiated from his eyes. She bit her lip and tried to still the trembling of her body as she took *him* in. There was no question —this was the Duke of Frostmore.

He was not pretty, as some men tended to be. There was certainly nothing angelic about his face or form to bring forth a sense of natural charm. Instead, he seemed to exist in a singularly masculine way that made her sit up and take notice. Fear and curiosity warred with each other as she continued to stare at him.

"Devil?" It was a foolish thing to say, but no other thoughts in her mind were coherent enough to say. The effect George had on her paled in comparison to this man. Fighting George, had it come to that, would have been difficult, but she could tell with one look that attempting to resist this man would be impossible. She swallowed hard and resolved to be pleasant, but not overly so, lest he think she was a woman he could take to his bed.

"Yes, my black-haired companion here. I spent a summer in the Bavarian Alps two years ago and brought him back with me. He's a rather new breed of dog, a giant schnauzer. Devil seemed a fitting name for the brute. He's torn many a throat from a careless man and even a few careless ladies." His tone was serious, but she thought—or rather hoped—she saw the glint of teasing in his eyes, a dark, cruel teasing.

"If that is so, perhaps the fault lies not with the beast but with his master," Harriet replied, meeting his gaze with courage, despite the fact that deep within she was quivering.

He's no different than George. You can handle him.

She tried to instill within herself a sense of confidence, but her right arm ached fiercely, and her head was pounding with a headache that made even the light of the fire sear her eyes. She had dealt with men like this, the kind who took pleasure in striking fear into a woman's heart. But Harriet was not so easily shaken.

Lord Frostmore crossed his arms and leaned lazily against the doorjamb, preventing her from escaping. She felt his eyes rake over her, as if he wanted to rip her clothes clean off her body and ravage her.

But much to her surprise, the power of those eyes was enough to send a whisper of a dark, forbidden thrill through her as well, something she'd never felt before. George had only ever disgusted her when he looked at her like that, but with this man...something was different. The anger and disdain mixed with lust in the duke's eyes seemed different. And there was something else in his gaze...shadowed not by evil, but rather by pain. Pain was something she recognized all too well.

The man snapped his fingers, and Devil trotted out of the room, leaving his master and Harriet alone.

"Might I ask, Miss...," he began.

"Russell, Harriet Russell." She blurted out her real name without thinking, but it was too late. She couldn't take it back. She could only pray that if this man indeed knew George, then

George would never have had a reason to discuss her, let alone call her by her name.

"Miss Russell, what are you doing in my house at this *ungodly* hour?" His lips curved upward as he said "ungodly," as though sharing some private joke. So she'd been correct in her assumption. He was the Dark Duke, the infamous Devil of Dover.

"My carriage overturned, and my driver was injured. I sought help from the man who answered the door." She took a small step back as the duke entered the room and shut the door behind him. She heard the sound of a key turning in the door before he faced her again. Harriet gripped her wounded arm to support it, while also attempting to look relaxed, lest she betray her wounded condition.

"So my man Grindle let you in, did he?" The duke leaned back against the locked door, eyeing her with increasing interest.

"Your Grace, I did not mean to intrude, but my driver is terribly injured, and the storm is worsening."

Thunder rumbled as if on cosmic cue, shaking the house around them. Harriet tried to remain calm as the duke came closer. He wore buff breeches and a loose white lawn shirt that billowed open at his chest, revealing broad shoulders and a sculpted chest so breathtaking the angels would have wept. His state of relative undress had escaped her attention while she'd been so focused on his face and his dog.

Harriet took another involuntary step back, her body warning her of the danger that emanated from him. She should not be left alone with him. Daring to look around, she tried to find a bell cord to pull that might summon a servant to protect her if her strength failed her.

"Are you all *alone* this night, Miss Russell?" The duke was only a foot from her now, peering into her eyes.

He cupped her chin, raising her face up as he studied her. She tried to retreat, but the settee was right behind her now, her calves pressed against the base of the cushions. Lord Frostmore reached up with his other hand to undo the clasp of her cloak at her throat. The thick fabric collapsed at her feet in ebony waves of coarse wool. Harriet felt suddenly naked beneath his gaze, despite the pale-pink muslin gown she wore.

"I am alone, save for my driver," she answered. He would know the truth in her eyes if she tried to lie, and she refused to be cowed by him. The duke's hand at her throat dropped slowly to her chest and then to the rising flesh of her breasts. His fingertips traced a burning line over her skin before he withdrew his hand.

"You should *never* travel my roads alone." Lord Frostmore released her chin and turned to face the fire, no longer looking at her.

"I am not afraid," Harriet declared boldly.

He chuckled softly. "You will be before this night is through." He said this to himself, as if his words were not a warning but a dark promise.

"You would not dare touch me." Harriet's tone remained steady, despite her rising concern. She wanted to convince herself that he would do her no harm, not with Mr. Grindle and the other servants as witnesses. The duke turned back to face her, a cruel kind of delight shining in his eyes.

"I would do more than *dare*, my dear. Do you not know in whose house you stand?" He returned his focus to the fire, but she knew his attention was still upon her, as though he waited for her to scream or faint dead away like some ninny of a girl.

"You are Redmond Barrington, the Duke of Frostmore." She did not think it wise to mention his other names. The duke gave a wide smile as the firelight played with shadows on his face. Had she made a mistake in coming here? But what choice did she have? She couldn't leave Mr. Johnson injured in the midst of a dangerous storm. She'd face this devil and do whatever she had to survive the night.

Three

"Tell me, do they still call me the Dark Duke?" the duke asked her, dark amusement coloring his tone. "Or have they adopted that other name, the Devil of Dover?"

Harriet inhaled sharply as he spun to face her.

"I see that they still do. Well, my dear Miss Russell, you have crossed a dangerous threshold. You have passed through the devil's gates, as they say." He gripped her shoulders tightly.

Harriet didn't have time to react at first as he shoved her down onto the settee. But a moment later she recovered her wits and struck him across the face. He recovered quicker than she expected from the blow, and her shoulder throbbed as punishment for the effort. He caught her wrists and pinned them against the cushions of the seat.

She screamed loudly, more from pain and fear than anger. "Unhand me!" Harriet shouted. She wouldn't be able to stop him, wouldn't be able to do a bloody thing if he...

Flashes of memory, of fighting off George and his men, only made her scream louder. This man could easily do what three men had struggled to manage only hours ago. The nightmare, it seemed, wouldn't end. Exhausted, she gasped for breath as her lungs burned.

"Go ahead, scream. No one will come. This is the house of a devil, and you've strayed too far from safety." He chuckled and released her. She whimpered as pain rolled in waves through her shoulder. The duke stepped back. His eyes narrowed as she clutched her injured arm to her chest. "I couldn't have hurt you that badly—I barely touched you," he muttered, half to himself.

She closed her eyes, waiting for him to start on her again, to hurt her further, but when she opened her eyes, he was staring at her with...concern?

"You didn't... I..." she panted, breathing through the pain. "The coach overturned, as I said...and my shoulder took the brunt of the fall." Why she felt the need to explain herself she wasn't sure.

He continued to stare at her. "Why don't you come upstairs, and I'll have a look at you." He spoke so softly that she was tempted for a moment to trust him, this man who until today she'd known only by his terrifying, legendary reputation. His focus was still on her arm, and that need to trust him, to trust *someone*, started to grow. Until his eyes rose to hers and she saw the desire in his gaze. And then her father's advice to never let her guard down resurfaced.

She couldn't trust him to play the gentleman for long. The man was a devil. It was clear in his face what he desired from her.

"If you try to remove me from this room, I demand an attempt to defend myself with honor." She raised her chin and stared at him defiantly with every bit of her remaining strength.

"So...you will not submit to me if I decide to ravage you?" He seemed strangely amused at the indignation in her tone, and his own voice sounded like he was teasing, but no decent man would tease a lady about such a thing. He leaned down toward her, placing one hand on the settee and the other on her good shoulder, pinning her in place.

"Of course not! You have no right to touch me!" She struggled, trying to loosen his hold on her shoulder, but he kept her still with apparent ease. Rather than giving in to her own fear, she embraced her anger. She was a petite woman, but she was not weak. She'd become an expert on evasion around her stepfather, but there was no evasion possible in this moment. She would have to use her wits as a weapon until she was able to get her hands on something else she could wield.

"No right? My dear Miss Russell, rights have nothing to do with this. You have trespassed into my domain. My rules govern here, no one else's." He abruptly bent to press his lips against hers in a harsh kiss. The sudden sensation overwhelmed her for a moment—the heat of his mouth, the taste of his lips, and his warm breath that made her body stir to life. A moment later, reality crashed back in on her as she felt the gentle scrape of his teeth on her lower lip. Seizing the opportunity, Harriet bit his lip, drawing blood. He jerked back with a snarl. She braced for a blow, but it never came. He released her uninjured shoulder and stepped back, glowering at her.

"Damn you, you little minx!" He licked at the blood trickling down his bottom lip. Lord Frostmore then wiped at his mouth with his fingertips. He suddenly chuckled and shook his head, then muttered something that sounded like "Serves me right, I suppose."

Harriet quivered with rage now. Rage felt so much stronger than fear, and it seemed to clear her head of the dull ringing from the pain from the accident.

Her eyes rose to the wall behind his head. Two fencing foils hung on the wall in a decorative style. If she could but reach them, she might yet fight her way out of the room. Lord Frostmore noticed her staring intently at the foils and smiled, his ill humor replaced with devilish delight. He reached up and took one off the wall, swishing it near his ankles. It seemed a careless move, but she saw the deftness with which he handled the foil. He seemed as intimately familiar with such a weapon as she was. Harriet rose from the settee and darted behind it as the duke approached her at a leisurely pace, teasingly waving the foil in the air. She needed to get to the other if she was to fight him off.

"I do not suppose you would permit me to defend myself as an equal?" she asked, her eyes darting to the second foil. Perhaps he would underestimate her and not realize her skill until it was too late—if only she could convince him to hand her the weapon.

"I will not simply hand it over. I should like to make a wager."

"A wager? On what?" She had never been the sort to frequent gambling establishments, but she was not remotely surprised that he was.

"I will give you the other foil, and if you can best me, I will accost you no further this night. You can sleep safely, knowing the devil does not linger at your door. If I win, you come up to

357

my bedchamber and I will take a look at your arm, whether you like it or not."

She did not trust him one inch. His eyes and smile betrayed him, but Harriet could not refuse the opportunity to gain possession of the foil.

"And the terms of this match?" she asked, wondering if there might be some devious catch in his plans.

"The first to draw blood. Just a scratch will do—no doubt as a woman you are familiar with such meager defenses."

The devil was provoking her. She was tempted to run him through instead, but if she could not make her ship to Calais by dawn, she would be surely caught and executed for murdering the duke, even if he was the devil.

"First blood? That I can agree to." She had moved around the settee now, her back to the wall with the foil as he pursued her slowly across the carpeted floor. If she'd felt better, she would have smiled. The duke didn't know she was the daughter of a renowned fencing master. He was going to lose.

Harriet spun quickly, taking advantage of the distance between them to jump up and rip the second foil off the wall with her good arm. Even though she was right-handed, her father had trained her to use both hands equally well in swordplay.

She turned just in time to deflect his first well-placed thrust. With a flick of her wrist, she changed the engagement of his blade's position and was able to shift her footing, leaving herself able to retreat back a few more steps. Harriet steadied her feet and raised her sword arm. The thrill of the fight dulled the pain in her right shoulder and arm enough to keep her moving quickly. She then took two fast steps and lunged. He parried and she danced back, just out of reach of his responding lunge.

"Someone has taught you some skill with a blade. A lover, perhaps?" He leapt for her again.

Harriet countered with a circular parry and then riposted with perfect technique, but he had anticipated that and evaded her through a classic disengage. He feinted a thrust and dodged back, only to surge forward again. She feinted this time and managed to cut through his loose shirt near his stomach, but he moved back too quickly, and she did not even graze his skin.

"Perhaps you ought to put that foil away, child, before you hurt yourself," he mocked cruelly.

"Careful, Your Grace, or next time I will slash deeper," she warned without the slightest bit of fear now. She would injure him if she had to, and damn the consequences.

His tone remained flippant. "Be serious, my dear. You would not dare do more than a scratch. Young ladies such as yourself are always so shocked to see blood."

Harriet wanted to growl, just as the giant black dog had done, but she couldn't lose her concentration. The duke seemed ready to abandon the rules as he vaulted over the settee, which she had so carefully put between them again. He stood on her crumpled cloak now, and Harriet smiled. She dove for the ground, grasped the cloak's edge, and ripped it out from under his feet. He fell onto his back, his foil rolling away from his hand as he looked up at her, astonished. He almost seemed ready to laugh with hearty amusement rather than scorn. Harriet advanced on him, blade tip poised at his throat. She forced him to look up and meet her gaze. Never in her life had she felt the thrill of having a man under her power like this, but now she understood why her father had warned his pupils to be cautious. One could be careless when one anticipated an easy victory.

"To first blood?" she asked with a wicked smile. There was something about this man, as frightening as he was, that drew out her own wickedness. A strange, wild need to prove she wouldn't stay afraid of him.

His eyes narrowed to slits. "You wouldn't dare…"

"I would do more than dare." She flung his own words back at him with far too much enjoyment. She flicked the blade's tip down, slashing his shoulder, tearing cloth and skin, but the line of blood was faint. A scratch, just as he'd said she would, but not because she feared blood—rather, out of respect for his talent with a blade. Her father had taught her much about fencing, but honoring one's opponent was one of the most important lessons.

"Your rules may govern here, but so does a sword," she added with a confident smile. She knew her father's trade well enough to keep this devil at bay. Lord Frostmore rolled up onto his feet now, brushing his pants before he looked at her again, this time more critically and with far less anger.

"It seems a sword's tip provides enough persuasion for me to offer you dinner while we await your driver's rescue and a room is prepared for you tonight. Would you permit me?" He unlocked the door and gestured for her to precede him into the hall. She kept her sword raised, expecting him to change his mind at any moment and pounce on her.

"You may go first, to show me the way." She was not foolish enough to offer him her exposed back.

The duke led her back down the hall and into a large dining room. He summoned a servant to light candles and bring wine and food. Harriet took the seat farthest from him at the opposite end of the long table, putting her foil on the edge of the table within easy reach. Her shoulder still ached fiercely, but she masked any hint of pain.

"You said that your name is Russell? You would not be kin to Edward Russell, the fencing master? Does he still teach?"

"I am his daughter. He died six years ago." She watched his hooded eyes for any reaction.

"The man was a fine tutor to many a lad at Cambridge. I am pleased he taught you his trade as well." The duke's lips twitched in a small smile. "What brings you through Dover? Your father had a home in the Cotswolds, if I remember correctly."

"We lived there before he died. I was on my way to Calais to join his family." She didn't mention her mother; even thinking of her brought such fresh pain.

"You have my condolences," the duke replied. There was a strange sincerity that seemed out of place as he said it, but it was brief, and his eyes soon glinted again with a cavalier attitude that spoke of a man who indulged in dark pleasures and cared not one whit about anyone judging him for it.

A servant entered the dining room, bearing a tray of hastily prepared food and a bottle of wine. The duke ate immediately and without concern, sampling all of the dishes as though to show her he had no intention of poisoning her. Harriet was famished after the long evening, and she ate probably more than was wise, but while tending to her mother for the last few weeks, she'd barely been able to eat, her grief and worry too overpowering.

Lord Frostmore watched her eat with an air of amused satisfaction. "Miss Russell, permit me to ask a question." Harriet saw no harm in allowing it; she could always refuse to answer if the question was offensive to her.

She took a sip of wine. "What do you wish to ask?"

"You are not married?"

It was an unexpected question, and she gulped uncomfortably. "Married? No."

"Why not? You are a beautiful woman." The duke leaned forward in his chair to prop his elbows up on the table. Harriet knew she should be concerned with where this conversation might be going, but she felt oddly at ease with answering his question.

"I…" She paused, choosing her words carefully. "I remained with my mother when my father died. I was but fourteen when my mother remarried. The man…my stepfather…did not allow us much time to be out in society. I didn't have a chance for love." She knew it must sound ridiculous to a man like him, to speak of love and other such romantic notions, but she'd often wondered what her life would have been like if she'd met a young man in Faversham and married. Would she now be hosting a gathering to celebrate the arrival of a babe? What might her life have been like?

He set his fork down on his plate of venison and studied her. "And now? Do you consider yourself interested in love?"

"I believe so. If the right gentleman comes along, a man with honor." She wanted to marry someone like her father. A good man, a man with laughing eyes and a warm smile and a heart full of love.

"A man of honor? There is no such thing. We are all scoundrels and demons—some are merely better at hiding our horns than others." Lord Frostmore smiled wryly, his fingers toying with his still full glass of wine.

Harriet did not say anything; though she was tempted to point out that he seemed not to care that she could see his horns, and even his tail and pitchfork.

"The man doesn't have to be a saint," she added, quietly thinking it over. "But I could never marry a man who seeks to check my character at every turn like some willful pet. Despite the current laws of England, I am not property and would never marry a man who treated me as such." She hadn't given much thought to love and romance since her father died, however.

361

She'd been living under George's shadow for so long that she'd locked that part of her dreams away.

But now, as she was thinking about it, she knew deep in her heart that she could not agree to marry a man unless he kindled some fire in her blood. She believed herself to be a woman of wild passions, and she needed a husband who would embrace that, not condemn her for it. It would not do to stifle her unpredictable nature by marriage to a man who would ruin her vivacity.

Harriet reached for her wineglass to take another drink, but her movements seemed slower than before, as though her strength was finally failing her after the ordeal of the night.

"Not all men treat their wives as property. Some men dare to love and to dream, even when it costs them their very souls." The duke pushed his chair back from the table and got to his feet and began to walk toward her.

Concerned by his slow, predatory progress in her direction, Harriet reached for her sword. Her fingers curled around the smooth metal of the handle, and she felt safe again.

"Please do not come any closer, Your Grace. I do not... I do not trust you." She pushed her chair back and stood up, but her head reeled with an unforeseen bout of dizziness, and words became suddenly harder to form.

Her sword arm wavered, the blade tip falling a few inches. She blinked; her vision doubled and swirled slowly. Harriet fell against the table for support, nearly dropping her foil since she had but one good strong arm to brace her weight with. As Lord Frostmore reached her, he attempted to gently wrest the blade from her, but she whipped it up in an arc at him. But her action was too slow, and he caught her wrist and squeezed lightly.

"Drop it," he ordered. The sword clattered to the floor. Harriet swung her free fist at his face, then screamed in pain as her shoulder twinged violently.

"You little fool," he muttered. "I didn't want you to hurt yourself." His voice was soft and gentle, and for a second she wondered if he cared about her, but how could he care? He was a devil.

Lord Frostmore caught her in his arms, and the pain lessened as whatever was happening to her deepened even further. It was as though some sorcerer had cast a powerful sleeping spell upon her. Would she wake in some distant tower, cobwebs covering her form as she woke to a kiss from a prince? Her mother used to read her fairy tales as a child, and now…now it was all she could think about. Princes…dark towers and enchantments…endless sleep.

"How…did…you…do it?" she murmured drowsily. Lord Frostmore had done this to her, whatever it was, and she clung to her consciousness, wanting to know how.

"The wine, my dear. I never drank it. I thought for sure you'd notice." His soft laughter stirred her hair as his arms tightened about her waist.

"You are the devil," Harriet said in an angry whisper as she sagged against him, now barely able to stand.

"The worst is yet to come. Luckily, you will not remember much of this night come dawn," the duke assured her.

His arm encircling her waist was the only thing keeping her upright. They exited the dining room and entered the entry hall near the stairs. Harriet latched on to a small table by the stairs, digging her fingers into the wood. The duke tugged at her weary body, but when she refused to budge, he pressed her up against the wall, letting her feel his strength as he pressed his lips to her ear.

"Now, my dear, be reasonable. Do you wish me to tend to you here? Or should I see to you in a more private location?" One of his hands drifted down her back and over the curve of her hips, gripping the thin pink muslin gown at her waist. Harriet struggled to understand. Was he going to…?

"No…please!"

The duke kissed her forehead, brushed his knuckles over her cheek, and then released his hold so that he could bend over and wrap an arm about her legs and back, picking her up and carrying her like a child in his arms.

Harriet's head fell back, her eyes mesmerized by the spinning ceiling and the dancing light of candles that created a flaming crown around the duke's red hair. Her eyes fell shut and did not open again until her body sank into a soft bed. She forced her eyes open, just in time to see Lord Frostmore coming toward the bed. He seemed to be a dream, like a pagan god forged of light-ning and moonlight, a powerful Zeus transforming from a swan to mortal form so that he might take his pleasure from the beautiful human Leda.

Harriet tried to sit up, only to collapse back onto the bed. Then she struggled to turn over and crawl away from him, but he caught her and gently settled her back in the middle of the bed.

"Stay," he commanded, then left the room.

Harriet closed her eyes, her lids simply too heavy to stay up any longer. She surrendered to whatever he had mixed into her wine. As she slipped into the darkness swallowing her up, she vowed that she would kill him if she survived the night.

Four

Redmond stared at the wisp of a woman lying in his bed, trying to stop himself from feeling the guilt of his actions. She had been badly hurt—she still was—and it was made abundantly clear by the tip of her rapier that she did not trust him at all, and he couldn't blame her, given how he'd behaved. He also feared that she may have been a bit mad with panic. Surely only a woman half out of her mind and desperate would enter into his den, given what was said about him.

He'd not wanted to drug her, but as the evening wore on and her distrust showed no sign of easing, he'd had the cook slip laudanum into the wine. No doubt when she woke, she would be furious and vindicated in her distrust of him, but at least she would be well rested, and her arm would be cleaned and healing.

He had grown used to acting like a wicked man, threatening ravishment of more than one young lady foolish enough to come to his door. Not that he would have done it, but sometimes it took quite a lot to scare a marriage-minded woman away. But this one? She'd had a fear unlike the others in her eyes, as though she'd felt the fear of a man forcibly taking her before. It had shocked Redmond, and he had changed tactics, allowing her to take a sword in defense, only to have her best him like a master fencer. He'd been confused at first by her obvious skill with a blade and wondered what made her so desperate to draw upon it first in defense. He hated to think a woman like her, with such wit and bravery, would have faced something terrible like that.

So, Edward Russell's daughter was in his bed... He shook his head and moved for the door, resolved to think on the mystery of how she'd ended up here later when he had a chance to talk to her after she woke up.

Redmond met his butler in the hall. "Ah, Grindle. Did you find Miss Russell's coach?"

Grindle's face was lined with weariness, and he scrubbed a hand through his hair as he faced Redmond.

"I did, Your Grace. The grooms brought the horses and the driver back. It was as she told me. The coach was overturned and the driver badly injured. A broken leg, as far as I can tell."

"Summon the doctor. They may remain here as long as needed. I give you permission to see to the driver's needs. And Miss Russell must also be seen to when the doctor arrives. Have him set the man's leg first and then come directly to my chambers."

Grindle nodded, weariness etched in his features. "Yes, of course, Your Grace."

"One last thing, Grindle."

His butler waited expectantly.

"You and the rest of the staff are to go to bed once this is all settled. No need to rise early on the morrow. Sleep a few hours extra. You all must be half-dead from tonight's events."

Grindle's shoulders relaxed, and he offered his master a genuine smile. "Thank you, Your Grace. We would appreciate it."

The butler headed back downstairs, and Redmond paced the corridor, his boots hushing against expensive oriental carpets as he debated how best to proceed.

When he could put it off no longer, he returned to his bedchamber and sat on the edge of his bed to examine the girl again. The laudanum and alcohol had worked its magic, and she was fast asleep, no pain marring her lovely features. She was not what one would call a classic beauty, but he found her pleasing to look at, the soft curve of her cheek, her dark-gold lashes and wet blonde hair that looked like liquid ropes of burnished gold where it clung to her face and shoulders. He reached out with a trembling hand to touch her forehead. She was still damp and slightly cold. He scowled at the wet clothes she wore. The girl needed to be put into something much warmer, but it was not his place to do so. He knew he was tempting himself by putting her in his chamber, but he couldn't seem to accept the idea of sending her away to one of the dozens of other rooms. It felt…wrong.

Redmond pulled the bell cord. When his valet, Timothy, arrived, he sent him to fetch one of the upstairs maids.

Maisie, a sprightly Scottish lass recently hired on as an upstairs maid, arrived a few minutes later. "You sent for me, Your Grace?" She was hesitant in the way that a maid would be when summoned to the master's chambers after midnight, especially given his reputation. But his staff had nothing to fear.

"Rest easy, Maisie. I have need of your assistance. This way." He led her into the bedchamber and pointed at Harriet. "This is my guest, Miss Russell. We need to get her out of her wet clothes. The doctor has been sent for, but until he arrives, we need her dry and warm. Do we have any of my late wife's nightgowns?"

"Aye, we do, Your Grace."

"Good. Fetch one at once."

Maisie bustled off to hunt down a nightgown, while Redmond carefully began to undress Harriet, starting with her boots. Her feet were small, dainty, and as he unlaced the boots he marveled at her form. She was slender, as he had noticed, but she wasn't without curves. A pretty form, even when she wasn't threatening to cut his throat. Redmond couldn't resist a smile as he set her boots down and began to roll down her stockings. He was glad she was not awake and in a position to claw his eyes out. He draped the stockings over the nearest chair by the fire to dry them out.

Maisie returned, and between them they were able to remove the simple muslin gown, and then he turned his back as Maisie removed the stays as she finished undressing Harriet and helping her into the diaphanous nightgown.

"She's all warm and dry now," Maisie announced with satisfaction, and Redmond turned around to see her.

He expected to feel unsettled by seeing another woman wearing a nightgown he had bought for Millicent, but in truth he felt…nothing. At least nothing that turned his heart to stone. Rather, he was strangely content. Yes, *that* was the word. In the last seven years since Millicent had passed, he'd felt discontented. The empty castle, the sense of something left undone, or perhaps left behind, constantly nagging at the back of his mind. But as he looked at the little hellion in his bed, he felt strangely at ease.

"May I do anything else, Your Grace?"

"No, not tonight. Thank you, Maisie." He waited for the maid to leave before he pulled back the covers of his bed, and then with a tenderness that surprised even himself, he tucked Harriet beneath the covers and then sat down by the fire to wait for the doctor.

It was nearly an hour before there was a knock at his door. Grindle had brought the doctor to him.

"Your Grace, this is Dr. Axel."

The doctor was a young man with a great intelligence in his eyes that came with being intimately familiar with illness and death. "Your Grace."

"Thank you for coming, Doctor. As I'm sure Mr. Grindle informed you, we are taking in a pair of travelers from the storm."

"Yes, I've just seen to the driver of the coach. It was a clean break, and his leg was easy to set."

"I'm glad to hear that."

The doctor's eyes strayed to the bed and his brows rose, but he made no comment other than "Now, what ails the young lady?"

"I'm not entirely sure. She's bleeding a bit from a small wound on her head, and she's favoring her right shoulder. I gave her laudanum to relax her. She's unconscious at the moment."

Dr. Axel set his black leather satchel on the foot of the bed and pulled back the covers. He pressed his head to Harriet's chest and closed his eyes.

"Heartbeat is steady," he murmured to himself. Then he looked at Redmond and Grindle. "I need to examine her shoulder. Her gown must be pulled down a little."

Redmond joined the doctor and unfastened the silk ribbons at the throat of the gown, his hands trembling. Then he stepped back and looked to the doctor rather than Harriet as the doctor bared her right shoulder.

"Ah... 'Tis dislocated. But I can reset it." He lifted Harriet's arm in a series of slow motions and then swiftly popped it back into place. The sound made Redmond's stomach lurch. He was now thankful for having drugged the poor woman. Then Dr. Axel fixed her nightgown and examined her forehead, where he applied salve to a cut.

"She should have this." He passed Redmond a small blue glass jar. "At least once a day on the cut. The shoulder will need looking after. Should be tender. Use more laudanum if she continues to have pain, but small doses and only when absolutely necessary. No need to create a habit with it."

"Understood." Redmond accepted the salve and took an extra bottle of laudanum when the doctor offered it to him.

"If she or the driver should worsen, don't hesitate to summon me."

"Thank you, Doctor. Grindle will see you out."

Redmond turned his focus back on Harriet once he was alone with her. She stirred briefly and murmured broken fragments of sentences that tore at his heart. What had she suffered that had left her all alone and frightened of a man's touch? A woman her age who was unmarried shouldn't have been without a chaperone. Something terrible had happened to her, and he would find out what it was.

"Who are you, Harriet? What frightens you?" He reached out to touch her face and paused. After a moment of indecision, he brushed his knuckles over her pale cheek, then settled in his chair by the fire to wait out the long night with only the shadows for company.

"Harriet..." A woman's voice pulled at Harriet in the quiet darkness of deep sleep, drawing her into a waking dream. Harriet stirred in the large bed, puzzled by the strangeness of it. It was not her bed, not the one she'd slept in at Thursley Manor for the last six years. That bed had been a small piece of furniture with sensible linens and a pale-blue faded coverlet. This was a tall four-poster bed with dark wood and red damask curtains. It was a bed of beauty, of seduction, even. How had she come to be here?

Firelight from a hearth across the room cast shadows on the

bedchamber, illuminating the figure lying back in one of the chairs. The man was asleep, his long, muscular legs stretched out and one arm limp over the armrest.

"Harriet…," the feminine voice called again, and the crackling of the fire seem to slow down. A sliver of moonlight detached itself from the thick milky beams pouring in from the windows.

Harriet blinked, awestruck as the moonbeam seemed to gather within itself like shimmering stardust as it became something she recognized. A willowy female form.

"Harriet…" The syllables of her name were dragged out in a fervent murmur as the figure raised a hand and pointed to the man asleep in the chair. Her face was so melancholy, so full of sorrow, that Harriet's throat closed up and she choked down a sob.

"Wait," she whispered, but the phantom was already drifting away, melting into a tapestry of a pair of stags in the woods.

Blinking again, Harriet noticed the crackling fire was back to normal and the rain was plinking against the windows. She sank back against the pillows of the bed. Her mind, so clear just moments ago, was now fighting sleep again. As she closed her eyes and burrowed deep into the blankets and inhaled the dark, masculine scent of the sheets, she swore she heard one last distant call.

"Harriet…"

REDMOND JERKED AWAKE IN HIS CHAIR AT THE SOUND OF A SOFT cry. He leaned forward and saw that Harriet was twisted in his bed, her face lit by the dusky light of the fire. Tears coated her cheeks, making her skin shine.

"Miss Russell." He had assumed she was awake, but she did not respond to him. He rose from his chair and tossed another log onto the fire before he came over to the bed. She was tangled up in the bedclothes, her body's position clearly uncomfortable.

"Wait… Don't go…" Harriet's murmur was so full of loss and pain, he wondered who she was dreaming about.

He wiped the tears from her face with a handkerchief, stunned by his desire to be gentle with the stranger who had trespassed in his domain. Ever since Millicent and Thomas had died, he had demanded solitude, a quiet house to himself so he could bury himself in regret and guilt. It was no less than he deserved.

Suddenly the hairs on his neck rose, and he felt the faintest caress of something over his skin, like cool fingertips. He sensed it, sensed the presence that often came to haunt him just after midnight. His grandmother would have called it the hour of the wolf, where the sleepless were haunted by their deepest fears, when ghosts and demons were at their most powerful. He looked around as he always did but saw nothing.

"She doesn't belong here, not with me." He spoke softly to the room, not sure why he needed to speak at all, or what otherworldly thing might be lingering in the shadows.

Harriet grasped his hand, which had brushed against her cheek.

"Please don't leave," she murmured, her eyes still closed. "Please… I'm so cold."

Redmond gasped as he tripped and fell onto the bed. He would have sworn it felt as if someone had just pushed him. But it was madness to think such a thing, wasn't it?

Harriet burrowed closer to him, and before Redmond could extricate himself, he found himself holding Harriet. He could have done anything he liked to her, she was that helpless, still under the hypnotic sway of the laudanum. But he was not a monster, not the monster he pretended to be, at any rate. Whatever cruelty she had endured elsewhere, he would not perpetuate any on her here.

He pulled the coverlet up again around their bodies, not caring that he was still fully clothed. He had slept many a night in worse conditions in the last seven years, and perhaps it would help assure her that he had not taken advantage of her vulnerable state if she should regain her senses too soon. He closed his eyes, wondering how Edward Russell's daughter had ended up here in his arms.

Redmond had been one of Russell's students more than a decade ago, just after he left Cambridge. He had felt a bond to the fencing master, like he would have to an older brother. The man had been honorable, amusing, and openhearted. To hear of his death tonight had shocked Redmond, but he had been so angry at having a young woman here disturbing him that he hadn't processed the fact that Edward Russell was dead.

And now here he was, holding the man's daughter, a daughter who was lonely and tempting. She was also the same tender age as his late wife. Pain seized his heart, and he squeezed his eyes even tighter, hoping he would sleep soon because he was not going to cry about the past.

Not again.

GEORGE HALIFAX SMILED SMUGLY AS HE LEFT THE BEDSIDE OF HIS wife, who now lay cold and lifeless. He'd slept late after dinner, and by the time he'd returned to Emmeline's bed, she'd finally drawn her last breath. It'd taken her long enough to die. Now he was clear to get what he wanted, what he had craved for so many years. He walked down to the room his men had taken Harriet into, and his grin widened at the sight of the locked door. She was inside, waiting for him, waiting to ease his needs. If she resisted, as he expected her to, he would call for his men to assist him in subduing her. She'd always been such a willful creature, no doubt because she had wasted her time learning the art of fencing when she should have been practicing needlepoint or some other frivolous activity. But it had made for a fiery creature he would delight in bedding and breaking until he molded her into what he desired.

He pulled the heavy brass key from his pocket and inserted it into the keyhole. He opened the door, his heart pounding with excitement, anticipating the chase. He waited for his caged pet to fly at him in a rage, but there was no movement in the dark room.

"Harriet?" he murmured. "Your dear mother has passed, and your father has come to comfort you."

More silence. He stepped into the room and retrieved a lamp, lighting it with a pair of strikers he found on the side table. He waved the lamp around the room, casting its light over every corner as a black rage built up inside him. The room was empty. The window was open, with a trail of bedsheets knotted together dropping down to the gardens one floor below. His pretty little bird had flown away. When he caught up with her, she would regret ever escaping him.

Five

When Harriet woke, warm sunlight illuminated the lavish bedchamber she was in. She blinked in confusion, expecting to see watery pale sunlight fogging up the glass windows of a room in Thursley Manor, yet she found herself in the same room she'd dreamt about.

Not a dream…

She shifted in the bed and groaned as every muscle protested. She winced and put a hand to her head as memories from the night before trickled back.

She had fled Thursley while her mother lay dying. The coach had overturned during a terrible storm. She had fought the Devil of Dover with a fencing foil…and won? Yes, but then the memories grew fuzzier, like thick wool blanketing a window she desperately wished to see through. She remembered dinner, and her shoulder in pain, and then… She gasped.

Lord Frostmore had drugged her, and now she was in a bedroom. She lifted the blankets and found she was wearing a nightgown of fine quality. She had never touched something like this before, let alone worn one. With trembling hands, she pulled her gown up but saw no bruises, no blood on her thighs. Had he not taken his pleasure, then, while she lay helpless?

The bedchamber door opened, and a lovely young woman with dark hair and light-brown eyes entered. She was humming to herself but paused when she saw that Harriet was awake. She glanced down at the tray she was holding and lifted it up slightly as she looked at Harriet.

"Good morning, miss, my name is Maisie. I'm to tend to you as a lady's maid while you're staying here. His Grace thought you might be hungry. May I come in?"

Harriet nodded mutely, and the girl came in to place the tray on the bed. Toast, a jar of marmalade, a hard-boiled egg, and some peaches were all set on a pale-blue-and-white pattern set of china. A tiny vase of chrysanthemums filled the air with their sweet floral perfume. The duke must have a hothouse on his grounds somewhere. It was far too cold for anything to grow outside this time of year.

"Tea or coffee?" the maid asked.

"Er... tea, thank you."

"A bit of orange pekoe, all right?" Maisie's lilting Scottish accent was bright and cheery. It managed to put Harriet at ease a little.

"Orange pekoe? I've never heard of it."

"It's from Denmark."

"Does it taste like oranges?" Harriet asked as the maid began to prepare a cup.

"His Grace says it's not a flavor, but a reference to the noble house of Orange-Nassau, who brought the tea to Europe a hundred years ago. He says the pekoe is the top bud of the tea plant." The maid handed her a hot cup of tea, and the scent was divine.

"And how did you come to learn so much about it?"

Maisie chuckled. "I often pester His Grace, when he's in a mood to talk. He knows quite a bit about a lot of things. He's traveled all over the continent, even as far as Bavaria."

"Oh?" Harriet found herself wanting to know more about him, but she was afraid of him, and the fact that she couldn't remember fully what had happened the night before between them only strengthened those concerns.

"He's..." The maid paused as she retrieved Harriet's muddy muslin dress off the floor. "Well, he's quite gentle and scholarly, when he's not in a black mood." Maisie eyed the clothes in her arms thoughtfully. "Oh, dear. You cannot wear these again. Too torn up to repair, not with my poor sewing skills. I'll see what I can find for you."

"Oh, please, I don't want to be any trouble, and I really must leave, at any rate. Did Mr. Grindle find my coach driver, Mr. Johnson? He was injured when I came here last night."

"Oh, aye. A pair of our grooms found him. Mr. Johnson's leg is broken, but Dr. Axel set it, and your man is resting in the servants' quarters. The groom who found him happened to say you had no luggage?" Maisie asked.

"I didn't." Harriet lay back against the pillows, feeling suddenly very tired again.

"Never you mind then, miss. Like I said, I'll find something for you to wear. Now eat up and sleep." The maid turned to leave.

"But—"

Maisie halted and looked over her shoulder. "Yes, miss?"

"The duke... Did he...?" She blushed and stared down at the bedclothes she clutched hard enough that her knuckles were white.

"Did he what, miss?" Maisie inquired, her tone softer now.

"I don't remember much after dinner. He gave me something... Laudanum, I think."

"Aye, he did. Your shoulder was badly out of joint, and His Grace said you were close to hysterics. He had the cook put a bit of it in the wine and carried you up here. The doctor set your shoulder and tended to your cuts. I changed your clothes myself." Maisie gave her a meaningful look of reassurance.

"Then he didn't...?" She still couldn't voice her fears.

"No, miss. That's not his way. He's..." Maisie hesitated.

"He's what?"

"It's no' for me to say, miss."

"Please tell me. Surely you know of his reputation."

"Well that's the thing, miss. He's more bark than bite. He was hurt once, a long time ago, and he does not let anyone get too close anymore. But he's a good man, once you get him to trust you. At least, that's been my experience."

Harriet watched the maid collect her wet stockings from over the back of a chair, her pensive expression brightening a little as she faced Harriet again.

"Ring the bell cord by the bed if you need anything. I'll be back with clothes once I find something that will suit you."

"Thank you, Maisie."

"You're welcome, miss."

After the maid had gone, Harriet's appetite returned, and she ate her breakfast and had two cups of the orange pekoe tea. Then she lay back in the bed, half-asleep, and focused on the sunlight creeping across the room.

Her gaze fell upon the radiantly colored tapestries of the woods and the stags within them. Had she really dreamt of a lustrous silver figure stealing into them, then evaporating like an errant pool of mist? She remembered quite clearly the figure raising a hand to point at a man asleep in the chair by the fire. It had to be the duke, and the scorching flames had illuminated his masculine form into a black, haunting silhouette that stole her breath. Had she really been visited by a spirit last night? If she had, what did it want? What was it trying to tell her by pointing at the duke as he slept?

Exhaustion tugged at her limbs, pulling her back down into the bed again, but her fear and unease from the night before was fading quickly, and she no longer feared falling asleep.

Harriet carefully lay upon her left side and closed her eyes. When she woke, it must have been a number of hours later. A haze of dappled sunlight lit the wooded tapestries as though it were a real forest where the stags might have raised their long, elegant limbs with ease, stepping clean out of the threaded world sewn around them. The magic of the room—with the added scent of someone, most likely the duke—lingered strongly here. Had he come to see her while she slept? The idea unnerved her, but there was very little fear left at the thought. Maisie was right, he was like that intimidating black dog of his, Devil. All bark and no bite.

She sat up, pushed the covers away, and slipped out of bed. The stones beneath her feet were cool, but not cold as she expected. Harriet went to the fireplace and added a few logs, despite the fact that her shoulder still ached, but the pain was far more manageable. She studied the cut upon her brow in a mirror and washed her face in the white porcelain basin. The cold water felt good and woke her up a bit. Weariness still tugged at her limbs, but she was content to keep moving, stretching her legs and regaining some of her mobility. Maisie returned to find her practicing some fencing positions, ones she could execute without requiring her right arm.

"Miss?" Maisie tilted her head. "Are you well? I'm not certain you should be out of bed."

"Yes, I'm quite well. I needed to move or else I'd become stiff." Harriet returned to the bed. Maisie carried over a large white box and set it before her.

"I found this up in the attic. Been stored there and was never worn, as far as I know." She opened the box and pulled out a beautiful gown.

"Oh... It's lovely. I couldn't possibly wear it," Harriet protested.

"Nonsense. You will look fetching in it, miss. I've dried your stays and have a clean chemise ready for you."

Maisie helped to remove her nightgown, and she was dressed in fresh undergarments before Maisie helped her don the dress. It was made of green silk, and it had an open robe with a matching underskirt of white silk. It was what her mother would have called a 'greatcoat' dress.

The turned-down collar with patterned lapels gave the appearance of a man's military coat, yet there was a feminine elegance to it. Harriet glanced down at the outer skirts and saw the ends of the side panels had been stitched back, which gave the illusion of additional panels in the same slightly masculine fashion, as though she were wearing a full-length military coat. But there was nothing masculine about the dress. The bright-green and cream silk called to mind the colors of summer lawns and clouds. Tiny pink flowers were embroidered along the hem and the bodice, making it look as though Harriet had rushed into a field of wildflowers and rolled about until her gown was covered with them.

Maisie brushed her palms over her skirts and nodded to herself in approval. "Very fetching."

"I still think I shouldn't wear this." Whoever had owned this dress deserved it more than she did.

"We have a mountain of clothes that are still boxed and unworn. The duchess—"

"These are the *duchess's* clothes?" Harriet tried to remove the dress. Maisie pushed her hands away.

"His Grace had them ordered as a wedding present, but she didn't much care for them."

"But... They're so lovely." Harriet felt like a queen in the gown.

"Yes, they are. Her Grace simply had different tastes. You are nearly the same size as her in the bust and hips, though she was a little taller. I can tailor the unworn gowns if you like. I have skill enough for that."

Harriet bit her lip and looked at herself in the looking glass. "It won't upset him to see me in these?"

"I dinna think so," Maisie admitted honestly. "He ordered the gowns, but when she chose her own instead, he was sad. It may do him good to see these worn by a lovely woman." Maisie's gaze had moved to her hair. "Shall I style it better for you?"

"Oh, could you? I haven't had it done in ages. I wasn't allowed to have a maid at Thursley."

Maisie's eyes widened. "Thursley? That's in Faversham, isn't it?"

"Yes, but please don't speak of it to anyone. I must insist."

The maid's expression turned thoughtful, and she bit her lip. "Are you in some trouble, miss? I'm sure His Grace would protect you if you were."

"That's just it—I'm quite certain he wouldn't." She took a chance to trust Maisie. "My father died when I was young, and my mother married a terrible man. That man is hunting me now, likely this very minute. He is an acquaintance of Lord Frostmore's. I don't want the duke to discover he's harboring a fugitive from someone he considers a friend. He may choose to turn me over to my stepfather."

The maid ran a brush through Harriet's hair and was silent a long moment. "What is your stepfather's name?"

"George Halifax." Harriet was almost afraid to breathe it aloud lest she summon him like some demon.

"I can say in all honesty that we haven't had anyone by that name visit here. His Grace rarely goes into town. And we are a ways from Faversham. Of course, I've only worked here a few months. Could be that I'm wrong, but is it possible your stepfather lied to you?"

Harriet wanted to believe her, but she was afraid. If she was wrong, George might catch up with her and... She shuddered and tried not to think about what he would do.

"It's possible, but I do not wish to risk it."

"Then I shall keep silent, miss."

"Thank you, Maisie." The two of them shared a smile.

"Come on. The housekeeper, Mrs. Breland, will want to show you the house. I told her I would fetch you once you were dressed."

"Mrs. Breland? I didn't meet her last night."

"Most of us were in bed when you arrived." Maisie giggled. "She gave Mr. Grindle quite the dressing down this morning for not waking her, but if you ask me, he let her sleep because he fancies her."

"Does he? Is she lovely?" Harriet asked.

"She is, but she tries to act severe. But when she thinks she's not being watched, she smiles and lights up the room."

They continued to gossip about the staff as Maisie escorted her downstairs to the great hall on the ground floor. A tall woman with auburn hair threaded with silver was busy issuing orders to a pair of footmen. She turned at their approach and offered a polite but reserved smile.

"Miss Russell?"

Harriet nearly dropped into a curtsy at the housekeeper's regal beauty. She wore a black dress made of fine silk, and the cut was simple but elegant. "Yes, that's me."

"I am Mrs. Breland. I regret I was not able to assist you last evening when you arrived. I trust you are feeling better this morning?"

"I am, thank you. Maisie has been wonderful looking after me."

"Maisie is a good girl, though I hope she did not talk your ear off." Mrs. Breland nodded at the maid, who smiled encouragingly at Harriet before leaving her alone with the housekeeper.

"Now, I will take you on a quick tour of the house so you won't lose your way. At night the corridors can feel much the same, and it can be very easy to get lost."

For the next hour, Harriet followed Mrs. Breland and became acquainted with the rambling old manor house with its progression of stately rooms. There was a great hall, which had once been the toast of kings, at least according to the house-keeper. Now it was a room full of marble busts and sculptures. The timber beams along the walls had been removed twenty years before and replaced with fluted stone Doric columns that reflected a pure Italian Renaissance style.

Harriet had never seen such a grand home; it dwarfed Thursley Manor. There seemed to be a magic that had settled into the stones, sometimes a dark and frightening magic in the shadows of some rooms. But at other times, when sunlight streamed through high windows, it painted brilliant colors upon walls covered with damask silk wallpaper or intricately woven tapestries, creating a light, joyful enchantment. In those moments, she felt love burning clear through her, almost overwhelmingly so. This house had seen much over the centuries. Heartbreak and blinding love in equal measure.

Harriet's heart swelled as Mrs. Breland next ushered her into a portrait gallery. At its entrance stood a tall suit of armor. The metal was polished to a shine, but there was evidence of nicks and scratches on its surface. Whoever had worn this armor had seen battle. It had tasted the bite of a blade. She looked at the helmet and swore she could feel the grave gaze of a medieval ghost staring back at her. But the armor said nothing. It was a mute, stalwart guardian over the gallery of portraits just beyond.

Mrs. Breland gestured down the massive corridor. "This is the long gallery."

Filmy red curtains caught the light, so as to prevent the sun from fading the abundance of oil paintings that covered the walls. Harriet strained to see each and every piece. In the center of the room, three portraits were hung close together. There was a man in the middle, flanked by another man on the left and a woman upon the right.

"A fair likeness, I think," Mrs. Breland mused next to Harriet.

"That's the duke in the center?" She knew it was—there was no mistaking his eyes and the red flame of his hair. He stood with quiet intensity, posing for the artist without flair or pomp. Harriet's eyes drifted to the other man. He was beautiful, his features perfect in every way, and there was a glint of humor about his mouth that made him instantly likable. "Who is that?"

"That is Thomas, His Grace's younger brother. He passed seven years ago."

Harriet desperately wanted to ask how, but she dared not upset Mrs. Breland.

"And that next to them is the late Duchess of Frostmore."

Harriet focused on the pretty woman with graceful features and dark hair. A tingle of foreboding rippled like quicksilver beneath her skin. She had no doubt that this was the woman she had dreamt about.

"Mrs. Breland, how did she die?" She regretted the question the instant she spoke it.

"It was a terrible accident near the cliffs. She fell. His Grace and his brother almost perished as well."

"His Grace was present when she died?"

"He was." Mrs. Breland's brusque tone warned Harriet that she would have no more luck in obtaining answers on the subject. Mrs. Breland showed her the rest of the house, including the library. After that, the housekeeper left her on her own.

Harriet trod softly now on the carpets in the corridors as she returned to the great hall, where she found the duke engaged in a game of tug-of-war with his giant schnauzer. Devil was growling and tugging hard on a large knotted rope. Devil thrashed his head from side to side, trying to wrench the rope away from his master, but without success.

"Come on, boy. I won't let you win that easily!" The duke's laugh was deep and hearty, not the cold laugh she remembered from last night. Harriet lingered in the shadows at the top of the stairs, not wanting to intrude upon the happy scene. Finally, Lord Frostmore relinquished his hold on the rope, and Devil trotted off to another room with his prize. Harriet chose that moment to come down. Lord Frostmore's back was to her, but he spoke as she reached the last stair.

"I trust you slept well, Miss Russell?" His tone was soft, carrying a slight sensuality that made her think of beds and activities other than sleeping. She froze. She hadn't made a sound on the steps, yet he had sensed her.

"I slept tolerably well, but my head still pains me. No doubt a parting gift from the laudanum you gave me," she replied coldly as he turned to face her. He wore no coat, only buff breeches, a white shirt, and a silver waistcoat. Seeing him dressed like this, more free to move about, made her stomach flutter with nerves. For a long moment his gaze swept over her, and she wondered what he could be thinking as he saw her in his wife's old gown. But his contemplative look revealed nothing of his thoughts.

"I gave you only a little laudanum. I wouldn't wish your pain upon anyone, and you were in terrible pain."

"You could have asked me," she argued.

"You have my deepest apologies, but you wouldn't have trusted me. We battled only minutes before."

Harriet stiffened as he approached her. "Because you threatened to ravish me."

"My solitude had been disturbed, and I was angry. I would never have harmed you." He stepped closer into her space until she came level with his shoulders.

"And how was I to know that?"

He shrugged. "You couldn't have, not with my reputation and the rather theatrical weather outside to enhance your mistrust. Hence my course of action. As frightening as it seemed at the time, I assure you my intention was only to assist you." His topaz-colored eyes searched her face for something; for what she wasn't sure, but it made her feel small and feminine in a way that excited her.

She couldn't deny her attraction to him now. He lacked the finesse a London dandy might possess, nor did he have the angelic beauty of his brother. But there was a raw, untarnished purity in his looks that made him physically admirable. With his red hair and proud patrician features, he was beautiful in his own way.

He clasped his hands behind his back. "You are welcome to stay for a time. I've decided it has been good for my staff to have someone else to fuss over."

"But I can't. I must leave for Calais."

Lord Frostmore placed a palm on the banister next to her. Her heart jumped wildly, and her mouth went dry as he leaned in toward her. A strange yet exciting magnetism held her still as he peered at her. Other than her stepfather, she'd never been the focus of a man before, and she found that she liked the duke's attention, even if it was a little frightening.

"What awaits you in Calais?"

The pit of her stomach tingled, and she couldn't help but stare at his mouth, the full lips that looked impossibly soft. "My father had family there," she whispered as his focus drifted down along the length of her body. The duke disturbed her in ways she had never imagined, yet he inspired more longing than fear in her. Such an attraction was nothing short of perilous, yet she could feel it building within her.

"Stay." He spoke the word as a mixture of a command and a plea.

"Why? We are strangers, and hostile ones at that," she reminded him.

His lips twitched. "Oh, nonsense. I greet everyone like that." He leaned in slightly, enough that the heat of his body emanated off him, warming her in the most delicious way.

"With a sword fight?" She almost smiled, damn him.

"No, that was only for you. But everyone who visits tastes my lack of charm and overall displeasure. You see, I'm a wicked man. A wicked man with wicked desires and a terrible past that is only whispered about in the shadows. But I'm sure you're familiar with the stories."

"I have heard…," she admitted.

With their faces so close, there was a brief and wild moment she thought about kissing him, thought about how it had felt last night even when she'd been afraid of him. What would it feel like to kiss him now when she wasn't?

"Tell me, what do the villagers say of me these days? The stories seem to be getting positively Gothic as of late."

His scent enveloped her as he raised her chin so their eyes locked. She could smell leather and rain. Had he been outside recently?

"They say…you killed your brother and your wife."

He blinked and dropped his hand from under her chin, looking away, his eyes suddenly distant. "Some days it feels like the truth."

"It isn't?" she asked, then immediately regretted it.

"Not in the way you probably believe." He stepped away and began to leave. Harriet stared after him, utterly baffled. She couldn't let him walk away with her questions unanswered, but neither could she pry directly. She decided to follow him at a discreet distance, to see if he would volunteer more information, but he never did. It was only when he stepped into the library that he spoke.

"Either come in or find your amusement elsewhere, Miss Russell. I'll not have you stalk me like a black cat in the shadows."

A little ruffled, she came into the library and watched him collect a few volumes of political treatises and set them on a nearby reading table, which he then sat down at. The light coming in from the windows lit his hair like flames.

"I did not take you to be an avid reader, Lord Frostmore."

He arched a brow as she settled down across from him and stole the next book in his trio of chosen volumes.

"Given the brief duration of our acquaintance, I could say the same of you." His tone was half-amused, half-frustrated. Harriet suspected he was not accustomed to conversation.

"Well, I do like to read."

"And fence," he added.

She blushed. "My father used to take me to his lessons with the young lords. I learned much. My father believed women ought to have as much physical activity as men. My mother was very healthy until…" Her breath caught in her throat, and pain tore through her. How had she so easily buried thoughts of her mother?

"What? What's the matter?" Frostmore observed in concern.

"I…" She bit her lip and closed her eyes. When she opened them, the duke had risen from his chair and came over to kneel at her side. He offered her a handkerchief. She accepted it, feeling so very silly to cry and even sillier when she glimpsed a stag's head crowned by briar roses embroidered on the cloth. His family crest, no doubt. The Devil of Dover had given her his personal handkerchief.

"When I left my home, my mother was dying. I think she must be gone now. She was already so close before…I had to leave. I managed not to think of it until now. And that makes me a wretched daughter."

Frostmore watched her, his eyes suddenly warm. He reached up and covered one of her hands with his.

"You were injured and ill. Your mother wouldn't blame you for that. Dry your eyes." She dabbed at her tears and drew in a shaky breath, then returned the handkerchief to him. He tucked it into his trouser pocket. "Tell me, why did you leave?" Frostmore leaned back on the edge of the reading table beside her. His question caught her off guard, and she was tempted to answer openly and honestly, but she still didn't trust to tell him the truth, at least not all of it.

"Do you know a man by the name of George Halifax? He owns Thursley Manor in Faversham." She held her breath, waiting to see if her fears would be confirmed.

"Halifax?" He thought it over, then slowly shook his head. "No, I don't know the man. I spend little time in Faversham, and since my wife and brother died, I haven't been there except perhaps once or twice a year." His face held an honesty that she decided she would try to trust. If he was lying, she was doomed, but if he wasn't…she might find an ally.

"My mother remarried after my father died. But the man she chose was vile. That man is George Halifax. While she was healthy she kept him away from me, but when she fell ill he saw his chance, and my mother told me to flee. So I did. I left her alone with him…" She feared deep down that George may have hastened her mother's death.

She wasn't sure what she expected Lord Frostmore to say, but he simply picked up the book she'd been about to peruse and handed it to her.

"You did as your mother wished. You did not fail her." Then he sat down and opened his book again. After a long moment, he spoke. "And I do like to read. It is one of the few pleasures I allow myself to indulge in."

She'd never been one to be overly open, and it seemed Lord Frostmore was the same, yet she didn't feel lonely sitting here with him. He knew she was in pain, both of the body and the spirit. He'd offered comfort and kind words, but he hadn't pushed her to speak of it again. It was a relief not to be pressed about it.

They both read in silence until the shadows stretched across the library.

"You truly wish for me to stay here?" she asked.

Frostmore raised his eyes from the page. "I do. Christmas will be here soon, and the Channel will be full of icebergs. You don't want to make the voyage, even one so short, in poor weather. Wait until spring."

"But I only have enough money to pay for my voyage and a few days beyond. I must find work in order to pay for lodgings and food."

The duke steepled his fingers, looking at her in silent contemplation. "Stay here until spring. You need not pay me anything."

"Your Grace, I cannot—"

"Oh, what are you concerned about? Scandal? Who would care? No one comes on my lands. No one would know you are here. Consider my home a private refuge until you are ready to voyage in the spring."

"May I have some time to think upon it?" she asked. He answered with a nod and then stood and left the room. This time she didn't follow him.

How strange that she would find refuge with a man whom so many others feared. Perhaps he was less of a devil than they believed—at least, that's what she hoped.

Six

Redmond strode out the front of Frostmore and whistled sharply. Devil bounded into view and joined him outside as a groom brought his horse forward. The white Arabian mare, Winter's Frost, was his favorite. Many men favored stallions or geldings, but not Redmond. He had purchased her after burying his wife and brother, and her gentle spirit and exceptional speed were a balm to his soul. He rode her for miles, especially when the weather was fair, and it helped him feel like he was escaping his sorrows, if only for a little while.

As he mounted her and rode out across the lands of his home, he watched the fall leaves turn from gold to brittle brown, a sure sign that winter was on the way. The promise of snow was carried upon the wind, its bite bringing Redmond's thoughts more clearly into focus. Had he really asked Harriet to stay through the spring?

In truth, he admitted he wanted her to. She was rash, bold, and uncompromising, but she wasn't like the other women who had come to him. The ones who came to tempt him into offering marriage. Marriage was far from Harriet's thoughts. It was her mother she was grieving for, a loss deep enough that it rattled the cage he had placed around his own heart.

Her tears today had tugged at him, beckoning him closer to her. Perhaps because her grief was genuine, as his own had been seven years ago. To lose a wife and brother had emptied his heart of feelings and left him in a dark, cold abyss. Seeing Harriet face that same dark pain as she realized her mother was likely gone, and that she'd not been there to help her...

He felt a sudden chill inside. How long had it been since he'd felt something, *truly* felt something? All it had taken was a hellion to attack him with a blade and then weep over her mother's death, and all of his own pain, which he'd thought long buried, had come flooding back.

A desperate desire to see the cliffs drove him in their direction. When he finally pulled back on his mare's reins, he was but twenty feet away from the edge where he had tried to end his own life seven years ago. He always rode this close—the cliffs called to him, asking him to take the leap he had promised back then. But he didn't dismount, didn't do anything but stare out at the wintry sea beyond the edge.

Heavy clouds rolled in, and whitecaps topped the waves. The pull toward the edge faded. Instead, he felt an invisible thread tied to Frostmore Hall, and a glimmer of hope seemed to fill it with a pulsing energy, like a guiding light on the shore. Devil barked suddenly and began to jump, though there was nothing around to be seen. Redmond's mare danced back and forth uneasily.

"Quiet, Devil," Redmond commanded.

The dog barked at thin air for a few seconds longer and then stopped. Just then, Redmond swore he saw something out of the corner of his eye. Something that made no sense, something that wasn't *possible*. He had seen Thomas. And just as quickly, that sense of someone being there on the cliffs with him was gone. Devil became docile again, and the horse steadied herself.

Redmond dug his heels into her flanks and rode back to the manor house. The turreted structure stood proud beneath the overcast skies as sunlight surrendered to the approaching winter storm. The gates stood open, and he raced past them to the front door. A groom met him to collect the horse's reins. Devil darted up ahead of Redmond and into the house.

As Redmond jogged up the stone steps and entered his home, a flash of soft crème and green caught his eye. He froze as he watched her stunning gown illuminate her gold hair and paint her like a nymph who had escaped the woods she had been born into.

He'd once believed Millicent should have worn that dress,

but now he was glad she never had. He could imagine no other woman but Harriet would do it justice. He wanted to run up the stairs, catch her waist, and bury his face in her neck, covering her throat with kisses before he stole her lips and…

What is happening to me? He was losing his mind, that was what. His attraction to this woman was overpowering. Perhaps he'd simply been alone for too long? Or maybe it was something more, something that scared him because he couldn't open his heart again.

"Your Grace." She came toward him with tentative steps, the slight train of her gown whispering over the stones of the hall.

"Miss Russell." He gazed upon her with longing.

"I would like to stay through the spring, if you still wish to extend the invitation." She drew her bottom lip between her teeth in a show of nerves, and he was powerless to resist her. She could have demanded a thousand stars and he would have tried to give them to her.

"Yes, that would be very good. I'll have Grindle ask the cook to serve supper in an hour, if you wish?"

"Thank you." She paused. "I should speak to Mrs. Breland about moving to a new bedchamber. I am feeling better, and you should have your chambers returned to you." Her cheeks blossomed with a tender blush that quickened his heart. There was an innocence to her, one that he suspected would always remain within her. Yet she wasn't naïve or silly like others he had met. She had seen pain, felt loss, had her heart hurt by both, yet she hadn't given over to anger, hate, or cloying despair as he had. Redmond envied her that strength of character.

"Very well. Tell Mrs. Breland I recommend the Pearl Room."

Something akin to hope flashed in Harriet's eyes. "Would you show me the way? I believe Mrs. Breland is speaking to the kitchen staff right now, and I would hate to disturb her. If you don't mind, that is."

Strangely, he didn't. His instincts should have been to run from her and from this entire situation, but instead he nodded and held out his arm to her. She tucked her arm in his, and they ascended the stairs together. He remembered escorting Millicent up like this, both of them still in their wedding clothes. He had been so elated, so overjoyed to have a wife, to have someone to belong to him. Yet there had been a tightness around Millicent's eyes and a hint of worry that had darkened her brow. He'd mistaken it for a bride's wedding nerves. How foolish he'd been not to see her anxiety for what it was, not to see that she loved his brother.

"What's the matter, Your Grace?" Harriet's question forced him out of his thoughts. He looked down at her, frowning slightly.

"I beg your pardon. I was lost in thought." He was not about to admit that he was thinking of another woman, or the mistakes he had made.

"Oh…" He could sense the disappointment in her tone.

"I'm sorry, Miss Russell. It's just been a long time since I was in a position to entertain company, and it seems I'm out of practice."

"Yes, of course," she replied, and her lips hinted at a smile. "That does happen when one routinely chases away one's visitors."

Redmond found his chuckle had become rusty from disuse. "Yes, I suppose you're right."

They went up the curving staircase until they were one floor above his bedchamber. He stopped in front of an ornately carved door and opened it for her.

"This is the Pearl Room." He waited for her to enter ahead of him.

"Why is it called that?" Harriet asked.

Redmond followed her inside, admiring her figure from behind. "See for yourself."

She pulled her arm free of his to go and explore the room. A tall four-poster bed was decorated with curtains of black velvet embroidered with silver and gold. Pearls were sewn into the curtains, creating patterns like falling rain amid the embroidered silver and gold stars.

"It's a shower of stardust," he said, reaching out to touch the curtains. "That's what my grandmother used to call it."

Harriet's eyes were wide with awe as her hands joined his to brush over the velvet.

"It's the most beautiful thing I've ever seen. No, I cannot stay here. This room is more suited to a…" Her voice trailed off.

"A duchess? Yes. It is. Please, stay. A room like this should not remain empty."

Her blush vanished as she suddenly paled. "Did your wife stay here?"

"Millicent? No, she stayed in the Green Velvet Room, or my bed when I…" He swallowed hard as shame colored his tone.

"When you what?" Harriet looked up at him with an innocence that made him want to hold her close in a way he'd never expected.

"When I asked her to. She was not fond of sharing my bed." He wasn't sure why he admitted to such an intimate detail of his life, but he didn't want her to think he and Millicent had had a perfect marriage. He wanted… What did he want? For this woman he barely knew to see how empty his life had been of love? To pity him?

To love him?

"You have a lovely bedchamber, Your Grace. Forgive me for saying so, but I don't think the duchess should have slept apart from you."

"You don't believe in separate rooms?" That intrigued him. Most of society expected separate rooms.

"No, I don't. When it's a love match, I believe a man and woman who love one another should share a bed. Perhaps my view is affected by my childhood perception. My parents were not aristocrats, and our home in the Cotswolds was small by comparison. My parents shared a bedchamber, and I believe it kept them in love, to be so near to one another."

Redmond touched a pearl on the nearest curtain. He'd longed for a love match and had foolishly thought Millicent was his.

"I agree. The intimacy of sleeping beside another person is remarkable. Few barriers exist between two people who choose to share a bed, to share dreams and midnight whispers." He thought of how Harriet had slept in his bed last night and how he had wished to hold her, to sleep beside her. How could he long for that in a way that seemed so much deeper than it had ever been with Millicent?

Because Millicent had never truly been his. She'd belonged to Thomas from the moment they had met. But Harriet? She was someone who might yet belong to him and he to her. The thought surprised him, but he did not deny it. After seven years, he wished to shed his solitude, yet he was still afraid to trust in love again. And so was she.

"I shall light a few of the lamps for you. Please, make yourself comfortable. Maisie will continue to see to your needs for as long as you stay. I'll have a footman come up shortly to light the fire."

He caught her hand and bowed over it, kissing her fingertips. She didn't pull her hand away, which at least reassured him that she no longer feared him in any way. He left her alone and carried that little bit of hope with him back down the spiral stairs.

HARRIET SPUN AROUND IN THE PEARL ROOM LONG AFTER Redmond had gone. She felt giddy and excited staying in such a stately, dreamy room. The brooding duke she had feared was fading like a mirage before her eyes. She no longer saw him as a devil, but as a lost soul. A man still lost and still in pain.

She wished she knew the truth of what had happened to his wife and brother. That was the only mystery that still worried her. But perhaps she would soon coax that story out of him. She also admitted that she could not envision this man as being friends or even acquaintances with her stepfather now that she was coming to know him. When she'd first arrived last night, she'd refused to trust him, but now? She felt it might be possible.

Maisie knocked on the door a few minutes later and entered with a stack of boxes in her arms. Timothy the valet followed behind, carrying a set of even larger boxes.

"We emptied the attic, with His Grace's approval," she said as she put the boxes on the bed. Timothy added his load to the pile, and with a wink at Maisie, he left the two of them alone.

"A bit of a rogue, that one is." The maid giggled as she eyed the valet's retreating form.

"Who? Timothy?" Harriet asked as she helped Maisie open a few of the larger dress boxes.

"Aye. He's courting me. We only got permission from Mrs. Breland yesterday. Normally that sort of thing is forbidden, but,

393

well, the Christmas spirit seems to have taken over the house in ways it hasn't in years."

Harriet couldn't help but smile. "That's wonderful to hear."

"What about this one?" Maisie lifted a deep-rose-colored silk evening gown from a pale-blue box.

"Oh, that's far too pretty." Harriet shook her head at the sight of the silken gown that exuded elegant decadence.

"Well, I've got a potato sack down in the kitchen you might prefer."

Harriet's eyes widened, unsure of how to respond. Had the brash comment come because she had somehow caused offense? "P-pardon?"

Maisie covered her mouth as she held back a burst of laughter. "I'm just saying, miss, that you can't spend your life turning down things being offered just because you think they're nice."

"Well, no. I suppose not."

"You should have seen the look on your face just now, miss."

"Well, I'd never heard a servant speak so...boldly before."

Maisie smiled. "Bold? Aye, that's one way to put it. I suppose in any other household I'd have been sacked by now. Mrs. Breland's had words with me on more than one occasion. Course, it's not easy finding people to work here, so that works in my favor."

"Perhaps that's the real reason she approved of Timothy courting you?" Harriet said with a hint of a smirk.

"What do you mean, miss?"

"Well, maybe Mrs. Breland believes that if you're wed Timothy will help keep you in line, become a respectful and dutiful wife?"

Maisie considered this. "Oh, well, aren't they in for a surprise then?"

They both broke out laughing at this, to the point where Harriet had to wipe the tears from her eyes. When their laughter died down, Maisie removed the dress completely from the box and held it up to Harriet.

"I never speak my mind to be rude, miss, but because I care. This was the second time you tried to refuse something because you thought it looked too nice. Now what does that say about how you see yourself? Nothing good, if you ask me. If you keep saying things like that, sooner or later you'll start to believe them."

"You're right," said Harriet, bowing her head in appreciation. "You have my thanks."

"Now, I'm no expert, but I'd say this is perfect for you. Let's get you dressed for dinner."

Once she was wearing the gown, Harriet stared at her reflection in the mirror. The sheer overskirt carried a dreaminess of romanticism and was embroidered with delicate glittering gold leaves. Heavy satin pink ribbons bordered the hem and made the bottom of the overskirt thick and billowy in a way that would have suited a princess. A matching pink sash around her waist was tightened into a bow at the back, which drew one's eyes to her waist. She looked nervously at the low scooped neckline, and the sleeves of the gown rested on the edges of her shoulders. The décolletage was scandalously low. She'd always worn high-necked gowns at Thursley, fearing what George might say or do if he saw her wearing something so revealing.

"Are you certain they won't fall off?" she asked in a hushed tone as she stared critically at the sleeves.

Maisie fluffed the sleeves into delicate puffs and chuckled. "They won't. The gown's bodice is tight enough. It's designed to rest against the bosom and have the sleeves just barely drape off one's shoulders, like so." The maid plucked at the sleeves, but they remained firmly in place just barely on the edges of her shoulders.

"I've never worn a gown like this before," Harriet admitted.

"Trust me, miss. This gown will do what it was intended to do."

Harriet touched her naked throat and frowned as she pulled on the long white kid gloves. "And what's that?"

"It will draw his eye and show him how lovely you are."

Harriet's belly flipped. "Wait. Was this dress Lord Frostmore's idea?"

"No, miss. It was mine."

"But why?"

"Because His Grace has been thinking terrible things about himself for so long that he's come to believe them. I know what you must be thinking, but I'm not trying to match you, honest. I just think you both need a chance to believe you deserve to have nice things from time to time. Even something as simple as having dinner with an attractive companion."

Harriet considered the maid's words. Did she want the duke to see her as lovely? *Yes.* She did. The realization surprised her. She'd never wanted to feel beautiful before. Beauty had meant danger; it had meant that George would be watching her with those covetous eyes that gave her nightmares. It was different when Redmond looked at her. His hungry gaze excited rather than frightened her. And she realized that Maisie was right—for too long she had denied herself even simple pleasures, and she had begun to think she did not deserve them.

Maisie flashed her a warm smile. "I'll unpack the rest of the clothes for you during dinner."

"Thank you, Maisie. For everything."

As Harriet stepped into the corridor, she heard a distant gong ring out two floors below. She clutched her skirts in one hand and proceeded down to the entry hall. Lord Frostmore waited for her at the bottom stair. He looked exceedingly attractive in his blue superfine coat, gold silk waistcoat, and maroon trousers. His face lit up, and for the first time in her life, she felt the way a woman ought to when she entered a room. That a man's appreciative gaze was a thing to make her shine and not something to fear.

"You look…" He hesitated, and she thought he might be as nervous as she was. "Good, very good."

"Maisie thought you would approve of my wearing these?" She lifted the skirts and waved them a bit.

"She was correct. Besides, they were going to waste where they were. It felt like a crime to let the moths get hold of something so…" He paused, and she saw him ever so discreetly swallow. "Lovely."

"You have wonderful taste, Your Grace. I am honored to wear the dress. I've never worn anything so expensive before."

"Redmond, please call me Redmond." He reached for her hand. "Or Red, if you like. Red was my nickname as a boy. My brother, Thomas, was a few years younger than me and couldn't say Redmond, so he called me Red. I suppose it was because of my hair." He chuckled at the distant memory, and Harriet's spirits lifted.

"Would you call me Harriet then, Red?"

"Harriet." He said her name like he was tasting an expensive brandy and found it to his liking.

They sat down to dinner, the large table set so very far apart, which meant Harriet had to try to speak to Redmond from the farthest end of the table, where a trio of large bouquets kept him almost hidden from view.

"How do you find the dinner?" Redmond's voice echoed loudly as he almost shouted down the length of the table.

Harriet peered around the edge of the vases, trying to see him better. "I...quite good..."

"What?" he called back and leaned forward in his chair.

"I said, quite good, Your Grace. I think—"

"This is bloody nonsense!" Redmond growled and shoved his chair back quite forcefully, which startled Harriet. Then he collected his goblet of wine and plate and came over to sit down directly beside her. A footman scrambled to collect the duke's silverware and bring it over to them before dashing back into the corner of the room to wait to serve the next course.

"Much better." Redmond looked at her with a grin, and she found herself smiling back at him.

"Indeed."

"I suppose I'll have to tell the footmen to set our plates beside each other at meals. Tradition be damned."

"I would appreciate that." She couldn't help but think back to last night when she had dined with him. How he'd sat at the far end of the table, watching her with dark, hooded eyes, while she'd kept a sword within reach at the table. Not that it had mattered. He'd drugged her and carried her up to his bed, where he'd tended to her wounds with the doctor. How different last night had been compared to this. The man who had frightened her beyond reason was gone. In his place was a man with a kind smile, a guarded heart, and a haunted soul. He was a man she wanted to know everything about.

They dined on soup and salmon, making pleasant conversation throughout the evening.

"Did you enjoy your ride? I saw you from the window earlier. I hope you don't mind—I explored the house for a bit after Mrs. Breland gave me a tour."

"Yes, I did. Riding is one of my favorite pursuits, in addition to reading. Do you ride?"

"When I was a girl, I rode a neighbor's pony once or twice, but until the night of the storm, I'm afraid I hadn't ridden a horse."

"And yet you made it here. Impressive."

"Heavens, I didn't even think. I simply jumped upon the beast and came here. What else could I do?" She blushed and chuckled at herself. Her desire to help Mr. Johnson had overridden all common sense.

"It is as I suspected," Redmond said thoughtfully.

"What is?"

"You are brave. Incredibly so."

"I wish that were the case. But in truth, I'm afraid of *everything*." It wasn't entirely true, but it seemed like so much had given her cause for fear of late.

"You have no need to be afraid here." Redmond reached out to catch her hand, and the connection sent a tingle up her arm. She didn't pull away. It felt good, more than good, to feel his warm, strong hand on hers.

"Would you tell me about your family and your life here?" She hoped he would open up to her, just as she was opening up to him. She stared at his hand, the long strong fingers, then the way his shoulders strained slightly against the confines of his tailored coat displaying his well-developed body.

Harriet thought again of the contrasting portraits in the hall, the beautiful angelic brother and the duke, who seemed unremarkable by comparison at first. But now it became clear how handsome he truly was. The intelligence in his eyes, the compassion in his features, and the hard-won smiles that seem to burn her body hotter than any of the fires in the great marble hearth behind them. She wanted to know him, to feel that she could call him a friend.

"My family has lived here for three hundred years. We were given these lands by Queen Elizabeth when my ancestors did her a great service. My grandmother told me that the queen even visited us once and stayed in the Pearl Room where you sleep now. We thrive on the wealth of the tenant properties to the north and on investments I made twelve years ago in shipping companies that sail out of Dover. It was how I knew the port would close due to the storms."

"And your family? I know your wife and brother are gone, but what about your parents?"

"My mother died a few weeks after giving birth to Thomas. He was two years younger than me. My father followed her six years later. I was raised to the title of a duke at a very young age and had the help of my father's steward, Mr. Shelton, who resides in London most of the year to look after the estate's interests there." He paused and then squeezed her hand.

"I knew your father, Harriet, though only briefly. He trained me and Thomas one summer when I was just out of university. I liked him very much. I didn't meet your mother, and I am sorry for that." His melancholy smile softened. "If I had continued to work with him, I might have met you. Perhaps I am a villain." He said this last more quietly to himself.

"Why?" She didn't understand.

He looked to her now with a mix of determination and uncertainty. "Because I want you, Harriet. I want things I have no right to have."

She wet her lips with her tongue, afraid and excited all at once. She understood what he meant, but her only experience with desire had been her stepfather's predatory gazes. Redmond was nothing like George, and her body seemed to recognize that.

"That makes you human, Red. We all…want things." Her eyes focused on his lips. For all of his hardness and intimidation that night they first met, his lips had remained soft, inviting, even mocking at times, but their sensual promise had never left them.

"I have a tenuous grip on my lust, Harriet. But I could manage one kiss, if you have no objections."

She didn't have a single one. She leaned closer to him as he cupped the back of her neck and lowered his head to hers. She surrendered to the dangerous promise of life-altering passion he carried with him wherever he went. The desire inside her grew so strong it almost felt like a fury.

Heat uncurled in her abdomen, and she moaned as he parted her lips and his tongue flicked against hers. She hadn't known a kiss could be like this. She felt as though she could leap from the cliffs of Dover, spread her arms, and find white feathered wings that would carry her away upon the winds.

Redmond placed his other hand on her leg, raising her skirts above her knees. She whimpered as he met the bare skin of her

LAUREN SMITH

inner thighs and tickled her with gentle, exploring fingers. Heat built within her womb, and wetness pooled between her thighs. He deepened the kiss, leaning more over her, and she leaned back in her chair as he continued to touch her.

"I want to devour you," he breathed against her lips. She didn't fully understand his intentions until he pulled her up to her feet and set her on top of the dining room table. The two footmen in the corner of the room scurried out into the hallway and closed the door behind them.

"Red, what are you?"

He silenced her with another kiss. His hands roamed over her body, skimming over her hips. She wanted to feel his palms all over her, touching her in places that seemed to awaken with newly found desires. Harriet sighed against his lips as he held her close, capturing her as he wound his arms around her back, yet she didn't want to be anywhere else in that moment.

"I want you, Harriet. I want to drown in your eyes," he murmured between slow, drugging kisses that made her body sing.

She clutched at his shoulders, feeling his strong, hard muscles beneath her hands. "I want...you too." The heat of his body seeped through the fabric of his shirt.

"Then trust...trust me to give you what you need."

She nodded, and he stole another lingering kiss. Then he lifted her skirts up to her waist, before he lowered her back to lie on the table. Then he bent over her prone body. The wine she'd had with dinner made her dizzy in a good way as he pressed a kiss to her inner thigh and then set his mouth over the most sensitive part of her. If she hadn't been so full of need for his touch, she would have been shocked at the scandalous position they now found themselves in, but she couldn't find it in her to care. She never wanted him to stop what he was doing.

Anticipation pulsed through her as she watched the wicked duke do exactly as he'd promised—give her what she needed. His tongue flitted out against her sensitive folds, and she gasped and moaned and writhed. She closed her eyes and gave over to the sensations of Redmond's mouth on her. His tongue and lips kept her his sweet prisoner as he tortured her.

A building need that she'd never experienced before sent her breath into fast pants, and her vision spiraled. His lips found the small bud of desire within her and sucked on it. She screamed. Pleasure like she'd never felt, frightening and dizzy, hit her like lightning, and her back arched beneath him. His soft laughter cooled her hot flesh as he teased her with his mouth, and then he stroked his hands down her outer thighs and pulled her dress back down. She lay still on her back, panting and trying to understand what had just happened.

"If you"—she breathed hard—"are a villain for that, I may well play your victim anytime you desire."

He laughed and helped her to sit up. She suddenly felt very shy, open, and vulnerable after experiencing such violent pleasure, but he did not give her time to be nervous. He scooped her up in his arms, and they left the dining room. She curled her arms around his neck, taking in his rich scent. She bit her lip to hide a smile at feeling so protected by a man who'd just devoured her in one scandalous moment. He carried her up the stairs to the library, where they settled into an overlarge chair by a healthy crackling fire. He kept her close to him, and she tucked her head beneath his chin as they listened to the logs pop and snap in the hearth.

"You are very brave." He kissed the crown of her hair. "Very brave indeed."

Part of her was still reeling from the pleasure she'd felt in the dining room, but she wanted to speak honestly with him, this man who was in so many ways still a stranger.

"And you are wonderful, Red. *Wonderful.*" She wished he could understand that he had given her a precious gift tonight.

He had stripped away her fear of desire. He had shown her that such intimacy could feel good, could feel safe and yet exciting. It wasn't always frightening, wasn't always fierce looks and greedy hands in the dark. She had the sudden desire to tell him that she wanted to stay here forever, to never sail to Calais, but she couldn't...not unless he asked her to. So instead she breathed and relaxed into him until she fell asleep in the arms of the Devil of Dover.

Seven

"*Harriet…*" That ethereal voice drew her from sleep again. She opened her eyes and saw lightning flash against the windowpanes. The lamp on the side table burned low, illuminating the pearl-adorned curtains. She was in the Pearl Room, wearing a sheer nightgown of fine silk.

How had she gotten here? Why was she alone? Hadn't she fallen asleep in Redmond's arms in the library? Disappointment settled in a pit in her stomach. She had hoped that Redmond would have stayed with her after what transpired between them.

"*Harriet…*" The mournful call of her name lifted the hairs on the back of her neck.

"Who's there?" she asked, her body shaking as lightning flashed once more and thunder crashed against the manor house, making the bed frame rumble around her.

The pearls winked and sparkled like frozen drops of dew on the black velvet. She blinked, wiping her face with her hands.

Then she saw it. Saw *him*.

A man in the corner was watching her. He was beautiful, but the sight of him filled her heart with such anguish she never wanted to leave. He raised a hand as though to touch her, even though he was across the room.

Harriet couldn't breathe. She clawed at her throat, and the beautiful man, now wreathed in shadows, looked on, watching with sorrowful concern. She reached her hand toward him, gasping for breath.

Then she wasn't in the Pearl Room anymore. She was in another bedchamber. One with more masculine furniture, but it wasn't Redmond's room.

A woman appeared before her, wearing a dressing gown and shawl. She stood facing the man who'd been in her room.

"Do you think he meant it, Thomas?"

She recognized him now. Thomas, Redmond's brother. Harriet watched the man embrace the woman. Love was evident upon their faces. A pure, honest love that made Harriet's heart ache.

"He meant it. Red loves me, and he would do anything for me." Thomas cupped the woman's face in his hands. "But I've hurt him, Millicent. *We* have hurt him. What we did, what we're doing, is wrong."

"I know, but he agreed to seek an annulment. The scandal will be terrible, but isn't it better to be together? We can face anything." Millicent curled her arms around Thomas's neck, and he stroked her dark hair, cradling her against him.

"I want you," he said to Millicent. "But I cannot lose my brother. He's been like a father to me ever since ours died. I cannot leave him alone after this. Let me speak to him again." Thomas cupped her face and kissed her passionately before leaving the bedchamber.

Harriet, invisible to them as if she were the ghost, was drawn by unseen forces behind Thomas down the corridor to another room. Redmond's room.

"Red?" Thomas eased the door open when no one answered his knock. "Red, please, I need to speak with you." The bedchamber was empty. Thomas quietly slipped down the main stairs and headed toward Redmond's study, but he froze when a cold draft caught his attention. He moved into the main hall, where he caught sight of the open front door. The lightning outside revealed a tall, distant figure. It was Redmond, and he was walking in the direction of the cliffs.

"Millicent! Wake Mr. Grindle and Mrs. Breland. Red's headed for the cliffs!" he shouted back up the stairs, hoping Millicent would hear him.

"What?" Millicent appeared at the top of the stairs. "Oh heavens, I'll wake them at once!" She vanished from sight. Harriet, still bound up in this infernal dream, followed close at

Thomas's heels as he raced across the rain-soaked grounds toward the distant cliffs.

"Red!" Thomas shouted as he raced through the violent rainstorm.

"Stop him!" Millicent's cry joined his as Redmond took a decisive step over the edge.

Thomas grabbed Redmond's shirt from behind and pulled him back away from the cliff, stopping him from plummeting to his death.

"Red, what the devil are you thinking?" Thomas demanded, shaking his brother hard.

"Redmond… Don't ever do that again, please." Millicent touched his cheek as she started to cry.

A moment later, the ground beneath their feet shook and crumbled away. Millicent vanished from sight. Thomas and Redmond fell onto the ground, narrowly avoiding her fate.

"Millicent!" Thomas lunged for the edge, but Redmond dragged him back.

"No, you can't." Redmond pinned him to the ground. "She's *gone.*"

Suddenly Harriet was drawn into Thomas's head, seeing and feeling what he felt.

Thomas's heart stopped at the words. Time ceased to have meaning. Just moments ago—a lifetime ago—he had believed he would be with her forever, And he had believed that he would find a way to win back Red's trust. And now…the love of his life was dead.

Thomas stared at his brother, wanting to hate him for coming out here. Millicent would still be alive if not for him. But the rage faded as misery overwhelmed it. Red had only come out here to die because of what Thomas and Millicent had done to him.

"I'm sorry," Red murmured. "I'm so sorry."

But Thomas was the sorry one. His gaze turned to the sea, to the battering waves. There was no more light in his world, no more purpose. All had gone dark.

Harriet woke to the sound of a man shouting her name. She blinked, wiped her wet face, and gasped. She saw that she was but a dozen feet away from the cliffs. Icy wind tore at her body, and fresh snow burned her bare feet. How had she gotten out here? Had she followed a phantom to her own doom?

"Harriet!" Redmond's shout startled her. He grabbed her, jerking her into the safety of his arms. He half carried her nearly twenty feet until they were a safe distance from the cliffs. Harriet couldn't stop shaking from the fear and the cold.

"What in blazes were you doing? You could have died!" Redmond growled as he scooped her up in his arms, carrying her freezing form back to the house. Grindle and Timothy met them at the door.

"Have a bath prepared in my chambers at once. And a tray of food and wine."

"Of course, Your Grace." Grindle and Timothy left the pair alone.

"I can walk," Harriet whispered in mortification.

"I'm sure you can, but if it's all the same, I'll feel better keeping you in my arms." Redmond carried her back to his room, and only then did he settle her down in a chair by the fire. She shivered as he covered her with a heavy blanket, then added more logs to the flames. She sensed the tension building inside him.

"What happened, Harriet?" he asked.

She covered her face with her hands. "I… I'm not sure if you would believe me." Only when he gently pried her hands away did she meet his gaze. She wanted to curl up and hug her knees like a small child might, but she couldn't escape the question in his searching face.

"*Please*, Harriet. Tell me. What drove you to want to take your own life?"

"I didn't—" she protested, then drew in a calming breath. "I didn't mean to. I was asleep in my bed, and then I awoke. I heard someone say my name."

"Maisie must have—"

"No," she said, cutting him off. "It wasn't Maisie. The first time… It was *her*. The duchess. She stood behind this very chair and pointed at you while you slept last night. I thought it was merely a strange and fantastical dream, but tonight… *He* came."

Redmond curled his hands around hers as he continued to kneel in front of her. He didn't say anything, but she could see in his eyes that he knew who she meant.

"I woke tonight to find your brother standing in the corner of my room. He terrified me. Suddenly I couldn't breathe, and then I was in his room with the duchess. They were talking about you." She paused, trying to ascertain whether she ought to continue or if it would pain him too much to hear.

"Go on." His face had gone from concerned to still and somber, like a statue.

"They were speaking about how you had found them together. They spoke of a divorce by annulment. Thomas said he'd hurt you and hoped somehow to make amends. He was so upset, Red. I wish you could have seen his face." She couldn't forget Thomas's brokenhearted look.

"I found them in his room that night," Redmond whispered, almost to himself. "I offered Millicent a divorce...and told them I never wished to see them again."

Harriet pulled one of her hands free to touch his face and stroke his hair. The firelight made it look dark and warm as brandy, and the strands were soft and wet beneath her fingertips.

"Thomas went after you to talk and found you on the cliffs."

Redmond nodded and closed his eyes. "I wished to end my life."

"But he stopped you, and Millicent was there. I saw her fall."

His eyes flew open. "How could you have seen all this?"

"I don't know. But he was there, Red, your brother. I think..."

He shook his head. "Don't say it."

"They're both still here." Harriet leaned forward and kissed his forehead, and he dropped his head into her lap, heaving out a deep, shaking breath.

"They cannot be here," he muttered. "Have I not suffered enough without them haunting me?"

"I don't believe in ghosts," Harriet said, "but I must believe what I saw. How else would I know what happened here?"

"Someone could have told you. Mrs. Breland, perhaps."

"You know full well she would not break your trust like that." She gave a gentle tug on his hair, and he lifted his face. For a moment they stared at one another, and she tried to puzzle out the mysteries of this grief-stricken man. He'd been frantic for her, and the wild panic was still there, shadowing his warm hazel eyes. She brushed her hands through his hair, soothing him as best she could, and oddly it calmed her too.

"You should try to sleep, Red." She was worried more about him than herself. Weariness lined his eyes and mouth.

He shook his head. "Not until you're warm and fed."

Later, Harriet emerged from the hot water of the tub and cocooned herself in a dressing gown. She joined Red, and they ate in silence. His face was dark and unreadable as he drank his wine and she hers.

"I should return to my chambers." She rose from her chair, but he caught her arm.

"Wait. Stay here... With me. In my bed." There was no hint of seduction in his eyes. She saw only the raw need to keep her close. She felt the same way.

"Red, I don't think—"

"Please. I will only worry about you if I don't have you in my arms."

Harriet didn't like the idea that she was being seen as an object of pity, but he did want her in his arms, and she readily admitted that she wanted that as well.

He added more logs to the fireplace while she pulled back the covers of his bed. She climbed in, and he settled beside her. Harriet shivered as she realized she was almost naked. He had but to remove the robe she wore...

Redmond brushed her cheek with the back of his hand and touched her shoulder where the robe slid down a few inches to expose it. His eyes gleamed in the dim light, and Harriet wanted nothing more than a moment to forget her fear, to feel safe in his arms, but she also wanted him.

She reached up to part her robe and rolled onto her back. He gazed down at her, at first confused, then surprised, and then, at last, desire glowed in his face, making him beautiful to her.

She curled her hand around his neck and drew his face down to hers. "Please, Red." She didn't need to say anything else. Her mouth met his hungrily. After a moment he moved his mouth down her body, kissing her collarbone, her breasts, his teeth scraping against sensitive skin and nipping until she was hot and flushed. His hands roamed her body, exploring her hips and thighs. She arched and hissed as he slid a finger into her wet folds, but soon she was rocking against his hand.

Harriet clawed at his shirt until he removed it. Redmond moaned as she slid a hand down between their bodies and stroked his erection through his trousers. She tried not to think about how this man seemed to rob her of all good sense, but the need she felt was half physical and half emotional, overpowering everything else.

"Please," she repeated, and he rolled away from her to remove his trousers.

Then he was on top of her, gently parting her thighs. After settling into the cradle of her body, he kissed her fervently as she melted beneath him. He shifted, and she tensed as he started to enter her. But he kissed her again, and before she was ready to worry about it, he thrust inside her. The pinch she felt made her gasp, and she gripped him tightly by the shoulders. He remained still, and she drew deep breaths as she tried to adjust to feeling so full.

"Better?" he asked against her lips.

"Better," she agreed and raised her hips in encouragement.

What followed was the most memorable experience of her life. Redmond joined his body with hers, their mouths fused in a seemingly endless kiss as he claimed her. Harriet never wanted this moment to end. She had tasted pleasure before, but now it was so much more. Her breasts rubbed against his chest and the smattering of hair there. She had never seen that before, the remarkable naked chest of a man. She ran her palms over him, adoring the feel of him beneath her hands. He pushed inside her over and over, the sensation stealing her breath and making her mad with desire. They moved without words, with nothing but the candlelight and the sounds of their breath surrounding them.

Passion for him and other deeper emotions pounded through her blood into her heart as she shattered beneath him. The searing need she'd felt moments before softened into the sweetest sense of contentment. Redmond tensed as he growled her name against her neck and then relaxed into her, a soft look of wonder in his eyes that made her eyes burn with tears. It was as though he hadn't known what they'd shared could be like this. Was what had happened between them so different? Somehow more special than it was with others? Her heart cried out that it was, but she could not speak to it the way he could. Yet she dared not ask him. Instead, she cradled him to her, his head resting against her breasts until he withdrew from her and rolled onto his back.

"Come here," he urged, and she sidled up against him. He tucked her head beneath his chin and wrapped one arm around her waist.

"I must confess something," he said. "It's important that you hear."

She nodded tentatively, unsure of what he meant to say.

"I loved Millicent," he said softly. Her contentment and pleasure at being in his arms quickly faded into the shadows. She tried to pull away, but he held her still, not letting her escape.

"Please listen, Harriet. I loved her, but I think now it was more the *idea* of love that I loved." He sighed, trying to find the right words. "My brother was the fair one, the one with all the charms. I hoped Millicent would love me, would choose me. But she didn't. Her father convinced her that I was the better choice for her family. All along she had loved my brother, but I was so ready for love myself, so ready for a family and happiness that I failed to see she didn't want me. She cared about me, of course, but it wasn't the same as how she felt about Thomas."

Harriet hugged him tightly to her as her heart clenched in pain for him.

"What we have shared in the past few days has been infinitely more than I ever felt with Millicent. That's what I meant to tell you. There's something about you that soothes me. You don't need to ruin a pleasant silence with speaking, but when we talk it's genuine and interesting. You're pure, and I don't mean that in a carnal way. I mean..." Again, he struggled for words. "You speak to me not as a woman who is interested in a duke, but as a man. As myself."

"I understand," she assured him. For some reason, she had never wanted to think about his title. He was her Red. A man who feared love and yet craved it just as strongly. She understood that all too well.

Redmond played with a lock of her hair and held Harriet close as she relaxed into him. For the first time, she felt she could truly rest in this house. Perhaps the ghosts—for she now couldn't doubt they existed and that they were speaking to her—had wanted this. She had felt their love for each other, but also their love for Redmond.

"Red, what happened to Thomas? I saw you save him from falling over the cliffs. How did he die? He didn't show me everything...just what happened on the edge."

"He..." Redmond paused and swallowed audibly. "He took his own life after we buried Millicent. He couldn't bear to live without her."

"I'm so sorry, Red." She kissed his chin, and he hugged her tighter.

"I never understood before about a man loving a woman with his whole heart, but now... I think I might."

She heard the words, and her heart raced wildly with hope. It was almost a declaration of love. *Almost.* But was love possible for strangers like them? She wished it could be. But he'd lost so much, and she might have to leave for Calais. George wouldn't stop looking for her, and the last thing she wanted to do was put Redmond in any more danger. He may be a duke and have a duke's power, but George was evil, and evil always found a way to hurt good people. She couldn't let Redmond get hurt because of her. That meant she owed him the truth of what she was starting to feel in her own heart.

"I think I might feel the same...about you." She smiled sadly. "I know we barely know each other, but I feel like something fits in place when I'm with you."

Redmond's eyes were warm as he kissed her before he blew out the candle. They fell asleep with the storm outside and the warm fire within.

REDMOND WATCHED THE FLAMES BURN LOW IN THE HEARTH AS HIS worries plagued him. How was it possible that Thomas and Millicent were still here? They should have shed their mortal coils, yet somehow they'd left some part of themselves behind at Frostmore. What did these ghosts want? Revenge against him? Or were they trying to help him somehow? He honestly didn't know.

"Thomas?" He whispered the name, feeling foolish as he did so.

The curtains at the foot of the bed stirred as if an invisible hand plucked at them. Red held his breath, stunned to see that whatever presence lingered here in his home was trying to communicate with him. It had to be Thomas. They'd shared an unbreakable bond as brothers. If anyone could have found the will to stay behind and watch over him, it would have been Thomas. A thrill shot through him at the thought that he was talking to his deceased brother, yet it also unnerved him. Tonight his brother's phantom had nearly killed Harriet—perhaps not intentionally, but she'd almost died just the same.

"I care about her." He looked down at Harriet. "Please don't risk her life, if you can understand me at all. *Please*." He closed his eyes, almost disbelieving that he was trying to speak with a ghost.

A chilly wind blew the windows open violently. He left the bed and rushed to the window and latched them shut again. Then he returned to the bed and pulled Harriet closer in his arms.

"Red…" She murmured his name in her sleep, and his heart clenched as a fierce sense of protectiveness swept through him. He knew she had fled from a dangerous home, and he had a feeling that any man who had his eyes set on Harriet would not easily let her go. For the first time in seven years, he was glad that his ghoulish reputation kept people away from Frostmore. But would it be enough to stop whatever ghost haunted Harriet's steps? A ghost not of his making, but dangerous nonetheless.

Eight

The next few weeks passed in a blur for Harriet. She fell into a comfortable routine of breakfasting with Redmond each morning, and then she and Devil would accompany him on a snowy walk around the grounds of the estate as they were doing now.

She never got tired of watching him play with the imposing yet regal dog. The giant schnauzer would stand perfectly still when Redmond threw a red ball deep into a snowy field until Redmond gave a sharp whistle. Then the dog would dash through the snow, questing for the ball, and upon finding it, he would return it to them.

Devil dropped the ball at Redmond's feet each time and then came to Harriet, who bent and curled her arms around the dog's neck and kissed his furry brow. Devil would start to pant, his pink tongue lolling out of one side of his mouth with sheer delight as he waited for the ball to be thrown again.

"You're spoiling him," Redmond admonished in a teasing tone. "I want him to remain a fierce attack dog. Before you came, he used to delight in chasing women away from my door. I remember one time a young woman and her parents attempted to impose themselves on me. Devil chased them all the way to the gates." Redmond chuckled. "The young woman screamed like a banshee."

Harriet hid a laugh behind her glove. "You're terrible, Your Grace."

Redmond put an arm around her waist and gave her a playful squeeze. "I certainly am."

As they walked back to the house, Harriet looked up at the gargoyles at the gates with different eyes. The menacing faces of the beasts seemed more ancient, more protective than threatening now. Even the house with its turrets and towers, so reminiscent of a medieval fortress, seemed more lonely than frightening. How strange that such strong impressions of a place could change with time. She was glad for it. Frostmore was no longer the foreboding nightmare she'd heard whispers about for so many years. It was a place full of people who longed for love.

"Red... Would we be able to decorate the house for Christmas?"

He arched an eyebrow. "Decorate?"

"Yes, you know, garlands on the banisters, wreaths upon the doors, perhaps even a kissing bough or two?"

His lips slid into a seductive grin. "Suggest a dozen kissing boughs and I'll agree."

Laughing, they entered the house and shed their winter cloaks and gloves, handing them to a waiting footman. Mrs. Breland and Mr. Grindle were conversing about the dinner menu for that evening.

"Ah, good, you're both here," Redmond said as he saw them. "Harriet's had a splendid idea. We should decorate Frostmore for the holidays. What do you think?"

"That is a delightful idea, Your Grace." Mrs. Breland smiled, and Harriet noticed that Mr. Grindle watched her with barely concealed interest. Maisie was right. The butler was infatuated with the housekeeper. Downstairs romances weren't often permitted, but perhaps Harriet could convince Redmond to allow it since his valet had been given permission to court Maisie?

"Excellent. Make what changes you need, and send to the nearby villages for whatever we do not have," Redmond ordered.

"We'll see it done," Grindle promised and gave Harriet a quick smile.

Redmond caught Harriet by the waist. "Well, I have some letters to write in my study. Shall I find you later?"

It had become a ritual for him to find her wherever she was in the afternoon, and more often than not they ended up on the nearest flat surface, clothes scattered about. She couldn't get enough of Redmond or his irresistible touch.

"Yes, please. I'll most likely be in the library." She'd grown obsessed with the vast collection of books he had there.

"Good." He cupped her chin and brushed the pad of his thumb over her lip. The way he stared at her mouth made her tremble and ache. He truly was a wicked man, one who knew exactly how to kindle her darkest desires.

She watched him and Devil head for his study before she ventured into the library. A happy grin spread over her face as she collected several books and sat down to read in her favorite wingback chair by the fire. As she turned the pages, she daydreamed about Christmas at Frostmore and the magic it would bring back into her life and Redmond's. They had both grown so wary of love and trust that neither of them had felt alive in far too long. Her stepfather had turned her from a girl who had enjoyed life into a young woman who feared being used, being *controlled*.

I'm safe here with Red, for now. Safe.

Yet even as she thought the words, she had the eerie sense of something dark and terrible on the horizon, coming for her.

REDMOND SETTLED INTO HIS CHAIR IN HIS STUDY, AND DEVIL SAT at his feet, gnawing on a thick bone the cook had saved for him. Redmond ruffled the short-cropped hair on the dog's head before reaching for the nearest stack of letters. The first were several reports on the shipping companies he held interests in based out of Dover, followed by a few from the sheep farmers who had tenant properties on his estate. Finances were tight for the farmers at the moment, so he would move some money from the shipping accounts to tide over the farmers and their families until spring.

The last letter in the stack had a fancy red wax seal. He broke it and unfolded the paper to read the contents. His heart stuttered in his chest, and he crumpled the edges of the paper. A black rage rose up in him like a violent summer storm.

It was a letter from Harriet's stepfather, George Halifax, and he was searching for his beloved daughter who had stolen his coach and his driver.

How dare this man write to him? They had no acquaintances, no social connections. Redmond read the rest of the letter, his hands clutching the paper tight.

He professed that the young woman was mad, a danger to herself and others. Her mother had recently died, leaving the girl with no one in her life to mold her into respectable feminine behavior after she had become so dangerously willful. George requested that if Redmond knew of her whereabouts to write to him at once so he could come and collect her and bring her home.

The rage that had come upon him so swiftly began to fade as a hint of doubt crept in. Much of what George had said could easily be taken as the truth. Harriet had pulled a sword on him. She'd walked out in the snow in nothing but a nightgown and nearly walked off the cliffs. She not only believed she'd seen ghosts, but she had seen the past through them.

Yet he'd seen the curtains move in his chamber that night they'd first made love. He'd felt that unnatural chill associated with the spirit world and had sworn he caught a fleeting glimpse of his brother. But everything he had experienced could be dismissed with rational explanations, whereas her experiences could not be explained. The edge of doubt remained, a sliver of whispering darkness in his mind.

Redmond stared at the page a long time, weighing what he'd come to know of Harriet against the claims in the letter. He had, luckily, one more witness to ask on the matter. He set the note down and left his study, Devil following on his heels. He entered the service area belowstairs, startling his poor cook and sending two footmen and a scullery maid dashing out of his way. He found Mr. Johnson in the servants' dining hall, finishing his noonday meal. The man had remained here at his estate, along with George's coach, while the driver's broken leg healed.

"Your Grace." Mr. Johnson reached for his crutches, which were leaning against the edge of the table next to his half-eaten soup and bread.

"Please, stay seated. I have a few questions for you."

Mr. Johnson waited, his hands fluttering in his lap as he toyed with his napkin. "I'll answer as best I can."

"I need only the truth. Nothing you say will have you removed from my home, nor have you face any other trouble. Is that understood? You may speak freely without fear of repercussions."

"I understand, Your Grace," the driver answered.

"Harriet's stepfather, George Halifax. What sort of man is he?" When Mr. Johnson hesitated, Redmond encouraged, "The truth, please."

"He's not the best of men," Mr. Johnson began. "He has a sharp tongue, and he's been known to strike a servant a time or two."

"And what of Harriet and her mother? How did he treat them?"

"He was nice enough at first, I suppose, like lots of men are when they want something. Miss Emmaline was such a sweet lady, but she had a desperate look about her. Mr. Halifax saw that and took advantage. Miss Harriet was still a girl when she and her mother moved in. Thursley was bigger than anywhere they'd ever lived before, and they weren't used to being waited upon. It was rather nice, the way they thanked us downstairs staff for anything we did." Mr. Johnson's face reddened. "Not to say I needed that. It's my job, after all, but it's nice to be appreciated for hard work once in a while."

He cleared his throat before he continued. "Well, after a year or so, my master started to show his true self. Miss Emmaline was able to handle him, even the few times he struck her, but she was more worried about Harriet. You see, when Miss Emmaline married my master, he convinced her to sign a guardianship agreement. Until Harriet's twentieth birthday, he has full rights over her. That was meant to protect her, but recently the house realized it also meant he could control her, hurt her, starve her, prevent her even from escaping by marriage. All without consequence. The staff did their best to look out for her. The cook would put a light sleeping draft in the master's food to make him tired on those nights when she saw the evil gleam in his eyes."

Redmond could barely contain the rage bubbling inside him. A wave of self-loathing followed as he recalled how he had tried to frighten Harriet. He had been no better than her stepfather, though he'd had no intention to hurt her, let alone ravish her. But she hadn't known that.

"Do you believe he will come after her?" Redmond asked Mr. Johnson.

"Yes. I'm surprised he hasn't tracked us here already. I knew the moment I helped Miss Russell escape him that I would lose my employment there. He will no doubt accuse me of stealing the coach and have me imprisoned."

"Mr. Johnson, consider yourself under my employment. Once you're healed, your duty will be to watch out for Miss Russell." He started to go but paused and asked the driver one last thing. "When does she turn twenty?" Redmond wished Harriet had trusted him sooner with all of this. He could have been taking measures to protect her. As a duke he had some power, but he wasn't sure he could override a guardian without facing a magistrate.

"January seventh, Your Grace."

"Thank you, Mr. Johnson." The driver bowed his head as Redmond left. He had to find Harriet, if only to assure himself that she was safe. As he entered the great hall, he couldn't shake the feeling that he was being watched. But not by living eyes…

"Thomas, please," he murmured, feeling foolish again for talking to the air. As the feeling began to fade, he exhaled in relief. He had a real, living, breathing demon now to defend against. He could not afford to worry about ghosts in the shadows.

HARRIET HAD FELT THOSE SPECTRAL EYES UPON HER AGAIN. SHE shivered, but when she looked up, she saw only Redmond watching her, not a ghost. Her body began to hum as she noticed the intensity of his gaze.

She put her book down and started toward him. "Red?"

The duke acted fast, grasping her waist and pinning her against the nearest bookcase. He held her tightly to him, one hand wound around her back and the other fisting gently in the coils of her hair as he inhaled her scent and kissed her neck.

"I'm glad I found you," he said. His words sounded odd, as though he had not expected to find her at all. It made her wonder if that was indeed what he meant.

What had begun as a gentle hold turned harder for both of them. The bookshelf creaked as Redmond pressed her against it, and she gasped as bolts of arousal shot through her. The duke's desire was evident, but she was too short for him to easily reach down to kiss her mouth. She tried to curl one leg around his waist and cursed her cumbersome skirts. She dug at his coat, pulling it off him as he playfully nipped her shoulder.

She loved his possessive grip on her body as he lifted her up and set her down on the ledge of the bookshelf. He hiked up her mauve silk skirts to her waist so she could part her legs. Redmond was an excitement she had never imagined possible. Her hands tangled in his flaming hair as she quested for deeper kisses. Redmond groaned against her mouth, and his hands drifted down her back to her backside. He clenched her hard, urgently, pulling her tightly to him.

"I want you, Red," she whispered frantically. "*Here.*" She didn't care if anyone saw them. All she knew was that she wanted his body against hers. He dropped a hand to the front of his trousers as she pushed aside her underpinnings.

His eyes were the color of wheat fields, burning with a golden intensity as he stepped into the cradle of her thighs and slid one hand down to her core. He stroked her with his finger-tips, teasing her until she wanted to scream at him for not being inside her.

"Please, you're teasing me," she growled, and he shifted his hips, penetrating her now, filling her up.

She moaned, her head falling back as he withdrew and thrust back into her. She bucked against him, delighting in their almost violent union, and she reveled in the pleasure that seemed to rebound between them. Redmond breathed hard as he plunged deep and fast. It almost hurt to feel him enter her over and over with such vigor, but she liked the exciting edge of uncertainty that came with making love to him. He was a man of intensities: intense passion, intense tenderness. Yet she knew he would never hurt her. She spread her legs more, clinging to him as he claimed her relentlessly. Then she pulled his mouth back to hers, her arms twining about his neck as he rocked back and forth.

The shelf behind her shifted with the force of their lovemaking. His hard length filled her, prolonging her desire to come. His strength was all-encompassing, his passion beyond words. It was like she was making love to a sun god, not a dark devil. He was all fire and pleasure. She gave in to the sinful force of their bodies colliding and could not imagine ever leaving him.

Redmond's eyes glinted as he stared down at her, knowing full well the pleasure he was giving her. It only made him move faster, filling her body with his. His rough and possessive drive threw her over the edge into sizzling sensations of obliterating pleasure. She cried out. He covered her mouth with his, swallowing her scream and kissing her until she was quivering, feeling only the sensations of pleasure rioting through her body.

He gasped, holding her tightly as his muscles went rigid. Then he seemed to recover, and he rocked inside her, tender and sweet now as he pressed kisses to the crown of her hair. Her body clenched around him as aftershocks of pleasure made her womb tighten. She wrapped her arms around his shoulders as he shuddered, his body trembling almost as hard as hers. She wanted to hold him and never let go.

Her breath was shaky as she placed soft kisses against his neck. He stroked her hair, the ferocity of their almost frantic coupling settling into the sweetest of moments. The duke, with all of his near brutal seduction, was a masterful lover, and she was bound to him now, bound by adoration and fascination. She realized then—as he stole a deep, lingering kiss that made her toes curl—that she was falling in love with him.

You fell in love with him weeks ago, a voice murmured inside her head. She could not find a way to deny it.

When Redmond withdrew from her, she missed him instantly. He fixed his trousers and then put her dress to rights before he lifted her up off the shelf and set her on her feet. She almost collapsed into him on her shaky legs.

"Sorry," she said shyly.

"Don't apologize. A man likes to think he's a good lover, and when he leaves a lady weak-kneed, that's solid proof." He caught her hand and pulled her toward one of the fainting couches near the windows and lay down, pulling her on top of him. She almost protested at the intimate position, but considering how they'd just made love against a bookshelf in the middle of the day…

His lashes fluttered down as he sighed and relaxed beneath her. She shifted to tuck herself in between the side of the couch and his body. He wrapped an arm around her, and she laid her cheek against his chest. The slow, steady beat of his heart was an unexpected intimacy. She stole one more look at him, counting the ghost of freckles upon his nose and cheeks in the bright winter sunlight.

"You should rest," he said with a small chuckle. Blissful delight moved through her as slow as molasses, and she grinned sheepishly, even though his eyes were still closed and he couldn't see.

"Red…" She spoke his name tentatively. "Can I stay with you?"

"Stay?"

"Yes. I don't know what awaits me in France. I was so desperate to escape before, but now I feel safe here with you. I don't want to leave in the spring." She held her breath, knowing how very mad she was to beg him like this. "You don't need to change anything. I don't expect… I just wish to stay, in whatever way you would let me."

He opened his eyes. "You would be content to be my secret lover?"

She drew in a deep breath. "As long as I can love you, that is all I require."

He cupped her cheek and sighed. "You truly are the sweetest little creature I've ever met. Where were you seven years ago? Why couldn't it have been you?" he uttered, his voice a little hoarse. She understood. Seven years ago, he'd pledged his heart to another woman, and he'd been hurt. Betrayed. He wished he could go back; it was clear in his eyes. He couldn't erase the years that had passed by or banish the ghosts in the shadows.

"Sleep," he said.

She laid her head on his chest, fighting tears over the fact that he hadn't said she could stay. She would give him time, and she would wait to see if he changed his mind.

Just as she closed her eyes, surrounded by the warmth of his body and the sunlight streaming through the windows, she thought she heard him whisper, "Perhaps I will keep you."

Nine

Harriet wasn't sure how long she had slept, but when she woke, she was alone on the fainting couch. Redmond must have draped a blanket over her and cradled her head with a soft blue velvet pillow. Redmond's scent was still there, that faint hint of the woods and snow. She breathed in deeply and blinked slowly, rubbing her eyes with her fists.

She was usually such a light sleeper, so she was surprised that she hadn't woken when Redmond had slipped her off his body. Where had he gone to? He probably had more ducal estate matters to concern himself with, but nevertheless, she *missed* him.

Stretching her limbs, Harriet dropped the blanket from her body and took stock of her appearance. Her gown was dreadfully wrinkled, and her hair was quite mussed, but did it matter? No one was here to see her or judge her other than the servants, and she knew that they liked her. More importantly, they liked her being with Redmond. Their time together was changing him for the better. Mrs. Breland had confessed the previous week that he was finally starting to act like the man he'd been seven years ago. That thought alone made Harriet's heart fill with joy.

Harriet felt wonderful, spectacular, better than she had ever felt before in her life, though that probably had something to do with their rough-and-tumble lovemaking against the bookshelf. She bit her lip to stifle a fit of giggles when she noticed the massive pile of books that had fallen off the top shelf. Their lovemaking *had* been earth-shattering.

She climbed off the fainting couch and walked over to try to clean up the chaos. After putting the books away, she stepped back and looked at the shelf in satisfaction. No one would guess what she and Redmond had done here. She exited the library to find Devil waiting for her just outside.

"Well, hello there. Are you looking for Redmond?"

Devil rose from a seated position, holding a long knotted piece of rope, and then he crouched defensively, clearly ready to play.

"Oh, I see. Redmond is busy, and so you've come looking for me." Harriet laughed, catching the end of the rope and tugging it hard. Devil thrashed his head back and forth, trying to shake her hold free, just as he did with Redmond. After several minutes, Harriet was breathless as she let him at last have his triumph and pull the rope free of her hand.

He trotted to the far end of the corridor and paused to eye the end of a runner rug before he dug furiously in an attempt to bury the rope. Then he returned to her, a decidedly smug canine expression on his face, as though he was convinced he'd successfully hidden the rope from her. He continued to follow her around the house as she explored Frostmore room by room once again. It was a vast house, with many darkened chambers and locked doors. Servants bustled around her when she came upon them, and they offered warm smiles. She'd come to fit into life at Frostmore in the last few weeks.

Harriet paused in the long picture gallery, admiring Redmond's portrait. She preferred the real duke in person, but while he was busy in his study, she found this portrait of him comforting. She shook her head and looked down at Devil.

"I am unaccustomed to wishing to be with someone so much, especially a man." She scratched the dog's folded ears, which felt soft as velvet. She felt like she could confess anything to her attentive companion. "I'm in love with him, you see, and when I'm with him I feel strong and brave. Does that make me silly?"

The dog cocked his head to one side, as if considering her question. Then his tongue flopped out of his mouth, destroying the thoughtful expression.

"Not so silly, then?" The dog barked once, and she giggled. "Where is your master? In his study, I suppose. Does daylight offend his demon sensibilities?" She'd come to call him her demon lover sometimes, because he had been so wicked upon their first meeting, and now... She was spellbound by his carnal hungers and couldn't resist teasing him for them.

Devil licked her hand.

"Let's go bring him some tea and biscuits." She gave Redmond's portrait a lingering look before they left the hall of Redmond's ancestors. She felt a dozen gazes coming through the centuries of painted oil faces as she passed them by. She only hoped the ghosts caught within the canvases would find her worthy of Redmond.

REDMOND HELD THE LETTER FROM GEORGE HALIFAX AGAIN, staring down at the words that had sent him running to find Harriet a few hours ago. Then he cast it into the hearth across from his desk and watched it burn.

Grindle appeared in his study doorway. "Your Grace... You have a visitor."

"Oh?" Redmond straightened in his chair. He wasn't expecting anyone. "Who?"

"Mr. George Halifax." Grindle's somber expression warned Redmond that Grindle recognized the name and was as displeased as Redmond was to hear it. He'd shared with Grindle just a short while ago that Halifax was Harriet's stepfather and that Redmond didn't trust the man at all. He'd confided in Grindle that he could even pose a danger to Harriet.

"Bring him to me. But first, find Harriet. Take her to my bedchamber and keep her there. I do not want him to know she is here."

"A wise decision, Your Grace." The butler left, and Redmond rubbed his temples as his head began to ache behind his eyes. All he wanted was to be back with Harriet in the library. He regretted leaving her sleeping so sweetly without him. When they had lain there together, she had snuggled up against him so tenderly, it was as though she meant to keep him as close to her as she could. Whenever he'd taken Millicent to bed, she'd always wished to return to her chamber afterward. It had wounded him to be denied the intimacy of holding her in his arms, feeling connected. Now he had found that connection with Harriet, and if he wasn't careful, it could all be stolen from him.

George Halifax was soon shown into Redmond's study. The man was tall and muscular, but fairly thick and most likely not in peak physical condition. Redmond couldn't help but measure himself against the man, and he decided with certainty that he could best him in any form of combat. He stood up and nodded for Halifax to take a seat.

"Thank you for agreeing to see me, Your Grace. I know we have not been formally acquainted, and I hate to impose upon you, but I sent you a letter a few days ago. Did you receive it?"

"I did, though I confess I only just read it this morning."

"So you know that it concerns a grave matter. My ward, Miss Russell, is missing. Her mother has passed away, and I find myself in the position of being Miss Russell's sole guardian. I have been worried sick over her whereabouts. You are a bastion of strength to Dover. I knew I could trust you to help me once you heard of my plight." Halifax's expression was earnest and open, but Redmond had learned long ago that people could pretend to be something they weren't. Still, even if the man was full of lies, those lies might unwittingly reveal a truth.

"I am listening, Mr. Halifax."

"I married Miss Russell's mother six years ago and raised her daughter as my own. She was a willful child, and while I admire spirit in young ladies, it was clear my Harriet was far more spirited than is tolerable."

Redmond curled his hands into fists beneath his desk when Halifax said "my Harriet," but he let the man continue.

"Her mother fell ill and has only just passed away, but before she died, Harriet ran away and stole my coach and driver in the process. Her mother wished for me to continue as her guardian until after her birthday, but I fear it may have to be longer than that. She is vulnerable, and I believe prone to fits of madness."

"Fits of madness?" Redmond asked quietly.

Halifax's tone turned graver still. "Yes. She's capable of violent outbursts and spinning fantastical tales. To run away from the shelter of my home while her mother lay dying? That is proof enough to me that she needs special care. I only wish to have her back under my roof to protect her from herself."

The man was a remarkable actor. If Redmond hadn't had

the instinct so deeply ingrained in him to mistrust people's motives, he would have been tempted to believe Halifax over Harriet.

"I put my faith and trust in you, Your Grace, that you would tell me if she was here."

Redmond didn't miss the slight hint of an accusation in Halifax's words. He must have suspected that the only logical place a woman could find shelter in the surrounding area would be his home. He was tempted to call Halifax out for suggesting he would lie, but he *was* going to lie about Harriet.

"I would, but she is not here. I do, however, have your coach and your driver." Redmond thought quickly on his feet. "We encountered the vehicle broken down upon the road a few weeks ago. He made mention of helping your stepdaughter, but he said the moment the coach overturned she abandoned him. He suffered a broken leg, and a doctor from nearby has been assisting in his recovery. He is still not able to move on his leg and must continue to convalesce here a few more weeks, but I can have your coach horses ready to leave in an hour if you wish to take them home. I would have contacted you sooner, Mr. Halifax, but my business has kept me away, and I have only just returned to learn of the incident this morning from my butler."

Halifax nodded, as if Redmond's excuse was quite believable. "I would be glad to take the coach and horses now, and I trust if my daughter appears on your estate, you will take the necessary steps to return her to my care?"

Redmond wanted to punch the man so hard his jaw broke, but the game was still afoot, so instead he smiled and held out his hand to shake Halifax's.

"Of course. She sounds quite disturbed and would benefit from a firm, caring hand."

"Thank you, Your Grace. In the meantime, I have already begun the paperwork to have her declared disturbed. The magistrate in Faversham will be signing the papers any day now." Halifax smiled, and this time, a bit of his true desires slipped out. A hint of a triumphant gleam lingered a moment too long in his eyes.

"My man, Grindle, will show you out now."

Halifax exited the study, and Redmond sank back in his chair, a knot of concern tightening in his stomach. He had no doubt that Harriet was still in danger, now more than ever. He didn't trust Halifax to stay away from his lands. It was clear from the man's sharp gaze that he thought Redmond was lying. Halifax had likely searched both Dover and Faversham already. Frostmore was the most logical choice for a woman to hide. That meant Harriet wasn't safe here. She would never be able to leave the grounds, possibly not even the house. She would slowly wither away from being closed off from the world like that. The thought that had lingered darkly at the edges of his thoughts now returned and was unavoidable. Harriet could not stay. She needed to leave, to go somewhere permanently out of Halifax's reach.

Or she could stay…if you weren't such a coward to marry again, a dark voice whispered inside him.

But it was the truth. He was afraid to marry again, afraid to tie his life to another person's after the betrayal he'd suffered the last time. What if he was wrong about how Harriet seemed to feel about him? What if she didn't love him the way he hoped to be loved? He couldn't bear to have another Millicent situation; this time there wouldn't be anyone to stop him from stepping off the cliffs and answering that frightening call of the void and the death that would follow.

If she stayed and he married her, he'd face legal ramifications in the courts, but at least Harriet would be his. But it would be easier—and safer for his heart—to send her far away from here where she could be free of her stepfather.

And I can go back to being alone.

A deep ache settled inside his chest as he left his study. He heard Grindle say goodbye to Halifax, and he waited just out of sight until the door closed.

"Did you find Harriet?" he asked.

"Yes, Your Grace. She is in your room."

"Thank you." He paused. "Have a groom trail that man's coach as far as he can without being seen. Have him stick to the woods if possible, then return. I wish to know if Mr. Halifax takes any detours."

"Yes, Your Grace."

Redmond hurried up the stairs and burst inside his chambers. Harriet stood ready to fight, a fencing blade at the ready and Devil by her side.

"Oh, heavens, Red, you frightened us! We heard footsteps on the stairs and thought…"

Redmond came to her and gently removed the sword from her hand and let it clatter to the floor. Devil barked once and then trotted over to the carpet by the fireplace and settled down, resting his head on his paws.

"It's all right. He's gone." Redmond wrapped his arms around Harriet, stunned at how the strong, brave woman only drew out his fiercely protective side.

She buried her face in his neck. "I cannot go back, Red. You don't know what he's like." She whispered the words so softly it seemed as if he might've imagined them.

"I know." He brushed a hand down her back and cupped her head with his other hand, feeling her golden hair like sunlight warming his fingertips.

"You do?"

"Mr. Johnson warned me about him this morning. He told me about Halifax. Harriet… Your mother is gone. Halifax told me she passed."

She burrowed deeper into his arms. "I knew it. I sensed it, the way a heavy storm finally clears and pale watery skies replace the gloom. I couldn't feel her pain in my heart anymore." She sniffled. "There's a bleak emptiness there instead."

"You *aren't* empty," Redmond reassured her. Once, long ago, he'd dreamed of being close like this to his wife, to offer comfort and love, yet he had never been given the chance. And now Harriet, the woman who could have offered him so much, the woman he could have given anything to, could not belong to him.

"What if he learns I'm here?" She pulled back to look up at him. "I won't be safe anywhere. He's not afraid of anything."

"You think he'd come onto my lands to try to hurt you while I'm here?"

Harriet answered with a slow nod, her eyes full of a weariness that worried him more than he wished to admit.

"Even if I stayed here, and had all the protection a duke could offer, I don't think it would be enough, Red. He won't stop coming after me, and I don't want to put you or the staff here at risk."

He wanted to disagree, to tell her that she was safe, but it would be a lie, and he didn't want any lies between them.

"You're right. He's a dangerous man. The only way to keep you safe is for you to go. You must leave tomorrow morning. We'll ride to Dover and find you a ship. The Channel has not yet become too treacherous for a winter crossing. I'll see to it you have money for clothes and food. You'll have plenty to set yourself up with in Calais or Normandy where your father's family is."

Harriet's eyes filled with unshed tears. "You want me to leave?"

"I would give *anything* for you to stay. But fate has other plans, I fear. I don't trust Halifax either."

"Even having escaped him, George has managed to outfence me," she muttered. "He has still won, even if he does not possess me, because he has denied me happiness, and I must leave the second place in my life that truly felt like home."

"Yes, you must," Redmond agreed. "He means to prove you are mad or disturbed so as to retain guardianship over you, even after you would have legally escaped him. He's already begun the paperwork with the magistrate in Faversham."

Fresh terror struck her face. "Oh Lord, Red."

He held her fast, not letting her go as she trembled again in his arms.

"We'll arrange with Grindle and Mrs. Breland for you to leave tomorrow." The words felt bitter upon his tongue.

She was quiet a long moment before she raised her face to his. "Red, I don't want to leave."

"You must." *Even if it kills me to let you go.*

She tried to pull away, to turn her back, but he wouldn't let her. Instead he gathered her close again. Her slender hands twisted anxiously before they settled on his chest. Misery tore through him, leaving an emptiness inside his heart, except for a faint glow that she'd kindled weeks ago from a dying fire.

"I could arrange for you to have a home in France, but I couldn't come to you, not right away. He will have eyes following me, I'm certain of that."

"No, you cannot do that. He could find out somehow. Better if I go alone with no connection between us."

Her words, even though they were meant to protect them both, burned like a hot poker against his heart.

"I will fight him in the courts. I have influence over the magistrate in Dover, and I'm certain that with time, I could gain enough power in Faversham to find a way to reverse whatever ruling the judge makes if it's in Halifax's favor. I'll need time, time where I can know you're safe, far away from him."

"Oh please, Red." Her tormented tone pulled at him, and he knew that if he did not kiss her one last time he might perish. So he defied the agony and pain that formed an invisible shroud inside him and stole another kiss.

"We have but the fading daylight left, my darling." He brushed his nose against hers before pressing his lips to hers, soft but urgently. A powerful sense of awakening from a very long, terrible dream stole over him, one that had held him trapped for seven years.

Harriet kissed him back, her youthful passion and sweet ardor like a flash of brilliant light. It reminded him of when he had been a lad roaming in the attics. When he'd gotten bored, he'd thrown a few stones around and shattered a dust-covered window. The explosion of light had blinded him. It had been the single most glorious experience of his life, to feel the bright sun burning his body, reminding him of the joys of being alive, being outside and living in the world.

"Harriet," he murmured against her lips. "Against the will of my hesitant heart, I have fallen in love with you."

He didn't want to go another moment without having said these words. Yes, he would lose her. Yes, he would never find this feeling again with anyone else, but at least he would have said it. At least he would know that she felt the same.

Her blue eyes were soft like a sunny summer sky. "I love you too. More than is wise, but I love you all the same." Her melancholy smile echoed his own pain.

It was all that needed to be said between them as he carried her to his bed.

They took their time undressing each other. He memorized the slopes and curves that made her unique, that made her exquisite perfection. She was his light in the gloom, the piece of his life he'd thought lost years ago.

Redmond laid her down beneath him, covering her face with

kisses. He savored her shivers and sighs as he kissed his way down her body. She giggled as he nibbled on one nipple and then the other. Her hands dug through his hair in a way that made his entire body go rigid with pleasure. She scraped her nails down the back of his neck, which made him groan. Then he placed kisses on her stomach as he made his way down between her legs. She had become less shy these past few weeks, and he enjoyed how free she seemed to be with him, their passions equal to one another.

Now skin to skin, two joined as one, he entered her gently. It was an exquisite torture to make love to her like this, yet it felt like heaven. She locked her legs around his waist as she pulled his head down to hers.

"I never tire of kissing you," she breathed. Love and honesty glowed in her eyes, and it humbled him to his core. He shivered above her as he withdrew and sank back into her welcoming heat.

"In all my life," he whispered, "there has never been anyone like you, nor will there be again." Then he kissed her, deep, slow, his tongue playing an ancient game with hers.

The turbulence that had ruled his life for the last seven years had suddenly stilled into this most perfect moment of calm. Yet he was full of energy, full of joy, full of love, so strong his heart felt fit to burst. Their gentle rhythm quickened over time as their frantic need to taste each other, to share the pleasure of their love, grew stronger.

He delighted in drawing small gasps of excitement from Harriet as he claimed her. Redmond's own breath shortened as he came close to the edge. He slid a hand between their bodies, finding her bud of arousal and circling his finger over it until she arched beneath him and her inner walls clamped down around his shaft.

Then he was lost, his heart and soul pouring out of him and into her, and coming back again. A long moment later, he covered their bodies with the coverlet before pulling her to his side. He kissed her forehead and held on to her, closing his eyes.

If love was a heavy tome in his library, every page would have Harriet's face sketched upon it and poems about her written in a dozen languages. It would contain life's most powerful secrets, transcendental and far too enlightened for a soul like his. Yet if that book did exist, he would vow to read every page every night for the rest of his life until he was an old man, watching the sun set a final time. That way, he would never lose the memory of her. Harriet would be with him always.

Then he would be able to tell the ghosts that breathed within the walls that he had done one good thing with his time upon this earth. He had loved Harriet more than his own life, and he had been loved in return. There was no greater gift than that, and he would lose it forever come the dawn.

Ten

arriet buried her sorrow deep within her heart as she closed the valise Maisie had packed full of beautiful gowns. Gowns fit for a duchess. They didn't belong to her, but Redmond had insisted they belonged only to the Duchess of Frostmore.

He cupped her face and leaned in to whisper, "In my heart, there will be no other. You are *my* duchess."

She hadn't been able to deny him anything. He stole more kisses, his eyes rimmed with red as he dragged his hands through his hair as if he longed to pull the strands out in frustration.

She wrapped her arms around his neck, not caring that the staff were watching her. They had all come to say their goodbyes.

"Thank you for giving me a place to belong. A home." The words burned her throat, and she could barely speak. "Thank you for letting me love you." Whatever fate held for her now, she had been given the most precious gift a person could ever have. The gift of his love.

He wiped at her dry cheeks as she managed a bright smile. "No tears?"

"One cannot cry when one realizes one has been blessed beyond all measure." She stepped away from him, the action cutting her heart, but she dared not let him see how much. Instead, she knelt by his side to pet Devil, who watched in silence. As always, the dog seemed to sense her moods, and his brown eyes were heavy with reciprocal pain. She threw her arms around the dog's neck and hugged him tight, then stood and looked at Redmond again.

"You won't see me to Dover?" she asked again, needing as much time as she could with him before saying goodbye.

He shook his head, a rueful smile on his lips. "If I went, there is no way I would be able to stand by and let you board a ship."

She understood, even though it hurt. Better to make a clean break of it here where it still felt less real.

"Write to me once you're safe." His quiet request startled her. It would pain them both, but she would do as he asked.

"And you?" she asked. "You'll not go back into hiding? You promise to do as I asked?"

He nodded. That morning, as they had lain in bed, watching the pale sunlight stretch across the bedchamber, she'd made him vow not to hide from life any longer.

She touched his cheek one last time with a gloved hand, and he caught her wrist, holding it against his face for a long moment, their eyes locked.

Then he whispered hoarsely, "Go now… or I will lose the courage to let you go."

She turned and rushed out the door and hastened down the steps into the waiting coach. If she looked back, she knew it would break her soul, not just her heart. Redmond's driver helped her inside, and she leaned back against the seat cushions and drew in a shuddering breath as the coach began to roll away.

It was early evening as they reached the port, and she tried to keep herself busy by thinking about what she would do once she reached Calais.

"We're here, miss." The driver offered her his hand as she stepped down. The Port of Dover was quiet; only half a dozen vessels were docked. Their masts looked like an ancient forest, dead and quiet. Somewhere a bell clanged, and a man called out the change of an evening watch aboard one of the vessels.

"I'll go and see which boat you can book passage on," the driver said, and he headed into the nearest shipping office.

Harriet waited, her cloak hood pulled up against the chill. She watched the men on the ships in the distance as they saw to their duties.

Suddenly someone grabbed her shoulder, and something hard dug into her back.

"Not one scream, dear daughter," George hissed from behind her. "Not one, or I'll sink this blade into you."

Fear enveloped her as she closed her lips and nodded.

"Good. Move backward with me." He pulled her along until she was almost falling, then she was spun around to face his coach waiting in the shadows. George shoved her hard, and she stumbled inside. She tried to rush through to the other door to escape, but the two ghoulish men from his home were there, and they grabbed her, one pinning her arms to her sides and the other smothering her mouth with his hand.

"Bind her wrists and gag her," George snapped.

Harriet struggled, clawing and kicking, till George's knife-point pricked her chest, cutting through the rose-colored gown she wore. She stilled, and the men on either side of her bound her hands. One balled up a bit of cloth and forced it between her lips.

Unable to resist, she cast her gaze out the window of the coach, hoping Redmond's driver might see her. But her last hope failed her, and she sank defeated back against the seat.

"Do you have any idea the trouble you've caused me, little Harriet? Faversham has been flapping with gossiping tongues about where you've run off to. Your little adventure has brought shame upon my name and my home. You'll pay dearly for it, and Lord Frostmore won't be able to hide you this time."

Her eyes widened at Redmond's name, and it didn't escape his notice.

"Oh, I knew you were there. It was only the only place close enough, and it was too cold for you to be in the woods for long. It's quite clear that you're mad. Why else would a young woman run to a notorious wife murderer for help? Luckily for you, we have a doctor waiting at Thursley to declare you disturbed, and I have a local magistrate preparing to sign papers to the effect as we speak. Then I shall have a guardianship over you for the rest of your life. How long that is depends on whether or not you please me."

Harriet stared at him. Horror filled her until she felt nothing else. This man was a true devil, hidden behind a mask of caring and decency. She had hoped he would forget her in time, but his obsession ran too deep.

"Don't look at me like that," he snapped. "I rescued you from a murderer."

Of course he would paint himself the hero, rescuing her from the Devil of Dover, but he was the only devil in this tale.

"If you remain sensible, you may have the gag removed." He nodded to one man, who pulled the cloth from her mouth. They must be too far from Dover now for him to worry about her screaming. "We won't make it back to Faversham tonight. I have a room secured at an inn nearby. We shall sleep and proceed to Thursley tomorrow."

"One room?" Harriet asked, her voice cold, her body still numb.

George smirked. "Of course. I can't very well leave you alone in your own room. Not in your condition. We wouldn't want anything to happen to you."

She swallowed down a wave of nausea and tried to clear her thoughts. She would have to be smart, play as though he'd defeated her. Once his guard was down, she would fight to the death to win her freedom again.

"I can see you plotting and scheming, my dear. Whatever you're planning, it won't work."

The rest of the journey, George talked about his grand plans, how he would wait a respectable amount of time before marrying her, scandal be damned. She was, after all, only his ward and not his daughter. Harriet allowed herself to escape deep within her mind. She was back in Frostmore, exploring the old house, walking through the snow-covered grounds, running to Redmond and throwing herself in his arms. George could never lay claim to these memories. They were hers alone.

They reached the inn just after nightfall, and George told the innkeeper that they would take their meal in their room. Harriet sat across from him at the small table, eating reluctantly. She wondered if George would drug her, but she knew he would enjoy her screaming in pain and would likely prefer her to be fully aware of her powerlessness when he took advantage of her. He was obsessed with possessing and controlling her, the sort of man every woman feared, even the bravest ones.

George finished his meal and reached forward to clasp her

hand where it lay on the table. She tried to pull away, but his grip tightened hard enough to leave red marks.

"I want us to be friends, Harriet."

"And I want you to let go of me." She tried to keep her tone polite.

He rose from his chair and came to stand behind her. He stroked her loosely coiled hair, then dug his hand into it sharply, forcing her head back to look up at him. His other hand clamped around her throat.

"My dear sweet Harriet, do not anger me. I only wish to still that wild spirit in you. It will do you no good to fight." He loosened his hand on her throat just as her vision started to go black. She coughed violently as she gasped for air. But he wasn't done with her. He jerked her to her feet and moved her toward the bed.

"Come over here and rest. You may sleep soundly knowing that I will be here to watch over you."

His words sent an unholy wave of revulsion through her. She tried to wrench free of his hold. George struck, his fist catching her in the jaw. Blood blossomed in her mouth.

"You monster!" She tried to run for the door, but he crushed her body against it before she could lift the latch.

She elbowed him hard, and he collapsed against her. She slid out from under him and rushed to the table, snatching his dinner knife. Her father's lessons hadn't included training on short blades, but she felt she could handle it if it came to it.

George spun to face her with a growl. Harriet raised the blade, feeling her father's spirit inside her like a burning flame. She would fight him with everything she had. But her throat tightened with fear as she saw the pistol. He pulled the trigger and nothing happened. She exhaled in relief, but she had only a second before he charged at her.

REDMOND STARED AT THE DISTANT GATES TO FROSTMORE AND the black shape sitting there in between them. Devil had chased the coach all the way to the gates and then stopped, barking once or twice before he'd gone silent, still is a statue. He was waiting for Harriet to come home, and it broke Redmond's heart.

"Devil!" Redmond shouted from the front door, but the dog didn't move.

Redmond walked the distance out to the gates and stood beside his furry companion. Both of them stared down the road where Harriet had gone. Suddenly Devil spun to face the house, his hackles raised as he growled. Redmond turned as well and gasped in shock. A woman's face stared out of his bedchamber window. Even at a distance, he knew who it was.

Millicent.

"Red…" The whisper he heard was neither male nor female, and the way it caressed the air around him made him shiver.

The woman raised a hand, pressing her palm to the glass. *"Red… He has her…"*

Devil stopped growling and stood frozen, watching as the face in the window faded. The birdsong and wind blowing in from the cliffs soon came back. Only then did Redmond realize that everything had stilled while Millicent spoke to him. Her warning flashed through his mind again. His fears that the ghosts that haunted his home meant to bring him harm seemed to fade in that instant. They were warning him, helping him.

"Harriet!" He sprinted for the house, yelling for his horse.

"Your Grace?" Grindle rushed out into the hall as Redmond entered it.

"I have to go after her. She's not safe. I never should have let her go."

He ordered his horse to be made ready and went into his study to retrieve a pistol from his desk drawer and loaded it. Then he tucked it into his coat before getting on his horse. He rode for Dover, but as he reached the main road that split between Dover and Faversham as the gloom upon the land began to settle in, he saw something standing there, blocking the road to Dover.

Redmond stared at the phantom, which seemed to glow in the darkness. Redmond's lips parted, but he spoke no words. His usually gentle mare bucked wildly, as though sensing, perhaps even seeing, this supernatural vision.

Thomas.

His brother pointed toward the road leading to Faversham.

437

His pale form glowed from a light source deep within, leaving him a ghostly pearlescent version of his former self.

"The inn…" The words had barely left Thomas's lips before he vanished.

Redmond stared down the road to Dover, where he knew Harriet had gone, but then he looked down the opposite path his brother had pointed toward. Was he losing his mind to not only see but trust these visions?

He closed his eyes, breathing deeply. He had to trust them. He steered his mount toward Faversham.

"Show me the way, brother. Show me," he pleaded upon the winds as he raced on.

He saw the distant lights of an inn ahead. A vision filled his head, clear as day. *Harriet reaching for a knife, Halifax lunging for her.* Redmond didn't waste a second as he stopped at the inn and threw the reins of his horse to a stable boy. The inside of the inn was eerily quiet. A few men sat in a corner, drinking ale over hushed whispers. They eyed him warily as he strode in. Redmond ignored them and sought the innkeeper.

"I'm looking for a man named Halifax. He may have come in with a young woman. I will pay handsomely for full information." He slapped a small purse on the counter.

The barman's eyes widened. "They were here, stayed for dinner in one of the rooms upstairs. But they started shouting, and the woman ran out toward the cliffs. The bloke went after her." The man reached for the bag of coins.

The bitter taste of panic filled Redmond's mouth. Harriet was headed for the cliffs? What was she thinking? She could fall…like Millicent.

"Where is your back door?"

The man pointed over his shoulder, through the kitchen.

"Thank you." He ran to the door, his heart pounding as he prayed that he wasn't too late.

HARRIET CLAWED GEORGE'S FACE AS HE WRESTLED HER TO THE ground. The grass was wet with melted patches of snow. She had slipped as her boots caught on a slick spot of snow, giving

George the chance to catch up with her. Now she was fighting for her life. Her body ached with the weight of him atop her.

The meager moonlight darkened the shadows on his face. He snarled and hurled himself at her. He clubbed her savagely on the temple, and she lost her hold on his hands, which now curled around her throat. She struggled for breath, trying to reach for the small knife that lay inches away from her hand. His eyes were lit with the demonic lust for death as he held her down. It would be so easy to give in, to surrender and let go. Harriet was tired of running, tired of fighting. She wanted Redmond, to be back in his arms. Her vision began to dim, and she could hear her mother's voice.

"Harriet…fight…"

He laughed heartily, the awful sound of his joy jerking her back to her senses. Her fingers touched the tip of the blade, and she strained until she curled her fingers around it. Then she swung, jabbing it deep into his side. He threw back his head and cried out in pain. His hands released her, and she punched him hard in the throat, sending him stumbling back. The instant she was free, she tried to crawl away from the cliffs, but her head swam and she nearly fainted from the pain in her skull. When she turned to see George, he was a few feet away at the cliff's edge, staring at her in fury.

"You little bitch!" He pulled the knife out and stared at her. Then his face hardened, and he stepped toward her.

Crack!

George stumbled to a stop, looking down at his chest where a dark-red spot appeared on his white shirt, growing bigger every second.

Harriet stared in stunned silence as he then stumbled back toward the edge of the cliff. A second later the dirt gave way, and he fell into the darkness below.

"Harriet?" a voice called out. She clutched her aching head and turned to see Redmond there, a pistol raised.

Redmond had shot George, had stopped him from reaching her, or else she would've fallen over the edge too. She slowly crawled backward, afraid the ground beneath her would also give way. Redmond reached her a moment later and wrapped his arms around her, carrying her away from the edge, just as he'd done two weeks ago when he'd saved her life after she'd followed a ghost to the cliffs.

"Red…" She collapsed into his arms. They both fell into the grass, holding each other.

"Are you all right?" he asked, cupping her face.

She threw her arms around his neck, and he held her long after she stopped shaking. "Yes. I am now."

The clouds parted, and a full moon shone down, casting eerie beams of light where it reflected off the snow around them.

George was gone. The monster who had kept her in fear for the last six years was no longer there to haunt her. She started to close her eyes, but then she saw it. A flickering moonbeam that for but a moment seemed to be…*Thomas*. Staring at her and Red, a sad smile hovering about his lips before the moonlight vanished behind a cloud again. The specter of George's evil in her life was ended, and for the first time in a long while, she could breathe. She felt happy, safe…and now she was with Redmond again. She marveled at how it was even possible that luck would have brought her such a fate.

"It's over," Redmond said softly. "You're safe now. He can't hurt you anymore. I'll see that the magistrate in Faversham retracts anything he might have signed about you."

"You can do that?"

"Now that Halifax is dead and I can attest to his attempt to murder you, any paperwork put before a magistrate will be suspect given the man's motives to harm you."

Harriet leaned into him, relaxing for the first time in six years. It was over. George was gone. She was safe.

He kissed her forehead and pulled back to look down at her. "Are you ready to go home, my darling duchess?"

Harriet stared up at his handsome face, wondering how anyone could have ever thought him unattractive. He was perfect in every way.

But what had he just said? Duchess? He couldn't…

"Red, you don't have to…" He didn't need to marry her. She knew he might never again wish to marry after what had happened with Millicent. As long as she could be with him, that was all that mattered.

"You are my duchess. I thought I wasn't ready to marry again, but after almost losing you, I knew I couldn't let you out of my life again. So you'll have to marry me, Harriet. I won't have it any other way." He kissed her on the lips, a deep, sensual kiss that sent flutters through her lower belly. It banished all thoughts of the horrors she'd faced tonight, leaving only relief and joy.

"Is that so?" She felt so giddy that she couldn't resist teasing him. "Don't I have a say in this?"

Redmond smirked. "None at all. And if you resist me," he murmured seductively, "I may have to fight you for it. I'm not bad with a fencing foil."

She laughed and buried her face in his neck. "You're not terrible. But I'm better," she reminded him. "But perhaps I'll let you win."

"Would you indeed, minx?" He laughed, the cheery, open sound erasing all fear and heartache she'd suffered.

She was no longer losing him; she was going home with him.

"Come on, let's get back and hire a coach. Poor Devil may still be waiting at the gates for you."

"What?" They both stood and headed toward the distant flickering lights of the inn.

"He chased your carriage all the way to the gates and has been there ever since. He knows, like I do, that you belong at Frostmore."

"You know, he's really not a devil. Perhaps you can rename him? Angel, perhaps?"

Redmond laughed again. "He's a black guard dog. If you start calling him Angel, no one will fear him."

"Perhaps that would be a good thing?" She laughed. "For when the children come? We wouldn't want to scare the little ones."

Redmond jerked to a stop. "Children?"

She nodded, suddenly nervous. "Yes… I wanted to tell you, but then George came, and I knew I had to leave. My courses are two weeks late. I'm not certain, but"

She was unable to finish her sentence as he crushed her to his chest in a fierce hug.

"Children." He said the word with a boyish smile as he picked her up and whirled her around. When he finally set her down on her feet, he looked at her as though she was the answer to every question he'd ever had.

"Harriet. *My* Harriet." He pulled her close again. "I love you to the point of madness."

She nuzzled his throat and basked in the warmth of his body holding hers. "And I love you beyond all measure." It was a love that did not fill her with madness but rather a glorious, wondrous giddiness for life. It reminded her of when she'd been young, long before her father fell ill.

"Let's go home. We have the rest of our lives ahead of us." Redmond's voice was full of joy and hope. No more shadows, ghosts or otherwise, stood between them any longer.

"How did you know where to find me?" she asked as they reached the inn.

Redmond's eyes were serious again. "I'm not sure you'd believe me if I told you."

"Try me."

"Thomas showed me the way—after Millicent warned me you were in danger."

Harriet was quiet a long moment, thinking back to what the ghosts of Frostmore had shown her.

"I hope they can find peace together. They deserve it." She laid her head on his shoulder, and then he nodded.

"For once, I think I do as well. Frostmore shall be a place of joy from now on. A place of love and light."

"So long as we are together," she added.

"And forever beyond that." He raised her chin up to steal another kiss. Her heart was for none other than the Duke of Frostmore. He was no longer the Devil of Dover, because he had a pair of angels watching over him. And he was *her* angel.

Epilogue

Two weeks later

Redmond woke to a white Christmas covering the grounds of his ancestral home. Harriet lay in his arms, still sound asleep. He almost couldn't believe how easy it had been to deal with Halifax's death. The magistrate had set aside the papers Halifax had sent him, and Harriet had been awarded Halifax's estate in its entirety since he'd had no heirs. Harriet had made mention of converting the home into a fencing school, and Redmond had agreed it was an excellent idea.

He slipped from the bed and crossed to the window while he pulled his dressing gown on. The snow stretched out as far as the eye could see, all the way to the cliffs and the deep, icy blue waters beyond. For the last seven years, the winters here had been cold and depressing. But now everything was different. The halls were full of Christmas garlands. The upstairs maids hummed carols as they cleaned. The footmen had taken the placement of kissing boughs quite seriously. More than one maid had been caught unawares for a quick giggling kiss by the young men. Frostmore was a home once again, for everyone.

Harriet stirred in bed, reaching for him. "Red?"

"Here, my darling." He rejoined her and leaned down to kiss her. She laughed in delight.

He tapped the tip of her nose. "Why don't you get dressed? It's Christmas."

She rolled her eyes. "Someone is anxious for his presents."

"I certainly am. We haven't had a proper Christmas here in seven years."

Her eyes darkened with emotions. "Oh, Red…"

He shook his head. "None of that. Now come down and meet me in the long gallery once you're dressed. I must see Grindle and Mrs. Breland and see how the preparations for tonight are coming along."

He gathered his clothes and went to change, but he took the time to steal one more kiss before he headed downstairs.

The staff were bursting with their preparations for the evening celebrations. Tonight they would be hosting a Christmas ball, where he would officially ask Harriet to be his wife.

"Grindle?" He found his butler ushering in the orchestra that would play during the event. Old friends and local families had been invited, as well as his tenant farmer families. He wanted to restart his life, to embrace being a part of the world again, thanks to Harriet. When they'd mailed out the invitations, he'd been worried that no one would come, yet the positive responses had poured in within days.

Grindle smiled broadly. "We're almost ready, Your Grace."

"Good, good." He patted his pocket nervously. It held the present he'd chosen for Harriet. "Oh, and Grindle." He caught his butler before the man left.

"Yes, Your Grace?"

"You have my permission." The confusion on Grindle's face was almost comical. "To court Mrs. Breland. Should you choose to marry, you may retain your positions here with no qualms from me."

Grindle only managed a respectful nod before rushing off to show a few straggling musicians where to set up. He was far too professional to let more than that slip past his reserve, but his thanks was clear.

A few hours later, Frostmore was full of people and music filled the house. He'd spent the hours before with Harriet as they'd talked of everything and nothing while having a late luncheon in his study. Then she'd gone back to her room to dress for the ball. Redmond greeted all his guests, including Millicent's parents.

"Your Grace," Millicent's father, Henry, greeted solemnly.

"I'm glad you came, Mr. Hubert."

Henry and his wife, Maria, both smiled a little sadly. "We're glad to be here. It's been too long." Henry proceeded into the room, but Maria remained behind.

"I hope... I hope you find happiness again, Your Grace. It's what my Millicent would've wanted." She paused, her eyes misting. "We know the rumors weren't true. We know you loved her, and we have no quarrel with you. The past is the past, and we've put it all behind us." She squeezed his hand and offered a genuine smile.

Redmond's eyes burned as he thanked Maria. He never thought that they would say that they believed him. When he'd told them of Millicent's death all those years ago, they'd left his home heartbroken, just as he had been. But he had feared, as the years passed, that they might have believed the rumors that he'd killed her. But they hadn't. They were here to celebrate Christmas, moving forward.

He cleared his throat and glanced toward the main stairs. His heart stopped. Harriet descended alone. Her satin gown was the color of ivy, and the hem and bodice were embroidered with gold ivy leaves. Her skirt split apart to reveal a red petticoat down the middle, and a thin layer of gold netting was draped over her outer skirts. Her blonde hair was pulled back, and a duchess's coronet, one that had belonged to the women of Frostmore for two hundred years, was nestled in her artful coiffure. She hadn't wanted to wear it, not until she was officially a duchess, but with a little help from Maisie, she'd been convinced to wear it. She moved as though she were in a dream. He went to her, catching her hand as she reached the last step.

"Happy Christmas, darling," he whispered as he led her to the crowd of people gathered in the hall. Then he made an announcement for everyone to follow him into the long portrait gallery. There was no formal ballroom at Frostmore, but the gallery was long and wide. Musicians inside struck up a merry waltz, and couples began to form for the first dance. Redmond pulled Harriet into his arms.

"Harriet?" he said as they began to dance beneath the candlelight.

"Yes?" She gazed at him with luminous eyes that saw into his soul.

"Marry me. Tomorrow. I have a special license from London. Marry me and become my duchess." They stopped dancing, and he pulled out the small box with his mother's ring inside, inlaid with a large brilliant ruby, surrounded by small diamonds.

"Oh, Red," she gasped. "Of course I will. Yes!"

He slipped the ring upon her finger, and the couples who had witnessed the proposal broke into applause. He held her close, wanting to kiss her, but he had caused enough of a scandal for one night.

They began to waltz again. As the couples around them joined back in, Redmond's heart caught in his throat as he recognized two figures dancing in the crowd. Their pearly luminescent glow was otherworldly as they spun between the other guests, unseen by all but him. He swallowed hard as he watched them smile and twirl before they both looked his way. His heart stopped as he recognized quite clearly their pale faces, which were full of joy. A moment later their forms transcended time itself as they faded into shimmering stardust before his eyes.

"Red? What's wrong?" Harriet asked, her worried eyes fixed on his face.

"Nothing. Everything is finally, *truly* fine." He smiled as he focused on his future wife.

If love truly was a book, then he had turned the first page, and all he saw was Harriet's face. Whatever spirits had haunted Frostmore were at peace now. And for the first time in seven years, Redmond looked toward the future instead of the past, with the love of his life dancing in his arms.

THANK YOU SO MUCH FOR READING DEVIL AT THE GATES! IF you loved this story be sure to visit my website to discover more passionate romances: https:// laurensmithbooks.com/

About the Author

USA Today Bestselling Author Lauren Smith is an Oklahoma attorney by day, author by night who pens adventurous and edgy romance stories by the light of her smart phone flashlight app. She knew she was destined to be a romance writer when she attempted to re-write the entire *Titanic* movie just to save Jack from drowning. Connecting with readers by writing emotionally moving, realistic and sexy romances no matter what time period is her passion. She's won multiple awards in several romance subgenres including: New England Reader's Choice Awards, Greater Detroit BookSeller's Best Awards, and a Semi-Finalist award for the Mary Wollstonecraft Shelley Award. She was a 2018 RITA ® Finalist in the Romance Writers of America Contest.

To connect with Lauren, visit her at www.laurensmith-books.com

Scandal In The Snow

NADINE MILLARD

Prologue

Dearest Readers

It would appear as though the rumours are true.

Sir A. D's pockets are well and truly to let. While the beleaguered baron and his long-suffering wife Lady C have been desperately keeping up a charade of wealth, we have heard ever-increasing stories of servants being let go, and the family silver turning up in disreputable establishments in the wrong side of Town.

One can only assume that Sir A's penchant for gambling has finally led to his demise.

It has been said that the family will remain in London for Christmastide rather than returning to their comfortable country seat in Essex.

Can it be that the baron can no longer afford to run two homes? This writer certainly thinks so.

And one can only wonder as to what will become of the man's two daughters. Will their dowries survive this shocking change in circumstances? Will their names survive the humiliation? And will their mother ever be able to marry them off now?

With both ladies out, it would be prudent for Lady C to try to bring at least one gentleman to heel. And it's no secret that the eldest girl has caught the eye of the rather dashing and obscenely wealthy Lord F.

The man's reputation isn't exactly spotless, of course. And no self-respecting mama would want her daughter attached to a man whose penchant for opera singers, and dancers is legendary.

But then, one supposes, beggars cannot be choosers.

What's to become of them all?

As soon as we have an answer to these questions, so will you.

One

"This is a bad, nay, a terrible idea. I've told you that a hundred times," Olivia Darington hissed at her sister Jane as they hurried through the icy streets of London. Their satin slippers would be quite ruined by the time they arrived at Lord Fincham's townhouse. Not to mention what was left of their tattered reputations.

"And I told *you* that if you don't like it, you don't have to come. You weren't even invited in any case."

Olivia merely scowled at her irascible sibling. Though Jane may be two years older, she certainly wasn't two years wiser. If anything, she seemed to be getting ever more idiotic with age.

Bad enough that those nasty scandal sheets had dried up their social calendar faster than a drought in July. There was no need to add to the gossip by flitting about London with one of its most sought after bachelors.

Well, that was just fine.

If Jane wanted to flit and flirt with Lord Fincham then Olivia would be there to watch her. Judgementally.

What Jane even saw in the scoundrel Olivia didn't know. Perhaps he was conventionally handsome with his broad shoulders, and sable hair, distractingly green eyes, and chiselled chin. But he was also irascible and wicked and altogether dangerous to be around. Olivia knew this from experience. And so did Jane, come to that. Years spent growing up on a neighbouring if far more modest estate to the late earl's had taught Olivia that

453

Alexander Stratford was as pleasant as cow dung. But for some reason Jane seemed to have forgotten a childhood spent being tormented by the arrogant earl and his odious friends. Olivia would never forget.

Even now, all these years later, she could still feel the worms in her hair, the dirt in her boots, the spiders in her bed...

If she were inclined to being fair, she would admit that the earl and his circle had been among the very few people who hadn't turned their backs on the Daringtons when Papa's gambling had essentially had them unceremoniously dumped from the *ton*. But regardless of it being Christmastide, and therefore the season of good will, she *wasn't* inclined to be fair, and so her mood remained foul, and her nerves remained frayed. She would continue trying to get her sister to back out of this less than salubrious house party that the earl was hosting, no doubt for the very dregs of Society. People did like to mix with their own kind, after all.

"You've made your feelings about this party, and Alexander come to that, quite clear," Jane continued now. "And –"

"Alexander?" Olivia interrupted. "My, aren't we cosy?"

Jane rolled her eyes.

"We've been friends since childhood, Livvy."

"I think you'll find we've been *enemies* since childhood, Jane," she countered fiercely. "How can you forget the things he did? It took me almost two days to unstick my fingers from that teacup."

Olivia narrowed her eyes as a sound suspiciously like a laugh emanated from her older sister.

Why would Jane suddenly decide that Alexander Stratford was friend rather than foe?

It can only be that she's developed a tendre for the cad.

The sudden twist in her stomach at the idea of Jane and Lord Fincham forming an attachment to each other took Olivia by surprise.

It must be sisterly concern for Jane that had her feeling so – so uneasy about the idea.

After all, Jane's memory might have been befuddled by a pair of emerald eyes, but Olivia's certainly wouldn't be.

She needed to keep her focus. She needed to get Jane to forget this foolish endeavour to be friends with Fincham's set. To forget this troubling tendency to throw caution to the wind and risk her good name just because of a little mishap with father's finances. Well, a rather *large* mishap to be frank.

Yes, Jane needed to forget all this nonsense.

And Olivia needed to forget this odd feeling in her stomach when she thought of the earl and his eyes…

Jane came to a halt while Olivia was still having stern words with herself, and they both stared up at the imposing white stucco building before them.

The sisters were unlikely to know anyone here.

What little friends they had retained since father's embarrassing demise at the end of the Season when his debts were no longer secret had already retired to their country seats for the Yuletide.

For the first time in Olivia's memory, they hadn't received an invitation anywhere, not even for a dinner or a card evening at a country neighbour's house.

Both Mama and Jane had found that hard and humiliating enough. But it was when Papa had announced that they wouldn't return to their seat in Essex at all and would in fact remain in Town until he "set things right" that Mama had taken to her rooms and Jane had started to become rather wild.

Both were protesting their circumstances in their own ways, it seemed. And neither way was exactly helpful.

For the first few weeks, Olivia had tried to rally their spirits with talk of how magical London would be during Christmastide. But it was no use and eventually she'd given up entirely since all her efforts were now spent on acting as a nanny to her sister.

Her life had become utterly ridiculous. Thanks in no small part to Alexander Stratford.

Olivia cast a critical eye over the people sweeping towards the steps of the earl's townhouse.

Not quite the *demi monde* she feared but not much better. She didn't recognise most of the faces and the ones she did weren't exactly in the same circle of the Darington family. At least, they hadn't been until their fall from grace.

Olivia glanced toward her sister, noting Jane's flushed cheeks and sparkling eyes.

Well, she conceded wryly, *she* was falling from grace. Jane seemed to be leaping enthusiastically from it.

"Ready?" whispered Jane.

No, I most certainly am not *ready to see that blackguard Fincham again,* Olivia thought.

"Yes," was the only answer she gave.

It was one house party after all. How much could possibly happen in such a short space of time?

"DID YOU INVITE THE DELECTABLE DARINGTON GIRL?" Alexander scowled at Elliot's lascivious tone.

Yes, he'd invited Jane Darington. Elliot did mean Jane. He hadn't yet met the irritating little termagant, Olivia. And Alexander absolutely didn't want him to.

Loathe as he was to admit it, Alex knew that the description of delectable applied to Olivia Darington in spades. Something that annoyed the hell out of him, frankly. She should look like a withered old hag to match that personality of hers.

Granted, he hadn't seen her in years. She'd never been 'at home' when he'd made the obligatory house calls in deference to their parents' friendship and their being neighbours whilst at Fincham Hall. Not to him, in any case. And while Jane Darington had happily accepted every invitation thrown her way since Sir Alfred's disgrace, Olivia hadn't ventured outside the door of their townhouse. Not that Alexander had been watching out for her.

Of course, since the Darington's demise his mother had disassociated herself from the family faster than Alexander could blink. But that didn't surprise him. In the grand tradition of the *ton*, nobody cared about men's vices if the façade remained intact. Once they could all pretend not to know about gambling, whoring, and hell-raising in their glittering ballrooms they could do as they pleased.

"I did, as I said I would."

Alexander cast a glance around his own ballroom. It wouldn't be a crush. Most families of Quality had returned to the country. He remained because his mother had gotten it into her head to host a house party at Fincham and Alex could think of nothing worse than having single women thrown at him with gleeful abandon by his mother and her cohorts. Despite the countess's pleas, demands, and guilt trips, he'd merrily waved her off to spend her party explaining his absence from his own home.

In truth, he didn't mind spending some time in Town this Christmastide though it wasn't his favourite place to live. He liked his other homes. Preferred Fincham Hall to the rest. Even though the neighbours were intensely annoying. Well, one neighbour, he conceded.

Granted, the last time he'd seen Olivia Darington he hadn't exactly acted the gentleman. But in his defence, the bloody chit had started it! Bad enough she'd attacked him with snowballs. But snowballs with rocks in where more vicious than necessary to his way of thinking. Gluing her teacup had been childish though. He knew that.

London with Elliot would be nice and relaxing. Or should have been if not for this blasted ball.

The last thing he wanted was a party. He was only throwing the damned thing because he'd needed an excuse to stay in Town to stop his mother whittering on at him. And when he'd mentioned it to his sociable friend, Elliot had been unsurprisingly enthusiastic.

As the second son of a notable marquis, Elliot St. Clare rarely if ever turned down a party of any kind.

He was rich and handsome, with entrée into the best of Society because of his family name, and no expectations on his shoulders. He had nothing to do *but* attend parties.

Alex didn't usually mind them too much, either. And mercifully, his mother's ilk had departed Town already. Those who remained where by and large less staid and therefore, more fun.

Plus, Jane Darington had grown to rely on him for any sort of social life. And much as he despised the hellion she was related to, he found that he'd warmed to the more genteel, less fiery Jane.

Judging by Elliot's leer, he had too. But while Alex's affection was that of a sibling, Elliot's was very much not.

And while Jane Darington was none of his business, Alexander felt compelled towards protecting the chit.

"Just behave yourself, St. Clare. The girl has had a tough time of it. She might be – vulnerable."

What he meant of course was that she would be easily seduced by the compliments of a man who could drag her from the genteel poverty she so obviously struggled with.

"Vulnerable? Why, that's my favourite kind of lady."

Alexander opened his mouth to threaten bodily harm but a small furore at the entrance to the ballroom caught his attention.

Sure enough, there was a new round of people approaching.

Alex watched Elliot through narrow eyes and was about to issue another warning.

Half a second later, the small crowed at the door parted and suddenly, the most breath-taking woman he'd ever seen stepped into his view.

Alexander's heart just about stopped beating in his chest.

That couldn't be Olivia Darington, could it? He quickly scanned the other people who'd entered. That was Jane taller, and coolly beautiful. And the similarity between the ladies was unmistakeable...

He looked again.

The vision that walked through the door had stunning sable hair swept away from the most breathtakingly beautiful face he'd ever seen.

He remembered Olivia Darington from three years ago. She'd been a pretty thing, even if he had felt at the time that the devil himself had spawned her. It was doubtful that time had changed her personality, but good God, time had been very kind to her looks.

Alex's mouth went dry and his heart, strangely, began to pound.

What the hell was wrong with him? He'd never been so affected by the mere sight of a lady. Especially one he despised.

He suddenly thought back to three years ago, when he'd been quite madly tempted to kiss her. He'd dragged her out to the garden of her father's modest estate to get to the bottom of her recent machination. When he'd gone to the village that morning, he had been besieged by Miss Sophie Fogers, the brashest, loudest, giddiest, and stupidest woman in the county. Alexander, along with every other man in the vicinity, had been avoiding the girl since she'd been in long skirts. He quite literally hadn't been able to walk from one place to the next without her squealing and throwing herself at him. She'd pretended to faint, so he'd catch her outside the apothecary's, trip outside the bakery and tumble headfirst into parts of him he wanted to remain very much untouched by any part of Sophie Fogers and been forward enough to almost bring him to blush. He'd always garnered plenty of female attention being titled, wealthy, and, he thought, rather smugly, not too bad to look at. But this! This had been something else.

It had only been when he'd finally managed to get inside the local inn that he'd gotten to the bottom of it. That bloody doe-eyed nuisance Olivia Darington had taken out an advertisement in the local newspaper, claiming that Alexander was madly in love with Sophie Fogers but far too shy to go about courting her and was hoping that she would bold enough to make the first approach.

Alexander had known straight away that it was Olivia. It had her written all over it. She was smarter and viler than her sister. And took their enmity far more seriously. Where Jane had always been happy to carry out simple tricks that were mostly harmless and had an immediate impact, Olivia's schemes were always well-planned manipulations and war strategies, the likes of which Nelson himself would be proud.

While the sympathetic innkeeper had been helping Alexander to make his escape through a back door of the inn, Alex had been planning dastardly ways to get back at the chit.

Arriving home on horseback, he'd seen her sitting on a bench that bordered his estate, quite alone which had suited Alex just fine. He'd dragged the impertinent hoyden off to a more private spot deep in the hedgerows where he'd delivered a furious set down without having to control his temper or his volume. The two had been toe to toe, arguing at very nearly the top of their lungs. Alex had been, admittedly, rather insulting about the girl; she had been more so, claiming that it wasn't her fault the village idiot seemed to have taken a liking to him. It was when she'd said that she should perhaps set up a charity of sorts, to help poor Sophie and other women cure themselves of their lack of taste in men that the last of his control had slipped.

To this day, Alexander had no idea what had possessed him to grab the infuriating woman and pull her toward him. In the split second before his sanity had returned, he'd gazed into those pretty brown eyes and lost all sense. Even now, every so often, most especially in the still, dark night, Alex remembered the feel of her soft, slender body against his own. He remembered the gasp of surprise. He remembered the scent of honeysuckle that reminded him of her to this day. Most of all, he remembered how, after her initial resistance, she'd melted against him as though she belonged wrapped in his arms and turned her face towards his.

Unfortunately, he also remembered the moment she'd reared back and smacked his face, the sound reverberating around the quiet gardens...

The sound of a shout of laughter brought Alexander crashing back to the present and to the fact that he was staring at the girl, practically drooling where he stood. Worse still, his friend was doing the same.

Alex darted a look at Elliot, wondering if his friend would be fooled into thinking Olivia Darington was anything other than an utter shrew. And he didn't like what he saw. Elliot's eyes were on stalks. And it shouldn't surprise Alexander to see the effect Olivia had on the other man. It *didn't* surprise him. But it damn well bothered him.

Alexander had the sudden urge to plant a facer on his friend's jaw, or at least cover the other man's eyes. Which was nonsensical. Why should he care who admired her? Why should he care that she was slowly, torturously, removing a deep green, velvet cloak, revealing smooth, supple skin, a delicate décolletage, and curves to make a man weep.

All right. That was enough. Alexander took a subtle step in front of Elliot, blocking the other man's view.

He'd clearly been more than a little obvious since Elliot's chuckle sounded gratingly behind him. Alexander turned to scowl at him.

"Looks like you're in a spot of trouble my friend," Elliot smirked causing Alex's temper to rise.

"Do be quiet, St. Clare," he responded darkly, but his eyes never left the door where Olivia Darington stood oblivious to him and the confusion she had caused.

Two

OLIVIA'S TEMPER WAS SOARING, and she hadn't even set eyes on the blasted Fincham lout yet. She'd just been hearing Jane's tale of her encounter with the Elliot character and his scandalous words to her. How dare Mr. St. Clare make her sister feel like some sort of lightskirt? Though Jane was worryingly unoffended.

"He told me I was the most beautiful creature he'd ever seen. He told me he wants to kiss me, Livvy. How wonderfully romantic!"

Olivia had missed the exchange since she'd been hiding in a corner trying to avoid Alexander Stratford.

It did seem a bit of a waste of her best ivory gown. She had taken an age to pick it. She wanted to look her absolute best so that she was fully prepared to meet Lord Fincham again. Not that she cared what he thought of her, of course. Why should she?

And speaking of Fincham, Olivia had yet to set eyes on the man.

She had asked if her sister if she had seen the man when Jane had finally come hurrying over to find her, eyes flashing, cheeks flushed. But her Jane's head had been so filled with this St. Clare character that there hadn't been any mention of Fincham.

Then she'd had to sit tight while Jane rabbited on about the scandalous Elliot St. Clare and romanticised the fact that he was clearly a rake of the highest order. Jane had been adamant that they were lucky to be included in tonight's event and would be the epitome sophisticated young ladies for the duration. Olivia heartily disagreed. They would rise above old childhood foolishness, Jane had demanded, and thank Lord Fincham profusely for the honour of the invitation.

The only thing Olivia wanted to rise above was her hand over her head so she could deal out another slap or two to the arrogant earl's face.

"I am not," Olivia responded hotly, "calling him 'my lord' and bowing and scraping at him. Lord only knows what he'll do with that kind of ego elevation."

"I understand your – ah – issues with the earl, Livvy. But we are ladies with little to no prospects. And this is an opportunity. We mustn't waste it by holding on to childish grudges." Jane folded her hands on her lap in that annoyingly ladylike way of hers.

And Olivia felt suddenly weary of the whole thing. She'd been living on nervous adrenaline all day, awaiting the moment of confrontation with Alexander Stratford, and the horrible man hadn't even had the decency to turn up.

"You are far too trusting of that St. Clare fellow, Jane. You really should be careful," she said tiredly. She wanted to go home. Yet she couldn't in good conscience leave Jane alone. And so, she was stuck in this blasted house until Jane agreed to leave.

At that moment, Mr. St. Clare appeared at the sisters' side. Jane made introductions, and Olivia tried not to scowl too much as she eyed the man's lecherous countenance.

What on earth did Jane see in the man? He was quite revolting as far as Olivia was concerned.

Handsome enough, perhaps. But his blonde hair was a little too perfect, his blue eyes a little too cold.

Olivia did her best to supress a shudder as he bent over her hand.

She answered all his chit-chat with rigid stoicism and then watched in consternation as he swept Jane away with a hand scandalously low on her waist.

Glancing around the ballroom, Olivia realised that she didn't know a single person in attendance. And Jane had left her quite alone. Judging from some of the leers pointed in her direction, she was attracting attention unwanted attention standing here all alone. It would be safer elsewhere, Olivia decided. And so, sneaking away from the party, she wandered aimlessly around the darkened hallways of the house, eventually finding her way to the darkened conservatory.

The conservatory was blissfully quiet but unfortunately it wasn't the best choice of rooms, given the biting cold outside.

Shivering, Olivia went to peruse the shelves of potted plants; most of them sadly empty at this time of year. But some were filled with shrubs and winter flowers, and they gave the room a pleasant, fresh smell.

Much as she tried to stop it, Olivia couldn't prevent her mind from wandering back again.

She had come to her own conservatory all those years ago after that confusing moment with Alexander Stratford in her father's garden. She had been furious; with him for daring to act as though he would kiss her and with herself for wanting it so much. What the blazes was wrong with her? He had been the enemy, and she had turned to a shameless mess in his strong arms. Thankfully some tiny semblance of common sense had slipped through the unexpected haze of desire and saved her from Lord Fincham. Nay, from herself.

Her embarrassment had been acute as had been her confusion. Usually, she would have gone straight to Jane to discuss such an event. But *usually* she wouldn't have allowed herself to be touched by the beast, let alone pressed so wantonly against him! She'd almost been kissed by him! By the arrogant, cocky, Alexander Stratford.

As time had gone on, however, and she had replayed that almost kiss over and over in her mind, she began to naïvely think that perhaps Alexander cared for her. Hard as it was to believe, there was no way he could have held her like that if he hadn't wanted to, was there?

So it was, that in the space of thirty minutes, Olivia had managed to convince herself that Alexander Stratford had been secretly, desperately in love with her all this time, and *that* was why he'd put worms in her bedchamber and rotting kippers in her bed. The poor soul hadn't had any outlet for his feelings.

And, if she were being honest with herself only, she could admit that as much as she hated him, there was a small but persistent part of her that didn't hate him at all... that felt quite the opposite.

Most of the gentlemen of her acquaintance were far too young and immature. Or far too intense and inappropriate. Not one of them held even a flicker of interest for her.

But Alexander; Alexander was always so laid back, so relaxed about things. He had a charming manner, a wicked smile, and a penchant for never really taking anything seriously. That had been a heady combination to a young lady in the first flushes of adulthood.

Olivia looked around the conservatory, seeing it as her own had been that day. Hot and humid and filled to bursting with exotic flowers, their colours and smells combining to make her head spin.

Stupidly, she had allowed her mind to wander so far that she could practically hear church bells ring as she and Alexander walked down the aisle, her in a confection of satin and lace, him looking devilishly handsome in wedding clothes fit for a king.

A sudden noise behind her brought Olivia back to the present day, and she whirled round to see the source.

Oh, how she was brought back down to earth with a bang.

As though her memories had conjured him up, there stood Alexander Stratford in all his conceited, handsome glory.

Olivia was horrified at the jolt of lust she felt upon seeing him. Had she learned nothing in the past few years?

It had been three years; here was her chance to show him how sophisticated and singularly unaffected she was by him.

"What are you doing here?" she blurted out, sounding petulant and very much unsophisticated.

"I live here," he drawled in response, and Olivia ruthlessly pushed away her reaction to his mellifluous voice.

"Here in the conservatory?" she snapped back. "Quite a tumble from lord of the manor."

He smirked in response.

"I see time has not mellowed the viper, though it has improved you drastically in other areas."

His heated gaze travelled leisurely down her body and back up making her feel as though she were slowly catching fire. She didn't know whether to slap him or throw herself at him.

"I would thank you for the compliment, but since it's you, I can only assume there was an insult in there somewhere."

This time his smile was a full blown grin, and Olivia almost staggered back at the impact.

The dratted man! He had no business making her stagger.

"If you must know, I followed you in here," he spoke now, stepping closer to her, his voice quiet and deep and wicked.

"How could you have followed me in here? Nobody knew I was even coming in here, and you weren't at your own ball."

"I was at the ball. And I have been watching you all evening."

Olivia gulped.

If anyone else had said such a thing she probably would have worried for her life. But as awful as Alexander had been over the years, she'd never actually feared him. Rather than make her afraid, therefore, his words made her positively combust.

Stop it, Olivia, she scolded herself, *remember how he has tormented you.*

Deciding to ignore his words, because really, what sort of answer could she give to that, she focused instead on the reasons for his shadowing her.

"Why did you follow me?" she demanded.

"Perhaps I'm hoping for a repeat of the last time we were alone."

His words, spoken so softly, had the effect of rendering Olivia entirely speechless. And that was a first.

"Come now, Olivia, do not pretend you have forgotten." He smirked wickedly, stepping closer to her.

"I-I don't know what you mean," she stuttered, desperately wanting to back away from him but refusing to give him the satisfaction.

"Oh, you don't?" He quirked a brow and Olivia had the ridiculous urge to reach up and run her finger along it. She, who had never been particularly attached to eyebrows in her life.

"No," she said forcefully, hoping to remind herself, as well as he, that they were sworn enemies, and this was highly inappropriate.

"Hmm. I must admit to a rather bruised ego," he said with a rueful grin that was much more endearing than it had a right to be. "Perhaps I should pick up where I left off."

Yes, her body cried out.

"No," her mercifully more logical mouth said. "You should not."

Olivia thought she saw a flash of disappointment in his jade-green eyes but that was madness of course.

He stepped back, and she schooled her features not to show the disappointment she felt.

"What do you really want?" she asked, desperation tingeing her tone now. Her reaction to him was wildly out of control.

She wanted to run away from him, gather her scattered wits, and set about finding Jane and removing her from that lout, Mr. St. Clare.

Biting her lip, she looked up at him and waited for his answer. Her question seemed to take him aback slightly. His eyes widened infinitesimally, before his brow furrowed.

"I'm starting to think I have no idea," he said roughly.

And once again, Olivia was speechless.

WHAT THE HELL WAS WRONG WITH HIM?

Alexander hadn't been lying when he'd told the delectable Olivia Darington that he'd been watching her all evening.

In fact, he'd taken rather a lot of ribbing from his neglected guests because of it.

And yet, he hadn't been able to stop himself.

He'd been held in rapt fascination by the hints of red in her hair when she stood just so in the nearby candlelight, by the furious flush upon her cheek as she spoke to her sister, by the heart-wrenching, huge brown eyes as they stared with some bemusement as Elliot fawned over her. Something that Alexander was less than happy about.

Mostly, he was base enough to admit, he'd been held captive by the sway of her hips as she walked, the curve of her lips as she spoke, the way her dress clung, then swirled away from her body, causing him no small amount of discomfort.

Of course he'd watched her. He'd be a fool not to.

She was silently waiting for him to actually tell her what he was doing here, so he forced himself to concentrate.

In his own defence, he had had genuine reasons for following her in here. He'd noticed that Jane Darington was becoming dangerously besotted by Elliot. And he wasn't remotely convinced that Elliot's intentions towards the girl were honourable. He didn't want Jane hurt by Elliot. And, he realised with a start, he didn't want Olivia's family hurt by the actions of his friend.

He didn't want Olivia hurt by anything.

And that errant and insane thought was enough to scare some sense into him.

It was time to bring this encounter to a close lest he do something idiotic, like kiss her witless or, worse yet, ask her why she hadn't been as tempted by that first encounter as he had been.

"I think it's fair to say that after years of enmity between us, a truce is not something you would be agreeable to."

Alexander, for one mad moment, wished for her to deny his words, to say she wanted nothing more than to end the feud. Perhaps to even begin a relationship which would be the exact opposite of a feud...

Her unladylike snort was all the answer he needed, however.

"So then, you wouldn't be thrilled to learn of my older friend's sudden enchantment with your sister?"

He watched as a frown creased her brow, her chocolate eyes snapping.

"Enchantment?" she scoffed. "Hardly. The great big oaf will cause her utter ruin given half the chance. Half a chance he will *not* get if I have anything to do with it. And you can tell him from me," She stepped forward, her finger prodding his chest, "that if he so much as looks at my sister again in a manner that she finds anything less than respectful, I shall—"

"You shall what?" Alexander interrupted, his temper flaring. "You shall screech at him like a common fishwife?"

Her jaw dropped open at his words and then snapped shut. Alexander could actually hear her teeth grinding together.

"How dare you?" she finally gasped, her outrage doing terribly distracting things to the low-cut bodice of her satin gown.

"I dare because your foolish sister is no less interested in whatever this is between them than St. Clare is, only she doesn't know what she's doing," he snapped. "Which is exactly why I wanted to talk to you. I knew he had an interest. But I'm beginning to think that Jane is getting in over her head."

He watched emotions dash across her expressive face while some internal battle or other raged. Finally, after what seemed like an eternity, she closed her eyes, took a deep breath, and then levelled her gaze at him.

"Alright. What is it you want to talk about then?"

Alexander gritted his teeth at her imperious tone but made no comment.

They'd been at this to-ing and fro-ing long enough as it was.

"It's fairly obvious that Elliot has taken a shine to your sister," Alexander started. The hypocrisy of his words did not escape his notice. Elliot's 'shine' to Jane couldn't have been any less than his own to Olivia this evening. Only Elliot's made more sense because the object of *his* interest didn't have the charm of a spitting, feral cat as Olivia Darington did.

"Are you deaf?" she interrupted, raising his hackles yet again. "Did you not hear me when I said he wouldn't - ?"

"I heard you," Alexander interrupted through clenched teeth. "But as shocking as it is, he hasn't stopped bloody watching the chit all night and that presents a problem."

"You have just admitted to staring at me all evening, Alexander. Why should Jane and Mr. St. Clare be cause for concern?"

Well, she had him there. Alexander steeled himself against the wave of pleasure at hearing his name on her lips. Her distractingly plump lips, one of which she was currently nibbling.

"Because," he croaked. "Because I have the good sense not to do anything. Elliot, well I'm not so sure about him. I don't even know if he possesses any good sense."

She looked mightily affronted at his words. But really, did the little shrew think he would be pleased about this inexplicable desire he had for her?

"Pity, then, that you didn't possess the same good sense three years ago when you accosted me in my father's garden," she answered with a frown he tried not to find adorable.

The reminder of their proximity, of his reaction to her, the memory of her soft, supple body pressed so firmly against his own, was enough to make Alexander want to run from the danger of her.

"Olivia." He tried for his most reasonable tone. "Do you want your sister bedded by my friend?"

Her gasp of horror was answer enough.

He knew he shouldn't use such coarse language around her. But he couldn't help it. She brought out something base and animalistic in him.

Best not to think along those lines when discussing the subject of tupping with her. The sudden discomfort in his breeches was proof of that.

"I'll take your silence as a no. Now, unless you want Jane ruined entirely, you're going to have to help me do something about it."

He watched as yet again as myriad emotions raced across her face.

It really was a lovely face.

She didn't deserve it, the little harpy.

"Fine," she eventually bit out, bringing his thoughts back to the problem at hand. "I shall help you. What do we do?"

Three

OLIVIA ROSE EXHAUSTED FROM a distinct lack of sleep the night before.

Why had she allowed Alexander Stratford to bother her so, when she had promised herself that it wouldn't happen?

He was an arrogant cad, but he was so handsome. She had known, even flirted with plenty of handsome men. Well, some. Well, one. But he hadn't compared to Alexander, unfortunately. Worse still, he didn't seem to possess whatever magical powers Alexander did that drew her in.

Until he'd almost kissed her that fateful day, Olivia had carried a healthy dose of dislike for the man.

But that one moment of closeness had changed more than she liked to admit, even to herself.

Now the hatred she felt for him was based on the humiliation she had felt upon overhearing that conversation he'd had with his mother afterwards.

A knock on the door heralding the arrival of the one upstairs maid Papa had retained distracted Olivia from her dour musings, but whilst Ellie set about dressing her hair with a pink ribbon to match the long sleeved, pale pink muslin she wore, Olivia couldn't help but worry about Alexander's words the previous night.

Could it really be that Jane was in danger from Mr. St. Clare?

Impossible. Jane might be a little infatuated, but she wasn't so stupid as to get herself completely ruined, was she? A few months ago, Olivia would have said not. But father's gambling had made Jane reckless. Still naïve however, wherein lay the danger. Alexander had promised to keep an eye on his friend but had warned that it would be far too easy for the cad to seduce Jane should he really put his mind to it. Jane knew better though. She had to. She would never allow herself to become embroiled in anything so damning.

Yet, she appeared to be blinded when it came to Mr. St. Clare. Olivia had gotten the measure of him from the off. But Jane – Jane seemed to think there was a chance for real affection between them.

It wasn't long before Ellie had pulled Olivia's hair into a creation of twists and curls that Olivia had paid no attention to. Good or bad, it would do. She hadn't time to be worrying about such things, in any case. She needed to ascertain whether or not Jane was in danger.

There was no one in Jane's room when Olivia rushed in there however, so she could only assume that her sister had already gone to break her fast. Unusual in and of itself. Jane never surfaced before noon if she could help it. Especially on a cold, grey December day.

Stepping back into the hallway, Olivia collided with the family's ageing and long serving butler.

"My apologies, Miss," the old butler wheezed, the silver tray in his hands wobbling alarmingly.

"No apology necessary, Sterling, it was my mistake," Olivia answered with a smile, reaching out and steadying the tray.

"The Earl of Fincham sent a footman this morning Miss and asked that I deliver invitations to you personally."

Olivia took the proffered envelope from Sterling with her thanks, ignoring the old man's frown of disapproval then dashed off in the direction of the breakfast room.

She tore open the envelope. Fincham should know better than to send her invitations! But if it would help Jane, then she shouldn't complain. And while Sterling might not approve, he was fiercely loyal and would never spread gossip about Olivia.

Meet me at Hyde Park, by the tree where you pushed me into the Serpentine. I'm sure you remember the scene of your crime. I'll be there at eight.

Don't be difficult about it. Tis for your sister's sake. We might have a problem. A.

Olivia's temper boiled over at the imperious words and if the dratted man had been standing in front of her, she would have done bodily harm to the oaf. As it was, she scrunched up the paper and threw it at the wall with a shriek of annoyance.

He was going to drive her to Bedlam. Or Newgate if she murdered him which felt like a distinct possibility.

She would ask Jane to come with her, not least because she couldn't very well go meeting a man alone in the middle of Hyde Park.

Olivia glanced out the window at the dull, grey day. It looked freezing out. Frost still coated the roads and rooftops. Hmm. It was unlikely that anyone else would be mad enough to walk in such weather. And so close to the dinner hour. But needs must. And she wasn't going to risk being alone with Alexander Stratford.

Besides it would give them a chance to talk since Jane had been suspiciously quiet in the carriage that Lord Fincham had insisted the ladies take last night to return home. Jane had thanked him profusely. Olivia grudgingly.

If Jane agreed to come with her this evening, she would be able to determine if Alexander's concerns were legitimate or just another way for the man to cause Olivia trouble. And it wasn't as though the sisters had invitations to anywhere.

Bursting into the dining room, Olivia found Jane sitting at the table, as she had assumed.

"Jane, I wondered if – what's that?"

Was that a blush?

Olivia felt a little as though the wind had been taken out of her sails as she watched Jane hastily fold a letter of her own, a furious blush staining her cheeks.

Had she received her own missive from Alexander? The thought made Olivia's stomach twist painfully.

Last night she'd wondered if Jane was developing feelings for the earl. But when she'd seen her sister with the lascivious Mr. St. Clare she'd assumed that's where Jane's interest lay.

Was Jane interested in Lord Fincham? Was – Olivia had to swallow a sudden lump – was Alexander Stratford interested in pursuing Jane? Was that why he was so insistent on keeping her from St. Clare?

"What is it, Livvy?"

"Er – I wondered if you' like to join me for a walk this evening in Hyde Park? I-I thought a stroll in the cold night air would be refreshing," Olivia managed to mumble.

"A walk? At night? In Hyde Park?"

Jane's scepticism was understandable.

"Er, yes?" Olivia answered feebly. "Why not?"

Jane frowned at her for a moment before her expression cleared. "Well, I can't this evening, Livvy. I – I need to – to, um, write to an old acquaintance."

Olivia's stomach churned once more.

Jane was a terrible liar.

"Writing to an old acquaintance? Surely that can wait!"

"It can't. I've put it off for far too long. Just take Ellie with you. I won't be needing her services. If you'll excuse me."

Olivia kept her mouth firmly shut as she watched Jane stand and hurriedly leave the room.

She lifted the cup of coffee that had been poured for her when she'd entered the room. Though she was loathe to admit it, Alexander was right. Something needed to be done.

Now she just needed to figure out if he was part of the problem.

"ARE YOU OUT OF YOUR MIND?" ALEXANDER ASKED, MAKING sure his tone reflected his outrage.

He was worried about Jane. Not because he wanted to protect Olivia from gossip and upset. Of course not that. She didn't want his protection and he didn't want to give it.

He didn't.

But Scandal Lane was no place for an innocent lady and Elliot knew that.

The place had earned its moniker because it was notorious for secret assignations and debauchery among the *ton*. Many a married lady had engaged in illicit affairs there, many a gentleman had met a mistress, an opera singer, a dancer – and many a foolish young lady had met her demise.

Elliot merely grinned and shrugged his shoulders in response.

"What do you think you're playing at?"

"I'm not *playing* at anything. Not yet anyway," Elliot grinned, every inch the rake.

"Please, spare me the details of what you do when you're alone with a woman."

"Why should I? You could pick up some tips."

Alexander snorted.

"The day I need tips from you on what to do with a woman, is the day hell freezes over."

Elliot didn't respond with a witty rejoinder the way Alexander expected him to. He watched Elliot closely.

Something was… off.

And he suspected it had a lot to do with the innocent Jane Darington.

"Elliot," Alexander began hesitantly, not entirely sure how to broach the subject. "You're starting to seem – almost obsessive about the lady. Like your interest lies in something other than mere trifle."

Alexander watched a flash of something dark flare in his friend's eyes before Elliot schooled his features into impassivity once more.

"You're wrong," he said softly, and his tone told Alexander more than anything else that he was most definitely not wrong.

Damn it all to Hades. This was a bloody disaster.

Olivia would be fuming when she found out that Elliot had seriously dishonourable intentions toward Jane Darington.

Alexander groaned aloud and shook his head, knowing that somehow the little nuisance would find a way to lay the blame at his feet. He'd introduced them, after all.

"Just make sure that you don't do anything to ruin the girl, St. Clare. Because -."

"Oh, calm down Alexander. You are becoming hysterical." Elliot was enjoying this more than he should.

Alexander snatched the tumbler of brandy that Elliot held out to him and downed the contents in one gulp.

"You're asking me to turn a blind eye while you seduce an old friend, St. Clare. There's only so much I'll tolerate."

Elliot's smile widened.

"Come now, what's brought on this hero complex, old friend? I was rather thinking that you could keep the girl's watchful sister occupied."

Alexander managed a strangled sound of protest but not much else.

"You're not going to try and make me believe it will be a hardship? A whole Christmas season of moonlight, darkened corners, nobody around to witness your actions?" Elliot asked cajolingly. "I've seen your interest in her, Alexander. The way you watched her last night. You may as well have a sign painted."

Alexander suppressed a shudder.

"Usually, I wouldn't hesitate to agree with you wholeheartedly, Elliot. But the lady we're talking about is Olivia Darington. Moonlight, darkened corners and no witnesses is not only a perfect setting for seductions..." Alexander swallowed noisily, "...it's also perfect for a murder."

Scowling at Elliot's raucous laughter following his statement, Alexander turned his back to look out of the window that overlooked the gardens. And stopped dead.

Was that Olivia?

He squinted and stepped closer to the window.

Sure enough, there were her lustrous curls bobbing up from the bushes.

What on earth was she doing?

He watched in amused captivation as she spied him standing by the window and raised a hand to beckon him outside.

"What has caught your attention?" Elliot asked, stepping over to stand at Alexander's shoulder.

Alexander watched as Olivia's eyes widened a split second before her head disappeared once more. He could assume, then, that she didn't want his friend knowing she was out there.

Biting back a grin, he turned to Elliot to make his excuses.

"Nothing, I just fancy a walk."

Elliot's eyebrow rose in disbelief.

"You? Walk?"

"Yes, me walk," Alexander huffed. "It's not that bloody unusual."

Elliot frowned but thankfully didn't question him any further, and Alexander swept from the room and dashed toward the garden.

Just what was the little hoyden up to now?

"WHAT TOOK YOU SO LONG?" OLIVIA SNAPPED MORE SHARPLY than she intended. She'd been trying to get Alexander's attention for an age, watching furtively from the bushes like a thief in the night, not to mention getting tangled in twigs and branches.

"A thousand apologies, my lady," he responded sarcastically, "but I couldn't very well announce to Elliot that there was a young woman desperately awaiting me in the bushes, could I?"

Olivia's temper flared at his tone.

"How nice for you, to finally have a woman actually *want* your attention," she said sweetly.

His answering grin could have melted the frost surrounding them and Olivia suddenly felt unaccountably warm.

"Believe me, sweetheart," he said softly, "I've never had a problem with women not wanting me."

The arrogant swine.

This ridiculous conversation had gone on long enough.

"Much as I enjoy tales of your exploits whilst stuck in your shrubberies, I would rather speak plainly, farther away from the house," she bit out snippily, refusing to acknowledge his inappropriate and wildly flirtatious comment. "And I'm not your sweetheart."

He seemed to know he'd affected her however, as he chuckled softly before offering Olivia his arm.

Olivia placed her hand lightly on his bottle green superfine and fought valiantly to suppress the shiver of awareness that coursed through her body.

Gracious. This wouldn't do. The last thing the man by her side and his ego needed was to be made aware of her reaction to him.

They walked in silence until they reached the walled garden beyond the shrubs and flowers.

This would afford them privacy to talk. *Just* talk.

"So." Alexander was the first to break the silence. "Why were you watching me from the bushes?" he asked casually.

Immediately, Olivia's teeth were set on edge.

"I was not 'watching' you," she responded hotly. "I was trying to get your attention to discuss *your* idea about the problem."

"Hmm and you were so desperate to see me again you simply couldn't wait until tonight. I'm flattered. So, does that mean that you admit that your sister is a problem?"

Olivia dug in her heels, forcing him to stop walking and spun to face him, snatching back her hand.

"'Tis ·you and your odious friend who are the problem, Fincham. *Not* my sister. And the only person desperate here is you. Just what are you about sending secret missives to Jane?"

His face was a picture of confusion.

"I saw her hide it," she continued, ignoring the ridiculous sting of hurt. "And I don't know what you're about, sending us *both* letters and – and trying to throw me off your scent by pretending she's in danger from that St. Clare fellow. But if you think to distract me while you – while you –"

Olivia trailed off, suddenly feeling embarrassed.

She could hardly just blurt out such things with Alexander Stratford.

"While I what?" he pressed, grinning. He knew, the blighter. He knew she was discomfited.

"While you seduce her into engaging in activities entirely inappropriate for a single man and woman to engage in," she finally answered, quoting directly from the lectures of comportment her mother had made her attend after the almost-drowning-him-in-the-Serpentine incident.

Alexander looked at her in surprise for a moment before throwing back his head and bursting into laughter.

Olivia positively refused to let herself dwell on the strength of the muscles in his throat, or the husky sound of his laugh, and chose instead to be furious at his laughing at her.

"Where did you hear such a thing?" he asked, still grinning widely.

"I don't know what you mean?" She sniffed.

He raised a brow and bent slightly to look directly into her eyes.

"There is no way such virtuous drivel came from the

hoydenish Olivia Darington," he said softly.

Blast the man. He was right, of course.

"I am a grown woman, Alexander," she spat, not noticing she'd slipped and used his Christian name. "Not a little girl any longer. And I know, 'how to conduct myself in a manner befitting a young lady of good breeding,'" she quoted again before coming back to her point. "As does Jane. And you and your debauched friend — well, you are trying to make her conduct herself in a manner absolutely *not* befitting a young lady of good breeding."

He grinned again at her convoluted sentence.

"I'm not interested in anything to do with your sister Olivia, save keeping her safe. Besides, I shouldn't worry too much if I were you. After all, our encounter in the gardens all those years ago didn't steer you down a path of destruction, did it?"

The mention of that day seemed to suck all the air straight from Olivia's body.

Why had he brought that up? She wasn't prepared to speak of such things, especially with him.

She glanced up into his distractingly green eyes and was immediately irritated by the smug, knowing look in them.

The man had an ego the size of Westminster.

It was about time someone deflated it a little.

Giving her best, most believable innocent expression, she answered as sweetly as she could.

"I hardly think one, insignificant, thoroughly forgettable embrace would be enough to send me down a path of destruction," she said with faux innocence. "Why, nothing even happened for heaven's sake."

Later, Olivia would wonder how she hadn't noticed the sudden, dangerous glint in his jade eyes. She would wonder why his growl of frustration hadn't been warning enough of his intentions. But she had paid no attention to these things, and so, when he suddenly reached out and grabbed her in his arms, pulling her body against his, she had been taken completely unawares.

As his lips had descended toward her own, his whispered words sent shivers down the length of her spine.

"Perhaps it's time something *did* happen," he said before crushing her lips beneath his own.

Four

ALEXANDER KNEW THAT THE second he felt Olivia's lips beneath his was in far more trouble than he had ever been before in his life.

He felt every one of her emotions, even while his lips were pressed against her own. He felt her gasp of shock, following by her heavenly capitulation as her fingers moved to wind in his hair, pulling him closer still.

He almost combusted when her tongue tentatively reached out and mirrored the movement of his own.

Had he been in any sort of control over himself, Alexander would have wondered what the hell he was doing kissing the girl senseless in his garden.

But the second he'd tasted her, all thoughts, coherent or otherwise, were swept away by the tide of passion he was currently drowning in.

Had anything ever felt so perfect?

Damn but the girl had a way of getting under his skin. He'd kissed her out of sheer frustration. She got under his skin like no other. And the fact that he'd been walking around in a permanent state of lust since he'd clapped eyes on her again didn't help to temper his actions.

Something was shifting between them. Subtly changing. Becoming more than a battle of wills. More even than an intense, fiery attraction.

Alexander was starting to feel perilously close to caring about the girl.

Caring far, far more than he should.

This thought finally brought Alexander crashing back to the reality of the situation they were in. Reluctantly, he pulled his lips from hers, grasping her shoulders and gently pushing her from him.

Olivia gazed up at him, her eyes glazed with passion, a look of wonder in them, and Alexander felt his heart stutter at that look.

"Damn," he whispered softly. He had no clue how to deal with this.

To his surprise, she smiled ruefully.

"My sentiments exactly."

Alexander cleared his throat, suddenly as nervous as a green lad his first time with a lady.

"Yes, well, we — we cannot stand about all day doing — well, doing, or not doing something. Or nothing. Wait, what?"

Olivia was staring at him as though he had run mad, which he very probably had.

He was tying himself into knots, stammering nonsensical gibberish. And all because his blood had travelled considerably farther south than his brain.

"Alexander, what exactly are you talking about," she snapped impatiently.

Her acerbic tone and its familiarity served to bring him back to himself somewhat.

He heaved a sigh, got his scrambled thoughts into some sort of order, and then, finally, was able to answer with equanimity.

"You drive me to bloody distraction, Olivia Darington. More than anyone I've ever met. And you, a mere slip of a girl."

Olivia's mouth dropped open, and Alexander could have kicked himself. Why had he gone and confessed such a thing?

"But that is neither here nor there," he hurried on before she issued what would no doubt be a caustic rejoinder. "Now, why don't you finally tell me what you wanted me for?"

Olivia didn't answer for some time, choosing instead to gaze at him as though he'd grown another head. He couldn't blame her really.

Finally, after what seemed like an age, she shook her head

slightly, and he noted the glint of battle sparkle in her chocolate-brown eyes.

They really where beautiful, those eyes. She didn't deserve them. He'd never paid that much attention to them before, but he was captivated by them now. Of course, they had been more beautiful when they'd been rendered blank by his ministrations but—

"Fincham!"

The screech of his name brought him back to earth with a thud. Oh right, she'd been speaking.

"Are you quite alright?" she demanded, hissing out a frustrated breath. "Because if discussing strategy is a little beyond your mental capabilities, I'll just deal with this myself."

Ah, there was the little hell-cat he'd come to know and lo—

Alexander felt his eyes widen in horror. He was going nowhere near the end of that thought.

"What in God's name is the *matter* with you?" She stomped her foot and Alexander was disgusted with himself for finding it rather endearing.

"Forgive me. I — ah — over imbibed last night," he said quickly." And did you just stamp your foot at me?"

He grinned at her sudden obvious discomfort.

"O-of course not," she stammered. "Ladies do not stomp."

"No," he responded feeling much more the thing now that he was teasing her again. "But then, I never said a lady did it."

She growled in response, and it was all he could do not to pluck her from her stomping little feet and carry her off somewhere to do something about all that frustration.

Yes, indeed. He was in very big trouble.

NEVER, EVER BEFORE HAD OLIVIA DEALT WITH SUCH AN ARRAY OF emotions in such a short space of time.

She was already exhausted; mentally wrung out, and they hadn't even begun discussing what they should do about her irresponsible sibling.

Alexander was acting as though he had run mad, and she

couldn't deal with his madness. Not when she was trying hard not to descend into the same state herself after that kiss.

Good Lord. He'd kissed her. And she'd let him.

This was not good. Not good at all.

How could she stand in pious judgment of Jane when she went around kissing Alexander? And he was far more irritating than his friend, she was sure of it.

Pressing a hand to her temple, she tried desperately to claw back some semblance of normality.

There would be plenty of time to mourn the loss of her sanity later. And plenty of time to guiltily enjoy the memory of that toe-curling kiss and what it did to her insides.

She watched the man in front of her now, as his green eyes finally focused on her.

He seemed terribly distracted. And that wasn't very flattering really. It seemed that even with a kiss involved, she couldn't hold his attention.

"If you didn't write to Jane then it must have been St. Clare," she started through gritted teeth, ignoring the feeling of relief that swept through her, "and given that she gave me an insultingly awful excuse not to join me in the park this afternoon, I'm guessing he asked her to meet. Obviously, he's lying to get her alone. And—" This was the part she hadn't wanted to confess, but Olivia had always been the honest sort. "—and she didn't seem too averse to the idea."

"And?"

Olivia frowned. Whatever did he mean, 'and'?

"And he's obviously an utter rakehell," she said firmly. "So, we need to stop them from spending any alone time with each other."

He remained silent so long that she was contemplating slapping him. And not just because she'd rather enjoy it.

Finally, he sighed and looked at her with those direct, probing eyes of his.

"I have some bad news. News that I was going to share with you. At eight," he added.

Her jaw dropped open again. He was the one who'd warned her about this! He was the one who'd wanted to meet today in the first place.

"What does it matter if it's now or at eight?" she shouted.

"No need to shout."

"I did not shout," she shouted again.

Alexander smiled his maddening smile.

"Allow me to guess; ladies do not shout?"

Olivia squeezed her head at her temples again.

"Alexander," she began as though talking to a particularly dim child. Which he was. If an overgrown one. "Remember that we are both concerned about Jane. Though quite why you're involving yourself is beyond me. But I cannot stand idly by and allow my sister to be hurt by your friend."

She watched as some emotion, something akin to panic, flittered across his face.

"You assume he means to hurt her?"

She wanted to feel his forehead to see if he were feverish, but she couldn't trust herself to touch him without tackling him to the ground and ravishing him, so she kept her deviant hands to herself.

"Considering you were concerned enough to want to meet only hours from now, and it was your idea to step in and do something about this in the first place, I rather think my assumption is an accurate one."

Alexander swallowed hard and Olivia averted her eyes from the muscles in his throat lest she do something crazy like press her lips to them.

"I think," he said rather gruffly. "I think it's possible that he means to meet her in Hyde Park." That didn't sound so bad. But he wasn't done. He heaved a great big sigh before continuing. "He means to take her to Scandal Lane. And she has agreed to go there with him."

Olivia felt a pang of shock.

She had been thinking that Jane was starting to care for Mr. St. Clare, especially considering her carry on at breakfast.

But she couldn't believe that Jane would allow herself to be taken to such a place. A place where, if rumours were to be believed, ladies of their night shared their wares with anyone who possessed a spare guinea. Where gentlemen fought duels. Where ladies lost far more than their good name and standing. She wouldn't believe it. No good could come of it. For her or for Jane.

If Alexander's friend ruined Jane because he had brought

him into their lives, then the Daringtons would never see or speak to him again. He'd be gone from their lives like so many of their old friends.

Steeling her heart against any sort of compassion for her silly, innocent sister, and any stupid, idiotic feelings of hurt the thought of not seeing Alexander again evoked, Olivia raised her chin and made sure to look absolutely fierce.

"Stuff and nonsense," she said with a laugh. "Jane might be naïve enough to be forming an attachment to the cad, but she would never be so foolish as to be seduced by someone of your ilk."

"What the hell is that supposed to mean?"

"Only that your friend is a deplorable blackguard, and you know what they say. You are the company you keep."

She could practically see the wheels turning in his pretty head, trying to work out where the bitterness that she could not disguise was coming from.

"What is this really about?" he demanded; his voice low.

Olivia huffed out a frustrated breath. This wasn't how she had wanted this conversation to go. They were supposed to be discussing how to keep Jane and St. Clare apart. Now, he was questioning her anger. And that was a question she really didn't want to answer. Because she'd have to confess that she'd heard what he'd said about her all those years ago after their almost kiss. When he'd told his mother what he really thought of her, while she'd been convincing herself that he cared…

Raising a brow and making every effort to appear utterly nonchalant, Olivia gave another, brittle laugh.

"It is about stopping Jane from making a colossal mistake. I thought we *both* agreed on that."

For a moment, it looked as though he would argue with her. But finally, he sighed, the sound wearier than any she'd ever heard from him and shook his head.

"We do agree. It would be a mistake. For many reasons. So, what do we do?"

Five

I T WAS EXHAUSTING, OLIVIA decided hours later, planning strategies of war with her arch nemesis, instead of against him.

When she'd insisted on marching straight inside to his odious friend and giving him what for, Alexander had threatened to carry her bodily from the property. And because she believed that he'd do it, she mutinously agreed to leave and meet him later this evening as previously arranged.

"We have a better chance of talking some sense into Jane when she sees how bad things can get around there," he insisted. *"If you go running in there now, they'll only get sneakier about meeting. And don't forget, there are a pair of them in this. It's not only Elliot."*

She hadn't been able to argue the toss because he was right. Jane was seemingly just as eager for her complete ruin as Mr. St. Clare was to provide the means.

The sky was already dark at this hour. And snow had started coating the ice-hard road beneath her boots.

She shivered in her velvet winter coat, wishing she hadn't mutinously refused to wait in the earl's carriage with blankets and a warming brick.

"You're freezing," Fincham's voice sounded close to her ear and this time her shiver was very much *not* from the cold.

"I'm f-fine," she answered stubbornly, but it was ruined somewhat by the chatter of her teeth.

Jane had tried to sneak out of the house unnoticed earlier,

but Olivia had been on to her. Papa was presumably at another gaming hell, thinking he was going to save them all but more than likely pushing them further toward utter poverty.

Mama was having an attack of the vapours in her room.

An ordinary day in the Darington house.

As soon as Jane had slipped out, so too had Olivia. She dashed to the corner where Fincham had been waiting with an un-crested carriage as promised and jumped inside the luxurious interior. And now here she was. Freezing to death.

"Why don't you just go and warm up. I made sure the carriage can't be seen from the path. We can easily get you in there without anyone seeing."

Olivia counted to ten before realising it didn't help so she turned to glare at him, ignoring the way his eyes glittered brightly in the moonlight.

"I'm not going to get into a darkened, anonymous carriage with you, Lord Fincham."

He rolled his eyes.

"I will stay out here and await the arrival of your sister and Elliot. You will get warm. I don't want you falling ill."

Olivia studied his face. He seemed sincere. As though he really cared about what happened to her.

But he had hurt her three years ago, and then he had infuriated her earlier today so she couldn't let herself think he cared about her. It was too dangerous.

She pulled the edges of her cloak tighter and mutinously turned her back on him, ignoring his long-suffering sigh.

"If you think I'm going to run away like a meek little girl while you swoop in to save *my* sister, you are very much mistaken," she snapped.

She had been snapping at him all evening, she knew. Or at least for the hour they'd been standing here. At one point, she'd been afraid she'd freeze over fully. But Olivia was ready for action.

If Elliot St. Clare thought he could drag his sister down Scandal Lane and ruin her, he had another think coming.

Olivia just prayed Alexander would actually help her.

She still didn't fully understand his commitment to saving Jane but seeing the goings on around her scared her enough to be very grateful that he was here. Though she'd die before she'd admit it to him.

Taking a deep breath, ignoring the scent of sandalwood that had been driving her slowly mad, and ignoring the heat emanating from where he stood only inches from her, she cast her gaze around once more.

Such an innocuous place.

Olivia didn't know what she'd expected really. Maybe something more flamboyant like the mazes and dark walkways of Vauxhall, or the back streets and cobbled danger zones of The Seven Dials. But it was just a lane. Not that she knew much about the place, having only heard snippets of whispered conversations deemed too inappropriate for a young debutante's ears. It was quite pretty, in fact. Set far enough away from the main walkways that one could escape prying eyes if one wished, the trees that gave it its privacy were dusted with snow and oddly beautiful.

She'd been shocked when she'd first seen the women who looked like they should be standing by the docks and not in the middle of Hyde Park. Confused when she'd seen the young men standing about in much the same manner.

Then appalled when she'd seen a friend of her father's stumble toward the darkness with a girl who couldn't be older than Olivia herself.

And all the while, she was mindful of Alexander's eyes watching her. He hadn't been at all enamoured with the idea of her being here. But none of this was any of his business. Not really. So she ignored the disapproval coming off him in waves and was secretly pleased that he was standing here with her while she waited. And watched. And was secretly glad of his company.

ALEXANDER RELEASED THE DEATH GRIP ON HIS FLASK OF WHISKEY and turned to glower at a drunken idiot who had begun eyeing Olivia from across the small pond near the entrance to the Lane.

The later it got, the more hedonistic things would get around here. And he didn't want her around it.

Elliot and Jane hadn't yet made an appearance and

Alexander was worried that Elliot had lied to him or taken Jane elsewhere when he realised Alexander hadn't been joking when he'd warned Elliot to behave himself.

He didn't know how long they'd been standing here. Him fussing like a damned mother hen every time he spotted a shiver from Olivia.

Once again, he pressed the flask into her hand and once again she tried to shove it back at him.

"Brandy is about the only thing that's going to keep you warm now, Olivia," he said softly, one eye still on the dandy weaving his way toward them.

Alexander didn't recognise the man which was a very good thing. He didn't want anyone in his circle knowing Olivia was here.

"Fine," she muttered before lifting the flask to her lips and gulping from it.

Immediately her eyes filled with tears, and she coughed and spluttered as she thrust the flask back at him.

"Ugh, that's ghastly," she complained.

"Well, you weren't supposed to down it like a sailor," he laughed.

Screwing the lid back on, he tucked it into the pocket of his greatcoat and turned and walked the couple of feet to see that his carriage and driver were still in position tucked behind a huge holly bush.

He'd told his coachman to sit inside when the snow began to fall in earnest. One of them might as well have the chance of getting out of here before freezing to death.

If they had to wait much longer, he was going to throw Olivia over his shoulder and carry her to the damned thing.

Turning back around to tell her so, his temper flared as he watched the blackguard who'd been watching her salivate all over her lurching into what he assumed was supposed to be a bow and pawing for her hand.

If he touched her one more time, Alexander would launch himself at the bastard and strangle him.

The evening was dragging, the brandy was having no good effect on his temper whatsoever, and now he was going to have to murder someone.

Alexander watched Olivia's face closely as he ambled over.

He wanted to give the appearance of being calm and casual lest the blackguard turn out to be a decent pugilist. Alexander wanted the element of surprise on his side.

Olivia suddenly looked over at him, directly into his eyes and all thoughts, violent or otherwise, fled from his mind.

Dear God in Heaven. She was extraordinary. A goddess. And his heart, he knew, had never been in more danger.

Olivia raised a brow, as though daring him. To do what, he had no idea, but it made him determined to win whatever this battle between them was. He could only hope, rather desperately, that she was going to be his prize.

Alexander made no effort to release Olivia from his gaze. He knew he probably looked brooding and intense, a look that had frightened many before her, but he couldn't look away. Didn't want to.

His desire for her seemed a tangible force, reaching across the short distance between them to wrap her in its web. Her eyes widened and her lips parted.

This wasn't what they were here for! He had brought her here like some damned knight in shining armour yet here he was fantasising about seducing her just as he was trying to prevent Elliot from doing so to Jane.

More and more, Alexander was becoming sympathetic to Elliot's desire. If his friend felt for Jane even a fraction of what Alexander was starting to feel for Olivia…but that was just it. Elliot wasn't falling in love with Jane Darington.

And surely Alexander wasn't falling in love either?

Lord knew, he was starting to feel like he'd tear a man limb from limb if he attempted to keep Alex from being with Olivia. Was jealousy an indication of love? Was lust? She annoyed him and amused him in equal measure.

And at times, he'd genuinely feared for his life around the little termagant.

And yet -

All of this ran confusingly through his head as he finally came to a stop before Olivia and her drunken admirer.

The blasted idiot still had his left hand on Olivia's person. This time, he was touching her upper arm, his thumb brushing along the velvet of her cloak.

Alexander's tenuous grasp on his temper snapped.

"If you're fond of that hand of yours, I suggest you remove it from the lady," he said softly watching with a grim satisfaction as the young pup's eyes widened.

"I'm not sure I follow," the little upstart said now, but he had removed his hand from Olivia's arm.

"Oh, I'm quite sure you do," Alexander retorted softly.

He was gratified to see the other man's throat bob wildly.

There was an uncomfortable silence which Alexander made no attempt to break since all his efforts were focused on giving the man one of his most vicious scowls.

Finally, the drunkard put up his hands in a symbol of surrender and started to back away.

"My apologies," he said. "I didn't know she belonged to anyone."

Olivia gasped; no doubt angry at being spoken about as though she were a piece of property to be owned.

But Alexander was too distracted to contradict the lout. Too shocked at the feeling of desire that crashed into him. Not just the lust that he was coming to expect in her vicinity. But a desire to have her belong to him. And he, her.

He watched in silence as the man stumbled away.

"I don't think they're coming, Alexander," Olivia's soft voice broke the stilted silence.

"No, I don't think they are."

"So – should we go home?"

Home.

It sounded right. It sounded wonderful. Olivia and him. Going home together. Sharing a carriage, sharing a bed…

Alexander pulled out the flask and finished the contents in one, giant gulp.

He'd come out here thinking he would save Jane Darington from trouble. He hadn't realised that the one who needed saving was him.

OLIVIA SAT BACK AGAINST THE PLUSH CUSHION OF ALEXANDER'S carriage and let out a sigh.

"Damn and blast," she whispered softly.

"Tut, tut, my beauty. Ladies surely do no swear."

Alexander's voice from across the carriage caused the most delicious of shivers to run down her back.

Olivia swallowed and turned her head to glare at him.

"We've utterly failed you know. This entire evening was a waste of time."

"I don't know about that," he said cryptically. "I found it – informative."

The look in his eyes heated the very blood in Olivia's veins.

Oh, Lord. This was not good. Not at all.

Her heart was thudding most oddly, and Olivia had a sinking feeling in the pit of her stomach.

She was starting to genuinely fear that what she felt for this man wasn't ever going to go away.

As Olivia turned her head away, Alexander reached out and grasped her chin, pulling her face back around to face him.

She felt the impact of his touch right down to her freezing toes.

"You look incredible," he said simply. "I don't think I told you that."

Olivia didn't want to be thrilled at this simplest of gestures. But she was. And she knew then; she was lost.

Six

"**W**HAT ARE YOU DOING?" Olivia pulled her face from his gentle grip, but he merely reached out and clasped her hand instead.

It probably wasn't a good thing that he noticed how perfectly her hand fit in his, but he was starting to think he was doing them both an injustice.

Why fight something that felt more and more right by the second?

He'd agreed to wait another thirty minutes but only if she agreed to warm up in the carriage. The coachman had been sent off to find an inn and a hot toddy for himself. Alexander had told him to return in an hour. And so, he and Olivia were alone. He knew he shouldn't be in here with her. Just as he knew he shouldn't be thinking of all the delicious ways he could warm her up. He was very close to being besotted by her. Her! Olivia Darington. The shrew.

The problem was that Olivia was completely focused on separating Jane from Elliot. And if she didn't want her sister with Alexander's friend, then she certainly wouldn't want Alexander for herself. Especially because she would blame Alex for Jane's demise.

Alexander grinned.

"I'm trying to warm up your hands."

She watched him suspiciously as he reached out and grabbed her other hand. Both their gloves were a hindrance he didn't want, and he wondered what she'd do if he removed them. Probably slap him again, he conceded. Though it would be worth it.

Alexander chuckled at her scowl.

"What are you at, Fincham?" she asked. Well, demanded.

Alexander placed a hand to his heart.

"I am wounded," he pronounced dramatically. "There I was trying to be gentlemanly, and you suspect my motives."

She scoffed in a very unladylike manner and looked out of the carriage window.

"I very much doubt anything you want to do to me is gentlemanly."

Alexander's entire body froze. She couldn't know what her words meant to him, couldn't know how they sounded coming from her innocent lips. Couldn't know how torturous it was to hear them and imagine how they could be spending their time together in this carriage.

Was he truly no better than Elliot St. Clare?

The thought should repulse him, but he couldn't think coherently in the face of her innocent words.

"Olivia," he said softly, bringing her eyes back to his once more.

She sighed and threw her eyes to heaven, muttering under her breath.

"What?" she snapped.

"I—" Alexander hesitated, wondering what to say. It was odd; most of his conversations with the woman sitting across from him now had been teasing or insulting. Never had he wanted to just *talk* with her. Until now. "I think perhaps we should get you home."

Her beautiful eyes narrowed in suspicion.

"This was your idea," she reminded him softly.

Alexander sighed and ran a hand through his hair, a sign that he was agitated. The last thing he wanted was to get her home. Which was exactly why he should.

"I know, I know. But—" He reached out and clasped her by the shoulders. God, how he loved touching her. "It's better – for you – for both of us, to just leave here now. We can figure out what to do about your sister and Elliot tomorrow. Away from here."

She was gazing up at him, a frown of consternation upon her

brow, and Alexander had to fight the urge to pull her against him and kiss her the way he wanted to.

"Do you want people to see you here? With me?" he asked, a nervous energy coursing through him. "You've been so worried about your sister's reputation. But what about yours?"

"I don't care," she answered mutinously. "I know you won't hurt me." His chest swelled with pride at her trust in him. "But I don't know that he won't hurt Jane."

"If someone you know should see you –"

"Why do you care?" she blurted. "About any of this, I mean. At first I thought that perhaps you'd – you'd developed a *tendre* for Jane. But you've said you haven't and – and you k-kissed me. So – so why? Why, when you despise me?"

Alexander felt suddenly nervous.

She hadn't pulled herself from his hands yet and he tightened his grip on her upper arms.

"Isn't it possible that two people who have long considered themselves enemies could find themselves, well, the opposite?"

"I want to believe it is," she said softly. "But I think—"

He felt her hesitation, but he also felt her desire as though it reached out to collide with his own.

Tightening his grip further still, he lifted her from her seat and pulled her onto his lap, almost groaning at the sheer pleasure of just having her sitting there.

"You think too much," he said, lowering his head slowly toward hers.

"You only say that because you don't think at all," she argued but she tilted her head just so.

"You talk too much," he responded, so close to touching her lips with his own he could almost taste her.

"Well, you—"

Alexander didn't give her a chance to argue, yet again. His lips found hers, and he set about trying to remove any thoughts that weren't of him from her busy mind.

THEY WERE GOING TO MISS JANE AND IT WAS ALL HIS FAULT!

Olivia desperately clung to her irritation. It was just the

defence she needed against the unrelenting, soul-consuming love for him that was lurking inside of her, waiting to pounce.

She couldn't allow herself to love him.

No matter how many seductive words he said, or how heart stopping his kisses.

Self-preservation was key.

They were once more standing in the freezing cold only this time she was draped in his greatcoat as well as her cloak, and brain was the consistency of mush thanks to his shenanigans in the carriage.

If he hadn't set her away from him with a black oath and an insistence that he needed to cool off in the freezing air, lord only knew what she would have ended up doing with him.

"What if we missed them?" she muttered crossly.

"Does it really matter?" Alexander asked from behind her.

Olivia swung round to glare at him.

"I've already told you that it matters," she barked.

Alexander sighed and ran a hand through his hair, causing a stray jet black lock to fall over his forehead.

She wanted to brush it back from his face.

And then she wanted to cut it off because it had no business making her feel like she wanted to push it back.

God, this was infuriating; him, her feelings for him, his hair now too, apparently.

It was all far too much to deal with. She was confused and tired and freezing. and solve riddles at the same time.

"Can't you just speak to her tomorrow?" he asked. "After all, it's far too cold to engage in anything to ruinous this evening. Trust me."

He was right, she knew.

She really didn't want to get into an argument with him again. Especially because their arguments lately were ending with kisses, and they were confusing and wonderful and really, terribly inappropriate.

"I don't want her heart broken," she answered feebly.

Alexander studied her for a moment as though he were searching for something in her gaze. After an age, he took her hand and turned her toward the carriage.

"Come. Let's get you home."

"I'm not going home."

"I'll come back and search for them properly. I'm not bringing you down that lane with me," he said in a no-nonsense tone that got her hackles good and raised.

"And how do I know you'll come back?" she demanded, digging her heels into the frozen ground.

"Can't you just trust me?" he asked with a disarming smile.

Oh, how I wish I could.

"I trust you about as much as I trust Mama's pet dog. And that's a vicious, irritating thing as well," she said then stalked ahead of him.

HE WAS EITHER GOING TO THROTTLE HER OR KISS HER SENSELESS, Alexander decided as she marched away from him, imperious as a duchess.

She was driving him bloody well mad.

After that explosive kiss in the carriage, he'd thought that maybe she'd begun softening toward him.

But Olivia still had a heart of solid rock; he was convinced of it. For while he was caught up in flames just by looking at her, her demeanour remained colder than the frigid air around them.

He needed to remember how dangerous she could be.

Anyone who looked so doll-like and angelic, and still managed to wreck the havoc she did, was not to be trusted, even for a moment.

"You really do need to do something about that temper of yours," he called as he caught up to her.

"I have no problem with my temper. I have a problem with you."

"Why?"

He distinctly heard several whispered curses before she spun back around to him.

"Because you're distracting and — and flustering. And I cannot think properly when you stand so close."

Her words where music to his ears.

"And you can rid yourself of that smile. It's *not* a compliment."

Seven

.

"DON'T YOU WORRY SWEETHEART. I'M NOT SO STUPID AS TO THINK YOU'D EVER COMPLIMENT ME. AT LEAST, NOT ON PURPOSE."

Olivia ignored him and continued toward the lane way.

Suddenly, Alexander was there. All six feet of him looming over her.

"You're not going down there, Olivia," he said in a tone that brooked no argument.

So naturally she argued.

"I beg your pardon?"

Alexander crossed his arms looking as intimidating as he was handsome.

"I said, you're not going down there. There are people out there who are a lot less palatable than me, shocking as that might be to you. And I'm not having you exposed to them."

"And what if Jane is there with that scoundrel?"

"I suppose you want to chase after her? And what if you find them tupping? What will you do?"

His words brought a scarlet heat to her cheeks, she could feel it. And was grateful for the darkness that would disguise it from him.

She should be offended by his use of such vulgar language. But wanton hussy that she was, she only felt strangely exhilarated.

Olivia took a deep, steadying breath.

She'd never been the type to admit defeat. Never.

But sometimes, one had to recognize that there were things which could not be controlled. And she very much did *not* want to stumble on – well, that.

She glanced up at Alexander, feeling her heart do its usual gallop in the face of his harsh, masculine beauty.

She would never tire of looking at his face. Which was a problem, admittedly. But at least it was a problem with a nice view.

"You said it was too cold for that," she mumbled.

"And I still believe it is. But there's a world of pleasure that one could engage in, unhindered by the cold."

Olivia's breath quickened.

"And you're an expert on such things, no doubt," she quipped, but her tone lacked its usual bite.

Alexander grinned wolfishly.

"Oh, I hope so."

Olivia couldn't seem to form a response, especially when she caught the predatory glint in his eyes.

He dipped his head toward her own.

"Shall I prove it to you?" he whispered close to her lips.

Olivia could think of no way to answer, except to close the final, minuscule distance between them.

She loved him. She knew that now. Perhaps she always had. What she didn't know was what on earth to do about it.

ALEXANDER MADE A HERCULEAN EFFORT TO PULL HIMSELF AWAY from Olivia.

She was utterly irresistible, but he was conscious of the fact that they were in public and in the cold.

Much as he wanted her, he didn't relish the idea of making it a spectator sport.

He studied her face for a moment, drinking in her heart-stopping beauty.

The sooner he got her to the carriage and in a semblance of privacy, the better.

"Come," he said softly, taking her hand and walking toward

the vehicle. They walked in silence; Alexander was lost in his own thoughts, and he assumed Olivia was lost in hers.

Still, she didn't move her hand from his and he was surprised at how happy that simple act made him. It felt right somehow, to be holding her hand, as though she had always belonged right there, walking beside him.

"Are you warm enough?" he asked her quietly, not wanting to speak loudly and ruin the perfect stillness that surrounded them.

Olivia smiled wryly.

"Not really," she confessed.

He wasn't surprised.

The sky was bright and cloud free; the stars and full moon gleaming, illuminating the park with a brilliant white light and though it was beautiful to see, it certainly made it chilly.

There was already frost forming on the grass beneath their feet.

All of a sudden, he was filled with a need to protect her, to keep her safe always.

It was a heady feeling but one which was more than a little confusing.

They got to the carriage, and she turned to look up at him, her eyes deep enough to drown in, her body swamped by both his coat and her cloak.

She'd never looked so serene. She'd never looked so beautiful.

It was a moment of perfection, and he was starting to want a lifetime of them.

She was surrounded by his scent, and it was exquisite.

Furtively, Olivia clasped the lapels of the black greatcoat and inhaled. It smelled of soap, sandalwood, and Alexander. It was heavenly.

Alexander wasn't speaking much and nor was she.

His chivalrous act, his concern for her wellbeing, and of course his kisses, were forces too strong for her to fight.

She might as well embrace the fact that she loved him.

Then, when he rejected her as he had three years ago, she could go away and lick her wounds in peace.

But wouldn't it be nice to just let herself enjoy his company?

"Let's get inside and get warm," Alexander interrupted her thoughts.

She looked guiltily at him.

"Oh, Alexander, you must be freezing," she said, starting to remove his coat. Here, take—" her words trailed off as she looked at him, really looked at him, since he'd given her his coat.

Now that they were standing directly in the moonlight, away from the cover of the trees, she could see more of him and what she saw was enough to make her mouth dry and her heart gallop.

She could see the muscles of his arms through the material of his navy-blue superfine. They looked so defined, so big.

And his jacket had very obviously not been padded like that of some of the dandies of the *ton*, given the size of his shoulders and the breadth of his chest.

"Olivia?"

Her eyes snapped up to his, and she was mortified by the light of amusement in them. He knew, the arrogant swine. He knew the effect he was having on her.

"You were saying?" he continued with a smug grin.

"I thought you might be cold. I was g-giving you back your greatcoat," she murmured, refusing to meet his amused gaze.

"Keep it," he said, chuckling softly. "I do believe your heated glances are enough to keep my blood warm."

Olivia gasped in outrage. How dare he embarrass her so?

"I beg your pardon," she exclaimed. "I was not giving you heated glances you great big oaf."

He laughed again then bent to give her a swift kiss.

"You are one of a kind, Olivia Darington. Come."

He leaned around her and opened the door of the carriage before holding out a hand to help her up.

Rather than take his hand, however, she shoved the greatcoat at him and inelegantly scrambled up into the carriage without his help, trying hard to ignore his laughter behind her.

When she'd landed herself in a graceless heap on the bench, she looked up to see he'd already entered the conveyance, smoothly of course, and was sitting opposite her with a heart-stopping smile on his face.

"Olivia, can't you just ease up and have a little fun?" he cajoled.

"Yes, when I've removed my sister from your friend's dastardly clutches," she bit rather than acquiesce.

He sighed and shook his head.

"So busy worrying about everyone else," he whispered reaching out and stroking her cheeks softly. "But what about you? And your happiness?"

His words were so hypnotising, his touch intoxicating.

"I don't understand you, Alexander," she admitted hoarsely. "For my whole life you've despised me, and now – now you act as though, well – I just don't know why you're doing it."

"Isn't it obvious that I'm doing it because I want, quite desperately I might add, to spend time alone with you? That I want to explore this thing that's growing between us?"

Olivia's heart was hammering so loudly she was surprised he couldn't hear it. "I suppose that makes me no better than Elliot," he suddenly said, a frown of disgust marring his brow.

And Olivia immediately wanted to comfort him. Because even though they were at the notorious Scandal Lane, and even though she very much wanted to do exactly what she was trying to save Jane from, she knew instinctively that Alexander was nothing like his friend.

"That's different. I mean, he wants to, to bed her, and -" she trailed off in confusion.

"It's not different," he said. "Believe me."

Olivia froze as his words crashed through her mind.

He stared into her eyes. And she knew that if she told him to take her home this second, he would do it. Just as she knew that she *should* tell him to take her home this second.

Perhaps there was something about this place. This infamous part of Hyde Park.

But suddenly the consequences of her actions seemed unimportant. The price of taking this step with Alexander a pittance compared to the pleasure she knew she would experience at his hands.

Knowing that she was the very epitome of a hypocrite, but in that moment being unable to dredge up any shame for it, Olivia reached up and removed Alexander's hands from her face.

Wordlessly, she pulled off her gloves, then reached up to untie the ribbons of her bonnet, then her cloak.

He watched her, his eyes glittering in the moonlight streaming through a gap in the curtains.

The only sound was the gentle noise of their breathing, and the unsteady thump of Olivia's heart in her ears.

When she was free of her garments, she stood and before she could lose her nerve, placed herself firmly in his lap, her knees either side of his thighs.

Alexander's hiss at the contact was all the encouragement she needed, and she leaned forward to boldly press her lips against his.

For a brief moment it seemed that he froze, and Olivia had a split second of panic.

Had she misread his desires? Did he not want her?

But before her self-doubt could truly catch hold, he muffled an oath against her lips, and he took immediate control of the kiss. Without hesitation, his tongue plunged into her mouth. One hand pressed her against him, the movement causing them both to groan with pleasure. His other hand he buried in her hair, sending her pins flying and her dark curls tumbling down her back.

"Christ, Oliva," he growled, pulling his lips from her own to trail kisses down her neck, nipping and licking her sensitive flesh. "You drive me wild."

Olivia had lost the ability to speak coherently, too caught up in the maelstrom of desire he'd awakened in her.

"Please," she whimpered, her breathing ragged and broken. "Please, Alex."

She had no idea what she was pleading for. Only that there was an ache inside her that was growing by the second.

"I know, sweetheart," he whispered. "I know."

She felt the sudden loss of his hands keenly but before she could issue a protest, they were back. He'd taken the time to remove his gloves and the feel of his skin against her own was divine as he cupped her neck, positioning her head so he could once more plunder her mouth.

Olivia was a puppet in his hands. She could do nothing but

press herself wantonly against the rigid length of him, rejoicing in his growl of approval, in the surge of his hips against her own.

The ache inside her was building to fever pitch and she wasn't sure how to soothe it. She didn't think anyone could. Anyone but Alexander.

Before she could once again beg for something beyond her reach, she felt his hand reach under the bunched material of her gown.

They gasped in unison as his fingers met the smooth skin of her thigh, bare above her stockings.

Olivia wondered briefly if she should be scared or nervous or even horrified by the feel of his hand moving further up her leg, closer to her centre. But she only felt excited, intoxicated, enthralled by the pleasure he drew from her.

His lips moved from her mouth to her ear, his teeth pulling on the lobe before moving once again, down her throat, pausing at her hammering pulse, before travelling lower still.

The hand that had been cupping her nape moved suddenly to delve inside her gown and the feel of his flesh against her aching breast caused Olivia to cry out in bliss.

All the while his other hand was on the move.

It became too much for Olivia to stand, the pleasure bordering on pain.

He was a maestro, drawing the most beautiful music from her body.

She wanted to pull away. She wanted to press closer. She wanted it to end before she expired, and she never wanted it to stop.

Something inside her was twisting, tighter and tighter. His fingers stroked her once, twice, before one pushed inside her while his thumb pressed against her, and his mouth replaced the burning heat of his hand on her breast.

The twisting ball of desire inside of her exploded, shattering into a million pieces.

The power of it was blinding and Olivia became a slave to the feeling, her hips rocking against his hand, her head thrown back in wanton abandonment.

And through it all Alexander stayed with her, anchoring her, drawing every drop of heaven from her body, the creator of her torment, and the master of her pleasure.

Slowly, Olivia drifted back to earth.

It was all she could do to drop her head forward and rest it against his rock solid chest while she tried to catch her breath.

Alexander's arms came around her and he buried his face in her hair, dropping a tender kiss atop her head.

"Alex, I –"

Suddenly the carriage rattled, and Olivia let out a shriek of fright.

"Only me, my lord. The hour is up."

Alex let out a strangled laugh while Olivia buried her face in his shoulder, embarrassment warring with happiness inside her.

"I need to get you home," Alexander said softly, his arms still holding her close.

Olivia knew there'd be no ladylike way to extract herself from his grip, so she was happy to stay right where she was, nestled against him as he rapped on the ceiling and the carriage took off at a slow trundle.

Tomorrow she might regret every second of this interlude.

But tonight, she would just enjoy being so intimate with the man she loved.

SLEEP ELUDED OLIVIA AS SHE HAD KNOWN IT WOULD. SHE'D darted into the house, avoiding Sterling's frown of disapproval and Ellie's blatant curiosity. When she'd enquired after Jane, she'd been informed that her sister hadn't yet returned home.

So then she added a gnawing worry for Jane to the ever-growing pile of emotions crashing through her.

She couldn't believe what she had just done with Alexander. More than that, she couldn't believe how little she regretted her actions.

Shouldn't she be flagellating herself? Taking herself off to a convent or some such thing?

But instead of shame or mortification, she felt only happiness, only love.

All this time she'd worried about Jane's attraction to ruinous behaviour when she should have been worrying about her own.

Still, she could trust Alexander…couldn't she?

As Olivia readied herself for bed, wondering if she should tell Mama that Jane wasn't home, she heard the distinctive sounds of movement in Jane's bedchamber and heaved a sigh of relief.

She had no idea what had happened with Jane and Mr. St. Clare, but she couldn't question her sister right now. She needed to be alone to process what she'd done tonight.

That night as she tossed and turned, she started to regret her actions with Alexander.

She'd been so caught up in her desires that she'd convinced herself he was trustworthy. That he was enamoured of her as she was infatuated by him. But she'd made that mistake before and been humiliated for it.

Despite her best efforts, her mind would not be silenced, and the memories of that day would not be supressed.

After Alexander had almost kissed her, Olivia had been desperate to seek her sister's council.

Being unable to find Jane in her bedchamber, she had searched the house and had finally moved toward the voices she heard coming from the library.

It was only as she reached the partially opened doors that she realized one of the voices was male. Was, in fact, Alexander.

She shouldn't have really, but she settled in to eavesdrop. After all, she was full sure that Alexander had been about to confess tender feelings for her in the garden. She knew Lady Fincham was here to visit with mama. Alexander was bound to be telling his mother about it, perhaps even seeking her advice on how to proceed with a courtship.

What she heard, however, was decidedly *not* what she had wanted.

"You're going to pursue the Darington girl then?"

"What?" To Olivia's surprise, Alex had sounded horrified.

"Mavis saw you in the gardens, Alexander. Really, you should be more discreet. And I'm not altogether thrilled about the match either. She's a pretty thing and Lady Cynthia is a dear friend. But you are to be an earl. You can do much better than a baron's daughter."

The silence stretched so long that Olivia thought perhaps he meant to ignore his mother's insults altogether.

Finally, he answered, "You should tell your companion to have her spec-

tacles checked, Mother, there is nothing going on between me and Olivia Darington."

"Do you care for her?"

"Of course not. It was a joke. We're always playing tormenting each other, are we not?"

Olivia's face burned with humiliation.

"I do wish you'd stop with that immature nonsense, Alexander. But I'm glad to hear there won't be any sort of betrothal in the works. Perhaps you should keep your distance from the gel. Wouldn't want her getting any ideas, after all."

As her stomach churned with remembered humiliation, Olivia came back to the present with a terrible thud.

What was the point in all of this? She had barely gotten over her embarrassment then. Now, with her heart involved, she refused to take the risk.

ALEXANDER WATCHED OLIVIA'S FACE AS A MYRIAD OF EMOTIONS flitted across it. He was throwing another party, this time a smaller dinner, just so he could see her again. He watched in amusement as she stifled a yawn. She'd never been able to hide her feelings, even when they were children.

It was one of the things he loved the most about her.

His thoughts came to a screeching halt as the word burst through his mind, like fireworks across a darkened sky.

He did. He loved her, the annoying, sneaky, beautiful, stubborn little hell-cat.

He couldn't stop his sudden grin.

It seemed so obvious to him now.

He loved her.

They would marry and fill a nursery and she would be his countess and share his life with him. Her quick mind would be invaluable in the running of his affairs, and her sharp wit and sharper tongue would be a constant source of entertainment. And then of course, there would be the opportunity to hold her and kiss her and make love to her every second of every day.

It would be bliss.

Alexander was about to snatch her from the clutches of his

painfully boring solicitor to tell her all of this when she looked up at him and her expression changed once more.

She didn't look pleased to see him, or happy to be there. In fact, she looked miserable.

A feeling of trepidation dropped into his stomach and without acknowledging any of the nods or greetings sent his way, he cut through the room until he was at her side.

"Olivia—"

"Excuse me, my lord. Mr. Smith," dropping a quick curtsey to them both, she shook her head and moved towards the door.

He frowned in confusion.

What the hell was going on?

Alexander hesitated only moments before following her out of the room.

He found her once more in the conservatory.

"I heard you, you know," she spoke as though they'd been in the middle of a conversation. He could see the blush staining her cheeks, even in the moonlight. "All those years ago after we'd — well, after."

"I have no idea what you're talking about," he said carefully, not really knowing what her mood was or where this conversation was headed.

"No, I expect you wouldn't. The whole thing was rather boring and insignificant for you, I'd warrant. But it bothered me, I'll admit. And I haven't forgotten it."

Without saying another word, she turned and made to leave the room.

Alexander felt his temper flare, though he knew it was panic that was causing it.

Just like that, she was ruining all his hastily made plans. She couldn't just stomp off without explaining why.

"Would you care to expand, Olivia?" he called, rushing after her. "For I am at rather a loss as to what you are going on about."

"After our encounter in the garden that day, you were at such pains to laugh about me to your mother. To tell her about your decided lack of interest in me. To assure her that you would never be interested in me."

Damn.

"Olivia, we were young. We were enemies. You cannot think that things are the same now. After last night?"

"I can and I do. I can only hope that I can save Jane from making the same mistakes I did. I couldn't keep myself safe from a rake, but I can perhaps save her."

Alexander couldn't believe what he was hearing. The pain of hearing what she really thought of him was excruciating.

Was she really going to hold the sins of his past against him? He hadn't even meant what he'd said. He'd just had no idea how to deal with the visceral reaction he'd felt when touching her.

"Olivia, I didn't mean it. I was trying to save face. You have to understand."

"Oh, I do understand Alexander. I understand that last night should never have happened. I understand that if I wasn't good enough for you back then, I certainly shan't be now. Penniless and ruined."

"Can we please talk about this?" he asked desperately.

She sighed and looked suddenly weary.

"I'm tired and I have a headache. I'm going to find Jane and we can forget all of this ever happened. If you would be so good as to keep an eye on your friend, I'd appreciate it."

He watched as she walked away.

She couldn't leave it like this.

But she was leaving all the same.

Eight

Olivia,

   I refuse to allow a stupid mistake from three years ago come between us now. Meet me at Scandal Lane. Eight o'clock. Please, sweetheart.

   I'll send a carriage and meet you there. And if you don't come, I'll simply call on you at home. In front of your entire family. Don't think I won't. This is too important. You are too important.

   Alexander

T he man was a nuisance.

   But he was a determined nuisance, and Olivia knew he meant what he threatened. He would cause a huge scandal rather than allow her to ignore his summons. He really was that stubborn.

   And, truth be told, Olivia was worried that she was being rather ridiculous.

   After all, it was three years since that dratted day, and they'd shared more than an innocent peck since then.

   She certainly felt differently. Couldn't she trust that he did too?

   After she'd gone back to the party, she'd been surprised to see that Jane wasn't ensconced with Mr. St. Clare. Instead, she was alone in a corner and looking thoroughly miserable. The sight pained Olivia. Much as she'd been frustrated with her sister these past few weeks, she knew Jane was taking their fall to genteel poverty worse than she was.

Jane had jumped at the chance to go home so they'd scurried off, refusing his lordship's carriage and hurrying home in miserable silence.

Olivia sighed now and paced her bedchamber as she had been doing for hours.

She'd have to go to Hyde Park. She couldn't risk Alex coming here.

A knock sounded on her door and for one mad moment she was afraid Alex would be standing on the other side of it.

It was Jane who walked into her room, however, and perched on the edge of her bed.

Olivia snatched up Alex's letter from beside where her sister sat.

"Are you meeting Alexander?" Jane suddenly demanded.

Olivia didn't know what to say.

There was no point in denying it. Jane was clearly already suspicious, and she'd notice if Olivia suddenly disappeared.

"That's none of your concern," she said with a sniff rather than deny it.

"Do you realise this is Alexander?" Jane demanded, crossing her arms, ever the bossy big sister. "You despise each other. Sworn childhood enemies and all that."

"Do you realise you're being quite the hypocrite. What about Mr. St. Clare? Don't think I don't know that you went sneaking off to meet him the other day." Olivia shot back, hating feeling so defensive.

"Yes, well. You don't have to worry about seeing Mr. St. Clare again. He – that is, we – well, we are no longer friends."

Olivia saw the flash of hurt on her sister's pretty face and immediately felt contrite. It wasn't Jane's fault that Alexander Stratford had her tied in knots.

"I'm sorry to hear that," she said through gritted teeth. "What happened?"

Jane laughed though the sound wasn't exactly happy.

"And you accused me of being a bad liar," she quipped. "You're not sorry at all. But then, neither am I, I suppose. He turned out to be rather more dishonourable than I would have liked. Do you know, he took me to Hyde Park the other evening and tried to get me to take a stroll down Scandal Lane, as though I didn't know what it was. As though I would be depraved enough to go anywhere near that place or let him take liberties with me without so much as a proposal!"

Olivia felt suddenly rather ill as shame and confusion bubbled inside her.

There she'd been, piously judging her sister and she'd turned out to be the disgraceful one. She'd turned out to be the hussy.

Did the fact that she was desperately in love with Alex change anything? Probably not. Yet she couldn't bring herself to regret what they'd shared either.

What a mess she'd gotten herself into.

The clock chimed the quarter hour and Olivia realised she'd be late if she didn't get a move on.

"Well, I'm glad you've seen his true character and the error of your ways, Jane. Now you can concentrate on meeting a nice man who will truly care for you."

She knew she was practically shooing her sister out the door but if Jane didn't leave then Olivia couldn't leave, and that meant that Alexander would arrive on their doorstep.

Sending Jane off with a hearty 'chin up', Olivia waited until her footsteps padded down the hallway then swept quickly from the room.

ALEXANDER COULDN'T BELIEVE HOW ANXIOUS HE FELT AS HE checked his watch once again and resumed his pacing.

What if she refused to come?

Well, he'd meant what he'd said. He would bang her door down if he had to.

Of course, he wasn't quite sure what he'd do once he'd gained access. All his ideas very much involved *not* having her family around.

He couldn't believe that one stupid conversation three years ago had gotten them so off course. But he would fix it. Somehow, he would make her see what she had come to mean to him.

Too restless to stay inside his carriage, he'd jumped from the conveyance and started wandering aimlessly in the direction of Scandal Lane.

He'd come here in his youth, he had to admit.

There'd been a particular liaison with a very bored but very married marchioness that had nearly ended badly for him. And he'd often met Lucia, his Italian opera singer mistress here on a balmy summer evening.

Now, he didn't particularly want to be anywhere near the place. And he definitely didn't want Olivia near it.

But he was a sentimental sop and wanted to do this here, where he knew he'd fallen in love with her. Where he hoped she'd fallen in love with him.

Besides, as insalubrious as the place was, she wouldn't come to any danger with him.

Provided she actually showed up.

Biting back an oath of frustration, Alex turned to make his way back up the lane.

If she didn't come, did that mean he had no hope at all?

Well, either way he was determined to find out.

HE'D FORCED HER TO COME, AND HE WASN'T EVEN IN HIS dratted carriage to meet her.

Olivia scowled in frustration as she stood warily at the entrance to the notorious lane trying to avoid eye contact with the people going in and out. Some she recognised from the other day. Some, she didn't want to look at long enough to see if she recognised them.

Where on earth could Alex have got to?

"Why, Miss Darington. This is a surprise. A very, very pleasant surprise."

Olivia spun around, her heart hitting her toes as Elliot St. Clare leered down at her.

Judging from the smell, and the way he swayed unsteadily in place, the man was well and truly foxed.

"Mr. St. Clare, good evening," she answered with stilted politeness.

The man's grin only widened.

"You don't like me very much, hmm?" he asked.

"No," she answered pointedly. After all, she'd always prided herself on her honesty. "I don't."

"I know you'd be a tough nut to crack. That's why I reckoned I'd a better chance with your sister. Of course, she turned out to be a bit of a disappointment. But it seems as though you've more fire in you than she does. Perhaps we might get along, after all."

Olivia shuddered at the blatant lasciviousness in the man's gaze.

This was why she'd wanted Jane away from the cad. This was why she felt safe with Alexander and never would with one such as Elliot St. Clare.

"I have no interest in getting along with you, Mr. St. Clare."

"So, you're here to meet someone else, is that it? I didn't know you had it in you, my dear. It's not Fincham, is it? He always was a lucky bastard. Everything handed to him on a platter just because he's a firstborn. Bagged himself the right sister while I got stuck with the prude."

"Come on, let's have a drink."

He reached out and clasped the material of Olivia's cloak causing her to stumble towards him.

"Let go of me, I'm not going anywhere with you."

"Not good enough for you, hmm? Because I don't have a title? Come now, Miss Darington. We all know your father is ruined. Soon enough, you'll be begging men like me to take an interest in you."

Olivia knew she should be scared. But she was merely furious. Furious that he would say such things to her, furious that he would treat poor Jane so abominably. And furious that he would besmirch Alexander in such a fashion. Alex was nothing like this wastrel.

"If you don't let go of me this instance, I shall – I shall –"

"What?" he snorted derisively. "What shall you do?"

"Probably something like this."

Olivia caught a brief glimpse of Alex's murderous expression before his fist darted out and connected with St. Clare's face. She didn't see where he'd hit, but she heard the sickening sound of bone crunching seconds before St. Clare's hold on her loosened and he dropped to the ground, blood spurting from his nose.

She watched slack-jawed as Alex bent down and pulled his friend into a sitting position by the lapel of his coat.

"Your things will be removed from my home this evening. You are never to darken my doorstep again. And if you go anywhere near Olivia or her family again, I'll kill you with my bare hands."

When he was done speaking, he dropped the other man like a sack of potatoes and only then turned to face her.

"Did he hurt you?" he growled, and Olivia felt a shiver snake down her spine at the fierce look in his eyes. He would never hurt her, of course. But he looked rather intimidating all the same.

"N-no," she stammered.

She watched the intense relief flash across his face before he reached out a hand and wordlessly pulled her from where St. Clare lay groaning and bleeding at her feet.

"Why did you want to meet me?" she asked quietly as they walked.

This was the hard part, Alex knew, and he struggled to get his temper under control. Every time he pictured Elliot's hands anywhere near her, he wanted to go back and wring the bastard's neck.

But Elliot wasn't important right now. Nothing was except her.

Alexander had spent all deliberating over what he should say. Did he try to apologise again for what a fool he'd been that day three years ago? Or did he just admit that he was desperately in love with her, that he wanted more than anything to make her his wife?

And suddenly, the words wouldn't come.

He was as skittish as an unbroken horse.

He searched frantically for something to talk about, but it was so hard to concentrate.

Every time she touched him, even on the sleeve of his coat, it set his heart racing.

They'd arrived at the carriage he'd come in. He'd sent the

other home. Olivia gazed up at him, her beauty in the moonlight nearly bringing him to his knees.

How could it be that only days ago he'd thought he hated her? He should have known from that moment three years ago that he'd only ever be able to love her. It felt like she was the only reason he existed.

"I wanted to talk," he said feebly.

She raised an impatient brow, and he couldn't contain his grin. It was so very like her to be completely unaffected by being accosted by a blackguard then watching Alex knock the blighter down.

"Well, I assumed as much. Are you trying to figure out how to form coherent sentences? Because I'll probably freeze to death before you manage it."

Alex growled at her impudence, but in truth he was as enamoured of her feistiness as every other part of her.

And he would tell her so. But first, he would do something he'd been itching to do from the second he'd laid eyes on her again.

He threw everything he felt into that kiss, reaching up to capture her face in his hands, loosing himself in the feelings she brought out in him. Her response was immediate and intense, and it was only seconds before they were both caught in the storm of their desires.

Alex knew he could stay like this forever. As long as it was Olivia he was holding.

Nine

When he finally let her up for air, Olivia sagged against the carriage, her heart hammering, her mind utterly dazed.

"What has become of you, Miss Darington? Allowing yourself to be accosted by a man at Scandal Lane of all places?"

Olivia tried to match his serious expression, but she was just so terribly pleased to be with him.

"You've led me astray, Lord Fincham. Not content with ruining my childhood, it seems you're bent on ruining my reputation, too."

"Oh, I have many, many more ways of ruining that, love. Far more enjoyable than a mere kiss."

In an instant, he looked positively wicked, and Olivia's heart took off in response.

"Walk with me?" he asked softly.

She looked upwards, watching as snowflakes began to fall heavily from the sky.

"Alexander," she hissed, "it's snowing. We cannot go marching about Hyde Park."

"Where's your sense of adventure?" he asked.

He moved away from her and opened the door of his carriage. This one emblazoned with the Fincham crest.

To her surprise, he pulled out a giant, heavy blanket and threw it over her shoulders then reached back inside and grabbed a basket.

Olivia couldn't help but laugh.

"You've thought of everything," she said.

He turned and took a lantern from his smiling coachman then turned hold out his hand to her.

"What on earth are we doing?" she asked as she took his hand.

"You'll see. Have some patience," he scolded.

He was enjoying himself immensely, so it seemed.

So she would, too. If anyone saw her holding hands with Alexander Stratford at Scandal Lane, there'd be no recovering from the furore. And Olivia found that she simply didn't care.

ALEXANDER FELT LIKE A CHILD ON CHRISTMAS MORN AS HE LED Olivia through the darkened park.

It was freezing and the snow was already blanketing everything around them.

Perhaps this hadn't been such a good idea. He didn't want her falling ill.

Alexander glanced down at his companion and was pleased to see an excited little smile on her lips. She didn't look cold or miserable

She looked happy, even if it was freezing.

He drew them to a stop at the Serpentine and wondered if she recognised the spot.

Watching closely, he saw her eyes widened infinitesimally. "Ah," she said, a smile playing around her lips. "Back to the scene of my crime? Tell me, are you planning on drowning me?"

Alex laughed in response.

"No, sweetheart, though no doubt you deserve the payback. I'm planning something much better."

OLIVIA TRIED DESPERATELY TO KEEP HER WITS ABOUT HER, BUT IT was no use.

She'd been worried that Alexander had taken leave of his

senses altogether when he'd started walking them through a snowstorm. She could only assume they were at this particular spot for a reason. She hoped a wonderful reason.

She turned to look at Alexander and saw that he was watching her with a look of such tenderness that her heart almost flew from her chest.

Without giving it a second thought she reached up and threw her arms around his neck, nearly toppling him.

He chuckled in surprise before dropping the basket he held and lifting her clean off her feet and devouring her lips in a soul searing kiss.

When she finally needed to come up for air, he broke the contact, settled her on her feet and retrieved the basket before grasping her hand and pulling her the final few steps to the bench.

She sat atop the blanket trailing from her shoulders, making sure that she left room for him on it.

They were pressed so tightly together there was no room between them, and she wouldn't want there to be.

He whipped out a flask and two pewter mugs.

"Ugh, is that more brandy?" she asked.

His smile was heart-stopping.

"Cider," he answered. "For you."

He poured the liquid from the flask into one of the mugs and she wrapped her hands around it, grateful for the heat, and inhaled the spiced apple scent.

Another flask contained brandy for him, and they sat in companionable silence for a while.

When her cup was empty, Alex whipped it from her hand, dropping it and his own back into the basket, along with the flasks.

Then, before she could speak, he reached out and pulled her onto his lap. Olivia wrapped one hand around his neck, the other, she placed on his solid chest. "Thank you," she whispered softly. "Nobody has ever done something like this for me, and I shall never forget it."

For a moment, he didn't move, just stared into her eyes, then slowly, he moved her hand from his chest to place a soft kiss on the palm.

Even through her thick, winter glove she felt its impact.

"Olivia," he said, his tone gravelly and low. "If you would let me, I would spend my whole life doing things like this for you."

Olivia felt her jaw drop at his words.

He couldn't possible mean what she thought, could he?

"Y-you would?" she squeaked, hardly daring to believe it.

"I would," he confirmed with a self-deprecating smile that she found more endearing than any of the charm he'd bestowed on her previously.

"I love you, Olivia. I loved you from that first moment in your father's garden, three years ago. Back then, I tried to convince myself you meant nothing. That I hated you as I always had. That I had too much pride to care for a woman who set fire to my curtains and threw me into rivers," he grinned swiftly before he was all seriousness once again. "But pride is a poor substitute for the woman I love, and I won't let it get in my way again."

Olivia's heart soared at his words.

Dear lord, could he really mean it? Could she really be this lucky?

"This isn't a trick, is it?" she whispered, almost afraid to believe him.

He laughed softly.

"Of course it's not a trick! I adore you, sweetheart. I never thought it possible to feel as much love as I do for you."

"Alex," she sniffled, her eyes filling with tears that she made no effort to stop. "I love you, too. So very much. I'm so glad I didn't drown you in the river."

His laugh was short-lived as his eyes lit in triumph before he pulled her face to his for a heart-stopping kiss.

She could have this every day, Olivia realised. Every day, forever.

"Marry me," he finally whispered, his forehead pressed against her own. "I know how much you like to fight me but if you will concede on this, I promise to let you win every fight from now until we die."

Olivia laughed through her tears.

She thought her heart would burst from sheer happiness.

"Let me win, indeed," she scoffed but couldn't keep the smile from her face. "I will win whether you allow it or not, Alexander Stratford."

NADINE MILLARD

"Is that a yes?" he demanded, his hands moving ever so slowly to the strings of her cloak.

"That is a most definite yes," she gasped as he removed the garment and began to nibble wickedly on her neck.

"Finally," he growled as his mouth moved lower still. "We agree on something."

Epilogue

"Christmastide in London again. Your mother will be disappointed that we're not at Fincham Hall."

"She'll get over it," Alex drawled, pulling his wife onto his lap. "The children would be so very bored making the journey. Surely it's better to stay here where they're happy and settled?"

"That's an excuse and you know it," Olivia grinned.

Her heart stuttered as Alex's lips found the pulse on her neck, and he grinned against her skin feeling for himself the effect he had. Not that it should surprise him. Five years of marriage had done nothing to dull his effect on every part of her.

"We'll blame Jane, then," he said, his hands moving torturously over her body. "Say that she wanted us to be in London for her first yuletide season as a mother. After all, she married my solicitor. Christmas is a busy time of year for him."

Olivia was become very much past the point of coherent thought, and he knew it.

Suddenly he lifted her so he could reposition her, her skirts hitched up, her thighs either side of his own.

"I will never forget that night on Scandal Lane," he whispered gruffly. "In my carriage, you sitting on me like this, looking at me with those incredible eyes. I was in agony for wanting you so much."

Olivia smiled a wicked little smile as she lifted herself from him and moved her hands to his breeches.

"And I'll never forget how exquisite you made me feel, though if I remember correctly, you weren't exactly relieved from your agony."

"Just being with you was pleasure enough, my love."

Olivia leaned down to capture his lips, freeing him from the confines of his breeches, revelling in his groan of pure desire.

"I know we're not on Scandal Lane," she whispered against his lips, gasping as his skilled fingers found their way to her core. "But I think it only fair that you get your turn."

"Maybe tomorrow we can take a trip to the Lane when the children are in bed. For old time's sake," he winked. "For now, let's get some practice in."

In one deft surge, Alex lifted her so he could bury himself inside her.

"Look at that," Olivia quipped though she knew her laboured breaths ruined the acidity. "You've finally come up with a good idea."

Alex merely laughed and then set about rendering his sharp-tongued wife utterly incoherent.

The End.

Also By Nadine Millard:

The Ranford Series

An Unlikely Duchess

Seeking Scandal

Mysterious Miss Channing

The Revenge Series

Highway Revenge

The Spy's Revenge

The Captain's Revenge

The Saints & Sinners Series

The Monster of Montvale Hall

The Angel of Avondale Abbey

The Devil of Dashford Manor

The Saint of St. Giles

The Royals of Aldonia

The Hidden Prince

Protecting The Princess

Redeeming A Royal

Beauty & The Duke

Fortune Favours Miss Gold

The Rocky Valley Series

Can't Escape My Love

Can't Hurry Love

Coming Soon:

Can't Buy Me Love

Can't Help Falling In Love

About Nadine Millard

Thanks for reading!

Keep in touch with all things Nadine Millard at www.
nadinemillard.com

Nadine always loves to hear from readers!

Follow for updates at:

https://www.facebook.com/nadinemillardauthor

https://www.twitter.com/nadinemillard

https://www.intagram.com/nadinemillardauthor

Miss Pageant's Christmas Proposal

TABETHA WAITE

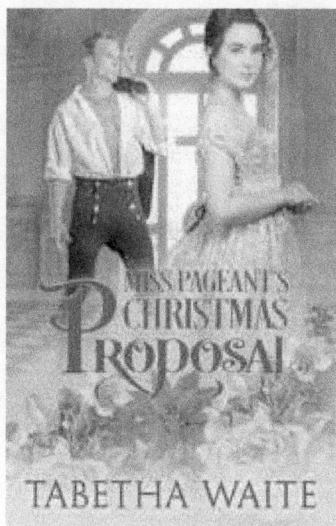

This story is for any girl who has ever wished on a star, picked petals off a flower, or prayed for her one true love. And may those men be worthy of that love.

One

London, England
December 1, 1815

Miss Emary Pageant studied her reflection in the mirror. She turned right, then left, then back again to make sure that everything was absolute perfection. Her white satin gown with its silver overlay had to flow precisely with her movements. Her hair was pulled into an elegant chignon, the style taking her ladies' maid nearly an hour to complete, but the efforts had not been in vain. A riot of sable curls framed her face and complimented her creamy complexion and expressive brown eyes. She'd even dared to apply a bit of color to her cheeks and lips, for she had to look her absolute best this evening.

The reason?

Lord Donovan Wainwright, Duke of Windwood, had arrived in town for his mother's ball, and *she*, Miss Emary Pageant, intended to be the one to bring the elusive bachelor to heel.

Satisfied with her appearance, Emary grabbed her reticule and headed downstairs. Her parents were waiting for her in the foyer, and when her mother spied her, she clasped her hands together over her bosom. "Oh, my darling, you look lovely!"

Emary grinned broadly. She could only hope that a certain gentleman would think the same. She wasn't nervous or worried about the upcoming encounter, because she knew that her chances of ensnaring the duke's affections were quite good. While some might think that sounded rather conceited, she had taken such painstaking efforts with her appearance that surely no other outcome could be ascertained. Not only that, but she had been told, quite frequently over the past several months, that she was one of the most sought after debutantes of the Season.

Throwing her purple velvet cloak around her shoulders, Emary climbed into the coach, placing her hands demurely in her lap as she sat across from her parents, the Viscount and Viscountess Armenton. They were only a couple blocks away from where the ball would be held, and while it might have been quicker to walk the short distance to the Windwood residence on Albemarle Street, the brisk, winter air would not have helped Emary's complexion. Besides, her father would have likely suffered an apoplexy at just the suggestion. When one was part of a well-to-do aristocratic family, one arrived in comfort and style.

Emary noted the endless line of carriages that preceded them, the process ensuring that they would be arriving fashionably late. When they finally stopped at the entrance to the large, Palladian townhouse, Emary gently placed her gloved hand in her father's grasp as he assisted her to the ground. She was careful to watch her step, so that the piles of dirty snow, mixed with the more unsavory aspects to be found on the city streets, didn't get on her shoes. It wouldn't do to have a pile of horse droppings clinging to her pristine slippers.

They handed their outerwear over to the footmen that were standing like a pair of statues on either side of the foyer, and waited patiently in the long receiving line. Emary was used to this for she had attended nearly every event in her debut Season thus far, and she'd had a fabulous time doing so. She had never been so flattered or complimented in all of her nineteen years. She could easily ensnare an earl or a marquess, so a duke shouldn't be any different.

Emary yearned to rise on her tiptoes to catch a glimpse of the golden head that everyone had been buzzing about for the past week, but she refrained from doing so. As it was, she felt as though she'd known the Duke of Windwood for years when they had never even met. She had heard that even though his father had forbade him to join the military, he had enlisted anyway and been awarded for his service in the Napoleonic Wars, that he had been named for some ancient Gaelic ancestor, that he liked two sugars but no cream in his tea, and that he was absurdly handsome.

With all of her knowledge about him, it was almost going to be *too* easy to capture a man like that. She would smile and use the charm that had brought more than one man to her parents' front parlor on bended knee. But she had refused every offer of marriage thus far. It was going to take a special man to win her affections, and she had the feeling that Donovan was that one she'd been looking for.

A confident smile touched her lips as she drew closer to their host and hostess. Of course, Emary had met Donovan's mother, Caroline Wainwright, the Dowager Duchess of Windwood, on several occasions. She was a handsome widow in her mid-fifties with golden hair that had grayed and dimmed in brilliance over time. She was tall and willowy and had a rather demure composure. Since Emary was already in the dowager's good graces, it should be no hardship to capture her son's attention.

At that moment, Emary finally caught a glimpse of her quarry, and her breath caught. *Oh my.* 'Handsome' didn't seem like a strong enough word to describe him. His honey-colored hair was smoothed back from his forehead, the ends just brushing his collar. He was tall with a firm build; that much was easy to discern, and dressed in stark black and white with a ruby stickpin in the folds of his cravat. His jaw was square, his eyes direct and accessing as he greeted each of his guests. He didn't seem to favor one more than the other, but then, he hadn't yet made *her* acquaintance.

As she finally stood before him, Emary had to hold back a gasp. This close, she could see that he had eyes of the purest blue, but that wasn't what had caught her focus. A scar ran along the left side of his face, from his brow and down the side of his temple. While she had been told that he'd served in the war, no one had bothered to mention that he had suffered such a concerning wound.

Her heart abruptly began to pound, a sensation she'd never experienced before. She hadn't even felt this sudden anxiety when she'd been presented to the Royal Court. She forced herself to calm as she offered a delicate curtsy and a brilliant smile. Adding a slight flutter of her lashes that was sure to curry his favor, she said softly, "Your Grace."

"A pleasure, Miss Pageant." His deep voice was perfectly civil, but when she glanced at him to gain his reaction to her, he wasn't regarding her in the manner of a man who was impressed with her appearance, or admiring of her looks, but rather as though he were... *bored*.

Emary swallowed her shock. She couldn't move, stunned as she was by his flat reception. From the time she had arrived in London for her debut ball until this moment she had been admired by men and women alike. The men were entirely smitten by her appearance and manner, while the ladies, however envious they might be of the attention showered upon her, flocked to her simply to learn her secrets.

But this man with his hard gaze and tightly clenched jaw was different.

He was, in a word, *fascinating*.

There were more people behind Emary, waiting to come forward, but her feet wouldn't obey her command to move away. As she lingered, something shifted in his face. It was subtle, but she saw the annoyance all the same.

Her mother touched her arm, shaking her out of her sudden stupor. "Come along, dear. Let's not monopolize all of the duke's time."

Emary allowed herself to be led away, but she knew the duke wouldn't stray far from her thoughts. A man like that would be worth fighting for, and at the end of the battle, she intended to be the one who carried the title of Duchess of Windwood.

THE MOMENT THE LADY AND HER PARENTS WERE OUT OF earshot, Donovan's mother leaned near him to whisper, "Miss Pageant has caused quite a stir this Season. She is a lovely young woman and sought after by many gentlemen. The perfect example of a delicate English rose."

Donovan wanted to roll his eyes. "Not everyone can be the epitome of perfection all the time."

Caroline didn't reply until another young girl had made her curtsy and moved out of earshot. "Perhaps not, but she would certainly be an acceptable candidate—"

"No," he said firmly.

Her brows drew together into a delicate frown. "You didn't even know what I was going to suggest."

"Yes I did," he contradicted dryly. "You were going to ask me to give her a chance, to get to know her." He glanced at her. "Was I wrong?" She pursed her lips together, and he had to snort.

His mother sighed. "Just keep an open mind at least?"

"You know I will," he returned, although he knew it was a lie. He'd met a hundred debutantes so far this evening. As yet, not a single girl he'd met tonight had given him much cause to hope. While Miss Pageant was one of the more comely ones, he knew she would be the same as all the others. They looked at him as if he was some sort of hero who hung the moon, or else they were frightened of his scar. The truth was, he was nothing more than a battle-hardened veteran.

He'd never understood why soldiers were romanticized. There was nothing remotely appealing about a bloodstained battlefield where a man had to watch the men he admired, the ones he'd trained with and perhaps had even known for years, fall at his feet with lifeless eyes. The only thing he'd been able to think about during those dark times was their parents and how they must be grieving for a son who wouldn't be coming home for Christmas anymore, or perhaps a widow who was mourning a lost husband, the children at home crying for a father who would never have the chance to see them grow.

Emotion clogged his throat now, as it did whenever he found himself dressed in his ducal finery knowing that he was one of the lucky ones who had survived. Each day that he opened his eyes in the morning and stared at the canopy above his bed, now that the war was finally over, he couldn't figure out why he'd been spared. Surely it wasn't just so he could stand in the middle of an elegantly decorated London ballroom and be fawned over by countless, empty-headed chits that he could never even consider taking to wife.

And yet, that's why he was here. He was nearly thirty years

old. He knew his duty to his title, it was expected for him to marry and produce the requisite heir.

While he hated to be put on display, like a painting in the British museum, for people to observe and dissect with their approval or criticisms, he had his limits. He wasn't going to be tied down for life to a silly girl who giggled constantly and couldn't string two coherent words together, the only things that she cared about in life being fashion or needlepoint.

As another girl paused before him, her beaming parents behind her, he had to withhold a sigh.

It was going to be a long night.

EMARY BARELY REFRAINED FROM BITING HER NAIL IN contemplation as the duke began to meander about the room nearly an hour later. Since the duke's initial impression of her hadn't gone as planned, she was confident that her dancing skills would do the trick. So when one of her faithful, male admirers came over to claim a quadrille, she accepted with a brilliant smile.

Her form was perfect and she moved with an easy elegant grace. After hours of training, she could practically perform the steps in her sleep. But when she glanced about to gauge the duke's whereabouts, she found him engaged in an involved discussion with a group of men of Parliament, still completely unaware of her existence.

Because of her distraction, she actually managed to tread upon her partner's instep, something that had never happened before. "Oh, I do beg your pardon!"

"No harm done, Miss Pageant," the young man replied, but his slight wince told her otherwise.

As the rest of the evening droned on, Emary spent the majority of her time trying to catch the duke's eye, but whenever she thought to try and impress him with her elegance or wit, he was either swallowed up by the crowd, or in some sort of in depth debate. As far as she knew he hadn't even danced with a single lady in attendance thus far, but yet she still wanted to stamp her foot in frustration.

What am I doing wrong?

She was surrounded by her usual crowd of admirers, who showered her with so many empty compliments that it was all starting to set off a pounding behind her temples. She finally excused herself to get some air, hoping that the brisk night would help to clear her agitated mind. Normally she relished being the center of attention, but at the moment, all that praise only managed to annoy her further.

She was so focused on her hasty retreat that she didn't notice the man walking in from the terrace — until it was too late.

Emary awkwardly crashed into a firm chest.

The man muttered an obscenity under his breath, and once she righted herself she found out why. Windwood had been holding a cup of punch in his hand, but she'd managed to knock it askew, causing a bright red stain to taint the front of his pristine, white shirt.

The blood left her face in a rush, the dizzying sensation causing the room to swirl about her. "I'm s... so... sorry," she stammered. She *never* stammered.

The duke looked down at his shirt, and then flicked a glance at her. "I suppose it's nothing that a good wash won't fix," he said dryly, and Emary could tell by the look in his eyes that he wasn't pleased. "I should probably go upstairs and change."

She wanted to sink into the floor. If she'd thought she'd been mortified before, she was thoroughly humiliated now. Thankfully, after a quick glance around, she didn't think that anyone had noticed the mishap. Something of that magnitude would likely cause her darling of the *ton* status to shift drastically.

As he started to move past her, she panicked and grabbed hold of his arm. He paused and glanced down at her hand where she clutched a rather muscular upper arm "You surely don't want to walk through the crowd, Your Grace." She tugged him back toward the terrace. "Surely you'd wish to take an alternate route and save yourself the embarrassment."

Emary might have imagined it, but she thought she saw his lips twitch as he allowed her to pull him away from the crowded ballroom. She was quite sure that he could have refused her at any time, but she was grateful that he went willingly. "Something tells me that it's not my appearance that concerns you so much as your own standing in society," he drawled.

The blast of cold air that hit her beyond the glass door nearly had her teeth chattering, but it didn't stop her from turning to him with an innocent expression. "Why, what a rather cynical view you have developed of me in such a short acquaintance. I truly only have your best interests at heart, Your Grace."

He continued to eye her skeptically, and she knew that he didn't believe a word she said. While that knowledge didn't particularly set well, she refused to let it deter her. However, when a rustling from the bushes beyond froze her in place, Emary silently cursed her luck. How ironic that a couple returning from a tryst would bring about her ruin. The moment they spied the duke's current predicament, it would be all over the ballroom within the hour.

"We're going to be seen," she whispered, as if speaking aloud would draw their attention, when the couple was still well out of earshot.

She gasped when the duke took hold of her arm and led her over to a shadowed corner of the terrace. He turned her around where her back was against the cold, stone railing, but the instant his towering height enveloped her, she no longer felt the chill in the air, but rather the heat emanating from his powerful body.

"Then let's ensure that they leave us alone." His breath was a puff of white before him, his bright blue eyes sparkling with a sort of mocking resignation, right as he lowered his head and took her mouth with his.

Two

Brought *to heel by a cup of punch,* Donovan thought dryly. Then again, he was the one who initiated the kiss, so who was truly at fault here? Thus far, he'd done his best to avoid paying court to any one female, had even refrained from dancing for fear that offering his hand to one woman would be misconstrued as anything other than polite.

All night he'd had the sensation that his cravat was tied too tight, for he could imagine all those eyes boring into his back. He'd done his best to occupy himself with talk of politics and matters that had nothing at all to do with searching for a wife, but he knew it was inevitable. At some point, he would have to choose one of them. But just — not yet. Not until he'd gotten a chance to know a few of them better.

And then this raven-haired whirlwind had slammed into him and set his world on end. He knew Miss Pageant would be a force to be reckoned with the moment those delicious brown eyes met his, but he was smart enough to be waylaid by a pretty face.

Or so he'd thought.

He'd certainly allowed himself to be persuaded to kiss her with little provocation. He wasn't sure if it was her sudden vulnerability at being caught that appealed to him, or how her lovely curves filled out her dress, but either way, he'd been unable to resist the temptation.

As his lips moved over hers, he felt à stirring in his loins that had been absent ever since he'd returned from France. The horror of that experience had gone far in allowing him to avoid his lesser desires, but with this single embrace, he was finding that the need for female companionship that had been dormant for so long yearned to break free. He suddenly wanted to pull her upstairs and remove more than just his stained shirt.

He blinked. What the hell was he thinking? Miss Pageant was an innocent, not some courtesan that he could pay off with a few pounds or an expensive bauble for a mutually satisfying night together.

When he heard a soft snicker behind him, followed by the click of a closing door, Donovan knew that the threat had passed. He abruptly broke the kiss and moved back a step. He ran a hand through his hair and closed his eyes on a heavy breath. He was almost afraid to see the horrified expression that would likely be on Miss Pageant's face after taking such liberties.

At the sound of a delicate noise, he feared she might be crying, so he reluctantly turned to her, only to feel his mouth fall open at the sight before him. The chit was *laughing.*

"Well done, Your Grace." She had her hand over her mouth, but there was true merriment in those chocolate-colored eyes as her ebony curls danced about her face. "I commend you on your quick thinking to salvage such a delicate situation."

"Yes, uh…" Donovan rubbed the back of his neck. He seldom found himself at a loss for words, but when a man kissed a woman only to have her find *humor* in the aftermath… "I do aim to please," he muttered.

Once she had recovered from her mirth, Miss Pageant said, "I shall take my leave of you now. I think you can handle it from here."

He blinked. The woman switched from one emotion to another with the flick of her delightful tongue. He had trouble following along. "What?"

She gestured to his shirt, her gaze dancing. "You were going to change before you saved us from that rather unsavory mishap, I believe?"

Donovan glanced down at the red stain on his shirt. He'd nearly forgotten the punch incident already. "Indeed." He cleared his throat. "I will take the servant's entrance."

She smiled. "And I shall return to the ballroom."

When she would have brushed past him, he found himself

reluctant for her to leave, which was decidedly odd, to say the least. Hadn't it been just a moment ago that he decided he wasn't interested in her? "Miss Pageant?"

She turned back to him with an expectant look. "Yes?"

He opened his mouth, but then snapped it back shut as he shook his head. "Never mind." *Dear God, what is wrong with me?*

He was still shaking his head as he walked away and descended the terrace steps.

ONCE THE DUKE WAS OUT OF SIGHT, EMARY COLLAPSED AGAINST the side of the building and put a hand to her thudding heart. Oh, that couldn't have gone any more perfectly!

Thank goodness she'd been thinking quickly enough to remember to act as though his kiss hadn't affected her. It wouldn't do to play her cards too quickly. First, she had to entice him, and by the confounded look upon his face when he'd left her, he was thoroughly intrigued. Rest assured, she had made certain that she hadn't seen the last of the Duke of Windwood.

But how to keep him invested?

She tapped a thoughtful finger against her lips, pausing when she recalled the feeling of his lips on hers. For a first kiss, it had been absolutely delightful, but then she didn't really have anything to compare the experience with. But just the memory of his brilliant, blue eyes and that golden hair illuminated by the glow of the ballroom, his scar standing out in stark contrast giving him a dangerous air, made her sigh. Even now, she wanted to hug herself in pure joy, but she must refrain. She had learned enough about men in her short experience to know that not only should their pride be catered to, but they wanted to feel as though they were the pursuant when it came to choosing a potential bride. If Windwood were ever under the impression that she intended to marry him, then he would be gone as quickly as a lightning streak in the sky.

Going forward, she had to be careful in the extreme.

A smile tugged at her lips. It was time to enact Plan B.

Donovan returned to the ballroom nearly thirty minutes later, much to the chagrin of his valet who saw the shape of his previous shirt. He pulled the cuffs of his jacket into place as he walked down the steps into the grand room decorated with bits of greenery for the upcoming holiday season. He had never really thought much of Christmas, for it had never been full of the merry abandonment that some aristocratic families enjoyed. As the only son of the former Duke of Windwood, Donovan had always been raised with a firm hand. Frivolities weren't tolerated for the heir to such a wealthy and vast estate. In fact, the only gift that Donovan could remember receiving that was remotely enjoyable was a book, although it was a selection of treatises rather than a fictional novel which would have "rotted the mind," according to his sire.

It wasn't until after the big upset with his father that had Donovan charging off to France in a fit of temper and youthful exuberance, that things had changed. By then, it was too late. His father had died while he was away, and while his mother had tried to soften the blow upon his return, Donovan still considered such festivities to be exuberant and without purpose. He had relented this evening only to placate his mother and because he knew it would help to ease his way back into society so that he might choose a bride and fulfill his duty to his father. It was the least he could do. The previous duke might have been strict, but Donovan now knew it was so he might teach his son what was important in life — his title.

He quickly sought out the group of men he'd been discussing politics with most of the evening. Unfortunately, his mind wasn't on the topic at hand as it had been before. Miss Pageant was still flitting about through his thoughts like an annoying insect buzzing around in his brain. It was aggravating that a kiss that should have withered away shortly after it had happened had only intensified. Of course, the exuberance that had followed the embrace had been nothing short of vexing, enough so that he found himself scanning the room in search of that head of sable curls.

He found her quickly enough, surrounded by a group of

eager men and women. As he observed the scene, they appeared to hang on her every word, as if she was some sort of Biblical prophet who might lead them to the Holy Land. He snorted at the very idea.

"Is the proposed bill not to your liking, Your Grace?"

Donovan gritted his teeth as Miss Pageant strolled onto the dance floor without an apparent care in the world. Forcing himself to look away from her, he turned to the older gentleman who had addressed him, who also served in the House of Lords. "I doubt my opinion gives much weight on the matter. It's not as if I alone retain the ear of Prinny," he returned noncommittally. In truth, he had no idea what the other four men had been blathering about.

A few chuckles resounded about the group, giving Donovan the smooth exit that he'd apparently required. He went in search of his mother, but winced when he spied her speaking to a handful of matrons. There was no way he was going to brave so many hopeful mamas. He wasn't nearly that bold. Or stupid.

Once again, he found his gaze drifting to Miss Pageant, where she was currently being escorted back to her entourage at the end of a set.

Then again…

Adjusting his cravat, he reluctantly headed in that direction.

EMARY SENSED THE INSTANT THAT THE DUKE OF WINDWOOD paused before her group. Even if the sudden hush around her hadn't given it away, she could *feel* his presence there. She waited a moment, and then slowly turned her head to acknowledge him. His bright blue gaze instantly clashed with hers. "Miss Pageant." He inclined his head.

She dropped into an elegant curtsy and made sure to take note of his new white shirt with a slight curve of her lips. "Your Grace."

He paused, as if the next words he spoke caused him a great deal of difficulty. "Might I have the pleasure of the next dance?"

Emary glanced down at her dance card where all the spots were filled. Except one. That had been done on purpose with the

543

hope that a certain gentleman might claim her hand. She barely kept her mouth from twitching in delight, but no doubt her eyes shone when she replied, "I fear that the only set I have available is the waltz."

He appeared to weigh something in his mind. "Fine," he said rather curtly as he scribbled his name on the blank line. "Until then." He turned on his heel and walked away from her for the second time that evening.

Emary couldn't help preening a bit at the duke's departure, especially when Miss Parkhurst, one of her rivals, looked at her aghast. "Lord Timberton and I had just made a wager that Windwood wouldn't stand up with anyone this evening! However did you manage such a feat?"

Emary shrugged in a delicate fashion. "I am Emary Pageant." As if that said it all. A collective murmur of praise went up, and Emary grinned outwardly, careful to keep up appearances.

Inside, she was a perfect mess.

With the very real recollection of the duke's mouth on hers, she was finding the thought of being held in his arms to be rather enticing. The butterflies in her stomach were so demanding that she decided a brief reprieve to the ladies' retiring room might be in order.

"I should probably go powder my nose to prepare for such an unprecedented event," she purred. She was about to make her escape when Lord Hallwood's face fell.

"But this is our dance," the young heir nearly whined.

Emary sighed inwardly. She had no choice but to remain. She knew the man well enough to know that if she refused him he would likely kick up a terrible fuss at being ignored and then she would be forced to sit out the rest of the sets, and that just wouldn't do with the duke due to return.

At times she grew weary of such young, immature men of the aristocracy who believed that they were entitled. But mature men like Windwood who carried more experience and battle-weary scars...

She offered Hallwood a brilliant smile. "Of course. I shouldn't dare miss the opportunity to stand up with you."

He was satisfied when she took his arm, his expression one of a whelp who'd been handed a particular treat. It made Emary nauseous, but she laughed and flirted and did everything that a young lady in society ought to do because it was expected of her.

It wasn't until she found herself standing in front of Windwood yet again that she felt her carefully rehearsed bravado slip slightly. His eyes seemed to caress her as he held out a hand. "Are you ready?"

As she drank in his appearance, a shiver to ran up and down her body so fast that she trembled. She didn't dare trust herself to speak, so she merely nodded and placed her gloved hand in his.

He led her to the floor where they got into position, his right hand placed on the small of her back while she settled her fingers on his broad right shoulder. She took a deep, steadying breath as she glanced up, only to see him staring down at her as if she was a dessert that he fully intended to devour. She felt her heart skip a beat — and then the music started.

Three

Donovan realized, in that moment, that he was an idiot. He had faced adversaries on the battlefields in France, faced down the enemy with nary a blink, and yet one pretty debutante fluttered her lashes at him and he found himself practically falling at her feet. *No*, he corrected himself. In truth, it was worse than that. He wanted to slowly strip the clothes from Miss Pageant's body and drink his fill of her form before he sank himself into her, giving them both the pleasure that their bodies craved.

And like it or not, he knew that she wasn't immune to him. He wasn't so much of a war weary soldier that he couldn't recognize the signs.

He admitted that she'd had him fooled at first, but the hitch in her breathing, the slight flush on her face, and the sparkle in those deep brown eyes told the truth. She wanted him just as much as he wanted her. But the trouble with debutantes was that he couldn't satisfy his lust without being leg shackled at the altar. And while he might be attracted to Miss Pageant, he couldn't say that she was the one he wished to spend his life with. It wasn't something he could deduce in the matter of a few hours, which was the extent of how long he'd known her.

"Emary is a rather unique name," he noted abruptly.

Instead of appearing insulted, she merely smiled. "It's a combination of my parents' names, Edward and Mary."

"Ah." *Interesting.* "Tell me about your family."

With her charming grin firmly in place, she replied, "I'm here with my parents this evening, Viscount and Viscountess Armenton."

He raised a brow. "Any siblings?"

She shook her head. "I fear that, like you, I am an only child."

"I suppose that someday you wish for a large family to make up for what you didn't have," he guessed.

"On the contrary," she returned. "I don't particularly wish to marry."

His second brow joined the first. *What game was she playing at now?* "I find that rather hard to believe, considering your many admirers, not to mention that you're a well-bred woman."

She tilted her head slightly, sending her dark curls bouncing around her shoulders. "I rather enjoy the attention that I receive, so why should I wish to rid myself of it? Besides, what does my sex have to do with anything? Times are progressing and changing all the time, Your Grace. Personally, I prefer to apply a more forward approach when it comes to my future."

He laughed. "While I appreciate your candor, Miss Pageant, surely you don't expect to become a spinster?" He found this idea terribly intolerant. "Ladies are expected to marry. If they didn't, what a sad lack of people we would have." He stilled. "Unless you plan to conceive out of wedlock?"

She shook her head. "I would never subject a child of mine to such ridicule and ostracizing. I was thinking more along the lines of self-support."

While what she spoke of was quite unheard of for a woman, he found that his interest was piqued nonetheless. "Such as?"

Her lips twitched becomingly, the action making him urge to sample them again. "I was rather thinking of becoming a novelist."

He snorted. "It's perfectly normal to have aspirations, Miss Pageant, but surely you can see the folly of taking such imaginings to these extremes."

"Am I?" She tilted her head to the side, her gaze shrewd. "What about Ann Radcliffe and her successes?"

"She was a commoner and a widow," he pointed out.

"And Miss Jane Austen?" she countered. "She is an unwed, gentleman's daughter."

He smiled in a tolerant manner, while at the same time enjoying the way her nose bunched slightly when she was making a point. "She writes anonymously."

"But everyone knows who she is, regardless," she returned. "Just the same as Frances Burney."

"Miss Pageant…" He sighed. "I pray you don't take offense, but while I admire your determination, I can't believe that you will succeed. Without the backing of a male relative—"

"Might I suggest a proposal for you, Your Grace?" she interrupted smoothly.

Alarm bells rang off in his head and he narrowed his eyes. "What sort of proposal?"

Her brown eyes twinkled, but he could sense the steel behind that sweet gaze. "Let's put your theory to the test."

"How so?" he prodded. It was becoming clear to him that Miss Pageant was too intelligent by half. It was almost a shame that women couldn't be allowed to vote in Parliament. He was quite sure that she would make a formidable adversary.

"Give me three weeks to prove to you that a woman can be sufficient on her own monetary value. If I am able to sell a novel that I wrote and have it published in *my* name, then you have to admit that you were wrong. If I don't, then I will concede defeat to you."

"This sounds suspiciously like a wager," he murmured, distrustful.

"I suppose it is, after a fashion." She released a deep sigh. "As there *is* a catch."

Donovan winced. Wasn't there always when it came to the fairer sex? "And what might that be?"

She looked him directly in the eye and said, "You have to pretend to be my fiancé."

The bells turned into a firm clanging in his brain, yet he still found himself asking, "For what purpose?" *What are you doing? Stop this insanity this instant!* And yet, he continued to listen to her asinine reasoning.

"I can't very well sequester myself in my room to write a novel and send it off to a publisher in three weeks' time when I am disturbed by continuous afternoon calls and hopeful suitors every hour. I should get nothing accomplished. I need *you* to be a diversion."

Every hour? "I'm not sure…"

"Come now, Your Grace. Surely you're not afraid of a brief engagement?" She fluttered her lashes. "Rest assured at the end of three weeks, once our wager has come to an end, I will cry off and you will be free to continue your search for the perfect duchess yet again. It's only a slight delay and you are still relatively young." Her eyes widened. "Surely you can still sire children at your age?"

He clenched his jaw, tempted to prove to her exactly how *virile* he still was. "I'm hardly in my dotage."

"Of course, not." She smiled a little too innocently. "So the only question that remains is, do you agree to my terms?"

He had to give the woman credit. She was damned persuasive when it came to something so incredulous. But it was the fact he was actually *considering* her proposal that was verging on madness.

He allowed his gaze to drop to her mouth. If he had Miss Pageant all to himself for the next three weeks, it could be rather dangerous indeed. He'd only been around her for one night and already she had him so befuddled that he couldn't think straight. That was probably why he opened his mouth to refuse, but found that the opposite came out instead.

"Very well, Miss Pageant. Challenge accepted."

EMARY HAD TO WORK TO KEEP HER SURPRISE FROM SHOWING. She couldn't believe that he'd actually taken the bait!

She thought she might have gone too far when she'd questioned his virility, for his blue eyes had flashed dangerously. She'd only said it to rile him, for she knew very well that men much older than him were more than capable of fathering children. And she had no doubt that he would be able to… *perform* the task quite admirably.

Just looking at him did strange things to her body. She could only imagine if they were involved in a more sordid act…

Stop it this instant! Such musings would not assist her cause but only push him away from her. She had a plan, a certain path that she must traverse if she were to succeed and win a true proposal by Christmas, so she mustn't stray to perilous territory and allow her desires to overrule her common sense.

The music came to an end, and Emary allowed a brief, victorious smile to touch her lips. "That settles it then. Shall we have the banns read this Sunday? For appearances sake, of course," she quickly added.

The duke swallowed visibly before he offered a bow. "I will take care of it." When he straightened, he held out his arm to her and escorted her back to her circle of admirers with a bow. "Miss Pageant."

Once he'd taken his leave of her, Miss Parkhurst wasted no time in demanding everything that was said between them.

Emary merely looked at her and said rather coyly, "You'll find out soon enough."

Several hours later, Emary was headed home in the carriage with her parents. She carefully stifled a yawn with her gloved hand. She was tired and ready to climb into her bed and sleep for what few hours of nighttime that she had remaining. Of course, she wouldn't have to rise before noon if she didn't wish to. Her mother was rather forgiving that way when it came to certain events. She always said that it wouldn't do for Emary to traipse about town in the afternoon with dark circles under her eyes.

"I am given to understand that this evening went well," her mother remarked.

"And who said that?"

"The Duchess of Windwood herself," the viscountess returned. "She seems to believe that her son might harbor a certain interest toward you. You were the only one he stood up with this evening, after all. And the look he gave you when we left…" Her mother's hand fluttered. "Why it was purely sinful. If he calls we shall have to make sure you are thoroughly chaperoned."

Emary had to hold back a satisfied grin. "I'm sure I'm just a passing fancy, Mother. No doubt he will forget all about me by morning."

Her father, who had been silent until that point, gave a snort. "I doubt it, my dear. I do believe that you might have snagged yourself a duke for a husband. Well done."

Emary felt tears prick the back of her eyes in the face of her father's praise. All of her life she'd known what was expected of her, had been raised to carefully observe the proprieties and walk a straight line, but nothing compared to her parents approval. She felt like a... *daughter*, instead of just a society debutante. "Thank you, Papa. I hope you're right."

"I know I am," he returned firmly. "Mark my words. There will be a proposal by Christmas."

"Perhaps even sooner than that," her mother added.

Emary said nothing. They would find out in two short days when the first of the banns would be read.

That is, if the duke followed through on his promise.

THE NEXT AFTERNOON, EMARY WAS IN THE DRAWING ROOM working on some needlepoint when her mother rushed into the room waving a paper in her grasp. "We have been invited by the duchess and her son to attend church with them on the morrow at St. Paul's Cathedral!" she announced, nearly out of breath.

Emary hid a pleased smile behind her frame. "How delightful."

When her mother didn't respond, she glanced up to see Lady Armenton eyeing her curiously. "Is there something I should know, Emary?"

Emary shrugged. "I shouldn't think so." In truth, she wanted to giggle with glee, but to spoil a surprise of this magnitude would just be too awful. It would be best to see her parents' faces light up when the first of the marriage banns were read. While the duke didn't imagine it was anything more than a harmless lark, she intended to make it real by the end.

Unfortunately, as London was wont to do, the drawing room soon filled with ladies who wanted the full *on dit* behind such a special invitation, as nothing was secret in the *beau monde*. Emary played her part, laughing gaily and making them all wonder as to the reason behind it all, never once letting on that she knew anything about it. She would have loved nothing more than to return to her needlepoint or even escape to the solitude of her room, but she forced herself to sip her tea and present the correct appearances.

When the last of the guests had finally taken their leave, Emary slumped back in her chair, the strain of sitting so stiff and poised for hours upon end having taken its toll.

"My gracious," her mother remarked as she sat across from her daughter with a similar pose. She had opened her fan and was waving it madly in front of her face. "I don't believe that we've ever had that many visitors in one afternoon! It never ceases to amaze me how fast word travels in London, especially when I was under the impression that it was a *personal* correspondence."

"Servants are the web of the city, Mother," Emary pointed out. "Not to mention the buzz the duke caused last evening by choosing to solely stand up with me, and for the waltz at that."

"Yes, you're right, of course," Lady Armenton murmured. She rose to her feet. "I suppose I should go to the kitchens to make sure Cook has everything prepared for supper. I'm nigh on famished after such an invasion."

Emary couldn't help but laugh as her mother took her leave. She stood up as well, but she didn't get the chance to return to her neglected needlepoint before the butler entered with a card upon a silver salver. "You have a guest, my lady."

She wanted to groan. *Another one?* She didn't even glance at the card, just waved her hand. "Send them in, if you please."

He hesitated a moment before he bowed and took his leave.

Emary took the opportunity to stretch the kinks out of her back. She raised her arms above her head and sighed in delight as her muscles loosened. She heard a strange sound, like some sort of groan, so she lowered her arms and turned to greet the caller. Her grin widened when she spied the duke standing in the doorway, but when she noticed the look of torture on his face, his scar standing out in stark, white contrast, she felt her smile falter slightly.

This didn't bode well. "Your Grace." She greeted him with a curtsy, and then asked cautiously, "Are you quite well?"

DONOVAN WANTED TO BURST OUT LAUGHING. *WAS HE WELL?* Pretty damn far from it, actually. He *had* been rather well and composed — until he'd walked in the room and saw Emary with her arms up in the air, back arched, with those enticing, full breasts thrust forward, barely contained by the pale yellow silk of her gown. A surge of lust had immediately rushed through him with enough power that it nearly knocked him to his knees and stole the air from his lungs.

He'd met countless French forces on the field of battle, yet he knew it was this

slip of a woman who was going to be the death of him. After having some time to consider her proposal, he had been fully prepared to call on her and put an end to this foolish charade. It was the reason for the church invitation, not because he had intended on going through with the banns being read, but because he *wasn't*. But one look at her tempting visage now and every bit of his carefully prepared speech vanished into thin air.

She looked so damned delectable standing there, uncertain of what he might say, when she really should have been concerned over what he intended to *do*.

Without a word, he reached her in three long strides. He cupped her face in his palms and crashed his mouth into hers. She stiffened slightly at first, but then her body eased into the embrace. She clutched his shoulders and moaned deep in her throat. Donovan instantly went hard.

He deepened the kiss, coaxing her lips to part with his tongue. When she opened to him, he delved inside, determined to taste her. She was sweet, like honey and tea and smelled like fresh, ripe peaches. He forced himself to go easy with her, not taking any more than she would allow, but according to her urgent response to him, her tongue daring to sneak forward and mate with his, he knew that wasn't an issue.

Donovan dared to slowly slide his hands farther down her body. He paused when he reached her ribcage. He boldly reached out and ran the pads of his thumbs across her firm nipples, which were eagerly pressing against the material of her dress. How he yearned to expose those enticing mounds of flesh to his gaze, to feast upon them properly, but he managed to tear himself away before he found himself acting upon the impulse. He took a full step backward.

His breath was heavy as he looked at her. Her brown eyes were glazed over with unrequited passion that lay dormant beneath the cloak of an innocent. Her lips were swollen and damp from his kisses. It made him want to return for another sampling, but he wasn't sure he would be able to stop there if he gave in a second time. The first was nearly his undoing.

"If that's how you say hello," she whispered huskily. "I should wish for you to call upon me every day."

He gave a chuckle, however strained it might have been. "In that case, I daresay you'd enjoy it when I said good morning." Her eyes widened slightly, and he had to look away from the curious anticipation he read there.

She blinked several times, finally regaining enough of her composure to sit down while gesturing for him to do the same. He took a seat across from her. After taking a deep breath, she said, "I can call for some fresh tea if you wish." She gestured to the teacart in the corner. "We've had a particularly busy morning entertaining guests, so I fear what's left will be cold by now."

He waved a hand. "There's no need to trouble yourself, truly. I realize that I'm calling later than is usual. I just…" He paused. He searched her lovely face, and just like the night before at the ball, he said the exact opposite of what he'd planned. "Wanted to see you." He cleared his throat. "Before tomorrow. To make sure that you weren't having any last minute reservations about our deal."

She reached up and put a hand to her chest as if trying to calm her heart, and then dropped it back to her lap. "No, I'm not. I have a point to prove and I intend to follow through on my promise."

He felt a reluctant smile tug at his lips. "I expected nothing less." He leaned back against the settee and crossed one leg over the other, folding his arms across his chest.

"Are *you* having reservations, Your Grace?" she said it evenly, but Donovan heard a hint of challenge in her voice.

"Not at all," he lied. Without wishing to dwell on the panic that had threatened all morning, he changed the subject. "Tell me about this story you're planning to write."

"And ruin the surprise of having you read the book when it's published?" she returned rather coyly. "I should think not."

He rolled his eyes, and then glanced about the room. When he spied the abandoned needlepoint in the corner, he had to snort, recalling that had been one of the things he'd despised about searching for a wife — women and their empty pursuits. "I wonder if you will even have enough time to complete the task at hand when there are so many other feminine pursuits for you to finish."

She clasped her hands in her lap. "As I explained before, Your Grace, that is where I shall need *your* assistance. As it stands, I can't possibly find any time to devote to pen and paper, but once our sham engagement is announced, that will put an end to most of the events I must attend as a lady in search of a husband."

He lifted a brow. "You are still that determined to prove me wrong?"

Her lips lifted in the corners. "You'll find that I am determined about many things, Your Grace. The ability that women can support themselves independently is just one of them."

He tapped his thumbs together, digesting her words. "Very well, Miss Pageant." He blew out a breath. "Let the games commence tomorrow at St. Paul's Cathedral." He rose to his feet.

She did the same. "And I shall endeavor to bring along the appropriate writing utensils."

He laughed. "To keep tally of your victories?"

She grinned. "I would never be so presumptuous, Your Grace."

As Donovan took his leave and strode down the front steps, he couldn't help but laugh at the entire situation he'd found himself in. And for the first time in his life, he had to wonder if he hadn't just met his match.

Four

The church of St. Paul's Cathedral was a mammoth, domed baroque structure situated on the banks of the Thames. It rose high above the rest of the city, as it had for centuries and had truly withstood the test of time. It had been destroyed and rebuilt due to the English Reformation starting with Henry VIII and the Great Fire of 1666. Its final design was courtesy of the architect Sir Christopher Wren and was announced fully completed on Christmas Day in 1711.

But while the exterior was breathtaking, it was the arches, sculptures and hollowed ceilings inside that truly caused Emary to stop and stare. It was the first time she'd crossed the threshold of the ancient church. Normally she attended services with her parents in the village near her father's estate, or at Westminster Abbey in London. Her mother had chosen that location since it had close ties with the monarchy. But she found that, while both were beautiful, she preferred the classic elegance of St. Paul's.

As her eyes lit on the duke speaking with someone in the middle of the aisle, she had to wonder if the true appeal of the church came in the form of a historical structure, or rather a towering man with a devilish scar who was in attendance.

Emary had worn her best dress today. At least, it was in her opinion. A pastel blue velvet, it complimented her creamy complexion and sable hair. More than one person had told her how beautiful she looked in it, but it wasn't until Windwood dragged that piercing blue gaze down her form in approval that she finally believed it.

She stood off to the side and admired her future betrothed as he greeted her parents. He wore black and white yet again; the only color he'd allowed being a deep crimson waistcoat and the ruby stickpin. In the lighting from the candles in the cathedral, the glow setting off the golden strands of his hair, he appeared as though he were a fallen angel descended from the heavens.

When he finally turned to her she couldn't help but fantasize that what was about to happen this day was real, that he was in love with her and they would soon become husband and wife. Although, if everything went according to plan, she could very well be a duchess by Christmas.

"Miss Pageant." The duke's voice was low and deep and it curled her toes.

She dipped a curtsy. "Your Grace."

He offered her his arm and led her over to a pew where his mother was already seated. Emary's mother took the spot beside her, followed by her father, the duke and herself. It wasn't long before the rest of the congregation was settled, giving way for the bishop to take his place.

For most of his sermon, Emary was more aware of Windwood's firm thigh pressed up against her own rather than anything that was being said. She chided herself for her inattention, but with that scorching kiss from the day before still quite vivid in her mind, she found it hard to concentrate when he was so near. Even the clean, male scent of him tantalized her senses. She clenched her Bible in her lap and took a calm, steadying breath, praying that she could keep her reserve until the end of the service.

"It is now my responsibility to announce that the following couples have declared their intentions to marry."

Emary instantly sat up straighter as several people were listed off. She bit the side of her cheek anxiously until she heard her name mentioned. "Miss Emary Pageant is currently betrothed to the Duke of Windwood, Donovan Wainwright. They are to be wed in three weeks hence on the twenty-fourth of December of our Lord God eighteen hundred and fifteen."

Emary released the air she'd been holding, but then found herself breathless when a warm, masculine voice whispered in her ear, "If I didn't know better, I might have thought you didn't hold faith in me to follow through on our bargain."

She turned to him and forced a smile. "I never had a doubt, Your Grace."

When they were dismissed, her mother instantly accosted her. "How could you keep something of this magnitude from us, you sly girl!" She drew Emary in for a hug, which she returned.

"We wanted it to be a surprise, Mama." Emary returned evenly, pushing aside the twinge of guilt that her words invoked.

"Well, it is certainly that," Donovan's mother said stoically with a level look at her son, which he returned evenly. Emary wasn't sure she even wanted to interpret that silent conversation. Holding out her hands to Emary, the duchess added, "Welcome to the family, Miss Pageant. I daresay I had nearly given up hope of my son ever settling down and starting a family. I'm so pleased that he chose you."

Once the well wishes had been spread throughout the members of the congregation who had come up to express their pleasant surprise, Emary finally walked out into the cool day on the arm of her fiancé. It was odd to imagine that she was an engaged woman with the matter of a few spoken words, but she reminded herself that she was supposed to break it off before the ceremony took place. If the duke thought that she had no intentions of doing so, she had no doubt he wouldn't ruin her reputation by breaking it off himself. He would no doubt be rather angry at her deception, and she couldn't blame him if that were so. While he believed she had three weeks in which to finish a novel for publication, the truth was, she had only three weeks to convince him to fall in love with her and to make their engagement one in truth.

The question was, could she do it?

She glanced at the man at her side, admiring the strong line of his smooth shaven jaw, the oceanic quality of his gaze, and even the rakish air of his scar, and prayed that this was one wager she would win.

"WHAT ARE YOU PLAYING AT, DONOVAN?"

He glanced up from his desk at the irate tone of his mother. "I regret that you have me at a disadvantage, Mother."

Once they had returned home after Sunday services, he'd gone into the study to catch up on some correspondence. He didn't know that his mother had intended to brave the lion in his own den, or enter without so much as an invitation.

"You know exactly what I'm talking about," Caroline returned firmly. She stood across from his desk and looked down at him, as if the pose might intimidate him. Fortunately, he was a man grown at nearly thirty years of age, so her tactics that might have chastised him when he was a boy no longer worked.

He sat back in his leather chair and crossed his arms over his chest since it was apparent he would have to listen to whatever it was she had to say before he could get back to work. "I suppose you're referring to me and Miss Pageant."

"That's precisely what I'm speaking of!" she returned in annoyance. "I don't want you playing with that girl's affections. I can't imagine what made you even consider something so outlandish as having marriage banns read after only one encounter!"

He held up a hand. "Actually, it was *two*. I called on her yesterday afternoon, if you recall." He shrugged. "Besides, it's not so unheard of. People in history who suffered from an arranged marriage seldom even met before the day they were wed."

"This is not Medieval times!" she snapped. She laid her hands on the desk and leaned forward, the blue eyes that mirrored his own, bright and direct. "End this ruse now before it gets out of hand."

Donovan didn't like his honor being taken into question by anyone, even his mother, but her heartfelt plea kept him from reacting too harshly. "Who says it's a ruse?"

The duchess was slightly taken aback. "How can you claim the opposite? I know you well enough to ascertain that you haven't formed an attachment to Miss Pageant in such a short acquaintance. Why, the night of the ball you made it abundantly clear that you weren't to have anything to do with her, and now this!"

He lifted a brow. "Can I not change my mind? I seem to recall that you do it frequently enough."

She eyed him steadily for a time, and then stepped back. "Very well. I can see you are set upon this course, but I implore you, as my son, do not do something that you will regret. I am truly fond of Miss Pageant and don't wish to see her get hurt simply because of your stubbornness to back down. The Bible says, 'Pride goeth before a fall.' Your father could never let go of his. Don't make the same mistakes he did."

As his mother left, Donovan scrubbed a hand down his face. Any mention of his father was a sore subject, which his mother knew quite well. Whenever she thought he was being unreasonable, she always played that hand.

However, if things kept progressing as they had between him and Miss Pageant, he wasn't sure she would be the one in danger of mending a broken heart when it abruptly ended.

THE FOLLOWING WEEK, EMARY WAS BOMBARDED WITH SO MANY calls that she hadn't had a spare moment to devote to her fictitious novel, nor add a single stitch to her poorly neglected needlework. At this rate, she feared she'd never have the opportunity to finish her basket of flowers, as surely the entirety of fashionable London had walked through her parents' front door.

When she said something to that effect to her mother, Lady Armenton had merely shrugged. "What did you expect? When the darling of society becomes covertly and rather *suddenly* engaged to the heroic Duke of Windwood, people are bound to be curious."

Emary hadn't missed the emphasis her mother had put upon *suddenly*. Her parents, while pleased about the abrupt turn of events, hadn't been happy with her about keeping such a monumental secret. But when the duke had arrived later that Sunday afternoon to finalize the marriage contract with her father, her subterfuge had been swiftly forgiven.

Unfortunately, since that day, Emary had not seen nor heard from Windwood. He was supposed to be assisting her, so she couldn't help but wonder what was delaying him. It wasn't as if he could back out of their arrangement after the first of the banns had already been read.

Unless…

Emary refused to even contemplate the idea that he meant to take this charade all the way to the end of the altar — and *leave* her there without a groom. She would be in such disgrace afterward that she would have no choice but to retire to the country with her parents and live out the rest of her days as a spinster.

At least I would have enough time to write the book I'm supposed to be working on now, she thought rather uncharitably.

When Windwood was finally shown into the drawing room later that afternoon, a surge of relief so powerful hit Emary that she was somewhat lightheaded from it. She held her breath, hoping that he might dare to take her in his arms and kiss her again, but with her mother present this time, the chances of him doing so were probably rather slim.

Her mother greeted him fondly and he bowed in turn. "My lady." His head turned and he sought Emary out. She wanted to believe that his eyes softened slightly when they lit on her. "Miss Pageant."

"Oh, surely there is no need for such formality now that you are betrothed." Lady Armenton gushed. "You're practically family, Your Grace. You have leave to call my daughter Emary."

"Of course," he concurred. "As she should call me Donovan."

"Well, I'll leave you two alone to get better acquainted." Her mother gave Emary a quick wink before she quietly took her leave.

Emary shook her head and noted dryly, "To imagine that a week ago she would have been horrified to learn that I was here alone with you without my ladies' maid present."

She could have sworn she heard her fiancé mutter something along the lines of, "I'm not so sure it's a good idea now," before he walked over and sat down beside her. "I'm sorry I've been so inattentive of late. I know that having my presence here was part of the deal, but I'm afraid I had some urgent estate matters to take care of."

She frowned. "I hope that everything is well."

"For now." Donovan winced. "But I'm afraid I may have to leave London again rather soon."

Emary smiled in an effort to put him at ease, although she felt a rush of panic. She couldn't persuade the duke that she was the perfect woman for him if he wasn't around to convince. "You're here now. That's all that matters."

His brow smoothed out a bit to allow a half-hearted grin. "So tell me about your writing. If you still intend to put me in my place, that is."

"Oh, that hasn't changed," she replied primly.

"Indeed?" His voice seemed to turn a bit huskier. "Then I suppose that means you still won't give me any sort of hint?"

She shook her head; her dark curls bouncing about her shoulders. "Now what would be the fun in that, Your Grace?"

Emary's pulse fluttered when he ran the backs of his fingers across her exposed upper arm. "I thought we agreed that you would call me Donovan."

Emary swallowed heavily, too distracted to form a coherent sentence when he was sitting so close to her. She could feel the heat from his body burning into her side. It was so intense, like sitting too close to an open flame, and it caused her palms to sweat. It was no wonder she couldn't put together a coherent thought. Everything this man did scrambled her senses.

"Say it," he demanded softly.

She shivered.

"Say my name," he repeated, his hot breath caressing her ear.

Emary wet her dry lips and finally managed to whisper, "Donovan."

He released a shaky breath and then reached out and cupped her cheek. His eyes were burning with a blue flame. "Someday, very soon, you will be saying my name while in the throes of passion, where rapture so consuming causes your body to tremble. I look forward to that day, sweet Emary."

Me too, Emary sighed to herself. He leaned forward and licked her earlobe, the sensation causing her lower abdomen to contract and her eyes to slide closed.

Emary sat there for several moments, heart pounding as she waited for him to kiss her, but it wasn't until Lady Armenton entered the room that the spell was broken and Emary realized that she was alone. The duke had left and she hadn't even known.

Her eyes popped open almost guiltily when her mother said, "Your future husband has invited us all to the opera to share his private box on Drury Lane this evening. This will be your first public engagement as a betrothed couple," the viscountess noted. "Just remember that you are not yet married, so there are still certain proprieties that shall still be observed in society."

Emary nodded her understanding while her face warmed and the butterflies in her stomach fluttered furiously with the idea that in a few short hours she would once again be on Donovan's arm. She could hardly wait.

$\mathcal{F}ive$

The Theatre Royal on Drury Lane was a fixture of London society, as much as Vauxhall Gardens and Hyde Park. The aristocracy enjoyed their entertainments, and the stage was no exception. Emary had been several times, as her parents also had a private box for viewing. She had always admired the theater's famed Rotunda and Grand Saloon, but when she entered now with Windwood by her side, any other time she'd traversed the Royal Staircase had been uneventful. She knew this night was the only one that would linger in her memory for years to come.

Amid a flurry of fans and curious, or in some cases, envious glances, followed their progress all the way to the Windwood box. It was situated directly in the middle of the large interior of the theatre and faced the red curtain that would be raised when the performance began. It was, quite literally, the best seat in the house.

Emary glanced over the edge of the balcony and noticed that nearly the entire lower half of the seats were already filled with people anticipating the upcoming entertainment. The buzz of the crowd around them was nearly deafening. It was likely to be a sold out performance. She was thankful it was going to be an intimate affair with the five of them — her and Donovan, his mother, and her parents — although there was room for several more people if they were so inclined.

Emary had been extremely careful with her appearance this

evening. She had wanted to make the duke yearn for her the way he'd left her yearning for him in her drawing room earlier. She still trembled when she thought of the little love bite he'd given her ear right before he had departed, leaving her breathless for more.

However, from the way he kept shooting heated glances at her from the moment he'd arrived in his ducal coach with his mother to pick them up to right now, as he took his place beside her, Emary knew her efforts hadn't been in vain. Her maid had styled her hair into an elegant chignon and left several curls to dangle across her slim neck. She wore an empire style gown of white and red striped silk with short puffed sleeves. Her white, elbow length gloves reached just past her elbow and teased the senses with just a bit of exposed skin. While Donovan was equally resplendent in a white cravat, gold waistcoat, and royal blue cutaway jacket and trousers, it was no wonder they had drawn the attention of several attendees.

Once they were settled, the duke leaned over to whisper in her ear, "You look delectable this evening, Miss Pageant."

She had to compose herself before she could respond appropriately, "Thank you, Your Grace." She turned to him with a slight smile. "You look rather handsome yourself."

The scar running down the left side of his face drew her attention to his eyes, which seemed to burn intently. "How is your writing going?" he asked as the lights began to dim, signaling that the show was about to begin.

"Very well, I should imagine," she lied easily.

His lips twitched. "That's it? I'm not even to be granted a title?"

"Oh, I think I will grant you that boon, Your Grace." She looked at him through her long, dark lashes. "I believe I shall call it, *A Seduction at Christmas.*"

He adjusted his position in his seat and gave a soft groan. "I'm sorry I asked."

She laughed lightly and then turned to face the stage when the curtain was drawn.

DONOVAN FELT CONFIDENT THAT HE COULD STAND UP AND WALK about during intermission without embarrassing himself. In truth, he was rather thankful for the reprieve when he left to fetch Miss Pageant some punch. He could certainly do with the chance to control his raging body. He'd hardly been able to follow along with the actors on stage for his preoccupation in entertaining some rather lascivious thoughts about the woman at his side.

In such a short acquaintance, she had managed to bewitch him, weave some sort of magical spell over him. It was certainly the only explanation, for she made his head spin. He'd never had this problem with any other woman before. So what made Emary so different from the rest? If it was merely lust, surely he could contain those urges. He was nearly thirty years old, but the way he was acting around Emary, it was as if he was a green lad. He couldn't seem to keep his hands — or his thoughts — off of her.

When he returned to his box, he had to pause on the threshold when he found Emary surrounded by her usual gaggle of admirers. He clenched his jaw at the sight, his vision clouded with some foreign emotion. He didn't want to admit that it was actual jealousy rising to the surface, but when some young buck congratulated Emary on her recent betrothal, and then went a step closer to kiss her gloved hand intimately, Donovan couldn't hold back any longer.

"I'm back, darling." He handed her the glass of punch. "I hope you didn't miss me too much."

She turned those adoring brown eyes on him and accepted his offering. "I daresay I was nearly inconsolable from your loss," she teased.

Donovan grinned. He couldn't resist the sudden urge to bend down and brush his mouth against hers, not only because she was tempting beyond all reason, but also as proof to everyone else that she was spoken for. Which was strange, since this entire engagement was supposed to be nothing but a sham, a proposal that wasn't supposed to go any further than three weeks.

So why did he feel as though she was already his?

Six

E mary sat in her sitting room the next morning and tapped her quill impatiently against the top of her writing desk. She stared at the accusatory blank sheet of vellum before her and blew out a disgusted sigh. For a woman who was supposed to be proving her worth as a female writer, able to survive by words alone, she was sadly lacking in motivation.

Christmas. Think Christmas… Emary closed her eyes and rubbed her temples with her fingers, willing the inspiration to strike. Unfortunately, her mind remained stubbornly blank. With a sigh, she set down her quill and began to pace the room. Perhaps a story might surface if she was active.

She thought back through the years when she was a child and tried to bring those happy memories to the forefront of her thoughts. She remembered countless Christmas mornings at her parents' estate when she would wake up to the snow coming down in giant flakes. She recalled that sensation of youthful exuberance when she opened the door and bounded outside, only to fall on her back in the midst of that cold, white powdery fluff and move her arms and legs to make an angel. As those bits of frozen crystal fell from the sky, they clung to her eyelashes and tickled her nose, and she didn't think anything else could be so wonderful.

Now she knew differently.

She instantly brought Donovan's face to mind and winced at a pang of guilty conscience. He had been so charming at the theatre the night before, attentive and entirely… *perfect*, while she'd had to force a smile to her face knowing that their sham of an engagement was a farce in itself.

So, this morning, in an effort to at least *try* and add some truth to the lie, she fully intended to write — *something*. The problem was that the words just wouldn't come.

Emary sank down on her bed and put her head in her hands. Perhaps this was her penance for being too confident in her abilities to ensnare the title of duchess. Not only did she risk forfeiting the duke's attentions if her subterfuge was ever revealed — the one man who'd ever managed to make her heart flutter and her pulse to accelerate when he was near — but she would be forced to return to her father's estate in shame, living the rest of her days with no one to talk to but the servants and the mirror on her wall that reminded her of everything she'd had — and lost.

She clenched her fists in her lap. She would *not* allow herself to end up that way. A singular existence might work for some, but she required attention. It was almost necessary for her as breathing. She craved it. She *relished* in it. And while it might be stifling at times (she certainly detested the strict rules of society), she knew that if she had to leave the city in disgrace, the solitude would eventually destroy her.

Emary rose to her feet. At times like this, there was only one thing to do that could ease her mind, so she rang for her maid. When Althea arrived with a quick curtsy, Emary announced, "We're going shopping."

Thirty minutes later, Emary was browsing the different bonnets with their colorful ribbons and fashionable feathers and adornments at her favorite millinery, when she happened to glance out the front window and spied a familiar towering figure crossing the street. Emary couldn't help but stop and stare at the handsome picture that the Duke of Windwood presented with his black greatcoat flowing behind him, his top hat sitting at a slight angle on his head.

He quite literally took her breath away.

She thought for a moment that he might have noticed her parents' carriage out front and intended to seek her out, but he didn't even glance at the coach as he continued purposefully down the sidewalk and disappeared from her view.

Emary, instantly curious, abandoned her own fashion perusal and went outside. She glanced in the direction he had gone, spotting his towering frame some distance away. She tried to casually follow the duke's progress without it being too obvious that she was doing so, her maid trailing a few paces behind. Finally, after a couple of blocks, the duke went inside a perfumer's shop. Emary blinked, surprised, and wondering what his purpose might be for going inside a store that was clearly meant for ladies.

She realized that, were he to exit the building at that moment, she was rather standing out in the open, so in an effort to remain covert, she quickly ducked into a shaded, narrow alleyway. She peeked around the corner of the brick, keeping her gaze on the perfumer's, not bothering to look about her to make sure that she was alone.

So when a filthy hand was abruptly clamped over her mouth, she was caught off guard. "Wot's a pretty thing like ye doin' sneakin' about?" a gravelly voice whispered next to her ear. She shivered, but it wasn't with the anticipation that she felt with the duke. No, this man's hot breath on her nape caused her eyes to widen in fright.

Thankfully, Emary wasn't one to suffer fools for long. She caught a slight movement out of the corner of her eye and knew that Althea was going to prove enough of a distraction for her to act. His grip slackened just enough at the gasp of her timid maid hovering at the fringes of the alley, that Emary was able to slam her elbow backward into the man's ribs. He grunted slightly and his hold loosened even further so that she was able to break free. She'd already laid her eyes on something that she might be able to use as a weapon, so she quickly picked up the broken, wooden board and turned around and swung with all of her strength.

The plank struck him in the upper arm and he instantly howled in pain. "Ye crazy bitch!" he shouted, although he didn't bother to stay and see how she might react to that insult. He ran off in the opposite direction and was lost to the shadows.

Emary was breathing heavily from her exertions. Her hair was starting to escape from her pins, and she began to shake in the aftermath of the assault now that the shock was wearing off.

When she felt a gentle hand on her arm, it didn't even register in her mind that it might not be a foe she was spinning around to confront. She just swung with the wood that was still clutching tightly in her grasp.

The Duke of Windwood caught it just inches from his temple.

The instant recognition was in place, Emary was flooded with relief. She let the wood clatter to the cobblestones as she nearly threw herself into her fiancé's arms. She hardly noticed it when her bonnet fell backward and her ebony curls fell around her shoulders. Nothing mattered other than the fact Windwood was something sturdy and familiar to cling to after she'd just faced down such a rotten miscreant.

The duke murmured something to her maid, but while Emary couldn't make out everything that he said, it was something along the lines of retrieving the carriage. When they were alone, Donovan pulled back slightly and looked into her eyes in true concern. "What happened?"

"I was… accosted." Her voice wavered slightly.

He instantly scanned the shaded area around them, his eyes almost lethal in their intent, but when he didn't appear to detect any further threats, he lifted her chin with his finger and softened his gaze. "Are you hurt?" he asked softly.

She slowly shook her head, and suddenly, something shifted between them. His blue eyes seemed to darken with awareness, and she found that as long as she was with him, nothing else mattered. She was safe in his arms. "Kiss me, Donovan," she whispered boldly. "Make me forget it all."

He didn't even hesitate, but lowered his head and placed his mouth on hers. Emary instantly wound her arms around his neck. He guided her backward until she was against the building, but even the coarse brick against her back didn't keep her from greedily taking everything that he was offering her. It was an escape, the freedom to share her worries with him. With this kiss, it was as if he was vowing to save her, protect her, but more importantly, to love her.

And she wanted it all.

DONOVAN HAD HEARD THE COMMOTION IN THE ALLEY, AND WHILE he knew it wasn't his place to get involved, he couldn't resist the urge to intervene. Perhaps it was his nature as a gentleman, or perhaps the ingrained need to vanquish an enemy, a profession that he'd been taught in the service of his country. Either way, he certainly hadn't expected to see Emary there, daring to fight off an adversary. He would have interceded if she hadn't temporarily stunned him with her abilities. He didn't think a well-bred woman like Miss Pageant, the daughter of a viscount, could defend herself with such precision and bravery.

Only after the threat was gone, did he notice the vulnerability beginning to seep into the slump of her shoulders and the tension of her hands as they clutched the wooden beam as if it was her only lifeline. He'd approached her cautiously, had been prepared for the blow that she would try to deliver. But what had really shaken him to his core was the complete sense of trust and solace that had appeared on her face when recognition had flooded her vision.

He wanted to do anything to wipe that fear off of her face, so when she'd asked him to kiss her, he had been unable to resist. He was quite sure that he wouldn't be able to deny her anything that she wanted of him, for he knew that he was already halfway to being in love with her. If he hadn't been confident of it before, as his mouth moved over her sweet lips, he certainly knew it now. No other woman had ever made him feel this way before. Others might look at him as if he was some sort of hero, as if he'd hung the moon, but with Emary, he could truly believe it.

The second of the banns would be read the next day, and Donovan admitted that after he'd dropped her back home after the theatre it was time he stopped trying to act as though she didn't mean anything to him.

Even before she'd come up with this asinine plan of hers to stage a mock engagement, he realized that he wouldn't have chosen anyone else. At some point, he would have been introduced to Emary and eventually asked her to be his bride. Some things were just inevitable. And it wasn't just her comely appearance, although he'd dreamt of that sable hair and those deep brown eyes in the throes of passion more than once. No, there was more to Miss Pageant than just a pretty face. She was intelligent and perceptive and had a depth of character that was equally proper and mischievous. In spite of her nature, it would have taken more than flowers and love poems to win this woman's heart.

He gently ended the embrace when he heard the sound of footsteps behind him, although he didn't release Emary. The way she looked now, her lips parted slightly as if silently begging him to return his mouth to hers, her dark hair cascading over her shoulders, her eyes partially closed — it was an image that would haunt him for years to come. "The carriage is here, Your Grace," her maid said quietly.

He threaded Emary's hand through his arm. "Allow me to see you back home, my lady." She nodded, offering no resistance as he handed her into the carriage. "I'll be back in a few minutes." He collected his horse and led it behind the coach and saw to it that the gelding was tied to the back.

He climbed inside the coach and sat beside Emary, where her maid had managed to put her hair and bonnet to rights while he'd been absent. Emary instantly clasped his hand with hers and leaned her head against his shoulder with a sigh. The sound shot straight to his groin, but with her maid sitting directly across from them, it was rather hard to ravish Emary. Instead, he leaned his head back against the squabs and enjoyed the feel of her nestled next to him as he tapped the roof of the carriage to let the driver know they were settled.

EMARY WAS DRAINED BY THE TIME SHE WAS DEPOSITED AT THE front steps of her parents' townhouse. Thankfully, the duke stayed by her side the entire time, giving her the courage to explain to her mother and father what had transpired. "It's a miracle you were there, Your Grace," her father said sincerely.

"Unfortunately, I can't take the credit, Lord Armenton. Your daughter is a force to be reckoned with." He glanced at her with a soft smile, and then regaled them with the events that he'd witnessed.

After he was finished, the viscountess looked at her daughter with a horrified expression. "Wherever did you learn such tactics?"

Emary could feel her face heat slightly. "From the village blacksmith."

While she feared her confession might cause her mother to fetch her smelling salts, her father merely laughed heartily. "I'm not surprised in the least. Old Fred was one in a million. I daresay I'm grateful for his teachings, or today might have turned out rather differently."

"Indeed, my lord." Donovan concurred. "Those were my thoughts exactly."

"I imagine you wish to lie down after such a harrowing ordeal," her mother noted.

"Actually," the duke interjected smoothly. "I was hoping to have a moment alone with Emary."

Emary's stomach tightened, for his gaze promised so many deliciously wicked things. "Of course," she said before her mother could intervene. "Shall we go to the parlor?"

She preferred the drawing room to the gold and pink color scheme that her mother had used for the front parlor, but it was the closest room where they could be alone. She even dared to shut the door behind her for privacy, but since her parents imagined that a wedding would be taking place in little more than two weeks, they didn't mind allowing them a few moments of solitude.

The moment she turned to face him, she was in his arms, his mouth crushed against hers. It wasn't until she was moaning for more that he ended the kiss and looked at her with a crooked smile. "I couldn't wait to do that again."

"I couldn't wait *for* you to do it again," she returned, entranced.

He chuckled, and then stepped away from her. He reached into his pocket and handed her a gaily-wrapped package. "This is for you."

Emary accepted the gift with a surprised smile. She untied the pretty bow and removed the paper to uncover a small bottle of perfume. She stared at it for a moment, realizing that when she'd been distrustful of the duke's actions, he had merely been shopping. For *her*.

"Do you like it?"

She swallowed her guilt and looked at him. His scar stood out in stark contrast to the rest of his face, his jaw clenched with uncertainty. "I love it," she said honestly. "But how did you know this is the fragrance that I use?"

His eyes instantly warmed. "Because you always smell like peaches."

She had to laugh. "You seem to know me rather well, Your Grace. Pity I can't say the same." She had been close enough to him to catch a spicy, earthy scent, but she couldn't put a name to it, other than it was wonderful and uniquely... *him*.

He lifted a dark gold brow. "Oh, I intend for us to know quite a bit more about each other in the coming weeks."

She felt her mouth fall open slightly, for she had *no* idea how to interpret such a promise. He bent down and brushed his mouth over hers, and then with a rather wicked wink, he was gone.

Seven

E mary was rather unsettled the next morning when she dabbed the perfume from Donovan on her wrists and behind her ears as she dressed for church. Each Sunday the banns were read she was invited to join the duke and his mother for services at St. Paul's to show a united front. In turn, she was surprised she didn't burst into flame the moment she stepped over the threshold for all her subterfuge.

Each day she continued to stare at that blank sheet of paper with nothing to write on it, but then, she'd never truly thought about becoming a writer. It was simply the only excuse she'd been able to come up with on such short notice. It was a profession that would be both credible and appropriate for a single woman of society.

Unfortunately, she'd never considered that writing was a talent that would be considerably lacking within her.

Emary shook her head, intending to put such trepidations out of her mind. She could worry about the 'words' tomorrow. Today she would simply enjoy being on the arm of the Duke of Windwood as he picked them up in his carriage.

Donovan was standing by the door to personally help her mother inside the fashionable coach with the Windwood coat of arms emblazoned on the side. It wasn't until her father entered that Donovan caught Emary's hand before she could follow suit. Emary's face heated as she looked into her affianced handsome face with that rakish scar. She didn't think she would ever tire of looking at him.

He bent his head toward her. "You look beautiful as usual, Miss Pageant." He kept his voice low, but his eyes spoke volumes as he slowly allowed his gaze to travel down her body and back up again.

She offered him her gloved hand, turning it to where her wrist was facing upward. "I'm wearing the perfume you gave me," she whispered mischievously.

He breathed in the scent deeply, and then kissed the delicate, exposed skin. She gasped when she felt the tip of his tongue lick her lightly, the sensation shooting all the way to her mid-section. "So delectable," he murmured.

Emary had a hard time catching her breath. She tried to tug her hand away, but he held her fast. His eyes were pure temptation when he looked at her, blue sparks of fire swirling in his bright gaze. And again, she felt his tongue dart out and taste her. The air left her lungs in a rush. "Donovan, please…" Again, she tried to tug her hand away.

He let her go, but not before he leaned closer and said softly in her ear, "Someday, my dear Emary, I will taste every inch of you."

She closed her eyes to imagine the erotic images his words evoked, but then remembered that she was on the street where anyone could see them, her parents and his mother waiting only a few feet inside. "You're a wicked man," she returned firmly, although her voice had a shallow quality that belied her words.

"Indeed," he returned, nonplussed. "And very soon, you will join me in this land of debauchery and I promise that you will enjoy every minute of it."

With that, he leaned back, leaving Emary feeling hot and flushed. But at least what he said was true. She couldn't wait to begin his tutelage.

DONOVAN DISCOVERED THAT HE LOVED TO TEASE MISS PAGEANT. Perhaps a bit *too* much. But he found that there was nothing else he'd rather do than to keep that charming blush on her cheeks and the sparkle of passionate interest in those expressive, dark brown eyes.

He was still entertaining some rather lascivious thoughts about the woman at his side, and was surprised he wasn't struck with a lightning bolt the moment he walked into the sanctuary.

They took their seats and Donovan managed to hear at least half of what the man in the pulpit was saying, even though he was more aware of Emary's soft, curvaceous body right next to him. When the second of their marriage banns were read, he glanced over at Emary to gauge her reaction. She appeared perfectly calm and composed, but he could sense a certain tension in her.

He leaned over and whispered in her ear. "Having second thoughts already?"

She turned to him and bit her lip rather becomingly. "Of course not." She paused. "You?"

He dared to wink at her. "Never a doubt." He was pleased to see that caused her lips to twitch into a slight smile. She also seemed to relax slightly.

After the service was over, they made their way outside. After being closed up in the dim confines of the church, the sunny December day was nearly blinding. He lifted his hand to shade his eyes and turned to his fiancée. "You haven't said anything about your book recently. How is it coming along?"

She sighed heavily and looked at him from beneath her becoming straw bonnet. "I'm afraid it isn't."

"No?" he asked. "Won't it be rather hard to put me in my place without anything to use to do it?"

"Don't you think I realize that?" she snapped, slightly annoyed. "I just can't seem to find the right..." She waved her hand in the air as if searching for the appropriate description. "*Words*."

"I see." Donovan studied her slightly dismayed face. Perhaps it was a reaction that was ingrained in most men to lift the spirits of downtrodden women, but suddenly he wanted to be her champion. "Perhaps I might be of assistance."

She snorted. "Surely not. That would be like giving your enemy the advantage."

He winced. "I'm not sure I would have put it quite that way. And it's not as if I'm offering to write the story for you," he pointed out. "It seems only fair that, given the brief amount of time you have left to write this novel, that I give you a fighting chance, as it were."

She tilted her head to the side and considered it. "That does seem quite reasonable, Your Grace."

"Capital." He grinned. "That settles it then. I'll see you later this afternoon."

EMARY WAS IN THE DRAWING ROOM TRYING TO CONCENTRATE ON her needlepoint, having changed into a pale pink muslin, when the duke strode in. Since her mother knew that he was going to call, she promised that she would entertain any guests that might drop by in order to give them some additional time alone. Emary had been grateful for her mother's intervention, but at the same time, she had wanted to wring her hands in anticipation of Donovan's arrival.

Was it so terrible that she wanted to kiss him again, instead of discuss some book that she would no doubt, never even write?

But since this was all part of a web of deceit of her own making, she decided that she had no choice but to play along. Then again… She tapped her finger against her lips in thought. This might work out to her advantage, and she knew just what to do. It would be rather devious, but it would likely be worth it. And if all went according to plan, she would have a story *and* that kiss.

Thus, when Windwood entered, she had to keep a smile from spreading across her face. Instead, she rose with a curtsy. He bowed in turn, and after a brief greeting, for they both knew why he was there, she walked over and sat down on the settee, nearly bemoaning the fact that he took the seat across from her. But she told herself it was only a slight deterrent.

"I think I may have had a breakthrough, Your Grace," she announced proudly.

"So soon?" His left brow inched upward, causing his scar to stretch slightly, roguishly.

"Most certainly." She clasped her hands in her lap in apparent excitement. "I do believe I already told you that the title shall be 'A Seduction at Christmas.' Of course, it shall be a romance."

"A romance?" he echoed, seeming to consider the idea.

"Indeed. And this afternoon it suddenly occurred to me that the motivation I've been lacking has been right in front of me all this time."

"Oh?" He grinned.

It's a shame he looks so hopeful... "Yes. I thought of the idea after I returned home from St. Paul's. I shall make my hero a country vicar!" She clasped her hands together. "Isn't it delightful?"

His face visibly fell. "Uh...of course."

"You don't like the idea?" she asked, trying to appear discouraged, but on the inside she was filled with glee. He was falling perfectly into her trap.

"It's just rather..." He cleared his throat lightly. "That is to say, I was given to understand that I might have inspired you."

She laughed lightly at the slightly bemused expression on his face. "Why, you certainly aren't vicar material!" He seemed to be relieved at this assurance, but then she took it one step further and tapped a finger against her lips somewhat thoughtfully. "Then again, when I was developing his nature, you were rather similar in character."

He frowned. "How so?"

Oh, this is just too fun. "It's nothing detrimental, I assure you. But now that I think upon it, he is rather... stuffy."

He nearly choked. "*Stuffy?*" Those blue eyes narrowed. "Madam, are you daring to claim that I'm dull?"

"Not you!" she hastened to say. "But rather the *vicar* in my story."

"But you just said we were similar!" He nearly growled. "That I was practically the model for this dim-witted imbecile!"

She sat up straighter and lifted her chin a notch for effect. "Well, you *did* get rather upset when I accidentally bumped into you the night we met and caused your punch to spill."

A muscle abruptly began to twitch in his jaw and Emary feared that she might have pushed him too far. When he spoke, his words were even and carefully pronounced. "It rather felt like a deliberate attempt to gain my attention."

Emary crossed her arms as if offended, when in all honesty, it was rather too close to the truth. "Are you insinuating that I *purposefully* drenched you in punch?"

He shrugged. "If the boot fits…"

"I daresay I wish there had been a plausible excuse for my clumsiness!" she retorted. "I was mortified. Besides," she sniffed. "You'd made it abundantly clear that you weren't interested in me."

"And yet," he pointed out softly, "here I am."

His eyes pinned her where she sat, and the room abruptly filled with tension. The sudden awareness caused the fine hairs on the back of her neck to stand on end.

"Since you say this novel shall be a romance," Donovan said smoothly. "Tell me about this vicar's lady love."

Emary hesitated. She had only meant to torment the duke with the idea that he was a dry simpleton so that he might move to the settee and prove her wrong, but instead, he had somehow turned the tables and challenged her to invent a non-existent heroine. Unprepared for this counterattack, she blurted the first thing that came to mind. "She's blond."

He waited for more, but when she remained silent, he said, "That's it?" His voice was deep and nearly caressing when he added, "That just won't do. It's terribly bland, and yet—" He scratched his chin. "—I suppose such an unremarkable character shall be perfect for a dull vicar."

Emary gasped. "I beg your pardon!"

He lifted an inquiring brow. "Do you have something to add?"

She wracked her brain for another adjective. "She's nice?" *Oh, this is terrible.*

His lips instantly lifted in the corners and Emary felt as if she was in the presence of a deadly snake. One wrong move and it would surely strike. "Come now, you can surely do better than that." His voice was silky now, and full of veiled secrets. "Tell me, how did this boring vicar and this nice, blond lady meet?"

"They… uh…" She froze. He was running his thumb across his lower lip and she quite forgot what they were even talking about.

"Emary?"

She swallowed. "Yes?"

"Do you think it was such a good idea to tease me?"

"But I wasn't," she lied breathlessly.

He grinned, the action making the scar on his face appear even more sinister. "I believe you were. And you know what I think?" She didn't dare ask, although he told her anyway. "That was rather naughty of you. I may just have to punish you." When he rose to his feet and moved to join her on the settee, she found that her wits abruptly scattered. Her heart thudded madly in her chest when he reached out and cupped the back of her neck. "Tell me, isn't this what you truly wanted when I called this afternoon?"

He nuzzled her cheek, her earlobe, her neck, but never once did he kiss her on the mouth. She wet her lips, eager for him to claim her, but she knew he was making good on his promise to punish her. And oh, what sweet torture it was!

It wasn't until he dared to cup her breast through her gown, flicking his thumb over her nipple, did she suck in a breath. "Donovan," she sighed, her eyes sliding shut of their own volition.

There was a slight tug on her dress. A slight breeze brushed across her skin, sending gooseflesh across her upper arms. Her eyes instantly popped open at the realization that he'd freed one of her breasts from her corset, but when she saw that golden head dip to take that bit of flesh into his mouth, she no longer cared that he'd exposed part of her to his view. He was doing such amazing, wicked, *pleasurable* things to her that the only thing she could do was run her fingers through his hair and silently urge him to continue.

When he freed her other breast, kneading and licking and caressing them both, Emary rather imagined she would melt completely from the heated sensations that were pinging through her body. She was lightheaded and burning with an ache that she knew only he could assuage.

"God, Emary, you're driving me mad."

She was quite sure that was the other way around, but she didn't argue. And when he gently pushed her back on the settee, she laid down without complaint. She wound her arms around his broad shoulders and relished his weight on top of her. It made her feel feminine and secure.

But when she felt his hand brush the inside of her thigh, perilously close to the slit in her drawers, she tensed slightly.

However, the moment he nipped her earlobe, she was lost to the torment yet again. With the first flick of his fingers at her core, her hips bucked upward, almost involuntarily. He continued to touch her, caress her, driving her to the brink of something wonderful, something almost magical. Just as she was about to tumble off the edge, he finally took her mouth with his. She moaned as her lower body contracted and shattered into a million different prisms of sensation. It was if for that brief moment, she was ethereal and no longer tethered to the earth.

She was still floating on a glorious cloud of hazy oblivion when the duke adjusted her bodice and sat back to smooth her skirts back into place. He touched her fevered cheek. "You are amazing, Miss Pageant. My very own goddess divine, even if you do enjoy tormenting me."

Emary looked at him through heavy lids, a sudden lethargy taking over her entire being. "You are…" She couldn't even think of the appropriate words, as usual, so she merely sighed in contentment.

He chuckled low in his throat. "I'll take that as a compli-ment." He lightly kissed her lips. "Rest now. I'll see you this evening."

Emary could only sigh once more as her eyes fluttered closed.

Eight

"I trust you slept well this afternoon?" Donovan immensely enjoyed the blush that stole across Emary's lovely face that evening. Once again, he had escorted her, his mother, and her parents to another society event. This time it was a Christmas musicale.

It had been rather daring of him to come so close to ravishing Emary in her parents' drawing room, but once it became clear to him that she'd merely been trying to get a rise out of him he couldn't resist the opportunity to return the favor. Yet it had nearly been his undoing. He'd wanted nothing more than to unbutton his breeches and thrust into her wet heat, but he wasn't so debauched that he couldn't wait to make her his without a proper bed. Less than a fortnight remained of their sham engagement, but by the time Christmas Eve arrived, he was determined to make their union a reality.

He realized now that he was grateful she'd spilled that punch on him the night of his mother's ball. If she hadn't, he likely wouldn't have even taken a second glance at her, thinking that she was just like the rest of the debutantes in London. The ones who prided themselves on their many accomplishments, the least of which being that they didn't have a mind worthy of intellectual conversation, something that didn't just involve the weather or fashion. But Emary was possessed of all that and more. She was witty, charming, and smart — his perfect match. She would make an excellent duchess.

He escorted her to their seats and sat beside her, enjoying the way Emary gasped when his thigh inadvertently brushed hers. Or, at least, that's what he made her believe.

All through the performance, Donovan was hard pressed to tear his gaze away from her. As someone on stage sang a lovely Christmas carol, his eyes had drifted down to the edge of her bodice, where a hint of those lovely breasts began to curve. He had the urge to lick his lips, just imagining the sensation of those tempting globes in his mouth. He was starting to get hard just thinking of other places he'd like to lick and suckle on her body. It had been her uninhibited reaction earlier that day that almost made up for the discomfort in his groin that he'd had to endure after he'd left her, the ache that still thrummed with desire.

He cleared his throat lightly and shifted in his chair, determined to ignore his body's response to the woman at his side. At this rate he might have to procure a special license, for two weeks was going to feel like a bloody lifetime.

EMARY COULD FEEL THE DUKE'S HUNGRY GAZE ON HER. WHILE she ought to be outraged that he was eyeing her so boldly in a public setting, a part of her wanted to shout her victory. It was obvious that the duke was becoming quite enamored of her, and she would certainly be lying if she claimed that his feelings weren't reciprocated.

After her brief nap in the drawing room, she'd gone up to her chambers to take a bath. There, she'd dreamed about how the duke had touched her so intimately. She dared to mimic the same actions, although the outcome was sadly unsatisfying. It just wasn't the same without *his* fingers bringing her to the heights of such ecstasy.

Ever since then she'd been wracking her brain trying to figure out when she might allow him to touch her again. Hopefully, it would be soon, for she was already eager to repeat the experience. She had never imagined that a woman's body could feel such amazing things. She knew, of course, that men arrived at some sort of completion in the marriage bed, or else how would the human race ever go on?

She'd considered speaking to her mother about the sexual act, but she hadn't yet had the courage to approach her. And if she was being completely honest, Emary rather enjoyed the instruction that the duke was providing.

She opened her fan and lightly waved it in front of her suddenly warm face.

Her mother leaned over to whisper on her other side, "Emary! It's nigh on freezing in here as it is. You shall catch your death if you continue stirring up the air."

"I'm sorry, Mama." She reluctantly shut her fan and placed it back in her lap, although her body still pulsed with renewed fervor.

When the final performance was over, Emary clapped her gloved hands together. As the crowd began to disperse, she jumped slightly when she felt the duke's hot breath on the nape of her neck. It caused a shiver to skate down her spine. "Have I told you how enchanting you look tonight, my lady?"

Emary's pulse quickened. "I believe you have, Your Grace." She turned her head to look at him, their mouths only inches apart from one another. "But I never tire of hearing it."

He smiled, reaching out to toy with one of her dark curls. "Then I shall never cease to tell you."

"Your Grace?" A masculine voice interceded. "I do hate to intrude, but might I have a word with you?"

Donovan didn't appear to be grateful for the interruption, but he reluctantly stood and bowed at the older man. "Of course, Lord Corderly." He turned back to Emary long enough to whisper. "I'll be back shortly."

Emary watched those broad shoulders and that towering height depart with a wistful sigh. She blinked abruptly. Dear Heavens! If one didn't know better, one might think that she was in *love* with the man, romanticizing about him like she was.

She shook her head at her own silliness until she actually paused and considered the possibility. It was true that she found Windwood absurdly attractive and her body thrummed with awareness when he was near, but to go so far as to claim such a strong emotion?

Unsettled, she stood and headed for the ladies' retiring room, suddenly wishing for a bit of solitude. On the way there, she was waylaid by one of her rivals for the duke's attentions.

Ever since Emary's engagement had become common knowledge, her former entourage had dwindled considerably. While Emary was still the darling of the *ton*, now that she was spoken for, some of her enticing luster had faded, but female enemies could still be found about every corner in catching such a prize.

"You seem to be rather cozy with Windwood," Miss Parkhurst noted evenly as Emary passed, causing her to pause. The other woman strode toward Emary with a smirk. "I'm quite impressed with how easily you've brought him to heel."

Emary glanced around them to make sure they weren't overhead. "I daresay you make him sound like a hound, Miranda," she drawled.

The other girl tossed her blond head, her green eyes flashing mockingly when she said, "And here I was under the impression that's what you liked about him, Emary dear. Your ultimate goal was to see him fall at your feet, after all." She clapped her gloved hands. "Well done. After such a rather non-existent courtship, I'd say you succeeded."

Emary didn't care for her condescending tone. She crossed her arms. "If I didn't know better, I would think you were jealous."

"Jealous?" Miranda laughed gaily. She stepped closer. "On the contrary, since you are off the market, my admirers have grown considerably. It won't be long before I'm the one every man is after, and all the ladies run to for advice."

Emary forced a smile. "I'm glad to hear it."

"Are you?" Miss Parkhurst murmured. "For it seems to me if anyone is jealous, it might just be you." She tapped Emary on the nose with the tip of her finger. "Very soon you are going to be spirited away to the duke's country estate waiting in solitude for an heir to be born. If you're lucky, he might just stay with you long enough for you to give birth to make sure you bear him a son before he returns to town to seek the delights of a mistress."

She shook her head sadly, but Emary knew she was anything but remorseful. *Spiteful* was a better word to describe the woman before her.

"I daresay I shall miss seeing you in London when that occurs, but I will endeavor to keep the duke company while you are whiling away the hours as a forgotten wife."

"And what makes you so sure that will happen?" Emary challenged.

"Because we both know that it always does," Miss Parkhurst returned smoothly. "How foolish of you to believe otherwise."

"Perhaps we shall be the exception," Emary pointed out, although Miranda's words were starting to make an impression, the ring of truth to the unions she'd witnessed in her time in the city proving her claims. "My parents are quite happy in their marriage."

Miranda laughed. "Keep telling yourself that you've found the fairy tale the rest of us only dream about. But when it all crumbles to dust, I should hate to say I told you so." Miss Parkhurst walked away, and while Emary didn't want to give that viperous tongue any further consideration, Miranda *did* have a point.

In Emary's quest to win over the duke, she'd never once thought about what might happen if she actually succeeded in marrying him. She knew her parents didn't have any amorous pursuits outside of their own marriage, although it was rather common for gentlemen of the aristocracy to keep a mistress. So when the honeymoon was over, *would* the duke become one of those men?

Emary clenched her fists. Damn Miranda for putting these doubts in her mind! She had been perfectly content before now, remaining oblivious to what lay beyond a wedding day that wasn't even supposed to take place. Or, at least, that's what she had been trying to make Windwood believe. Or was she trying to convince herself all this time?

Emary put a hand to her suddenly aching head. All this subterfuge was starting to become rather confusing. Lately, it was hard to tell the truth from the falsehoods.

"Miss Pageant?" She dropped her hand to see Donovan's mother standing in front of her. "Are you unwell? You look rather pale."

Since she didn't wish to alarm the dowager, she forced a smile. "I'm fine, thank you."

The woman was obviously wiser than Emary gave her credit for, her shrewd blue eyes so like Donovan's and seeing far more than Emary was comfortable with. She reached out and took Emary's hand and gave it a sympathetic pat. "Come with me."

Her future mother-in-law led her down the hall to a closed door. She opened it to reveal a library. With a look around to ensure that it was vacant, she shut the door and led Emary over to a pair of chairs near the glowing fireplace. With an expression that had turned abruptly serious, she said, "I don't wish to add to your troubles, but I feel it is my responsibility to tell you that I know this engagement is nothing but a sham. I also don't believe that Donovan has any intention of marrying you."

Emary had to work to keep her surprise from showing. "How do you know?"

The dowager's expression was wry. "Come now. I should know my son better than anyone, I think." She released a heavy breath. "I know I shouldn't interfere when it isn't my place, that this is something between the two of you, but I couldn't live with my conscience if I didn't at least warn you." Her blue eyes were sincere when she added, "I respect you, Miss Pageant, and don't wish to see you injured by my son, whose reasons for this farce are yet unknown to me."

Emary didn't know if it was the interaction with Miranda that suddenly loosened her tongue, or if it was her own conscience that she wished to unburden, but she suddenly found herself bursting into tears, truly distressed. "Oh, it's all my fault!" She covered her face with her hands.

The duchess apparently misread her upset, for she said softly, "My dear, you mustn't blame yourself—"

Emary lifted her head and sniffed. "You don't understand," she whispered brokenly. "This entire sham betrothal was *my* idea." She put a fist to her chest for emphasis.

Understanding finally dawned on the dowager's face and she slowly sat back in her chair. "Perhaps you should explain."

Emary clenched her fists and explained everything from the proposal she'd put to Donovan at the ball, up until her interaction with Miss Parkhurst. "I admit it rather started out as something of a lark, a chance to prove myself to the duke, but things are… different now." When she was finished, she looked down at her lap, unable to see the condemnation that was surely on Caroline Wainwright's face. "I can only imagine what you must think of me."

The lady was silent for a moment, before she said, "How are things different?" When Emary's throat closed up with renewed emotion, preventing her from speaking, the dowager came to her own conclusions. "Have you fallen in love with him?"

Emary hesitated, and then shook her head miserably. "I'm… not sure. Of course," she added hastily. "I will break off the engagement at once—"

"You will do no such thing!" the duchess interrupted firmly.

Emary blinked, both puzzled and stunned by her reaction. "Surely you don't wish for this to continue now that you know the truth?"

Caroline tilted her head to the side and studied her. "I believe that you have a kind heart, Miss Pageant. While this may have started out as a simple proposal, it is my hope that it will become genuine." She sighed heavily, her expression turning sad. "Not only was my husband a firm hand when it came to raising our son, but Donovan was grievously injured in the war, and not just physically. He needs a strong, brave woman that will love him unconditionally."

Emary certainly didn't feel very courageous at the moment. "Are you sure that person is me?" she asked hesitantly.

"Yes," the dowager said matter-of-factly. "I do." She rose to her feet. "I'll leave you to compose yourself." She walked to the door but paused and turned back to face her. "I would truly be honored to have you as a daughter-in-law, Miss Pageant. You're a strong woman, and these days, that is a rare quality."

Emary sat back in her chair and stared into the fire after the dowager left, contemplating all that had been said. Even after the duchess knew the level of subterfuge that Emary had been willing to partake in to ensnare a duke — her *son* — she still thought that she was worthy of his love. It was humbling, to say the least.

Emary stood and walked over to a nearby mirror. She withdrew a handkerchief from her reticule and wiped the last of the tears from her face. She tucked it away and pinched her cheeks to add some healthy color. When she was finished, she was satisfied that her appearance was just as fresh as before, even if her eyes were slightly puffy.

Putting a smile in place, she returned to the party.

Donovan took longer conversing with Lord Corderly than he would have liked. While he wasn't averse to speaking about politics, when he had a beautiful woman waiting for his return, Emary was the right choice every time.

But when he returned to the parlor where several people were still milling about and discussing the musicale, Emary was conspicuously absent. Several minutes later, when she finally appeared in the doorway, a wave of relief washed over him. He hadn't realized how much he'd missed her until she wasn't there. It was a thought that was both thrilling — and highly unsettling. He was starting to believe that this hole, which he'd dug for himself, was going to get so deep that he wouldn't be able to climb back out.

"You look quite besotted, Your Grace," a feminine voice said at his elbow. He turned to see a blond woman standing next to him. She wore an expression that could only be deemed as innocent, but he rather thought the opposite was true. "If you don't mind me saying so, of course," she added.

"Have we met?" Donovan asked, knowing that he sounded curt, but unable to keep the irritation out of his voice. *Am I so transparent with my emotions?*

"We have." She inclined her head. Her green eyes were shrewd, although her voice was perfectly polite. "I am Miss Miranda Parkhurst. Although I doubt you would remember me. Even the night of your mother's ball Miss Pageant had quite turned your head. But then," she shrugged. "Emary always made it her objective to charm any suitor. I daresay she was quite out of sorts when you initially brushed her off. But she has always been resourceful. But even *I* wouldn't have thought to spill punch on someone to gain their notice."

Donovan didn't want to be pulled into whatever game she was playing, but he found himself narrowing his eyes and asking her all the same, "What are you talking about?"

Her mouth fell open slightly, as if she was surprised, but Donovan was rather confident that she knew exactly what she was doing. "Didn't she tell you that it was all part of her grand plan to ensnare the unattainable Duke of Windwood?"

Donovan clenched his fists, both in annoyance at her attempt to discredit Emary, and for her encouragement toward his own misgivings. "No."

"It doesn't matter now, I suppose. It all worked out in the end." She turned those keen green eyes on him. "By the way, I never did congratulate you on your engagement."

She smiled slightly as she walked away, although Donovan didn't even acknowledge her withdrawal. Emary was moving toward him through the remaining guests, shooting a narrowed glare at the woman that had just departed. "What did Miss Parkhurst say to you?" she nearly demanded when she reached him.

"Quite a bit, actually." Donovan was pleased that his voice was so calm and controlled when inside he was roiling with anger.

"I hope that you didn't believe a word of whatever she told you. Miranda has long been jealous of my successes this season."

He finally turned his full gaze upon her. "Meaning me?"

Her face instantly blanched of color. "No! That's not what I—"

"I think it's time to depart, Miss Pageant," he interrupted firmly. Even he knew this wasn't the place to air their disagreements where it could be discussed in drawing rooms across London the next day.

He forced himself to ignore the hurt in those brown eyes as he turned his back on her. Once they had collected his mother and her parents, they climbed into the carriage. He was thankful that the dowager and his future-in-laws carried the conversation on the way back to the townhouse, for he was in no mood to engage. He kept his gaze firmly fixed out the window, staring off into the darkness.

He didn't want to believe that Emary was some calculating pretender who had only set her sights on him because he was a duke, but Miss Parkhurst's claims had unnerved him more than he cared to admit. He knew he shouldn't allow some envious debutante to make him rethink everything he felt, and yet, her words had revived the doubt he'd happily ignored until then. While it was too late to remove his heart from Emary's grasp, he had to know how things stood between them.

When they finally stopped at the Armenton townhouse, he turned to Emary's mother. "Might I have a private word with my fiancée?"

Lady Armenton acquiesced after a slight hesitation. But then, she was under the impression that her daughter would be his wife in less than a fortnight. "Of course. But only for a few moments." She turned to the dowager. "Perhaps I might show you the heirloom china I was speaking of earlier?"

His mother glanced between them, and then offered Emary's mother a slight smile. "Certainly."

Once the two women had departed, with Emary's father following silently in their wake, Donovan turned to Emary. She was sitting patiently across from him, likely waiting for the axe to fall.

Donovan wanted nothing more than to reach out and caress the silky softness of her cheek, to ease her concerns, but he forced himself to refrain. "Why do you want to marry me, Emary?"

She blinked, as if surprised at the question. "I... I..." she stammered.

He clenched his jaw, feeling as though something inside of him was ripping apart. If she could have only said she loved him, it would have been enough for him to take a risk on this crazy venture, no matter what Miss Parkhurst had said.

But she'd hesitated.

It was a split second pause like that which made all the difference on the battlefield between life and death.

He blew out a heavy breath. He knew things had been progressing entirely too fast between them, and because of his consuming desire for Emary, he couldn't think straight. Perhaps it was time to take a step back and evaluate how he truly felt, if only to reassure himself that he wasn't about to make a terrible mistake, that he wasn't confusing lust with... something else. He needed to put a wedge between them, to gain some space to think.

"I'm returning to my estate in the morning," he announced bluntly. "I have some things that I need to take care of, that need my personal involvement."

He could read the disappointment in her shimmering gaze, but she merely nodded. "Will you be back on Sunday?" she asked softly.

He heard what was left unspoken. ...*when the last of the banns are read?* He frowned lightly. "I'm not certain."

"I see." She visibly swallowed.

Without another look at her, he stepped out of the carriage and held his hand out. After a brief hesitation, she set her hand in his. It wasn't until she'd stepped to the ground that he looked at her. His heart instantly stuttered in his chest, she looked so beautiful in the moonlight. Her breath left her slightly parted lips on a little white cloud, the cold night air already starting to turn her pert nose a charming pink. Her ebony hair shone like a night full of stars, while her brown eyes shimmered with a mixture of swirling emotion. Unable to resist, he bent down and brushed his mouth over hers.

He saw the moisture well in her eyes when he pulled back. "I wish you didn't have to go, Donovan."

He was torn by her unspoken plea and his own need for distance, but in the end, self-preservation won out. "Goodbye, Miss Pageant."

Donovan caught the glisten of a tear in the moonlight as it coursed down her cheek before she turned and disappeared into the house. It didn't escape his attention that she didn't look back at him.

He told himself it was for the best, but as he climbed back into the carriage, he couldn't ignore the stab of guilt that followed.

When his mother joined him a few moments later, she looked at him in horror. "What have you done? Miss Pageant is quite upset." She stilled. "Please tell me you haven't called off the engagement."

He glared at her. Now that Emary wasn't there to distract him, he found that his ire was piqued at his pride being questioned. "Not yet." He tapped the roof of the carriage.

Caroline crossed her arms as they set into motion. "Surely you're not going to believe some envious chit's ramblings over what you already know about Miss Pageant's character?"

He clenched his jaw but didn't reply.

She shook her head. "I never pegged you for a fool, Donovan. Don't make me rescind my decision now."

He felt his irritation spike higher. "I asked her why she wanted to marry me," he stated firmly. "She couldn't give me an answer."

She lifted a brow. "Did you tell her why you wanted to marry *her*?"

He ground his teeth. "No. But then I wasn't the one who has been resorting to games and trickery to become a duchess!" His voice had risen throughout his tirade. He shoved a hand through his hair.

Instead of chiding him for his loss of temper, his mother merely sighed heavily. "I won't pretend that she could have gone about this entire situation differently, but don't we all make errors in judgment from time to time? She's young and impressionable. She had a large role to fill as a diamond of the first water—"

"Yes. And used *me* in the process," he growled.

His mother tilted his head. "Are you going to tell me that you didn't use her as well?"

He frowned. "What the devil are you talking about?"

"You never wanted to marry. It was only through *my* constant coercion that you even agreed to hold that ball. Yes, Emary may have decided that she needed a plan to get you to notice her, as most women do. But didn't you also use her to delay choosing a bride?"

Donovan couldn't deny that claim, for he knew it was true. "That doesn't excuse her actions."

"Perhaps not, but doesn't she deserve a chance to explain herself? Or would you rather condemn her without the benefit of a trial first?"

He turned his head to stare out the window. "I just… need some time. Surely you can't fault me for that, at least?"

His mother was quiet for a time. Finally, she relented with, "Of course. Just make sure you don't take too long to come to a decision. A woman like Emary Pageant doesn't come along every day."

Nine

Donovan's absence left a hole in the middle of Emary's chest. She couldn't believe how much she ached for someone after such a short acquaintance. But then, he had made her feel things that she'd never imagined were possible.

So why hadn't she been able to tell him what he'd wanted when he'd asked? What had kept her from throwing her arms around him and confessing her love — the feeling she had long known with every fiber of her being?

All her life, when she'd dreamt of the day she would meet the man she intended to spend the rest of her life with, did she ever picture a man like Donovan Wainwright. But truly, in her eyes, there was no other man who could equal him. And it wasn't the fact he was a duke, or because his scar gave him a roguish appeal, or how she melted under those piercing blue eyes, but it was the man himself. The more she knew about Donovan the man, the more fascinated she became. Not only was he a man of honor, a war hero who had fought valiantly in the war with France, but he took his responsibilities seriously. She knew he wouldn't hesitate to speak out against injustice in Parliament, nor would he fail to take action in public if he thought he was fighting for a cause that was right.

It was *him*, and not his title, that had stolen her heart.

But as the days slowly trudged along and Sunday morning arrived with no word from her affianced, Emary began to fear

595

that this was one vow that he might not actually follow through on. But then, he'd made no promises. All along, their betrothal was supposed to be nothing but a sham. And honestly, she knew she had no one to blame but herself if things turned sour. She'd embarked on this foolish endeavor, one that might very well bring about her own ruin.

And wouldn't Miss Parkhurst crow about my downfall, she thought rather uncharitably.

"My lady, you have a caller."

Emary lifted her head from where she'd been hunched over her writing desk. At least she had accomplished something during these past six days of misery. The dreaded words that had been absent had finally arrived. The ink that stained her fingers would attest to that.

Emary quickly checked her appearance in the mirror and then nearly flew down the stairs. But when she walked into the drawing room, it wasn't Windwood that she saw, but rather the dowager duchess. And according to Donovan's mother's solemn expression, any hope that Emary had been retaining for the duke's return abruptly dwindled.

Nevertheless, she offered a brief curtsy and a warm smile. "Your Grace."

In return, Caroline didn't waste any time in announcing, "My son sent along his regrets this morning. I fear that he won't be able to join us for church, as estate business detains him in the country."

Emary felt a slight buzzing in her ears, a warning for what was to come, but she did her best to keep her disappointment from showing. "He is a busy man," she deferred. "I'm sure he would be here if he could."

The older woman sighed heavily. "Do you truly believe that?"

Emary threaded her hands together before her. There was no use skipping about the matter at hand. "I suppose he's rather angry at me."

"I don't think he's angry so much as... confused," the dowager returned gently.

Emary sank down onto the settee. "Don't you think it's time I put an end to this farce—"

The dowager's blue eyes widened in horror. "Absolutely not!"

she returned vehemently. She walked over and sat beside Emary, taking her hands in hers. "I believe that you love him, do you not?"

Emary nodded. There was no use pretending otherwise when in her heart she knew it was true.

"And you wish to be his wife?" her future mother-in-law persisted.

She swallowed thickly. "Yes."

"Then as I see it, you must go to him at once. You have to make him see reason."

Emary's jaw went slack. "But, I can't... I mean, my mother would never allow—"

"Let me worry about that," the dowager countered. "As long as you take your maid with you, the proprieties shall be observed. Your parents and I shall go to services this morning to present a united front, while you take my carriage to Basildon. My driver knows the way to Windwood Hall located just on the outskirts of town."

Emary bit her lower lip, tempted, and yet... "What if he refuses to see me? What if it's all for naught?"

Caroline's face softened. "I know that you are genuine in your affections, Miss Pageant, however it all may have begun. But if you wish to see Donovan waiting for you down the aisle at St. Paul's on Christmas Eve, you must convince him that you are serious in your regard." Her blue gaze was imploring. "My son has suffered much, both in his youth because of his father's stern hand, and later upon the battlefield. He feels that he isn't deserving of love, but I know in my heart that he truly cares for you. The question is, are you willing to risk it all for him in return?"

Emary hesitated, but she knew there was no doubt in her mind regarding which course she would take. In truth, it had been decided from the first moment she glimpsed that towering blond head in the crowd. "Yes. I will."

And she knew just what to do.

DONOVAN REINED HIS MOUNT IN AT THE TOP OF A HILL. THE wind was cold and brisk today with the threat of snow on the graying horizon, but from here, he could look down at his massive, limestone estate and appreciate everything that went along with his title, his role as a servant to the Crown and his country.

A wave of pride washed over him — followed by a swift burst of guilt. Of course he knew the reason for that, for it was the true reason he'd had to escape his study, so he wouldn't be staring at the clock on the mantel and thinking about what was happening in London. The last of the marriage banns between him and Emary were likely being read at this very moment — and yet, here he was, hiding out at his estate near Basildon instead of facing his fiancée. *Coward*, his inner voice chided, and he blew out a heavy breath, because he knew it was true. He might have faced down those French frogs and carried one of the highest ranks in the aristocracy, and yet, one sable haired chit had managed to break through his reserve with one glance of those mesmerizing chocolate-colored eyes.

Love at first sight. He had to snort, but yet, it seemed entirely too accurate.

He clenched his fists on the reins, causing his horse to prance nervously beneath him. He forced himself to relax, although his mind was still in turmoil. Even after seven days in relative seclusion, he still hadn't been able to focus on anything but Emary and how he'd love to see her lovely body lain out like a sacrificial offering upon his bed.

He released a heavy breath. Nothing good could come from such musings. He desired Emary to the point of distraction, that was true, and he knew that these emotions rolling around inside his chest were foreign to anything else he'd ever felt before, but he was also smart enough to know that it took more than attraction and lust to make a marriage survive. The truth was, he was a broken man, who still suffered from the nightmares of a battlefield, not to mention his distrust in everything around him. So could he, in all good conscience, inflict that sort of life on an innocent who thought he was capable of a normal existence, when he would likely be plagued with such turbulent thoughts for the rest of his days?

If war had taught him anything, it was loss. While it might

cause his chest to ache with a raw pain unlike anything he'd known before, even the burning slash of the sword across his face, he had made his decision. In the short time he'd known Emary, he had come to respect and admire the woman she was. He'd even made his peace with the fact that although he might have been singled by Emary in the beginning, she had been determined and resilient enough to ensnare him. And ensnare him she had, both heart and soul.

Donovan suddenly narrowed his eyes as he spied a black coach in the distance. He set his jaw. No doubt it was his mother coming home to give him one of her many lectures. He could only imagine how she would react when he told her that he intended to put an end to this engagement. He urged his horse into a canter. It was best to get it over with now.

He reached the gravel drive at the same time the carriage came to a halt, but when he would have greeted his mother with a note of derision in his tone, it wasn't the dowager who alighted…

EMARY SMOOTHED HER HANDS DOWN THE FRONT OF HER PURPLE velvet pelisse and touched the brim of her matching bonnet once the coach rolled to a stop. She had no idea what she might even say to Donovan when she saw him. And if he flat out refused to see her? Perhaps he might at least look at what she'd brought him.

Caroline had taken the lead and been able to convince Emary's mother to allow her to remain home from church. After the dowager had told her parents that Donovan wasn't going to be in attendance, Emary's mother had paled considerably, thinking the worst. When Caroline went on to explain that Emary should stay behind to give the appearance that they were somewhere else together, Lady Armenton had reluctantly agreed.

As her parents and the dowager were leaving, Caroline had given Emary one last speaking look over her shoulder. The moment the door shut behind them, Emary flew upstairs and grabbed Althea. Once she'd told her maid what she had planned, she'd grabbed her manuscript and shoved it in a satchel and they were on their way.

Thankfully, Althea had been gifted with little conversational skills on the way to Windwood Hall, for Emary had been a bundle of nervous energy. She'd had nearly two hours to think upon what she might say to Donovan, and yet she was no closer to finding the right argument to convince him that they were meant to be together. Who would have thought that three simple words — *I love you* — would be so difficult to speak aloud? But then, it was the genuine meaning behind them that was the hardest to relay. Would he even believe her claim? Or would he scoff at her confession and turn her away? After that viperous Miranda had caused his head to fill with doubts, she wasn't sure she could convince him that she was sincere. But she knew she had to try.

Emary was still conflicted when the door to the carriage opened and a footman helped her alight.

She gasped, for before her stood a massive golden stallion, a coat so shiny and brilliant that it nearly glowed, even among an overcast December sky.

But it was the man who sat atop the mount that truly caused her heart to pound.

Donovan was casually dressed in a pair of navy blue trousers that disappeared into a pair of black Hessians. His white, cambric shirt was open at the throat and rolled up to his elbows with no waistcoat or cravat to speak of. With his golden hair tousled and his blue eyes sparkling, the white scar a stark contrast against his lightly sun-bronzed skin, he quite literally stole her ability to speak. He was normally so put together, but surrounded by the relaxed atmosphere of his country estate, he was more devilishly handsome than if he were fully dressed in a London ballroom.

It wasn't until she glanced up and met his gaze that she felt her heart wither in her chest. His jaw was hard and unrelenting, his blue eyes frosty chips of ice as he said curtly, "I suppose my mother set you up to this." He dismounted abruptly, handing the reins over to a waiting groom — and then he turned his back on her, his intentions quite clear.

Emary couldn't move, her legs were frozen as shock and dismay overwhelmed her. All of the carefully rehearsed speeches she'd run over and over in her head dissipated like smoke in the face of his painful desertion. Up until that point, she'd believed that she'd meant more to him, that he really had come to care for her and would forgive what she'd done. She wanted to be mad, to rant at how unfair he was being, but instead, when she opened her mouth, a broken plea emerged. "Donovan, please... I'm sorry."

She feared that he would keep walking, but he hesitated with his foot on the first step leading to the entrance of his grand manor house. His butler was standing with the door open, waiting for his master, but slowly, Donovan lowered his head and finally turned around to face her. The butler, along with the rest of the assembled servants around them, gradually melted away, as if they realized a delicate conversation was about to take place.

Emary's throat burned with remorse as they were left alone. She knew she couldn't keep standing there like some sort of statue, so she took a tentative step forward. "It was wrong of me to treat you as some sort of prize to be won," she began sincerely. "I daresay I got so caught up in the social whirl, so intent on proving my worth to the *ton*, that I didn't think of all the repercussions, of how everything would... end up."

She glanced down at the ground. "All I can say is that, for a village girl who was thrust into the gilded world of the London aristocracy, I was enchanted by it all." She dared to look at him. He hadn't moved from where he was, but at least he hadn't gone inside and dismissed her pleas either. Emary took that as a positive sign. "I was charmed by the gentlemen and their endless compliments, and I enjoyed outwitting the other debutantes. I suppose it became a game of sorts, but please believe that I never meant to hurt you. I never imagined that..." Her throat closed up, so she shook her head and held out the leather satchel. "I brought something for you." Tears pricked the backs of her eyelids, but she refused to let them fall. "It's my story, but I fear it's not quite finished. I was actually hoping you could help me with the ending. You see, my vicar is about to become married, but his fiancé betrayed him, used him quite ill actually. He has to decide whether to show up at the altar, or send her back home in disgrace."

At long last, the duke slowly moved toward her. He accepted

her offering, his turbulent eyes searching her face, but said nothing. Emary swallowed down the raw emotion clawing its way up her throat and turned toward the carriage, unable to take anymore, but a hand on her arm caused her to pause.

She closed her eyes, waiting.

Donovan's breathing was harsh when he said, "It takes two to err, Miss Pageant. The truth is—" He gently turned her around to face him. As he lifted her chin, she opened her eyes. "—you have nothing to be sorry for. Something in your eyes captured my soul from the very first moment I saw you. I allowed myself to be captured. And were I to have the choice, I wouldn't change anything, because I *want* to be with you."

Emary's pulse leapt. "Are you sure? Because—"

"You talk too damned much," Donovan nearly growled, right before he kissed her. Time was endless as he held her close to him, their mouths fusing, their bodies melting into one. When they parted, as her body was tingling with renewed hope, Emary decided it was time to enact Plan B.

With a tentative smile, she grasped his hand and bent down on one knee. Looking up at him, she said, "I would ask that you consider marrying me in truth. Will you, Donovan Wainwright, Duke of Windwood, make me the happiest woman in England and consent to be my groom?"

His amused laughter rang out and lit her up from within. He bent down and joined her on the ground, reaching out and touching one of the curls that was visible from beneath her bonnet. "I thought this sort of proposal was only allowed on leap year."

She shrugged, a hint of a smile curving her lips. "I never was very conventional."

His eyes shone with mirth as he tugged on her hand, catching her off balance and straight into his waiting arms. "You can say that again. And thank God for it." He brought his mouth down on hers yet again, and Emary felt it all the way to her toes, warming her blood with renewed anticipation. When he pulled back, he rested his forehead against hers, his breathing labored.

Emary sighed softly. "Does that mean yes?"

He nibbled her mouth and murmured, "Yes, you maddening woman, I humbly accept your proposal, even if you may come to regret it someday."

Emary's chest bloomed with elation as she reached out and traced a gentle finger down Donovan's scar. "Never," she whispered. "Whatever storm may brew on the horizon, we will face it together." Finally, the words that she'd long held back tumbled forth. "I love you."

He instantly cupped her face in his hands, his blue eyes intent and filled with an emotion that she couldn't name, but one that made her heart soar even higher. "My dear, sweet Emary, I never thought it was possible to feel love, but you've opened my eyes to the prospect of true happiness. Letting you go would have been the greatest mistake of my life, but it wasn't until you stepped out of that carriage just now that I realized just how important you are to me. I love you to the point of madness. You are the air that I breathe, the blood in my veins, and the reason my heart has started beating again. Rest assured, there is no one else on earth that I'd rather share my life with."

Emary was crying at this point, but it wasn't due to sadness.

It was pure joy.

Ten

Christmas Eve
One week later

"Y ou look beautiful, Emary."

Emary turned at the sound of her mother's voice, followed by some rather suspicious sniffles. She instantly closed the distance between them and put her arms around her. "Don't cry, Mama. Today is my wedding day. It's supposed to be a celebration."

"Of course, it is," Lady Armenton agreed. "But you're *still* my daughter even if you are about to become a wife and a duchess." She wiped at her eyes with her handkerchief. "And I meant what I said. You are a truly beautiful bride."

Emary glanced down at her cream silk gown, embroidered about the hem with greenery and holly berries. The design was actually her husband-to-be's idea, for he'd remarked that it was fitting for the occasion, as she would be the only present he'd look forward to unwrapping this night. Her face had instantly heated several degrees — as did certain other areas of her body.

A knock at her chamber door interrupted Emary's musings. Althea walked inside and curtsied. "The duke's carriage has arrived."

Emary put a hand to her stomach where hundreds of butter-flies were fluttering madly, but she let her mother guide her downstairs, the long veil of her matching satin bonnet flowing behind her. Her father was waiting in the foyer to escort her down the aisle once they arrived at St. Paul's, and he looked regal in his formal black and white attire.

He smiled broadly at Emary. "Didn't I tell you that you had snagged a duke?" He teased, bending down to kiss her cheek. "You look lovely, my dear. Windwood is a lucky man."

Emary beamed with his praise, and took his arm as he escorted her into the carriage. She heard bells somewhere in the city proclaim the hour of ten o'clock in the morning. While they weren't a great distance from the church, she didn't want to be fashionably late for her own wedding. But no matter how long it took them to arrive, she was confident that Donovan would be waiting for her at journey's end.

After Windwood had accepted her proposal, she had returned to London with a warm, fuzzy feeling in her chest. The moment she'd walked in the front door, she had reassured her anxious parents — who had found her hastily scribbled note about where she'd gone — that the wedding would be taking place as planned.

The next day, Donovan returned to town and called on her with her manuscript in hand. They had sat down in the drawing room and he'd handed her the satchel, his blue eyes warming as he regarded her. "This was quite an enchanting story, Miss Pageant. I think you might truly win our wager."

"I don't care about that anymore," she'd said honestly. She'd reached out and took his hand in hers. "I have everything I want right here. Besides," she'd shrugged. "I told you that I don't know how it ends."

"I disagree," he'd countered, reaching out to bring her hand to his lips for a sensuous kiss, his blue eyes nearly glowing with promise. "I think you know exactly what happens next."

Considerable warmth flooded her cheeks. "I can't possibly write *that* into a novel."

"Why not?" he'd urged with a mischievous grin. "I can only imagine it would sell rather well."

She'd merely rolled her eyes at him. "You're a wicked man."

But that evening, Emary mulled over what Windwood had said. So she'd returned to her desk and scribbled furiously long into the night. It was nearly three o'clock in the morning by the time she'd finished, but she sat back and grinned at what she'd written.

Who would have thought that two simple words — *The End* — would hold so much exhilaration!

After a few hours of sleep, Emary had woken bright and early the next morning, dressed in her light blue velvet gown, and her fur-lined sapphire blue cloak and walked down to the first publishing house she'd come across. After being forced to cool her heels for nearly an hour, Emary had walked into the editor's office with purpose and set her finished manuscript on his desk. "I wish to publish this story by Saturday."

The man's bushy, gray sideburns and heavy jowls had shook as he'd laughed. "You're mad! Leave my office this instant!"

She had been prepared for his reaction of course, so she'd took a small purse from her reticule, the pin money she'd been saving for some time, and plopped it on the desk. "This should expedite the process and make it well worth your time."

While the jingling of coins had gained his attention, he was still unconvinced, especially after he read the scandalous title and understood that she wished for it to be printed under her name and not a pseudonym. "Why… this is unheard of! A woman doesn't write these kinds of stories! It will never sell."

He'd started to push the pile of papers back across the table, but she'd set her hand on top of it. With a steady glare, she'd said, "I disagree, but what does it matter, since I'm taking all the risk?" She'd gestured to the purse still sitting between them. "That should more than compensate you for any editing services I might require, as well as all the printing costs, with enough to spare." She'd stood up straighter. "I don't expect it to be a huge success, nor do I wish to have more than a few copies made. I just want it available to the public and in Hatchard's by Christmas."

Emary had noticed the moment when he went from incredulous to annoyed resignation. He'd reluctantly dragged the pages back to him, flipping through them once more, but this time, in a professional manner. "This will take me two days to go over and another two for printing, that is if I pay my staff to work overtime..." he'd muttered. But it wasn't until he'd glanced at the heavy purse on his desk that he'd scrubbed a hand over his face and regarded her somewhat curtly. "Very well, Miss Pageant. You have a deal."

Emary had smiled broadly and stuck her hand across the desk. He'd hesitated a moment, and then accepted the offering. "It's a pleasure doing business with you," she'd said brightly, although she knew he wouldn't claim the same.

The instant she'd walked out into the sunlight, even the cold air couldn't dampen her spirits.

Now, as Emary walked up the front steps of St. Paul's on her father's arm, she couldn't keep the satisfied grin from her face. Not only was she a published author with her name on the leather bound cover of *"A Seduction at Christmas,"* but she was about to marry the love of her life.

As if proclaiming the blessing of God and His angels, a softly falling snow began to fall. Emary lifted her face to the heavens just as the doors to the cathedral opened. With her head held high, she walked down the aisle to begin her new journey as the Duchess of Windwood.

ONCE THE WEDDING BREAKFAST WAS OVER, DONOVAN STRODE UP to his wife with a hungry look in his eyes that Emary couldn't fail to interpret. "It's time we departed, my dear."

She returned his eager gaze with one of her own. "I thought you'd never ask." Although Emary retained a touch of maidenly nerves, her need for this man overwhelmed all else. She couldn't wait to be alone with him and seal this new bargain they'd made. From the moment she'd walked down the aisle and spied him in his red formal regimentals, she'd been hard pressed to keep her adoring gaze off of him. It was hard to imagine that this handsome man truly belonged to her.

Donovan held his arm out to her, but before they could make their escape, the dowager intercepted their retreat. "Leaving so soon?" she said with a tilt of her elegant, blond brow. Her son snorted as Emary likely turned twenty shades of red. "Might I have a moment with your lovely wife before you spirit her away?"

Donovan acquiesced, but Emary could see that he wasn't altogether pleased about being detained. Once he stalked off, Caroline turned to her with a curve of her lips. "You'll find that Donovan is more bark than bite."

Emary wasn't so sure about that as she recalled all the little love nibbles that he'd bestowed on her in the past week that had set her pulse racing, but she wasn't about to comment on *that*. Again, she felt her face heat rather traitorously. To distract herself from such wayward thoughts, she clasped her hands together and said, "I feel guilty for sending you out of your home for the evening."

"It's my son's townhouse, not mine," Caroline corrected, although not unkindly. "But not to worry. Your parents have always made me feel quite welcome when I'm in residence. Today won't be any different. Besides, your mother and I get along quite well. But I digress." She brought forth an object that Emary hadn't noticed until then. "I only detained you because I was hoping you might sign my copy of your novel."

Emary gasped in pleasant surprise. "I would be honored. But you know I would have gladly gifted you a copy."

As Caroline handed her a quill, she said, "And deprive the greedy women of London the chance to whine for more? I think not."

Emary frowned. "What do you mean?"

"Didn't you know?" The dowager smiled broadly. "I got the last copy from Hatchard's. It turns out your story is quite a success. It's creating quite a buzz about the city."

Emary's mouth fell open. "Truly?"

Donovan returned to wrap his arms around her waist. He put his chin on her shoulder and asked his mother, "Are you quite through monopolizing my bride?"

"I suppose so." She rolled her eyes. She reached out and set a hand on each of their cheeks. "I'm so happy for you both." With tears shimmering in her blue eyes, she turned away.

Donovan took Emary's hand. "Let's go, my love." Threading her arm through his, he led her outside and to his waiting coach. Once he tapped the roof and they departed, he wasted no time taking her into his arms. "Finally," he breathed, as he devoured her lips with his own, his assault so provocative and demanding that when they arrived at his townhouse a short time later, Emary was quite disheveled and burning up from the inside out.

The butler opened the door upon their arrival, but Emary didn't have time to greet him or inspect her surroundings, other than the black and white checkered floor at her feet, as the duke scooped her up into his arms and carried her over the threshold.

With a bubbling giggle of mirth escaping her lips, Emary wound her arms around her husband's neck as he strode purposefully up the stairs until he reached a slightly ajar door at the end of the second floor hallway. He kicked the door open fully and shut it behind them. Only then did he set her on her feet.

Emary was breathless as they fell into each other's arms.

Only once, when they parted briefly, did she ask, "Shouldn't I wait for Althea to attend to me?"

His blue eyes instantly sparked with fire. "I shall play your ladies' maid this day, my lovely wife."

Emary felt a shiver chase across her skin, yet it wasn't from fear, but eagerness. In reply, she unpinned her bonnet and tossed it aside and then turned her back to him. "Then let's not delay."

She thought she heard him groan as he made quick work of the row of buttons on her gown. As it fell into a puddle of silk at her feet, he turned his attention to unlacing her stays. She thought he heard him mutter something about a "damned woman's undergarments," before it too, fell away.

It wasn't long before the rest of her clothes were discarded, as well as his. She marveled at the hard planes of his chest, the broad expanse of his shoulders, the muscles bunching and clenching in his arms. He was truly magnificent to behold, and Emary couldn't resist reaching out and running her hands along his powerful form.

With an almost feral growl, Donovan lifted Emary into his arms, eliciting a squeal of delight, and laid her gently on the raised, canopied bed. But his eyes were serious when he brushed a strand of hair away from her cheek, "Tonight you will be mine in every way."

"Yes," Emary sighed.

His mouth suddenly kicked up at the corner. "I hope you

know that if you ever wish to offer me another proposal, I'd be more than willing to accept."

She couldn't help but grin. "In that case…" She wrapped her arms around his neck. "I propose that you make love to me."

He grinned wickedly. "On that, my dear duchess, I would be more than happy to comply."

He brought his mouth down to hers, and they loved one another until the early morning hours of dawn.

Thank You

I'd like to thank you for purchasing this book. I know you could have chosen any number of stories to read, but you picked this one and for that I am humbled and grateful! I hope that the romance captured your heart and added a smile to your day. If so, it would be awesome if you could share this book with your friends and family and post a review! Your feedback and support will help improve my writing and help me to continue growing as an author. You can find all my links on my website - *authorta-bethawaite.wix.com/romance*

Cheers! xo

About the Author

Tabetha Waite began her writing journey at a young age. At nine years old, she was crafting stories of all kinds on an old Underwood typewriter. She started reading romance in high school and immediately fell in love with the genre. She gained her first publishing contract with Etopia Press and released her debut novel in July of 2016 - "Why the Earl is After the Girl," the first book in her Ways of Love Series. Since then, she has become a hybrid author, transitioning into indie publishing. She has won several awards for her books.

She is a small town, Missouri girl who continues to make her home in the Midwest with her husband and two wonderful daughters. When she's not writing novels filled with adventure and heart, she is either reading, or searching the local antique mall or flea market for the latest interesting find. You can find her on most any social media site, and she encourages fans of her work to join her mailing list for updates.

www.authortabethawaite.wix.com/romance

Also by Tabetha Waite

Love's Frozen Kiss

Love Out of the Ashes

Tempting the Scoundrel

TRACY SUMNER

Prologue

An evening when young love is in the air...
Tavistock House, Mayfair
July 1808

The girl captivated him from first sight, fascination a delightful little shiver along his skin.

As she had every night he'd been in residence, she huddled in the veranda's dark corner, book in hand, an oil lamp illuminating the page she brought close to the tarnished glass globe. A housemaid, she read in secret. And hungrily.

He could feel her determination, her daring, from his perch one story above.

Determination matching his own.

Christian Bainbridge braced his hands on the ledge of his bedchamber window and leaned into a spill of moonlight, releasing a half-laugh at his foolishness. There was nothing poetic about this night, this house, or his circumstances. The air reeked of coal smoke and charred meat, rotting vegetables and the Thames, familiar even in its wretchedness. Cousin to the Earl of Tavistock, whose home Christian currently occupied, he was stuck in the slender crack between the aristocracy and the middling classes, welcome in neither.

The loneliest place to wedge oneself, he'd come to find.

619

After the recent death of his beloved brother, Christian was alone in the world except for the earl, a man rumored—and, regrettably, the rumors were true—to have several significant deficits of character.

To Christian's mind, the worst being that he failed to maintain his timepieces.

Christian glanced back to the pocket watch parts spread across the desk, candlelight dancing over metal coils, serrated wheels, the blunt edge of a screwdriver. You could tell much about a person from the way they tended their treasures.

The earl tended his poorly.

Tavistock had little care for his belongings, his tenants, his staff, or his hapless fifteen-year-old cousin. Leading Christian to make the rash decision to accept an apprenticeship he'd been offered with a prominent watchmaker in Cambridge. He had another term at Harrow to complete, but there were no funds, not one farthing left to sustain further education. And Christian was not willing to accept additional charity from a man he'd come to loathe.

The situation was actually as it should be because Christian had never been interested in anything but the art of repairing timepieces.

And when he was ready, designing his own.

Before this girl, only gears and coils and springs had captured his attention.

He'd asked a groom, a footman, and finally, the housekeeper for her name, because he'd felt he must learn it before leaving the estate at dawn. Raine Mowbray, he'd been told.

A young woman who now held a unique position in his universe.

Love at first sight did that to a boy.

There was something elemental about his reaction to Raine, more extraordinary than mere appreciation for her loveliness. Lust, he supposed, but it felt like more. He had little experience with women, so he couldn't accurately categorize his response.

He'd only seen her once up close, no words exchanged, no eye contact made, as she rushed through the walled garden and into the kitchens, the aroma of roses overpowering until the subtle scent of lemon and lavender clinging to her skin swept in and knocked all else aside. Blew every thought from his mind and left him stranded, like a withered leaf dangling from a limb.

It sounded melodramatic, but his heart had raced inside with her.

While she hadn't paused or blinked or seemed to notice him at all.

Which was a good thing. Christian was leaving, he was destitute, lacking in funds, family, or friends. Too young to matter, too old to indulge. His future, which was going to be bloody *brilliant* he pledged to himself right there in the cloying twilight, lay in Cambridge, not London.

He was going to make his way on his own, his awful cousin be damned.

The girl on the veranda moved the book into the light, turned a page with a delicate shift of her wrist, smiled softly at a twist in the story. He wished with everything in him that they'd been able to talk, he and Raine Mowbray. Even once. For a moment. About anything. Her voice was a mystery to him, and for that, he was genuinely sorrowful, because she looked as lonely as he felt.

Willing himself to turn away, Christian returned to his cousin's watch and his promise to restore the neglected timepiece before he left London. When repaired, it would provide an accurate accounting for a man who didn't deserve precision.

But such was life.

Christian placed the loupe against his eye and plunged into his task.

Preparing to walk away from one fascination and toward another.

One

A morning long after love had been forsaken…
Hartland Abbey, Yorkshire
June 1818

Raine stared out the duchess's drawing room window, the oilcloth in her hand forgotten. Her intention to dust the sashes and neat white frame forgotten.

There was something unusual about the tall, strikingly handsome man who'd arrived at the estate and now stood on the crushed-stone drive talking with Lord Jonathan, the Duke of Devon's eldest son. She gave the baseboard a punishing buff, searching her memory.

He seemed *familiar*, which was absurd.

Raine cataloged his features, trying to solve the puzzle. Square jaw, dark, disheveled hair, tastefully elegant suit of clothing, polished Hessians glinting in the sunlight. A curl of amusement about his lips, lines of delight streaking from his eyes, he looked rather like a man who held a secret close. A hint of mischievousness beneath an almost bookish air. Spellbound, she watched him gesture to a passing footman who'd unloaded a bevy of cases from a landau and was struggling to carry them inside the house, the man's regard for his belongings—which didn't look like the customary sartorial fripperies the *ton* dragged to Yorkshire—possessive and intense. Whatever was in those gleaming wooden cases mattered to their visitor. His gaze followed the boxes up the marble stairs and into the house with the longing one usually reserved for a paramour.

"They say he refused a knighthood."

Raine flinched, the oilcloth dropping from her hand to the Aubusson carpet. Ellen Bruce, one of the other housemaids, giggled and winked. In the duke's employ since she was a child, Ellen knew everyone and *heard* everything, while Raine had only been on the estate for six paltry months.

Therefore she knew almost nothing.

"A knighthood dangled before him for repairing the Prince Regent's fickle pocket watch," Ellen murmured with a sly glance cast toward the drive. "Can you imagine such a thing? Royalty be daft, Prinny especially. That's what I think, if anyone asks me, which they likely won't."

"Who are you referring to?" Raine stooped to pick up her cleaning cloth, hopefully hiding her curiosity about the intriguing stranger, inquisitiveness that a house servant of a magnificent house such as Hartland Abbey should not have about a guest.

"Mister Christian Bainbridge, that's who. Friendly with Lord Jonathan since his school days, he's stayed here one or two times in the past." Ellen pranced over to the grand fireplace and gave the intricate trim a passing swipe with her duster that in no way accounted for housework. She laughed, throwing a playful look over her shoulder, knowing she had a captive audience. "It's said he designs the most accurate timepieces in England, and you know the duke cannot stand to be late for any appointment. In this house, nothing but a Bainbridge will do."

Wordlessly, they watched the celebrated watchmaker stroll past the drawing room, his footfalls echoing off marble, providing another brief look that confirmed he was as appealing inside the house as he was out of it.

"A most eligible bachelor but a duke's daughter would be reaching too high. Although he's here to court timepieces, not unmarried ladies," Ellen whispered, breathless with delight at the opportunity to impart this much gossip in one sitting. "He has more money than half the peerage what with their silly extravagances and base business sense. And so attractive, too." She turned, her duster poised like a sword, and gave it a little jab. "He'll get one look at you, and poof, be smitten! It happened with Nash in seconds flat. You could have knocked him over with a feather after meeting you that first time." She sniffed and returned to her half-hearted dusting. "As if you would dally with a groom. Poor besotted Nash. This one, however, is *no* groom, but a dangerous man. According to the broadsheets, Mister Bainbridge only cares for wenches and watches, so don't say I didn't warn you."

Raine held back a spurt of laughter and circled the room to check the water level in the many vases scattered about the charming parlor. It was no wonder the space smelled like one stood in the middle of a rose thicket. Wenches and watches, indeed. She wanted nothing *less* than to unwittingly capture another man's attention, for her life to be dictated by his whims, weakness, or unfed appetites. Even if the newly-arrived scoundrel *had* imparted a slight quiver in her knees, thankfully well hidden beneath her skirt.

For now, she wanted, *needed* hard work and solitude. And a vast library where she could read to her heart's content without being accosted.

Nothing more, nothing less.

Ellen gave the hearth another unproductive bit of consideration. "Our duke likes to rescue people, he does. Give back in reward for his good fortune. Like he did with Miss Abigail, who has a new life. A new husband! Such a lovely conclusion, don't you think? A merry bit of matchmaking if I do say so myself."

Raine paused by the escritoire desk sitting in a darkened corner. *Ah*, Miss Bruce had a motive after all. Raine would have liked to argue that she hadn't needed rescuing, but she was nothing if not practical. She could admit the truth if only to herself. If not for the Duke and Duchess of Devon, she'd still be working at Tavistock House, living under the wicked, abhorrent thumb of the earl. Shoving a bureau in front of the attic door each night to keep him out. "My eldest brother is acquainted with Thomas Kingston, the duke's footman, and he recommended me for the vacant maid's position. The earl was reducing his staff due to financial constraints. It's as simple as that."

Of course, it wasn't, but why discuss an unfortunate situation when a resolution had been so generously offered? A resolution humbly but promptly taken.

Ellen stilled with a reluctant release of breath, her gaze going molten, her tears apparent from across the room. "Whatever your story, you're safe now. This is the finest household in England. The most generous of families to serve."

Raine sighed and turned to gaze out the window, noting Mister Bainbridge's landau was still parked in the drive. *What color are his eyes*, she wondered. How did one design a watch to be the most accurate in the country?

And why had she felt as if she recognized him the moment he stepped from his carriage?

CHRISTIAN UNPACKED HIS TOOLS IN THE PANELED STUDY THE Duke of Devon had graciously assigned to him, the niggling hint of unease he'd experienced since arriving decreasing with each treasured instrument he touched. Some items he'd purchased years ago when he'd had to decide between a new screwdriver or food for the week. Tweezers, pliers, oilers, files, calipers. A small, French wheel-cutting engine. The velvet-lined box of crystals sat at the bottom of one case. He breathed a sigh of relief; he hadn't forgotten them. Devon had mentioned a cracked face in one of his messages.

Christian wasn't used to traveling with his equipment. He rarely made home visits—but the man *was* a duke.

And *he*, Christian Bainbridge, could have been a knight, which verified the insanity said to roam the halls of Carlton House. He prayed he didn't have to visit Prinny again this year.

Gordon Pennington, his trusty partner, stumbled into the room, swearing beneath his breath, and kicking the study door shut behind him. "Did you truly need all of these? Enough gadgets to repair every device in Yorkshire. Didn't we discuss learning to work with less?" He deposited a trunk to the floor with a thump and a groan, then sent Christian a look that said, *don't say a word*.

"Some business associate you are," Christian murmured with a smile he made sure to cast away from the man who was, in reality, his best friend. His only friend.

"I'm a guard, Kit, not a business associate." With a grunt, he went to his knee, produced a knife from his waistcoat pocket, and proceeded to pick the trunk's lock.

Christian rolled his eyes. "I have the key, you know. And remember, Penny, to the *ton*, you're my valet." Although broad-shouldered, ham-fisted Penny looked like no valet Christian had ever seen.

"No need for a key. Your *valet* trained in the back alleys of Whitechapel in preparation for his duties protecting the most expensive timepieces in Christendom. And the watchmaker who created them. Thievery, lockpicking, forgery. Gordon Pennington, at your service." He snapped the knife shut and slipped it in his pocket. "I'm ill-used in this role, to put it plainly. But the pay is ample, the attire first-rate, and the danger slight. Women like the valet title, too, I've found. Makes me seem refined."

Christian laughed and situated his tools in a neat row on the duke's rather imposing mahogany desk. "I thought it a good idea after you saved me from being gutted on the docks all those years ago to repay the favor and offer you a more enviable position. Plus, weren't we both surprised to find that you're the best book-keeping in the city? Larceny certainly fostered a talent for addition and subtraction. I'd be lost without you." He shifted to remove a folio from his satchel, unwittingly releasing a hint of jasmine. A strong enough presence to brush aside the aroma of leather and bergamot currently occupying the study. Katherine liked to scent her letters, and he'd crammed one in his bag as he rushed from his Berkeley Square townhome. "By the by, did you have the necklace delivered?"

Penny snickered and collapsed into an armchair, sending his long legs into a sprawl before him. "Your typical parting gift with me as solemn messenger, you mean? Then, yes, I did. Lady Wheaton was composed but furious. Slammed the door in my face. *After* snatching your expensive settlement from my hand." He yawned and stacked one glossy boot atop the other. "Why not give them a watch when you've decided enough is enough? I'll allow you a steep discount and even have it engraved for free. Your jeweler is robbing you blind with these tokens of lost affection."

"Not going to happen," Christian said and perched his hip against the desk, the folio spilling open in his hands, Katherine Wheaton's letter peeking from behind a bent page to mock him.

His watches were personal; he'd poured his whole bloody *existence* into their creation. It was like giving a part of himself away when he sold one, which he realized was ridiculous for a man of trade.

The first time he'd taken a watch apart and put it back together had been the only time, aside from the girl on the veranda who'd knocked the breath from him years ago at Tavistock House, when his heart had wholly ruled his mind.

When he fell in love, *if* he ever fell in love, his wife would wear one of his watches. Which would mean more to him than any ring ever could. He would wait to find the woman who would understand that. Who would know without him having to tell her.

He slammed the folio shut, feeling the sting of dissatisfaction.

That was not happening as he'd given up on love.

At the moment, his loneliness was palpable but hidden, thriving despite the adoring mistresses he surrounded himself with. He'd tried, repeatedly, but there seemed little point in searching for what was not *there*. Had only been there that one time, a spark he'd extinguished by leaving before he even spoke to the girl.

"You're getting that sullen look again," Penny murmured from the chair, his lids low, close to sleep if Christian had his guess. "And we have no women, not yet, to lift you from your melancholy."

Christian shook himself from his stupor, slipped a letter from the folio, and flipped it between his hands. "I'm worried about the translations, which I'd hoped to work on during my time here," he lied, tapping the envelope against his palm. "A German watchmaker I'm in contact with tried to build a detached escapement caliber, but it failed, and he sent me details on the design in the event I'd like to have a go. But German's not my area of expertise, and English not his. Parts of the missive are incomprehensible, at least to me."

"I took care of it, whatever an escapement caliber is," Penny said with another yawn. "I discussed your dilemma with Miss Miller, the housekeeper, upon our arrival. A lovely thing with the bluest eyes you've ever seen. Like the sky in the middle of summer. Delightful. But back to the problem. There's a maid, new on staff, talented with languages." He settled his linked fingers over his belly and stretched his shoulders. "Assisting the governess with those subjects or some such. Unusual skill for a housemaid, isn't it? I guess this one loves to read and taught herself several languages. Imagine, a blue-stocking residing in the wilds of Yorkshire." He toed one boot off, then the other, preparing for the kind of serious slumber only Penny could fall into, anywhere, anytime. "Starting tomorrow morning, nine sharp, you have a translator. One hour per day for the duration of your stay if you need her. You're welcome in advance."

"What an amazing valet you are, Penny."

"It's a gift."

Christian dipped his finger beneath the flap of the envelope and broke the wax seal. "Does the bluestocking have a name?"

"Mowbray," Penny whispered, definitely on the edge of sleep. "Miss Mowbray."

The name danced through Christian's consciousness, sending goosebumps zinging along his skin. He forced his hand from its punishing clench on the envelope. "Her first name, do you know it?"

Penny opened one eye, a lazy blink. "Raine. Is that French? I only remember because of Miss Miller's eyes. Like rain falling from the clouds. Isn't that poetic? I may try to use that."

Christian's breath caught, the letter sliding from his grip to bounce off the toe of his Hessian. "Whose house did Miss Mowbray recently arrive from?"

Penny dropped a bent arm over his face, shrugged. "An earl's, I believe it was. A household going through a spot of trouble. A reprobate."

"Holy hell," Christian breathed, his heart kicking into a swift rhythm. There could be no one else with that name working for an earl with an appalling reputation. The coincidence was simply too much.

It was the girl he'd spent the summer watching. The summer dreaming of but never talking to. Years cursing himself for not trying, at the very least, to make her acquaintance. To be her friend when it seemed neither of them had been so lucky as to have one.

Her image, faded like it had sat too long in the sun, rotated through his mind. Hair the color of a shiny gold coin, dark eyes, shy smile. Slender and lovely and *connected* to him in a gut-sure way he couldn't explain.

Had never been able to explain.

He turned to gaze at the verdant slice of lawn outside the study's window, his chest tight, his fingertips tingling.

Tomorrow morning, he was finally going to meet the woman he'd been in love with for ten years.

Two

Raine adjusted the mobcap that never seemed to contain her unruly mass of hair, and with an anxious exhalation, blew the ruffled brim from her face. She stood before the door to the duke's study, ten minutes late for her translation session because she'd volunteered to assist Miss Miller with a chore a kitchen maid should have taken on. She'd been delaying the inevitable because she was nervous. Agitated for no good reason. Trying to squelch the adolescent butterfly-tingle in her belly. Appalling when she was far removed from—

Then he was there, the cause of her belly-tingle, opening the door, watch in hand. As if he'd been about to check the hall to see if she'd arrived. He was out of breath, dark hair tousled, cravat off-center. But not vexed as most men of her acquaintance would be by her tardiness. Instead, Christian Bainbridge, lover of wenches and watches, standing so close she could smell the delicate scent of citrus and ink drifting from his skin, had a tender, very fetching, very charming smile on his face.

And his eyes, because she'd wondered about them all night...

Oh, *heavens*, were his eyes a dazzling portrait, as blue as the delphiniums in the duchess's garden.

"It *is* you," he whispered beneath his breath, a statement she had no idea how to decipher. Had Miss Miller told him to expect her? Had he been expecting someone else? Had she mistaken the arranged time?

Discomfited, she smoothed her apron, the newest in her

possession, and stayed from reaching to adjust her cap. The plain, somewhat dour dress assigned to the staff she could do nothing about. Although it looked better on slim figures than it did on curvaceous ones, so she could tally this benefit. When benefiting the imposing man standing before her in dark, finely-tailored clothing was absurd to contemplate.

His smile grew as she fidgeted, creating a tiny dent in his cheek. A glorious imperfection in an otherwise extremely hand-some face. "Miss Mowbray, I presume," he said and gestured for her to enter the duke's study. "I can't express how delighted I am to meet you."

Oh. He seemed quite enthusiastic about the translation session. She hoped her German was on par with his needs. She gazed up into his face because he was tall enough that she had to. "Sir, I—"

"No." His expression shifted in an instant. Hardened, a flash of emotion confirming there was more to him than the bland smile and a compelling dimple. "My name is Christian," he managed, then laughed and shook his head, leaving the door properly ajar behind them. An escape route should she need one. "So easy, and yet, ten years overdue."

She entered the room, clearly missing some element of the situation. The *ton*, an exclusive group Christian Bainbridge was welcomed into, at least in part, were an eccentric lot. In her years of service, she'd grown accustomed to bizarre behavior. And become skilled at ignoring it.

On a table by the window sat a stack of books that hadn't been there when she cleaned the study yesterday. A band of sunlight waterfalled over them, glinting off the gilded script on the spines. Christian took his place behind the duke's desk as Raine moved forward like a pulley had drawn her. Brand new treasures, releasing nothing but the delicious scent of leather when she lifted one volume to her nose. No mold, no dust, no stained pages. Not yet. Her heart tripped. Books were her one indulgence, her grand passion in a life lacking any other. But they were costly and often out of reach.

As were most things she desired.

"I just finished the one on top. Austen. Two novels are included. Her last, sadly. You're welcome to it."

She streaked her finger along a groove in the cover, delighted but trying hard not to show it. "I couldn't possibly."

"Really? You couldn't possibly? Why not?"

Raine turned, a spike of impatience racing through her. A sentiment that had gotten her into trouble her entire bred-to-be-subservient-but-at-times-unable-to life. What she found was Christian Bainbridge's gaze centered on her, or more specifically, on her finger, which still lovingly caressed the spine of Jane Austen's final tome. His eyes were heated when they met hers; there was no way to hide it. She removed her hand from the book and tangled it in her apron to hold back the tremor.

The man affected her like no other.

She wondered suddenly, alarmingly, why she quite *liked* the way he made her feel. The way his attention put her on a pedestal she'd never inhabited. Made her *want* in a way she never had, skin tingling, mind whirring, heart thumping. She felt alive. Swallowing hard, her throat clicked. "I cannot because a gentleman does not loan books to a servant in a household he is visiting. It's simply not done."

Christian tugged on a length of twine surrounding a stack of envelopes he'd taken in hand, his gaze sweeping the length of her. "Who says I'm a gentleman," he whispered, his expression caught between professor and pirate.

She frowned and walked toward him, settling in the leather armchair situated before the desk. The same chair she'd huddled in as the duke offered her a reprieve from a dreadful situation, offered her a new life. A new life she must carefully guard. "This is a ridiculous conversation. You're an esteemed guest of the Duke and Duchess of Devon, and I'm here to help you translate." She pushed a breath past her lips. *We're not on the same level, and we shouldn't converse as if we were.* "I have one hour before I'm expected upstairs. Can we begin?"

"Of course, my apologies for any transgression. But know this." He dropped his eyes, slid a letter free from the envelope, and ironed his palm across the sheet. "I'm the youngest son of a vicar who used God's word most brutally. I was lucky enough to find my talent at an early age, a profitable talent, admittedly, and thank God for it because there was nothing else for me. I, too, have worked for everything I have; I've been given nothing. If you and I are going to spend time together, I simply wanted you to understand we're not so far apart." He sighed, his gaze touching hers before roaming to the window and that enticing stack of books. "As recompense for assisting with the translations, I thought it proper if you took the book. Any of them," he added, dragging his hand through his hair, leaving it in charming spikes atop his head.

His distress, and his generosity, sent a jolt through her. Not many kind men populated her world. She drew a breath that smelled faintly of the duke but more of the man across from her. She knew, instantly, the difference—and which scent she preferred. "I suppose I could borrow it. The Austen. With its return, what's the harm?" Shrugging, she curled her toes inside her worn slippers, letting the way her body sang in his presence capture every sense while vowing to deny it. "I love nothing more than reading."

His head lifted, his smile blinding.

She was lost.

And vexed that he'd so easily won their first battle.

HE WAS LOST. CHARMED, INTRIGUED.

Relieved. To know the girl he'd been drawn to so intensely years ago was a woman worth knowing, worth loving. Worth fighting for, should the situation come to that, which it would. He wasn't afraid to act on impulse—and he *always* trusted his gut. Like the swift decision to take the apprenticeship in Cambridge that had changed his life, Christian knew what he wanted.

And he wanted Raine Mowbray.

Her finger trailed across the page, a tiny, concentrating fold centered between her brows. Her nose was pert, her cheeks lightly freckled, her jaw sharp, used to being stubbornly set, he'd bet. Her hair, as golden as the butter he'd spread on his breakfast scone, fleeing the silly domestic's headpiece he'd love to yank from her head. She was slender. Delicate. As poised as any lady roaming any ballroom he'd ever been invited into. Whip-smart, when intelligent females who *admitted* being intelligent, were a rare commodity.

And, *ah*, was she beautiful.

She nibbled on her thumbnail and hummed beneath her breath, scribbling translations on a sheet of foolscap. Christian held back a groan—and the urge to tip her chin high and pour his frustration into a fiery kiss. His body was pulsing with the fantasy, every *inch* of it.

"Am I interrupting your work?" she asked without looking up, a subtle smile tilting the corners of her mouth.

He wasn't sure what he'd done to bring about amusement, but he'd go with it. They only had ten minutes left together, and Christian wanted Raine's conversation more than he wanted details on how to build a detached escapement caliber. And that was a first. "I'm sorry, I got distracted. Devon's watch repair may require a part I neglected to bring."

Her long lashes lifted, revealing eyes he'd thought were brown but had turned out to be an enchanting shade of hazel. She hesitated before asking, "Did you truly turn down a knighthood?"

He opened his mouth, closed it. Ran his tongue over his teeth while searching for what he wanted to tell her. The truth was probably best. In any case, his cheeks flushed, saying it before he could.

"Heavens above, you did. You turned down a knighthood!"

The Prince Regent is cracked, Christian wanted to say. The watch in question was a piece of Austrian junk, not worth the expense or the bother. Annoyance, and a ragged little thread of panic, almost drove out the pulse of desire controlling him. Raine would never find him suitable if she believed a meaningless knighthood stood between them. "It was a lark," was all he came up with.

She tapped her quill pen against the desk, considering. "Did Prinny think the proposal a lark?"

He placed his tweezers on the desk, removed the loupe from its nestle against his eye. "What else have the chattering ninnies been saying?" Gossip had followed him his entire life because he presented such an intriguing subject, stuck as he was in that graceless spot between the aristocracy and everything below. A man of industry when men of industry weren't revered.

Her smile broke, spreading across her face. So exquisite, it stole his breath. "Watches and wenches," she said through her glee.

A winding wheel dropped from his fingers and rolled across the desk, coming to a stop against the duke's inkwell. "*What?*"

"All you care for, that is."

His cheeks got so hot, they stung. "My work is my passion. I treasure this"—he gestured to the tools, the watch parts, spread across the desk—"more than, well…more than any…" *More than any wench. More than I could any woman except you, I'm coming to suspect.*

But that didn't sound right *at all*. And she'd never believe him anyway.

Raine dropped her head, laughing softly. "I'm sorry. I'm being unkind. Teasing you when I should not dare to."

Christian slumped back in his chair, uncertain where she was going with this. Women seldom admitted being unkind, especially when they were being unkind. "You are?"

"I don't often get to converse in this manner." She folded her arms along the desk and rested her chin atop them, giving him a candid perusal typically only circulated inside a bedchamber. "You see, clever conversation isn't expected of a humble housemaid, isn't requested or required. Just because I'm passive by necessity doesn't mean I am in *life*." Her lids fluttered with a sigh that almost had him reaching for her, which would be a mistake. He wanted to be her friend first. Needed to be her friend first. There was a reticence about her he feared had come from the debacle that had sent her fleeing from Tavistock House.

But Christian knew one thing. If he found out his cousin, a man he hadn't talked to in ten years and barely knew, had touched Raine Mowbray against her will, he would kill him.

Calming himself, he picked up a winding wheel and flipped it between his fingers, better to have something to do with his hands than placing them on her person. "You can talk to me as I adore clever banter. I'll not require but certainly request."

Her gaze danced away from his. "I miss those conversations. I miss engaging my brain. My former employer, Countess Tavistock, let me attend lessons with her governess from the time I was in leading strings. Later, I acted as an informal tutor to her children in certain subjects. My education is lacking for a peer but advanced for a maid. Languages, reading, came easily." Lost in thought, she chewed on her bottom lip, increasing his enchantment and his physical discomfort. "I think…I'm finding it easy to talk to you, which should not be.

Or rather, doesn't need to be for me to assist with your translations."

He slid his hand across the desk, unable to check the impulse. His heart had begun to thump, images of what he'd like to share with her—mind, body, soul—flooding him.

She was watching, wide-eyed but accepting, about to let him touch her.

"Kit, have I found the most unbelievable—" Penny burst into the room, took one look at the intimate scene, and bumped back against the door. "Sorry. I've interrupted."

"*Kit*," she mouthed with a grin that lit Christian up inside. Then she flipped one of the five watches on the desk over and viewed the time. "Oh, goodness, I have to go." Making a note on the letter to mark her place, she collected her papers in a tidy pile and laid the quill pen on top. "I'll be back tomorrow. Same time. I don't think it will take me more than three days, maybe four, to translate them. There are a few words I'm not sure of, colloquial speech, but the duchess has a German-language text in her materials for the children's lessons which may help."

Christian was out of his armchair like a shot and heading to the stack of books by the window. He knew Penny was watching the scene unfurl with undisguised interest, but Christian couldn't worry about that *and* deliver Jane Austen. A bit winded from his effort, he intercepted Raine at the door. "You forgot this," he murmured and pushed the volume into her hand. She wasn't wearing gloves, and neither was he, and his thumb brushed her wrist, a desperate, exhilarating feeling flowing up his arm and into his chest. And settling. "Please," he added when he'd never begged a woman for anything in his life. "We had a deal, remember?"

Her shoulder lifted, that ridiculous cap on her head bobbing as if she was going to refuse when her fingers closed gently around the book. Then she left him standing there, the sensation of touching her bare skin engraved on his senses like his name was engraved on his watches.

Penny stepped behind him, following his gaze down the deserted hallway, the only thing remaining Raine's teasing scent. That, and the images racing like feral dogs through his mind. Some of them lewd, he'd admit.

How soon could he make *that* reality, he wondered?

"That gorgeous creature is our bluestocking?" Penny asked in dazed incredulity. "Remind me to consider the brainy ones in the future."

"*My* bluestocking," Christian corrected.

Penny jammed his broad shoulder against the doorjamb. "So that's the way of it? Soft heart like yours, I knew it was coming at some point." He sighed, the sound genuinely mournful. "Well, now we're doomed."

Christian looked away before his face betrayed him. His severe upbringing and everything he'd had to do to succeed had beaten any sense of benevolence out of him.

He didn't have a soft heart. A generous heart.

Slightly more generous than Penny's perhaps.

But for the girl on the veranda, he was willing to expose his— even if he lost it in the process.

Three

Christian was waiting for her the next morning, lounging in the doorway of the duke's study like a panther stalking his prey. Teacup in hand, he took a leisurely sip and let his gaze roam the length of her and back. His calculated study was the most erotic thing she'd ever experienced—and all without being touched. She kept her expression placid, she hoped, as her chest flushed beneath starched cotton.

My, what would being kissed by the man, which she'd spent half the night contemplating, be like if his straightforward but pointed scrutiny scorched?

Most likely, it would be a disappointment, as the two careless kisses Raine had experienced to date had been.

"Are we ready to proceed with the project?" She halted before him, amazed her voice sounded steady with such wild anticipation seizing her. A stunned breath struck as she looked into his eyes and understood she felt much more than she should have. This was dreadful, an attraction between them a breach of an elemental tenet of servitude. A domestic did not, could not, foster feelings for a guest. A guest in a *ducal* home. A man notorious enough to be written about in the gossip sheets. A man known for his profligate lifestyle and his magnificent timepieces. A man well above her station.

A man who would break her heart into a thousand pieces if she let him.

He raised a dark eyebrow and sipped from his teacup. "Are you done?" he asked and turned to move into the study.

She tilted her head in question. "Done?"

"Your face, just then, was like one of my watches when I crack open the casing. A lot of moving parts." His deep voice drew her into the room, where he added with a cunning look thrown over his shoulder, "I apprenticed with a very brilliant horologist who once told me, deliberation can arrest innovation."

She settled in the armchair before the desk, her stack of translation materials where she'd left them the day before. Christian's tools were perfectly placed, as well. A precise row, an exact arrangement from largest to smallest. Interesting. A conscientious man with the things he cared for. "Go with your gut. Is that what you were supposed to take from that charming bit of horological wisdom? For a man, I'm certain that's excellent advice. Women are not often afforded the opportunity to rise to such a challenge, Mister Bainbridge."

His burst of laugher had her glancing up from the letter she'd spread across glossy mahogany, another opportunity to dive into the blasted blue of his eyes. Another opportunity to note the wicked dimple denting his cheek. "Let's agree," he said, sliding a cup of tea across the desk when a man had never poured tea for her in her life, "that within the walls of Devon's exhaustively regal study, you're afforded every opportunity to rise to such a challenge."

She pressed her lips together to hold back a smile. "So I'm to speak freely. And this benefits you how?"

Christian popped the loupe into place against his left eye, picked up a small screwdriver, and turned his attention to the metal parts spread before him. "That, Miss Mowbray, is still to be determined."

The hour passed quickly, quietly, contentedly. There was an ease in being around Christian Bainbridge, which Raine understood was not customary or conventional. His regard warmed her, brief strikes when he stretched or took a sip of tea, that made her feel like a thick, woolen shawl had been placed about her shoulders rather than a sharp blade edged along her skin, as masculine attention usually brought. She was attractive, and men were weak. Indeed, her appearance was a drawback rather than a source of good fortune, as beauty was for a woman of highborn birth. Thinking of the times she'd had to push the scuffed bureau in front of the attic door at Tavistock House suddenly came to her, and she frowned. Placed her quill on the desk and leaned back in her chair to watch Christian work.

Five minutes at her leisure, she decided with a glance thrown at the mantel clock Christian had modified earlier, a device that had never before kept accurate time. Fascinated, she watched him adjust the wheel of a pocket watch, pause, then go in for another alteration.

"There's nothing faulty with the piece. Just a loose hairspring." One side of his mouth kicked up. "It's aging, like skin that starts to sag. Springs lose their elasticity, as it were."

"It's lovely," she murmured, unable to look away from the long, slim fingers manipulating the tool with true artistry. He was gifted. More talented than anyone she'd ever known. Foolish, to be this attracted to a man so far from her reach. To be compelled to know him better, to share the scant, uninteresting bits of her life with him.

"A Bainbridge open-face duplex chronometer, to be precise." He removed the loupe, leaving a shallow dent where it had pressed into this skin, and slid the watch across to her. "Take a look. It's a superb model. Probably the one I'm best known for."

"The most accurate," she said and grasped the watch, the metal casing warm from his touch.

He tilted his head, his lips curving in pleasure. "The chattering ninnies included that bit, did they? Sometimes gossip is as precise as my timepieces."

She rotated the watch, the silver filigree chain sliding through her fingers. "This is beautiful. I've never seen the like."

"A silversmith in France makes them. Unique to my pieces."

"Gorgeous," she murmured.

"*Yes.*"

She stared at the watch, unable to meet his gaze, wondering what he wanted from her. Her intuition told her it wasn't what most men of her acquaintance had. Or not all. There was hunger in his attention, yes, but there was also an affectionate, enveloping kindness that even his sardonic banter couldn't quell. He was a better man than he believed if she had her guess. It frightened her that she was beginning to trust him, to understand, like his timepieces, what made him tick.

"There's a spare length of chain, slightly damaged, that has no home." He nudged a length of filigree into her line of vision. "It would make an excellent bookmark."

She shook her head. "No more gifts, Mister Bainbridge."

"There've been no gifts. Miss Austen is returning to me, is she not? And the filigree has no use, consider it rubbish."

She blew out an exasperated breath. *Impossible man*, she reasoned and reached for the chain. It glimmered against her skin, a flawless fragment, not an imperfection in sight.

"Rise to the challenge in our safe space, Miss Mowbray. Tell me what's circling through your astute mind."

"I'd rather serve as a maid my whole life than be beholden to anyone," she said in a rush, the words tense, hard, shaded by a forlorn past and an uncertain future. She thrust the delicate silver across the desk. "That's what I'm thinking."

Christian cursed softly beneath his breath.

She looked up, startled to see how stunned he seemed by her words. "Sorry you asked? An honest woman isn't always welcome."

"No, God, no. I want to hear anything you wish to tell me." He scrubbed his hand over his face. The eyes that met hers were apologetic, beseeching, an indigo sea she wanted to plunge into. "I imagined it would be days before we got to this topic. You see, I'm a devotee of actions over words, and if I speak before you've had time to *see*, I'm not sure you'll believe me. I hadn't planned on this, on ever meeting you. Of course, I had things I wanted to say should it ever occur, but life never goes the way you plan, does it?"

Her heart stuttered in her chest. Could her intuition have deceived her this appallingly? Was he a devious man, after all? "You've been withholding something from me. Something I should know."

His beautiful lips parted, closed, parted again. "No, yes, partially."

"You're betrothed," she whispered and rose shakily to her feet, the notion sending a dart of grief through her. Grief she had no right to feel. No *place* to feel. How many times had she seen aristocratic men take advantage? Was she going to betray herself and fall prey as well? Over a man who had the most arresting voice she'd ever heard, the sweetest smile, the gentlest laugh? A man who was intelligent and cunning and even a little shy? A man who seemed to know her, who she seemed to know right back.

Was that what it took for her to fold? To fall?

Bracing his hands on the desk, he shoved from his chair, fury tightening his stubbled jaw. "If you think I would betray you in this manner after I've sat here for two days consuming you with my eyes, panting like a dog over a bone but holding my feelings inside for both of us, then there's no chance. I'm a scoundrel, fine, admitted, but I don't play with people's happiness nor seek to increase their challenges. When I can see you're challenged. And alone. But I'm alone, too, Raine. For years, *centuries*." He yanked a hand that trembled through his hair and exhaled sharply. "This is coming out wrong. I'm not gifted in the art of sustaining relationships. Or fostering them."

"Not according to the chattering ninnies," she returned, realizing they were arguing. Although she had no idea about what. So what if he had a mistress? A fiancée? Or one of each. It should mean nothing to her. But, *oh*, it did.

"Bringing up the gossips rags? Really? The lady doesn't fight fair."

She leaned across the desk, closing in until the gray flecks in his eyes shot into view. "You're mistaken. I'm not a lady. I'm a housemaid, and that's all I'll ever be. You're here"—she held her hand high, then lowered it—"and I'm here."

"I won't let you evade this discussion that easily. As if the tiers of society mean a damned thing to me." He grasped her hand, unfurled her clenched fist, and angrily dropped the length of chain into it. "As if they mean anything to you. I'd be very disheartened if they did."

Miss Bruce's high-pitched voice intruded, a strident call from the hallway.

Raine backed away from him, bumping into the armchair, her fingers closing around the filigree. "I have to go."

"Meet me tonight. Ten o'clock. At the stone bridge over the pond. I've been walking every night to clear my mind. It's quite lovely. And safe." He held up his hands. "I won't touch you. I'll explain everything, though I'm sure I'll muddle it up. Hopefully, I can figure out what to say between now and then."

"The truth will do nicely."

When Miss Bruce's voice again flowed between them, he sighed and gave Raine a resigned wave toward the door. "That's what we'll go with then. I only ask for tolerance in advance. Men are, you must remember, simple, foolish creatures. We often stumble along doing the best we can."

Raine strode from the study with Christian's gaze stinging her back and his delicate filigree chain marking her palm, confused and agitated, thinking somewhat crossly that she'd never met a less simple, foolish creature in her life.

CHRISTIAN HADN'T BEEN LYING WHEN HE TOLD RAINE HE WASN'T very good with women.

Success had brought them to his Berkeley Square doorstep in droves, and he knew, after diligent practice, how to satisfy. For a night, a week or two. A month. He was skilled in transitory pleasure; the mechanics of tupping weren't hard to perfect when one liked working parts and the microscopic details that accompanied them as much as he did. He was patient. Meticulous. Generous in bed, as his last mistress had shared with a level of surprise that let him know most men *weren't*. A fast pace had its time and place. As did a slow one.

He liked both and everything in between.

But he knew nothing, absolutely nothing, about quiet conversations over tea. Intimate discussions about family and politics and art while thoughts of making someone happy *out* of bed swirled through his mind. Thoughts about love filling his heart. He'd only loved two people, his brother and mother, and they were both long gone. Maybe three, if he counted Penny, which he felt he could in a brotherly, best friend fashion.

Moonlight slithered across the boundless woodlands as choppy pianoforte chords, compliments of a regrettably untalented Devon guest, flowed over him. Christian sighed and kicked at a patch of overgrown grass. Raine was late, likely not coming. Reading Austen in her narrow bed in the servant's quarters, tucked in and away from him. Or, maybe she'd taken the book and the length of entirely serviceable silver filigree he'd gifted her on a whim and shoved them under his door, a determined rebuke. A mild breeze ripped through the pitch night, the temperature, for a Yorkshire evening, balmy and ideal. A perfect night for—

Christian halted, flipping the worn compensating balance wheel he'd replaced on one of the duke's watches from hand to hand. A perfect night for *what*?

Not an assignation.

As much as he wanted Raine beneath him on any available surface she'd agree to share, he wanted her friendship, her opinions, wishes, dreams, past, present, future, *more*. He wanted the one person in the universe he felt could ease his loneliness.

The one person he might have a chance to make happy in return. Why he imagined he could, he wasn't able to explain; he only knew it to be true.

The wheel tumbled from his hand to the grass. With a growl, he went to one knee to retrieve it. This was trouble, even if he welcomed it. Dire and unpredictable. He was in love with the woman in the duke's study, not only the girl he'd mooned over at his cousin's estate.

The sound of a branch cracking had his gaze reaching into the night, his body flooding with anticipation.

She was late. But she'd come.

Strolling across the lawn, that unflattering dress whipping her long legs, flaxen hair unbound and flowing down her back, something he'd yet to see. He clenched his hands into fists and rose unsteadily to his feet. This is how she'd look in his bed. A little untamed, a little unsure.

All *his*.

She appeared nervous when she reached him, her cheeks ashen in the creamy moonlight, her bottom lip tucked firmly between her teeth. Tugging at her threadbare shawl, she gave him a cautious smile, a tilt of her head that said, *I'm here, now what?*

He extended his hand, watched in trepidation as she glanced at the offering, caught her breath in indecision, then slowly linked her fingers with his. It was a sweetly intimate gesture, and he was unable to remember holding hands with anyone except his mother.

With a smile but no conversation, not yet, he tugged her along, over the stone bridge to a secluded spot on the other side

645

of the stream. The plink of the pianoforte rippled through the night, the only sound aside from their hushed breaths and the distant chirp of crickets.

Penny, a romantic at heart though he'd deny it to his death, had secured the blanket and the candles. Christian had charmed the bottle of wine from the cook, Mrs. Webster, who certainly suspected he planned to use it for nefarious purposes, which for the first time, he didn't.

Raine moved ahead of him, halted, and he stumbled into her. *Bloody hell*, her body was warm, soft. He tucked his nose in her hair, his inhalation sending the scent of lavender through him.

"What's this?" she asked with a searching backward glance.

Christian gave her a gentle nudge away from his body before it provided proof of her ardent effect on him. "A moonlit picnic among friends. I'll sit on the far side of the blanket, not even the tip of my boot touching the hem of that most unflattering garment Devon has you wear. The candles add a certain sense of propriety, am I right? With those and a close-to-full moon, we're as illuminated as we'd be in the duchess's drawing room. You see, I remember my promise."

A laugh burst from her, sending her shawl fluttering to the ground. "You think two tallow candles will style this a proper situation? Mister Bainbridge, I'm astounded by your lack of prudence and your optimism that the wind won't blow them out. Also, a gentleman never tells a woman her clothing is unflattering, even if it's the absolute truth."

He dropped to his haunches to retrieve her shawl and gestured to the candles that had defied his will and indeed remained unlit. "Go on. Please. You're ruining the most romantic undertaking of my life. And it's Christian. Not sir, not mister. I'm neither of those things, not to you."

"That's just as well," she said and wandered to his celebration beneath the stars, arranging herself on the blanket with all the grace of a queen, "because I prefer Kit."

He hummed beneath his breath, unsure what to say. His nickname on her lips sent a jagged, desirous pulse spiraling through him. Of longing. And strangely, of loneliness. No one aside from his brother and Penny had ever called him Kit. He wouldn't have allowed it if they had. The name brought too many painful memories, ones he'd sealed in a box and buried deep in his heart. This endeavor, he realized as he settled across from her, was going to test him.

Test that promise he'd so boldly made not to touch her.

Silent, he poured wine into the tumblers he'd guessed would make the trip more safely than wine glasses and handed her one. Rucking his knee high, he dropped his arm atop it and watched her tongue peek out to catch a drop of wine on the rim. His fingers clamped around the crystal as his body tightened. God, looking and not touching was *torture*.

"I wish Lady Adam's pianoforte skills were enhancing this enchanting summer evening, but alas, she's quite horrible," Raine murmured after taking an engrossed sip, as if she didn't often get to taste wine. "If she starts singing, I may have to plug my ears."

Her calm certainty about his honorable intent threw him off balance. "You're not frightened to be out here with me?"

She paused, her gaze, black in the muted light, narrowing. "Should I be?"

He took a leisurely drink, then shook his head. "No."

"You're a gentleman. A *gentle* man. Known more for your reputation than the truth. I know the difference; I've encountered the difference."

Imagining how she knew sent a jolt of anger through him. "Your beauty is tempting, but your mind even more so."

"Beauty is fleeting. And no man has ever taken the time to know my mind."

He blew out a breath, frustrated with himself. And her. "You effectively paint me in a corner when I'm not even sure it's your intention. I've never had a partner verbally joust and outman me so well. Or so easily."

That charming little dent pinged between her brows as she frowned. "What do you mean?"

"That I unhappily join the ranks of the fleeting and frail. Because I, too, find you incredibly beautiful. My captivation started when I had little notion what was in your mind, just like those toffs you describe with disdain," he admitted, forging ahead despite her obvious shock. "I only knew you had a great love of books, nestled in the corner of the veranda night after night, lamplight flooding over you as you tuned the pages. I'd never wanted anything more than I did to hear your voice. And, I suppose, yes, to touch you. My only justification is that I was a fifteen-year-old fool."

"Tavistock House," she breathed.

He nodded with a long pull of his wine, wondering if he was going to be forced to chase her over the bridge and across the lawn if she decided to run. Because he *would* chase her. To the ends of the earth. She simply didn't understand that yet—and he was just beginning to.

She placed the tumbler by her side and rose to her knees. "Who *are* you?"

"You're waiting for me to lie, aren't you? Maybe I should, but I won't. The Earl of Tavistock is my cousin, a very distant relation. Even more distant in terms of our acquaintance. After my brother died, he was the last relative I had left. I spent three weeks with him one summer before I removed myself from his household for an apprenticeship in Cambridge. I was already on my future path, already had a reputation for repairing capricious timepieces." Soothing a bout of nerves, he polished off the wine in his glass and reached for the bottle. "There was nothing for me at Tavistock House except the girl on the veranda, but I was in no position to fend for myself, to fight for more. I was a child still in many ways. Vulnerable in mind and heart from the previous months, losing my family. The earl was horrid. Belittling. Callous." He paused, the idea of his cousin touching Raine blackening his vision at the edges. "Which I fear you already know."

Her gaze lifted to roam the woodlands, the lawn, the bridge. Anywhere but on him. "That's why you seemed familiar. How you knew about the books."

"Yes."

Through moonlight the color of a tarnished coin, her gaze found his. "Why didn't you talk to me? Your bedchamber must have overlooked the veranda, and I went there every night. Mainly to escape the earl. He would come to the attic and select a maid, willing or not, it didn't matter. Not every night. Or even every week when he was in residence. You never knew, just heard his footfalls on the stairs. At that time, I was young enough, fourteen maybe, to escape his attention and my father was the head gardener, my mother his housekeeper, so—"

"I may not be able to hear this," he said between clenched teeth.

Her blinding smile, a most contrary reaction, rocked him where he sat. "Oh, no, Kit, he never…" She pressed the tumbler against her cheek as if it could cool her skin, then sighed and took another drink.

He wanted to tell her to slow down or risk becoming tipsy, but he said nothing, just sat there consumed with relief that his cousin had never gotten his filthy hands on her.

"My brother is friendly with Thomas Kingsman, the Duke of Devon's footman," she said after a charged moment of silence. "He spoke to the duke, who offered to pension me off, of sorts, from your cousin. He said my language skills were needed, his governess not equipped. Tavistock was deeply in debt, reducing his staff, so his attraction to me meant much less than the coin in his pocket and one less mouth to feed. All this delicacy, instead of my up and leaving in the middle of the night, was done so my father and mother could remain at Tavistock House until they are ready to retire, possibly with a modest cottage retained on one of his country estates. The countess is quite lovely, and my parent's positions lofty enough to make her home a fine place to live, the earl notwithstanding."

"I could kill him for making you feel like you had to run away, for making you leave your family. For making me flee to Cambridge, alone in the world with a hardened heart."

Raine stilled, placing her tumbler on the grass. Leaning on an outstretched arm, she brought her face close to his, her body moving in until Christian caught the scent of her skin, her clothing, her hair. Starch, lavender, lemons. *Raine*. Mixing with the teasing aroma of a country summer, bringing his blood to a boil. "I wish you'd talked to me. Let me know you were up there watching." She pressed her lips together, her lids lowering, teasing him, teasing them both. She had power over him, and he wondered if she was becoming courageous enough to use it.

"Don't," he warned, "not now. Not yet."

Why, she mouthed, breathless, as affected by him as he was by her.

If he had to do so little to convince her, they were both lost.

He shifted out of reach, an awkward move when he wasn't an awkward man. "Because I'm afraid kisses are all you'll give me. All you think we're suited for. And then you'll use them as proof that it's all I want."

"You engineered this"—she gestured to the wine, the moonlight—"and you're not even going to kiss me?"

"I feel caught," he said, stumbling. Then he went ahead and told her, making a fool of himself. "You know I want to. Since the first moment I saw you ten years ago when I didn't even know how to kiss! That would not have been pleasant, for you anyway."

She laughed and reached, catching his jaw, her thumb sweeping over his cheek and drawing every bit of air from his lungs. "It would have been wonderful and very sweet if you'd tried, because I didn't know how to then, either."

"Now, you do."

"Don't get cross, Kit Bainbridge. Not with your unsavory antics. I've been kissed twice. Both disappointments." She went to lower her hand, but he placed his over hers, trapping it against his cheek. "Honestly, one was acceptable. Boring but acceptable."

"I feel challenged because I've never been boring." He dipped his head, pressed a soft, searching kiss to her wrist. "I believe in accurate timepieces. Tepid summer nights and blueberry scones and first-rate Scotch. Tangled sheets and damp skin. Bottomless kisses." She made a low purring sound and leaned in, her lids fluttering. He waited until she opened her eyes before he continued, "I believe you can meet someone and *know*. I always have. The girl on the veranda is why no one has been able to touch my heart. I've been waiting for her, for *you*, my entire life."

She didn't stop him when he tunneled his hand through her hair to circle the nape of her neck. Didn't stop him when he went to his knees and fit her against him, chest to chest, hip to hip, capturing her mouth beneath his. Didn't stop him when he tilted her head, kissing her more soulfully, giving more of himself than he'd ever given. Didn't stop him when he palmed her waist and pulled her in, letting her know in graphic detail exactly what she was doing to him.

Her lips were soft, her sighs sweet, her skin moist, her body perfect. Her arms rose to circle his shoulders and bring them closer, like hot wax on parchment, a seductive, molten press.

Following timelines and building trust and maintaining control slipped away. He let his lips slide to her cheek, her jaw, a sensitive spot beneath her ear as she released a heavy breath against his neck.

Dutifully, he would record everything she liked, every little thing.

Starting now.

"You're *mine*," he whispered, his voice sounding like it had been cut with jagged glass.

And that's when she stopped him.

Rocking back off her kneeling pose, she broke his hold, landing on her bottom in the middle of the blanket.

He blinked, dazed, shaking his head as if the movement would return thought. "I'm sorry, I lost control. I don't know what happened. I swear, I only wanted to talk to you, get to know you better and admit seeing you years ago, an admission that had started to feel like a betrayal of our fledgling friendship."

She pressed her palm to her brow. "You don't have to be sorry. I wanted you to kiss me. It was everything I imagined it would be. I didn't push you away because I didn't like it. I liked it *too* much."

The hot lick of temper that had gotten him in trouble many, many times rolled through him. He wasn't practiced at accepting things he didn't want to hear. "This was a delicious taste, a glorious start. There's much more, Raine, and God do I want more, but why do I have the feeling you're going to tell me that can't happen?"

She jerked her head up, her own temper sparking. "Because it can't! There's a pleasant young man on staff. Nash. A groom with a promising future, someone who occupies *my* world, Kit, someone who has intimated—"

"Oh, no, Raine Mowbray." He grasped her wrist, giving her a gentle shake. "If you're marrying anyone in this lifetime, it's bloody well going to be me. I claimed the right ten years ago, even if you didn't know it. Even if I didn't fully know it. The thousand dreams I've had about you since then confirm the decision, make no mistake."

Her eyes widened, her cheeks leeching color until he feared she would swoon. Then they filled with rosy-red fury. "Marriage? Should I have you admitted to Bedlam? I'm a housemaid, and you were just offered a knighthood! A union with me would be preposterous to consider when you could climb so much higher. You have patrons who would drop you and your accurate time-pieces before you took your first matrimonial breath."

He settled back on his heels, releasing her as if her skin had scorched his hands. "What did you think I was doing out here with you?"

Guilt raced across her face, and he realized what she'd thought: that he was toying with her as she'd been toying with him. His chest constricted, and he closed his eyes to fend off the crimson haze. To her, he was just another feckless aristocrat when in truth, he'd never fit anywhere except his lonely crevice. A crevice it seemed he was never to crawl from.

When he'd imagined creating his own universe with her in it.

A Latin phrase he recalled from school rolled through his mind. *Contra mundum.* Against the world. He'd wanted his future to be the two of them against the world.

"Go inside, Miss Mowbray. Before I say something I'll regret. I have a lamentable disposition that's landed me in more than one brawl. Ask Penny if you need proof." He grabbed the bottle and lifted it to his lips, the taste of wine washing away the taste of *her*.

"I've hurt your feelings," she said, her voice cracking. "Kit, I would never…that is, I…"

"Mister Bainbridge, if you don't mind. Sir works, too." He sprawled to his back, his arm going over his eyes to hide what-ever might lie in their depths. He wasn't accomplished at hiding his emotions, as those many scuffles Penny had rescued him from attested to. Raine witnessing his dismantling would serve no further purpose; her rejection was already stripping him bare. "Leave me to my plans to climb higher in society by means of an advantageous but loveless marriage. My plans to seduce a maid beneath a"—he shifted his arm and stared at the tree above them—"towering elm."

She muttered something he didn't catch, then said clearly, "I'll leave as you're not willing to discuss this rationally, when you know I'm right. I wish I *weren't* right, do you not know that? I'm sorry, I would never do anything to hurt you. We're becoming friends, and I've never had many of those." She sounded close to tears, and he felt close to them.

He heard her rise, shake out her skirt, hesitate, when he wanted, suddenly and desperately, to be alone. "It looks like I'm going to have a lot of time to devote to creating a detached escapement caliber, and I need you and your German, Miss Mowbray, so don't think about wheedling out of finishing the translations for me."

There. Well done. If he made her mad, she'd bolt.

Women tended to do that; he tended to make them.

She cursed beneath her breath, a most unladylike sentiment, and stalked away, the sound of her footfalls lessening until halting pianoforte notes and a chorus of bleating crickets were all that surrounded him.

He was going to finish the bottle of wine and slumber beneath the stars. Stagger into Devon's agreeable abode at dawn and sleep until supper. Let the entire household think him a mad artiste because perhaps he was. Penny could make excuses for him *and* supervise the translations, while Christian spent the rest of the week repairing the duke's timepieces in seclusion.

Then he would bolt for London himself.

Because his heart was breaking.

Raine didn't believe that love could happen instantaneously. Intuition or fate or destiny, whatever one wanted to call it.

And there was nothing he could do to *make* her believe.

Like the nick of a blade against tender skin, his dilemma was painful but uncomplicated.

For years, he'd loved someone who, when given a chance, wasn't willing to love him back.

Four

Raine huddled beneath the starched sheet in her attic bed, tugged a counterpane of higher quality than Tavistock had ever provided for his staff to her chin. Moonbeams, the same that had tumbled over Kit so generously an hour ago, poured in the small window, highlighting the dust motes drifting through the air and the despair filling her heart.

He might not talk to her again, except for his bleeding translations, a project she'd been dragging out to spend more time with him. What if he woke at dawn and decided to return to London? What if he woke at dawn and decided wenches were much less trouble than obstinate housemaids?

She sighed and touched her lips, still tingling from his kiss. Wasn't that what she'd *told* him to do? Leave her to an independent future, a footman who may or may not ask for her hand. A man she considered a friend but nothing more. A man who'd given her nothing more than a tiresome kiss.

She didn't want to live the rest of her life with tiresome kisses.

Not when there were ones powerful enough to melt copper if she only dared to accept them.

She closed her eyes and swallowed against the sting of tears. The hurt in his gaze had pierced something deep within her.

He was going to be doubly mad that she'd alerted his valet— who looked like no valet Raine had ever seen—to his possibly drunken state out there on the edge of the parklands. Where foxes and grass snakes and she wasn't sure what else roamed at night. Maybe it wasn't safe. Maybe he would get cold. The clouds had looked tempestuous like a storm might be rolling in. And…

Damn and blast. This felt like what she'd imagined falling in love would. Astonishing and distressing. Like stripping naked and diving into a calm pond. Glorious, until you looked to the shore and realized you weren't alone and everyone was watching.

Kit might love her, too. Or imagine he did. That timid girl had made an enormous impression on him. Hard to believe when she'd been so lonely and fearful. But he'd been lonely and fearful, too. Like recognized like. It made her breath catch to imagine that brilliant boy gazing down from his window above and wishing he had the courage to talk to her.

Something he'd said when he met her shimmered through her mind.

So easy, and yet, ten years overdue.

A tear rolled down her cheek, and she scrubbed it away. His odd comment now made all the sense in the world.

If she tried, she could almost picture him. She remembered a young man visiting that summer. Quality clothing covering a gangly body, one in the midst of splendid promise. Beautiful features too big for his face.

Of course, he'd grown into them, into everything, beautifully. Become a gorgeous, talented, thoughtful man. A man suited to a highborn lady, someone who would add every advantage to his life, to his business. Even in Raine's class, marriage was rarely about love and often about necessity or accessibility, property, or monies. She'd never expected love.

When Kit expected *everything*.

She snuggled deeper in the bed, her toes chilled, her skin clammy. There were a thousand reasons for her to push Kit away and only one reason not to. If she let herself love him, and someday he regretted his choice, as she assumed he would, she'd curl into a ball and die. Simply die. A marriage of convenience was one thing, but a marriage where only one person was happy…where only one person was in love…

Better to be alone than suffer such torment.

She pressed her face into her pillow, deciding to take the coward's path.

CHRISTIAN FELT THE TIP OF A BOOT NUDGE HIS HIP. AT THE third nudge, he snarled, "Leave me be, will you? I'll head back to the house with the sun. Go away."

"You're a disaster. I can't take you anywhere." Penny dropped to his haunches beside Christian and seized the empty wine bottle with a groan of dismay. "I was afraid of this. Women aren't clocks. Nothing reliable about them."

"I tried, can't you see? Romance. It didn't work."

"Perhaps the traditional approach would be better. In London better. Rides through Hyde Park, strolls along Bond Street, two scandalous waltzes in one night, done. Marriage to someone who means something but not everything. Everything is not required, Kit."

"It is for me." Christian elbowed to a wobbly sit. A gust of wind whipped in from the east, sending his hair into his eyes. A storm was brewing. He rubbed his aching chest; his argument with Raine had taken a piece of him and shattered it like china against marble. He didn't feel whole at the moment.

Penny sat next to Christian, stretching his legs out across the wrinkled blanket. "I feared this."

"Wonderful, add prophecy to your list of talents. Have your flask handy?"

Penny grimaced and yanked the dented tin from his coat pocket, thrust it toward Christian. The etched metal caught a streak of moonlight and sent it shooting across their Hessians.

Christian took a long pull, the Scotch adding weight to the wine he'd consumed in a way he knew would distress him come morning. "She's not going for it," he said with a sinking heart. Even with that scorching kiss standing between them, she hadn't considered it. Or him.

Penny's blistering gaze swept him, the judgmental cur. "Did you mention marriage?"

"I did," Christian said with another drink, "and she's out."

"Maybe we rehearse, and you can try again. You're not the best with these things. Remember what you said to Lady Leadbetter about her gown? She stills get pink in the face when we see her."

"I thought she'd accidentally dressed for a costume ball, I honestly did!" He coughed and shoved the flask in Penny's direction. "Did you see that silk catastrophe? I was trying to save her from embarrassment. 'Go home and change before anyone sees you' type of thing. You dressed for the wrong event."

"What I'm hearing is that you applied your standard finesse to the proposal tonight."

"It wasn't poetic if that's what you're asking."

Penny took a drink and wiped his mouth with the back of his hand. "Ah, I've read this play before. You bumble, then Miss Mowbray says something you don't want to hear, and boom, a sulking, insolent man appears, stage left."

Christian stacked one boot atop the other and hung his head back, his gaze going to a sky that looked like it was going to unleash havoc at any moment. "A congenial groom got to her first. Someone by the name of Dash or something. Certainly the more appropriate choice. Another maid told her about that knighthood offer from cracked George, so she believes we're leagues apart. If she only knew what it was like growing up with a wastrel for a father, a revered vicar the entire household was terrified of. My upbringing was less than noble. Likely less noble than hers in many respects."

"So she declined because of societal disparity and this illustrious groom…"

"Then I got angry, and that sulking, insolent bloke you mentioned joined the party. It wasn't pretty."

"Your temper is truly your downfall." Penny polished the flask on his sleeve and slipped it in his pocket. "We're lost if we can't upstage a humble groom, however."

"It's more complicated than that." He groaned, digging his heel in the soil. His cheeks had gotten hot, always a bad sign. "Remember that girl I fancied? The one at Tavistock House?"

Penny whistled beneath his breath, tilted his head in meditation. "The paragon on the veranda. Yes, I remember, because you bring her up every time we're deep in our cups. She's mysteriously ruined every relationship you've tried to sustain, if I may be so bold as to judge. Let me guess, she's in your head along with your lovely bluestocking and you don't know—"

"She *is* my lovely bluestocking."

Christian held back a grin as shock whipped across Penny's

impossible-to-alter countenance. At least he was getting *some* joy from this dreadful experience.

"Well…" Penny rummaged in his pocket for the flask, apparently deciding another chug was in order. "Consider me stunned." He issued a humorless grunt, his gaze locking with Christian's then dancing away. Penny was his best friend in the world, but discussing emotions was hard for men. God knows what tender sentiment was shining in Christian's eyes. "Almost gives me a chill along my spine. I don't believe in fate or fanciful events, or love, but damn, that's incredible. Are you sure?"

Christian nodded. He was sure.

"Then you must make her understand. All these years. She's your…she's the…"

"You're going to have to finish the translations."

Penny crawled to his feet with a curse. "I'm the best soldier-cum-manservant in England, and I'm dutiful, but I'm not crazy. And I'm *not* sitting in that stifling, regally-oppressive room with a vexed woman you inelegantly asked to marry you." He collected the edge of the blanket in his fist as raindrops began to strike the ground, yanking it from underneath Christian. "I'm scared of angry women. And tired of dealing with yours. This is your dilemma to solve, my friend." Grabbing the candles, he stuffed them under his armpits, and kicked the wine bottle in the bushes. "If you can look her in the eye and tell her you don't want her, if you mean it, then I'll pack up our gadgets and tools, and we ride back to London. If you can't, maybe your job's not done. And I don't just mean the watches. I guess I'm asking you to stop and think and not let your temper lead."

"Feels hopeless," Christian said and rose unsteadily to his feet, the rain coming down hard, soaking his clothing and sending tiny rivulets of water into his eyes.

Penny took off across the bridge, throwing over his shoulder, "That's the liquor talking." He halted on the rise, just before he dipped down on the other side, lost from sight. "And she cares. At least a little. How do you think I found you? Your lovely blue-stocking was worried about you out here in the wild, three hundred feet from a ducal manor, which I didn't point out. Came to get me. To get *you*."

Christian sank back against the bridge's pillar, his mind awhirl. Thunder rumbled in the distance, but he barely acknowledged it. It would serve him right, getting struck during a fit of masculine pique.

Raine cared about him.

She'd almost admitted that. Not wanting to hurt someone equaled caring, didn't it? Her kiss, while untutored and endearingly guileless, spoke of attraction. And curiosity. Which could lead to love. With their tempers, he expected a lifetime of senseless arguments and fierce lovemaking.

She was everything he'd dreamed of. Clever, perhaps too much so. Beautiful and serious-minded. Attentive. Kind. Unconventional in the most enchanting way. He didn't care that she hadn't been born a lady. He simply didn't *care*. He'd never wanted anyone else, not ever. Had been in love with her since the first moment he noticed her sitting beneath a dusky summer moon, even if no one—except, incredibly, Penny—believed it.

He would find a way to make her forget about that ridiculous knighthood.

About her enthusiastic groom.

He would find a way to make her choose *him*.

Five

hristian was late for the morning's translation session.

Penny had overslept, which meant he'd overslept. There'd been no time for anything but a quick freshening up with tepid water from the washbasin and a guzzled cup of lukewarm tea. He was unshaven, cravat askew, waistcoat buttons, he noted as he looked down upon entering the duke's study, misbuttoned. He'd decided to forego his coat and had his sleeves rolled to his elbows. He wasn't going to play the part of the supposed aristocrat Raine had turned down—because his tailor *was* the best in London, and it showed in his attire—when the real Christian Bainbridge was an informal man.

He would be himself with his bluestocking and see how *that* went.

She was there, dependable to a fault, settled in the massive armchair that swallowed her petite frame, head bent, glorious hair stuffed in that horrid cap. After they crawled from bed the morning after their marriage, his second duty was going to be tossing those pathetic pieces of cotton and lace in the hearth. His first being making love to her until neither of them could see straight. He gave a mental sigh and made himself circle her to the desk. He had no reason to touch her even if his fingertips tingled with the temptation, his stomach twisting with the *need*. He'd dreamed about her most of the night, their kiss lingering on his lips like mist on the moors.

As he collapsed in the duke's chair, his fingers stumbled over his waistcoat buttons, a quick repair when there was no way to hide the shape he was in.

Raine glanced up from her folio, took him in with one of those penetrating reviews that set his skin aflame, her lips lifting in a wry smile she didn't try to conceal. With a slight shake of her head, she pushed a teacup across the desk, then returned to her work.

The tea was blessedly hot, strong, no milk, one sugar. Just as he liked it. This trivial thoughtfulness combined with the rosy tinge lighting her cheeks eased the spiral of tension in his belly. She wasn't unaffected by him *or* his graceless proposal.

It was a start.

He popped his loupe in place, collected his tools, and dove into his work, content to be with her amidst a most companionable silence. The Duke of Devon had proven to be an excellent client over the years, his watches all coming from Christian's shop. The one he worked on now was a particular favorite, a piece Christian had relinquished with what felt like despair, the substantial blunt in his pocket not enough to ease the pain of surrendering his design. Perhaps making him an artist if not an able businessman.

Christian smoothed his finger over the etchings on the sterling silver case, the whirring wheels, the coiled hairsprings. Clicking and spinning in a flawless tempo, with maintenance able to provide the most reliable part of the duke's day for the rest of his life. His son's life. Christian's timepieces would live far beyond him, a notion which gratified whenever he imagined it.

The heat of Raine's regard hit him, and he looked up in time to see her green-gold eyes focused on his hands, the flushed streaks beneath her cheeks etched in deeper than before, her face glowing in the muted illumination flowing in the window. The sounds of an awakening house vanished as their gazes locked, the scent of tea and books and ink beaten down beneath the weight of his longing, his desire to climb across the desk and finish what they'd started the night before.

His chest constricted, his body tightening.

The quill pen slipped from her fingers to the Aubusson rug beneath her feet. She must have felt it, too.

He rose, intent on rounding the desk and convincing her in a way he suspected he easily could when the notion came to him.

With a secreted smile, he settled back in his chair. His joy knew no bounds.

Because he'd stumbled across the key to unlocking Raine Mowbray's sealed heart.

Christian was used to employing stubborn persuasion—used to getting his way. Used to convoluted business negotiations, and in some instances, convoluted personal ones. He called the shots and expected to prevail while playing by his rules. Raine was used to none of this. A housemaid had limited opportunities to express an opinion. Little freedom to *choose*. Like they'd agreed at the beginning of this journey, within these four walls, he would be her friend first. Let her drive the carriage. A gift he'd guarantee no one had ever given her.

A gift he'd never given.

He flexed his fingers and held back a grin as she fidgeted as surely as if he'd trailed his lips over her skin. "Would you like to see the inner workings?" He gestured to the watch. God above, she should imagine he meant something else.

His body throbbed at the thought.

When, of course, he meant something else.

But he was willing to ride this out and show her the bloody watch.

Pushing aside the letter she was transcribing, she rested her elbows on the desk and leaned in, her simple, elegant scent skimming his senses. Soap and rosewater and the lightest hint of lemon, free of conceit or enticement, like the woman. Her eyes lifted to his, then dropped to the timepiece. "It's exquisite," she murmured and went to touch, then halted, thinking better of the impulse.

He smiled, rooted to the spot, his love for her confirmed that second if it hadn't been already. "Here." He took her hand, extended her index finger, and lightly touched the watch, letting her feel the whisper-kiss movement of the wheels against her skin. "Nickel motor barrel bridge. Winding wheel. Crown wheel. Regulator. Escapement wheel." With each item he listed, he tapped her finger gently on the part.

"This timepiece will be in the duke's possession, his family's, for centuries. He'll likely gift it to Lord Jonathan. Perhaps another to Lord William. And they will gift them to their sons. Or, one can hope, to their daughters."

Christian's heart skipped, a full second before it kicked into rhythm again. He exhaled, his hand trembling where it rested over hers. "That knowledge gives me such pleasure, such pride, that it makes it easier to let them go."

She sighed, a low, melodic echo he would hold in his memory forever when he'd once wondered so savagely what her voice sounded like. Snaking her hand from beneath his, she said, "You're possessive."

He knew they weren't talking about his watches. "I've had to fight for everything I have, and I do mean everything, Raine. I don't easily share. Or give up."

"Is that a challenge?"

He shrugged. "I don't know. Is it?"

"Stubborn," she added, humor chasing the declaration.

Taking his teacup with him, he sprawled in his armchair, his gaze locked on hers as he sipped. "Flaws aplenty."

"Kit, you're brilliant. And irritated only because I didn't tell you what you wanted to hear."

He rolled the rim of the cup along his bottom lip and felt intense satisfaction when her gaze tracked the movement. "You're the most forthright person I've ever met. It's strangely humbling. And punitive."

She laughed, such a joyous reaction he jostled his cup, spilling tea on his wrist. "I like talking to you. It's been ages, forever, I think, since I could speak my mind or anyone cared to listen. It's addictive. Like I feel when I'm close to figuring out the mystery in a book. I'm so ready to get there."

"You're killing me. You know that, right?" He blew a fast breath through his teeth, slapped his cup to the desk, and leaned in until he got close enough to see the flecks of gold swimming in her eyes. His body was alive with yearning, absolutely pulsing. "I'm happy to feed your compulsion. Any of them. Try me."

Her eyes widened, her lips parting on a spent, ragged sound that tore him up inside. "You don't know me well." She drew her hands into a prayerful fist and rested her chin atop them. "I'm headstrong. A horrible cook. An abysmal seamstress. My only talent languages, words, books. I'm independent and outspoken, a nightmare for most men. No one you would truly want to involve yourself with. I'm uninterested in parties or fashion or gossip. I'm happy with my novels. A cat would be nice. A dog even. A horse. And children." Her eyes flicked to his, then to the desk. "Someday, children."

He coughed to cover his mirth, but like smoke it slid neatly into the study, surrounding them.

"Why are you *smiling*, you beast?" she asked between bared teeth. "You know, I used to punch my brothers for teasing me like this."

"Because this diatribe is enlightening as all hell, Raine darling. You're talking yourself out of this, out of me, because you know I've already decided. I decided ten years ago. Somehow, this rambling list of excuses about why I shouldn't want you is very, very good news. In the few hours between last night and this morning, you've decided we're a 'maybe'." He snapped his fingers with a grin. "My horse has moved up in the odds."

"I haven't…that is, I am…I'm not…" With a growl of frustration, she shoved to her feet. "Oh, bother!"

He was out of his chair, catching her wrist before she could storm from the room. Walking her back against the door, he used her body to close it with a soft snap. "I'm going to say this once, then we'll sit, have tea, and finish my translations. No more teasing, no more verbal fencing. I'll not address the issue again unless you want me to." He leaned and whispered in her ear, "You're in control, Miss Mowbray, how does that feel?"

Her shoulders rose and fell on a hushed breath, her arm quivering in his hold. "You know how it feels. In a world built for men, it feels wonderful."

He braced his hand against the door, palm flat, fingers spread. He wanted to be steady—and he wanted her to listen. "I'm in love with you, Raine. My first and only love." When she went to lower her gaze, he tipped her chin high with his free hand. He'd never realized how much taller he was, how slim and delicate she was. He felt empowered and frightened by his depth of feeling. To protect, to possess. "Penny told me if I could look you in the eye and tell you I didn't want you, I was on the right path. I could leave Hartland Abbey and never look back. Well, I obviously can't do that. And I won't leave without knowing I told you everything that's in my heart and my mind. A silly misunderstanding is not going to be the reason you run from me." He smoothed his thumb over her bottom lip as she blinked, fighting, he could see, the impulse to look away. "My father was a harsh taskmaster. Cruel. My mother tried to assuage his temper, which made for a most miserable existence. Walking on broken bits of china, always. Cholera decimated our village when I was fifteen, and within two weeks, I had no one. My beloved brother, who'd hoped to go into business with me, gone. My mother, everyone, gone."

Tears sparked her eyes. "Kit, you don't have to tell me this."

"Oh, yes, I do. I absolutely do. You said we don't know each other well, so here I am. Like my tools, laid out on the duke's desk, ready for inspection." He curled his fingers into a fist against the door. "Tavistock House was a desperate destination, though I had nowhere else to go. The earl not far from my father in temperament, unfortunately, which I could no longer countenance. I knew within three days of arrival that I couldn't stay. He was wretched and...I loathed him almost as much as I feared him. I'd been offered an apprenticeship with a watchmaker, one I decided to accept without delay." Laughing, he pressed a playful kiss to her cheek. "Then, I saw you. The very night I sent the note to Cambridge announcing my plans to arrive, there you were. In that darkened corner, bathed in moonlight, pressing a book against the globe of an oil lamp. I was like a butterfly caught in a net, immediate entrapment. Visceral. Gut-deep. Final. You must believe me. I beg you to believe me when I say I knew in one second that you were the only woman for me. It sounds like something out of a fairy tale, but it was true for me."

She slipped her hand over his lips, but he simply kissed her palm, this caress not playful, bringing a needy sound from her that shocked them both.

Drawing her fingers to cup his cheek, he leaned in until his lips grazed hers. "I didn't have the courage to stumble down the marble staircase at Tavistock House and introduce myself to the girl on the veranda. So I'll do that now. Christian Emory Bainbridge, pleased to make your acquaintance. Now that that's over, will you please marry me?" Then he slanted his head, his lips covering hers, taking possession, branding her as she'd branded him on a lonely night ten years ago.

Tunneling her fingers in his hair, she gave the strands a tug, her nails gently scraping his scalp. Touched her tongue to his and shyly began an erotic dance. Stepping between her legs, fitting himself as close to her as he could while standing, he murmured an approving hum that mixed with another of those enchanting sounds she freed when she liked what he was doing.

He would enjoy learning what she desired. Needed. *Loved.* What made her heart race, her skin flush. Like his watches, he'd study her until he could disassemble the unique pieces of her to find the glorious, perfect fit.

He'd spend a lifetime making sure happiness and pleasure were never far from reach.

Predictably, the door opened as they were losing themselves in each other, sending Raine stumbling into Christian. Penny peered around the open space, one brow rising, a trick he'd perfected in his chipped mirror until he had it down, only putting in the effort because women appreciated it and invited him into their beds that much quicker.

Penny took them in with a flat smile, snorting as Raine danced away from Christian.

She straightened her sad mobcap, smoothed her dress, and tugged on her apron before throwing up her hands in mortification and slithering through the doorway without a backward glance.

Penny shoved Christian back a step when he tried to follow. "Get a grip on yourself, man. I don't know what's happening in that usually gifted brain of yours, but if you don't want to ruin her position in this household, ruin your relationship with Devon, you should let your able manservant assist with this scandalous post-encounter as you look like you've been dipped in something sticky and are not yet dry. And she looked about the same."

Christian muttered an oath and yanked his hand through his hair. "I asked her again, much better this proposal, romantic even, and then there you were, barreling in." He brought his knuckle to his mouth, winced. "Cut my lip on her tooth when she bumped into me. Your timing is impeccable, Mister Pennington, utterly impeccable."

"At your service, sire." Penny gave Christian's cravat a rectifying yank. "You didn't allow for much time between proposals. A tad desperate, isn't it?" He yawned, stretched his shoulders like he'd just woken from a nap. "You think she'll accept?"

Slapping Penny's hand away, he growled, "How should I know?"

His valet's brow rose, that odious trick again. "You couldn't tell from the kiss? My, you *are* losing your touch." He released a sardonic smile and leaned lazily against the doorjamb. "At least marriage means I won't have to deliver any more necklaces to departing mistresses. No joy in that task. Remember that crazy countess who pulled the pistol on me? Can only be thankful she had no idea how to use it." He crossed the room and collapsed in the chair Raine had recently vacated, gave the air a little sniff as if it still smelled of feminine delight. "I've had enough of enraged women to last a lifetime. For my sake, I'm hoping the bluestocking says yes."

Christian strode to the window, braced his forearm on the ledge, and let his mind sink into their kiss. They'd been entangled, the scent of her storming his mind, the touch and taste of her devastating his body. His soul. When her eyes had opened for one brief moment and caught his, he'd seen something authentic and profound shimmering in their golden depths.

Christian gazed across the duke's sloping lawn, clouds the color of pewter releasing scant light, the evergreens and hedges coated in a blustery mist. "She's going to say yes."

"Again, let's hope," Penny murmured in a drowsy voice, "after you've made a cake of yourself. *Twice*."

"She loves me, too." *A little. I think.*

"So, it's love. Couldn't go for one of those advantageous but loveless marriages, could you? Not your style, I suppose." The grunt his valet released sounded resigned and mournful. "Well, well, well, you've let yourself be caught, my friend. This should prove enlightening. To me, in any case. Ways I can avoid the trap."

"I want to be caught," Christian whispered too low for Penny to hear, realizing it was the sincerest statement he'd ever uttered.

He wanted, for the first time, to own and be owned. Wanted to give Raine everything she'd dreamed of while securing *his* dream.

For the girl on the veranda to finally be his.

RAINE DASHED DOWN THE HALLWAY, EMBARRASSED, OVERJOYED, panicked. Her body blazed like one of the kitchen's ovens, throwing off heat until she feared anyone close to her would feel it. She skidded to a halt before she entered the main hall, Mrs. Webster's smooth voice gliding from the pantry. The scent of baking bread and roasted meat joined the dusty air rolling in the open gallery windows, though when she lifted her hand to her nose, all Raine could smell on her skin was Kit. Sandalwood and the faint scent of bergamot that must be in the soap he washed his hair with. She'd had her hand tangled in the dark strands, her lips open beneath his, their legs entwined like holly circling an elm trunk.

It had been, for one electrifying moment, what she imagined lovemaking was like.

Except, they'd been standing up.

Her face flamed, turning what she knew was an unbecoming shade of pink. Dear heaven, the man could kiss, quickly finding the way to unlock her passion. And, somehow, she'd seemed to know just how to follow along, his ragged sound of pleasure the most sensual thing she'd ever heard in her life. It had been natural, touching him, body melting against his, hands clutching to bring him closer.

When it had been impossible to get closer.

I love him. I do. I love Christian Emory Bainbridge.

Now, what to do about it?

Raine was riddled with uncertainty, debating between telling the adorable man yes or hiding until he'd repaired all the duke's timepieces and retreated to London when Charlotte Webster, Lady Ann's personal maid, stepped from the pantry. Newly married to Phillip, the cook's son, Charlotte glowed like a lit candle rested inside her, her pleasant personality. She had a devilish wit that came out in only the loveliest of ways, no cuts involved, which in Raine's experience was rare.

Charlotte would understand her dilemma; her marriage to Phillip was a love-match.

"Raine, dear, you look like you've seen a ghost." Charlotte wiped her hands on the cloth she held and tilted her head in consideration. "Are you unwell?"

Raine knocked the frilled edge of her cap from her eyes, wondering if she looked like she'd been ravished. She felt like she had. "Do you have time for a walk? Through the gardens, perhaps? The flowers are in bloom and quite lovely." She tangled her hands in her apron and groaned. "I have a question. A concern. About a man. A vexing, tempting, wonderful man. I'm confused and excited and, oh, so many things!"

Charlotte's green eyes widened, and she choked back a laugh. "How could I say no when this sounds like it will be the most entertaining conversation of my day? I'd rather talk about men than new gowns. And I'm not due to assist Lady Ann and the modiste for another hour."

"Likely a very entertaining conversation," Raine muttered and turned down the main hall, heading to the servant's entrance at the rear of the house. Kit, as a guest of the duke, would use the main entrance. She used the rear. This difference in their lives was what she'd been trying to tell him, to no avail. He didn't seem to care, and she wondered if she should.

But what woman didn't want to be an asset to her husband?

She couldn't see what she had to offer when he had so much already.

The morning was a warm one for Yorkshire, the somber sky casting dappled light across the path they took over the lawn. In the distance, she could see the bridge she'd traversed last night, falling in love by the time she arrived on the other side. When they reached the gardens, Raine inhaled the scent of lilacs and hibiscus, bees and butterflies flitting around her. She didn't have a green thumb like her father, although she'd spent many a day with him in Tavistock's gardens, listening to his advice about how to make his beloved plants flourish. Usually, the thought of family brought a stinging sense of loneliness, but instead, now, she imagined Kit beside her—and felt empowered.

Charlotte crossed to a marble bench surrounded by a riot of colorful blooms, stretched her arms over her head and sighed. "I love summer. My favorite season." She patted the empty spot next to her. "Come tell me about this tempting, vexing, wonderful man. I admit I can't wait to hear the story. A certain groom has taken quite a fancy to you if gossip is accurate."

Raine settled beside Charlotte, plucked a daisy from its stem, and twirled it between her fingers. She hoped Charlotte wouldn't be irritated to learn the man she wanted to discuss wasn't Nash

Cartwright. "How did you know? With Phillip? That it was love?"

Charlotte clicked her tongue against her teeth, selected her own daisy, and lifted it to her nose. "He's called me Lottie since we were little, but there was this shift, and the next time that nickname rolled from his lips, my world expanded. I felt a glow. Like I was lifted from my slippers. It suddenly occurred to me that we weren't simply friends anymore." She dusted the petals against her palm. "And there was an impressive kiss. That, too."

Raine laughed and gave her daisy a spin. "Ah, a blinding kiss. That sounds about right."

"He was funny and charming, a bit naughty. Handsome. Frankly, he was everything. When I knew he loved me, too…" She shrugged, a dreamy tilt curving her lips. "There was no question."

"So you can just know," Raine whispered. "In an instant."

Charlotte nodded. "Sometimes, yes, of course. However, Phillip and I took years to get around to it. We aren't a perfect example."

"It's complicated. This man I speak of"—Raine laid the flower on her apron and glanced into Charlotte's eyes, then back at her worn slippers—"he's not a servant. It won't advance his life, his career, his holdings in any of the ways another marriage, to someone more appropriate, wealthy or highborn, would. But he doesn't care about that, and I'm not sure I should care so very much."

"Does Mister Bainbridge love you? Do you love him? I think these are the questions you should ask yourself. That you should consider above any other. Not if he's listed in *Debrett's Peerage* or needs funds for his watchmaking business, which I can assure you, from what I know, he does not."

Raine's heart dropped to her knees. She swiveled on the bench, marble snagging her dress. "How did you know?"

Charlotte chewed on her lip, her smile when it broke through positively wicked. "You crossed the main hall yesterday on your way to the kitchens. You were reading a book and almost walked into a wall. Mister Bainbridge was at the front door with Lord Jonathan, and his gaze followed you until you were lost from sight. His expression…" She fanned her cheeks and trailed the daisy across them. "His expression was a study in dazzled befuddlement. He had to shake himself out of a stupor as if he'd had a sudden rush of blood to the head." She pointed her flower at Raine, shrugged a slim shoulder. "He's been here before, and certainly, there have been rumors in the scandal sheets, men will be men, but he's always seemed lonely to me. Remote, without anyone except that scamp of a valet, Mister Pennington, by his side. So, my dear Miss Mowbray, what you can offer, if he loves you, is *you*. Not funds or property or a silly title, but you. And *you* are the only you he'll ever be lucky enough to find."

Raine watched a ladybug crawl along the bench and, with a flicker of its wings, drift from sight. The anguish in Kit's voice when he spoke of having no one after his family died whispered through her mind. Even with the wenches and the watches, she suspected he *was* lonely. In a way only someone just as lonely could understand. "Will the duke be incensed if I agree to marry Mister Bainbridge and move to London? He did go to such trouble to secure my future and get me away from Tavistock House."

Charlotte giggled and threw her arm around Raine's shoulder, sending their daisies tumbling to the grass. "He's a romantic! Do you see the way he looks at the duchess when she doesn't *know* he's looking? He'll be extremely happy for you. Just think, we can have another wedding in the chapel! This is the most glorious year ever!"

Abigail Frank and Rex Ableman had gotten married in the estate's chapel just after Raine arrived at Hartland Abbey, and Charlotte and Phillip had married there one month ago.

"Are you going to say yes?" Charlotte asked. "Tell me you are. I'll help you plan, and we can have a dress made and…"

Raine smiled softly and ducked her head, Charlotte's excited chatter flowing over her, the image of taking Kit's hand in the enchanting Devon sanctuary too wonderful to imagine.

She only had to find the courage to seize her heart's desire.

It was as simple as that.

Six

Hartland Abbey was tranquil, hushed, servants above and below stair asleep, duties complete. Kitchens cleaned, wicks extinguished, floors swept, beds turned, basins freshened. Raine tiptoed down the hallway, halting at Kit's bedchamber door. It had been easy, a remark about the delivery of a letter that didn't exist, to find out which room was his. She placed her hand on the walnut door as if she'd be able to feel his presence, then laughed at herself for such lovesick foolishness.

She stood there for a minute, perhaps two, the tick of a mantel clock Kit had likely recalibrated signaling the passing of time and her increasing cowardice.

"Damn and blast," Raine whispered and tapped on the door. How hard was it to tell a man you loved him? Wanted to marry him. Live the rest of your days watching him fiddle with his timepieces. Translate his ridiculously intricate chronometer designs and have his undoubtedly gorgeous children.

She pressed her hand to her quivering belly.

Very hard, indeed.

The knob squealed, and the door inched open. Raine exhaled, then caught herself, and clamped her lips shut as Christian moved into view, perching his shoulder on the doorjamb with a look of surprise, pleasure, and finally, uncertainty. She took him in from head to toe. *Heavens*. Trousers hanging low on his lean hips. No shirt, no shoes, no stockings. A dusting of hair on his chest that trailed down and into his wrinkled waistband. His body was lean but layered with muscle. A body she wanted to press into service, to warm like clay with her hands and *sculpt*. Her skin flushed, a steady, unfamiliar pulse settling between her thighs.

She'd never seen a man in such an unclothed state—but she presumed from her response that she rather liked it.

He allowed the perusal, patient, relaxed, a wry smile turning his lips, that enchanting dimple denting his cheek. "Do I pass muster?" he murmured after a charged pause, rotating the tiny screwdriver he held in his hand.

She nodded to the tool. "Do you work at all hours?"

He glanced at her bare toes peeping from the hem of her dress with a raised brow. "It's what I have, Miss Mowbray. It's what I have."

She flushed, not about to tell him she'd raced from her attic bedchamber to his door without stockings or slippers. "Are you going to send me away?" she asked because he seemed to be guarding the room.

In response, Christian trailed the pointed tip of the screwdriver from the end of her ring finger to her wrist. She sucked in a gasp, her hand flexing, her knees trembling beneath her skirt. "Are you going to marry me, Raine? Not to sound missish, but if you want this"—he nodded to the bedchamber—"you're going to have to marry me to get it. My body, mind, and soul are yours if you'll agree to take them. But I won't ruin you. I won't. And I can't share any more of myself and wonder if I'll get it back. I'm in too deep for that." He swallowed hard, his sapphire eyes darting to the floor, and she knew with such sweet simplicity that her roguish, complicated, brilliant watchmaker was as delicate of heart as she. "You fear being beholden, but what if I were to tell you I would be wholly beholden as well? What if *we* are worth more than any promise you made to yourself?" His gaze lifted, his earnestness smoothing away her fear like a plane to rough wood. "I won't own you in any way you don't own me."

Encouraged by his passionate focus, she wiggled the screwdriver from his grasp and trailed it along the line of hair on his chest, over his ribs, halting at his navel. He blew out a startled breath and whispered her name beneath it. Two could play this game, she thought. And she'd always loved games. "You've decided then?"

His muscles quivered beneath the cool metal. "In 1810, as a matter of fact."

She laughed, freely, joyously, astonished by her boldness. "What about the wenches?"

With a quick look down the thankfully deserted hallway, he grasped her wrist and dragged her into the room. "No more wenches. You, my lovely bluestocking, are more than enough for this lifetime."

Turning, she rested against the door, the taper on the bedside table throwing a golden glow over a space that held his scent so firmly she felt a quiver run through her. *Bluestocking*. How odd. How enchanting. "Kit Bainbridge, if I tell you I love you more than I imagined possible, that I don't want to be without you for another moment, that you are the most incredible man I've ever met, can I have a modest token of appreciation before the wedding? Our wedding." She pressed her lips together, holding back her smile as he absorbed her adoring confession. "A kiss, perhaps. Like the one in the study earlier today. That little thing you did, when you nibbled on my bottom lip. Heavenly."

"I think I can arrange that," he whispered and reached, tugging her mobcap from her head and dropping it to the floor. Removed one hairpin at a time until her chignon collapsed over her shoulders in a golden shroud. "Your hair is divine. Never restrain it. Beautiful things should be able to follow their own will." He filled his hand with the strands, trailing his fingers up the nape of her neck and bringing her against his hard body.

She caught his shoulders and swayed, melting into him. His skin was warm beneath her questing fingers, a smattering of hair on his chest, a mottled scar on his shoulder.

Tipping her head high, he captured her lips beneath his and circled her, once, twice, like they waltzed across a ballroom. He breathed into her mouth, used his tongue to engage and attack, unleashing her rabid hunger. Bowing into him, she threaded her arms around his neck and put every part of her lonely soul into the kiss, without hesitation or fear. Within moments, they were lost.

Obliterated, shattered.

When her hip bumped the bed, he halted, a fierce exhalation

racing from his lips, his dazed eyes meeting hers. "Will that suffice? For the token of appreciation?"

Gazing at him, she searched her heart for what she wanted.

Not what society expected or what anyone would advise her to do. She searched for what *she*, Raine Mowbray, wanted. Obedience be damned, she thought. Presenting her back, she swept her hair over one shoulder, bowed her head. She could feel his moist breath against her neck as he leaned in but didn't touch. Her awareness of another human being had never been this potent, desire connecting them as if the emotion held its own lifeforce.

"Undress me, Kit," she whispered with a teasing look thrown back at him.

"Are you sure?" His pupils flared, a flood of dark black. "We have time. Thousands of nights."

She closed her eyes as the screwdriver slipped from her hand to the carpet. "I love you. And I want our life, the 'we' you spoke of, to start right now."

Goosebumps exploded along her arms as he went to work on her practical gown fit for summer servitude and nothing more, loosening the tie at her neck, releasing the hook and eyelets at her waist. The material drooped, and Christian swept his hand around her hips, pulling her back against his aroused body as his lips fell to her neck. Teeth nipping, tongue soothing, her muffled sigh expressed her arousal, her *impatience*.

"A slim form such as yours does not need a corset," he said into the curve of her shoulder.

She turned in his arms, letting her dress puddle at her feet. "Just how well do you know women's apparel, Kit Bainbridge?"

He cupped her cheek, tilted her face up. "I can't recall anyone before you. You're all I desire. My heart, my soul. There's no one else. Really, there never has been."

He was skilled, even if she wished he wasn't, removing her frayed petticoat and chemise while kissing the very life from her, until she stood before him in a pool of spent clothing, longing forging a persuasive path from her inflamed mind to her tingling toes. When she shivered and made to cross her hands over her chest, he held her arms by her side. "Oh, no. You are breathtaking, more beautiful than I'd dreamed, and I've spent many nights dreaming, Raine. But let's level the playing field, I agree.

Where you go, I follow." Stepping back, his fingers went to the fall of his breeches, unbuttoning as her heart raced. He wore no drawers, and when he flicked open the final button and kicked aside the garment, there wasn't a stitch of cotton or linen between them.

She hadn't known what to imagine, but *he* was the beautiful one. Lithe and lean, his skin golden, a body in ideal balance. Her gaze traveled below his waist. A prolonged breath escaped through her teeth as he took himself in hand and stroked, slowly, his eyes locked on hers.

"Are you certain you'll fit?"

"Trust me, love, we were made for each other." Smiling, he gave her a gentle push that sent her across the feather mattress, where he then flooded over her. His serene patience evaporated the moment his skin met hers, his hands roaming as his lips reclaimed.

It was an assault, sure, steady, relentless.

Hunger, reckless passion.

Desperation.

With a hoarse murmur, she gripped his hip, his shoulder, nails scraping his back, hardly knowing how she'd come to be squeezed into this molten, quivering mass of flesh, not one whit of intent beyond a maddening race for pleasure. His hand cupped her breast, thumb sweeping her nipple, circling, and sweeping again. Her back arched off the mattress, and she let out a frayed sound, interrupting a kiss she could no longer sustain.

"Duly noted," he murmured and tugged the peaked nub between his lips, biting lightly until she felt the hard pinch in her fingertips, the soles of her feet, the backs of her knees. Her rough moan shattered the stillness, her hands falling from him to twist in the counterpane, her body curving into his touch. A sharp gust ripped in the open window and swept her, cooling skin reheated moments later. Stunned, she lay there as he kissed one breast and palmed the other, switched, then switched again, until she could absorb nothing but their gulping, ragged breaths, walled inside a house of pleasure.

"Your heartbeat is racing beneath my lips. I'm crazy for the feel of you." He shifted his hips with a groan, his cock settling against her warm folds, a natural, flawless fit. They moved together, creating a rhythm he echoed with his tongue when he captured her mouth beneath his.

Awash in sensation, her fingers rose to tangle in his hair as she begged for more.

He snaked his hand between their bodies, palming her thigh, delving between her legs. He queried lightly, gently, sliding a finger inside her, a leisurely effort that left her trembling, strung tight, expectant. *Wanting.* This was *nothing* like what she'd done to herself on those solitary nights in her bed, her knowledge of her body slight but her yearning fierce.

It was as if he knew her better than she knew herself.

Knew exactly where to touch her, *how* to touch her.

"There. More, oh, Kit," she whispered against his shoulder as he inserted another finger, biting his skin to emphasize her plea. "*There.*"

When she went to touch him, feel his rigid length for the first time, he lifted her arm high over her head, stretching her body out like one of his chains beneath him. "My bluestocking arrives, wild and greedy. I would love to have your hands on me, but if that happens now, I'll come in seconds." Rising over her, he braced his weight on his forearm, never releasing his hold on her, below the waist or above. "Look at me, love."

When she did, she found his gaze stunned, brow moist, cheeks glowing, lips parted—truthfully looking as devastated as she felt. "What?" she murmured, lost, trying to catch what she'd missed. "Why did you stop?"

He grinned, laughed softly, looking so boyishly handsome her heart stuttered. "I love you, Raine, with everything inside me, and I'll thank God every day for sending you to me again. I just wanted you to know before I took you." Astonishing admission released to the night, he positioned his body and slid inside her, just enough. Not nearly enough. The feeling of fullness was astounding, frightening…magnificent.

He caught her thigh, angling her leg over his hip and stroked, taking calm possession until they were locked, hip to hip. Tunneling his arm beneath her, he set a fundamental rhythm, a cadence neither reckless nor rushed. An elegant tempo of slick skin, seeking hands, broken, uneven kisses. Half-breaths and fractured moans. She answered his earnest questions—*is this okay, does it hurt*—his aroused murmurs a bottomless tremor in her ear. And he followed her instructions—*faster, deeper, there*—with almost perfect devotion.

She moved against him, drove him, drove herself, with confidence born of instinct.

Any pain was fleeting, minor, and after a few moments, nonexistent. The world constricted to his frantic directions, his clutching hold, his weight, the salty taste of his skin. The tart scent of them riding the air, the sheets, their bodies.

She tried to tell him what was happening inside her, the creeping sensation of being swept away on a roaring tide, but the tremors racking her made speech challenging and rational thought impossible. But he understood, reaching between them, a final, prolonged touch between her legs all it took to unleash her climax. An endless release that drew reason and breath from her until she was boneless, floating on a sea of twisted silk bedding, helpless to do anything but allow passion to take her.

His answering groan and thrust deep, deep inside her confirmed he'd reached this wondrous place, too.

They gasped and clung, lips touching, chests heaving, brow to brow, cheek to cheek. He tried to say something but finally shook his head and collapsed to his side, bringing her with him. Wordlessly, he tucked her against his body. She opened her mouth, feeling she must say *something*, but he shook his head again and whisked his finger across her lips. *Not yet.*

Before she could take another breath, her solicitous, remarkable intended tumbled into an exhausted sleep.

She could only sigh, laugh, and join him, her heart lighter than a butterfly's wings.

SHE WASN'T ALONE.

The panicked realization ripped through Raine's mind before she remembered. Blinking, she rose to her elbow, her hair a flaxen shroud falling over the man whose shoulder she'd been using as a pillow. Christian's breathing was even, his lids fluttering with dreams she hoped she inhabited. She looked to the window, determined it to be an hour or so before dawn. She'd need to leave him soon, creep back to the attic, and pretend she'd been there all night.

Instead of what she'd been doing, which was planning her future.

Raine dropped her cheek to her hand, allowing herself a moment to watch him. Record every inch of him as she'd been too occupied during the night to do. The sheet was tangled about his long legs and drawn judiciously to his trim waist. His belly rose and fell with his breaths. She trailed a finger up his chest, traced a crescent scar on his neck, marveled at eyelashes that looked like the tips had been dipped in amber.

He wasn't perfect. He had a temper. He was impulsive. Even a little arrogant. But he was also generous. Considerate. Shy, unbelievably. And so talented he made her proud when she'd no reason to claim the sentiment.

He was a sincere man in a society of impersonators.

And he was *hers*.

"Your scrutiny is lighting me up like you pressed a glowing ember against my skin," he whispered and rolled over her, their bodies settling flawlessly into place. "I'm a watchmaker without a timepiece. How long do we have?" He gazed to the window, chewed his bottom lip in deliberation. "I have an appointment with Devon at nine, the courtesy of informing him of our upcoming nuptials before any bit of nonsense about us is repeated. In light of your father not being here for me to ask. Though once we return to London, it's my first task."

Her heart squeezed. Love was a powerful drug, indeed. "We have ten minutes, maybe fifteen."

He nodded, the keen glow in his eyes sending a serrated pulse through her. "I'll make it work."

"We'll see," she said as he dipped his head to nibble on a sensitive spot beneath her jaw. Both times during the night had taken longer, *much* longer.

"Oh, love, just watch me." His hand swept low, his fingers, his tongue, his teeth following just behind, turning her world upside down. "And you know what they say. Third time's a charm."

So, she did. And it was.

Seven

Christian was rarely nervous.

However, the Duke of Devon's regard across the breakfast table was unflinching, rather like Christian had felt upon being summoned to the headmaster's office at Harrow. Which, due to his tenacious nature, had occurred often.

After escorting Raine to her attic chamber without incident just before dawn, he'd taken a stroll around the estate, nerves snapping, pulse drumming. Nervousness was allowed; it wasn't every day a man publicly professed his love and intention to marry the woman of his dreams. Across the sloping lawn, over the bridge, and past the spot where he and Raine had shared the first of what would surely be many arguments, he'd considered his future and his extreme good fortune.

He was, after all, gaining a passionate wife.

And passionate women didn't always do what their men wanted them to.

When the sun had risen high enough in a vivid blue sky to designate it appropriate, he'd gone in search of James Hampton, the fourth Duke of Devon. Surprisingly, Christian was directed to the breakfast room, where His Grace, an early riser unlike most of the useless fops in the *ton* according to the footman, was having tea while reviewing an ironed edition of *The Times*.

To say His Grace's glittering green gaze could cut glass as he waited for his watchmaker to get to the point would be apropos. Christian sipped his tea when he much preferred coffee and practiced his entry into the conversation. *You see, Your Grace, ten years ago…*

"Let me expedite the process as you're about to splash tea on your waistcoat. You've come to alert me to the fact that Miss Mowbray will not be in my employ for any longer than it takes you to finish calibrating my clocks. Does that adequately summarize the situation?"

Christian's cheeks stung, emotion flowing freely across his face an embarrassing predicament since he was a child. And then it occurred to him that someone in the house may have seen them sneaking through the halls this morning, fingers linked, faces aglow. "I don't… that is to say, Miss Mowbray…"

The duke laughed, bringing his napkin to his lips to hide it. "You've not been caught if that's your concern. And if it is, I'm heartily glad you're making the expedient decision to offer for the girl." He dusted his lips with the linen square and laughed again, truly the first time Christian had known the man to show such cheerfulness. Being a source of entertainment was starting to nip at his self-esteem as much as embarrassment had his cheeks. "Calm down, my man. Miss Mowbray spoke to someone in the household, a request for feminine advice, I believe. It traveled from there, quite swiftly, into my ears. I'm a fair taskmaster, Bainbridge, so my staff talks to me. I know it's unheard of in some aristocratic families, but I prefer it to surviving on a bolster of fear and intimidation."

Christian placed his cup on the saucer before he dribbled tea as the duke had predicted. "The particulars aren't valuable to anyone but us, but I've loved her for ten years. This isn't a chance occurrence for me, random temptation or some such. Happening upon her here, in your employ, is nothing short of a miracle. I'll go to any length to secure her happiness. You have my word."

A boy raced into the room and threw himself at the duke. "Father! You must come and see what I've built. It's simply marvelous. Miss Daisy said it's the best castle she's ever seen!"

Devon ruffled his son's hair and gifted him with a loving smile. "I'll come straightaway, Nicholas. Just give me a moment to finish my discussion with Mister Bainbridge."

Nicholas turned to Christian with an impish smile. "You're the watchmaker."

"I am indeed. I wasn't much older than you when I started taking timepieces apart and putting them back together." He pulled a center wheel from his waistcoat pocket and offered it to the boy. Nicholas snatched it from Christian with a gasp of delight. Christian's heart softened, thinking of a child with Raine's golden eyes someday staring up at him. "I'm working on Philip Webster's pocket watch this morning. If you come to your father's study in one hour, if your governess allows it, I'll show you exactly where it fits within the other parts. Maybe I'll even, if you have a very steady hand, let you tighten a case screw."

Nicholas traced his finger over the wheel. "I have a steady hand like no other. I'm a Devon."

Christian grinned, charmed. "Well, then, you'll be an ace at it right off."

The duke gave his son a nudge. "Back to the nursery. Tell Miss Daisy one hour, in my study, for a watchmaking lesson. Thank Mister Bainbridge for the wheel."

Nicholas bowed dutifully and offered his thanks before bolting from the room.

"You're good with children," Devon said with a speculative look in his eye.

Christian fiddled with his silverware, his gaze going to a dour landscape hanging on the wall behind the duke. "I want a family. As it is, I have none."

The duke wiped at a smudge on the table, then placed his napkin in his lap. "I can speak with Vicar Rawley if you'd like to have the ceremony here. My chapel is exceedingly lovely if I do say so myself. We've recently hosted two weddings, and it didn't take long to arrange either. Then, you can get started right away on that family you're seeking."

Christian blinked, stunned by the offer. He would have to speak to Raine, but he'd like nothing more than to secure her hand before they returned to London. "Is marriage easy?" he blurted out, having no idea this would fall from his lips.

The duke's teacup and saucer rattled as he bumped them, glee splitting his cheeks. "Who told you that balderdash? Easy? What woman have you ever found to be easy? But the easy ones, my friend, are also *boring*. You want to avoid monotony at all costs. My duchess has never bored me a day in my life."

"Oh, Raine's far from boring. Or easy, come to think of it."

He frowned as he recalled their argument beside the bridge, the way he'd had to practically beg her to marry him. "Very intelligent but rather stubborn, not to place too fine a point on it." Suddenly, the way they'd challenged each other with bold, teasing touches and stimulating conversation until dawn clouded his mind and tightened his body.

"She sounds perfect. And from the smile on your face, I'd say you agree."

Christian rose and gave the duke a shallow bow. "Far from perfect, Your Grace, only perfect for me."

Then he went to find the perfectly stubborn woman who would be his wife.

Epilogue

A romantic morning two months later…
Berkeley Square, London

"Kit," Raine said as she stumbled over a wrinkle in the carpet, "I'm going to trip. Let me see."

He laughed, a sound she would never tire of hearing, his hand shifting from where he held it over her eyes, allowing a burst of sunlight to sneak in and dust her face. His body was pressed against hers as he guided her down the hallway of their London townhouse, and she gave her bottom a little wiggle to throw him off his mark.

"Oh, no, my lovely bluestocking. You're not using that trick on me. Penny nearly walked in on us in the morning room last week, or have you forgotten? The man doesn't knock and you're insatiable. Cross purposes I'm left to safely coordinate."

"I thought you *liked* that I'm greedy where you're concerned."

Christian halted, tilted Raine's chin, and covered her lips in a heated side-kiss that left them both dazed. "Where was I headed again?" he murmured against the nape of her neck once his breath had settled.

Raine lifted her gaze to his bottomless blue one, love a rushing tide through her veins. "It's a surprise, so I don't know!"

"Ah, yes." Christian nudged her toward a paneled door at the end of the hall. "I remember now. Your touch is finally loosening its hold on me."

"But this is your new study," she said and glanced back at him. "You had the carpenters in all week. I haven't stepped inside, not once, as you requested, though I don't know what trouble I could have—"

He reached around her and opened the door.

She peeked inside, then leaned back into him with a low sigh. "Oh…*Kit*."

"Go on." He gave her another nudge, pushing her into the room.

She looked around, turned a full circle in wonder. The space was perfect.

It was her. And *him*.

Sunlight a bold wash over furnishings in shades of blue and green, her favorite colors. A magnificent globe showing the constellations, because she and Kit liked to gaze at the sky during their walks through their lush Mayfair garden. A set of stately library chairs situated before a blazing hearth. A brocade chaise in the corner, fresh flowers in a vase on the table beside it. Kit knew she liked to read and nap, and that she loved the sweet scent of wildflowers. Floor-to-ceiling shelves housing more volumes than she could read in a lifetime seized her imagination as she walked into the room. Crossing to the mahogany book-cases, she ran her finger down a stiff leather spine and drew in the refreshing scent of new books. "You're spoiling me. New clothes and my very own phaeton. A personal account, a staff at my disposal. I'm completely ruined for life."

He closed the door to the library—*her* library—and leaned against it. "You're right, I am. And, damn, I'm enjoying it."

She turned to face him, propped her hip against the book-shelf, and willed her heart to quiet its mad romp. She searched her mind for what to say, how to thank him, how to *tell* him. But only tears came, in great, heaving gulps.

He reached her in seconds and pulled her into his arms. "Raine, don't. This is meant to be the happiest of places. Almost from the first moment at the duke's home, I've dreamed about creating this spot for you. Don't cry. Please, you'll have me on my knees in moments."

She melted into him, his heart thumping beneath her cheek.

"I love it. I love *you*. But you don't have to…do so much." She sniffled, unused to emotional displays when she'd been profoundly expressive since the day of their wedding at Hartland Abbey five weeks earlier. "Give so much."

He tipped her chin high, his smile contrite. "This next bit may not help your tears subside."

"*What?*" she breathed. "There's more?"

He reached in his trouser pocket, retrieved a small wrapped parcel with a hand that shook. "I'd like to say this is nothing, but it's everything. More than the sapphire on your finger, more than this library and the phaeton put together." Tapping the package to his chest, he whispered, "This is my heart."

She unwrapped the parchment, knowing before she looked inside what he'd given her. The watch was delicately crafted, smaller, and more elegant than his usual pieces; the silver case etched with roses interwoven with her initials. The chain was one she recognized. "I thought I'd lost this," she murmured and brought the timepiece to her chest.

"Too fine to be a bookmark, I agree."

"There was never anything wrong with the filigree, was there?"

He shook his head. "No. But like my heart, I knew it was yours. There's an inscription on the inside."

Snapping the case open, she saw the words and felt her heart drop: *at first sight*. "Kit…" Her eyes stung, and she blinked rapidly. "I will treasure this forever."

He pressed a tender kiss to her brow, her temple, her cheek. "Darling, I'm a watchmaker. This can't be that much of a surprise."

"But you've never," she sniffled again and tucked herself into him, "the wenches."

His chest rumbled with his laughter. "Never have I given a wench a watch. You are the first. The only."

"That's good," she said into his now-damp linen shirt. "Because when the *ton* sees this, every woman in London will demand one. Prinny will have you make one for Maria Fitzherbert, you can certainly bet."

"I'll avoid that if I can." Taking her shoulders, he moved her back a step and reached into his trouser pocket.

"Oh, no more, Kit." She backed away, shaking her head

until her hair fell like a shroud around her face. "My heart can't take it."

He grinned, a wicked, knowing turn of his lips. "This gift, the third and final for today, is perhaps more for me." Crossing to the door, he fit a key into the lock and turned the tumblers with a snap. "The sturdiest bolt in England, or so I'm told. Enough to keep out even the most inquisitive of valets."

"Penny doesn't have a copy?"

Christian pocketed the key and leaned against the door with a licentious smirk. "No, and he'll never get one. This room is *ours*."

She tilted her head toward the chaise lounge. "That looks sturdy."

"Hmm, very. I selected it myself."

Giving her watch a swift glance, she crooked her finger, beckoning. "Do you have time to assist me with a project?" She flipped a button on her bodice. "A particularly knotty one, requiring a most refined touch."

Everything he felt for her swept his face, filled his eyes— matching every wondrous thing filling hers. Pushing off the door, he moved to her. "Darling, I thought you'd never ask."

The lock held.

And the love lasted.

Afterword

Thank you for reading Kit and Raine's love story! I learned so much about love AND watchmaking while writing this novella! Please sign up for my newsletter for a steamy free read (*Chasing the Duke*) and receive exclusive updates about releases, sneak peeks, sales and giveaways!

https://www.tracy-sumner.com/newsletter/

And my latest release, *The Wicked Wallflower*. The hero, Xander Macauley, has a Bainbridge watch in his collection!

Happy reading, always. xoxo

Lightning Source UK Ltd.
Milton Keynes UK
UKHW040641011122
411449UK00003B/138